"I'm going to Georgia, Hank,
I'm going to see Roselawns!"

Andrea's voice was filled with wonder and
elation. "Hank, pinch me so I'll know
I'm not dreaming!"
    Henry didn't pinch her. Groaning, he
pulled her into his arms and held her so close
that the trembling of his body transferred itself
to hers. He couldn't bear to let her go!
She was so filled with dreams about Georgia and
all the glory that had been part of the
Beddoes family until the war had changed things.
She'd marry the scion of some aristocratic family
and never come back to him in Texas.
So Henry kissed her, a kiss that shook her
to the core of her being, and Andrea felt a wild,
almost uncontrollable impulse to tell him that
she would stay and marry him. And then,
just as her senses began to reel, something
inside her cried out in frantic, wing-beating protest.
There ought to be more to life than marrying
a boy you'd known all your life, even if you
loved him. Life was out there, just beyond the
horizon, waiting for her with its untold
romance and adventure . . .

DESIRE AND DREAMS OF GLORY

Books by
Lydia Lancaster

Desire and Dreams of Glory
Passion and Proud Hearts
Stolen Rapture

Published by
WARNER BOOKS

Desire and Dreams of Glory

by

Lydia Lancaster

WARNER BOOKS

A Warner Communications Company

WARNER BOOKS EDITION

Copyright © 1979
by Lydia Lancaster
All rights reserved.

ISBN 0-446-81549-7

Cover art by Tom Hall

Warner Books, Inc.,
75 Rockefeller Plaza,
New York, N.Y. 10019

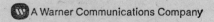 A Warner Communications Company

Printed in the United States of America

Not associated with Warner Press, Inc.,
of Anderson, Indiana

First Printing:
February, 1979

10 9 8 7 6 5 4 3 2 1

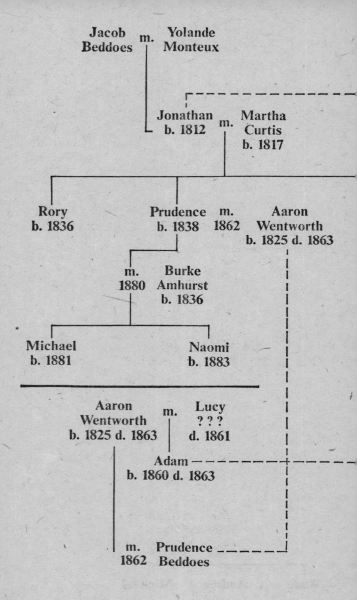

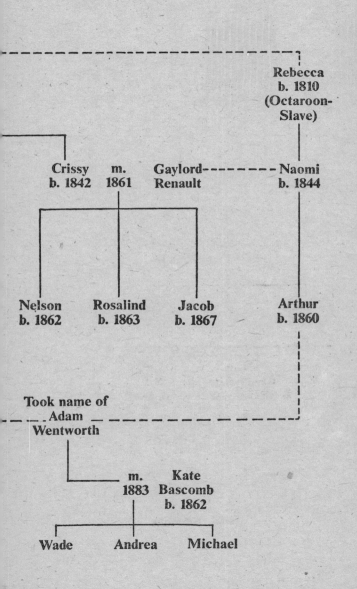

TRAIL'S END

1

By eleven-thirty in the morning, Kate Wentworth was so exasperated with her daughter Andrea Marie that she was ready to shake her! This was unusual for Kate, whose equanimity was seldom ruffled, but today was different; it was the fifteenth day of May, 1906, and Andrea's eighteenth birthday. Trail's End, the enormous ranch that Kate and Adam had built up in the Chinati Mountain region of the Big Bend country in Texas was very close to becoming a second Bedlam.

It wasn't the fault of the servants, who were working with every ounce of their energy to make Andrea's birthday party that evening the biggest and the grandest party the Chinatis had ever seen, a party that would be talked about for years. It wasn't the fault of Wade, Andrea's twenty-two-year-old brother who with Adam had made himself scarce by riding out to the south range to check fences; or even of Mike, Andrea's year-younger brother who was usually her shadow, aiding and abetting her in any deviltry that she was up to. And it certainly wasn't Kate's fault, because she had everything well in hand.

It was Andrea herself, darting from one room to another, who was getting in everyone's way. Andrea, demanding that the Chinese lanterns strung from the rafters of the barn and from lines run between the barn and the venerable cottonwood trees be lowered, or raised, that more be added here, those two moved, at least four more hung on the patio. And Andrea, popping up in the forty-foot living room to push furniture around, poking at the flowers that Kate had spent so much time arranging, then darting off to the kitchen to bedevil Manuella and her crew of helpers by sticking her fingers into the perfect icing of the four-tiered birthday cake, and by demanding for the twentieth time whether Manuella was sure she'd baked enough hams, made enough potato salad, baked enough bread and rolls, and shaped enough tortillas.

Kate stiffened as a howl of rage echoed from the kitchen, followed by a torrent of rapid Spanish. She turned from restoring some sort of symmetry to the flowers Andrea had been fussing with only a moment before, as Andrea darted into the room and almost knocked her off her feet eluding Manuella, who was three feet behind her wielding a rolling pin.

"Doña Catherine, she did it again! Fingermarks in the icing, the beautiful cake ruined! How can I get things ready with her poking her finger in the icing? If you don't keep her out of my kitchen there won't be any party! *Por Dios,* what a day, she's turned into a demon! She should be spanked!"

"I'm sorry, Manuella. I didn't mean to do it, that pink icing just looked so luscious I couldn't resist! If you'll stop shaking that lethal weapon at me I'll fix it."

"No, no no no no! Stay out of my kitchen!" Manuella's voice rose to a shriek. "I'll fix it myself. Go and take a bath, take a nap, are you eighteen years old or only eight, to be so naughty?"

"For heaven's sake, Dria, light somewhere and stop being such a nuisance!" Kate demanded. "Everything is under control; the party will be perfect if you'll just calm

12

down and behave yourself." Her voice was severe, but there was tenderness in her eyes as she looked at this daughter she and Adam had created, this girl whose beauty and wildness of spirit had already caused disruptions among all of the young men of the Chinati region.

Wade, their firstborn, was Adam all over again, tall, lithe, his hair almost the silver-blond that Adam's still retained, only a little dulled by all of his years under the Texas sun.

Michael was cut from a different piece of cloth. Shorter than Wade, as lithe but of slighter build, his hair was as flaming red as Andrea's father's had been, the Babcock Scotch-Irish blood dominant. Mike was nothing like as handsome as Adam and Wade. His face was square and there was a pugnacious set to his chin and devils in his eyes, in spite of the fact that he was invariably good-natured. In fact, he was so easygoing that sometimes Kate wondered whether he'd ever settle down to the serious business of ranching that Wade took to as naturally as breathing. It was fortunate that Trail's End had so much help that Mike's wasn't needed, because if he and Andrea weren't off somewhere together he was off alone, sometimes for days at a time, visiting friends who were mostly of Mexican peon stock, equating himself with them, preferring their company rather than that of the other stockmen's sons or helping Adam and Wade run the ranch.

And then there was Andrea, born almost exactly a year before Mike had been. Andrea, with her cloud of raven hair from that touch of Apache that came from Kate herself, but with a fair, creamy skin that even the Texas sun couldn't tan, and eyes as blue as Adam's. Andrea, who was almost an exact replica of Kate herself, so beautiful that she was already becoming a legend in the Chinatis.

Thank heaven that Andrea was eighteen at last, although to Kate it was incredible that the years had passed so quickly. Eighteen, old enough to marry Henry Stockton if she ever got around to making her mind up to it, and to settle down and raise a brood of grandchildren for Kate and Adam to dote on.

Nothing would please Kate and Adam more. Of all

the young men who buzzed around her like bees maddened by nectar, Henry was the one they preferred, and he'd been trying to pin Andrea down for the last two years. Only Wayne Bradshaw came a close second in Andrea's favor, although Kate suspected that this exasperating daughter of hers used Wayne to keep Henry on tenterhooks for all that he was by far the handsomest of all the young men in the Big Bend. Half Spanish because his father, Clay Bradshaw, had married a Mexican girl, as had so many of the other ranchers in this district back when there were no other women available, Wayne's catlike grace and striking coloring came from his mother while the other half of him had all of the overbearing arrogance of his barrel-chested, belligerent father.

"Where's Mike?" Kate asked now, turning back to the vase of flowers as Manuella waddled back to her own domain, every round inch of her quivering with indignation. "Why don't you and he go for a ride so you can work off some of that over-excitement? You'd still have time enough to rest and bathe and dress before the first guests arrive."

"Mike's gone up to the mining settlement again. If I know him, he probably won't even show up for my party!" Andrea reached out to move a rose and Kate slapped at her hand.

"Then for pity's sake find something else to do! I've never seen you so wild, Andrea."

"But, Mother, I'm eighteen! Didn't you feel like this, on your eighteenth birthday?"

The look on her mother's face, although it was replaced immediately by a serene smile as Kate shook her head, made Andrea contrite. "I'm sorry, Mother. I forgot, just for a minute. I guess you couldn't have felt like this, could you?"

"Hardly." Kate's voice was dry. "When I was eighteen, I was coping with a ne'er-do-well father who fell into the bottle too often for comfort, and I'd never had a party in my life, nor even been to one. But there's no need to feel sorry for me, Dria. Those days are long past. I have your father now, and Wade and Michael and you, and

Trail's End. What happened to me when I was your age no longer matters."

She lifted her head again as she heard hoofbeats outside the house. "Oh, dear! Don't tell me someone's already arrived, and it isn't even noon! Go and see, Andrea, and if it's an early guest you'll just have to entertain whoever it is. At least it'll keep you out from underfoot."

Andrea went out onto the deep, vine-shaded patio that ran along the entire front of the Spanish-styled adobe *casa* just as Henry Stockton pulled his horse to a stop. Her hand went to her hair automatically. It had to be a mess, after all the running around she'd done all morning.

"Henry, darn it, why are you here so early?"

Henry sat there looking at her for a moment before he swung off and handed the reins to a barefooted Mexican boy who ran to take his horse. Flushed with excitement, her hair disheveled around her shoulders, she made his breath catch and his heart swell with almost unbearable pain just to see her. If he loved her any more, he'd die of it, and that was God's honest truth.

He'd loved her for years, even before he'd been old enough to fully realize what love between a man and a woman was all about, ever since he and his family had come to the Chinatis when he'd been only a gangling boy and Andrea a long-legged filly, as wild and free and beautiful as any unbroken colt on the range. They'd grown up together, as much as children could grow up together in this country where the ranches were so many miles apart. She was as much a part of him as his arms and his legs.

"I knew you'd be busting out of your skin. I thought we might ride, to help you pass the time till your party."

Kate appeared in the opened doorway, and she drew a breath of relief.

"Yes, Dria, for goodness sake do! Henry, keep her away from the house for two or three hours, before she drives us all insane. Have you brought your clothes? Just put them in Mike's room; you can get ready for the party there. You must have second sight, to show up just when we need you!"

Henry's eyes, a clear hazel under sun-bleached brows that matched his brown hair, looked at Kate appreciatively. Andrea would look like that, years from now, once she'd matured and lost that wildness of hers that drove him frantic. Unruffled in spite of the party preparations, not a strand of hair escaping from the loose French knot at the nape of her neck, Kate was still breathtakingly beautiful, and it was his good fortune that Andrea looked exactly like her.

"But Mother, I have to see about the paper streamers in the barn, and make sure the men are watching the barbecue pit, and—"

"You're going riding," Kate said, her voice final. "Now scat! Henry, you'd better take a fresh horse from the corral; yours would never be able to keep up with Runner after it's come so far, and the mood Dria's in, she'll take some keeping up with."

"Right," Henry said. "I'll keep a rope on her and see that she gets back all in one piece."

As busy as she was, Kate took the time to stand on the patio and watch as Andrea and Henry rode off, Henry on the fresh horse she'd suggested and Andrea on her own Roadrunner, the Appaloosa that Adam had given her for her sixteenth birthday. Runner's hindquarters were the most perfectly mottled of any Appy that Kate had ever seen; his muscles rippled with power, his vertically striped hooves were capable of outrunning any horse on the place except Adam's own Beau Noir, whom even Andrea had never been permitted to ride. Adam had chosen Runner to be as much horse as Andrea was a girl, and that was saying a lot.

Kate only hoped that in her present mood and with Runner under her, Hank would be able to keep up with her. Then she smiled and shook her head, going back to all the details that still had to be seen to to assure the success of this party. Nothing would happen to Andrea. She'd all but been born astride a horse, and Henry would make sure that she didn't come to grief, no matter how wild a mood she was in.

16

Astride Runner, her hair stuffed up any which way beneath her white Stetson, Andrea let the horse have his head, exulting in leaving Henry behind as Runner caught her mood and flattened out into an all-out gallop. If Hank had been on his own horse, and it was fresh, she'd have had a harder time outdistancing him, but this time, as an extra, added birthday present, she would win the race with no effort. It was exactly the way she felt today, her eighteenth birthday, that no one could catch her, that she was as free as one of Texas's golden eagles. Eighteen was the most wonderful age in a lifetime, more wonderful even than being twenty-one because twenty-one was too old, too grown up, while eighteen was the promise of everything that was to come, old enough to grasp every delight that life had to offer and not too old to enjoy it.

She drew up at last and sat laughing while Hank caught up with her, his lean face filled with exasperation.

"Dria, cut it out! Kate'll be darned put out with me if I have to carry you back to Trail's End with a broken leg!"

"Pooh!" Andrea swept off her hat and let her hair fall free, and Hank's breath caught, choking off the rest of what he had been going to say. This was the way he loved to see her, with her hair free and her face flushed with excitement, with her eyes shining and her mouth parted with laughter, deliciously curved, soft and warm and ripe with her awakening womanhood, although God knew that Dria had been woman enough for him or any other man since she'd been sixteen.

"Just because it's your birthday and Adam and Kate are throwing you the biggest shindig that the Chinatis have ever seen is no reason to act as if you've taken leave of your senses."

"Pooh!" Andrea said again. You're only a man, so what would you know? A man isn't grown up until he's twenty-one but a girl's grown up when she's eighteen."

"I'm twenty, almost twenty-one, and I won't go hog-wild on my twenty-first birthday. If you're so all-fired grown up why don't you act it? Right now you look about fourteen." The heck she looked about fourteen. It was all he could do not to climb off his horse and haul her off

17

Runner and treat her like the woman she claimed she was. But Dria didn't like being hauled around and manhandled, it made her so mad there was no controlling her and only made him lose ground instead of advancing his cause whenever he lost his head enough to try it.

So he kept a firm rein on his emotions, holding them in check. "Dria, I came over early because I want to talk to you. You're right about being grown up. I haven't pushed you too hard up till now because you were so young, but you're old enough now to start settling down. It's about time you gave me an answer."

Andrea's face tightened with annoyance. "Hank, don't go spoiling things, today of all days! I'm not ready to get married. I'm only eighteen!" The fact that she was contradicting what she'd just said about being grown up didn't enter her mind. "I don't want to get serious about anyone yet, even you."

Henry's face also tightened, but with pain rather than with annoyance. "I love you. I've loved you ever since I can remember. I can't go on waiting forever. Your mother and father would be tickled if we let them announce our engagement tonight, at your party. You know as well as I do that I'm the one they want you to marry. We've always known it would happen, ever since we were kids."

"Maybe you have, but I haven't!" Andrea faced him defiantly, hating the tell-tale flush that gave away that she was lying. "There's more to life than getting married and raising a herd of children, a whole lot more! I guess getting married doesn't mean that much of a change for a man, but for a girl it's the end of everything. A girl is tied down the minute she lets that ring be put on her finger, with housework and cooking and having babies, and never another minute she can call her own as long as she lives."

"Housework and cooking!" Henry stared at her, torn between laughing and anger. "A heck of a lot of housework and cooking you'd have to do! Our place is staffed almost as well as Trail's End, we can't turn around without stumbling over a servant, so where's all that housework and cooking you're complaining about?"

"There's still the babies. A mother is just a mother, she isn't herself any more, she's a wife and a mother."

"Kate's a wife and a mother. Do you think she feels like that? My mother doesn't, and Kate doesn't, either. It's what a woman's supposed to be, Dria. You can't change nature to suit yourself, even if you are Andrea Wentworth!"

"And that's why I'm in no hurry to tie myself down! Hank, do you realize that I've never been out of Texas in my whole life? I was born right here at Trail's End, and there are places to go and things to see and things to do that I'd never get to go and see and do once I was married and started having babies. I couldn't bear it, I couldn't. Not even for you."

That last was more of an admission than she'd meant to make. She did love Hank. He was a part of her life, so much a part of it that she couldn't imagine him not being a part of it. She supposed she'd marry him some day, but not yet, please not yet! There was something inside her that cried out that she hadn't even lived yet. Why, she'd scarcely scratched the surface! If she married now, she'd feel all the rest of her life that she'd been cheated, that she'd let life slip through her fingers without making an effort to grasp it and hold it and savor it to the last drop.

"Hank, don't!" she said. "Don't spoil things for me today, please don't. I'm just not ready." She *was* ready—at least half of her cried out that she'd never be complete until she and Hank were married, until they could have more than the kisses, the caresses, that they indulged in whenever she'd allow it, whenever that wild yearning inside her let Hank hold her in his arms and show her a little of what it would be like to have it all. But the other half still strained at the bit, wanting to be free, wanting to soar, wanting to know more of life than just marriage and babies.

"And in the meantime, every unmarried man in this territory is trying to undercut me, to take you away from me! Wayne Bradshaw's hell-bent to get you, and sometimes I think he's succeeding, and I can't take much more of it."

"Not Wayne, either, any more than you! And don't you dare to start a fight with him tonight, or I'll never speak to you again as long as I live!"

Henry's face tightened even more. "Then he'd better stay away from you. It isn't as if every other girl in the Chinatis isn't after him. He can have his pick, as long as it isn't you."

"Why do you have to be so jealous?" Andrea cried. "I don't tell you who you can see, what friends you can have!"

"I'm jealous because I love you and Wayne's out to get you. I'm sorry if it bothers you, but that's the way it is." Looking at her face, filled with fear that her party might be spoiled, he softened. "All right, Dria. I promise I won't pick a fight with him if you'll promise not to encourage him."

"Why should I have to make any promises at all? I don't belong to you, Hank Stockton, even if you think I do!" Andrea jammed her hat back on her head and kicked Runner, who needed no further encouragement to take off again, his Appaloosa stamina not in the least depleted because of their earlier run.

Sighing, his mouth tight, Henry set off after her. He'd waited for Andrea to be eighteen for a long time, but now it looked as if he was going to have to wait some more. He just couldn't seem to lasso her; she always managed to elude him, to refuse, at the last moment, to be branded and tamed. His disappointment was a sharp ache inside of him. In the excitement of this day, he'd had a real hope that Andrea would admit that they belonged together, that she'd promise to marry him, and that the marriage would take place sometime in the reasonably near future. It wouldn't be as hard to wait if they were engaged, if he was sure of her.

But there she was, putting Runner to his fastest pace to get away from him again, to keep from being cornered into giving him an answer. If this party of hers tonight had turned into a combination birthday and engagement party, he'd have been the happiest man in Texas. No, dammit, he'd have been the happiest man in the world! He felt like catching her and shaking her until her teeth rattled; he felt like holding her and kissing her until her bones melted and every drop of resistance drained out of her. Instead, he contented himself with keeping up with her, making sure that she got back to the *casa* all in one piece, as he'd promised Kate.

He had no idea that keeping just far enough ahead of him so that he couldn't catch up with her, Andrea's heart and mind were in turmoil. Damn Hank Stockton, damn him anyway! Every time he looked at her the way he'd looked at her just now, every time he kissed her, she came nearer to throwing caution to the winds and accepting him. Just looking at him did something to her insides that frightened her, because she wasn't ready for it yet. There'd been times, more times than Hank had ever guessed and that she liked to think about, when she'd been so close to giving in that it wasn't funny. If Hank had been a different sort of man, one who'd press his advantage when her resistance was at its lowest, she'd have already been committed to marry him because she'd have lost her virginity. Why was being a girl so hard, why did a girl dream and long for more than nature ever intended for her to have, a man, a home, children?

Hearing her daughter storm into the house, seeing Hank follow close on her heels with his face set and grim, Kate sighed. Like Hank, she'd hoped that tonight Andrea would make up her mind to have him, so that she could set her mind to rest about this daughter of hers and no longer have the fear that Andrea would make the wrong choice and ruin her life. It wasn't to be, at least not tonight. But it was Andrea's life; both she and Adam were careful to allow all three of their children all the freedom they could, including the freedom to make their own choices. Right at the moment there was nothing she could do except hope that whatever Dria and Hank had quarreled about, it wasn't serious enough to spoil Andrea's party.

21

Jacob Renault, Adam's younger half-brother, detected uneasiness in Kate's eyes as she made her way to where he stood in the archway to the living room, his height and his broad shoulders making it easy for her to spot him even through the crowd of people that filled the room.

Kate was wearing garnet satin, and the color became her creamy skin and dark hair. The gown had been sent from Worth's, made to her exact measurements, but she wore no jewels outside of her wedding ring and the strand of perfectly matched pearls that Adam had given her when they were married. Kate didn't need jewels, she was the jewel, even though her lack of them astonished the other wealthy ranchers' wives, knowing as they did that among his other assets Adam still owned a fine jewelry store in Boston, part of his inheritance from his father. Lord, but she was beautiful, her figure as good as it had been when Jacob had first known her when he'd come west to join Adam way back in '85.

"Jacob, Wayne Bradshaw is here, and he and Henry have been circling each other like two hostile dogs, and Dria's upset because she knows that both of them are going to ask her again, tonight, if they can corner her, to marry them. If we get through this evening without an explosion, it'll be a miracle!"

"Now, Kate, Dria just isn't through kicking up her heels yet, she's still only a filly. Henry'll throw a rope over her yet. I wouldn't worry about Wayne if I were you, she has too much sense to tie herself up with that arrogant, conceited young bast—" Jacob bit off the last of the word he'd almost said and looked at Kate apologetically. "Well, if we're going to be technical, he isn't because his mother and father are married, but all the same you know what I mean. But I wouldn't go borrowing trouble, Kate. Even Henry and Wayne will have better sense than to cause trouble on a night like this. And I'll keep a sharp eye on them, just in case."

He spoke with more conviction than he felt. Kate was right about the trouble that might erupt before the evening was over, with both of those young hotheads after

22

Dria like dogs after a bitch in heat. Dria was trying to walk a tightrope to keep them from each other's throats, but she was so determined not to let Henry stampede her into saying yes that she didn't use her common sense when it came to showing him that she could pick and choose.

Jacob's roving eyes caught Wade, as Kate's oldest moved up to Henry to talk to him. Now there was a fine-looking boy, and Jacob was proud to call him nephew. Right at the moment, he couldn't locate Mike in the throng, let alone Wayne Bradshaw, so he started edging his way through the guests to where Wade and Henry were talking to see if either of them knew where Wayne was. With Kate so worried and his own mind far from at ease, he'd like to know where everybody was at any given moment so he could keep his eyes peeled for trouble.

He'd no sooner worked his way through to them than his daughter Natalie threw herself against him, her pointed, nine-year-old face alight with excitement.

"Daddy, you got here! Did you get him? Can I have his pelt for my room? Can I?"

"Now, Nattie, what's your mother told you a thousand times about your grammar? May I!"

"Well, can I?"

Jacob ruffled her curls, as fair as his lovely wife Barbara's. He'd been late in arriving because he'd been hunting the *lobo* that had been preying on the young stock for a few weeks, a particularly big and cunning one that the stockmen had named Big Black. "Sorry. Burke's already laid a claim to it."

"That's all right, then. He'll give it to me if I ask him." Natalie couldn't stop jumping from excitement. "Burke always gives me his stuff if I ask him, he isn't like that selfish old Ron! Why did I have to have two brothers, anyway? Burke's the only one I need."

"Where's the birthday girl? I haven't seen her yet."

"She's dancing with Wayne, I think, out on the patio."

Beside Jacob, Wade's fair eyebrows went up, and Henry's darker ones increased their scowl as his expression turned black. Most of the younger people had already gravitated to the patio, where half a dozen guitars were furnishing music for them to dance by under the light of the paper lanterns. Excusing himself, Henry headed that way, barely nodding in apology to the older people he was forced to jostle in his rush to see if Dria was actually dancing with Wayne.

Natalie giggled, the sound high and shrill. "It won't do him any good to go out there. Dria isn't going to dance with him, she told me so. She's mad at him because he told her she mustn't dance with Wayne."

"It's none of your business, Nattie. Why don't you go find your mother, or some of the younger children to play with?"

"I'd rather go outside and see the fight," Natalie said, her eyes sparkling with anticipation.

"There isn't going to be a fight. This is a party." But Jacob was already shouldering his own way through the crowd, and Wade was right behind him, taking advantage of the wake he created with his shoulders. Somebody ought to shake Dria's teeth loose! If she was determined to punish Hank by not dancing with him tonight, then she ought to have more sense than to dance with Wayne. His face set, Jacob barged through the smiling, talking guests without seeing them, intent only on getting out to the patio before all hell busted loose.

As fast as he and Wade moved, Natalie was ahead of them, because she was so small that she could wriggle through where they had to force a passage. By the time Jacob and Wade stepped out onto the vine-enclosed patio, Natalie was already jumping up and down with an excitement that surpassed her excitement of a moment before.

"There they are, Daddy, see?"

It wasn't necessary for her to point. Anyone could see, because the other young couples had all stopped dancing and were holding their breath as Henry and Wayne, with furious, white faced Dria between them, glared at each other in a pregnant silence broken now only by Wayne's contemptuous drawl.

"Stockton, you heard the lady. She doesn't want to dance with you, so why don't you climb on your horse and go on home? You aren't wanted here."

Wayne's arm was around Dria's waist, insolently

possessive, and that was all that Henry needed to make him explode.

"Get your hands off her! Dria, you come with me, we have something to settle!"

"We haven't anything to settle, Henry Stockton, and you stop making a scene!"

But Henry was too far gone in his anger to hear her. The sight of Wayne's arm still around the girl he'd loved ever since they'd been yearlings made the patio dissolve in a red haze in front of his eyes. He lunged forward like a maddened bull and grasped Wayne's arm and threw it off Andrea with such force that Wayne staggered.

"Here now, you two young hotheads, quit it!" Jacob bellowed.

"Henry, Wayne, come on inside and have a drink and cool off!" Wade's authoritative voice backed his uncle up.

They might as well have been talking to the wind. Recovering his balance, Wayne lashed out with his balled fist and Henry staggered as it clipped his jaw. If he hadn't seen it coming and jerked his head he'd have been down and the fight would have been over.

A dozen girls in billowing, pastel party dresses screamed with real or feigned fright while their partners surged forward, some of them intent on breaking up the fight while others egged the two combatants on. Fight! Nothing was dearer to the hearts of these young Texans, and this fight was a relief from circling the patio with even the prettiest of girls, perspiring in their unaccustomed suits and ties and feeling like fish out of water at being on a dance floor instead of on the backs of their horses.

In the commotion, Natalie was knocked down, but she scrambled to her feet again, screaming along with the older girls, completely oblivious to the fact that both of her knees were skinned and bleeding all over the ruffled dress that her mother had spent all of last week finishing in time for this party.

"Hit him, Henry! Knock him down and stomp him!" Natalie shrilled.

The two rivals needed no encouragement from the onlookers. One of Wayne's eyes was already swelling shut, and blood dribbled from Henry's split lip. As fast as he

25

moved, and he moved with incredible speed considering his size, Jacob, the biggest man in all of that section of Texas, couldn't reach the original combatants before half a dozen other young mavericks had plunged into the fight. Side by side, he and Wade dived into the melee to reach the core of it, Jacob to wrap his gorilla-like arms around Henry and drag him off, Wade to try to control the equally maddened Wayne.

"That's enough!" The voice lashed out like a steel-tipped whip. "I want this patio cleared in five seconds, and I mean all of you! Henry, Wayne, just calm down. I'll have no fighting in my home, and you'd better believe I mean it!"

Tall, panther-lithe, as dangerously powerful as he'd been in his youth, Adam's authority broke through even Henry and Wayne's fury. They still glared at each other so venomously that Jacob was thankful that no one had worn guns to this shindig, but they stopped struggling against their captors as the other disappointed combatants also fell apart, grinning sheepishly while they nursed their own black eyes or wiped dribbles of blood from their faces.

Only Dria disregarded her father's lashing voice. "Darn you, Henry Stockton! You've ruined my party, you've ruined everything! Go home, get out of here, I never want to see you again!"

In spite of his swollen eye and a rapidly swelling bruise on his cheek, Wayne grinned. "You see? You should have got on your horse and made tracks out of here when I told you!"

Andrea turned on him now, her eyes blazing with such fury that he took an involuntary step backward and trod on Wade's foot. "And that goes for you, too, Wayne Bradshaw! I never want to see either of you again! Go on, get out of here so the rest of us can enjoy my party!"

Kate was there by then, standing beside Adam, completely in control of herself. "Andrea, you'd better go and bathe your face, you're flushed. And Henry and Wayne, I think you'd better take my daughter's advice and leave. At the risk of being a poor hostess, I suggest that you'd both better stay away for a few days until Andrea has had a chance to calm down."

The patio began to clear, the girls to gather in one group to talk excitedly about the fight, some of them to wish, secretly, that it had been over them instead of over Dria, and the young men heading for liquid refreshments to drown their disappointment that the fight had been broken up so promptly. With Adam escorting Henry to his horse and Wade escorting Wayne, it looked as if the excitement was over, at least for this evening. Adam, not being a fool, instructed two of his vaqueros to escort both Henry and Wayne home to make sure that they didn't tangle again before they reached their respective ranches. Wayne had come to the party alone, but Henry's mother and father and two sisters had no intention of being cheated out of such a gala affair, so they were content to let Henry go on home without them, laughing about the ruckus as if it were only natural.

Natalie sighed. Golly, in another minute Henry would have licked Wayne, and she wished that her father and Cousin Wade hadn't broke it up. It wasn't every day that you got to see a good fight. Being only nine years old, she hadn't seen nearly enough of them to satisfy her, unless she counted the fights between her brothers, and they weren't anywhere near as good.

She jumped as a heavy hand descended on her shoulder, and then she laughed up at her father. "There! Didn't I tell you there was going to be a fight, didn't I tell you? You shouldn't have stopped them, you spoiled all the fun!"

Jacob was speechless as he looked down into his daughter's innocently joyous face. "Go find your mother," he finally managed to get out. Lord, if he didn't miss his guess, there'd be hell to pay as soon as Henry and Wayne came face to face again. And just wait till this imp of a daughter of his grew up to Dria's age! He didn't relish the prospect.

Sighing, he headed inside himself, shooing his reluctant daughter ahead of him, in search of some of what the younger men were drinking to calm themselves down after all the excitement.

2

Henry wasn't sure of what kind of a reception he'd receive when he rode over to Trail's End three days after Andrea's birthday party. Just as likely as not, not only Dria but Kate and Adam would tell him to turn his horse around and haul out of there, without even letting him through their front door.

But he couldn't let things rest the way they were. Andrea had been angry with him before, more times than he could count, but this was by far the most serious rift they'd ever had. He had to at least try to make it up with her before she decided that now he was gone, she could do without him. Even as it was, Wayne might have gotten there ahead of him.

He was therefore pleasantly surprised when Dria herself met him as he stepped up onto the patio. All signs of the party had been removed; not even a paper streamer marred the neatness of the grounds.

Andrea was dressed for riding, wearing a divided

skirt and one of Mike's shirts because she insisted that men's shirts were better because they had longer tails that didn't work out, an annoyance that only women had to put up with. Henry's mouth almost fell open with surprise at her greeting.

"Hank! I was just going to ride over to see you, and here you are!" She linked her arm in his, as companionable as if their quarrel had never happened. "No, you won't need a fresh horse. I have to talk to you, so we'll only go as far as the orchard."

What the devil! But Henry went along with her. It was obvious that she wanted privacy for what she had to say, and his heart began beating rapidly. Had she come to her senses, was she going to tell him, at last, that she would marry him?

Adam's peach orchard was famous throughout the entire Chinati region. The trees bore abundant fruit, not only for the table but with enough left over to make peach brandy that a good many people said was the best they had ever tasted. It was one of their favorite places, sheltered out of sight of other people, affording complete privacy when they wanted to be alone. She and Henry had spent a fair part of their lives there, sometimes quarreling, sometimes simply talking, and sometimes ending up with Henry having to use every ounce of control he possessed to leave Dria's virtue intact before they left for some safer place where temptation couldn't be so easily given in to.

Now they sat with their backs against the trunks of the old peach trees, the leaves already mature enough to offer welcome shade. It was more romantic earlier in the spring, when they were in bloom, but Henry wasn't going to complain about the lack of the sight and scent of the blossoms if Dria was going to tell him what he wanted to hear.

He waited. It never paid to try to hurry her. She didn't like to be pushed, even if it was into something she intended to do anyway.

Andrea wrapped her arms around her knees, looking at him with her face flushed with some inner excitement but with an odd reluctance in her eyes that made Henry feel uneasy.

"Hank, I was going to ride over to tell you that I'm going away."

A ball of cold settled around Henry's heart. Going away? But that was crazy. Where could she go? If she were younger he'd be afraid that Kate and Adam had finally succumbed to the trend of sending daughters east to some fashionable school for young ladies, but she was eighteen now and this was the beginning of summer, not of a school term. It wouldn't have been likely, anyway. There wouldn't have been much left of one of those fancy schools after Dria got through with it; she'd give the teachers fits.

Andrea waited, and when there was no immediate response, she lost her patience.

"Haven't you anything to say? I'm going away, Hank, I'm going to Georgia, I'm going to Roselawns!"

"Roselawns?" In his shock, Henry couldn't think, and Andrea had to prompt his memory.

"Roselawns, the Beddoes plantation! I've told you about it a hundred times, and so has Uncle Jacob. Why, all my life I've dreamed of going there, of actually seeing it for myself!"

"But why?" Henry remembered that Dria had talked about it a lot, but he'd never thought that she'd actually go. "Why would anybody want to go to Georgia when they could stay here in Texas?"

"Henry Stockton, you make me sick! Why, our family is all tied up with the Beddoeses and with Roselawns—it's where our roots are! My great-aunt Prudence is there, and her husband Burke, who Jacob's Burke is named after. And my cousin Naomi and my cousin Michael. Half-aunt and half-cousins, actually, because Prudence is only Father's half-aunt; his mother was Prue's half-sister. It's all terribly involved, but it's family, and Roselawns is a genuine Southern plantation, it's been in the family for generations and Aunt Prue has been begging and begging us to come, and now we're going to do it."

"Roots! Your roots are right here, in the Chinatis.

Your father and your uncle built their places up from nothing, they came here when the region was hardly even settled."

"I know. Uncle Jacob never gets tired of telling us about it, how he came out here in '85, when Dad and Mother were hardly moved into the big house. How it was all wide open, with state-owned land going for a dollar an acre and watered land for two dollars and timbered land for five, and all anybody wanted to lease for four cents an acre. And Dad had already slapped his brand here on a hundred thousand acres, where springs guarantee a sure water supply and the land is so fertile it'll grow anything."

She closed her eyes, remembering, because she never tired of hearing about it any more than Jacob tired of telling it. There hadn't been any law then, and there'd been wild longhorns all over the place so that any man who could latch onto them and keep the ornery critters from busting loose and taking off yonder could get a start with nothing but his two hands, a good rope, and a branding iron.

There hadn't been any barbed wire, or any windmills to draw up water to fill huge watering tanks. Uncle Jacob had been a cocksure, green-as-grass kid from Georgia, and he'd taken his lumps until his greenness had been knocked out of him, helping Adam establish Trail's End, and then he'd gotten his own place and married Aunt Barbara and had Burke and Michael and Natalie.

It had been the year of the Big Die that Jacob had come out, hell-bent to join the half-brother he worshiped as a hero, a real Westerner who'd punched cattle and been in gunfights. Jonathan Beddoes, Adam's grandfather and Jacob's, too, had come with him in spite of being so old that he'd fought in the Civil War when he'd been in his forties.

Every mile they'd traveled, Jacob and Jonathan had been appalled by the sight of dead and dying cattle, by gaunt-faced men going down to defeat after having spent all their lives building up their ranches and battling sun and rattlers and rustlers and everything else Texas could throw at them, only to be forced out, at the last, by a drought that seemed to have no end.

"The Big Bend? Man, you're *loco!* No sane man would go in there, much less try to settle there. If your grandson took his wife in there he must be stark, raving insane!"

If they'd heard that once, they'd heard it a dozen times, until they'd almost been afraid to look at or talk to each other for fear of what they'd find when they finally reached their destination.

"Why, man, that country's so crazy you have to dig for wood if you want to get warm, and climb for water if you're thirsty! There's nothing there but rattlers, *lobos,* javalina, cactus, and Mexicans who can't afford to pull out!"

But then, at their journey's end, they'd found this place, the Chinati Mountain region. They'd found Adam's ranch, that he'd named Trail's End even if it was such a common, ordinary name, because it meant exactly how he felt about the place after his years of wandering, feeling himself an exile from all the rest of humanity after that old scandal had knocked his life from its foundations and exploded in his face.

Situated hell and gone from nowhere, almost impossible to get to, the Big Bend country comprised seven million acres of canyon, mountains, and desert, cradled in the big bend of the Rio Grande in western Texas, jutting down into the Mexican states of Chihuahua and Coahuila.

It had still been largely populated by Mexicans. The American men who had the fortitude to reach the Big Bend and settle there had nearly all married Mexican women. Even their trading had to be done in Mexican settlements across the border because any settlement worthy of the name on the American side was too far to travel to.

Outside of that, the old-timers who'd warned Jacob and Jonathan about the area had been dead wrong. It was true that wood was scarce in the lower regions, and their story of having to dig for it was because the roots of the mesquite ran for incredible distances underground in search of water. But there was wood and water enough in the mountains, in sheltered valleys. It was far enough south so that it escaped the devastating blizzards the northern Texans had to fight; it was high enough so that it escaped the equally devastating heat of Texas summers. And the men who had the courage to find it and settle here carved out vast ranches for themselves, created individual empires to hand down to their children and their children's children.

There weren't any longhorns any more; it was all Herefords now. Adam had been the first to bring them in and then to see the need for fences to hold them. The open range was gone; barbed wire took its place. But Hank was right about one thing. Andrea's roots were here, and they went deep, and she was as proud of her father and Uncle Jacob and other men like them as Henry was of his family's part in it. Trail's End covered five hundred thousand acres now, and Uncle Jacob had two hundred and fifty thousand acres and the Stocktons as much.

Kate had helped build it, too; she'd worked like a man, she'd headed a trail drive before the railroad came, when Adam was laid up, she'd flapped her slicker in the faces of stampeding cattle to turn them, she'd hunted *lobos* and panthers, and she could still bring down one of the golden eagles that preyed on young stock, dropping it from the sky with a single rifle shot even if she hated having to kill something so beautiful and free.

She'd stretched fence, she'd run the place single-handed when Adam had been off chasing rustlers, she'd fought down neighbors' opposition when she'd taught Trail's End's vaqueros and their families to read and write. She'd nursed the sick, she'd stood her ground and shot and killed a charging javalina when she and Adam had been hunting and Adam's gun had misfired, and then got off another shot to kill the sow that was charging in right behind the boar.

And she'd had three children in between times, before the ranch had been so well established that she could remain at the *casa* and let her hands become soft and white, Doña Catherine now, the lady of the hacienda.

It was a heritage to be proud of, and Andrea was proud of it, so proud that it made a lump come into her throat whenever she thought about it. But there was Rose-lawns too, Roselawns! All the romance of the antebellum period, all the glory of the Civil War, all the agony of the Reconstruction. Trail's End's *casa* was beautiful, but how could it possibly be as beautiful as the white-pillared house at Roselawns that Uncle Jacob had told her about ever since she was old enough to listen; how could her heritage here be anywhere near as romantic as the story of Martha, who'd married Jonathan and then gone back to Massachusetts and become a famous abolitionist? Or as romantic as Prudence, Martha's daughter, who'd had to wait for years, until she was old, in her forties, to meet Burke again, the man she'd loved for all those years, and marry him? Or as romantic as Rebecca, Andrea's great-grandmother, who'd left Roselawns and ended up, as a very old lady, in France, the Countess de la Roche and one of Paris's most celebrated hostesses, invitations to her salon eagerly vied for by the most important of people?

"I never can keep it all straight, all that about Rose-lawns and Swanmere, back there." Henry frowned.

"You could if you'd paid as much attention to Uncle Jacob's stories as I have. I love Trail's End, Hank, and I love the Chinatis, but all of my life I've felt as if I'm only half a person, that the other half of me has never existed because I've never seen Roselawns, and Swanmere, where Uncle Jacob was born and lived until he was in his teens, because I've never been back to where the other half of me came from."

"If you're so all-fired to go back there, we could go there on our honeymoon," Henry told her stubbornly. "I'd take as much time as you wanted; there's plenty of money and Dad could spare me."

Andrea's eyes turned darker, filled with pain. "But it wouldn't be the same. Can't you even try to understand? It wouldn't be the same at all, if I were married. This is something that belongs to me alone. I have to live it, or I'll never be satisfied."

In his hurt at the shattering news that she was going

away, Henry exploded. "Who on God's green earth could have done more living than you've already done right here in Texas? You're the most alive person I've ever known! You never would stay put the way a girl's supposed to, you were always into something, getting in trouble. Don't you remember how you and Mike decided to go into the high mountains hunting, when you were only twelve and thirteen? Adam and Wade had gone but they wouldn't take you two, so you threw some grub into your saddlebags and took off all by yourselves. Your mother was nursing some of your vaquero's children who had the measles, so she didn't know you'd gone, but I happened to ride over and I trailed you and never came up with you till the next morning. You were both scared half out of your wits after listening to *lobos* howling and panthers prowling all night and half dead from lack of sleep because you'd kept a big enough fire going to burn the whole darned woods down! But you wouldn't admit you were glad to see me, not for a minute."

"And Mother met us, halfway down, looking for us herself, and she didn't even give us a licking because she said we'd been punished enough by being frightened. She just made us promise never to do it again."

"Maybe you never did that again, but there were plenty of other things you did do! Like Mike catching that rattler and trying to tame it, just to see if it could be done. You were helping him poke meat to it in that cage Mike had built when I caught you, even if you both knew darned well that it wouldn't eat anything that wasn't alive."

"I was mad at you for weeks for shooting it!" Andrea remembered, laughing.

"Dammit, those fangs came within a quarter of an inch of your hand when you were trying to feed it! All I could think was that you might have been bitten, you might have died. Of course I shot it! What did you expect me to do, let you go on taking your life in your hands?"

"We were monsters." Andrea admitted. "And you were always having to get us out of trouble. Do you remember when Mike and I decided to dig a cave, and it caved in on us? If you hadn't been with us that day, Mike wouldn't have got out alive. I never could have pulled him out by myself."

"I told you two idiots that it would cave in, but you insisted on going right on digging anyway," Henry said, his voice showing his disgust.

"All the same, you didn't have to slap me so hard once we got Mike out! My face had a red mark on it for two days!"

"I was mad. And you deserved it. I'd have hit Mike, too, if he hadn't still been spitting out sand and dirt."

"We were as crazy as loons. I don't know why you put up with us. I don't know why you still do, but I'm glad you do. When I think of all the times you saved our lives, there just isn't any way to thank you. What would I have done if Mike had managed to kill himself, with my help?"

Andrea's tone reflected the special love she had for her brother. Mike was special to her; there was a bond between them so strong that they might have been the twins that Hank had used to call them. The Terrible Twins, he'd say, when he was particularly angry with them.

"Dria, don't go! I have a bad feeling about it, I have a feeling that you'll never come back."

"That's silly. Of course I'll come back! And I'd have to go even if I didn't want to, because Mother and Dad have decided that if they don't ship me out for a while you and Wayne, or even some others, will end up killing each other over me. They want me to have time to think, away from here so that I can make up my mind whom I want to marry. They think that being back there will gentle me down so I won't always be in the center of some storm. Mother's going with me, of course. They wouldn't dream of letting me go alone. And you know that Mother will come back to Dad, so of course I'll come back, too!"

"All the same, I don't want you to go." Henry rose to his feet, his eyes more bleak than Andrea had ever seen them. He reached down and pulled her to her feet as well, so that she was facing him, and then he had her in his arms. He was kissing her savagely, violently, with all the years of dammed-up emotions breaking out at the thought of her

36

going away, because he had this gut feeling that she'd never come back to him.

For a moment, all the strength seemed to go out of Andrea's body, and she clung to him, returning his kisses as if she were as afraid of never seeing him again as he was afraid of losing her. Maybe he was right, maybe she was crazy to go, when she could settle all the controversy over her by marrying him right away.

He held her pressed against the entire hard length of his body. His hands were possessive, demanding. She belonged to him, she always had, he wasn't about to allow her to go away, he had to make her see it. Her hat fell off, and her hair, as usual simply tucked up under it when she was in too much of a hurry to plait it for riding, fell in a tangled halo around her shoulders. She felt lightheaded; she couldn't breathe. It would be so easy to surrender, and then her whole future, all the rest of her life, would be safe and assured right here where she had been born.

But then she would never know what lay beyond the horizon that had tantalized her ever since she was a child. Some combination of genes inherited from her ancestors roiled in her blood and kept her forever restless, reaching out for more and still more. She had to know it all, experience it all! One lifetime wasn't long enough to do all the things and see all the things and experience all the things that something inside her demanded that she do and see and experience. No matter how much she loved Hank, no matter how much a part of her he was, she'd always feel cheated, feel that she had thrown away her only chance.

At the last possible instant when withdrawal was still possible, she gathered her strength and pushed at Hank's chest, struggling to free herself from his arms.

"Hank, stop it, stop it this minute! You aren't going to get around me that way. You always think you can make me do whatever you want just by kissing me till I can't think straight. It isn't fair, I'm not going to let you get away with it! We have all our lives ahead of us, we don't have to get married this minute. I won't be cheated of this trip. If you love me as much as you say you do, you wouldn't want to cheat me of it!"

In another moment she was in her saddle, lifting Runner into a headlong gallop toward home. Seeing her daughter's stormy face as Andrea rushed into the house and to her own room, Kate caught back the question she had been going to ask, how Henry had taken the news that they were going away for the summer. Obviously he hadn't taken it well, and they'd quarreled again. It was just as well that they were going to be separated for a while. Maybe by the time she came back, they'd both realize how much they meant to each other, and Andrea would be ready to marry him and settled down at last.

Three days later, they were ready to leave. Wade had gone into town the day after the party, to send a telegram to Roselawns and wait for an answer. Their luggage had gone to town in the buckboard yesterday. Adam and Mike would escort Andrea and Kate, on horseback, to town to take the train that would start them on their journey.

Andrea was in her room, making sure that her hair, plaited and pinned at the back of her neck, would stay reasonably in place. Kate was always so neat, so perfectly groomed, that Andrea didn't want to disgrace her on such an important occasion as this.

She told herself, for the hundredth time, that she didn't care if Hank had made no attempt to overtake her during her mad gallop back home after their quarrel in the peach orchard. She told herself that she was glad he hadn't come to Trail's End to try to persuade her not to go, since then.

But she'd been so sure he'd come! Angrily, she poked at a strand of hair that persisted in trying to escape its severe restriction. She wasn't going to cry, she refused to cry! If that was the way he was going to be, then it was a good thing she'd found it out before it was too late. Imagine being tied for life to a man who wanted to own you and boss you as if you had no rights of your own!

Mike rapped three sharp raps on her bedroom door, his own private signal meaning that if she wasn't decent she'd better throw a wrapper on in a hurry because he was coming in.

"Hank's in the orchard. He'll wait for you, if you want to see him." Mike didn't tell her that he himself had ridden over to the Stocktons' to persuade Hank that Andrea really wanted to see him before she left. "You'd better hurry, you don't have much time."

"He can wait forever, for all of me!" Andrea snapped. The gall of him, waiting until the last minute like this! She wasn't going, she wouldn't give him the satisfaction of thinking that she'd come running every time he whistled! But her face flushed and in another second she'd dashed past her brother.

"I saddled Runner for you!" Mike yelled after her. "Don't be too long."

He grinned, his Irish face filled with satisfaction. There was no way he'd been going to let Dria go off to Georgia without making up with Hank. He couldn't do without either of them, and they had to be together.

Henry watched her coming, not quite believing that she'd actually come. He reached up to help her dismount, and then she was in his arms, crushed against him, her bones almost grinding with the force of his embrace. His mouth came down over hers, and she began to cry even while she returned his kiss with every ounce of feeling in her.

"Dria, why do we do this to each other?" Henry demanded, only to kiss her again before she could answer.

She couldn't have answered him anyway, because she didn't know. It just seemed that sparks began to fly of their own accord whenever they were together. It had to be her fault. She loved him, but there was this contrary streak in her that she couldn't subdue; it always came to the surface and spoiled things. But this last time had come near to being a disaster.

"Promise me you'll come back! Promise me, Dria!"

"Of course I'll come back! Oh, Hank, all of a sudden I don't want to go! I don't want to leave you. . . ."

They sank to the ground, their bodies still crushed against each other, their mouths, their arms, their hands frantic with loving each other, with wanting, frantic because of their imminent parting. The earth and the peach

39

trees that sheltered them and the sky seemed to dissolve around them, as if they were suddenly suspended in time, in some place that had nothing to do with the world that they had always known. The pain of their need for each other was an agony, but an agony so sweet that they wanted it never to end.

Andrea had no will of her own left; the last drop of it had been burned away by the rush of love for Hank that engulfed her, all but consuming her. How could she leave him, how could she bear it?

"Dria!" Hank's voice was agonized, she could feel him trembling with a longing that merged with her own. "Dria, please . . ."

If Mike's voice, shouting at them as he approached the orchard, hadn't jolted them back to reality, it would have been too late. "Dria, Mother wants you back. We're about to start."

Andrea felt dazed as Hank released her, his arms falling from her reluctantly, his eyes dark with pain. Her own eyes were dark with the same pain. Why couldn't she know what she wanted, why couldn't she be sure who she was?

But then Mike called again, his voice urgent. And Andrea rose to put her foot in Runner's stirrup, mounting by instinct because her eyes were blurred with tears.

"I'm coming," she called back, her voice choking. "Hank, don't come with me, I couldn't bear it. Just be waiting for me when we come back."

ROSELAWNS

3

"Well, Kate!"

Prudence Amhurst, née Prudence Beddoes, Adam's aunt, faced Kate in the drawing room at Roselawns, and her still brilliant hazel eyes were warm with pleasure. "It's been a long time, but we meet each other at last!"

Kate had evaluated Prudence within minutes of descending from the train in Savannah, where Prudence and Rory had met her and Andrea Marie. Everything Adam had ever said about her was true. Prudence was beautiful, even now when her hair, which had been a rich brown in her youth, was snow white, and there were unmistakable age lines around her eyes. Prue's figure was still good in spite of her being in the early sixties, and the traveling dress she'd worn to meet Kate and Dria had been well chosen, plain and tailored but vastly becoming, its spring green accenting the green of her eyes. But it was her smile that had most impressed Kate, a smile so full of warmth and welcome that she had felt immediately at home in spite of the fact that she was farther from the Southwest than she had ever been before.

It wasn't that she and Adam hadn't been well able to afford to travel. They could have traveled around the world and never missed the money that such a venture would cost. But Kate and Adam had been content where they were. Adam had already traveled extensively, both to England and the Continent. The only necessary ingredient for her happiness with Adam, was their world, the world they had built together, Trail's End.

"Aren't you tired after that long trip? Would you like to go to your room and lie down until dinner?"

"Tired? Not at all. The train cars were as comfortable as being in my own living room." Kate spoke the literal truth. Adam had booked the most lavish drawing rooms for her and Dria for the entire journey, lush with mahogany panelling, red plush hangings, polished brass lamp fixtures and comfortable padded chairs and the softest of bunks. Their accommodations had been thickly carpeted, the food excellent, everything they needed either at their fingertips or available within minutes by pushing a bell. "But I confess that I had no idea, until this trip, that the United States is so big! It seemed to take forever before we got out of Texas alone!"

Prudence laughed, and Kate marveled at the sudden youthfulness it brought to her face. Yes, Adam had been right. When Prudence smiled or laughed, her whole face came alive with a beauty that was startling. He'd told her that he'd heard that Prue's mother, Martha, had had that same quality, that people on meeting her for the first time had thought her plain until she had smiled, and then they had been awestricken by her sudden radiant beauty.

"Well, Texas is the largest state in the Union; it's little wonder that it took a long time to cross it, even on a train! And now you're here, and I can still hardly believe it. Kate, your Andrea Marie is lovely! I don't believe I've ever seen a girl as beautiful. Isn't it marvelous that she and Naomi took to each other on sight, the way they did? Goodness, we couldn't get a whole sentence in, all that long ride here to Roselawns, for their chatter! I had the feeling that we were trapped in a small room with a couple of magpies!

That in itself is remarkable, because Naomi is usually so quiet that you forget she's there."

"It would have been pretty uncomfortable if they hadn't liked each other. I was a little worried about it," Kate confessed, and once again Prue flashed her wonderful smile.

"And no wonder! Now, there's no need to feel embarrassed, but you had every right to worry that Naomi would be consumed with jealousy the minute she laid eyes on Andrea! But you needn't have fretted; there isn't a jealous bone in Naomi's body, there never has been. She's just her own quiet self, and the fact that she isn't the traditional Southern beauty has never bothered her. I seriously doubt that it's ever entered her mind."

"But Naomi is lovely! She doesn't look anything like Andrea, of course, so there's no basis for comparison, but her smile makes her whole face light up so that she shines, it's the first thing I noticed about her."

"Yes, she has my mother's smile. She looks like Mother, too."

"And like you. Adam's told me, often, about you. I wish I could have known Martha. She was everything I admire in a woman."

Prudence nodded toward the fireplace, where an oil portrait hung over the mantel. "There she is. Father had it done years after she died, from a miniature he had done of her when they were in New Orleans, before she went back to Massachusetts to embark on her anti-slavery campaign. The artist caught her perfectly, even though he'd never seen her in person."

"Jonathan." Kate's eyes warmed with memories. "I loved him, Prudence. I've always been grateful that he was able to come out and visit us in Texas. My life would have been poorer if I'd never known him."

Although Prudence had liked Kate, a liking that she knew in her bones would develop into the love of one sister for another in spite of the difference in their ages, she warmed still more toward Adam's wife, of whom her father, Jonathan Beddoes, had told her so much after he'd returned home from escorting Jacob to Trail's End.

It had been so long since Prudence had seen Adam!

But then, she knew that she was fortunate that she had ever seen him again at all, after what had happened right here at Roselawns so many years ago.

All of his life, Adam had believed that Prue was his stepmother, that he was the legitimate son of Aaron Wentworth, of Boston, a jeweler who had had so many other investments that he was extremely wealthy.

Prudence had brought her younger half-sister Naomi to Martin's Corners, in Massachusetts, her mother, Martha's, original home. Naomi was the natural daughter of Jonathan and Rebecca, a beautiful octaroon slave at Roselawns, conceived after a disastrous quarrel between Martha and Jonathan because Jonathan and his father, old Jacob, had sold two slaves to buy Martha a string of pearls after the birth of her first child. Naomi had been brought up at Roselawns after Martha had left Jonathan and returned to Massachusetts to become an abolitionist.

Rebecca left Roselawns, and dropped from sight. And Naomi had been raped by Gaylord Renault, the scion of the neighboring plantation of Swanmere. Prudence had taken the young pregnant girl to Martin's Corners to bear the resultant child, to her mother's Aunt Emily. It was a tragedy when she and Michael, the young Irish immigrant she had married, had been caught smuggling an escaped slave toward Canada. Naomi and her husband had been killed by slave-hunters.

Aunt Emily had died shortly afterward. The Civil War had started and Prudence had been cut off from returning to Georgia. There was very little money, no funds from Roselawns were getting through, so she had attempted to sell Martha's pearls, which were now her own, to the Boston jeweler Aaron Wentworth, in order to receive enough to support herself and her half-nephew Arthur, Naomi's infant son.

Instead, Aaron had employed Prudence, allowing her to bring Arthur with her, as his housekeeper and companion to his young dying wife. The Wentworths had an infant son, of Arthur's exact age and coloring.

When Aaron's wife had died, Aaron and Prudence had married in order to assure both little boys a normal home. But Adam, Aaron's son, along with Aaron himself,

46

had died of fever while they were in Baltimore on business.

Prudence knew now, she'd learned with bitter agony, that she'd been wrong to take her own nephew Arthur back to Martin's Corners rather than to Boston and pass him off as Adam. Her intentions had been of the best. She'd adored her nephew, and she knew that kindly Aaron would have approved of her protecting him in this way from the disadvantage of his trace of Negro blood. They didn't return to Boston until the boy who was now accepted as Adam was old enough to go to Boston Latin School.

Adam had grown up into a remarkably handsome and intelligent young man, popular, sought after. It was the merest accident that a letter from Roselawns had arrived while Prudence was in England, and Adam had accepted the invitation, sent by Prue's brother Rory, to visit Roselawns. There he'd fallen in love wtih Rosalind, the daughter of Prue's younger sister Crissy and her husband, Gaylord Renault. Prue had barely arrived in time to prevent Adam from marrying his own half-sister, and the whole story had come out.

Stunned, his world shattered, Adam had left Roselawns, sold his Boston house, placed all of his affairs in the hands of agents and gone west, to wander homeless and exiled from all personal attachments until he met Kate Babcock. That in itself was a story of the utmost romance, because Kate, a quarter Apache, had been a virtual slave of a saloon owner who was forcing her to work off the debt left when her drunken father had overturned a lamp and burned his saloon. Adam had paid the remaining amount, had a brief and bitter-sweet affair with Kate, and moved on, still not willing to love again.

He'd been traced to San Francisco by a Pinkerton agent who brought him the news that a Countess Maria de la Roche, of Paris, had left him her large fortune. Intrigued by the mystery of why the woman should have made him her heir, Adam had returned to Roselawns to demand answers from Prue. He'd found Prue married at last to her girlhood sweetheart, Burke Amhurst, and the mother of Naomi, named after his own mother, and Michael, named after his mother's husband. He'd learned that the Countess Maria de la Roche had been Rebecca, his grandmother.

Adam had forgiven Prue at last, finally realizing that she'd deceived him because of her great love for him. But his heart was now in the wide spaces of the American West, and he'd gone searching for Kate, found her in jail for trying to kill a man who had tried to rape her, forced through a new trial with the best lawyers money could buy, married her, and taken her to the Big Bend country of Texas.

All in all, it was quite a story. Adam, completely involved with his ranch, had never visited Roselawns again, but his half-brother Jacob, Rosalind's brother, had come out to join him and he'd kept in touch, by letters, with Prue for all of the intervening years.

Looking at Kate now, the first time she had ever seen her, Prudence thought that her father, Jonathan, had been absolutely right about her. When Jonathan had accompanied Jacob to Trail's End, it had been love at first sight between Jonathan and Kate, and the old man hadn't been able to praise her enough. Kate was unique, just as Prue's mother, Martha, had been unique, and Prue felt a sudden, twisting regret that Kate and Martha had been fated never to meet.

"Being here is like a dream come true. But I can't help feeling that staying the entire summer is an imposition. Are you sure you don't mind?"

Prudence pulled a face that made Kate laugh. "Mind? Kate, you're kin! This is as much your home and Dria's as it is Naomi's. And if half of what Adam wrote me is true, it's high time that Andrea was taken away from Texas, before those two young suitors of hers end up killing each other. We may just keep her for a year, or even longer, even if you feel you have to get back to Adam."

"I'm afraid that half of the young men of the Chinatis are at each other's throats over Andrea, not just Henry and Wayne. It's been like that ever since her adolescence."

"Now that I've seen her, I'm not surprised. It's no wonder at all that she can't make up her mind, Kate. She has too many choices! A year's respite from all that rivalry over her is exactly what she needs. She has to have breathing space, a chance to think things over and make a sensible decision without being badgered."

The room they were in held such a quiet elegance

without any hint of ostentation that Kate could feel the traditions of generations of gracious Southern living seep into her bones. Only the most malicious of eyes would discern a certain shabbiness, the unmistakable signs of not being quite affluent enough to repair or replace things as they showed signs of wear. To everyone else, the patina of the proud Southern heritage more than overcame the expert darning of fabric, the thin spots in the rugs that wouldn't have been replaced even if Prudence and her husband Burke and her brother Rory could have afforded to replace them with pieces of equal worth. Everything about the room, the whole house, spoke of loving and meticulous care, of possessions so cherished that they were irreplaceable.

But above and beyond everything else in the room, Kate thought that Martha Curtis Beddoes's portrait dominated the surroundings. There was a quiet strength in her features, a quality of self-respect, that transcended even the beauty that radiated from the canvas. Integrity, Kate thought, that was the word. Martha had possessed an integrity of spirit that had forced her to leave Jonathan, the husband she had loved with all her heart, to work for the cause of abolition, the cause for which, in the end, she had laid down her life. Everything she could ever have wanted had been here at Roselawns, but she had left it all because of that integrity that would neither bow nor bend to her own wants or convenience.

"She was a wonderful woman," Prudence said simply. "I loved her more than I can say. When she died I felt as if my world had ended. But later, I had Adam, and then Burke and my children, and life has a way of going on, of bringing satisfaction, no matter what you have lost in the past."

"We each have a Michael," Kate said. "Adam didn't think you'd mind if he named our youngest Michael, even though you'd already given that name to your son. We were so many thousands of miles apart that it was unlikely that it would ever cause any confusion, and he wanted to honor the memory of the man who married his mother Naomi and gave him his name, even if it was later changed to Wentworth. He would have liked to name Andrea

Naomi, for his mother, as well, but that would have been carrying giving the same names too far, and even though our Mike wasn't born yet he was convinced that he'd have another son. So he settled for Andrea Marie, in honor of his grandmother."

"Rebecca." Prudence nodded. "Rebecca, who changed her name to Maria and then married the Count de la Roche. She would have been pleased, Kate. She, too, was a remarkable woman, in her way."

Kate knew the story well and was glad there was no bitterness in Prudence's voice. She was sincerely glad that Prudence had found happiness at last and that she and Adam were reconciled.

The two women were interrupted as a slender black girl brought in a tray of coffee and sandwiches and cakes. The tray was silver, beautifully chased, the coffee pot was Queen Anne, the cups and saucers of translucent china so lovely that the small chips and cracks only served to enhance their beauty. Kate felt honored, because she knew that this china was among Roselawns cherished heirlooms, used only on the most important occasions.

"Thank you, Bella." Nodding toward a chair for Kate, Prudence sat in the chair opposite with a small Chippendale table between them. "This should hold us till supper. Bella, will you tell Naomi and Andrea that if they're hungry, they'd better hurry before Kate and I finish every crumb? And you'd better locate Mr. Burke and Mr. Rory, as well, and tell them the same thing."

"Yes, ma'am." Bella's smile was friendly, and her glance at Kate filled with admiration and something a little like awe. There might even be, Kate thought, amused, a tiny hint of trepidation, because Bella was undoubtedly aware that she possessed Apache blood as well as coming all the way from the untamed West.

"There are only a few pieces of this china left," Prue told Kate, confirming her surmise. "It belonged to my grandmother, Yolande, and to her mother and her grandmother before her."

"Then if Andrea drops one of the cups, I'll spank her!"

50

"Not unless you can get her over your knee before I do!" Prudence laughed. "But she won't drop her cup, Kate. She's anything but clumsy. Kate, I'm so glad you're here, I can't express myself! If only Adam could have seen his way clear to come with you, I'd be so happy I don't think I'd be able to bear it! Is he as handsome as ever?"

"Every bit." Kate assured her. "I have to fight other women off with whips and guns." Her face was perfectly straight, but her eyes were dancing with laughter. "He's hardly changed, except for being very slightly heavier. His hair is still as fair as it was when I first saw him; the little bit of gray in it doesn't show because it's so light. He still moves like a man half his age, all strength and power like a—"

"Panther." Prudence finished for her. "How well I know! All the young ladies were mad for him. Thank heaven none of them snared him before he met you!" She and Kate smiled at each other, fully in accord, and their sense of affinity increased.

There was a clatter of running footsteps on the staircase, and Andrea rushed into the room, flushed and breathless, her face radiant with excitement. "Food! I'm perishing with hunger! Mmm, this cake is delicious!"

"Andrea, eat a sandwich first, and be careful with that cup!" Kate admonished her.

"Oh, my goodness! I'm afraid to pick it up, it looks as if it would crumble at a touch!" Andrea breathed, her voice filled with awe.

"It's survived for a good many generations, Andrea. I think it's safe to assume it will survive your gentle touch." Prudence smiled at the girl. "And here's Naomi."

Naomi entered the room a good deal more quietly than her cousin, although her face was also flushed with joyous excitement. Her resemblance to Prudence, and to the portrait of Martha, was striking. She had the same brown hair, the same hazel-green eyes, the same calmness of countenance that blazed into incredible beauty only when she smiled. Her voice was soft, her movements gracefully calm, and Kate felt strongly that the girl before her possessed in full measure her mother's and her grandmother's integrity. She couldn't have wished for a more desirable companion for Andrea if she'd been able to order one tailor-made from her own specifications. If being with Naomi for several months didn't exert a gentling influence on Dria, then nothing could!

"Where's that handsome uncle of mine? I could eat him up!" Andrea demanded. "I never knew that any man could be that handsome, except my own father and maybe Wayne Bradshaw, only Uncle Rory's more elegant. Talk about a genuine Southern gentleman, he must have been the original pattern!"

"No, my father was that. Rory's only a copy." Prudence laughed. "But he'll do very well, for all that!"

"I'll say he will! I still can't believe that I'm actually here! Mother, you should see my room! There's a bed with a canopy, and the bed's so tall that you have to use a footstool to get into it! And Naomi's room is just the same, only hers is pale green and mine is pink. I haven't seen yours, so I don't know what color it is, but I'll bet that you'll have to stand on a footstool to get into bed, too."

"Red." Prudence told her. "Naomi's room is the one that my sister Crissy and I shared when Father brought us back to Roselawns after Mother died. It was pink then, like Andrea's room is now, suitable for our tender years."

"I feel like I'm living back in history!" Andrea said. Her eyes were sparkling, and Prudence caught her breath, not for the first time since she'd seen her. It was a good thing indeed that Naomi wasn't inclined toward jealousy, or this visit from her unbelievably beautiful cousin would never work out.

"I want to see everything!" Andrea bubbled on. "I have this crazy feeling that I've been here before, that I'll know what lies around every corner. But that's because Dad and Uucle Jacob have told me so much about Roselawns, of course. I've dreamed of this house ever since I was old enough to listen to them. It's as if I've always known it."

"And that's the way it should be." Naomi spoke for

the first time since she'd entered the room. "After all, your roots are here, just as mine are. I was never so happy in my life as I was when Michael got married and brought Ardis to Amhurst and Mother and Father decided that we should move into Roselawns so they could have Amhurst to themselves. Uncle Rory wanted us to come here to live for years; he rattled around in this big house like one pea in a pod after he moved back in years ago to keep it from disintegrating. So now we all have what we want, and now that you're here, it's even better. It's wonderful having a cousin, Dria, and such a glamorous cousin, from Texas! All our friends are dying to meet you. I'm almost jealous, because I'd rather have you all to myself for a while."

"But I'm going to be here practically forever! And when I do go home, then you can come with me! She may, mayn't she, Aunt Prudence? We can't lose each other after it's taken us a whole lifetime to get to meet each other!"

"We don't have to decide any such momentous question today, Andrea. But I'm sure that if Naomi wants to go, when the time comes, Burke and I will have no objections."

Andrea picked up her coffee cup and looked at it, holding it reverently. Her voice was filled with awe. "Just think, Yolande herself drank out of this cup! And Martha. And Jonathan!"

"It isn't the Holy Grail, for all that." Naomi laughed at her. "Drink your coffee, Dria. I'm sure you'll find it tastes just the same as if you were drinking it from a tin mug."

"No, it doesn't. Coffee in a tin mug tastes sort of . . . well, tinny! I've drunk enough of it like that, around campfires, to know. This is like ambrosia!"

"Not ambrosia. Chicory. We still use it to give its own unique flavor to the coffee beans," Prudence told her.

"Well, I like it, and when we go home we'll have to introduce the custom at Trail's End, won't we, Mother?"

"If you say so. Adam might be pleased with the idea, at that." Kate fought down the sudden, almost overwhelming feeling of loneliness because she was separated

53

from Adam for the first time, except for business trips and trail drives, since they had been married. "And I know he'd be pleased to have Naomi visit us, for a year or five years or the rest of her life. Andrea, you don't have to gulp down every cake on the plate!"

"Yes, I do." Andrea's laughter turned to quick contrition. "Oh, I'm sorry! I didn't realize that I was hogging them all. There won't be any left for Uncle Rory and Uncle Burke!"

"I'll bring more." Naomi picked up the serving plate, laughing softly. "Come with me, Dria. You'll want to see the kitchen house, and everybody out there wants to get a better look at you. And if you're really starved, we'll sweet-talk Cleo out of some of her gingerbread. She always has some, only we thought we'd be a little more elegant than to serve it for your very first tea at Rose-lawns."

"Cleo!" Andrea jumped out of her chair so fast that she nearly did drop her coffee cup. "Oh, yes, Naomi! I have to get a better look at Cleo, too! Dad's told me about Cleo my whole life! To think that she's here, that I'm actually going to get to know Dad's Cleo, who helped bring him up, the very same Cleo who was Martha's personal slave and who helped bring up Aunt Prue and Rory and Crissy! It's like meeting someone historical, right out of the pages of a book."

Hand in hand, their faces alight, the eighteen-year-old girl and her cousin, five years older, left the room. Left alone again, Prudence and Kate also smiled. It was as if they had known each other all of their lives.

"Do you know, I think I'll buy one of those Eastman Kodaks we've heard so much about, and take some pictures to take back to Adam. He'll want to see Roselawns as it is now, and you can't imagine how pleased he'd be to have pictures of the house in Martin's Corners where he lived with you and Cleo when he was a little boy. I want a picture of Andrea in the doorway of that saltbox house. And pictures of all of you here, including Cleo. Do you think I can buy one in town?"

"I'm sure you can! Michael already owns one, he's

quite taken up with photography. Certainly you must have one, and he'll show you how to use it. You can ask him about it when he and Ardis come to dinner tomorrow night. Our only other guest will be Gregory Randolph. The Randolphs are neighbors; they bought up Swanmere after Gay and Crissy lost it. They're an old Georgia family, planters from way back, as we all are, but they lost their own plantation shortly after the war when so many of the old places ended up in the hands of the carpetbaggers. Fortunately, they recuperated a good deal of their fortune later, and Mr. Randolph, Greg's father, has restored Swanmere to its proper place as one of Georgia's showplaces."

"Do I detect a romance here?"

"Well, Naomi has been seeing a lot of Gregory. He's a personable young man, and we'd all be pleased if he and Naomi married."

"If he's right for her, it would be wonderful. It would bring Swanmere back into the family, wouldn't it? I only hope the young man is good enough for her!"

"There's no doubt of that. You'll see for yourself, when you meet him. Only, don't say anything about this to Naomi. It isn't official, and she can't seem to make up her mind to have him in spite of the fact that every unmarried girl in the county would give anything to snare him."

"Oh, dear, so you have problems, too!" Their eyes met with complete understanding. "Well, it's no good trying to force them. We can't live their lives for them, we can only hope that we've given them the wisdom to live them for themselves without ruining them."

"If both of them will be as happy as we are, no matter whom they choose, that's all I ask," Prudence said, and Kate nodded.

Burke and Rory came in to join them, and the way Prue and Burke looked at each other made Kate's heart swell. How wonderful it was that Prudence had finally found her happiness, after years of loneliness and heartbreak. Kate knew that Prue had only married Aaron Wentworth because she'd believed that her sister Crissy had married Burke while Prue was in Massachusetts with her great-aunt Emily. The war had just started, and Prue had received a letter from Crissy, passed from hand to hand so often and smudged until it was all but illegible, telling Prue that she had married, and from what Prue could make out she'd thought that her sister had taken Burke. It wasn't until a long time later, when Prue was already married to Aaron, that she'd learned that Crissy had married Gaylord Renault and not Burke Amhurst.

Prue and Burke had met again only when Prue had rushed to Roselawns to prevent Adam from marrying Rosalind. Burke, a doctor, had come to treat her after Crissy, wild with disappointment because her daughter wasn't to marry the Wenworth fortune, had shot Prue for passing Adam off as Aaron Wentworth's son. Burke, too, had married, and been widowed. Both marriages had been sweet and good, but their original love for each other had never died.

And now here they were, the parents of two fine grownup children, and as much in love with each other as they had been before the Civil War. Kate's heart ached with happiness for them. She couldn't think of any two people who deserved happiness more.

Andrea liked Michael and Ardis Amhurst. Michael was only a year older than Naomi, and Ardis a year older than herself, so that made three cousins in her own age group, riches indeed. Michael and Kate were in a deep discussion of cameras, and she and Ardis were as deep in a discussion of the latest fashions, a subject that Andrea felt she must learn a great deal more about, when Naomi interrupted them.

"Andrea, this is Gregory Randolph. Gregory, my cousin Andrea Marie, from Texas, who has arrived at last!"

Andrea looked at the young man Naomi had just admitted to the house appraisingly, anxious to form her first impression of him, which was very good. Gregory was everything that her romantic girlhood had dreamed of in a gallant young Southern gentleman. His hair was nearly as dark as Wayne Bradshaw's, but instead of brown, like Wayne's, Gregory's eyes were blue. He lacked perhaps half an inch of Henry's height, but his shoulders were as broad, and Henry never in his life could have worn a jacket with the same elegant ease that Gregory wore his, or spoken with such a natural, inherited grace of manner. Every inch of him spoke of generations of wealth and culture behind him, and she was glad that Naomi was all but engaged to him. As well as she liked Naomi, who fulfilled all of her expectations in a cousin, she wouldn't have been satisfied for her to settle for anything less.

Gregory's hand took hers not in a clumsy bear-clasp, such as the young Texans she knew would have used, but gently, giving her the warm satisfaction of knowing that he was fully aware that she was a lady.

"I've been looking forward to meeting you. Naomi's talked of nothing but your arrival ever since she heard that you were coming. My mother and father are sorry that they couldn't be here tonight to meet you and your mother. Unfortunately, they had a prior commitment, nothing less than my great-aunt Belinda's birthday, and to keep peace in the family they had no choice but to keep it."

"Of course they had to," Andrea said. "But I'm sorry they couldn't be here, too."

"You'll meet them soon, in any case." Gregory was smiling, and his smile was warm. "Mother told me to be sure to invite you and your mother and of course Naomi and Mrs. Amhurst to Swanmere tomorrow, and if I don't arrive home with your acceptance she'll have my head on a platter! May I tell her that you'll be there?"

"Greg, I'm sorry, but Dria and I have already promised to go to Amhurst tomorrow. Ardis asked us not five minutes before you arrived, and we promised her that we would. Andrea can hardly wait to see Amhurst, she has years of family history to catch up on."

"Well, we'll make it the day after tomorrow, then! It's a shame that you're leaving for Massachusetts so soon, Miss Wentworth, but Mother is already planning to have a party for you soon after you get back. There's nothing she likes better than the excuse to have a big party, and this is the best excuse she's had in years."

"A party for mother and me?" This was the stuff that Andrea's dreams had been made of. "That's very nice of her, Mr. Randolph. I can hardly wait to meet her and thank her for her kindness."

"You'll enjoy the party, you'll meet at least half the county. But that's so far in the future there's no use thinking about it. The day after tomorrow's another matter. You ride, of course? How could you not, coming from Texas? Maybe you'd like to ride over, you and Naomi, instead of coming in the buggy with your mother and Mrs. Amhurst. I'll come to escort you, of course. It won't take as long to make the trip and you'll be able to see more of the countryside than from a buggy.

"I'd love it, if Naomi agrees." She *would* love it. For as many years as she could remember she hadn't been this many days without being on horseback, and she was aching to ride again. There was just one thing. She and Kate had left Texas so quickly that there'd been no time to order her a proper riding habit such as ladies in Georgia wore. At home she rode, as did most of the other girls, in a divided skirt, and astride. Good heavens, how was she ever to manage a sidesaddle? She'd never been on one of those contraptions in her life! She'd probably fall off, or some other stupid thing, and be a laughingstock before her visit had really begun! It was lucky that she and Naomi were much of a size; Naomi could probably lend her a habit. As for the sidesaddle, she'd just have to do the best she could! After all, a horse was a horse, and she'd yet to come across one that she couldn't handle.

"I'll be here as early as you'll let me in, then," Gregory promised. His smile was so genuinely warm that Andrea's heart warmed in return. All the stories of Southern hospitality that she'd been brought up on were true, people here were as friendly as they were back home. If all of the other people she was to meet were as friendly as Gregory Randolph, this visit would come up to every dream she had ever had of it.

"Then you'll have to start way before dawn because

58

we'll be up and ready by full daylight." Naomi laughed at Greg. "I can hardly wait for Dria to see Swanmere."

"It will be my pleasure, I assure you." Gregory's laugh was as pleasant as his voice. "At first full daylight, then!"

The rest of the evening passed so pleasurably that Andrea felt that she was living in a dream. She had to pinch herself under the cover of the meticulously darned damask tablecloth to convince herself that she was actually having dinner in the restored dining room wing of Roselawns, the one that the Yankees had set fire to during the war, when the rest of the house had been saved only by the providential onset of a downpour. The table and chairs and the sideboard weren't the same as the ones that her grandfather Jonathan had been commissioned to buy for his mother Yolande on his fateful trip north when he'd met Martha Curtis, of course. They had been destroyed in the fire, but Prudence and Rory had replaced them with the nearest replicas they could find. Everything about Roselawns came up to her expectations, and even more, and now she was to see Amhurst and Swanmere as well! Texas seemed a very long way away, farther than it actually was, and that was almost a continent away.

She felt like hugging herself. She'd waited all her life for this and now it was actually happening, she was actually here. She smiled across the table at her mother, who sat in the place of honor at Burke Amhurst's right. How distinguished Burke was, how right he was for Aunt Prudence!

They'd waited a very long time for their happiness, they'd waited for years after the war, when they'd finally met again and found that they still loved each other. It was better than any romantic novel that Andrea had ever read, and she felt so proud of being a part of this Southern family that she could burst. And just look at her mother! Kate looked as if she belonged here every bit as much as Aunt Prudence herself. If she were any happier, Andrea thought, she wouldn't be able to bear it.

She took a long time getting ready for bed that

night. She was filled with an excitement that refused to admit the need for sleep. Brushing her hair at the dressing table, she tossed the brush down and drew a wrapper over her nightgown and went to tap at Naomi's bedroom door.

"Is that you, Dria? Come in!" Naomi too, was still awake, looking much younger than her twenty-three years with her soft brown hair in two plaits over her shoulders in readiness for bed. "I was hoping you'd come! I didn't want to go to your room in case you were tired and had gone to sleep. It's so wonderful to have another girl in the house to talk to. Michael is a wonderful brother, but a brother can't take the place of a sister and I never had one of those, any more than you did."

"I know just what you mean." Andrea laughed as both girls settled in the middle of Naomi's huge bed, their legs bent up under the sheet and their arms wrapped around their knees. "I feel like a schoolgirl again, the way I felt when Mother and Father let me visit another girl for a week and we sat up and talked and giggled half the night. Naomi, I like your Gregory Randolph. Are you going to marry him?"

Naomi's eyes shadowed, and Andrea couldn't interpret the expression in them. "I don't know. I'm not sure."

"Your mother and father want you to, I can tell. And where on earth could you find anyone more handsome, or nicer?"

This time Naomi smiled. "I don't know that either. I suppose I'll marry him sooner or later. Not only my parents, but everyone else in the county expects it. It would mean a lot to my family because it would be like getting Swanmere back. Aunt Crissy and Uncle Gay owned it once, you know."

"Yes, Father told me. It's like a novel, isn't it, that after its being lost to the family, now it will come back again through your marrying Gregory."

Naomi shook her head as if she were chasing cobwebs away. "I'm hungry again. Let's raid the kitchen. There'll be milk, and unless Cleo's sick, and she isn't there'll be more gingerbread."

"Yes, let's!"

Their wrappers pulled tightly around them, but their

feet as bare as the naughty schoolgirls they felt themselves to be, they crept down the stairs and through the covered passageway to the kitchen, so different from anything Andrea had ever seen before. Imagine having the kitchen entirely separate from the house, connected only by the covered passage!

There was milk, and as Naomi had promised, there was gingerbread. They were just helping themselves to liberal pieces when the door opened and Cleo came in.

"So it's you two. I might have known," Cleo said. "Especially since Andrea is Adam's daughter! As I recollect, he never spent a night under my roof in Martin's Corners that he didn't go sneaking down to the kitchen in the middle of the night for milk and gingerbread!"

"But Cleo, how could he help it when it's this delicious?" Andrea demanded.

The still sharp eyes in the long, homely black face regarded her as if they were looking backward through the years. Additional wrinkles appeared around Cleo's eyes, lost in the sea of wrinkles in her incredibly creased face. "Adam's daughter," Cleo said again. "I'm mightily glad you've come, child. I've missed that boy. Outside of Miss Emily, and Miss Martha and Miss Prudence, he meant more to me than anyone else in the world."

"And he still loves you, and misses you," Andrea told the former slave; just imagine, Cleo had been a slave! "He's told me a hundred times, at least, how loyal you were to the family, and how much they owe you. And now I love you, too!"

Impulsively, she threw her arms around Cleo and hugged her and kissed her cheek.

"A mouthful of gingerbread!" Cleo said. "If you aren't Adam all over again! He always did think he could get around me that way when he was a young 'un. But you're old enough to behave yourself, you and Naomi both. Go on, shoo! Take your gingerbread and your milk up to your room and let me get this kitchen neatened up again for morning!"

"Thank you, Cleo." Naomi, too, kissed the thin, straight-backed women, the woman who'd been her second mother ever since the day she'd been born. "We'll get out of your way. I'm afraid we're taking the very last bit of your gingerbread."

"I'll just mix up some more, come morning. Wouldn't want Adam to think I let his girl go hungry, now would I?"

Laughing, the two girls retraced their steps, and it was another hour before Andrea went back to her own room and to bed.

I'm happy, she told herself. I'm so happy I could die. She blew out the lamp and settled against her pillows, closing her eyes and fully expecting to drift off to sleep within minutes.

But sleep eluded her, and it had nothing to do with overindulging her stomach at such a late hour. Henry's image kept printing itself against her closed eyelids, looking so heartbroken that it made her writhe with guilt because she was so happy here while he was so miserable back in Texas without her.

Then the image dissolved and it was replaced by the image of Gregory Randolph. He certainly was handsome, but that was no reason for him to intrude on her consciousness when she wanted to sleep. If she had to think of any young man at all, it should be of Henry. She made a conscious effort, but she only succeeded in merging the two images so that neither of them was distinct.

Stop it, you ninny! she told herself. Stop it and go to sleep this instant! Gregory's taken, he belongs to Naomi, and I wouldn't have it any other way. What do I need him for, anyway, with Henry waiting for me back in Texas?

But Texas was a long way away, and she wouldn't be going back there for a long time. She wasn't even sure that she'd marry Henry when she did. How could she be sure, when he and Wayne Bradshaw were the only two she'd ever considered, when there might be someone else, some elusive and shadowy man she hadn't even met, in her future? Someone as handsome, as romantic as Gregory Randolph, only waiting for her to come into his life.

She slept at last, but it was no stranger whom she hadn't yet met who troubled her dreams. The face that refused to blot itself out as she struggled to banish it was Gregory's.

MARTIN'S
CORNERS

4

The departure for Massachusetts, first to visit Boston and Prudence's old friend Estelle Richards and then to go on to spend a month at Martin's Corners, filled Andrea with relief.

It wasn't that Andrea hadn't enjoyed herself at Rose-lawns. It was because she had enjoyed herself too much, and the main point of her enjoyment had been in Gregory Randolph's company.

It wouldn't do, she told herself at least a dozen times a day. She'd rather go back to Texas right now than do anything that would hurt Naomi. And before they left for Massachusetts, she had ample proof from every side that it was an accepted fact that Naomi and Gregory would be married. Her cousin Rosalind, who was her Aunt Crissy's daughter, had known Adam well. Not that Rosalind, either, dwelled on the subject of how well they had been acquainted, but Andrea had detected a mistiness in the still lovely woman's eyes when she mentioned

Adam, and eagerness to know everything that had happened to him, every detail about Trail's End and Adam's success as a rancher.

How strange it must have been for Rosalind to discover that Adam was a half-brother she'd never known she possessed, all those years ago before Andrea had been born! But like her full brother Jacob, it was evident that Rosalind held no resentment toward Adam Wentworth but that she wished only the best for him. Rosalind's eyes had lighted up with pleasure when she'd met Kate, as though she had had some private mental reservations that any woman could be good enough for Adam and now they were set at rest. And Rosalind had asked Naomi, specifically, when she was going to set the date for her marriage to Greg, a question that Naomi had brushed aside without appearing to change the subject. Rosalind, too, was happy that Swanmere, where she had grown up, would come back into the family when the marriage took place.

Yes, it was definitely Greg who bothered Andrea, who kept her nerves just enough on edge to take the last final sheen off her enjoyment of being at Roselawns.

Not that Greg had stepped out of bounds with her, or as much as hinted at it. He was attentive to her, but only within the bounds of the vaunted Southern courtesy, as was due a guest of his friends and neighbors. But every time he put his hand under her elbow to help her mount a horse, every time their fingers touched when he handed her something, and every time he touched her arm to draw her attention to something, she felt that uneasiness grow until she was almost overwhelmingly relieved to leave Roselawns and place hundreds of miles between them.

It hadn't been easy for her to keep her natural inclination to flirt, to bring every young man she met under her spell, in check. She'd had to watch herself constantly, even when she and Naomi weren't visiting at Swanmere or Gregory at Roselawns, for fear that she'd let some unguarded word drop that would trouble Naomi.

She was acting like an adolescent, like a calf-eyed schoolgirl the first time a boy asked her to dance, Andrea told herself with angry disgust. Gregory was only a man, like any other. He had two arms and two legs, and if fate had conspired to make him extraordinarily handsome and so charming that any girl who wasn't frigid would be stirred by him, he was still no more a man than Henry, or Wayne, or any of the other young Texans she'd flirted with and led around by their noses to the combined amusement and consternation of her elders. For all she knew, Gregory might be mean to his mother and kick dogs!

He wasn't, and he didn't, though. She was with him enough in the two weeks before they left for Massachusetts to know that Gregory was everything that he appeared on the surface to be, the very epitome of the fabled Southern gentleman. It really wasn't any wonder that he affected her so strongly; he was so different from any man she'd ever known, so cultured, so polished, so handsome, and so charming! When he drew out her chair to seat her at the table, he did it as naturally as he breathed, not red-faced and embarrassed the way the young Texans were, more used to roping and branding than to being courteous to young females. When he called her Miss Andrea, her heart melted. At home, whatever young man who addressed her was more likely to yell, "Hey, Dria!"

But he was Naomi's, and she wasn't going to lift a finger to change that fact, and besides, it was ridiculous to imagine that she was falling in love with him on such short acquaintance. If she hadn't been able to make up her mind about Henry, whom she'd known most of her life, how could she imagine that she could fall in love with a man she'd known for only a few days? It was only that he was so different, so completely outside anything in her previous experience, that her mind broke loose from the tight rein she tried to keep on it and took the bit in its teeth and ran away with her.

The soft, rolling landscape that they traveled as their train made its way to Boston fascinated her. The hills were so gently billowing that she imagined that she could roll in them like a featherbed. Everything was green; everywhere she looked was that bright, clear, fresh, green, its freshness untainted by dust, fed by the plentiful rainfall that amazed her as much as the softness of the land.

"How much rain do you get in a year?" she asked her Aunt Prudence, only half paying attention as she watched a small herd of placid cattle in a field, the grass so lush that it reached to their knees. But she jerked her head to look at Prue, and her mouth gaped open at Prue's answer.

"Georgia averages fifty inches, but sometimes we get a good deal more than that. And Massachusetts, I believe, averages around forty inches."

"Mother, how much do we get in Texas?"

"We're lucky if we get around seventeen inches in the mountains, and eight or nine in the lower regions, where we live. Other parts of Texas are more arid, and in Arizona and New Mexico, they sometimes have as little as three or four inches in a year." Kate, too, was enthralled at the lushness of the eastern part of the United States.

Seeing their bemused expressions, Prudence laughed. "It's beautiful in the summer, but you might not like Massachusetts so well in the winter! Boston often gets more than fifty inches of snow! And winter lasts a long time here; before it ended, when I was a girl in Martin's Corners, we used to think that spring would never come! Every part of the country has its own beauty and its own special advantages. That's why travel is so enjoyable. It's nice to see other parts of the world, to know firsthand what they're like."

Prudence herself had traveled extensively when she was younger. During her widowhood after her first husband, Aaron Wentworth, had died and she'd been raising Adam as her stepson, the Wentworth fortune had enabled her to go to England and France and Italy and Greece as often as she'd liked, and she'd taken full advantage of the opportunity. But since she'd married Burke the farthest she'd been was back to Massachusetts.

"Fifty inches! It's a wonder you don't all develop gills!" Andrea marveled, and beside her, Naomi laughed. "And back in Texas, it's a wonder you don't all dry up and blow away! But we've all managed to survive, haven't we, and I expect we'll go right on doing it."

There was an animation about Naomi that Andrea hadn't seen before, a soft glow in her eyes and a flush on her cheeks that was astonishingly attractive. There seemed to be an inner excitement about her, and for the life of her Andrea couldn't understand why. Naomi had been to Boston, and to Martin's Corners, almost every year of her life ever since she'd been old enough to travel. Was Boston so wonderful that it could bring this glow to her, as if she were on the threshold of some enchanted wonderland? If that were true, then it must be fabulous beyond all of Andrea's expectations.

Actually, the city came up to everything Andrea had thought it would be, except that the old buildings seemed to be dingy and dirty from years of accumulated grime. But that was no wonder, considering how old some of them were, and all of the coal and wood smoke that had all those years to stain them. Compared to Boston, everything in the west had been built yesterday!

The hustle and bustle of the narrow, often cobbled streets astonished her, and she marveled at the jostling crowds, so many people that they were, as Kate put it, packed between the rows of buildings like herring in a barrel. Andrea leaned out of the window of the hansom to marvel at all the sights, uncaring that her behavior wasn't too ladylike.

"It's so big! I never really realized how big it would be!" she said. "We hardly got to see anything of the other cities we came through on our way east, just the railroad station areas. My goodness, how many people live in this town, Aunt Prudence?"

"Nearly six hundred thousand." Prudence smiled. "And it's growing like a weed. When I was your age it had only about a hundred and fifty thousand, a mere village compared to what it is today. The Irish immigrants have accounted for a lot of the growth; whole sections of the city are Irish, and they do a lot to maintain Boston's prosperity. They're ambitious and hard-working people, an asset to any city."

69

"You have to see just everything before we go on to Martin's Corners," Naomi told her cousin. "Paul Revere's house, and the Common, and the Old South Meeting House, and Old North Church, and Faneuil Hall. The churches and Faneuil Hall are so beautiful it's hard to believe that they were built so long ago."

"There's plenty of time for everything," Prudence reminded them. "Right at the moment, I'll be content to get to Estelle's house on Beacon Hill! Kate, we'll be passing the Wentworth house, and I'll ask the driver to go very slowly while we're going by so that you can see where Adam spent his young manhood, as well as his early infancy. Better still, I'll have him stop so you can take some pictures of it with that camera you haven't been parted from ever since Michael helped you buy it in Savannah!"

She spoke the literal truth, because Kate was fascinated by the Kodak that she even now carried cradled in her lap, so as to have it in her hands whenever she saw something she wanted to preserve on film. She'd already taken several rolls of film at Roselawns, at Amhurst, and at Swanmere, and now she intended to capture every point of interest in Boston and in Martin's Corners as well. Already, she projected her mind into the future, when she and Adam would look at the results of her labor together, savoring how much Adam would enjoy the snapshots that would let him revisit the scenes of his childhood and early manhood.

"Why, the houses are built right up to the sidewalks!" Andrea exclaimed. "And they're so close together! What on earth do people do for elbow room and breathing space?"

"They simply ignore the lack of it," Naomi told her, her eyes twinkling. "It's all they've ever known, so they don't know the difference. Boston is built on an island, Andrea, and space has always been limited. There are back yards, though, some of them large, because people have always had to have horses and carriages and carriage houses and gardens."

"But you wouldn't believe the soot and the smoke in the winters, when everyone's burning coal," Prudence put in. "The snow turns black soon after it's fallen. And the slush, when it thaws, and the freezing sleet find their way down your collar and into your boots, when it isn't quite cold enough to snow. I love Boston, and I always will, but when winter comes, I'm always glad that I live back in Georgia now. There's the Wentworth house, Kate." She leaned forward to signal the driver to stop.

Kate and Andrea stared. The house, tall and narrow like all its neighbors, fronted the street, looming above them far larger than Kate had imagined, although compared to their hacienda, with its courtyards and patios, it didn't cover nearly as much ground space.

"Golly!" Andrea breathed. "Dad was a gol-darned nabob, wasn't he?"

"You could say that." Prudence smiled. They all got out, and took turns arranging the others in front of the house so that one of them could take pictures, while the driver waited patiently, assured that he would receive a tip for his trouble that would make it well worth his time. He was one of the Irish that Prudence had just told them about, his face good-natured even though his nose, a little redder than normal, spoke of a liking for the bottle. His horses were well cared for, showing no evidence of mistreatment, and that was what Andrea and Kate noticed and liked about him. As long as a man did his work and did it well he had a right to a nip when it was time for him to rest.

"I wonder who lives here now?" Andrea asked, her voice wistful. "Couldn't we knock, and ask to go through the house?"

Both Prudence and Naomi were astounded by her simple question, their faces registering shock.

"My dear girl, this is Boston! One does not knock on the door of a stranger and ask to be shown the house!" Prudence said, her voice verging into laughter at the naivete of the question. "It simply is not done! We've taken much too great a liberty just by taking those snapshots!"

"Then I think that Boston folk are mighty unfriendly! Back in Texas, anybody would be spitting mad if somebody who used to live in their house didn't stop and introduce themselves!"

"But this isn't Texas, Andrea. It's Boston. You'll find more stiff necks here than anywhere else in the world. Why, it must hurt most of the people here something awful just to have to nod to an acquaintance on the street. They probably have to go home and wrap warm flannel around their necks to get the ache out!" Naomi exploded into laughter. Then, contrite, she took Andrea's hand and squeezed it. "The Texas way is better, though. It must be wonderful to live where everyone is friendly, even to complete strangers. Georgia's like that, too, so I can understand your shock at Boston's staidness."

Andrea, after a moment of feeling ruffled, joined in her laughter. "I thought I was fairly well educated, the way Dad kept after me all the time, but I see I still have plenty to learn! But then, when you come to Texas you'll have a few things to learn, too! Like riding astride," she said, a glint of teasing amusement in her eyes. "You'll find that as different as I found getting used to these danged sidesaddles you use back here. If Greg hadn't been so blasted polite, he'd have laid down on the ground and died laughing at me! I'm glad Mother didn't get any pictures of me perched on that sidesaddle; Henry would bust his head wide open pounding it on the ground laughing!"

"Come, girls." Prudence urged them, firmly, back into the cab. Estelle would be mortified if any of her friends saw them standing in the street, laughing like hyenas! "It's time we were getting to Estelle's. She'll be wondering what's happened to us."

The Richardses' house was fully as imposing as the Wentworth residence, but not nearly as imposing as Estelle Richards herself when she came sailing across her drawing room to greet them.

Sailing, Andrea thought. That was the only word that could describe her, because Estelle was built on magnificent proportions. Now in her sixties, she had added a good many inches to the imposing girth she'd already possessed when she and Prudence had been friends back when Prue had still lived in Boston and traveled together every summer to England and Paris. She could even be described as massive, and she barged full steam ahead with all the power and assurance of one of the Cunard liners, to envelop first Prue, and then Naomi, in her arms and then turn to Kate and Andrea, scrutinizing them as keenly as a captain of such a liner would scrutinize threatening clouds from his bridge.

"So you're Adam's wife! I'm pleased, very pleased indeed, to meet you, Mrs. Wentworth. And Andrea, Adam's daughter! This is a pleasure I've long looked forward to. Adam was my darling, my absolute darling, yes, I adored him even beyond my own son, as shocking as it might seem. But then, he was such a handsome scamp, everybody doted on him, much less a middle-aged female who wished her own son were half as prepossessing!"

One thing Estelle was not, and that was stiff-necked. She radiated warmth and hospitality and made them feel so welcome that it was like meeting a long-lost member of the family. No doubt her reserve was as great as other Bostonians', with strangers, but Adam's wife and daughter could never be strangers to her, and she told them so, volubly and at great length.

"Prudence, you simply must come along to England with me this summer! I've heard all the excuses I'm going to. It's been years since we've traveled together. You have plenty of time to get ready; I won't be sailing until August, and we'll return in October, in time to escape bad sailing weather. You must all come! Think what fun it would be, all of us together! It would make me feel quite young again, and these girls certainly ought to see something of the world while they're still young enough to enjoy it!"

"You know it's impossible, Estelle." Prudence was indulgent of her friend's enthusiasm, but firm. "A month spent here in Massachusetts, away from Burke, is all I can possibly manage."

"Then Mrs. Wentworth and the girls must come with me! Andrea, I'll wager you'd love it, and I can show you everything that's worth seeing! Naomi, wouldn't you adore to be gowned by Worth, to see Paris? And this gorgeous Andrea! I still buy all my gowns there, but face it, on me they're wasted! But Catherine, and Andrea and Naomi, the modistes will go out of their minds with ecstasy just at the opportunity to gown them!"

"I'm afraid it's just as much out of the question for me as it is for Prudence." Kate smiled. "Six weeks or two months away from Adam is all I can bear. And our time is completely booked, at any rate. It seems that half of Georgia is determined to entertain us, and the other half have accepted the invitations to the galas. Whatever clothes we buy in Boston will cause as much furor in Texas as if they came from Paris, anyway."

Estelle's face fell, all of her chins along with it, but she brightened immediately. "Then I shall take you shopping in Boston and see that you're shown only the best!"

"We're really more interested in sightseeing, Mrs. Richards," Naomi told her mother's friend. "Andrea and Mrs. Wentworth's clothes are already fabulous." There was no need to tell Estelle that some of them were from Worth, made to their own measurements; it might break Estelle's heart.

"Of course! They must see everything. I'm devastated, simply devastated, that my grandson is already married!"

"I beg your pardon?" Kate asked, completely bewildered by the *non sequitur*. Surely she hadn't missed a connecting phrase somewhere?

"Because if he weren't married, then I might have captured your daughter for him!" Estelle said, as if it were perfectly obvious.

It was Prudence's turn to laugh. "Now, Estelle, you know perfectly well that if your grandson hadn't married that girl you chose for him, from one of Boston's most prominent families, you'd never have forgiven him! Besides, Andrea would have your friends in fits."

"Then they could have fits, it would have been worth it," Estelle declared. Andrea was entranced. Estelle was so different from what she had expected, and she felt drawn to the woman, already liking her as well as she liked friends of her parents that she'd known all her life. It was only a shame that all Bostonians weren't as friendly and natural as Estelle Richards.

74

"And anyway, Andrea's great-grandmother was a French countess!" Estelle added, vindicating herself, her voice filled with triumph. "And the great-granddaughter of a countess is entitled to give people fits!"

Kate, with Prue's help, changed the subject, and in another moment Estelle had forgotten the countess and was launched once again into trying to persuade them to sail with her in the late summer. That led into an argument as to their itinerary for the next few days, whether sightseeing or shopping was of more importance, and by the time dinner was over and they finally sought their beds, Andrea felt as if she'd been run over by one of those beer wagons she'd seen from the hansom.

"You mustn't mind Estelle," Naomi dimpled at her, as they prepared for bed in the room they shared. "Personally, I adore her. But she is rather much, for someone who never met her before."

"I adore her, too," Andrea reassured her cousin. One thing was certain; when Estelle was in the same room with her, she hadn't had a minute to think about her own problems, Henry Stockton back in Texas and her more immediate problem of Gregory Randolph in Georgia.

There was something approaching worship on Prue's face as she fitted the key into the lock of the saltbox house in Martin's Corners. The very way she touched the door jamb, while she was turning the key, spoke of adoration.

"This is it," she said as she pushed the door open. "My great-aunt Emily's house, just as she left it. Nothing has been changed or will ever be changed as long as Cleo and I have breath in our bodies."

"It's a pity that Cleo couldn't come," Kate said. "How she must miss not being able to make the trip any more!"

"Yes, she does. You know it's actually her house. Miss Emily left it to her for all her years of friendship and service. But at Cleo's age, there's no way she can keep on making the pilgrimage. I'm glad you have that camera, Kate. At least this time we can take her back a lot of pictures; she'll cherish them more than you know. I wish I'd thought of it years ago!"

There was a lump in Andrea's throat as she remembered the pride the aged ex-slave had exhibited when she'd pretended to decide that she wouldn't accompany them this time. "This house would fall apart without a firm hand at the helm!" the old woman had said. "Those no-account girls wouldn't dust or sweep and the kitchen would be a shambles, and what would Rory and Burke do without me to keep things going for them while you're gone? Somebody has to be here to see that there's decent meals put on the table for them, and on time! Girls aren't what they used to be, back when we could trust them to do things right with nobody standing over them to see they did it!"

They'd agreed with her, expressing their gratitude for her devotion to duty, their admiration for the way she, singlehandedly, kept the family from falling apart.

"And it's more nearly true than you might imagine," Prudence told them. "I don't know what we'd have done without her, those early years after I married Burke and Rory and Father nearly lost Roselawns. She was a tower of strength, she never let us falter or lose hope. It was almost like having Miss Emily back."

Andrea walked through the house where her father had spent so much of his youth, where he had continued to visit Cleo during his young adulthood. She touched a chair here, a picture there, feeling awe and something very close to tears in her throat. Roots! That was what this house stood for, as much as Roselawns itself. The huge kitchen fireplace was still in working order, although the shining black range was used for cooking now. The bedrooms still had the patchwork quilts, the braided rugs, that Miss Emily had made with her own hands.

Everything about the house and its small plot of ground was immaculate, perfectly cared for. One of the granddaughters of the original Tate family, neighbors of Aunt Emily's, whom her father had often told her about, came in to care for it regularly, airing it in the summer, building fires in the winter to keep out the damp, cleaning and polishing.

"I feel as if ghosts were walking up and down my spine, but it's a wonderful feeling, not scary," she confided to Naomi.

Naomi's face was radiant, far too radiant to be accounted for by this visit, because it was all familiar to her, a part of her life. And Martin's Corners itself was so small that Andrea was at a loss to understand what had brought about the change in her gentle cousin.

"Home!" Naomi said. "This is as much home to me as Roselawns, as Amhurst used to be. If I had my choice of all the places in the world that could be my very own, this is what I'd choose. This house, this little town."

"You'd trade Roselawns for them?" Andrea demanded, astounded.

Naomi bit her lip, and Andrea could see the effort it cost her to laugh and make a deprecating comment. "I'm just talking, of course. It's just that this place is so wrapped up in my childhood." But the shining light was still in her eyes, and Andrea was more convinced than ever that there was some mystery here. If Naomi didn't tell her pretty soon, she'd burst with curiosity!

Naomi didn't, after all, have to tell her. Andrea found out for herself, just by using her eyes, the next afternoon when the two girls walked to the center of the town, larger than it had been when Adam had known it but still a small town by any standards.

"That's the general store. The Hamiltons still own it. And there's the feed and grain store, the Blaisdels still own that, too. Things don't change much here; the same businesses go down from generation to generation in the same families," Naomi told her. "And there's the *Clarion*. It's the only major establishment in Martin's Corners that didn't go down in a straight line, because David Lawrence was a bachelor and there weren't any sons to leave it to. He loved our grandmother Martha, you know. It was there that she wrote all those articles against slavery, the ones that made her famous."

"Yes, Father told me quite a bit about it. She must have been a wonderful woman, Naomi. It makes me feel sort of humble, just to think about her."

"And so it should! She was a heroine, greater than most of the heroines you read about, because she was real! Grandfather never got over her death, especially the way it happened, her getting hit on the forehead by a stone a rioter threw at one of her lectures in Boston. He was there, in the audience; he'd come to bring her home to Rose-lawns even if he had to tie her up and carry her, but it was too late. The riot broke out, and everyone piled outside, and somebody threw that stone and it just happened to hit her and she died right there, on the sidewalk, in his arms."

Naomi blinked her eyes to clear away the tears that had gathered, and took Andrea's arm. "We'll just go in and say hello to Mr. Barnaby, the man who owns the *Clarion* now. Mother and I always call in there when we come to Martin's Corners."

Andrea had never been in a newspaper office before. It was Wednesday, the day the paper was printed, or, as Naomi told her with her greater knowledge, "put to bed." The clatter of the press from the back room, where the machinery was, was deafening. But it didn't seem to bother Naomi at all. She nodded to the middle-aged woman who sat behind the counter in the front office, and went right on through to the pressroom, taking Andrea with her. Andrea thought that she called the woman Bessie, but with all the noise she couldn't be sure.

Inside the back room, the clatter was even more deafening. But it stopped so suddenly that the silence was nearly as painful as the noise when the stocky man running the press looked up and saw them and turned it off.

"Miss Amhurst! I knew you and your mother were coming, but I didn't realize you'd already arrived! I'm going to have to shake up my news-gatherers!" Mr. Barnaby wiped his hands on his leather apron and came forward to clasp both of Naomi's in his. His eyes twinkled behind steel-rimmed bifocals. "The town will be rolling out the red carpet again, in honor of the daughter and granddaughter of our most illustrious citizen, Martha Curtis Beddoes!"

"We just arrived late yesterday afternoon, Mr. Barnaby. Mother and Aunt Catherine haven't stirred out of the house yet. All the same, I expect everybody in town already knows that we're here. They probably all thought that somebody else had already told you. There won't be any use of printing our arrival as a social item, the news will be stale."

"Bad reporting!" the editor-owner insisted, still smiling, but now his eyes turned to Andrea, and he stood waiting to be introduced. It took Naomi, whose own eyes were searching the rest of the big room, so cluttered with strange machines that Andrea was dazzled, a moment to realize that she hadn't remembered the amenities.

"Andrea, this is Mr. Barnaby, the owner of the *Clarion*. If we'd got here one day earlier, there'd have been a big article on the front page, telling of our arrival. Now we'll have to wait till next week to see our names in print, because Mr. Barnaby will print the piece anyway, even if it will be stale news by then."

"Not so!" Mr. Barnaby's face positively beamed with pride. "You're behind the times, Naomi. The *Clarion* now comes out twice a week, on Wednesdays and on Saturdays! And there'll be an article on the front page, all right. But you still haven't told me your friend's last name, or who she is, and that's no way to treat a newspaperman!"

Naomi's face flushed with embarrassment. Really, Andrea thought, her cousin seemed to be in some kind of a daze!

"I'm sorry! I'm just so excited at being here that I don't know what I'm doing. Mr. Barnaby, this is my cousin Andrea Marie Wentworth, from Texas. She's Adam Wentworth's daughter. You never knew him, but you've heard of him."

"Haven't I, though! Everybody in Martin's Corners who's old enough remembers Adam Wentworth, and they have nothing but good to say about him! This is an honor, Miss Wentworth, a real honor! Is your father with you, by any chance? By George, I'd like to talk with him! Texas! He could tell me enough to fill a whole issue!"

"I'm sorry. Father didn't come with us, but my mother is here, Catherine Wentworth."

79

Mr. Barnaby was already scribbling on a piece of notepaper. "Mrs. Catherine Wentworth, wife of Adam Wentworth, one-time citizen of Martin's Corners," he said, his tongue in the corner of his mouth. He licked the lead of the pencil and went on writing. "And his daughter, Andrea Marie Wentworth, accompanied Mrs. Prudence and Miss Naomi Amhurst. I'll give this to Bessie to write up, she'll be calling at your house to fill in all the details that everybody in town will want to know. Oh, here's Kelvin! Kelvin, come over here, Miss Naomi's back, and this time she has her cousin with her! Miss Wentworth, this is Kelvin Janson, my assistant editor and my good right hand."

"Miss Amhurst. Miss Wentworth. I'm very pleased to meet you. Miss Wentworth, and I'm pleased that you and your mother are visiting Martin's Corners, as well as that Miss Amhurst and her mother have returned again this summer."

What a nice young man, was Andrea's first thought. There wasn't anything overly handsome about Kelvin Janson. He appeared to be in his mid-twenties, maybe twenty-five or twenty-six. His hair was of a medium shade of brown. His eyes were brown, as well, warm and friendly and filled with a lively intelligence. There was a trace of a cleft in his chin. Her overall impression was of a lanky, pleasant-faced young man, one that she'd be glad to count among her friends.

"And we're glad to be here." She smiled at Kelvin, and she sensed that he liked her, too, although there was none of the instant, stunned look about him that other men of his age usually exhibited on meeting her for the first time. His eyes went instead to Naomi, and realizing that Naomi hadn't said a word since Kelvin had come into the room, Andrea looked at her, too.

So that was it! The mystery that had been puzzling her ever since they'd set out for Massachusetts was solved. Because Naomi, her face paler than usual, was looking back at Kelvin with an expression in her eyes that no other girl could ever mistake.

"We'll have to be going now," Naomi said. "I just

wanted to show Andrea where Martha Curtis Beddoes worked."

"Did you remember to show her Martha's picture, in the outer office?"

Naomi flushed. "I'm afraid I didn't. I'll show you now, Andrea."

Kelvin fell into step beside them as Mr. Barnaby went back to his press and the clatter started again, making Andrea want to put her hands over her ears. She was grateful when the door between the pressroom and the outer office closed behind them, although the noise was diminished only a little.

"There it is, Miss Wentworth," Kelvin Janson said.

The picture was hanging in the middle of the wall directly behind the counter where the woman called Bessie presided. It was a daguerreotype, in an oval frame, and there was a brass plaque under it inscribed with her name and the dates of her birth and her death.

"Martin's Corners' own heroine," Kelvin said softly, and there was worship in his voice. "The heroine of all of the Northern states as well, of course, because she became quite famous. But she got her start at writing her anti-slavery articles right here in this office, sitting where Bessie is sitting now. You might call her this newspaper's patron saint."

Andrea was moved, so moved that she felt close to tears. But at the same time, she was fully aware of the agitation that Kelvin Janson's presence caused her cousin.

"We'll all be seeing each other again soon, Miss Wentworth," the woman Bessie, her fingers splotched with ink, told her. "The Hamiltons will have a party in your honor. It'll be held in the church hall, as it always is, because no house in Martin's Corners could accommodate the guests. Mrs. Hamilton and Mrs. Blaisdel will be co-hostesses, as they always are when your aunt and your cousin come to visit. I'll let you know the minute they tell me the time and date. Of course, they'll both call on you by tomorrow, at the latest, and issue the invitation in person."

"That will be wonderful, Bessie. I'll feel like a celebrity!" Andrea smiled at her.

"And so you will be! It isn't every day that Adam Wentworth's wife and daughter come to Martin's Corners, much less another connection of Martha Beddoes! I'll see you there, if we don't see each other again beforehand. I wouldn't miss it for the world, nor would anyone else in Martin's Corners!"

"Naomi, you didn't tell me Bessie's last name," Andrea reproached her cousin when they were back out on the street.

"What? I'm sorry, I didn't hear what you said."

"Naomi Amhurst! Oh, all right, I forgive you. Now that I've met Kelvin Janson, I know why your head has been in the clouds these last several days! And you never gave me as much as a hint!"

Naomi's face seemed to freeze. "Andrea, you stop that! There isn't anything between Kelvin and me. We're simply old friends, we've known each other ever since I was a small child. I like him better than almost anybody else in the world, but there's nothing between us now and there never has been."

Andrea looked at her, her mouth all but hanging open. If Naomi wasn't in love with Kelvin Janson, then Andrea didn't know what the word meant.

"Don't tease me, please. It would upset Mother; it would upset everybody," Naomi went on, her face so pale that Andrea wondered if she might actually faint right here in the street. "Kelvin and I are like brother and sister, there's no more to it than that. We used to play together, when we were children."

Is she deliberately lying to me, or does she honestly not realize that she's in love with Kelvin, Andrea wondered. And what about Kelvin himself? He had not, by a word or a glance or a gesture, indicated that Naomi meant anything more to him than her cousin had just told her, but Andrea would have been willing to swear on a stack of Bibles that he loved Naomi, too. This East was a hard place to understand, and she wondered if she'd ever be able to. Back home in Texas, if people loved each other, they told each other so, and everybody else as well, and then they got married and that was all there was to it.

Looking at Naomi with complete puzzlement, Andrea dropped the subject. All the same, it was mightily peculiar! Unless, of course, Naomi felt that she was honor bound to marry Gregory Randolph just because it was expected of her!

And I, she thought, will just see about that! Because if I can make Naomi admit that she loves Kelvin, then I'll be blamed if I'll let her go marrying anybody else, even Gregory Randolph, and what people expect can go jump into the nearest lake!

5

Even before the huge party that the Hamiltons and the Blaisdels put on for them at the church hall, Andrea felt as if she'd known everybody in Martin's Corners all her life. Wherever she went, in company with Naomi or alone, people greeted her by name, asked her about her father, told her stories about Martha Curtis Beddoes. They told her their own family histories insofar as they had touched on either Martha's or Prudence's or Adam's, and they asked her about Texas, their amazement at both her extraordinary beauty and the fact that she had come from such an outlandish place taking precedence over their natural New England reticence.

Kelvin Janson, she learned right away, was a Tate, one of the descendants of the Tate daughters. Andrea knew the story well because it was one that had always amused Adam. It seemed that the Tates, Sam and his wife Mehitabel, had had one daughter after another, and never a son, until Sam had been fit to be tied. It had been a town joke, the way Sam had carried on, getting drunk at the tavern every time poor Mehitabel had presented him with another female child. It wasn't until his daughters had grown up and married that boys had appeared in the family. His daughters had run to having sons, with only a sprinkling of girls among them, but even that hadn't mollified old Sam because his grandsons, naturally, couldn't carry on his name.

As close as they were, Andrea couldn't draw Naomi out about Kelvin. She merely got a remote, touch-me-not look in her eyes and insisted that she and Kelvin were only friends. In the end, it was the young assistant editor whom Andrea was furious with, because she was convinced that he felt that he had no right to speak for her cousin because of her aristocratic family background. Not only was she a Beddoes, and a descendant of the Curtis family, while the Tates had never been more than blacksmiths and farmers, but even here in Martin's Corners people were aware that she was to marry into another aristocratic Southern family, the Randolphs.

"Naomi, I feel like shaking every tooth in your head loose!" Andrea finally exploded. "If you love Kelvin, go get him! Believe me, if I loved somebody, nobody and nothing on earth would keep me from getting him!"

"And maybe I would, if I were sure! But even if I were sure, I could hardly propose to him, could I? How can I know if he even wants me? He's never given the least indication that he thinks of me as anything except a younger sister."

Andrea threw her hairbrush so that it clattered against the wall of their bedroom in the saltbox house and had the immediate, creepy sensation that Miss Emily, who had taken such meticulous care of her possessions, would have disapproved.

"If you don't beat all! How are you ever going to be sure, unless you do something to find out? Naomi, it isn't the fact that the Randolphs have so much money, and that you'll end up with Swanmere, that's holding you back, is it?"

Naomi's face flamed with anger. For a moment,

Andrea flinched, sure that her cousin, who was normally so gentle that she could hardly bear to swat a fly, was going to slap her.

"No, it isn't! If you knew anything about Southerners you'd know that money isn't half as important as family name! Mother could have married Gaylord Renault, when he was the catch of Georgia, but it was Burke she loved, and the Amhursts didn't have half as much!"

"Then what in heck is stopping you from finding out how Kelvin feels about you?"

"It's easy for you to talk! Look at you, you're so pretty than any man would want you! I'm just a plain, mousy spinster. If Greg wants me, then I'm the luckiest girl in the world! But I certainly have no reason to think that Kelvin would want me, too! We were playmates, every summer since I was old enough to go tagging after him when we came here to Martin's Corners. And that's all I am to him, a friend, a girl who used to be a pest to him except that he was always too polite to tell me to go away and get lost! I'd rather die than tell him that I love him and have him take me because he's sorry for me the way he used to be sorry for me because I didn't have anyone esle I wanted to play with, I only wanted to be with him. Kelvin's like that, he's so kind he can't bear to hurt anyone. Both our lives would be ruined. So if he doesn't do the asking, then I'll just go back home to Georgia and marry Greg the way everyone expects me to. I don't want to be an old maid, I want a husband and children, especially children, and a home of my own."

She saw Andrea's expression and she jumped to her feet, her face blazing with a passion that Andrea had never seen there before.

"Don't you dare!" she cried. "Andrea Wentworth, don't you dare go trying to find out! Kelvin's nobody's fool, he'd know what you were hinting after in a minute! And don't go trying to tell me that you aren't thinking about it! I'll never forgive you, I swear I won't, not for as long as we live!"

"Don't you think I'm smarter than any mere man? I've been twisting men any way I want them to go ever since I could walk! He wouldn't have an inkling, I promise you!"

"No! You have to promise me. Promise, this instant!"

Andrea hated to give that promise. She was convinced that she could find out what she wanted to know without Kelvin's coming close to guessing that she was picking his brains. but Naomi was so agitated that she finally gave in. After all, it was none of her business. Naomi was twenty-three years old to her eighteen, and with her own emotional life so mixed up, where did she get the nerve to try to interfere?

All the same, during the four weeks they remained in Martin's Corners she gritted her teeth with frustration a dozen times a day as she saw the way her cousin neither sought Kelvin out nor avoided him, but only treated him like any other of her Martin's Corners friends. She would have sworn that Kelvin worshiped Naomi, but that he was too proud to ask her to give up everything she'd ever known, all of her expectations of a brilliant marriage, to cast her lot with a simple assistant editor in a small Massachusetts town. Back home in Texas people weren't that stupid; if they wanted something, and somebody else's brand wasn't already on it, they went out and threw a rope on it! Sometimes, the way she saw Kelvin look at Naomi, and the way Naomi looked at Kelvin when they thought the other one was looking at something else, she could just cry.

Two evenings before they were to leave Boston to begin their journey back to Roselawns, Prudence invited everyone to what she called an ice cream social, held on the lawn of the saltbox house. This, too, had become tradition, she told Kate and Andrea, a way of returning the hospitality for the party held for them at the beginning of their summer visit.

Andrea was intrigued with the idea of an ice cream social. Milk and cream were brought in from the Tate farm, and she took her turn at turning the cranks of the gallon ice cream freezers, borrowed from their neighbors and packed with cracked ice and rock salt, to freeze gallon after gallon, chocolate, vanilla, lemon, strawberry, all so delicious that she shivered with delight when she scraped the dashers after they were removed for the ice cream to set and harden.

With the help of Eunice Tate, who cared for the saltbox house during the rest of the year, the girls and their mothers baked more than a dozen cakes and strung paper lanterns from the trees and set up tables made of boards laid across sawhorses in the yard.

Andrea loved everything about the social. Everyone came, dressed in their second-best as this was such an informal affair. Children stuffed themselves between racing and screaming in games of tag that never seemed to end, and the girls were lovely in their light summer dresses.

Prue and Kate each wore their pearls, as they had at the initial party, Prue the same strand that had caused the first rift between Martha and Jonathan, and Kate the almost identical strand that Adam had given her when they were married. One day Prue's pearls would go to Naomi, and Kate's to Andrea, but Dria prayed that that day would not come for so many years that there was no point in thinking about it.

But even more than the novelty of this kind of a party, Andrea was avid with interest in Naomi and Kelvin. The two young people made no special effort to seek out each other's company, but Dria missed none of the glances they gave each other. If ever she'd seen two people in love, Naomi and Kelvin were the ones, and it was a shame that they didn't do something about it.

Her attention was diverted when Mr. Blaisdel stood up on a bench and bellowed that Snap and Catch'um was about to begin. What in the world was Snap and Catch'um?

"I want a couple for the center!" Mr. Blaisdel shouted. Eunice Tate and her husband immediately walked to a cleared space well illuminated by the paper lanterns and stood facing each other, each of them with their hands grasping the other's forearms very firmly.

"Now another couple. You, Nate Hamilton, and you, Miss Wentworth."

The game was simple, and Andrea thought it was

hilarious. Nate chased her around and around Eunice and Jack Tate, this way, that way, lunging, grabbing, while she fled from him, ducking and screaming and sidestepping. The reason for Eunice and Jack's firm grip on each other's arms was obvious, they took a real buffeting as Nate attempted to catch his quarry, his face flushed with determination.

There! He had her, and she had to pay the penalty, a chaste, quick kiss on her cheek. Nate then took Jack's place with Eunice, while Jack dropped out, and it was up to Andrea to choose someone for her to chase around them. No one knew the origin of the game, although some thought that it had been brought to Martin's Corners by an immigrant from upstate New York. It was fast and furious, good clean fun, with the spectators shouting and clapping encouragement.

Her hair disheveled, her face hot, Andrea chose Kelvin, hoping that he'd have sense enough to choose Naomi once she'd caught him and taken her place in the center with Nate.

Her ruse worked. Catching Kelvin took some doing. His legs were long and he was used to the game, but she finally grabbed his shirt and then she held her breath as Kelvin was apparently going to choose a Blaisdel girl but veered toward Naomi at the last instant.

Even being buffeted around as she was, standing in the center with Nate, Andrea saw that Naomi's face was radiant. She'd never seen her cousin's eyes shine like this before, never seen such a happy flush on her face. Naomi was transformed, she was so lovely that Andrea thought that Kelvin would have to be simple-minded if he didn't make an opportunity to be alone with Naomi before the evening was over and tell her that he loved her.

There! Kelvin had caught her, and Naomi turned her cheek for his kiss, looking as if she'd been transported to heaven. Kelvin's expression made a lump come into Andrea's throat as he hesitated for a fraction of a second and then kissed her as if he were kissing an angel descended from that same heaven.

But no one except Andrea seemed to notice. Kelvin

took Nate's place and Naomi, looking as if she were walk-ing in a trance, pointed out another of the Tate clan to play. And when they were both out of the game, they went their separate ways.

Darn them! What was the matter with them, anyway? Did they think that love like theirs grew on trees, that they could walk out into any yard and pick it? Didn't they know that winter was coming and soon there'd be no more leaves, and their opportunity would be lost forever?

Andrea's chin firmed. And a few moments later, she slipped into the shadows where no one could see her and deliberately worked at the heel of her slipper until it was loose. Then she returned to the crowd, and when Naomi glanced her way she pretended to stumble and turn her ankle.

"Oh, I've lost my heel, and I've hurt my ankle a little, too. Naomi, Kelvin, come and help me!"

They were both beside her in an instant, their faces filled with concern. "I'm all right. Just help me hobble out to the back where I can sit on the back steps and catch my breath. Besides, I want Kelvin to tell me more about when Martha was here in Martin's Corners and wrote for the same newspaper Kelvin works for, writing those anti-slavery articles."

She sank down onto the bottom step and sighed. "I hate having to leave here! I wish I could stay here forever. Don't you feel the same way, Naomi?"

Even in the darkness, the only light from the win-dows of the kitchen behind them, she could see Naomi's face pale. Say yes, Andrea willed, say yes, you idiot! Say you'd rather live here in Martin's Corners than any place in the world!

"Yes, I often feel like that." Naomi's voice was small.

"Oh, I've torn my stocking, and I must change into another pair of shoes. No, Naomi, don't come with me. You and Kelvin wait for me right here, and don't you dare go away until I get back!"

Before Naomi could protest, Andrea got up and was up the back steps and into the house. Left alone, Naomi and Kelvin looked at each other.

90

"Do you really like it here so much, Naomi?" Kelvin asked.

"Yes, I do. I've always loved it, you know that, Kel."

Kelvin's face was as pale as Naomi's. "But you have your beautiful plantation, and all that Beddoes tradition to go with it."

"We've as much tradition here as in Georgia, and I'm every bit as proud of it. Even more proud, because of my great-great-aunt Emily, and my grandmother Martha. Yes, I love it here, Kelvin."

Kelvin's hands knotted as he struggled to bring out the words that he'd wanted to say to her for so long. Did he dare, had he any right, or would it only distress her when she had to refuse him?

"Naomi, I . . ."

At that critical instant, a little lad no more than two years old wandered into the back yard, crying. Naomi got up to go to him. "Why, Billy, what's the matter?"

"I hurted my knee, and I can't find my mama," the little boy wept.

Naomi took his hand. "I'll help you find her, Billy. Kelvin, I'll be right back." What had he been going to say, just now? Could he have been, was it possible? She had to find Betty Tate quickly; her heart was beating furiously and her knees felt weak as she dared to let herself hope.

It gave Kelvin a breathing space. He took a deep breath, his face filled with resolution. He'd ask her. All she could do was say no, but what if there was a chance, any chance at all, that she'd say yes?

Voices came from the kitchen behind him, drifting out through the window that was open to the cool night air. It was Kate and Prue, who'd come in to slice and carry out more cake.

"When do you think Naomi and Gregory will be married? He's a fine young man, Prue. You couldn't have wished anything better for her."

"Yes, I'm happy about it. We all are. It will be wonderful having her live so close to us, at Swanmere. I suppose every mother dreads losing her daughter, but I'll hardly be losing her at all."

"She'll be a lovely mistress for Swanmere. And I can't think of any girl who deserves such good fortune more. I hope the engagement party takes place while Dria and I are still at Roselawns. Dria would love it, it's the sort of thing she's dreamed about ever since she was a little girl."

His face much paler than it had been a moment before, Kelvin rose and left the back yard. When Naomi came back a moment later, he was nowhere to be seen, and when Andrea joined her, thinking that she'd given them enough time and that if she didn't come back they'd grow suspicious of her matchmaking, Kelvin was nowhere to be found. He'd left the party, and Naomi's eyes were dark with pain, all the beauty and life she'd shown such a short time before gone out of her.

There was nothing Andrea could do to help her. Darn, she thought. Oh, darn, darn, darn! She had no idea of what had happened, but she knew that Kelvin and Naomi had lost their last opportunity to keep from ruining their lives.

ROSELAWNS

6

The air had turned thick and close, and black clouds were gathering. Andrea had never felt such uncomfortable heat, wet and heavy. It stormed in Texas, sometimes violently, but she'd never felt as though she were suffocating.

She and Naomi were visiting Swanmere. Gregory had ridden over to escort them early that evening. Eulalie Randolph, Greg's mother, was deep in the plans for the ball she was going to give in Andrea and Kate's honor, and she'd particularly wanted the girls to come so that they could help her iron out all the details. She had to know the color of the gowns that they were going to wear, for one thing, so that her decorations wouldn't clash with them. Andrea was both amused and amazed. In Texas, it wasn't what people wore that counted, it was how much fun they had! A barn dance was nearly always a lot more fun than a fancy party where everybody had to dress up and worry about whether their gowns clashed with the décor or with each other's!

They had been going to ride this afternoon, as soon as Naomi and Eulalie finished with the guest list. The girls were going to stay overnight, so there was plenty of time for Greg to give Andrea the grand tour of the plantation and the surrounding countryside. But now, with this storm lowering overhead, their plans had been changed. They were all in Eulalie's private sitting room at the back of the house when Greg looked up and saw the storm clouds through the long French windows that looked out over the garden.

"I'd better go to the stable and tell Jake to unsaddle the horses. This storm is going to break any minute."

"I'll go!" Andrea jumped up, eager to escape the stifling room and the endless discussion of names of people she'd never heard of. Once again, she thought of how much simpler things were back home, where if you were throwing a big shindig, you just sent out the word and everybody came!

She stepped through the windows before anybody could protest. The air was heavier than ever. and most of the light was gone, a strange, eerie light diffused by the clouds that seemed almost to touch the ground. There was a smell of ozone in the air, and a prickling ran along Andrea's arms and legs as if the atmosphere were charged with electricity.

All of a sudden she felt alive, ready to burst with animal energy, every nerve in her body quivering in anticipation of the coming storm as a wind sprang up. instantly drying her perspiration-damp body. She lifted her face to the sky as she faced into the wind and felt it lift her hair, cooling her forehead and the nape of her neck, savoring the smell and the feel of it.

Jake, the middle-aged Negro who took care of the saddle horses, had already led her mount back inside the stable, and now he was leading Naomi's his wary eyes also studying the gathering clouds. A lad of nine or ten was holding Greg's huge chestnut hunter, but he was having a hard time of it because the horse, like Andrea, felt the nerve-tingling quality in the air.

"Easy, you big old horse, take it easy, you hear?" the

boy coaxed, his eyes rolling as Jupiter tossed his head and began to prance. The lad's feet left the ground and he gave a yelp of fright as Andrea reached them and put her own firm hand on the bridle to bring Jupiter back down to all four feet and steady him.

Glory, but Jupiter was a magnificent beast! He was every bit as good as Adam's Beau Noir, the black stallion that was the envy of all his friends in the Chinatis. Beau Noir was the only piece of horseflesh on the ranch that Andrea had never been permitted to ride. The fact that neither of her brothers had ever been allowed to ride him, either, did nothing to mitigate Andrea's disgust. She'd have given her eye teeth to ride him but even her imperative cajoling had never been able to coax any of the vaqueros to let her sneak him out and try him.

But here was Jupiter, as sleek and powerful as Beau Noir, a hunter bred from generations of champions, prancing and still trying to toss his head to pull free from her and the boy who was holding him.

"Steady!" Andrea told him. And almost before the word was out of her mouth, she knew what she was going to do. Her hands moved with lightning-fast speed as she shortened the stirrups, and even as the lad cried out with horrified protest, she'd swung up onto the great beast's back and gathered up the reins.

"Missy, get offen that horse!" the boy begged, his face going gray under his natural pigmentation. "Get offen him, he'll kill you!"

Andrea laughed, the sound filled with wild exultation, and dug her heels into Jupiter's side, wheeled him, and headed for the paddock. She had to try him out, she just had to; she felt stifled riding around the soft Georgia landscape on a sidesaddle, at a sedate trot or a controlled canter. Lord, but it was good to feel the solid horseflesh between her knees again, to put her weight on the balls of her feet in the stirrups, to feel the thundering power of the stallion under her as she lifted him first into a trot and then into a gallop.

They gained the paddock and they'd just completed their first lap when a flash of lightning with an accompanying peal of thunder split the air, and Jupiter went crazy. Dimly, Andrea was aware that the stableman was running toward the paddock, shouting something that the wind tore from his mouth and blew away before it reached her, while the boy, his eyes rolling with terror, bolted for the house to alert Greg that the young mistress had taken his horse and was going to get her neck broken as sure as Judgment Day.

Andrea had no time to think about that. A new surge of exultation flooded through her body as she fought the horse that was determined to throw her, that had panicked and wanted only to streak back to the safety of its stable. Jupiter had never carried a woman; only Greg rode him, and there were times when even he was hard put to handle him, times when the powerful beast had even thrown him and come near to trampling him into the bargain. Every horseman in the county envied Greg that hunter, but few of them would have wanted to own him. He was just too much horse, too dangerous to handle.

Jupiter was plunging all over the paddock now, his head tossing, rearing up on his hind legs, his feet scrambling. Overhead, the skies opened up and the rain came down in a drenching torrent, further maddening him.

Andrea stuck to his back like a burr. Jake's knees nearly gave out under him, and he began to pray as if the devil himself had come down to earth in the storm, as he heard her exultant laughter as she fought to control the stallion. Lordy, lordy, she was going to be kilt, and he'd get the blame for not stopping her from taking that devil-horse!

Another shout was added to the noise of the storm as Greg came pelting through the downpour as fast as his long legs could carry him. Naomi, her hair and her drenched clothing clinging to her head and body, followed him as fast as her hindering garments would let her.

"Andrea, stop it! Get off!" Naomi screamed. The words that came from Greg's mouth were a great deal stronger, words that would have made Naomi flinch with shock if she hadn't already been too shocked at Andrea's mortal danger to hear them.

Andrea had never felt so alive in her life. Her spine was jolted, her head snapped back on her neck, as Jupiter fought her for control of the bit, jumping, bucking and turning, his head flailing, every ounce of his tremendous power intent on ridding himself of the burden on his back so that he could plunge into a blind gallop through the storm. His maddened eyes rolled and froth streamed from his mouth, and still Andrea kept to the saddle, her knees clamped to his sides so that it was impossible to dislodge her. She laughed again, neck-reining him with all her strength, her heels kicking him, urging him forward in a straight line instead of the circles he was going in, backwards, on his hind legs, his front feet scarcely touching the ground.

Naomi was crying now, Greg swearing more violently than he had before, and Jake was actually on his knees, his own eyes rolling and his mouth muttering prayers.

"Run, darn you!" Andrea cried. "Let's see how fast you are, you beauty!" She kicked him again, lifted the reins sharply, lifted him from his prancing and into a gallop. Straight at the paddock fence on the other side of the paddock, thundering down on it, and then up, up and over, to land still in full gallop, racing the wind that had torn her hair loose from its pins and sent it streaming out behind her.

"Yippee!" Andrea shouted, leaning forward, a part of the horse that was now galloping flat out, at one with him, two wild spirits that nothing could tame.

This was more like it! She'd had to bite her tongue almost in two, the first time she'd seen the flat, postage-stamp-sized English saddles, but there was something to be said for them after all. You could really get a grip with your legs; it was almost like riding bareback with the added benefit of stirrups, even such stirrups as these, little iron things that any red-blooded cowboy would laugh himself sick at.

Jupiter ran still faster, mane and tail flying in the wind. And Andrea felt as though she were flying, straight down the field beyond the paddock, straight toward another white-painted fence. They took the jump as if

99

Jupiter had wings and thundered on, Andrea's laughter lost in the wind that grew in force with every passing second. The rain was in her eyes, blinding her so that she had to narrow them to slits to see; her riding habit might have been molded to her body, but in her wild elation she hardly noticed.

Back at the paddock, Greg was shouting for a horse, even as he knew, despairingly, that no other horse at Swanmere had a prayer of catching Jupiter. Once that devil had the bit in his teeth, nothing could stop him, and Andrea didn't have a prayer of not being thrown. It would be a miracle if she weren't killed. He found it hard to credit that she was still in the saddle, that she actually seemed now to have the brute under control.

She did have Jupiter under control! Unbelievingly, his mouth hanging open, Greg acknowledged it even as his mind rejected the possibility. They soared over another fence, and then she turned him and they came thundering back toward the small group that waited in the teeming rain, the wind threatening to blow them off their feet.

There they came, the second fence jumped, the last one, Andrea riding like a Valkyrie, a myth come to life. And then they were in the paddock again, and Andrea pulled Jupiter down to a controlled canter and then a trot as she took him around another full lap, his neck arched, his head held high, his feet lifting in perfect rhythm as though he were in a parade prancing to the applause of a crowd. And then she brought him to a full stop and slid to the ground, her face alight with a radiant joy that made Greg's throat close as she shook her loosened, rain-soaked hair back from her face and led him, as docile as a gentle mare, toward him.

"Greg, he's wonderful! He's stupendous! You must let me ride him again, you just have to! But we'd better get him under cover now and rub him down, he can't be cooled out out here, it's like standing under a waterfall!"

The next thing she knew, she found herself folded in Greg's arms, crushed against his chest.

"Damn you! You crazy little fool, damn you for scaring the wits out of me like that! I thought you'd be killed, for sure! Oh, God, Andrea, I thought you'd be killed, and I wouldn't have been able to bear it, how could I have gone on living without you?"

Bemused, dazed by the rush of emotions that was shaking her to the core, Andrea looked up into his agonized face, streaming with rain, as wet as her own, and then his mouth came down over hers, and her arms found their way, of their own volition, around his neck. For a moment she thought she was soaring again, as wild as the storm, until at last they broke apart, looking at each other in stunned consternation.

Naomi, as quiet as a shadow, turned back toward the house and left them standing there in the rain, their eyes still locked and their faces pale with the realization of what had happened to them. She'd suspected this for days; it had only taken this incident, this wild, reckless prank of Andrea's, to bring it to the surface. Greg had fallen in love with her beautiful cousin, and Andrea loved him, too.

She felt no sense of loss, but rather a sense of freedom, a calm certainty that this was right, that at last things were as they should be. Her voice was perfectly calm as she entered the house and told a wide-eyed housegirl to begin preparing hot baths and to have dry clothing laid out for all three of them.

Eulalie, who had been standing in the doorway, her hands clasped so tightly that her knuckles showed white, looked at her with bewilderment. "Naomi, what happened? Was Andrea thrown, is she hurt?"

"She's perfectly all right, Mrs. Randolph, and so is Greg. Everything is perfectly all right," Naomi answered her, her voice serene. And then she went up the stairs to the guest room she was occupying and began, without haste, to take off her sodden clothing.

The news of the whirlwind courtship spread through the county like a swarm of wild bees. It was discussed in every parlor, in bedrooms between husbands and wives, talked about over teacups as ladies forgot their fancywork in this latest and juiciest bit of news that had come their way in a generation. Andrea Wentworth, that incredibly beautiful daughter of Prudence Amhurst's stepson Adam, had come from Texas and taken Greg Randolph right out from under Naomi Amhurst's nose!

"How's Naomi taking it, poor thing?"

"Like a lady, naturally. No one would as much as suspect that she'd ever cared a fig about Gregory! But then, she's a Beddoes, a Beddoes and an Amhurst. We couldn't expect that she'd take it any other way. Blood tells, every time."

Heads nodded in agreement as hearts bled for poor Naomi, to lose a catch like Gregory Randolph!

All of this bothered Andrea a great deal more than it bothered Naomi herself.

"Naomi, all you have to do is say the word, and I'll pack up and go straight back to Texas! I wouldn't have had this happen for anything. It was like a bolt out of the blue, when Greg told me he loved me. I'm still not sure how it happened, or even if it has at all!"

"Of course it's happened. I have eyes, Dria. It started even before we went to Massachusetts; I saw it even if you didn't realize it yourself. And I'm glad it's happened! Now I don't have to try to convince myself that I could be happy with Greg, when I knew all the time that it's Kelvin I love."

"If you love him, what are you going to do about it?" Andrea, still in a daze and feeling more than a little guilty because what had happened between her and Greg hadn't been as much of a surprise to her as she pretended, demanded of her cousin. She wouldn't feel half as guilty if Naomi and Kelvin got together, the way she'd been convinced all along that they should.

"I'll be going back to Martin's Corners next summer. And in the meantime, I can write to Mrs. Blaisdel and tell her that my engagement to Gregory is off. Once she knows about it, you can be sure that everybody in Martin's Corners will hear of it within a day. Then when I go back, Kel will know that I'm free, and if he doesn't ask me to marry him, I'll know that it's because he doesn't love me."

"A whole year! You ninny, why don't you pack up and go back there right now? But of course you can't do that, that would make everybody think that you were running away from a broken heart! But still, a year! How can you bear to wait that long?"

"I've waited all my life, Dria. Another year won't matter all that much. It'll give Kelvin a chance to be sure, for one thing." And that was all that Andrea could get out of her.

It was like a dream, as though she were moving through the pages of a book. Georgia Roselawns, Swanmere, Greg. Greg! She'd never known anyone like him, never dreamed that such a man could actually exist. All he had to do was walk into a room, and her pulses began to throb, her body to tingle. He was the embodiment of all the romantic heroes she'd ever dreamed about, and she still had trouble convincing herself that it was all true, that he loved her, that she wouldn't be going back to Texas this fall. She was going to stay right here at Roselawns, and they were going to be married at Thanksgiving, when her father as well as her mother could come for the wedding. The fact that such unseemly haste was a scandal made it all the more exciting, all the more like a dream.

She tried not to let herself think about Henry, who was counting the days until she'd return to Texas. There was a letter from him upstairs in her room, the first letter she'd ever had from him because they'd never been separated this long before. Henry's handwriting was black and strong, and his eloquence on paper had surprised her. He loved her, and it would tear him apart when he learned that she was going to marry someone else. She remembered the day she'd told him that she was coming to Georgia, when he'd said, his voice flat with despair, that she wouldn't come back, and she'd told him that he was being silly.

She was sorry that Henry was going to have to be hurt. She was so happy that she wanted everyone else in the world to be happy, too. But she couldn't let anything, not even her contrition because Henry was going to be hurt, spoil things for her.

Already, she dreamed of her wedding day, when she would float down Roselawn's staircase to meet her father at the bottom, with Greg waiting for her beside the minister in the drawing room, the house filled with hothouse flowers and guests. Thinking how her father would feel when he had to give her away to Greg, when he'd had his heart set on marrying Henry, was another thing that she refused to dwell on.

Kate tried to penetrate Andrea's trance-like state. She was happy for Andrea, because even though she'd known Greg for such a short time she had to admit that Gregory Randolph was everything that most women would want for their daughters. But at the same time she felt a sense of foreboding.

"Andrea, you have to be very sure about this. It isn't as if you've known Gregory long enough to be certain that this feeling you have for him will last. Any love that happens as fast as yours and Greg's for each other is just as likely to die just as fast, once the first bewitchment has faded."

"I can't believe that it's you saying that!" Andrea said, staring at Kate with amazement. "Haven't you told me, so many times that I can't even remember, how you fell in love with Father the first time you saw him? And he fell in love with you, too, else he wouldn't have gone back to get you!"

"That was different. We had a good deal of time, after our first meeting, to think it over."

"Well, what do you want me to do, get myself put in jail somewhere where Greg can't see me for months, so that we'll be sure of our love even after we've been separated?" Andrea's mouth quirked at the corners and then she burst out laughing.

She sobered at Kate's serious expression, her mother not returning her smile as she normally would. "Mother, it's going to be all right, I promise you! We'll have plenty of time to think it over, to be sure, before the wedding. But when you and Father get here, you'd better be prepared to see me get married, because that's the way it's going to be!"

Kate looked at her, this daughter of hers who was so lovely that she sometimes wondered how even Adam could have fathered such a glorious creature. It would be wonderful to have Andrea married, to have her safe, her wildness tamed. No more fights over her, no more danger of fatal duels or even crippling feuds springing up because of her beauty and her waywardness. If Andrea was sure, she should be content. But still her feeling of uneasiness persisted.

Andrea herself experienced no such feelings. It was as if she were walking on air, as if every dawn unfolded another page of a living dream that was too beautiful to be borne. Hardly a day went by that Gregory didn't ride over, and then he and she would ride out together, so right together that it was as if they had been destined, from the moments of their births, to find each other.

There were teas, garden parties, picnics. Andrea was examined by curious, sometimes slightly hostile and always a little envious eyes as both the young, unattached girls and their mothers evaluated her as she was introduced to all of the county society that mattered. The masculine portion of the county population had entirely different reactions. It was fortunate, Kate thought, remembering how it had been back home, that Andrea was already spoken for, or there might have been as much trouble in Georgia as there had been in Texas. Except that, thank heaven, Georgians didn't go around toting guns on their hips the way men did in Texas, at least not any more, not in these modern times.

All the same, she wished that Adam were here. She felt the need of his strength, of his decisive, analytical mind, as she seldom had before.

Still troubled in spite of the placid surface of things, she went to her room and began a letter to Adam. What would he think when she told him that Andrea was engaged, that plans for announcing the engagement, at a ball at Swanmere, were already well under way? Adam would be startled and not a little disturbed; he'd had the idea in his mind that Henry Stockwell was going to be his son-in-law for so long that it would be hard for him to accept that Andrea was going to marry a stranger.

She tried to keep her foreboding from coming through in her written words. Adam would have enough on his mind, accepting the fact that Andrea was to be married, and faced with the unwelcome task of telling Henry, without her adding to his problems.

Left to herself, Andrea was too restless to sit and read. With Kate busy at her writing desk, Aunt Prudence in the kitchen house supervising the putting up of preserves, and Naomi at Amhurst for the day, there was nothing for her to do, and she wasn't accustomed to being idle. She could go out to the back porch and help Cleo stem the berries that Aunt Prudence was so busily boiling down into jam. Cleo had been given that task under the pretext that only she would get all the hulls and stems off; actually it was to save her from working in the steaming kitchen house, a fiction that Cleo had accepted with dignity.

Ardis was suffering the discomforts of her first weeks of pregnancy, and Andrea felt ashamed that she'd decided to stay at Roselawns in case Greg might ride over. He'd already told her that it was unlikely that he could come today because he and his father were deep in some plantation business that had to be taken care of without delay. Still, she had hoped, only now it was obvious that he wasn't coming. It was already well after noon, and the distance between the two plantations was too great to make it worth while unless he started early in the day. If he was coming, he'd have been here by now.

It wasn't too late for her to go to Amhurst. Amhurst wasn't far and she'd have ample time to visit with Ardis and ride back home with Naomi. But even as she started upstairs to change into her riding habit, she changed her mind. She'd stay dressed as she was, in her cool lavender dimity, and take the buggy into town instead. There were several small purchases she needed to make, and it would be fun to be in town alone for the first time, to browse in the little shops that served the plantations and farms between their more major shopping expeditions to Savannah.

She helped the stableman harness up the gentle gelding to the buggy, enjoying the feel of the soft leather, kept soft and pliable by plenty of saddle soaping and oiling. Everything at Roselawns was beautifully kept, as it was at Trail's End. Her father would approve; nothing made him angrier than for good equipment to be neglected.

In spite of the warmth of the day, they made good time. The gelding was fresh and the light buggy, with only herself in it, was no burden to him. It was still early afternoon when she put out the iron weight to keep the patient gelding from straying and began her stroll down Jefferson Street, where all of the shops and businesses were located on two tree-shaded blocks. The amount of shade here in Georgia never ceased to amaze her. There were trees everywhere, and it was a good thing that there were, with the cloying summer heat.

She nodded and smiled at everyone she saw, whether she'd been introduced to them or not. A surprising number of people spoke to her by name. In a town as small as this, visitors at Roselawns were a subject of avid interest.

There was the Emporium, just across the street. Andrea's smile deepened. She'd go across and say hello to Grandfather Gaylord. He'd come to Roselawns a few days after she and Kate had arrived and had dinner with them, and she'd thought that he was the most handsome man of his age that she'd ever seen. Her father would look very much like that when he was old, she thought. Still straight and tall, his vitality was virtually unimpaired. She'd been sorry that Aunt Christine hadn't come, but her absence hadn't surprised her. Aunt Prudence had mentioned that Crissy wasn't well and that she seldom went anywhere socially. What a pity, she'd thought at the time, for such a vital man to have an invalid wife!

Gaylord, who was now half-owner of the Emporium, was measuring out a length of calico for a middle-aged matron when Andrea entered, blinking her eyes at the change from the bright street to the dimmer interior of the store. "I'll be right with you, ma'am." he said. And then he looked up and recognized her, and his face lighted up. "Andrea! What a pleasure to see you again! Is your mother with you?"

"No, I'm all alone. You might say I'm playing hooky." A dimple appeared in her cheek, close to her mouth, and the matron's breath caught. So this was Andrea Wentworth! No wonder everyone was raving about how beautiful she was. And not a bit standoffish, for all she wasn't a Georgian. Of course, Texas was a Southern state, too, even if it was far out west that it was hard to think of it as belonging to the Union. When Mr. Renault introduced them, Andrea's handclasp was as warm as her smile. The matron could hardly wait to get home to tell all of her neighbors that she'd been introduced to the girl from Texas and that she was every bit as lovely as everyone said she was.

"I'm really in town looking for gloves and talcum powder and hosiery." Andrea said. "And I thought it would be nice to keep business transactions in the family."

"Oh, you won't find what you want here! Mrs. Gibbon's shop in the next block is where all the ladies buy their gloves and hosiery!" the matron exclaimed, and then she flushed with mortification at her implied slur against the Emporium.

Gaylord only laughed. "Mrs. Farley is right, Dria. We don't carry the quality you want. You'd best take her advice and visit Mrs. Gibbon's shop."

"All right, then, but I hope I'll see you soon again. You'll be at the engagement party at Swanmere, of course. I do hope that Aunt Christine will be well enough to come, too."

"We'll see." There was a note of caution in Gaylord's voice, as though he'd prefer not to discuss it. But of course that couldn't be true, she was letting her imagination run away with her. "It depends on how she feels. But you can be sure that I'll be there, I wouldn't miss it for the world!"

Andrea found the gloves and hose at Mrs. Gibbon's

shop, and the talcum powder at the drugstore, and then she went into the ice cream parlor. The other patrons were mostly young people, girls still in high school, one young couple, still in their teens, holding hands surreptitiously under the table. It made Andrea feel mature, far removed from her own adolescence. The lemon soda she ordered was delicious. Ice cream was one thing that was still a treat in Texas. Being able to walk into a store and order it whenever you wanted it was a novelty to her, and she enjoyed it to the fullest.

But even as she savored the tart, lemony bubbles of the soda, she found herself musing over Aunt Crissy. Could it be possible that her aunt still harbored a grudge over Gaylord's youthful indiscretion, after all these years? Her great-aunt, she reminded herself, only that was so awkward to say that she'd fallen into the habit of calling great-aunt Prudence just Aunt Prue. Maybe that was why Crissy hadn't come to Roselawns to meet her and her mother, maybe she wasn't ill at all but rather didn't want to meet anyone who was related to her husband's illegitimate son. How could people be like that, Andrea wondered? It had all happened so long ago that it didn't even matter any more. Certainly Uncle Jacob had no animosity toward Adam; rather, he held his half-brother in the highest esteem, and his love for Adam was genuine. But it didn't follow that his mother would have the same attitude. Maybe Crissy was one of those people who believe that a sin, no matter how long ago it had been committed, should never be forgiven.

A glance at her lapel watch, one of her birthday presents, made her break off her brooding. She'd have to start back; her mother and Aunt Prue would be wondering where on earth she was. She'd forgotten to tell either of them that she was coming to town, and if they didn't think to ask at the stable they wouldn't have an inkling of her whereabouts. Besides, the gelding would be wanting his supper. She hadn't brought a nosebag for him, because she'd intended to be back before it was time for the horses to be fed.

She stroked the gelding's nose before she got into

the buggy, apologizing. "It's just that I'm not used to being turned loose in a pretty little town like this, all on my own!" she said crooningly. "Never mind, it won't be long before I have you back home, my pretty boy."

"Do you always talk to horses?" a teasing voice behind her asked.

Andrea looked up, smiling her gamine smile. "Of course I do, Grandfather! Their replies are more intelligent than I get out of a great many humans! Do you close your store this early?"

"No. My partner and I take turns going home for supper. It just happens that today is my early hour, and then I'll go back and hold down the store until closing time."

He didn't explain that there was a reason for his having chosen the earlier hour. The chances were that Crissy would have forgotten to prepare the meal, and he'd have to do it himself. It happened more often than he liked to dwell on. If anything had happened to upset her during the day, she'd have been at the wine bottle again. But his face betrayed nothing of his personal problems to Andrea. Gaylord Renault was used to covering up, to keeping his emotions hidden. God knows he'd had to be, with Crissy the way she was ever since she'd found out, all those years ago, that Adam Wentworth was his own natural son and that her dreams of his marrying their daughter Rosalind were impossible because they were half-brother and sister.

The revelation had almost killed her; for a while, she'd come close to losing her mind and had had to be watched and guarded constantly for fear that she'd make another attempt on Prudence's life.

Even today, the memory of that night when Crissy had stood with Old Jacob's smoking gun in her hand and Prue, her face registering surprise rather than pain, had fallen to the floor with a bullet in her shoulder, was as clear in his mind as it had been the day after it had happened. If it hadn't been for Burke, Prue would have died. Burke had always been a good doctor, one of the best, but his skill in removing the bullet and bringing the resultant fever down had been bordering on the miraculous. As it was, because of Burke's skill, they'd managed to keep the whole affair from seeping outside the confines of the family.

But even today no one, not even Crissy's friends, ever mentioned Prue, or Roselawns, to Crissy, because even if no one knew the real cause of Crissy's hatred for Prue, they knew that just to mention her name was enough to set Crissy off and send her into another drinking bout. They surmised it was because Rosalind and Adam had decided not to get married after all, and that Crissy was merely insanely jealous of her older sister, who had married the Wentworth fortune and who was Adam's stepmother. Crissy, they thought, must have some idea that Prue had discouraged the marriage, and blamed her sister for the broken engagement that would have made Crissy and Gaylord rich again if the marriage had taken place. The ones who'd known Crissy long enough knew that she'd always been spitefully jealous of her more fortunate sister, and so their surmises were reasonable.

"Get in. I'll take you home. I'd love to meet Aunt Christine, even if I can only stay a minute," Andrea urged. She felt slightly ashamed of her underhandedness, but if Crissy received her and was nice to her, it would set her mind at rest. Andrea wasn't used to having people dislike her, much less for such a silly reason, something that had happened almost back in the Dark Ages.

"I'm afraid she isn't feeling well today." Because he could hardly stand here in the street resisting Andrea's invitation to get into the buggy, he helped her up and then followed her, but there was no way he could take her into his house and introduce her to Crissy! "But thanks for the ride, anyway. It's welcome, after I've been on my feet all day."

It was Andrea's turn to hide her feelings, and she covered up her disappointment with a smile. It must be true, then, that Crissy still held a grudge against her father. But however disappointed she was that she wasn't to meet the almost legendary Crissy, she felt a lot sorrier for Gaylord. It must be miserable for him, having to live with a wife who was so unforgiving.

The Renault house was just off the main street, a white frame house with green shutters. A climbing rose-bush, she thought it was a Paul's Scarlet, rioted over the porch, and the deep lawn was neatly clipped, but the windowshades were drawn even though it would still be bright daylight for hours, now in the middle of the summer. Andrea had been bewildered at visiting the houses of some of Aunt Prue's friends and finding that their shades were kept drawn in the daytime, until Naomi had explained that it was to protect the carpets and upholstery from fading from the sunlight. Their adobe walls in Texas were so thick, the windows so deep set, further protected by deep, roofed patios, that there was no such problem back there.

"I'll see you at my engagement party, then," she said, as Gaylord got out and thanked her again for the ride. "Don't you dare forget! And tell Aunt Crissy that I'm sorry that she isn't feeling well." For her grandfather's sake, she mustn't let on that she'd guessed that she wouldn't be welcome in his home.

"I'll do that, Dria."

Gaylord bowed, a courtly man who swept his broad-brimmed white planter's hat, a habit from the past that he still affected, from his head, the picture of an aristo-cratic Southern gentleman. Andrea felt a lump in her throat. She didn't wish the Randolphs any bad luck, but there was certainly no harm in wishing that Gaylord still owned Swanmere and that the Randolphs had bought some other plantation. Maybe her grandfather was only a half-owner of a general store, but he was still every inch a Southern planter!

7

Neither Andrea nor Gaylord noticed the windowshade lift aside just far enough for someone to peer out at them as Andrea started off. The gelding set out at a sharp clip, knowing that he'd be given a measure of oats and then turned loose in the lush summer pasture as soon as he reached home. Andrea waved her gloved hand to Gay and and he nodded, his hat still in his hand, and watched until the buggy turned the corner and was lost to his sight.

My granddaughter, he thought, and Lord, what a beauty! Greg Randolph had better appreciate what he was getting. Adam had done mighty well for himself. After seeing Kate and Andrea, he wished that he could see his two Texas grandsons, as well, but Gay was used to appreciating what came his way without dwelling on what couldn't be. Just having been granted the privilege of knowing Kate and Andrea was enough.

Slowly, he walked up the path to the porch and let himself into the house, moving quietly so that if Crissy were asleep he wouldn't disturb her. She was apt to be shrewish when she was disturbed if she was sleeping, her head aching, her complaints ranging from the petty to the ridiculous.

But Crissy wasn't asleep on this late summer afternoon. He'd hardly opened the door before she confronted him, her face filled with a mixture of displeasure and curiosity.

"Who was that girl who drove you home? That's Prue's buggy she's driving!"

"Just a visitor to Roselawns, Crissy. She happened to see me on the street as she was heading back, and she was kind enough to offer me a ride."

"A friend of Naomi's?"

Gaylord, who had been casting around for some explanation that wouldn't be an outright lie, grasped at this straw.

"Yes, that's right. She's a friend of Naomi's. She and her mother are visiting Prue and Naomi."

"Well, it's a mercy you wouldn't have told me! I have to pry every last bit of information out of you! What do you care if I'm trapped here in this house year in and year out, that I almost never get to go anywhere or see anyone! A fine lot of friends I have, they almost never come to see me any more, much less invite me to their homes or their social affairs!"

"Is supper ready? I have to get back to the store." Gaylord didn't point out that it was Crissy herself who drove all of her friends away with her complaints and her constant insistence that because she hated her sister, they must hate Prue, too. And besides, they all knew about her tippling, and they never knew what condition they'd find her in if they did call on her. It was an embarrassment to them, and it was small wonder that they avoided her as much as their Christian charity would let them.

"No, it isn't. I don't feel well, I've had migraine all day, that's why I'm not dressed. Not that you'd notice that I'm still in my wrapper, you never look at me any more! You'll have to get something for yourself, I must lie down again. Bring me a fresh cold cloth for my forehead, the pain is excruciating!"

"Yes, Crissy. Right away." Wearily, Gaylord picked up the bowl of water that had turned tepid on the table beside the sofa and carried it to the kitchen. There was only a small lump of ice left in the icebox; Crissy had forgotten to put the card in the window again to let the ice man know that they needed another fifty pounds. He'd been thinking about a tall glass of ice water all the last couple of hours at the store, but now he sighed and put the little chunk of ice into the bowl of fresh water that he drew from the pump on the sink. Carrying it back into the darkened sitting room, he wrung out the cloth in the cold water and placed it gently over Crissy's forehead and eyes.

"Is that better?"

She murmured something that may have been assent or may not have been, and Gaylord's mouth tightened. It hurt to see Crissy as she was today, as she'd been, gradually deteriorating, for years. When she'd been a girl, she'd been a beauty, the most gorgeous piece of young womanhood he'd ever laid eyes on. If she'd been the elder, he might have picked her as his first choice instead of Prudence. Compared to Crissy with her golden hair and her magnolia skin and her huge blue eyes, Prue had looked like a little brown mouse. Only Crissy'd been too young and there'd been something about Prue that got under his skin, so that he'd been determined to have her. There was still something about her, that same quality that Martha had had, that made her more beautiful, more desirable, than any other woman in spite of their rather plain faces. It was their smiles, the light and warmth in their eyes, that caused the transformation that had set more than one man's blood to pounding through his veins.

Prue still had that quality, and there were many nights when Gaylord, unable to sleep, cursed himself for his youthful folly that had made him force Jonathan Beddoes's natural daughter, the girl Naomi, when he'd been angry at Prue and taken out his rage at her on her illegitimate half-sister. The fact that he'd been drunk out of his mind was no excuse, drunk because Prue had ignored him at his own birthday party and had spent the entire evening giving all her attention to Burke Amhurst, who wasn't half the catch that Gaylord was.

But all that was over and done with. You can't turn back time, no matter your regrets. And Adam had sprung from that night of folly, and now there was Andrea, and two grandsons that he had never seen, back in Texas. He couldn't honestly wish that as fine a man as Adam had never been born, or Adam's children, just because he regretted making the mistake that had forever kept Prudence from accepting him. Being honest now as he hadn't been when he'd been young, he admitted that Prue wouldn't have had him in any case, because she'd loved Burke even then, a love so steady and true that it had survived all the years until they had finally been reunited and married.

He turned away from Crissy and went back into the kitchen because he couldn't bear to see her as she was today. There was still a certain elegance about her, the carriage and self-assurance that comes from breeding, but the elegance was frayed at the edges, a little seedy. Her once golden hair had grayed, and often wisps of it strayed from her carefully arranged coiffure. Her creamy skin was fretted now with tiny lines, more from her drinking, which had ruined her health, than from her age, because Prue, who was several years older, looked years younger than Crissy now. She wore her clothes, good clothes for which he paid more than he could afford, with flair, but the lace at her collars was apt to be not quite immaculate, the ruffles at elbow or cuff raveling, her expensive kid shoes in need of polishing and run over at the heel because she forgot to send them to the cobbler for repair. And so much of the time, her eyes were red-rimmed and bloodshot, after she'd gone on another of her periodic bouts with the wine bottle.

The kitchen was in disorder, dirty dishes stacked in the sink and crusted food in pans still sitting on the range. Beulah Jones either hadn't come in today, or

Crissy had screamed at her to get out because she was making too much noise as she tried to wash up and clean. The Negro woman did a good job, when Crissy let her, but Gaylord could only afford to have her come in three times a week, and things got ahead of her. Methodically, Gaylord set the crusted pans to soak and then located a clean frying pan. There was a heel of ham left, old and unpalatable looking, but it would have to do. Luckily there were half a dozen eggs. He'd have two tonight with the ham and two for his breakfast in case Crissy still didn't feel up to getting it for him.

"Can I bring you something to eat?" he asked Crissy while the ham was frying.

"No! I told you that I don't feel well! Just leave me alone!" Crissy's voice was petulant. "And close the kitchen door, the smell of that ham is making me nauseous!"

The kitchen door closed behind him, and Crissy lay there with the damp cloth over her eyes, her mind racing. She was filled with determination to find out who it was who was visiting Prue. She wouldn't get any more out of Gaylord than she already had. Either he deliberately withheld things from her, or he was just too obtuse to know what was important. After all, what could you expect of a man who had turned out to be a mere clerk in a store? If she'd known, when she was a girl determined to snare Gay away from her sister so that she could be the mistress of Swanmere, what she knew today, she'd have drowned herself in Bartlet's Creek before she'd have married him!

To think that she, Christine Beddoes, who'd been the belle of the county, of all Georgia, could have been brought to this! Her husband a clerk, a common merchant, this house no better than a hovel, a slovenly, untrained cleaning girl three times a week! It was no wonder that she had migraines, that sometimes the pain was so bad that only alcohol could alleviate it. While Prue queened it at Roselawns, the leader of all the county society, living in the lap of luxury! There was no justice, no justice at all. She, Crissy, had been the pretty one, she, Crissy, should have had all that Prue had, and more! She couldn't bear to think of another family living at Swanmere, she couldn't bear to think of all she'd had, all she'd hoped to have, and lost!

The pain stabbed through her head, making her moan. Even if she'd been hanged for it, it was a pity that she hadn't killed Prue that night when she'd learned the truth about Adam Wentworth, Adam who'd been going to marry Rosalind and with his untold wealth restore Swanmere to all its former glory! Instead, here she was, the wife of a shopkeeper, living in poverty, only her name and her pride still intact out of the shambles that her life had become.

The girl in Prue's buggy had been pretty, extraordinarily pretty. Her young face had been radiant as she'd laughed at Gay, delighted with something he'd said. Who was she, exactly? She was rich, of course. Even the few seconds Crissy had had to study her had told her that. Those clothes hadn't come from any general store, they'd come from Boston, or New York, or even from Paris. There was always an air about wealthy people, an unmistakable air, and this girl had had it. Wealthy Bostonians, visiting Prue! Maybe there was a brother in the offing, maybe Naomi would marry into wealth and prestige, while her own poor Rosalind eked out a middle-class existence as the wife of a lawyer who'd never be a real success.

She went on speculating, and she knew that she was going to find out everything there was to know about Prudence's guests before another day had passed.

Gaylord was relieved to find her apparently asleep when he left to go back to the store, and more relieved to find her already in bed and this time actually asleep, her mind sedated by wine, when he returned after he'd closed the store for the evening. He too went to bed, but not to sleep. God grant that Crissy didn't find out who Andrea was, and in her spite do some irreparable damage! But there was little danger of that, he thought. None of Crissy's friends would be likely to mention the Amhursts' guests to her, and in a short while Andrea would be married to Gregory Randolph, her name no longer Wentworth, so that if by chance she was mentioned there'd be no way for Crissy to make the connection.

Crissy's eyes had dark circles under them in the morning. and she complained that her head still ached. Gaylord had no inkling that she wouldn't go back to bed the moment he left the house.

But Crissy had no such intention. As soon as Gaylord had gone she changed out of her soiled wrapper into a clean voile dress and arranged her hair with a semblance of her old skill and went out to sit in her back garden. her eyes glued to the back yard next door as she rocked restlessly in the wicker lawn chair. Bees droned around the flower beds; soft, fleecy white clouds drifted across the sky; it was a beautiful morning, but Crissy might have been sitting in a freezing rain for all her appreciation of it.

Her vigil was rewarded an hour later. She'd known that Danny, Beulah Jones's five-year-old son, would come out into the garden of the house next door because his mother would shoo him out from under her feet while she did Mrs. Farley's cleaning.

"Danny, come here."

Danny looked at her warily, apprehension on his dusky face. All of the black children were a little afraid of Miss Crissy; their elders said she was daft, and that they'd better keep clear of her or she might do something bad to them. They knew from experience, because Crissy had scant patience and less compassion for anyone who wasn't her social equal, much less for black people.

"Come here, I said! I'm not going to hurt you!"

Reluctantly, his feet shuffling, Danny approached her. He stopped several feet away from her, well out of her reach in case she got out of her chair and came at him. In all the time his mother had done for Miss Crissy, he'd never set foot in her house; Beulah knew better than to bring a child into the house with her, the way most of her other ladies allowed her.

"I want you to go and tell your mother that I want

119

to see her immediately, do you understand? Immediately!"

Danny was gone like a shot, only too willing to do as he was told as long as it took him away from the daft lady who was looking at him with such a wild expression in her eyes. Crissy leaned back in her chair. There was no use trying to pry information out of any of her friends or neighbors. They'd never tell her because they all knew how she felt about Prue. But Beulah would know. The black folk knew everything that went on in the county. And she'd get it out of Beulah if she had to pry it out of her. She knew ways to make servants talk; she hadn't been a Beddoes and then a Renault for nothing.

Beulah was a long time in coming. Uppity, that's what the black folk were these days, downright uppity; they didn't know their place any more. But she came, her face as wary as Danny's had been.

"You wanted to see me, Mrs. Renault?"

"Certainly I want to see you! I sent for you, didn't I? Beulah, who are the people visiting my sister?"

Beulah's face was expressionless. "I don't know, Mrs. Renault."

"Of course you know! I know perfectly well that you know! And you're going to tell me, this instant!"

"I'm sorry, Mrs. Renault. I just don't know."

"How would you like to have me call the sheriff and tell him that my cameo brooch is missing? Nobody else could have taken it, nobody else has been in my house for days! It turned up missing yesterday, right after you'd been in to clean."

"It isn't missing! I saw it right on your dresser, when I dusted, after you sent me upstairs because you didn't want me to clean the kitchen because of your headache! I put it in the little redwood jewel box where it belongs!"

"It isn't there now." Looking at her, hearing the timbre of her voice, Beulah blanched. If Miss Crissy said it wasn't there now, then it wasn't. Likely it was in her pocket, or pinned to her chemise so's it wouldn't be anywhere in the house if Miss Crissy called the sheriff and he searched. Beulah needed this cleaning work, and even if most people wouldn't believe it if Miss Crissy said she was a thief, the name would stick. Mud had a way of sticking, no matter how untrue it was.

"Well, Beulah? Are you going to tell me what I want to know?"

"Their name is Wentworth." The words came slowly, because Beulah hated to say them. Still, there couldn't be any harm in telling her. Miss Prudence's name had already been brought in, and people were only careful not to mention Mrs. Prudence Amhurst to Miss Crissy. There couldn't be any reason not to tell her that was worth being questioned by the sheriff and having everybody know it. She was just curious, that was all, she hated her sister but she still wanted to know everything about her and what went on out at Roselawns.

"Wentworth?" Crissy's voice was so sharp that Beulah took a step backward, a shiver of fear running through her body. "Did you say Wentworth? What are their first names?"

"The young lady is named Andrea. Andrea Marie. And her mother is named Catherine." Beulah was completely familiar with the names. The Amhursts' Clarice was Beulah's sister-in-law's niece, so Beulah had all her facts right from the source.

Andrea and Catherine. The names meant nothing to Crissy, but how could Wentworth be nothing more than a coincidence? "Do you happen to know the name of the girl's father, of Catherine Wentworth's husband?"

Beulah had to think a little about her. It seemed that she did recollect it being mentioned, but only once. It was the young lady and her mother, both so beautiful and so rich, and from Texas, that Clarice talked about. "I'm not sure. It might have been Andrew. Or Allen."

Crissy's voice now made Beulah wish that she were a hundred miles away. "Or Adam?"

"Yes, that's it. It was Adam." Beulah started to back away, but Crissy hadn't finished with her yet.

"How long are they going to stay?"

"I can't say about Mrs. Wentworth. The young lady isn't going to go back to Texas at all. She's going

to marry Mr. Gregory Randolph, sometime this fall."
Hung for a lamb, hung for a sheep. As long as she'd
already had to tell Crissy so much, there was no point in
holding anything back. Besides, what harm could it
do? Everybody in the county already knew about it; it
would only be a matter of time before Miss Crissy found
out anyway, even if she had to learn it from the society
column of the weekly newspaper. Beulah happened to
know that Crissy read that column; it was the only thing
in the paper that she was interested in. When some old
friend of Crissy's had a party, or a tea, and Crissy wasn't
invited, she was always in such a foul mood that Beulah
dreaded to go in and clean for her for days afterward.

Crissy was silent for so long, staring out of eyes
that didn't seem to see a thing, that Beulah thought
she'd forgotten her and started to edge away again.

"All right. You may go now. And don't forget to
come tomorrow, the house is a disgrace! I don't know
why we pay you to clean when you leave it in such a
shambles!"

It wouldn't do any good to remind her that she'd
sent Beulah packing yesterday before she'd had a chance
to do a decent job downstairs, it would only make her
mad.

"Yes, Mrs. Renault. I'll be here." Beulah never
called Crissy ma'am if she could help it. It was a petty
way to salvage her pride, and Crissy never even noticed
it, but it was better than nothing.

Crissy went back into the house, heading straight
for the side board and the bottle. She poured a liberal
amount into the same stained glass that she'd used yesterday, and drank it as if it were so much water. It might
have been water, for all the steadying it did to her shaking
hands. She poured more the second time and drank
that off as well.

Adam Wentworth! The girl in Prue's buggy had
been Adam Wentworth's daughter! And Gay hadn't told
her, he'd deliberately kept the fact that Adam's wife
and daughter were visiting Prue away from her!

Marry Gregory Randolph? Crissy's mouth curved in

a parody of a smile. Andrea Wentworth marry Gregory Randolph, the son of one of the oldest and most respected families in Georgia?

She began to laugh as she poured still another glass of wine and lifted it to her mouth. At last, at long, long last, she was going to take a measure of revenge on Adam Wentworth, and on Prue! It wasn't fair, nothing had ever been fair to Crissy, but this time Prue, and Adam, weren't going to get the best of everything!

She put the glass back on the sideboard, unmindful of the sticky ring it would leave on the finish, and went upstairs to change her clothes. She was wearing a morning dress, an at-home dress, and it wouldn't do. She must put on an afternoon dress and then send Danny to tell the liveryman to have a hired buggy here immediately. Her lavender hat with the pink roses and all the veiling was only a year old, it would do, and she needed her gloves; where were her gloves?

The gloves, when she found them and pulled them on, had a tiny hole in the right index finger, but there was no time to do anything about that. After what she had to say to the people on whom she was going to call, they wouldn't notice a little thing like a hole in the finger of a glove. They'd have something almighty more important to think about!

The parlor maid who answered the door at Swanmere much later that day was undecided about the lady who stood on the doorstep demanding to see her mistress. There was something a little strange about her. Then she recognized Crissy; everybody in the county knew Mrs. Gaylord Renault even if she didn't go out in society much any more, and she asked her to wait in the small morning room. No matter if Mrs. Renault was a little seedy, and by the looks of her more than a little tipsy, she was still a Beddoes and a Renault, still a lady, and she could neither be turned away nor left to wait on the doorstep.

Eulalie Randolph was as startled as her maid at hearing who was calling on her. "Mrs. Renault? Are you sure, Zoe?"

"Yes, ma'am. I'm sure."

Zoe hadn't been mistaken. Crissy was sitting on the cretonne-covered sofa, her hands folded in her lap, her head held high and imperiously, when Eulalie went to her.

"Mrs. Renault? How delightful to see you! I'll ring for tea, you must be weary after such a long journey from town!"

"No, I'm not tired, but tea would be lovely." Crissy, behaved as the lady she was, accepting the offer of tea graciously, as no more than should be expected.

"Lemon or cream?" Eulalie asked her, after they'd chatted of trivialities while they'd waited for the tea tray to arrive.

"Lemon, please, and sugar." Crissy had an insatiable desire for sweets, especially when she was removed from her wine bottle and she was agitated. "Three lumps."

"I prefer lemon, too." Eulalie smiled. "Cream seems to disguise the aroma of fine tea, don't you agree?"

"I do, indeed." Crissy sipped her tea and took one small delicate bite of the paper-thin watercress sandwich, and then looked directly at her hostess. "Mrs. Randolph, I understand that your son is to marry an Andrea Wentworth, who is visiting my sister."

Only Eulalie's breeding enabled her to hide her distress. Oh, dear, now she'd have to invite Crissy—there simply wasn't any way out of it—and what if Crissy made a scene? She was perfectly capable of it, Eulalie knew. Her animosity toward her sister Prudence was known throughout the county, and Eulalie had particularly noticed that Crissy's name had not been on the list of guests to be invited that Naomi had brought to Swanmere for her approval.

"Yes, he is. Such a lovely girl! I can't express how delighted we are that she's to become our daughter-in-law." Uncharitable as the thought was, Eulalie hoped that Crissy would fall ill on the day of the engagement party or, Lord forbid, be so drunk that she couldn't come. "Have you met her?"

"I've seen her." Crissy's head inclined just a fraction

of an inch. "She is beautiful, I admit. How much do you know about her background, Mrs. Randolph?"

"Why, I should say I know everything! She's one of the Boston Wentworths, even though she and her parents now reside in Texas. An impeccable family, Mrs. Renault. Not only a Wentworth, but there's a connection to the nobility, a countess, in her family tree, a French countess to be sure, but still!"

"The Comtesse Marie de la Roche." Crissy nodded. "Née Rebecca, a slave owned by the Beddoes family! Rebecca, my grandmother's personal maid!"

Eulalie's face paled. Everything people said, all the whispers over teacups, were true. Crissy Renault was quite mad.

"Rebecca," Crissy went on. "A beautiful woman. So beautiful that my father, Jonathan Beddoes, begat a child by her, a child called Naomi. Rebecca disappeared a few years later, and it wasn't until years afterward that we knew that she'd made a fortune running a nefarious house in New Orleans, and gone from there to England where she opened a gambling casino, and married an impoverished Italian count who was more interested in her fortune than her antecedents. She didn't take her daughter Naomi with her. Naomi was left with us, Mrs. Randolph, while Rebecca pursued her checkered career that ended with her taking up residence in France and giving the erroneous impression that she was a French countess by birth rather than an Italian countess by marriage. Her daughter Naomi was not only my half-sister, but she was my personal maid! And Adam Wentworth is Naomi's son, the illlegitimate son of an illegitimate slave!"

"Mrs. Renault, what are you saying?"

"Nothing but the truth, Mrs. Randolph. I felt compelled to tell you, otherwise a tragedy would have occurred! You'll no doubt want to do your own checking, but you'll find that every word I've told you is true. Andrea Marie Wentworth, for all her beauty and all her wealth, is part Negro, the descendant of Negro slaves! The tea was delicious, Mrs. Randolph. I really enjoyed it, but I must be leaving now. It's a long drive back to town."

Crissy rose and swept out of the room, her movements unhurried, every inch a lady taking leave of her hostess after a pleasant visit over afternoon tea. She left behind her a woman so stunned that she could only stare at the wall opposite her, her heart filled with despairing turmoil.

Slowly, like a woman who has received a mortal blow, she reached for the little silver bell on the tea table. When Zoe came in answer to her summons, her voice was hoarse and trembling in spite of a lifetime of training in keeping her emotions hidden in front of the servants.

"Zoe, have someone find Mr. Randolph and Hr. Gregory and send them to me, as soon as they can be located."

"Yes, ma'am."

Not until the maid, wondering what that daffy Mrs. Renault could have said to her mistress to make her look like that, had left, did Eulalie so far break down as to cover her face with her hands.

8

"It's ridiculous!" Naomi raged, her face so white that
her green eyes blazed like emeralds. "I never heard of
anything so ridiculous! How can one sixty-fourth Negro
blood make Andrea a Negro? Why, there's more black
blood than that in hundreds of this country's best families,
I know there is!"

"I expect you're right, Naomi." Prudence's face, too,
was white, white and drawn from the intolerable strain
she'd been under ever since Mr. Randolph had arrived
at Roselawns early that morning, so early that he must
have set out well before dawn, and closeted himself with
Burke and Rory in Grandfather Jacob's old office at the
back of the house. "But this is Georgia, and there's the
illegitimacy factor involved, as well. I'm afraid that to
the Randolphs, it makes Andrea's marriage to Gregory
impossible."

"I just can't believe that Greg will listen to them!
He loves Andrea, Mother! I've seen how much he loves

her; he'll never let her go for such a petty, stupid reason!"

"Naomi, strong language isn't going to change things. There won't be any wedding. We, both of the families, will explain that Andrea and Greg had a change of heart. Andrea and Kate will go back to Texas, and we can only pray that none of this will seep beyond the confines of the families involved."

"No! Greg will never permit it! He'll face his parents down, he'll face the whole blamed county down, just you wait and see!"

"Naomi, I wish I could believe that. I wish it with my whole heart. But don't set your hopes on it." Prudence was so tired that all she wanted to do was collapse. Crissy! Wouldn't you know that it had been Crissy who had exploded this bombshell, who'd ferreted out Andrea and Kate's identities, who had used her knowledge to strike back at her, and at Adam, through Adam's daughter!

Crissy hadn't cared that her own husband was involved, that now the Randolphs, at least, knew that Jonathan had sired an illegitimate daughter on their own slave Rebecca, and that Gaylord in his turn had sired an illegitimate son on Jonathan's daughter! Crissy didn't care whom she destroyed any more. They'd managed to control her, managed to make her realize that she would be as much disgraced as their father, as Gaylord, if the truth had come out that first time. She'd had enough sanity left, then, to realize that. Now, after more than two decades of bitterness, of brooding, of drinking, she just didn't care any more. How Gaylord was going to control her now, make her keep quiet and not broadcast the scandal to the whole county, Prudence couldn't imagine.

"Mother, Andrea's breaking my heart!" Naomi said. "She doesn't know what hit her, she looks as if she's been run over by a threshing machine! She can't understand why any of this is so important, why anyone would care! No secret was ever made of it in Texas, and nobody out there would have cared anyway even if they didn't broadcast it. They just never did anything to hide it simply because it is darned unimportant! She's so bewildered I can hardly bear to look at her. And Kate's heart is breaking for her." Naomi sat down abruptly and began to cry.

"Of course she is. Any mother's heart would break, to see her daughter so desperately hurt! My heart's breaking, too, just as yours is. But we must keep control of ourselves, Naomi. Crying won't do a bit of good; all we can do is prevent, if we can, any further life-ruining scandal from leaking out. We still have Rosalind to think of, and her children, as well as your brother and Ardis and the children they'll have. Like it or not, this is Georgia, and no matter how foolish we know it is, things like this still matter a lot to nearly everyone else."

She broke off as the sound of a horse ridden at full gallop reached her ears through the front bedroom window of the room that she and Burke shared. Whoever it was must be in a raging hurry. She couldn't remember when anyone had been in such a rush that he'd still have his horse at a gallop all the way up the drive.

Naomi had heard it, too, and as quick as a cat, she was out of her chair and at the window to see who it was.

"It's Greg!" she exclaimed. "His horse is all lathered, he must be almost out his mind to push Jupiter that hard!"

Even before she finished speaking, young Tad ran from where he'd been dozing in the shade in front of the stables, to take the reins Greg tossed him. Tad's face registered his own astonishment that Mister Greg would have misused a horse, as he started to walk the beautiful stallion to cool him out before he took him to rub him down.

Naomi was already out of her mother's room and tapping at Andrea's door. She didn't wait to be invited in but burst in to see Andrea, her face still white with shock, talking to Kate. Kate, too, showed the strain of these last several hours, although her face was carefully controlled.

"Andrea, Greg's here, and he'll want to see you. Shall I tell him that you'll come down?"

"Of course I'll come down!" Andrea walked over to the dressing table and inspected her hair and straightened the collar of her dress. She appeared calm; only someone as concerned for her as Naomi would have noticed the almost imperceptible tremble of her fingers as she tucked a strand of hair back into the loose Psyche knot at the nape of her neck.

"You can talk to him in Grandfather Jacob's study, nobody will bother you there," Naomi told her.

"Thank you, Naomi."

Andrea reached the foot of the stairs just as Bella was starting up to tell her that Greg was calling on her. The slender, sweet-faced servant pressed herself against the wall to let Andrea pass, her face filled with sympathy. Bella didn't know exactly what was wrong, but she did know that Mr. Randolph and Mr. Burke and Mr. Rory had been closeted in the old master's study for over an hour this morning and that everyone in the house was more upset than she'd ever seen them. Her intuition told her that the trouble, whatever it was, concerned Miss Andrea and Mr. Greg.

"Hello, Greg. I didn't expect you." Andrea was perfectly candid.

"Well, you should have expected me! Did you think I'd take this standing still? I've had it out with my mother and father. . . ."

Andrea's face, so pale and still a moment before, lighted up with a radiance that made Bella swallow.

"Let's go to the study, Greg. Bella, it won't be necessary to bring any refreshments. I'll let you know later if we want anything."

The instant the study door closed behind them Greg caught her in his arms, crushing her hard against the whole length of his body.

"It's infamous! That woman ought to be put away! But we won't let it make any difference, Andrea, we'll be married just as we planned. I'm not going to lose you, and that's all there is to it!"

"Your mother and father—"

"I told you I've had it out with them! I'm well over twenty-one, they can't dictate my life, not even if they disinherit me as they threaten! But it won't come to that. I have it all planned, darling, every detail. I'm going to go on a 'business' trip. I'll go to New York; there's nothing unusual about that, our factor is there and nobody will think anything of it. And a week or so after I leave, you'll pretend that you're going home to Texas, but you'll actually meet me in New York and we'll be married there."

"You mean we're to be married secretly, we're to run off like thieves in the night?"

"That's a nasty way of putting it, Dria! I only mean that we'll avoid all the unpleasantness that way. I have some money of my own, left me by my maternal grandmother, and your father will undoubtedly make you an allowance. We can manage until all of this blows over. I can always find some kind of work, if it comes to that. That crazy old alcoholic can't live forever. Gaylord Renault might even have her put away. People have been wondering for years why he hasn't already done it. In a few years, at the most, we'll be able to come back and take our rightful place at Swanmere. Once that old harridan can't make any more trouble for us, and we show up with a grandchild or two, my parents will relent and accept you. It isn't as if the scandal is going to get outside the family. Crissy Renault's the only danger, and Gaylord will see to it that she doesn't do any harm. We'll be together, we'll be married, I'll make a good life for you."

"By running away," Andrea said. She pulled herself out of his arms and looked at him, her eyes blazing like summer lightning in her white face. "You love me enough to marry me against your family's wishes provided that it's done with the darkest secrecy!"

"Yes, I do! Oh, God, Andrea, you know I do! Isn't that what I've just been telling you?"

"But you don't love me enough to marry me here,

in Georgia, to face your folks and everyone else down right here in the county."

"Andrea, be reasonable! How could I, under the circumstances? You know as well as I do that it would be impossible! My way is the only way!"

"No, Greg, you're wrong. There's another way, and that's to forget the whole thing, and that's just what I'm going to do."

Greg stared at her as if he thought she'd taken leave of her sanity and was babbling gibberish. "You don't mean that! Not when we mean so much to each other, not when we love each other so much!"

Andrea's eyes didn't waver, although her face went a shade paler. "But we don't love each other, that's just it. I thought you loved me, but if I'm not good enough for your family, if you don't love me enough to marry me right here, to have the big wedding we planned with the whole county here, then you don't love me at all! And I thought I loved you, but there's no way on earth I could love a man who wants me to run away with him, to skulk and hide until 'scandal' is in no more danger of breaking and disgracing you! I couldn't possibly love or want a man who'd be happy to see another human being die, or be put away in some asylum, even someone like poor Crissy, just to sweep a scandal under the rug and pretend that it never existed!"

"Andrea, you don't mean that! I love you, how could I possibly love you more than by wanting to marry you, no matter what your ancestry is?"

"No matter what my ancestry is!" Andrea's voice blazed with contempt. "The very fact that you'd say that proves that it does matter to you, that it matters a whole lot! But I'll tell you something, Gregory Randolph! I'm not a piece of tarnished goods, to be hidden away until I can be passed off as the real thing! I'm Andrea Marie Wentworth, part English, part Scotch, part Irish, part Negro and part Indian, and I'm darned proud of it! I wouldn't trade one of my ancestors for all the blue blood in Georgia! My blood is what this country's made of, what it'll always be made of, good red, rich blood that's worth more than all the watery blue blood of all you aristocrats put together!"

"Andrea, don't! I didn't mean, I never meant to imply that I'd be ashamed of you! You don't know what you're saying! Why, what would you do, if you didn't marry me?"

"I don't know what I'm going to do in the future, Greg. I haven't thought that far ahead yet. But I know what I'm going to do right now. I'm going to visit my great-aunt Crissy and thank her for preventing me from making the biggest mistake of my life!"

Gregory tried to catch her in his arms and hold her back by force as she started toward the door, but it was like trying to latch onto a whirlwind. She ducked under his arm, and her hand lashed out and left a white palm-print on his cheek, and when he still tried to restrain her she brought the sharp heel of her slipper down on his instep. Then she was through the doorway and she brushed past Naomi who had just come downstairs.

"Andrea, what on earth happened?" Naomi demanded. "Are you all right?"

"I'm fine, you'd better go and check on Greg. He may need a little first aid!" Andrea said. "I'm going out, Naomi. Tell Mother and Aunt Prue not to worry. I'm only going in to town, and I'll be back before dark."

Naomi found Greg still in the study, sitting in Old Jacob's worn leather chair nursing his foot. "What have you done to Andrea, what made her rush out of the house like that? What did you say to her?" she shouted at him.

"I asked her to marry me!" Greg told her, his face as white as from the pain of his throbbing instep as from his shock at Andrea's rejection of his proposals. "I told her that I didn't care who her father and her grandmothers were, that I'd marry her anyway!"

"There had to be more than that! No girl would have rushed out the way she did just because a man had proved how much he loves her!"

"She's unreasonable! How else could it be handled, except for us to slip away to be married and live in some other part of the country?" Greg demanded. "Naomi, talk to her! Make her see that it's perfectly reasonable, that it's the only way!"

Naomi was not a tall girl, but now she seemed to grow several inches as she withered Greg with furious, scornful eyes.

"Right at the moment, I'd swear that Andrea and I are the two luckiest girls in the world! When I think that I almost let myself be gulled into marrying you just because it was expected of me, I could throw up! And now Andrea's escaped from you, too! You're the most despicable, the lowest human creature that ever walked on two legs! When I think that you dared to ask Andrea to run away with you, as if she were something to be ashamed of, I wish I had the courage to take Grandfather Jacob's gun and shoot you! Any man worth breathing would be proud to marry her right here, the way it was planned; any man worth having Dria would take a horsewhip to anyone who dared to raise an eyebrow! You get out this house, Gregory Randolph, and don't ever come back!"

For the second time within five minutes, Greg felt the sharp impact of a hand against his face. And Naomi thought as she turned on her heel and left him, that at least now his cheeks matched. As for herself, she couldn't wait to pack up and go back to Martin's Corners. If Kelvin Janson thought that he was going to get away from her, he had another think coming! Compared to a skunk like Gregory Randolph, he was the only man in the world worth marrying!

9

Crissy lifted her head from her crumpled pillow as Gaylord turned the key in the lock and entered their bedroom. The bruise on her face stood out lividly even in the dim room, where the windowshades were pulled down almost to the sills, leaving only a couple of inches for what breeze there was to attempt to mitigate the heat of the late summer afternoon.

"It's about time you came to your senses and apologized!" Crissy said, her voice filled with venom. "Not that it's going to do you any good! I'll never forgive you, never as long as I live! If it wasn't for the scandal, I'd pack up and leave you so fast you wouldn't know what happened!"

"I came to see if you were all right," Gaylord told her evenly. "You've been too quiet for the last hour. I hoped you were sleeping, but as long as you've stopped throwing things and screaming, I'm satisfied."

Crissy's voice rose. "And why wouldn't I scream,

with my husband beating me! Beating *me*, Christine Beddoes! How dared you, you bastard, how did you dare raise your hand to me!"

"I dared because you damned well deserved it, you've deserved it for years and it's a pity that I didn't have the courage to do it way back when you were crazy enough to shoot Prue! You've been raising hell with all our lives ever since, but this thing you did yesterday was the last straw. That's my granddaughter whose life you just ruined, do you realize that? My granddaughter! Andrea never did a thing to you, she has nothing to do with what happened years ago when we learned that Adam is my son and all your plans for Rosalind to marry him and restore you to all the glory you thought you deserved because you're a Beddoes went down the drain! But carrying your filthy tales to Niles and Eulalie Randolph, deliberately wrecking the lives of two fine young people who never did you any harm, just because you've never forgiven me for fathering Adam and never forgiven Prue for keeping his identity a secret, is the worst thing you've ever done and there has to be a stop to it before you do any more harm!"

"I only told the truth! The Randolphs are one of the first families in Georgia. How could I stand by and let their son marry a nigger?"

Gaylord's face turned the color of dirty putty, and his eyes blazed with such fury that Crissy shrank back against her pillow in spite of her own anger. "That's a damn lie! She doesn't have enough black blood in her to make any difference anywhere in the world, and you know it! You only wanted to hurt Prue and me, you don't care whom you destroy just so you can exact your petty, spiteful revenge for something that happened half a lifetime ago! I warn you, Crissy, if you don't straighten out and begin acting like a reasonable human being, I'll be forced to have you locked up! And don't make the mistake of thinking I couldn't do it. You're an alcoholic; the whole county knows that you're half crazy; Doc Mason has told me, more than once, when he's had to come over here to treat you after one of your bouts, that you ought to be locked up for own safety!"

"And whose fault is it?" Crissy sat up again, her rising anger sweeping away her fear. "You're the one who did it to me, you and Prue! And that bastard, Andrea's father, that dirty nigger bastard who had no right to be born!"

"You just go right on like that!" Gaylord didn't raise his own voice, but it held a threat that was all the more deadly for that. "Keep it up, and I'll have Doctor Mason commit you! Andrea will go back to Texas where none of this will ever filter to, but Prue and Burke and Naomi have to go on living here, and so do our own children! Do you want to make Rosalind's life miserable as well as ours, do you want our grandchildren to be ashamed to face their friends and neighbors? Why can't you realize that once you start tearing something down, the innocent as well as the guilty are going to be crushed in the shambles?"

"I want a drink." Crissy's hand was at her throat, and her tongue ran over her dry, cracked lips. "Give me a drink, Gay. Just one, just a little."

"No. You're all through drinking, Crissy. I've been a fool to let you go on, just because it dulled your grievances and made you a little easier to live with. I'm sorry that you're going to suffer, and I know that you are going to suffer the torments of the damned. Doc's told me enough about it so I know what you'll go through before you begin to get well, but it has to be done. For my sake, granted, even more for our children's sakes, and Prue's, but for your own sake as well. You have to face it. It's either stop drinking and start to live like a normal human being again, or go to an asylum."

"You can't send me to an asylum! Where would the money come from? You, a storekeeper! Do you know what those places cost? You have to be rich, you have to be a millionaire, to go to one of them!"

"And that's one of the reasons I've never sent you, Crissy. Can't you get it through your head that it would have to be the State Hospital?"

He winced at the expression on Crissy's face, the sudden, wild fear of a trapped animal. "That's an insane asylum, not a sanitarium! Oh, God, you wouldn't do that, you couldn't! I'd die, it would be the same as killing me!"

"I doubt that you'd die, but you'd almost certainly wish that you were dead before they let you out again!" Gaylord's voice was heavy. "So no drinking, Crissy. I'll bring you some water if you're thirsty, or coffee, or milk."

Crissy's face twisted and her fingers began to twist the bed sheet, her knuckles white. "You're a monster! You can't just cut me off! You have to let me have just a little, to help me stand it!"

"I'm cutting you off because I'm not a monster. I'm a lot of other things, or at least I used to be. I was a monster when I was young and I thought that I was entitled to everything I wanted just because I wanted it, but a lot of years have gone by since then and I've learned a lot of hard, cold facts. I'll spend the rest of my life in bitter regret for the things I did, but at least I've learned that I have to go on living the best I can, and most of all never to hurt anyone else again. Now you have to start learning it, too. You can believe it or not, but I'm sorry for you. I'm sorry I hurt you; I'm sorry that my actions ruined your life. But we've come to the end of the road, Crissy. It branches right here. Either you stop drinking, you stop living on your hatred, or you'll have to be put where, I hope, doctors will be able to help you."

The metalic whir of the front doorbell broke into their quarrel, and Crissy stiffened. "Who can that be? I don't want to see anyone, don't let anyone in!"

"It might be Beulah. I sent her away this morning when she came to do the cleaning. I told her that you weren't well, but she might think you're feeling better by now."

"Well, tell her to go away! Do you hear me, send her away!" Crissy's voice rose hysterically. "It's bad enough being tortured by my own husband, without

138

having a black cleaning woman spreading the story from one end of town to the other!"

"You're going to have to let her in eventually, unless you want to do all the heavy cleaning yourself. I can't stay away from the store indefinitely. Beulah can be trusted. She won't spread any stories about us." His voice still heavy, but filled with an implacable determination that shriveled Crissy's last shreds of hope, Gaylord turned to go downstairs and answer the door.

It took so long for anyone to answer her ring that Andrea almost left, thinking that no one was at home and her trip had been for nothing. But just as she was turning to go back to the buggy, she heard heavy footsteps and the door inched open a crack.

"Grandfather! I didn't expect you to be here at this time of day!" Andrea's surprise was apparent in her voice.

"Andrea. Come in." Gaylord's surprise was as great as her own, and something more than surprise, a consternation that made Andrea feel sorry for him.

"You know, then," she said. "Did Aunt Crissy tell you what she's done?"

Gaylord led her into the sitting room. It was cluttered and dusty. Beulah had been sent away when she'd come to clean this morning, Gaylord told her, embarrassed that she should see his house for the first time when it was in such disarray.

"It wasn't Crissy, Andrea. Niles Randolph was here almost before it was daylight, to tell me what my wife had done and to ask me if there was any truth in it before he went to confer with Burke and Rory. I'm sorry, child. There isn't any way to tell you how sorry I am for the grief I've brought you!"

To his amazement, Andrea's smile held actual amusement. "You could scarcely have foreseen this, when you were indiscreet so many years ago, could you? But that's why I'm here, to tell you not to be sorry, at least not to be sorry for me! I'm glad that it happened! That Aunt Crissy spilled the beans, I mean. It enabled me to find out what Greg is really like, under all that charm of his.

He actually asked to me run away with him, to marry him secretly so that no one would have to know that he'd married so far beneath him!"

Gaylord's face went gray, and a muscle in his jawline throbbed with the anger that blazed up in him. "The blackguard! I ought to beat him within an inch of his life!"

"There's no need for that. Women don't use their fists, at least not if they're smart, but our tongues do just as good a job! You can be sure that he knows exactly what I thought of his proposal. Grandfather, may I see Aunt Crissy?"

"I don't think she'd want to see you, Andrea. She isn't . . . herself this afternoon." His eyes met hers, his own filled with shame. "I wasn't exactly easy on her, after Niles Randolph left."

"I won't tire her, but I do want to see her, if only for a moment. It'll probably be the only chance I'll ever have to meet her, and I want to thank her for what she did."

"Thank her!"

Andrea's chin went up, and Gaylord's heart twisted; there was actual pain in his chest from the constriction. What a thoroughbred she was, this granddaughter of his! He'd have given the last ten years of his life to be able to claim her publicly, to shout from the rooftops that she was his flesh and blood, to hire the town hall and stand up on the podium and tell everybody that she was his granddaughter, the finest granddaughter that any man had ever been blessed with.

But as much as he'd like to claim her in front of all the world, it was impossible. Even today, the scandal that would result from public announcement would reflect not only on Prudence, but on his own legitimate children. It wouldn't do his daughter Rosalind's husband's career as a lawyer any good if people learned that the lawyer's wife had a half-brother who was one thirty-second black, and Prudence would be sure to be condemned for having passed Adam off as her completely white stepson. This was still Georgia, no matter how enlightened a day and age it was. To say nothing of the effect that such widespread knowledge might do to Andrea herself! The Randolphs could be depended on to keep the secret, but in a great many people's minds Andrea's drop of colored blood, only one sixty-fourth, would be enough to brand her a Negro. So he had to let the fiction that Andrea was no kin of his stand, for the sake of everyone concerned.

He nodded, sure that letting Andrea see Crissy was a bad idea, but there was no way he could refuse in the face of her determination. "She's in bed," he said. "I think that if you insist on seeing her, we'd better just have you go on in. If I asked her for permission she might raise a fuss. She probably will anyway. You're prepared for that?"

"I'm prepared. She can't raise a fuss that would hold a candle to all the fuss I've seen, these last few hours."

The bedroom that Gaylord led her to, up the stairs with their frayed carpeting, was also dim, the shades drawn. There was a closeness in the room that was stifling. The windows were almost closed in spite of the heat of the afternoon, and the odor of stale perfume and cosmetics was heavy in the close air, along with an even more unpleasant odor that came from Crissy's own perspiration, brought on more acutely because of the stress she was under. Articles of women's clothing were scattered haphazardly over the backs of chairs and hanging from the bedposts, and a chemise and pair of hose lay in the middle of the room, with one shoe on top of them.

Crissy raised her head from her pillow as they entered the room. "What is it now? If you're going to shout at me again, you needn't bother! I'm not sorry I did it! They had it coming, all of them had it coming, they've had it coming for years, they ruined my life. . . ."

"Crissy, your niece Andrea is here. She wants to meet you," Gaylord told her heavily, his voice laced with apprehension.

"Andrea?" Crissy struggled to sit up, and even in the dim light Andrea could see a bruise on the side of her face, a fresh bruise made not many hours before, livid against the shrunken paleness of her face. She couldn't stifle her shocked gasp in time, and Crissy looked at her with hate-filled eyes, her voice filled with venom.

"Yes, he did it, your grandfather did this to me! He struck me, he raised his hand to me and struck me! Me, his wife, his invalid wife!"

Andrea looked at Gaylord, still disbelieving, but his guilt was there on his face.

"Yes, I did it. When Miles Randolph told me what she'd done, how she'd ruined your life, something exploded inside of me and I struck her before I knew what I was doing. I'm afraid our much-vaunted Southern chivalry has worn thin, in my case. I hope you won't judge all Southerners by me, Andrea."

"Me, your wife, you struck me over this little half-breed bastard!" Crissy hissed before Andrea could answer him.

"Aunt Christine, I am not a bastard. My father and my mother are legally married. I'm sorry that my grandfather struck you, but I can understand why he did it." Andrea's eyes were fastened on Crissy again, fascinated by the ruin of the once beautiful woman who was glaring at her with such naked hatred. "And if my father was a bastard, it was no fault of his. He's a fine man, a successful and respected man, and where we come from, there's not a person who would give his bastardy a second thought, or his bloodlines, either! There's nothing you can do to hurt my father, and there's nothing you can do to hurt me. I'm glad that you ran to the Randolphs the moment you found out who I am! You did me the greatest favor in my life, and I'll be grateful to you for it as long as I live. I only came here to thank you, and to tell you that you can go on hating me all you want to because I'm my father's daughter, but I don't hate you. I'd even try to like you if you'd let me. As you won't, I'll have to take it out in being sorry for you, because hating us isn't hurting anyone but yourself."

"How dare you talk to me like that! Gaylord, get this nigger daughter of yours out of my room! How dare you bring her into my house, the daughter of your bastard nigger son! Are you trying to kill me? I don't have to put up with this, I'm a Beddoes, I'm still Crissy Beddoes even if you have ruined my life, and I don't have to put up with having this little bitch in my house!"

Frenetic with rage, Crissy struggled out of bed, her face blotched with rage. She advanced toward Andrea, who stepped backwards with shock. Crissy's hands, her fingers curved into talons, reached out and would have grasped Andrea by her hair if she hadn't jumped out of her way quickly enough, her face filled with astonishment to think that this nearly demented woman would actually try to attack her.

Gaylord grasped Crissy's arm and brought her to a stop, helpless in his grasp, but she went right on struggling, trying to break loose to get at this hateful representative of everyone who had ever hurt her.

"What do you know of how I've suffered, of how that father of yours made me suffer! Everything was taken from me, everything! That bastard Adam should never have been born, and he has it all, everything that should have been mine! You, and your father, and Prue, you have it all!"

Her voice rose to a shriek. Gaylord shook her, deep white lines etched around his mouth.

"Damn you, Crissy, stop it! I'm not going to have any more of it, do you understand? I've listened to your ranting for over twenty years, I've let you ruin my life, but now you're going to stop it! My granddaughter is worth a dozen of you, a hundred of you, and so is Prue, and you know it, that's why you're bitter, why you hate them so much! Andrea, I'm sorry you had to be subjected to this. I warned you that it might not be pleasant."

"Yes, you did. But you needn't apologize. I've done what I came to do, and I would never have been satisfied if I hadn't seen Cristine. She'd have been a bugbear to me all the rest of my life, but bugbears have a way of being cut down to size once you come face to face with them."

Gaylord urged her out of the room. Andrea was

startled when she saw him turn the key in the lock from the outside. "Grandfather, you aren't keeping her locked in?"

"If I don't, she'll find a way to escape the house and get a bottle, and the state she's in now she just might drink herself to death. I've poured every drop we had down the sink, but I've done that before and she's always managed to get more. As long as she used any discretion about her drinking, I turned a blind eye to it, because when Crissy is crossed she isn't pleasant to live with. The doctor told me that there's no way of stopping people like her outside of putting them in an institution where they're kept under constant supervision, and locked up."

"You wouldn't do that!" Andrea's face was pale with shock.

"No, I won't do that." There was defeat in Gaylord's voice, but resignation as well, a determination to do the best he could. "Only for now, for at least a few days, I have to keep her locked in, for her own protection. I'll never send her to an institution unless it becomes absolutely necessary."

"Won't being locked in make her even angrier, even more bitter? Won't she be likely to spread this story around, out of revenge, when you do let her out? That would be hard on you, and on Aunt Prue and Uncle Burke and Naomi, and the rest of your family, your own children."

"If she does, she does." Gaylord's face was grim. "I reckon I can live through it, and others, too. We've lived through everything we've had to, up till now. There's no reason to think we can't go on doing it."

They stood facing each other after they'd stepped out onto the porch. "I'll write to you, Grandfather. I'll keep in touch," Andrea promised, her throat hurting. "I hope things work out for you."

"I don't have to wish that things will work out for you." Gaylord's voice was husky, filled with the emotions he had to keep under control. "I can see that you'll be all right. You have what it takes, Andrea, and I thank God for that."

She left him then, without looking back, the sound of Crissy crying in her locked room following her down the path. The sound made cold chills run up and down her spine and the short hairs at the nape of her neck stand up. There was something not quite human about the sound; it was more as if some animal were being tormented.

No matter what Gaylord Renault had done when he was young, Andrea felt nothing but compassion for him now. She could see something of Adam in him. Maybe there was something in all that talk about blood, after all. Maybe good blood would tell, given enough time. And like Gaylord, she was glad for herself that she'd inherited some of that blood. Yes, she'd be all right. Only it was going to take some time. The first numbness, the first rage, had worn off by now, and she knew that only those closest to her would ever guess that she was hurt, badly hurt, and that she wasn't going to heal overnight.

Her eyes blurred with tears that she brushed away impatiently before she picked up the reins and set the gelding in motion. Damn it, Greg, why couldn't you have been a real man, and not just a figment of my romantic imagination! she thought. If someone had come and told her that Greg was dead, that he'd had a fatal accident, it would have been easier to bear. Learning that the man she'd thought she loved had never existed was far harder to bear.

She lifted her chin and straightened her back, her mouth set into a firm line, and when she pulled the gelding to a stop in front of the stables an hour later, the lad who jumped to help her down from the buggy had no inkling that her world had been shattered.

"Did you have a nice ride, Miss Andrea? You got any parcels for me to carry up to the house for you?"

"No, Tad, thank you. I haven't any parcels. But it was a nice ride. It's a beautiful afternoon."

"Yas'um, it sure is! It sure is a pretty afternoon!" Which only went to show, Andrea thought, that nature doesn't give a hang if your life has been ruined; the sun will go right on shining and the birds will go right on singing no matter if your heart has been broken.

She let herself in and went directly upstairs, but Kate had been listening for her return, and came out of her room to intercept her, her eyes betraying her anxiety even though her face was calm.

"Are you all right, Andrea? Where did you go rushing off to after you and Naomi sent Greg out of here as if he'd come face to face with the devil?"

"I went to see my grandfather and Aunt Crissy. Grandfather's quite a man, Mother. At least he is now, even if he was a no-good skunk when he was young. I'm not ashamed to claim him."

Kate linked her arm with her daughter's and walked with her to Andrea's room. "Dria, what do you want us to do now? Shall we pack up and take the first train home?"

Andrea went to stand at the window, her eyes brooding, but there was a look of determination on her face when she turned to look at Kate again. "Home? No, I don't think I want that, at least for a while."

"But what else can we do? Everything you know, everyone who loves you is there! Think how glad Henry will be to see you. I don't mind telling you, now, that I never trusted this sudden love you felt for Gregory Randolph. Granted that he's handsome, and cultured, everything a girl could dream of, or at least we thought he was until he proved that he wasn't worth it. But it was all too romantic, too much the stuff that stories or dreams are made of, to be true. I know how much you're hurting right now, but I promise you that it will pass. Hank's worth a dozen Gregs, and he always was!"

"And you'd be happy if I'd go home and marry him, the way you and Father have always wanted. I'm sorry, Mother, but I can't do that. Even if he never found out what happened here in Georgia, even if I decided that I loved him, I'd always wonder if I hadn't married him just because there wasn't anything else left for me to do, just to smooth balm on my ego! And that wouldn't be good enough for me, or for Hank, either. Before I go home, I have to be very sure that I'm going home because I want to, not running home like a kicked mongrel with its tail between its legs."

"But what will you do, then?" Kate had never felt so helpless in her life. "I hardly think you'll want to stay on here for the rest of the summer. Shall we travel a little more? We could spend some time in New York, see the plays, and there are other cities we could visit."

"Mother, do you think that Estelle Richards would still want us to go to England with her?"

"England! Andrea, I can't go chasing off to England! I must get home to your father, I've already been away from him for too long."

"Then there's no need for you to go, but there's no reason that I couldn't, if Mrs. Richards would still have me. I'm going to write her right now, and send the letter out the first thing in the morning. It's what I want to do, Mother. I want to get as far away from both Georgia and Texas as I can, to give myself a chance to figure out what I want to do after that. I need the breathing space, I have to have it!"

Kate spread her hands. If Andrea's heart was set on this course, then she couldn't forbid it. Andrea was eighteen, and she had the same independence of spirit that both she and Adam had. She wasn't a child who could be rocked and coddled because she'd been hurt; her mother couldn't kiss it and make it better. It was something that Andrea had to work out for herself.

Estelle Richards was a completely respectable woman, and Andrea would be safe under her chaperonage. And Estelle had been terribly disappointed that she hadn't been able to persuade any of them to make the voyage with her. If she still felt the same way, then she'd have to let Andrea go.

"All right, Dria. We'll write to Estelle."

147

For a moment she thought that Dria was going to come into her arms and cry, but Andrea only said, "Thank you, Mother." She should have known better, anyway. Andrea hadn't come into her arms and cried since she'd been six years old.

MARTIN'S
CORNERS

10

Kelvin looked up from the copy he was setting in the pressroom of the *Clarion,* the composing stick tilting in his hand so that the loose type in it was in danger of spilling out onto the floor. He blinked, not willing to believe what his eyes told him was true. Naomi and her cousin Andrea couldn't be here, they were back at Roselawns, getting ready for one of the most socially prominent weddings ever to take place in Georgia.

But they were here. A phantom of the mind doesn't speak, at least not in such a clear, audible voice. The press was silent, waiting for the next issue of the newspaper to be put to bed, so he couldn't be mistaken about Naomi's voice.

"Hello, Kelvin. I decided to come back, to stay, this time. And Mother and Aunt Kate and Dria came with me, only they aren't going to stay. Dria's going to go off to England with Mrs. Richards in just a few days, and Mother will be going back home to Georgia. We dropped in to invite you to supper tonight."

The composing stick tilted still more as Kelvin continued to stare at her, his face a picture of bewilderment. Naomi walked across the room quickly, and took it out of his hand. Andrea busied herself by staring at the walls.

"The type almost fell out. Wouldn't that have resulted in what you printers call pi? All the letters mixed up so you have to sort them out? We can't let that happen, because it might make you late, and Aunt Kate's promised to make us a genuine Mexican meal, chili and tortillas. Only there won't be any tequila, of course, you can't get that in Martin's Corners."

Tequila, tequila. Kelvin's face cleared. Of course, that was some strong liquor, a Mexican drink. It couldn't matter less that it couldn't be had in Martin's Corners. He was already drunk, just from seeing Naomi, just from hearing her say that she'd come back to stay. He didn't drink, anyway. Not that he hadn't felt like it, when Naomi had gone back home just a short while ago, back to Georgia to marry Gregory Randolph.

"I'm afraid that I don't quite understand. You mean to stay here in Martin's Corners, alone?"

Naomi laughed. "Disgraceful, isn't it? I expect it'll be a scandal. All the same, I'm here to stay. I love it here, it's where I've always wanted to live, and I'm going to settle into Aunt Emily's saltbox house and never leave it again as long as I live. Will you come to supper tonight or won't you?"

"Of course I'll come."

"Then I'll tell Aunt Prue that she'd better get in more milk from the Tates," Andrea said, her eyes twinkling. "Mother's chili will burn your throat lining right out, and you'll need lots of milk to soothe it. Naomi, I'm going to go along now. I'll see you later."

"What's this, what's all this? You've come back to stay?" Mr. Barnaby, the *Clarion*'s editor, came bustling around the composing table, or the stone, as Andrea had learned they called it, where he'd been locking up

152

the form of type for the first plate of the next edition. His plump face was filled with astonishment.

Andrea linked her arm in his. "Come along, and I'll tell you all about it." She didn't give him time to protest, but started out of the room, literally dragging him along with her. "I'll make sure you spell all our names right, for your social events column. And Aunt Prue and Mother want you to come for a cup of coffee right now."

"But Miss Wentworth, I have work to do!"

"It'll wait. Work never goes away just because you turn your back on it." Andrea's voice was firm, and Mr. Barnaby had no defense against her. He looked back over his shoulder at Naomi and Kelvin, who were just standing there now looking at each other as if they'd both been struck dumb, and then Andrea had him outside of the building and was hustling him along, chattering a mile a minute as if taking an editor away from his pressroom in the middle of a working day was the most ordinary thing in the world.

Left alone, Kelvin finally found his voice again. "Naomi, I simply can't assimilate it. It doesn't seem possible that you'd choose to live here in Martin's Corners, and alone! You haven't quarreled with Gregory Randolph, have you?"

"Yes, I have, but that had nothing to do with my decision. Gregory and I broke off way before I decided to come back."

"But why, then?" Absently, Kelvin reached for the composing stick, but Naomi picked it up from where she'd set it on the stone and held it out of his reach.

"I have good and sufficient reasons. As I told you, I like it here; this is my home. Or it's going to be, from now on. I'm only sorry that I didn't make up my mind to live here years ago."

"But I still don't understand. You can't live all alone! You're too young. It wouldn't do at all; your parents would never allow it."

"I have no intention of living all alone for very long." Naomi couldn't control the blush that suffused her face, but her voice didn't waver. She hadn't come all this way to back down now! Kelvin was hers, and the sooner she let him know it, the better.

"You're talking in riddles. I don't understand you at all."

Now Naomi's face paled, and she had to take a deep breath before she gathered her courage to go on, but her eyes were steadfast as they met his and held them.

"Then I'll spell it out for you, Kel. I'm going to be married, and in the very near future, the sooner the better."

"But you just said that you've broken off with Gregory Randolph! And I can't see him leaving that magnificent plantation of his, back in Georgia, to come and live in a backwater like Martin's Corners, even if you hadn't."

"Martin's Corners is not a backwater. And it isn't Greg I'm going to marry, it's you."

She'd said it! She could hardly believe that she'd actually got the words out, actually proposed to Kelvin! Everyone she knew back in Georgia would be scandalized. How unladylike could you be, to propose to a man who'd never given the slightest indication, unless you could count that last time she'd seen him here in Martin's Corners at her mother's social, of being in love with her? And even then he'd run away and she never had found out why.

Her resolution hardened. She could be a whole lot more unladylike if she had to. Andrea would have done it, if she were in her place, and she admired Andrea more than any other girl in the world. Go get him! Andrea had said, and that was just what she was going to do, and if Kel thought he was going to get away from her, then he could just think again. She told him so, her voice steady and filled with conviction.

"There's no use in standing there with your mouth hanging open, Kelvin Janson. I'm not going to budge out of Martin's Corners until you tell me that you'll marry me. And even then I won't, because we'll be married and I'll have to stay where you are. If you don't say yes today, then

I'm going to chase you, I'm going to chase after you so hard that I'll make spectacles of both of us and the town will rock with the scandal of it.

"But you'd better say yes right now, because Mother has to get back to Georgia and Dria's going to sail for England and Aunt Kate has to go back to Texas, so we don't have much time. You might as well give in because you aren't going to get away from me anyway."

And then at the last moment she faltered, her voice wavering. "Kel, you do love me, don't you? There isn't someone else? I never saw you with anyone else, but you could have a sweetheart in some other town."

The type in the composing stick that she'd taken such pains to keep from being spilled went flying as Kelvin lunged for her, his elbow knocking it to the floor. Neither of them noticed as he caught her in his arms, his face alight.

"Naomi, I think you've taken leave of your senses, but promise me that you'll stay insane if that's what it takes to get you to marry me! Love you? I've loved you for years, I've loved you all your life, but I had no idea. . . ."

"Well, I did!"

Naomi broke completely, sobbing with near hysteria as she clung to him as if she were never going to let him go, which was exactly her idea. "Oh, Kel, if I'd married Gregory because I thought you didn't want me, I'd have been miserable all the rest of my life! All the magnificent plantations in the world wouldn't have made it up to me, not even the children I might have had, because they wouldn't have been your children! I never wanted anyone but you, but you just wouldn't ask me!"

"I would have if I'd thought I had any chance. How could I have thought I had a chance? You're quality, you were destined for something a lot better than being the wife of a country editor!"

"There isn't anything better. There isn't anything else in the world that I'd accept. Only you, Kel. When I think of the mistake I almost made, it scares me so much I want to hide my head under the covers and shake."

"I can't give you much. I don't even have a house to take you to. We'll never be rich."

"We have a house. We have the saltbox house. Cleo's giving it to me. It's hers, you know, my great-great-aunt Emily left it to her for being such a loyal friend to her and the family for all those years, right here in the same house ever since Martha brought her with her when she left Jonathan. And now it's going to be ours, and we will be rich, in every way that matters. And we have to be married right away before you change your mind and get some silly idea that you aren't good enough to marry a Curtis and a Beddoes and an Amhurst. After all, the Tates were here as early as the Curtises were, and that's what counts, not the amount of money a family's managed to pile up in the bank."

"Tomorrow?" Kelvin asked.

"Don't be ridiculous! That wouldn't give me anywhere near enough time to get ready."

Whatever else she'd been going to say was blotted out as Kelvin's mouth came down over hers. A few seconds later, when Bessie Courtland got back from her lunch hour and poked her head into the pressroom to announce that she was back, they were still kissing each other, pressed so closely together that Bessie's face registered complete shock.

"Miss Amhurst! Mr. Janson! Whatever are you doing?" Bessie gasped.

Kelvin stopped kissing Naomi just long enough to raise his head and speak.

"What does it look like we're doing?"

"But you can't do that here! This is a public place, a newspaper office! Miss Amhurst, consider your reputation!"

Naomi's smile was angelic before she lifted her face to Kelvin's again. "You consider it. I'm far too busy."

Bessie retreated. She sat down at her desk behind the long counter in the outer room and put her trembling hands to her face. Was she having a particularly vivid dream, or had the world gone mad? Kelvin and Naomi, when everyone knew that Naomi was engaged to a wealthy young planter down there in Georgia! She didn't understand it, she didn't understand it at all.

Just to make sure that it was really happening, she got up and looked into the pressroom again. Naomi and Kelvin still hadn't moved; they were still kissing each other. Bessie made a strangled moaning noise.

The sound made the two lovers break apart at last. "It's all right, Bessie. Kel and I are going to be married, and you're to write the most wonderful piece about it that you've ever written, so I can save it for our children and our grandchildren."

Bessie's face worked. She had to go back to her desk and sit down. And then she burst into the sentimental, aching tears of a middle-aged spinster who was starved for romance, even other people's. This was the most wonderful thing that had ever happened in her entire life. She'd guessed, long ago, that Kelvin, who was like the son she'd never had, was in love with Naomi, but she'd never dreamed that anything could come of it.

Married! She'd write a piece for the *Clarion*, all right, she'd write a whole column, two columns, she'd fill up a whole page! This wedding would be the event of the decade in Martin's Corners. Miss Naomi Beddoes Amhurst, the granddaughter of Martin's Corners' own heroine, Martha Curtis Beddoes, marrying Kelvin Janson and making her home right here! She wondered if Mr. Barnaby would allow a headline, but if she never wrote another piece in her life, this would be her masterpiece and she'd die content.

That evening, after a celebrating dinner, Naomi made it clear once and for all that she had no intention of going back to Roselawns for her wedding. She didn't need, or want, an elaborate affair. Besides, walking down the staircase at Roselawns, with half the county invited, would be in questionable taste so soon after two broken engagements to the same man.

"Dria wouldn't have time to go back with us and still get back to Boston in time to sail with Estelle, and I refuse to be married without her standing up with me. Besides, I

157

want to be married right here in the church that Aunt Emily and Martha went to. I'm going to live in their house, and I want to be married in their church. It'll be a big enough wedding right here. Mother, you'd better send Father a telegram right away, for him to get here as fast as he can to give me away."

She smiled at Kelvin, who still looked dazed, as if he was having a hard time believing that this was really happening. Her eyes glowed with love for him, and her inner happiness made her whole face glow.

"Now you see why I was in such a hurry to make you say yes. We simply haven't much time, if Dria's to be at our wedding."

"I only hope that with all this rush, people won't start counting on their fingers!" Prue said a little plaintively, and then she flushed, aware that what she'd been thinking had come out in words.

Both Naomi and Andrea broke into gales of laughter. "Mother! And I didn't even know that you knew the facts of life!" Naomi gasped. "Anyway, let them count. It'll liven up their lives and give them something to look forward to, won't it? Kel, you look about twelve years old when you blush like that. Never mind, we'll be good and not tease you any more. I think we're all just a little bit hysterical."

The next few days were hectic. In spite of the rush, Prue was determined that Naomi's wedding should be as beautiful as possible. They made a wildly hurried trip to Boston to have Naomi fitted for a wedding dress, paying a seamstress for engaging half a dozen helpers to have it finished in two days. Fortunately, Andrea already had a dress that would be appropriate for her role as bridesmaid, a summer pastel in a delectable shade of pink. It had come from Worth's, and Kate's wardrobe, even though she had packed very little for this quick trip, possessed a lavender chiffon that was perfect for the matron of honor.

The church was arranged for; Mr. Barnaby was to act as best man; all of the Tate clan, of whom Kelvin was a descendant, turned out in force, along with everyone else in town and Naomi's hastily sent for family. Dria and Naomi went into spasm of giggling as they wondered if the startled minister, Reverend Wilson, thought that the marriage was being rushed because of a delicate reason.

"But then I wouldn't be getting married in white, would I?" Naomi chuckled. "I wonder if the poor man has thought of that?"

Naomi was so beautiful when she was dressed for the ceremony that Andrea had to blink to keep from crying. It wouldn't do for the chief bridesmaid to have reddened eyes; this wedding had to be perfect. The delicate lace of the headdress and veil made Naomi look like an angel who had stepped out of a painting by some medieval master.

"It's almost time," Dria said. "Naomi, how can you be so calm? If I were in your place I'd be a bundle of nerves."

"There's nothing to be nervous about. I'm marrying Kelvin. I've always known he was the only man I wanted to marry."

Prudence tapped at the bedroom door. "Naomi, are you ready?"

"Mama, I've been ready for at least four years. But if you mean am I ready right now, yes, I am."

Prue came into the room, followed by Kate. "I have something for you," Prue said. "No, don't protest. You're to have them. It took a long time for them to bring me the happiness I finally found, but yours will begin immediately, and it's only right that they should be yours now."

Naomi's eyes misted with tears as she looked at the strand of pearls lying in the velvet case. The fabric of the case was a little matted now, the satin lining frayed a bit from age, but the pearls were as lustrous as they had been on the day when Jonathan Beddoes had placed them around Martha's throat, his gift to her for presenting him with his firstborn child, Rory.

Andrea felt her throat tighten for she knew the story of the pearls well, from both Adam and Uncle Jacob. Martha had been furious when she'd learned that two of Roselawn's slaves had been sold to finance the purchase. She'd said that every pearl represented a tear of an oppressed people, and she'd put the pearls away in the bottom of a drawer and never worn them again. Jonathan had given them to Prudence when he'd left Prudence with Aunt Emily, right here in this saltbox house, so that Naomi's child wouldn't be born at Roselawns, another slave although it would be his own grandchild. And now Prudence was fastening the pearls around her own daughter's throat.

Kate met Andrea's eyes, and her own were misty as she touched the strand of pearls around her own throat, the strand that Adam had given her at the time of her marriage. Adam had told her that pearls were a tradition in his family, and how true it was! Someday, Kate hoped that her own pearls would adorn Andrea's throat on Andrea's wedding day, but right at the moment it seemed that that would not take place for a long time. But sometime, please God, some day not in the too far future!

Naomi kissed her mother's cheek. "Thank you, Mother," she said quietly.

"Come now, Kelvin and your father are waiting at the church. And even at his age, I expect that your Uncle Rory is having to endure covetous glances from a few widows and spinsters, and he won't appreciate being kept waiting in such embarrassing circumstances. It's his own fault for being so outrageously handsome, but all the same, it makes him uneasy."

The church was banked with flowers. Everyone in Martin's Corners had stripped their gardens to make sure that enough honor was done to Naomi Beddoes Amhurst. Andrea had sworn to herself that she wouldn't cry, but she did. Her tears were of happiness for Naomi and of despair for herself. But she dried them quickly because nothing must mar the perfection of this day, the most wonderful day in Naomi's life. Would she ever be this happy, would she ever stand in front of an altar with the man she loved with her face as radiant as Naomi's when she lifted it to receive Kelvin's kiss? Hank, I was such a fool, she thought, and now you're having to suffer because of it just as much as I am.

She mustn't think about it now. She kissed Naomi and took her place in the reception line, her smile so convincing that no one except Kate and Prue realized how she felt inside.

"Dria, won't you change your mind and come home to Texas with me?" Kate asked her that afternoon, when she and Prue and Andrea were already on their way to Boston so that Naomi and Kelvin could have the saltbox house to themselves. "It isn't too late, Estelle would understand. Henry's there waiting for you, you'd make him the happiest man in the world if you'd come back with me and tell him you're ready to marry him."

"No, Mother. Don't ask me. I can't go back yet. I'm not ready. I know now that Hank's twice the man Gregory is or could ever hope to be, but I was going to marry Greg. I'm confused, I feel as if I've lost my way, but at least I know I'm confused, and I know that I have to find my way all by myself. I'd hate myself if I married Henry when I wasn't absolutely sure that that was what I want. He deserves better than that, and so do I. I need time to make sure of who I am and what I really want. I have to be very, very sure before I'll let some man, even Henry, give his whole life over to me. I think I've grown up a little. At least, I hope I have. But I'm still feeling my way. This trip with Estelle will give me time to think it out."

Kate managed to keep a smile on her face as she stood on the pier and waved as the ship sailed. Beside her, Prue reached for her hand and tried to give her comfort.

"She'll come back, Kate. And I'll come out to your Texas to see her married, and that's a promise."

"I'll hold you to that, Prue. Just help me pray that we won't have to wait too long!"

Hand in hand, the two women, so different and yet so much alike, turned away from the receding ship. Roselawns first, and then back to Texas, where Kate would have to wait for Andrea's return and bear the hurt in Henry's eyes every time she saw him.

She touched the pearls to her throat, seeking comfort from them as well as from Prue's presence. Some day Andrea would wear them, and on that day she'd be as happy for her daughter as Prue was for Naomi. In the meantime, there was nothing she could do but wait.

ENGLAND

11

Andrea's only consolation as she toweled herself dry at Sir Robert Cavindish's country house was that it wasn't raining. It had rained every day for the five days that she and Estelle Richards had been in England. Their shopping sprees had consisted of dashing from the shelter of cabs into the stores, then dashing back from the cabs to the shelter of the huge umbrella that the hotel doorman held over their heads. The British weather had matched her mood, serving to deepen her unhappiness and sense of gloom.

But this enforced visit to Lady Madeline and Sir Robert was the worst of all. She'd come to England to throw herself into an orgy of shopping, of sightseeing, of theaters and cafés and all the gaiety she could find to mitigate her roiling emotions.

To go back to Texas like a whipped puppy, eventually to turn to Henry Stockton because there was nothing else for her to do, had been more than she could endure. She'd snatched at the opportunity to come to England with her Aunt Prudence's friend Estelle as the only course that was left open to her, the only way to give herself time to heal, to find the courage to face the future after the debacle she'd left behind her in Georgia.

And then it had rained. The shops that would have delighted her a few months ago bored her; even the most enticing gowns failed to hold her interest. Estelle, as nice as she was, was still well past middle age and she was also boring, although Andrea was far too well bred to let her boredom show. The necessity of keeping her heartbreak and humiliation to herself had been such a strain that she'd actually wished that she'd gone home to Texas instead of making this trip.

And now this! Andrea shared none of Estelle's delight at the chance meeting with Lady Madeline and Sir Robert at the theater. The Cavindishes were old acquaintances of Estelle's from her previous visits to England, when her husband had had some sort of business dealings with Sir Robert. But there had been nothing she could do to avoid this visit to the country. Estelle was her chaperone, and common courtesy demanded that she accede to Estelle's wishes.

The rose-colored afternoon dress that Estelle had helped her choose at one of the shops in Piccadilly was already laid out on the bed. The soft, glowing rose complemented her fair skin and dark hair, made her look sweet and innocent, as innocent as she'd been before she'd gone to Georgia to visit her father's relatives there. Now the dress seemed a mockery as she pulled it over her head and smoothed the soft material over her hips. How Gregory's eyes would have lighted up if he'd seen her in it . . . before he'd found out about her ancestry!

The housekeeper had informed her that tea would be served in the large drawing room at four. It was still twenty minutes before four, but she was too restless to stay in her room. She hadn't even met Sir Robert and Lady Madeline yet. A manservant—she supposed that he was a butler—had admitted her and Estelle when they'd arrived from the station, and the housekeeper had shown them to their rooms. This was an added source of irritation to her. Back home in Texas, friends or neighbors who came to Trail's End would have felt darned unwelcome if her mother hadn't met them at the door, exclaiming with pleasure because they'd come. The prospect of spending several days in this Queen Anne house, as beautiful as it was with its façade of time-mellowed brick covered with decades of climbing ivy, of being trapped with her elderly chaperone, with a middle-aged host and hostess, made her want to scream.

Estelle wouldn't be ready to go down yet, she took ages to dress, so she found the broad staircase and went down without her. A startled parlormaid directed her to the large drawing room at the side of the house opposite her own wing, telling her at the same time that she was early for tea and that no one else was down yet.

A glance into the drawing room was sufficient. It looked big enough to ice skate in, and almost cold enough to do it. The fire had been kindled, but it hadn't burned long enough to take the chill from these last several days of rain.

She didn't even bother to enter the room. She'd go outside and examine the rose garden she'd glimpsed when they'd arrived. It at least would be warmer out there in the sunshine, and looking at the roses and memorizing their colors would give her something to write to her mother about. Kate's roses were famous throughout the Chinati Mountain region of Texas, but from what she'd seen from the carriage that had fetched them from the station, Lady Madeline's roses would put Kate's to shame.

The sun was still shining, and the scent of newly mown grass and a myriad of flowers wafted over her as she stepped outside. She'd have to remember this, too, and try to describe it in her letter. Her mother and father would be worried enough about her without her letting her despondency show through.

Her eyes widened as she saw something a good deal more unusual than green grass and flowers was directly in front of her, something that most definitely hadn't been there when she'd arrived. It was an automobile! She didn't know enough about automobiles to know what kind it was, but it was beautiful. She'd seen several of them when she'd been in Boston, but this was the first time she'd ever had the chance to examine one closely.

She approached the machine tentatively and reached out her hand to run her fingers across its sleek, shining paint. It had mudguards, and a coal-shovel hood, and its one seat was upholstered with leather. It had running boards and bright gleaming headlamps and a steering wheel and a windshield.

A long, low, and extremely appreciative whistle startled her so that her head jerked up. "Hallo! Admiring my buggy?"

The man was young, surely no more than in his early twenties. His head was bare so that the same sun that glinted so enticingly on his automobile made highlights in his light brown hair. He was dressed in tweeds, shabby enough to be recognized by Andrea as good ones. But it was his smile, eager and boyish, that made the most impression on her. It was a smile that demanded an answering smile, a smile that said its owner's heart would be broken if you didn't smile in return.

Andrea smiled in return, and her reward was to see his smile deepen into one that seemed to envelop him in pure delight.

"I'm glad you like my pet. That's what she is, you know, my pet. I groom her and feed her, and if I could I'd let her sleep at the foot of my bed. As my landlady would object to that, I have to settle for providing her with a nice cozy room of her own in the mews. I'm Reggie Mansfield, by the way. I don't believe we've met. A great oversight on my part, if you've been in England long. You're Aunt Madeline's younger American house guest, of course. You couldn't be the older one, a Mrs. Richards, isn't it?"

"Estelle Richards." Andrea nodded. "And I'm Andrea Wentworth."

"From Boston. Proper staid town, Boston. At least so I've been given to understand. I've never had the pleasure of seeing it for myself."

"From Texas." Andrea corrected him. "It's Mrs. Richards who lives in Boston. What kind of an automobile is it, Mr. Mansfield?"

"She's a Renault 8-C.V. She has a dashboard radiator and a 1-1-litre upright twin engine, a three-speed gearbox, and Renault's final-drive. She isn't the most powerful little buggy on the market, or the most expensive, but she's all mine and I love her."

Andrea caressed the bright red finish again. "I don't blame you. Does she have a name? I mean a name you've given her? You wouldn't call a dog Boxer or English Terrier or Shepherd, you'd give it a name, if it's your pet."

Lady Madeline's nephew had the grace to look abashed. "Do you know, I never thought of that!" But an instant later his face lighted up again, more delighted than ever. "That's a capital idea, and since you thought of it, then you must name her."

"Do I get to break a bottle of champagne over her front?"

Reggie was horrified, and showed it. "We mustn't scratch her paint, now must we? I have it! You name her, and I'll give you a ride in her! We just have time for a spin before tea. Ghastly boring, tea. We don't mind if we're slightly late, do we?"

"We don't mind in the least!" The idea of actually riding in this beautiful little automobile filled Andrea with an excitement she wouldn't have dreamed possible a few moments ago, and the idea of being late to tea was certainly more appealing than being on time for it. "But how can I ever think of a name that's worthy of her? Let me see. . . ."

She closed her eyes. Slowly, a smile transformed her face and Reginald Mansfield stood mesmerized, completely overwhelmed by the beauty of this young American visitor.

"I have it! How about Bella Linda?"

"It's perfect. What does it mean?"

"Beautiful beautiful." Andrea said with a peal of laughter. "But she is, you know, and that's the name I choose! Now do I get my ride?"

Before Reggie could move to assist her, his smile as delighted with their escapade as her own, she'd scrambled into the automobile. There were no doors to be opened so it took only one light step onto the running board and she was in. "How fast will Bella Linda go?"

"How fast do you want her to go? I've clocked her at nearly forty but it's pretty risky on these country lanes, and besides there won't be any A.A. people around here to warn us in case a constable's lurking in the hedgerows ready to run us in for speeding."

"A.A. people?"

"The Automobile Association. Every chap who has his own best interests at heart belongs to it. For two guineas a year you get all sorts of services, not the least of which is bicyclists wearing A.A. badges. If the red side's facing you, you see, there's danger ahead and it's best to slow down. It could be a sharp curve, or a hill, or an obstacle in the road. But most likely it's a constable intent on enforcing the ridiculous twenty-five-mile-an-hour speed limit that's been inflicted on us by our lawmakers. If the white side's facing you, then all's clear and it's full speed ahead. The constables dislike the A.A. people no end, but they're the motorists' best friends."

"But you don't think there'll be any around here, so we'll have to be careful. How careful?"

"How's your nerve?" Reggie was already at the crank and the upright twin engine roared into life. Another second and he was in the driver's seat beside Andrea on her right his whole countenance radiating adventure.

"There's nothing wrong with my nerve. Do hurry, before Estelle catches us!"

"Or Aunt Madeline." Reggie grinned.

They were off, and Andrea's heart began to race as the Renault picked up speed. It was a mercy that the wrought-iron gates were standing open, the gatekeeper's tea having been ready before he'd got around to closing them and his wife inclined to grow cross if he let it go cold after it was made.

Then they were beyond the gates, and Andrea had the impression that the automobile was about to leave the narrow road and soar over the treetops. The wind played havoc with her hair, loosening strands from the pins; it stung her eyes and brought color whipping into her cheeks, along with clouds of dust that made her blink and squint to see through it.

"Still have your nerve?"

Andrea nodded. "You can't frighten me! Only she can't go any faster than this, no machine could!"

Reggie promptly proved that she was mistaken, his grin as infectious as ever. The Renault took a bend in the road and swerved to the far side before he brought it back under control and urged still more speed from it.

Exultation was racing through Andrea's veins. Why, the best horse on her father's ranch, Beau Noir himself, couldn't begin to match this pace! The hedgerows blurred together as they sped past, and she gasped, a little frightened but not willing to call it quits. After all, the honor of the Yankees was at stake. If she asked Reggie to slow down, he'd think that all Americans were cowards. They took one bend after another without the slightest idea of what might lie ahead of them, going so fast that Andrea found it hard to breathe with the wind in her face.

"Reggie, look out!"

Reggie swore as he had to swerve wildly to avoid a farm cart that was directly in the middle of the sunken lane around the last curve, the shire horse in no hurry to move out of the way. Leaves flew into the air as the Renault grazed against the hedgerow, and they came within a hair's breadth of piling up against the steep bank. The farmer stood up in his cart and shook his fist after them, calling something that Andrea surmised it was just as well that she couldn't hear.

"Sorry. For my language, that is. Pokey horses and wagons, cluttering up the roads! It won't be long until they're as archaic as Roman chariots!"

The near accident hadn't even fazed him. He only slowed down when they ran into a particularly deep rut. "Something's going to have to be done about these roads! Now that the day of the motorized vehicle is here, they'll have to be improved to accommodate them. Can't have our tires mutilated. They don't last long enough by half as it is."

Half an hour later Andrea alighted in front of the Queen Anne house windswept, disheveled, her face still pink with excitement where the color could be seen through the grime and her fashion designer's dress well covered with dust. Even her hair felt gritty. She brushed her dress with her hands as well as she could, jabbed pins back into her hair, and wiped her face with the handkerchief that Reggie handed her. Estelle would be horrified.

Reggie offered her his arm. "We're late. Shall we march into the menagerie together and beard the lions in their den? I warn you, there'll be some growling and gnashing of teeth."

Now that her adventure was over, Andrea was fully aware of the enormity of her lapse of manners, going off without a word, with a young man she didn't even know, and failing to present herself to her hostess at the proscribed time. But what was done was done, and now she had no choice but to march into the lions' den, offer what apologies she could, and make the best of it. She only hoped that Estelle wasn't too angry.

Estelle's mortification at her protégée's behavior was evident when the two culprits entered the drawing room to find tea already in progress. "Andrea, where on earth have you been? We couldn't imagine what had become of you!"

Lady Cavindish smiled, and Andrea's apprehension lessened. Their hostess didn't seem in the least perturbed. She was a handsome woman, robust without being heavy, her tea gown looking as if it had been bought at a very expensive shop but not chosen for her.

"I might have known that my naughty Reggie was at the bottom of it." she said. "And from the looks of them, they've been tearing up the roads in that reprehensible autocar of his! How do you do, my dear. Come and meet my husband, and have some tea. You'll need some nourishment to restore your strength after Reggie has frightened you half to death."

"She doesn't appear to be frightened." Sir Robert had

risen to his feet when she'd entered the room, and now he bowed. "How do you do, Miss Wentworth. You look as though you've enjoyed your outing. Mrs. Richards, this young scalawag is my wife's nephew, Reginald Mansfield, and not an abductor of young women as you might have thought."

Reggie's smile was his most boyishly charming. "I'm sorry if you were worried, Mrs. Richards. But you know how it is. When I discovered this beautiful young creature admiring my autocar, I couldn't resist whisking her away for a spin. She was never in an instant's danger, I assure you."

Andrea managed to control the hoot of derision that rose to her lips. Reggie Mansfield could charm a bird out of a tree, much less her susceptible chaperone! No danger, indeed! Just look at Estelle, she was completely captivated by Reggie, her pique at Andrea's breach of manners already forgotten.

"Estelle tells me that you're from Texas. That's in the western part of the United States, I believe. Then of course you ride. I've a new mare I'd like you to see; she's quite good, and I think you'll like her if she isn't too frisky for you," Sir Robert was saying. "Will you join me in the morning for a canter? Always ride in the morning, there's nothing like a brisk canter to start the day off right. You, too, of course, Reggie, if you can tear yourself away from the motorized abomination that's smelling up my drive."

"I'd like that, thank you. I'm aching to be on a horse again." Andrea fought down the sudden wave of homesickness that threatened to overwhelm her. With the exhilaration of the automobile ride behind her, her depression was settling down over her again. She had a hard time swallowing a bite of scone spread with strawberry jam, even though the jam was as delicious as all of the British conserves she'd sampled. She had to help it down with a large sip of tea, which she detested. What she wouldn't give for a cup of Manuella's coffee right now, strong enough to prop up a dying man!

"If you've finished, I'll take you out to the stables and introduce you to the four-legged creature you're to

173

ride." Reggie's face was eager. Andrea had never known anyone who put so much enthusiasm into everything he did. "I suppose I'll draw that rawboned chestnut again. His trot's so high I always end up crippled."

Andrea hadn't finished, but she welcomed the chance to escape. If she stayed, Estelle would urge her to eat; Estelle was worried because, having no idea of the cause of Andrea's lack of appetite, she could only attribute it to some encroaching illness.

"Deuced attractive young woman," Sir Robert remarked as the two young people left the drawing room.

"Yes, Andrea's very lovely." Estelle beamed as she accepted another cake. "But then, her father is the handsomest man I've ever known, and her mother is also beautiful. I've known Adam Wentworth since he was a lad. With his background, it's little wonder that his daughter is so charming."

Lady Madeline and Sir Robert continued their discussion of their younger guest that evening as they were dressing for dinner. "American, of course, but she seems acceptable for all that," Sir Robert remarked. "She must be all right, if she's the daughter of friends of Estelle's."

"Yes, she's very attractive. And he and Andrea seem to have hit it off, don't you think?"

Lady Madeline jabbed another pin into her hair where it was threatening to come loose. "Wouldn't it be nice if something should come of it? It's time Reggie settled down. It worries me that he isn't married."

"Are you toying with the idea of doing a little matchmaking, my dear? It mightn't be such a bad idea at that. And if the gel has money, it wouldn't go amiss. Pity that your brother-in-law didn't leave him a bean. Not that I'd object to Miss Wentworth if she didn't have money, as long as she has the right background, but it would make things easier for them."

It was a pity that Reggie was so lacking in funds, Lady Madeline thought as she jabbed in another pin. Bother! Why couldn't Annie do her hair so that it stayed?

174

She had no hand for it herself. When it began to straggle, she never could get it back right. But then Peter Mansfield had never had a penny to leave to anyone, and if he had left his son anything, Reggie probably would have gone through it by now. Reggie didn't believe in stinting himself when it came to things he wanted, like that silly autocar of his. And Lady Madeline's sister's second marriage had turned out to be to a man just as impecunious, so there was no hope there. Dear Hattie did tend to choose the most impractical men! Educated, cultured, but with no flair for making money.

This young American girl, now. Lady Madeline smiled. After all, a good number of young men from the best families were marrying American money these days, and perhaps Miss Wentworth wouldn't mind that a title wouldn't come with the marriage, which was what most of the wealthy young American ladies seemed to be after.

In the meantime, it wouldn't hurt to cultivate the girl, even to ask her and Estelle to extend their visit in order to give Andrea and Reggie time to know each other better. It would be very nice to have Reggie settled. Lady Madeline doted on him; she loved him almost as much as she loved her own son Edward, who was too busy looking after Robert's affairs in London to come down during the week. That would give Reggie a clear field for several days; not that Miss Wentworth would be suitable for Edward, who would inherit the title. Unless Edward fell in love with her, of course. In that case Lady Madeline would have no objections. But she had her eye on Penelope Carruthers for her son, the daughter of the Honorable Archibald Carruthers.

A little ashamed of herself, because ordinarily she refrained from meddling in other people's affairs, Lady Madeline determined to question Estelle very discreetly as to Mr. Wentworth's financial standing. It was shameful to pry into someone's bank account, but she did want to be sure that the young people wouldn't have to live on Reggie's earning ability entirely, if something did come of it.

The little mare, Caprice, was a delight. She was sleek and fleet-footed, as frisky as a spring colt, with enough spirit to make riding her a joy. Reggie introduced Andrea to every bridle path and bylane in the vicinity, often challenging her to a race that she, with her Texas background of riding since she could walk, invariably won. The two of them were free to ride as far and as fast as they pleased, because in spite of Sir Robert's avowal that there was nothing like a brisk canter to start the day, he had not once appeared at the stables to accompany them.

After luncheon, Reggie persistently urged her out to Bella Linda, now dressed more appropriately for motoring in a long duster and a hat tied onto her head with a long, wide scarf, the ends fastened into a huge bow under her chin. Goggles that made her look like a gargoyle completed her ensemble. The fact that the duster, which belonged to Reggie, was much too large for her did nothing to detract from her enjoyment. In fact, she enjoyed the overall impression that she gave of a child dressed up for Halloween. She wasn't out to charm Reggie with her beauty and chic, she was out to have fun, to keep her memories at bay.

Together they explored every country lane to its end, stopped at country inns for English country teas of scones and strawberry preserves and clotted cream. All of the exercise and fresh air had restored her appetite in spite of nights spent tossing sleeplessly while she relived that last dreadful scene with Gregory, as exquisitely painful now as it had been when it had happened. She wondered what the upstairs maids thought when they saw her rumpled sheets, torn from their moorings by her threshing around.

They'd return barely in time to bathe and dress for dinner, and more often than not they'd beg off the inevitable bridge and Reggie would put a record on the Victrola and they would dance. Estelle and Lady Madeline and Sir Robert watched them with benevolent eyes and excused themselves early and left the young couple alone.

She and Reggie were alone most of the time, Andrea realized before she and Estelle had been there for four days. At the same time she realized, with burgeoning horror, that if the older people weren't matchmaking, they were giving a remarkable imitation of it.

The thought drew her up short. She wasn't ready for another romance; it would be a long time before she was ready, if she ever was at all. The Georgia debacle had left her too shaken to trust her heart to any man again, no matter how personable and charming he was or how much fun to be with. This wouldn't do, it wouldn't do at all! Panic rose in her, and her only thought was to escape. When Lady Madeline asked Estelle, on Friday, to extend their visit for at least another week, Andrea told them as firmly as she could without being impolite that it was impossible, that they still had a good deal of shopping and sightseeing to do, as well as plans to travel to the Continent.

"But Andrea, I thought you were having a wonderful time here! You and young Reggie seem to get along so well!" Estelle protested when they were alone. "Really, the way you cut me off from accepting when dear Lady Madeline asked us to stay on, I can't imagine what she thinks!"

"You stay if you wish, Mrs. Richards, but I'm leaving tomorrow just as we planned." The set of Andrea's chin told Estelle that no argument would change her mind. She must be getting old, Estelle thought, sighing. She didn't understand young people any more. She'd have sworn that Andrea was happy here, that she and Lady Madeline's handsome nephew were hitting it off. However, if the girl was determined to leave, then Estelle would have to go with her. She was responsible for her, and it was unthinkable to let her continue her tour unchaperoned.

Even Reggie's bewildered disappointment failed to shake Andrea's resolution. There was danger here, and she had to run. So their luggage was already being carried out to the carriage when Lady Madeline's son arrived for the weekend, and in the flurry of the departure Andrea had only the briefest impression of a man a year or so older than Reggie, an inch or so taller, and with hair a shade or two lighter and with keen, probing hazel eyes that evaluated her a great deal more thoroughly than she evaluated him. One young man was bad enough, let alone two. No, they must hurry, they mustn't miss the train that Reggie was all too patently trying to make them miss by none too subtle delaying tactics.

"If I'd known that we had such charming guests, I'd have managed to get down a day earlier," Edward Cavindish told them. "I'm sorry you have to leave just as I arrive. Will we have the pleasure of seeing you in the near future?"

Estelle opened her mouth to say that she hoped that he would, but Andrea cut her off. "I'm afraid not, Mr. Cavindish. Mrs. Richards and I plan to stay in London for only a day or two longer, and then we'll go on to Paris."

Estelle's chins quivered with indignation, but as Andrea was already propelling her toward the carriage there was nothing she could do. Two such personable young men, and her charge insisted in leaving! It was beyond her understanding. If the prospect of Paris with its unparalleled shopping hadn't been ahead of her, she'd have been bitterly disappointed. What a *coup* it would have been if her protégée had snagged not Reggie, as eligible as he was, but Edward Cavindish himself, and the title that would eventually come with him!

12

It took Andrea a moment to orient herself when she woke up in her luxurious bedroom at the Ritz, with the traffic noises of Piccadilly drifting up through the opened windows. The tapping at the door was persistent and annoying, and she gritted her teeth as she reached for her robe and slippers.

"Who is it? What on earth do you want?" she demanded.

"There's a delivery for you, Miss Wentworth." The voice sounded muffled, so that she had to strain to hear it.

"There's been a mistake. I'm not expecting a delivery."

"It's addressed to Miss Andrea Wentworth, and you have to sign for it."

Andrea gave up and unlocked the door, and then immediately stepped backwards, her mouth falling open.

He stood there grinning like a Cheshire cat, his eyes

dancing above the huge mass of hothouse roses that all but obscured the rest of his face.

"Reggie! What are you doing in London?"

"And where else would I be when you're in London?"

"Back with your aunt, of course, where I left you yesterday!"

"She threw me out."

"Liar!"

"Where I come from, ma'am, men have been called out for less than that. As you proffered the insult, I have the choice of weapons. Kippers, and a chop, porridge and toast. The customary rules will prevail; the first one to finish the last mouthful wins. Hurry and get dressed; I'm famished. And then, win or lose, I'm taking you on the grand tour of London."

Reggie had more gall than any other man she'd ever known, even Wayne Bradshaw, and Reggie wasn't anywhere near as handsome as Wayne! Granted, he was a lot more fun, but it was still outrageous. But outside of calling for help and having him forcibly ejected, which would cause a scene that Estelle would never forgive, there was no way to get rid of him.

In spite of her anger at having her plans to escape him thwarted, she had a wonderful time. How could she help it, with Reggie nattering on in imitation of a tour guide, saying such inane things, in a voice intended to carry so that all of the other sightseers stared at them, as "If Scots Mary had kept her head, she wouldn't have lost it" and "The guard has to be changed so often because their hats are so heavy."

The Tower, Buckingham Palace, Westminster Abbey and the Parliament Buildings, Drury Lane and Trafalgar Square, and Saint Paul's—Reggie knew London like the palm of his hand. Estelle had refused to come with them, protesting that she'd seen it all before and that she intended to shop. Andrea's protests at dinner that because she'd left Estelle alone all day she couldn't possibly leave her alone again that evening got her nowhere. Estelle was tired; she fully intended to retire early and get a good night's sleep. Andrea must most certainly go out with

180

Reggie; she mustn't waste any of the little time they still had in London.

Their destination turned out to be a flat in Soho, and Andrea was sure that Reggie was playing some sort of a joke on her.

"How can you have friends living here?" she demanded. "Reggie, if you're trying to find out how gullible I am, it won't work! I'll bet you're taking me to an opium den or something, just to see my reaction!"

For a moment, after Reggie had made a great thing of knocking at the fourth-floor walkup door with a special signal, four sharp raps, then one, then three, she thought that her guess had been right. When the door opened, her first impression was of almost complete darkness, and the scent of some exotic incense that added to the sense of mystery and evil.

Then a pair of plump arms enveloped in red chiffon wrapped themselves around Reggie's neck, and she wondered if even Reggie had dared to bring her to a house of ill repute!

"Reggie! Where have you been all these days? Up to no good, I'll wager!"

"Stop it, love, you're choking me! Besides, I've brought a lady with me and you're shocking her no end. Andrea, this is Caroline Byron, and that seedy-looking individual just behind her, the one who's grinning as if he's trying to imitate an ape, is Mortimer Byron, our unfortunate hostess's husband."

As Andrea's eyes adjusted to the murky atmosphere in the flat, the only illumination coming from a few candles stuck in the necks of wine bottles, she saw a pair of candid brown eyes in a round, innocent face, surrounded by a mass of ginger-colored hair. "It is a lady! Where ever did you find her, and what kind of a drug did you have to give her to get her here? Do you have a name, lady?"

"Andrea Wentworth." Andrea still wasn't sure what kind of a place Reggie had brought her to.

"Come and meet the rest of the zoo, Andrea. The ape, as Reggie said, is my husband. This is Eleanor Talbot, and that's Owen Fitzgerald, and Bruce Yarnell."

They were all young, in their twenties or early thirties. Only Caroline and Mortimer were married. Caroline was a poetess, "Because I had to be a poetess because of Mortimer's name, didn't I? As long as he isn't, then I have to be. He daubs."

"My good wife and helpmeet, I do not daub! I am a genius, the second Raphael, a budding Renoir!"

Caroline Byron ignored him. "Owen scribbles. Eleanor designs . . . women's fashions, as well as having designs on men. Bruce is a misfit; he's a junior partner in a publishing company, a mere wage slave, but we have to cultivate him because he might be able to talk the senior partners into publishing my deathless poetry, or Owen's rotten prose. Come and sit down. Mort, bring Andrea a drink. What do you do, Andrea?"

"She's a bronc-rider from Texas," Reggie said with a perfectly straight face. "She breaks wild mustangs."

Caroline screamed with delight. "A bronc-buster! Doesn't that mean that you ride wild horses? How many bones have you had broken?"

"Seventy-three," Andrea said. "But that includes all those tiny bones in my hands and feet, of course."

They surrounded her, delighted with their new acquisition. Was she really from the Wild West? Where was Texas, exactly? Had she ever killed an Indian? Did all Texans speak English?

She was a hit, she was accepted, she was one of them. These Bohemian friends of Reggie's adored her. She was plied with sour red wine as she sat on the cushions that were strewn around the floor because they were cheaper than chairs and couches. She was shown Mortimer's latest canvas, the paint still wet. Other canvases were stacked along the walls, so many that Andrea thought, and was sorry, that he couldn't be much of a success at his chosen profession. She didn't know enough about art to know if the paintings were any good, but she liked them and she liked Mort, too. Besides, he didn't look like an ape, he looked more like a beguiling, cuddly panda.

Caroline's poetry was incomprehensible, and Owen Fitzgerald's novel, the chapter that he insisted on reading to her, was probably good but she didn't understand it, either. It didn't matter whether what they did was good or not, or even if it were marketable. They were the most fun, the most exciting people Andrea had ever known.

Only one of them kept to herself, apart from the group that clustered around Andrea. Her hair was fair, almost the color of ripened wheat, and it was bobbed. She was the first woman Andrea had ever seen who had bobbed hair. It curled around her face in a halo of small, tight ringlets, emphasizing the classic contours of her facial structure. And in addition to the bobbed hair and her extraordinary beauty, she held a long jade cigarette holder in her hand, the cigarette's smoke drifting around her head. It was a mercy that Estelle had refused to accompany them, Andrea thought. She'd be so shocked that she might swoon and have to be taken back to the hotel and put to bed.

"You haven't told me what you do." Andrea looked at the young woman inquiringly.

Caroline jumped into the breach. "Oh, I'm sorry! Bea sculpts, and she's good. She made a head of Reggie that can almost speak to you! She's the only one of us who's a real success, she actually sells her work and doesn't have to depend on handouts from her family to keep tea in the pot and shillings in the gas meter when our luck runs out."

"A sculptress!" Andrea was awed. "I'd love to see your work!"

"Not unless you're interested in buying." Beatrice Langdon's voice was husky and it held a deliberate insolence. "My studio isn't a ha'penny tourist attraction."

An embarrassed silence fell over the group, and even Caroline seemed at a loss as how to cover up her friend's lack of manners.

"You aren't really a bronc-rider, though!" Mort accused Andrea so suddenly that she started. A paint-stained finger pointed at her just as accusingly. "Reggie made that up."

"I've helped break a few." Andrea's lips twitched at the corners in her effort not to break into what Uncle Jacob called her gamine grin. Maybe she didn't do anything glamorous and wonderful, as all of these people did, but she'd just like to see one of them handle a bucking horse!

"Like in the Wild West shows? I saw one once, a troupe from the United States. Do you fancy tricks on horses like they did?"

"Not exactly. But we do have rodeos, to show off our horses and skills."

Mortimer wasn't satisfied. "What do you do, in those rodeos?"

"Not very much. My father made me stop riding the bucking horses after I was thrown and was unconscious for several hours. Girls aren't supposed to ride the buckers anyway, but I stuck my hair up under my hat and wore my brother's clothes and said my name was Tom Atkins, from Montana, before anyone caught me out. If that critter hadn't thrown me, I'd have gotten away with it. Now I stick to fancy roping and barrel racing; Father still lets me do that because I get very ugly when I'm prevented from doing what I want to do. Some of our neighbors think it's a scandal, but we Wentworths never care much about what other people think."

"Barrel racing?" All of the faces staring at her looked blank.

Andrea laughed. "It's quite simple, really. Barrels are placed on end at various points around the arena. The riders run the horses around them to see who can cut the closest without knocking them over, and still make the best time to the finish line."

Caroline clapped her hands together like a child. "I wish I could see that!"

"Why not?" Reggie spoke casually, but there was a devilish gleam in his eyes. "There's no reason we can't get out and set up a few barrels tomorrow morning, is there? It'll be no trouble to hire a horse."

"Reggie, the horses have to be trained!" Andrea protested. "Barrel racing on an untrained horse, with an English saddle?"

"Are you afraid to try, then?" Beatrice Langdon's voice was filled with amused contempt and something else,

184

a repetition of her earlier hostility. Andrea felt an unaccustomed anger rise in her. Why did the sculptress dislike her, when they'd only just met?

The answer struck her so suddenly that she wondered how she could have been so dense. It was Reggie, of course. Of all the group, Bea was the only one without a partner. She and Reggie were supposed to be the twosome. She wished that she could tell Bea right out, without causing an unpleasant scene, that she had no designs on Reggie and that she'd only be in London another day or two in any case.

But Bea's eyes, regarding her derisively, made her chin come up. "All right. If the men set up the barrels, I'll ride."

Reggie's protest was immediate. "Andrea, if it's dangerous?"

"Don't be silly. I'd like to see the rental horse that I can't handle! Perhaps Bea would like to lay a small wager that I can't do it?"

Caroline and Eleanor looked distressed at the quivering animosity between Andrea and Bea, and except for Reggie, the men were embarrassed. Reggie seemed oblivious to the tension between the two young women.

"If Bea wants to lay that wager, I'll take it." he said. "If you say you can do it, I believe you. After all, I've seen you on Caprice."

"Not tomorrow, though. I'll have to find a costume. Even to bolster your faith in me, I'm not riding sidesaddle! Besides, Caroline will want it to look as authentic as possible, barring a Western saddle."

She spent the next morning with Reggie, who located a costume rental shop for her, and the afternoon at a riding stable where she tried out several different mounts and chose a steady young black that seemed the most intelligent of the lot. Two hours of testing him out, and she was satisfied that she'd give a good accounting of herself.

Caroline and Eleanor gasped with appreciation when Andrea alighted from a cab at St. James Park the morning the challenge had to be met. It was very early, and the dew was still on the grass. The hackman, already astonished

185

at the costume his fare was wearing, was even more astonished to see the barrels that the men had set up, and Reggie appearing on the black, his face alight and his eyes dancing. He decided to stay and see what was going on even though it meant missing another fare.

Andrea was wearing a divided Western riding skirt and a vest, cowboy boots that were only a little too large, and a wide white Stetson hat. Her long black hair hung down over her shoulders in two braids, Indian style. Standing a little apart from the others, Beatrice Langdon's mouth compressed.

Andrea ignored her. The barrels were set too close together, and she directed their removal to the proper positions. Then she swung up into the saddle and trotted the black a good distance from the first barrel before she reined him around and set him into a gallop.

Anyone with less experience would have come what the British called a cropper. The black shied away from the first barrel and she had to bring him back under control and start again. This time they rounded it, a little too far from it to qualify if it had been a genuine contest. They bore down on the second and cut much closer. Then the last; the barrel wobbled as the black grazed it but it didn't go over, and in a fraction of an instant she'd steadied him and turned him to retrace the course.

Elation at having done so well with a completely inexperienced mount flooded through her, and as she rounded the last barrel she stood up in the stirrups as she reined in and gave vent to a wild war whoop, sweeping her hat off and waving it at her audience.

Her audience! Where had all these people come from, at this hour of the morning? There were at least two dozen, including the hack driver, standing with their mouths agape.

" 'Ere now, 'ere now, what's going on? This is a public park, you can't put on a Wild West show 'ere! Where's your permit?" A red-faced bobby shouldered his way through the crowd, his voice filled with indignation. "Putting on a Wild West show, digging up the nice green sod with that beast's hooves, instead of staying on the

186

path as is proper! I ought to take you in, that's what I ought!"

"Officer, this young lady from Texas was only kind enough to show us how things are done there. We can't go around arresting visitors to our fair city, now can we? The American ambassador mightn't like it, and then there would be all sorts of diplomatic trouble, wouldn't there?"

"All the same, you can't put on any Wild West show in St. James Park! Get those barrels out of 'ere, and take yourselves off!"

"We'll do that, officer. We'll take care of it at once. Unless you'd like to see Miss Wentworth perform? You arrived just too late for the show. Perhaps if we were to ask her nicely . . . ?"

The bobby's face lighted up before he recollected himself and refrained from accepting the offer. Reggie looked sympathetic. The crowd dispersed, laughing and shaking their heads at the way Americans disported themselves, and an hour later Andrea and her new friends, along with Reggie, invaded a restaurant in search of breakfast. Only Beatrice Langdon failed to accompany them.

"That was wonderful! What on earth can we do for an encore?" Caroline wanted to know.

Andrea pushed her wide Stetson back on her head, oblivious to the stares of the other patrons in the restaurant at her unorthodox attire. "Go swimming in the Thames?" she asked innocently.

Reggie's studied look made her wish that she hadn't mentioned it. And two hours later, five otherwise respectable London citizens and one visitor from the United States of America were ordered out of the river, herded into a paddy wagon, and taken before a magistrate and given a caustic lecture about decent and prudent behavior.

It was inevitable that the less conservative newspapers should pick up the escapades of the American heiress who was shocking staid London. Andrea couldn't have cared less. She wanted nothing more than to be busy every minute, to rush from one madcap adventure to another, to fill her hours so full that she'd have no time to think.

Reggie and his friends filled her need. She was never in bed before three in the morning, she drank too much, she wore out three pairs of slippers dancing, and she and Reggie were arrested three times for speeding. These new friends liked her, they accepted her, she was one of them, and her lacerated pride reveled in the healing balm of their admiration.

The morning Andrea was arrested for inadvertently driving Reggie's Renault into a public pool with a fountain in its center, damaging the fountain and causing a water-spout, when Reggie had been giving her her second driving lesson, Estelle put her foot down.

"We can't have it, Andrea. It's disgraceful! Reggie, don't you realize that you're ruining Andrea's reputation?"

"I expect I am, but it doesn't really matter, Mrs. Richards, as we're going to be married, anyway."

"Reggie, stop that!" Andrea glared at him. "Mrs. Richards, I'm sorry if I've caused you embarrassment. It's just that I'm having so much fun! And I know you're dis-appointed because we aren't already in Paris. I've been selfish, keeping you in London when you're pining to get at those Paris shops, but I just couldn't seem to tear my-self away."

"All the same, it has to stop. I'm afraid that I'll have to insist that we leave London immediately."

"Certainly we're leaving London. We're going back to Aunt Madeline's. Oh, did I forget to tell you? She's expecting us tomorrow and we can't fail to show up, she's having a dinner party in your honor." Reggie's face was a picture of innocence.

"Reggie!"

Reggie ignored the warning in Andrea's voice. "We'd better get an early start. Mrs. Richards, I'm sorry that Bella Linda will only accommodate two, so I'm afraid that you'll have to make do with the train. Of course, Andrea could drive you and I could take the train. . . ."

Estelle blanched. "I'll take the train! How could you have forgotten to let us know we were expected? Andrea, we must pack at once." As enticing as Paris was, this was much better. Imagine being Lady Madeline's guest again!

Estelle would have a great deal to tell her friends when she returned to Boston. Few of them had ever been so fortunate as to be invited to stay with titled people as their house guests, and certainly not twice in one tour!

This was a turn of events that Andrea didn't like at all. Being in London with Reggie, almost constantly in the company of Reggie's friends, was one thing, but to be thrown with him as a twosome again, in the country, was something entirely different. It was on the tip of her tongue to refuse to go even if Lady Madeline was expecting them, but Estelle's next remark made her capitulate.

"I was going to insist that we return home immediately. I've found that I can't cope with Andrea's wildness. But perhaps a few days in the country will settle her down, and we'll be able to go on to Paris after all."

She couldn't go home! She wasn't ready. Everything she'd left behind her was still too close to her, too filled with humiliation and heartbreak. She needed time, a great deal more time, and so there was nothing to do but go back to the country.

Lady Madeline was indeed expecting them. In fact, she told Reggie severely, she'd expected them two days ago! If they hadn't arrived today, she didn't know what she would have done, with all their guests expected and the guests of honor not in evidence.

Andrea was stunned by the guest list. Lady Genevive and Sir Evan Morgain, the Earl of Argyle and his countess, Lady Constance, an assortment of local squires and their ladies, a vicar, as well as Edward Cavindish and the Honorable Mr. Carruthers and his wife Agnes and their daughter Penelope.

"Such a lovely girl! Reggie's done well for himself, I'm sure. I expect they'll be very happy," Andrea overheard Lady Constance remark to Mrs. Carruthers. She kept her smile plastered on her face as she turned to accept Lady Genevive's invitation to visit her and Sir Evan at their country house, to accent the vicar's wife's invitation to help with a jumble table at the church fair, to assure a ruddy-faced squire that she'd be delighted to see his shire horses and his blue-ribbon pigs. How had such a rumor ever got started? It was bad enough that Reggie had jokingly told Estelle that they were going to be married, but this was something that had to be stopped.

Her resolution deepened when Edward Cavindish singled her out a few moments later, his hazel eyes filled with probing concern. "Have you and Reggie set the date, Miss Wentworth? It seems that we're to become related to each other."

"No date has been set, because no marriage is going to take place!" Andrea told him, hoping that her face wasn't as flaming with anger as it felt. "Reggie's playing one of his jokes."

"It doesn't seem to be a joke." Edward's eyes probed into hers even more deeply. "I don't recall ever having seen him so serious about anything." He looked as if he were about to say something more, but Mrs. Carruthers claimed his attention and he had to excuse himself. It was a pity that Reggie didn't take more after his cousin, Andrea thought, still furious. Surely Edward Cavindish would never find amusement in spreading false rumors!

She knocked on Reggie's door before he was awake the next morning and demanded that he get dressed immediately so that they could ride out before anyone else decided to join them. He'd avoided her all last evening, except when she'd been surrounded by other people, so that she couldn't challenge him without causing a scene.

"You're putting me in an impossible position!" she burst out as soon as they were well away from the house. "I want you to put a stop to these rumors about our marriage, and don't pretend that you don't know what I'm talking about!"

"But we *are* going to be married! The only question is how soon you'll set the date," Reggie told her, looking so genuinely bewildered that she didn't know whether to laugh or to cry. Caprice wanted to run, and she had to hold her in. If she had her wish, she'd let the mare have her head, and gallop as fast as the wind anywhere at all as long as it would take her out of Reggie's reach, and everybody else at the house.

"We are not going to be married. I don't even want

to talk about it. Just tell them that it isn't true." Her eyes were dark with anger.

"I love you."

"So you say. I heard that from another man, not very many weeks ago. Only he changed his mind."

"That's impossible. No man on earth would be fool enough to change his mind about you!" Reggie was more bewildered than ever. "What possible reason can you have for telling me such a patent falsehood?"

Andrea exploded, all of her pent-up wrath and hurt and trampled pride pouring out. She had to lash out at someone to relieve the pressure inside her that was threatening to tear her apart.

"It isn't a lie! He found out about me, about my antecedents. He found out that I'm one sixty-fourth black, that I'm one-eighth American Indian, that my grandmother and great-grandmother were slaves, that my father was the result of rape on my grandmother. And now you know it, too, and tomorrow I'll go back to London, and from there I'll go to Paris, and you won't ever have to see me again and you needn't feel sorry for me because I don't need your pity, I don't need anyone's pity. I'm proud of who I am and what I am, and I want to thank you for all the fun we've had together, but that's an end to it!"

"But I don't understand. Why did this man, this idiot, change his mind about you?"

He didn't know. He honestly, truthfully, didn't know! The things she'd just told him meant less than nothing to him. Andrea felt the trap around her growing tighter.

"You're either incredibly naive, or you're semi-retarded! Your aunt and Sir Robert will explain it to you, if you're too insane to figure it out for yourself!" Wild with the panic that was sweeping over her, wild with the hurt that hadn't had time to heal, she dug her heel into Caprice's side and lifted her into a headlong gallop. She didn't know where she was going, she only knew that she had to put as much distance between herself and Reggie as she could until she had some sort of control over herself.

Above the pounding of her heart, she heard thundering hoofbeats behind her as Reggie sent his own mount to racing after her. She urged Caprice to an even faster pace, determined not to be overtaken. But it was apparent that all of Reggie's declarations about being an indifferent rider were false. As fast as Caprice was, Reggie's long-legged, rangy hunter cut down the distance separating them. Now he was abreast of her, cutting ahead of her, cutting her off so that she had no choice but to pull up unless she wanted to careen into him.

Reggie reached out and grasped Caprice's reins, and at the same instant he dismounted. Another instant, and he had literally hauled her out of her saddle. The man who loomed above her, his eyes blazing, was a complete stranger to her. He wasn't smiling, he had no quips ready to his lips, there was only that intense, commanding gaze from which she was powerless to tear her eyes.

"You're driving me out of my mind!" he said. "I love you, I have to have you, and I'm going to have you, so you might as well stop fighting me!"

She began to struggle, to try to pull herself free from his relentless grasp. His hold on her only tightened. Her hat fell off, and her hair came loose from its pins and tumbled down around her shoulders as she fought him.

"Stop it, Andrea! Stop it, I say! There's no use trying to get away from me. You belong to me, and I'm not going to let you go, not now, not ever!"

His kiss, demanding, exploring, exciting, made her bones turn to water. He was a man, a grown and extremely vital and attractive man, and she was a woman who'd been running away from life, running away from love, because she was determined not to be hurt again.

He loved her. He didn't care about her antecedents. He'd face his aunt, his friends, all of those wealthy and even titled people back at the Cavindish country house, and claim her as his own.

Still, she had to be sure. "A church wedding?" she demanded as soon as he had to stop for breath. "With everyone there? Your family, their friends, not just Caroline and Mort and the others back in London?"

"Aunt Madeline will get the bishop to officiate,"

Reggie told her. "The same one who's going to do for Ned and Penelope. She's already mentioned it."

She still wasn't sure. It was too soon. She'd thought that she loved Gregory Randolph; before that she'd been almost sure that she loved Henry Stockton, except that she hadn't been ready to marry before she'd ever seen anything outside of Texas.

Reggie had loosened his hold on her, and it gave her the chance she needed. She turned and began to run toward Caprice where she was cropping grass a short distance away. It was too soon; how could she be sure?

He caught her in a few strides, just as she tripped over a fallen branch and fell headlong, taking him down with her. He held her there on the ground, and fire ran through her veins and set her whole body ablaze as it took over from her mind. Above them, storm clouds were gathering, blotting out the blue of the sky, but they were oblivious to the first drops that fell. She heard Reggie's wild, exultant laugh as he held her captive, as he kissed her again and again until she was powerless to resist him.

Soaked by the sudden storm, their world filled only with the wild pounding of their blood, they had no idea that at that precise moment Edward Cavindish was facing his mother, his mouth set in a grim line.

"It isn't right, Mother. Miss Wentworth shouldn't be thrown at Reggie. He's never made anything of himself, although you've certainly given him every opportunity, even underwriting his education. He's singularly lacking in ambition. And it looks to me as if you're aiding and abetting him in rushing her into marriage before she can find out what she's getting into."

"Now, Ned, Reggie loves Miss Wentworth, and I'm sure that she loves him. If they decide to marry, it will be the making of him. He's never had any real incentive before. And your father has arranged for him to have a splendid position in that bank he helps direct. Marriage will settle him, you'll see."

Edward wasn't convinced. The last he'd heard, Reggie's affair with that sculptress, Beatrice Langdon, had still been going on. But one couldn't mention things like that to one's mother, and he was sure his father was already aware of it. And of course the affair didn't actually signify. It had started before Reggie had met Andrea, and any man in his right mind would prefer the girl from Texas.

Lady Madeline looked at her son severely. "Edward, if I didn't think that the marriage would work out, I wouldn't encourage the girl to accept him. I'm not an ogre, you know. I honestly believe that he'll settle down once he has such a suitable and charming wife. You should be happy for him. After all, he's your own blood cousin. Now run along so that I can get dressed, but remember what I said. Don't cause any trouble!"

Edward left his mother's bedroom, but he was still far from happy. However, as his mother had pointed out, Reggie was his cousin, and in spite of his disapproval of some of his actions, Edward was fond of him. No doubt the girl was old enough to know her own mind. In any case, he wouldn't be around long enough to cause trouble, as he was scheduled to go to the Continent in two days' time to untangle a particularly tricky legal snag in one of the family enterprises. And from all he'd heard, American girls weren't as sheltered as British young ladies; in all probability Miss Wentworth was fully capable of taking care of herself.

13

Kate and Adam scrutinized the crowd that was waiting for the disembarking passengers, but even Adam's keen eyes, used to picking out strays from miles of Texas scrub, failed to find their daughter.

"I don't understand it! Surely she knew that we were due to dock this afternoon!" Kate's voice was a good deal calmer than she felt. The cable from Andrea, apprising them that she was to be married to a Reginald Mansfield, had caught her and Adam completely by surprise.

It had taken Adam no more than two minutes to decide that in spite of the fall shipping that lay ahead of him, he could leave the ranch in Wade's capable hands. His one idea, and Kate's, was to get to England before Andrea could do anything as foolish as to marry a man she had scarcely met. If they liked this Mansfield, then they would have no objections to her marriage, provided that they were convinced that Andrea really loved him and that she wasn't rushing into this alliance in order to soothe her trampled pride. But not, even then, if they could convince her that she should wait for at least six months before she made such an irreversible move.

Adam's mouth was set in a grim line, the only sign of his displeasure. He, too, was keeping a firm grip on his emotions. Of all his children, Andrea was the dearest to him, because there was so much of both himself and Kate in her. She mustn't be allowed to make a mistake that could ruin her life.

They were through customs at last, and still there was no sign of Andrea. But even as Adam pondered on what move to make next, a distinguished-looking man singled them out and came forward with his hand outstretched.

"Mr. and Mrs. Wentworth? I was sure it had to be you, from your daughter's description. I'm afraid that those youngsters of ours are playing truant. Reggie's taken Andrea up to Scotland, along with a couple of friends of theirs, a young married couple, Caroline and Mortimer Byron, so it fell to me to meet you and escort you to our country place. I'm Robert Cavindish. Your friend Estelle Richards is waiting for you there; she didn't feel up to coming into London, and besides she and Madeline are running themselves ragged with the wedding preparations. I rather suspect that that's why Andrea and Reggie made themselves scarce; they were thoroughly fed up with lists and plans and they wanted a breather."

"Sir Robert," Adam said. His first impression of their host was favorable; Robert Cavindish appeared to be one of the solid pillars of British society. Beside him, Kate was experiencing the same reaction. If Reginald Mansfield was a family connection of the Cavindishes, then he must be acceptable. They'd find out more about it when they could talk with Estelle.

"I'm afraid we're rather rushing things, but the youngsters insisted," Sir Robert went on. A uniformed coachman was already gathering up their luggage and supervising its placement in a handcart to be taken to the carriage. "It must have taken you by surprise. You must have had a time of it, getting here so soon. Let's get

196

out of this press. I'll jolly well be glad to get back to the country. London isn't what it used to be. I never come in any more unless it's absolutely essential. I let my son Edward cope these days."

During the long train journey to Sir Robert's country estate, the English countryside was a delight to Kate. Her trip to Georgia and Massachusetts with Andrea had been the first time she'd ever been outside the Western states, but coming abroad filled her with even greater excitement. If it hadn't been for her worry about this step her daughter was taking, she'd have reveled in the ocean crossing on one of the Cunard line's most luxurious ships, in actually being in England with Adam. It would have been the honeymoon they'd never had, the one that Adam had promised her ever since they'd been married but that they'd put off from year to year because they'd been so busy, and so contented, at home. She had enjoyed the crossing; Kate wasn't one to forego pleasure in a new experience because of worrying about something that she couldn't do anything about yet, and being alone with Adam, having him all to herself without any pressure of ranch affairs, had been a delight. But still, she hadn't been able to entirely keep her well-controlled worry about Andrea from nagging at the edges of her mind.

Her first glimpse of the Queen Anne house, set in its spacious parklike grounds, further relieved her mind. She could feel a slight lessening of Adam's tension, as well. She and Adam had always been so close that there was no need of words for each of them to know what the other felt. But she scarcely had time to gasp at the beauty of the rioting rose beds that Andrea had written her about before Estelle was hurrying through the front door to greet her.

"Mrs. Wentworth! I can't tell you how glad I am that you're here! And Mr. Wentworth, as well. What a rush you must have had, and then those naughty children not even here to greet you! I'm really quite distracted! There's at least one more fitting to be done on the wedding gown, and Andrea not here to be fitted. How can she be married in a gown that hasn't been fitted perfectly?" Estelle's

197

distraction was evident in both her voice and her appearance. Her face was flushed, and all of her chins quivered. "Do come in, Lady Madeline is waiting to make you welcome, and tea is ready in the drawing room."

"Yes, come in, come in!" Sir Robert urged. "As for tea, I'm sure that Mr. Wentworth will welcome something a little stronger, for starters. I know I will, after the journey in to town! Makes me appreciate the country, that's one good thing. I wouldn't appreciate it half as much if I didn't get an occasional taste of what it's like in London these days! The mobs and the dirt and the smoke grow worse every year. Mr. Wentworth, after we've refreshed ourselves, I have some horses I'd like your opinion on, especially a mare, a recent acquisition. Your daughter's been riding her. What a horsewoman she is! I'd like to know whether you think as much of Caprice as she does."

If Sir Robert had impressed them favorably, Lady Madeline only added to that impression. Perhaps Andrea wasn't making as great a mistake as they'd feared, after all. It could be that their long-standing hopes that Andrea would marry Henry Stockton had tinged their apprehensions and made them darker than they needed to be. Telling Henry that they were rushing off to England because Andrea was planning to marry a man she'd met there had been one of the hardest things they'd ever done. Henry's disappointment when Kate had returned from Georgia without Dria had been bad enough. His eyes had looked positively sick when Kate had had to tell him, without, naturally, telling him why Andrea had made the decision, that Andrea had gone on to England with Estelle Richards and that it would be weeks or even months before she'd return to Trail's End. Henry had clung like a burr to his hopes that Andrea would come back to Texas with her romantic notions behind her and be ready to marry him and settle down. And now she wouldn't be coming back at all. Looking at him when Adam had broken the news to him had made Kate want to cry.

"You must have been stunned when you received Andrea's cable," Lady Madeline sympathized as she filled Kate's cup. "But there was no holding the children back. We only hope that you'll like Reggie as much as we like Andrea. Seeing my nephew married to a lovely girl has been my dream for quite some time, and Andrea is everything I could have wished for for him."

"Certainly they'll like Reggie, how could they help but like him?" Estelle demanded. "He's the dearest boy imaginable! Witty, charming, handsome. It's a perfect match, Mrs. Wentworth. I'm so excited about it all that I hardly know which way I'm turning. I never dreamed, when Andrea consented to accompany me to England, that it would prove to be so exciting."

"When do you expect them back?" Kate wanted to know. She kept her voice casual, but she was still a great deal more anxious than she was willing to let anyone know.

"Tomorrow, at the latest. I admit I'll be relieved when they get here. I know Reggie's a capable driver, but I still worry when they're out in that autocar of his." Seeing Kate's startled look, she hastened to elaborate. "Oh, they didn't drive up to Scotland together! It would hardly have been proper. They went by train, but then there's the drive down from London after they get back, and no matter how safe and reliable Reggie tells me that autocars are, I can't quite bring myself to trust them. Your daughter doesn't agree with me at all. Reggie's been teaching her to drive, and she's enthusiastic about it. These young people have more courage than I have!"

Andrea, driving a car! Still, Kate wasn't surprised. No matter how wild the horse, Andrea had always insisted on riding it. No matter how difficult or dangerous a hunting trip, Andrea had always insisted on going along. Thrills, excitement, danger, were the breath of life to her, and Kate could hardly have expected her to change in the few short weeks they'd been apart.

There was no use borrowing trouble, brooding over whether or not Andrea was heading for a crash in this precipitious marriage of hers. Tomorrow she and Adam would meet Reginald Mansfield for themselves, and if they didn't approve of him there would still be time to try to reason with her, to persuade her to wait until she was absolutely certain. If Reggie wasn't everything that his aunt and Estelle said, Kate had no doubt that Adam would be perfectly capable of handling the situation.

It was nearly dinnertime before Andrea and Reggie arrived the next day. Kate felt as jumpy as a cat that hasn't found a place to have her kittens, too restless to settle in one place, her resources taxed to their limit to appear calm until she should see Andrea and have a chance to judge Reginald for himself.

It was a little easier for Adam; Sir Robert had him out all day, riding around the estate and beyond, introducing him to their neighbors, whatever men do when they're first acquainted and each is interested in everything that pertains to the other. But Kate was confined to the house and garden, because Estelle insisted that she must be available every minute to approve the wedding gown, to approve the guest list, to discuss what they should wear to the wedding.

Looking at the all but completed wedding gown on its dress form in the sewing room, Kate felt a lump in her throat and a prickling behind her eyelids. In two short weeks, Andrea would wear this creation of antique satin and Venetian lace down the aisle at St. Margaret's in London. She'd be as beautiful as an angel, but all of her radiant beauty would be for the stranger waiting for her at the altar. She was losing her, a loss far greater than it would have been if Andrea had married Henry and gone on living in the Chinatis.

By the time a shiny red motor car raced up to the front of the house and stopped with a spurt of flying gravel, Kate was ready to jump out of her skin. Andrea, flushed and shining under the wide-brimmed hat that was tied on her head with a scarf and that had a thick veil to protect her face from the dust, scrambled out to throw herself first in her mother's arms and then in Adam's.

"Mother! Daddy! You got here! You aren't cross because I wasn't here to meet you, are you? Mother, this is Reggie. Dad, Reggie Mansfield."

They studied him, this young man who was determined to take their daughter away from them, to turn her into a British subject. Estelle's enthusiastic descriptions of him had been accurate; he certainly looked personable, and acceptable. Still, Kate had this feeling of uneasiness that she couldn't shake, and knowing Adam as she did, she sensed that he, too, felt a reserve about Reggie Mansfield.

There was something wrong, Kate was sure of it as she saw Andrea and Reggie look at each other, a question in their eyes. Reggie looked nervous, and even Andrea was nervous, something so unlike her that Kate's sense of dread deepened.

"We might as well tell them, Reggie. There's no sense in putting it off. Mother, Daddy, I'm sorry if you were looking forward to seeing us married in a big, beautiful church ceremony. It's a little late for that now. Reggie and I were married in Scotland."

"Reggie!" Lady Madeline's voice was stunned. "Oh, Reggie, how could you! All our plans, the church arranged for, the bishop himself to perform the ceremony, all the invitations accepted! Really, Reggie, this is quite too much, even for you!"

Sir Robert stepped forward to kiss Andrea's cheek. "If it's done, it's done," he said. "And I can't say that I blame them, myself. These big weddings are a strain, especially on the bride and groom. Eloping saves a lot of bother, even if you ladies have to be disappointed at being done out of your big day."

"Adam, how could she have been so foolish!"

Kate stood by the window in their bedroom. Everyone else had retired for the night, but Kate had only gotten as far as taking her hair down so that it hung thick and lustrous almost to her waist.

"As Sir Robert said, what's done is done. She's a grown woman, Kate. We couldn't keep her forever. You told me the same thing when you came home from Georgia without her, remember? She has to make her own life; we can't live it for her. If she's made a mistake, and I confess that I'm not sure that she hasn't, then she's the one who'll have to pay for it. All we can do is be ready to help her if she ever needs it."

"I still can't take it in. Andrea, married! And to do

it like this, to elope, when she knew we were coming, when she knew all the trouble it could cause Sir Robert and Lady Madeline, even if she didn't think of how we'd feel about it!"

"Easy, darling. Nothing could have held us back, either, at their age. She's too much like us, that's the trouble. But our marriage worked out all right, even if we have had our share of dust-ups."

"I'd say that we've had more than our share!"

"And why shouldn't we? I never knew a more stubborn, independent, pig-headed woman, and Dria's you all over again! That's what gives me some hope for this marriage, Kate. Andrea has enough of both of us in her so that we can be sure she'll never stand for being mistreated or made unhappy. She can take care of herself, and God pity the man who doesn't realize it!"

He shook his head, still, like Kate, not quite able to take it in. "Well, one of our brood's flown from the nest. Maybe we should be glad that Dria's married, Kate. It looks like Wade never will get married, as long as he refuses to settle for anyone but Constanza Alverea y Castello when he knows there isn't the chance of an icicle in hell that Don Felipe will ever let her marry him, and Mike spends all his time hanging around the mining camp instead of buckling down to ranch business the way he ought to. We sure hatched ourselves a nest of hornets when we decided to have a family."

"Decided? There was no deciding about it! The miracle is that we only had three!"

"And if we aren't darned lucky, we'll still make it four!" Adam reached for her with a sudden, overwhelming need and longing. "Damn it, you have no right to still be so beautiful, so that I can't look at you without wanting you! To heck with your children! Let them look after themselves. They'll have to in the long run, anyway, and there's nothing we can do about it. I have all I can handle just looking after you."

The real miracle, Kate thought as Adam's hands began to fumble with trembling eagerness at the fastenings of her dress, was that their love still flamed as burningly wild as it had when they'd first been married, that more than twenty years had done nothing to cool its searing fire. As eager as Adam, she helped him with the row of tiny buttons, her pulses beating with fierce pride that Adam still found her the most desirable woman in the world, and that her own ardor burned as bright as his so that she could still satisfy him beyond his ever wanting another woman. As long as they had each other, nothing that fate could throw at them could defeat them. A love like theirs could happen only once in a lifetime. Her only prayer was that her children, all three of them, would be as lucky as she and Adam.

Then she forgot her children, she forgot everything except Adam's arms around her, his hands caressing her quivering flesh, the explosive forces that drew them together and burned them with a fire that should have consumed them, reduced their bodies to ashes, only to renew them instead. In all the world, at this moment, there was nothing but the two of them and their love for each other, and that was the way it should be. If there were going to be more problems in their lives, they would have to wait. This moment was theirs, out of all eternity, and nobody else could share it.

In the room at the end of the east wing, the room that Andrea was sharing for the first time with Reggie, Reggie's kiss was tentative as he drew her into his arms.

"They took it rather well, don't you think? I'm afraid that I expected a scene, that your mother, at least, would cry or have hysterics, or your father might decide to horsewhip me."

Kate, cry or have hysterics? The thought was amusing enough to Andrea to make her smile as she settled herself more closely against Reggie's body in the bed. The fact that Reggie was so diffident about having persuaded her to marry him in Scotland instead of coming back and going through with the huge, formal wedding touched her and made her feel guilty. Reggie thought that it had all been his own idea, when as a matter of hard, cold fact, she had manipulated him as easily as if he'd been an adolescent boy in the hands of a beautiful, older and experienced woman set on seducing him.

It had been reprehensible of her, and she knew it. She'd manipulated Caroline and Mortimer, as well; they'd neither of them had the faintest idea that all of her enthusings about the countless romantic elopements to Gretna Green had been anything more than that, just dreamy, romantic talk. She'd directed their every thought and action just as a puppeteer directs his puppets, pulling one string here and another string there until they'd thought, Reggie and Caroline and Mort alike, that the idea of a romantic elopement of their own had originated in their own minds.

And she'd accomplished her purpose. She and Reggie were married, they were man and wife. Tonight wasn't even their wedding night, the night before last had been. She was a married woman of three days' standing, and she felt exultation flood through her as she realized how easy it had been for her to achieve her ends. Two nights in that rustic, almost primitive inn in Scotland, truly the stuff that romantic dreams are made of, but achieved with such a different purpose in her mind that even now she couldn't quite push her guilt into the background.

She'd done it, she'd given up the elaborate church wedding that she'd wanted almost more than she'd ever wanted anything in her life, for one purpose only. She'd been afraid, as the time neared for her parents to arrive, that Adam and Kate would find some way to stop her. She knew her own strength, but she also knew theirs, and faced with a confrontation she hadn't been absolutely positive that she would emerge the victor. And she had to marry Reggie, she had to go on living this new life that she found so wonderfully exciting, so satisfying, so fulfilling of everything she had ever dreamed of. It was what she wanted, what she had to have; she needed it as a drug addict needs his drugs. She couldn't be Andrea Wentworth any more, an innocent and conventional girl from Texas. She must be Mrs. Reginald Mansfield, the madcap heiress, rushing from one adventure to another, always busy, forever too busy to look back.

"You aren't sorry that I talked you into it?" Reggie's worried voice made her feel more guilty than ever. To quench the feeling, she wrapped her arms around him and kissed him, a kiss calculated to send all feelings of guilt into limbo. She felt Reggie's rising excitement and matched it with her own. She was a married woman, she was Mrs. Reginald Mansfield, she was going to live exactly the way she wanted to live and never feel a moment's regret, never again feel a moment's heartbreak or humiliation or doubt.

"Darling, I still can't believe it!" Reggie said, his voice hushed with awe and an underlying trepidation. "It isn't as if I have anything to give you. You're used to so much more, I'm afraid you'll tire of your bargain."

"Well, you'd better believe it! Because if you don't, then we're living in sin!" Andrea told him. She felt a moment of contrition. She'd had no idea that it worried Reggie that he wasn't wealthy. She held him more closely, trying to convey to him the depth of her affection for him, of her love. "You silly ass! There, see how much I love you, I'm already picking up British expressions! As if it mattered about money! You mustn't give it another thought. I love you, and we're going to be wildly happy, I know we are."

Reggie's response was more than gratifying. Andrea felt her blood begin to race as his kisses intensified, as his hands, gentle and almost worshipful but wildly exciting, explored her body. Reggie was a wonderful lover; he could bring her to heights that she had never dreamed of. She'd felt something of this when she and Henry had made love to each other in the privacy of the peach orchard at Trail's End, but she'd never been brought to completion, she'd had no idea of the wonder and the glory of it.

If this was any sample, then her life with Reggie was going to be happy beyond her wildest dreams. "Darling, darling!" she whispered, and her voice ended in a gasp as she learned that the delight gathered and burgeoned and grew. There seemed to be no end to it, until an explosion of ecstasy that went on and on plunged her into abject awe that such a thing could be.

Lying in Reggie's arms afterwards, almost purring

with contentment, Andrea reflected that Kate and Adam really had taken their elopement very well. After all, what else could they have done? If they were disappointed now, they'd be as happy for her as she was happy for herself when they saw how well it was going to work out.

They were off again early the next morning, in spite of Lady Madeline's protests and Estelle's bewildered shock and Kate and Adam's patent disappointment, to hunt for a place to live in London. They took with them a check from Adam, a wedding present that had made Reggie have to hold back his whistle of surprised pleasure. Fifty thousand dollars! Even translated into pounds, it was an amount that made his prospects look very bright indeed. His salary at the bank, once he actually started working there, would be a mere pittance, but fifty thousand dollars would enable him to live the way he wanted to live but had never been able to afford to until now. And there was the certainty that when the fifty thousand was gone, more would be forthcoming. He'd seen the way Adam looked at Andrea; the man doted on her, and he was wealthy beyond imagination.

Faced with an accomplished fact, their presence here no longer required, Kate and Adam made rapid changes in their own plans. They'd see everything that England had to offer and then go on to Paris, to Rome, to Greece. They'd return to England for only a few days, no more, to see that Andrea and Reggie were well settled, before they went on home.

Adam's brows raised with diabolical quizzicalness as he grinned at Kate when he laid their itinerary before her.

"After all, Kate, if you're going to be raped, you might as well relax and enjoy it!"

Kate knew what he meant. As long as all their plans had been laid to ruin by that strong-willed daughter of theirs, they might as well make the most of this opportunity and have their own honeymoon and savor every moment of it. In perfect accord with Adam's decision, Kate put her doubts and worries firmly behind her and turned her face to this new adventure, her long-delayed honeymoon with the only man in the world who mattered.

14

Andrea waited for her mother and father to finish going
through customs, her elation at their visit dulled by her
anger with Reggie. Reggie had promised her that he'd be
on hand to meet the ship. He'd even arranged with the
bank where he was a junior clerk to have the morning off
in order to go with her.

And then, less than an hour before they had to meet
the ship, he'd gone rushing off to see a Mr. McDouggal,
or a Mr. McGreggor, or whoever he was, just because
Owen had telephoned to tell him that the Scotsman was in
town for this afternoon only, and they were going to get
together to talk about engines. He hadn't even told her
that he was sorry; on the contrary, he'd taken it for
granted that she'd be as happy at this golden opportunity
as he was!

In the three years since their marriage Andrea had
had too many occasions to wonder why she'd rushed into
marrying Reggie without giving it more thought.

They'd been happy at first, wildly, almost insanely happy. For more than a year, it seemed as if the world was their oyster. Their flat in Mayfair was beautiful, exquisitely furnished, filled with expensive decorator items and with even more expensive guests as they entertained everyone they thought worth knowing.

Andrea's initial success in London, before she'd married Reggie, paled into nothing by comparison to the swath she cut after her marriage. There'd always been something novel, something exciting or even outrageous to do. Her name had appeared in the tabloids with gratifying regularity.

"Beautiful young American heiress shocks London by bicycling to the Ritz clad in men's trousers and demanding entrance to the dining room." "The vivacious and charming Mrs. Reginald Mansfield, née Andrea Wentworth, gave dinner for British notables and burned their throats with fiery Mexican dishes, after which she regaled them with an American country hoedown." "Mrs. Reginald Mansfield startled London by joining a troupe of Morris dancers at Drury Lane for the evening. The beautiful American heiress borrowed a colorful costume from one of the female entertainers and gave forth with song and dance, appearing to enjoy herself thoroughly as members of London's aristocracy watched with scandalized eyes while her husband and friends stood by and applauded, demanding encore after encore."

It had been a mad, breathless race to keep ahead of her memories, to do anything that came into her head or the heads of their friends, to convince herself that she was happy, that her life was full and exciting and satisfying and that there was nothing left to be desired.

Of the original group of their Bohemian friends, only Caroline and Mortimer Byron remained. Bruce Yarnell had married his senior partner's niece and become ultra-respectable; Owen Fitzgerald and Eleanor Talbot had begun living with each other openly, only to change partners and introduce them into the group and eventually drift away entirely while others equally unorthodox took their places.

Reggie was still thick with Owen and insisted on including him and his newest paramour in their social activities. The fact that Andrea found Claudette Drummand cheap and coarse had no bearing on the case as far as Reggie was concerned. Owen was his friend, therefore Andrea must accept Claudette, who claimed to be French and a descendant of a noble emigré family but whom Andrea suspected of being pure Cockney clawing her way up by using her only asset, her coarse and flamboyant beauty.

Strangely enough, throughout all that first madcap year of their marriage and the two years that had followed, Ned Cavindish had visited them regularly. Although he nearly always declined invitations to their parties, he dropped by at least once or twice every month to spend an evening with them when they were at home without other guests. Andrea had developed a tremendous liking for Reggie's quieter, more conservative cousin, and she knew that he liked her in return although he certainly disapproved of many of her actions.

Reggie's tolerance for his cousin was considerably less than Andrea's, especially when Ned warned him that he must slow down, that he was throwing money away as if the supply were inexhaustible.

"You're going to have to face it sooner or later, Reggie. You aren't a millionaire. The first thing you know, you'll be running into debt, and before you know it you'll be swamped. Most of those friends of yours are only using you. Not Caroline and Mort—they're fine people, none finer—but the others are worthless, nothing more than hangers-on. It's time you started cutting down on all this spending, before you find yourself in serious trouble."

"I can take care of myself, Ned, I don't need you to play nanny to me. The thing is, you're jealous because Andrea and I are so happy. You never did know how to enjoy yourself, even when we were boys. Why don't you marry Penelope and stick to your own stodgy circle of country bumpkins? Dria and I have our lives well under control, thank you."

209

But they hadn't. It was appalling how fast they'd gone through their wedding present money. Andrea realized how right Ned had been when the last of it was gone and they had to give up their flat and move into a much smaller one, even to sell some of their choicest pieces of furniture to satisfy creditors.

Reggie's reaction to these economies had both surprised and dismayed her. He'd actually expected her to ask her father for more money, and he'd sulked for a month when she'd flatly refused. But he'd come up against a blank wall. Andrea wouldn't budge from her stand; they weren't charity cases, and she wasn't going to beg. They'd live on what Reggie made, and they'd be happy. Caroline and Mort were happy, without scads of money in the bank to throw away on whatever took their fancy. In fact, Caroline, like Ned, had warned Andrea more than once that it was time to slow down, that she and Reggie were being almost criminally foolish.

It wasn't that Reggie wasn't still charming, amusing, and more fun to be with than almost anybody else Andrea could name. It wasn't even that they didn't still love each other. Reggie was still exciting, he still brought her to the heights of ecstasy when he made love to her, she still melted at his touch when he chose to bring her to the melting point. But the fact was, Reggie had never grown up. He might be twenty-six, but he acted more like a four-year-old with his first kite than like a grown man. Let it be pouring rain, let the wind be blowing a gale, let the house burn down behind him, he still had to get that kite in the air and fly it higher than anyone else had ever flown a kite. It wasn't that he lacked native intelligence, he simply let every current enthusiasm run away with him. The plain fact of the matter was that he was selfish to the core, that he had to have whatever it was he wanted the instant he wanted it. Any future consequences were of no importance, so long as he had the momentary satisfaction of doing or having whatever he wanted.

Adam and Kate were through customs now, and Kate embraced her, her eyes shining with excitement at seeing her daughter again.

"Andrea, you look wonderful! Life here in England

certainly must agree with you! Isn't she beautiful, Adam? I ought to be jealous, having such a gorgeous daughter, but I'm not!"

Adam's eyes, usually almost startlingly blue, looked dark as he regarded this daughter of his of whom he'd heard too much since her precipitate marriage to a young Englishman whom he'd never met. Kate was right about her beauty; if anything, she was even lovelier than she'd been at eighteen. Maturity became her. Her bust was fuller, her waistline even smaller, and her face had taken on character to enhance its once girlish prettiness, so now her beauty was so startling that even in this jostling crowd people turned to gape at her.

But he sensed something wrong. Dria wasn't as happy as she was letting on she was; something was worrying her. And even more to the point, here she was, going on twenty-two; she'd been married for three years, and there was still no sign of a child. Adam was convinced that Andrea wasn't barren. How could she be, with all of his and Kate's vitality, with all of the lusty vitality of all of her forebears running in her veins? Was it Reggie, then? Was her husband incapable of fathering a child?

That would be a hell of a note, Adam thought as he kissed her and then offered her one arm and Kate the other. Here he was, crowding fifty, or so close to crowding it that it didn't matter, and he had only one grandchild to his name! Wade's Constanza had presented them with a boy only three months ago, a fine, strapping boy, as lusty as Adam himself and, he thought pridefully, the image of him! Let Kate laugh at him, pointing out that as he was fair and Wade was fair and the Alvarez family was from that stock in Spain that ran to blue-eyed blonds; young Philip could scarcely help but be fair. As to the rest of small Philip's features, Kate teased him, the resemblance was all in his imagination. Philip was himself, and never mind boasting that he was a chip off his paternal grandfather's block!

"Tell me all about it!" Andrea begged as soon as they were settled in the cab. "However did Wade persuade Don Felipe to let Constanza marry him? I was convinced that Wade would go to his grave a bachelor, and Costanza a spinster, probably cloistered in some nunnery! And then you wrote that they were to be married, and now Wade's a father and I'm an aunt, and I still can't believe it."

"Darling, I wrote you all about it, just as it happened, every detail."

"I know, but letter-writing always leaves something out! Did Constanza actually go on a hunger strike?"

"She certainly did! Don Felipe was beside himself. She refused everything but water for ten days, Dria, and then she even refused water! Don Felipe was convinced that she'd die if he didn't give in, and you know how he dotes on her. So he finally promised that he'd give his consent, but still Constanza wouldn't eat or drink until he'd said it in front of witnesses! What a blow to his pride that must have been, his own daughter doubting his Spanish honor! She made him call their priest and swear to it, and then she took a little broth, and two months later, a scandalously short time, Constanza and Wade were married. She said they'd waited for years already and she wasn't going to wait any longer!"

Kate's silvery laugh brought a stab of homesickness to Andrea's heart. How she had missed it, all these years in England! How she missed everything she'd left behind her! But she fought it down; sadness had no place in this gala moment, with her mother and father here for the second time.

She felt a moment of trepidation as the cab pulled up in front of their new address. Her mother and father knew that they'd moved, of course. But they hadn't known, because she hadn't told them, that their new address wasn't nearly as smart as their old one, that their new flat was much smaller and the furnishings were from moderately-priced department stores rather than from exclusive galleries.

She fought that down, too. As if Kate and Adam would care about that! They weren't snobs, they didn't know the meaning of the word. They'd understand that Reggie wasn't wealthy, that he was a working man.

"It's cozy," Kate said, looking around. "I think I like it better than your other place, Dria. All that Chipendale and Hepplewhite made me uneasy, I was afraid I'd break something every time I moved." She was being too cheerful, and she cautioned herself to be more careful or Dria would guess that she was dismayed that their circumstances had been so reduced.

"We had to make the change. We were living way beyond our means." Andrea met her mother's and father's eyes without flinching.

"Well, it was a step in the right direction." Adam was blunt. "It showed common sense, Dria. I never thought that I raised any of my children to be fools, and going into debt in order to keep up appearances is as foolish as anyone can get!"

Andrea herded them both toward the compact kitchen, hardly big enough to turn around in. "Mother, I know you're dying for a cup of coffee, and Dad will want a drink. Don't worry about the coffee, I've learned to make it myself, Texas style! Dad, the makings are in that cabinet. And you can chip some ice from the icebox. I've never been able to convert Reggie or any other Englishman to having ice in their drinks, but they haven't been able to convert me not to, either!"

"I'll take it British style." Adam grinned, reaching for the bottle of Scotch. "No ice, just a dollop of water. Can't get into bad habits and shock people. When in Rome and all that."

"What your father means is that we had to do without ice for so many years that we got into the habit of not having it!" Kate laughed.

"Mother, what about the wedding? Was it as magnificent as you told me in your letters?"

"Even more magnificent! Once Don Felipe had committed himself, he went all out to let everybody know that Constanza was marrying with his full approval! He invited half the people in the Chinatis, as well as everyone of importance that he knows in Mexico. It must have been the most lavish wedding even Mexico had ever seen! Even President Díaz was there. If Don Felipe's heart was broken because his only daughter married a gringo, no one knew it. We were treated like visiting royalty. We stayed at Don Felipe's hacienda for a week. It's a fabulously beautiful place, but then he's one of the wealthiest aristocrats in

213

Mexico. His ranch is even larger than Trail's End. I never saw so many servants in my life!"

"I hope Mike behaved himself," Andrea said as she filled the coffee pot with water and measured in the ground coffee. "I'd have been afraid that he'd insult President Díaz, and start a war between the United States and Mexico! You know how he feels about Díaz, about all the fabulously wealthy Mexican aristocrats who grind the peons under their heels."

"It wasn't easy for him, but he kept himself under control for Wade's sake. That younger brother of yours is a firebrand, Dria. He thinks that the peons should revolt. He and Wade are at each other's throats about it. Not that Wade doesn't sympathize with the peons, but he maintains that not all of the aristocrats, the large ranchers, mistreat their workers. Certainly Don Felipe doesn't; even Mike could see that, and it helped him keep his opinions to himself and not disrupt the happy occasion. Besides, he knew that not only Wade but his father would call him to account if he did anything to mar the festivities."

"Is there any sign that he'll ever get married and settle down?"

"It's too soon to tell." Kate's voice was careful as she cut slices of bread and spread them with butter and jam. The British had a hand with jam, she had to admit. "There's a new girl, Lupe Mendoza. He only brought her home once. She's the daughter of one of the workers at the cinnabar mine. You know how Mike hangs around that settlement every chance he gets. The Mendozas haven't been on our side of the border very long. They came looking for work, like all the others."

"Is she pretty? Is Mike serious about her?"

"She's very pretty. She's tiny, with a mass of black hair and big brown eyes that could melt an ogre's heart. She's just learning English. I think she was embarrassed when Mike brought her to meet us, and she won't come again because she thinks we're rich *patróns* who are too good for her. I'm going to make a point of getting to know her better when we get home. Of course, she's very young, she's only sixteen. Mike will have to wait a while even if he is serious about her. For one thing, she'll be reluctant to leave her family. There's only her grandfather and a younger brother; her parents both died in Mexico and Manuel decided to bring Lupe and Jesus across the border in hopes that they'll find a better life in the United States."

There wouldn't be any real problem there, Andrea thought as she got cups and saucers out of the cupboards. Her father would find places for Manuel and Jesus at the ranch if Mike and Lupe got married. Her next question was a great deal harder to ask. Feeling a little ashamed for her subterfuge, she tried to disguise it by asking about two people at once.

"And Henry and Wayne? Are they still causing all the young female hearts to flutter?"

"Wayne's married," Kate told her, not in the least deceived. "Only last month, as a matter of fact. He married the Ingram girl, Paula Ingram." She didn't mention the fact that it had been a marriage of necessity. In her own opinion Wayne had been entirely at fault. Paula Ingram had been hopelessly in love with him ever since she'd been in pigtails, and desperate enough as she saw the years slipping by so that she'd have believed any lies he told her in order to have his way with her. "Henry's still playing the field, paying as much attention to any one girl as another."

And not too much of that, she added silently. Henry wasn't interested in any other girl; he was still in love with Andrea and he always would be. He came to see them at least once a month and he never mentioned Andrea, but he never left, either, until either she or Adam brought up her name and said something about her welfare. It was enough to break your heart, although Hank Stockton was the last man in the world you'd dare to feel pity for. He'd matured these last three years; he was every inch a self-contained man. It was a shame that things had worked out so badly for him. Some men were one-woman men, and Kate was afraid that Hank was one of them. It had only been boyish pride that had kept him from chasing off to England to try to stop Andrea's marriage to Reggie, and Kate suspected that he regretted that pride that had kept him from it. Not that it would have done any good, as Andrea had already been married before she and Adam got here!

"So Wayne's been lassoed and branded at last!" Andrea's laugh was slightly forced as she covered up her consternation at learning that Henry still hadn't found someone for himself. "It's a shame that Reggie wasn't able to meet you at the pier, but he'll be home in time for dinner."

"How is he doing at the bank?" Adam wanted to know. His question was too blunt, and Kate sent him a warning look.

Andrea laughed again, and both of her parents detected a hint of brittleness in the sound. "As well as might be expected. Sitting behind a desk doesn't agree with him. There's lots of chance for advancement, of course, but it takes time. These English are so conservative that they think someone has to work for their firm for twenty years before they're trustworthy enough to be considered for one step up the ladder."

"That's one thing about Texas," Adam said. He took a sip of his drink and found that the Scotch was good, probably better than Andrea should have laid in for him. "Out there, when your mother and I first settled, we didn't have to depend on anyone else. We were able to get ahead as fast as our strength and our brains let us. Things have changed considerably since then. These days there aren't many men who could make it without financial backing."

"It must have been wonderful!" Andrea said wistfully. "Dad, did I ever tell you how proud I am of you? Not for making it big, but for doing it all on your own, making Trail's End pay even though you didn't need the money."

"Your father would have died of boredom if he'd started Trail's End as a rich man's toy!" Kate told her scornfully. "He has to work, to do something significant. I expect that all of the really great men in the world have felt the same way, no matter how much money they might have inherited."

Reggie was late for dinner. Andrea, keeping her face

serene, said that they wouldn't wait for him. "If he thinks we're going to let this roast get cold waiting for him he's mistaken! Growing up in Texas spoiled me; I want my food hot! Father, you sit here."

The flat boasted no dining room. A small table was laid in the living room, in front of the now empty fireplace. The windows were open and the curtains crisp and clean, Kate noticed with satisfaction, blew gently in the breeze that found its way between the crowded buildings. She breathed in the fresh air with appreciation.

"I've wondered how you survive, during the winters when the air is so filled with coal smoke. Does it get as bad as I've heard?"

"We develop strong lungs," Andrea told her dryly. "Oh, Mother, you can't imagine how I long for one breath of clean wind sweeping across Texas, when those winter fogs close in and the air is so thick that I feel I'm suffocating! But here I am, still surviving. Dad didn't raise his children to be weaklings."

There was the sound of an automobile stopping in the street, and a moment later feet pounded up the stairs to the flat. Andrea's back stiffened in anticipation. Reggie was home at last, and he'd better apologize to her parents for being late, much less for not meeting them when they arrived!

But it was apparent that apologies were the furthest thing from Reggie's mind as he burst in on them. "Dria, Mother and Father Wentworth, come and see what I have! You'll never believe it! I couldn't turn it down, it was the deal of a lifetime!"

"Reggie, whatever are you raving about?" Andrea demanded.

"Come and I'll show you! There, you can see it from the window, but you've got to come down and see it close at hand!"

Andrea's back stiffened even more as she looked down into the street. There was no sign of Reggie's Renault. Instead, a strange car, not very large, was parked at the curb, with a rapidly growing cluster of youngsters around it, the boys' admiration evident even from this third-floor flat.

"It's a Mercedes!" Reggie told them, his voice running over with pride. "A genuine Mercedes! I got it for a song, Dria, the Renault and only a few guineas extra. It's second hand, of course, but it's in top condition; you should have seen me open it up when I test-drove it! Those Daimlers have speed, they're the fastest things on the roads!"

Andrea had had to listen to enough autocar talk from Reggie and Owen Fitzgerald, his fellow enthusiast, to know that the German makers of the Daimler had changed the name to Mercedes, thinking that they'd gain a wider acceptance in England. They'd chosen the name Mercedes after Mercedes Ellinek, the daughter of one of the company's officials, a wealthy banker and sportsman. But Daimler or Mercedes, she knew that they couldn't afford it, no matter how much of a bargain it was. It was all they could do to keep the Renault in petrol, and how many guineas did Reggie consider a few?

Furthermore, there was something decidedly fishy about this whole thing. Reggie had been complaining about Bella Linda for months, saying that the Renault was too old, that it wasn't fast enough, that its engine was shot. Owen's phone call this morning was just too much of a coincidence. She'd be willing to lay a sizable bet that the whole thing had been rigged, that Reggie had chosen today to bring home a new car because she wouldn't be able to make a scene about it in front of her parents.

"Stumbling onto it was a bit of luck!" Reggie rushed on, so filled with pride of ownership that Andrea's less than warm reception of his news passed right over his head. "If Owen hadn't told me that McDouggal was in town and I hadn't got there to see him, I'd have missed it entirely, because another chap came to talk with him, too, the one who owned the Mercedes, and he decided to get rid of it on the spot to buy another car with McDouggal's improved engine. He was good enough to take the Renault as part payment."

His story was so pat, so obviously rehearsed, that Andrea's suspicions turned into certainty, and her mouth thinned.

218

"It's very pretty," Kate said, somewhat inadequately.

"Pretty! Do you know what it can do? I hit sixty on my test run; that's why I'm late, I couldn't very well buy it without testing it out, could I? Sixty, and it's four years old! Why, the royal family goes in for Daimlers! Edward bought one for himself way back in nineteen hundred! I'm sorry it's only a two-seater. Mr. Wentworth, will you do me the honor of being my first passenger? Usually it's ladies first, but you'll know more what I'm talking about when I explain all the fine points. I'll take Mother Wentworth next, and Dria will have to be on the tail end. After this ride, you'll want to buy a new Mercedes for yourself and have it shipped back to the States. I'm going to give you the spin of your life!"

"Well!" Kate said helplessly when Reggie had literally propelled Adam out of the flat. "Is Reggie always so filled with enthusiasm?"

"Always," Andrea said flatly. "It's part of his boyish charm."

Kate looked at her closely. There was a definite trace of irony in Dria's voice, laced with a stronger trace of bitterness. It was as she had expected, things weren't going as well with Andrea and Reggie as she could have hoped.

"But he's a satisfactory husband in other ways?"

"Oh, he's a wonderful lover! I have no complaints on that score!"

"Andrea!" This time, in spite of her down-to-earth nature, Kate was shocked.

"I'm sorry, Mother. That just came out of its own accord. Yes, Reggie and I get along fairly well, as well as most couples, I suppose. It's just that he can't seem to grow up! We can't afford that car. We couldn't even afford the one he had, Bella Linda! I named it, did I ever tell you? It was the first time we met, and it was a kind of a joke. He wanted to know what it meant, and I told him 'beautiful beautiful.' Mother, it seems like twenty years ago, instead of only three! Has time gone crazy, or have I?"

"It's like that with everyone, at times," Kate reassured her. "As long as you and Reggie don't quarrel, I expect it's as you say, you're getting along as well as most young couples."

Andrea's mouth curved, half in amusement, half in despair. "Reggie won't quarrel, that's the hell of it," she said. This time Kate managed to hide her shock. "He simply refuses. He can't even see that there's anything to quarrel about! He looks at me as if he were a puppy I'd just kicked and he doesn't understand why! And then he goes on and does just as he pleases, and if I'm not as enthusiastic about it as he is, he sulks."

"Oh," Kate said, and once again she felt entirely inadequate. What do you do, when your daughter's marriage is in trouble? How can you help her?

She knew the answer to that. She couldn't help Andrea. Whatever the difficulties between her daughter and that charming young scamp she'd married, Andrea would have to work them out for herself. She felt the full futility of it, and she hated it, but that was the way it was.

"Well, we might as well finish our dinner," she said, sitting down at the table again. "There's no use in letting the delicious roast go to waste, just because men are more interested in engines than in good home cooking!"

Andrea pushed her own slice of roast around on her plate petulantly. "I don't want roast beef. I'm sick and tired of roast beef! What I want is a great big pot of chili, hot enough to burn my throat out."

"Then we'll make one tomorrow," Kate soothed her. "We'll simmer it all day, the way we do at home, and if it doesn't take all the skin off Reggie's throat, I'll eat his share without water!" Privately, she wished she could make it hot enough to burn that irresponsible streak right out of Reggie, but she doubted that there were enough hot chili peppers in all of England to do that.

It was almost dark, even now in the summer when England stayed light until late in the evening, by the time Reggie and Adam returned. Even then they didn't go directly back up to the flat. Adam's face was grim as money exchanged hands, enough money to pay off the remainder of what Reggie owed on the car.

My son-in-law is a damned young fool, Adam thought

220

disgustedly, but I can't have Andrea worried about his going into debt, for all that. Personally, he'd have been happy if Reggie had piled up this Daimler, or Mercedes, or whatever it was, and reduced it to a heap of rubble before he'd ever got home with it the first time, providing that he hadn't killed himself in the process. If he didn't get himself killed in it, or kill Dria, it would be a miracle.

The idea of any man being foolish enough to go into debt for something that went sixty miles an hour and threatened your life every time you got into it was beyond him. It looked as if Andrea hadn't got herself any bargain in her husband. Not that he'd thought she had, three years ago when he'd first met the boy! He'd had doubts then, in spite of Reggie's charm and his obvious love for Dria. And like Kate, he felt a sense of futility, because there was nothing he could do about it.

As for Reggie himself, he was not in the least perturbed when both his mother-in-law and his wife refused to go out that evening for a test ride in his latest acquisition. He played the charming host, a role he loved, to the hilt, replenishing drinks, asking intelligent questions about ranching in Texas and about the state of American financial affairs. He complimented Kate extravagantly about her beauty, declaring that when he took her and Andrea out to lunch everybody would think that she was Andrea's sister and rib him because there was no way he could have married both of them without being put behind bars for bigamy.

"But how could you help but be beautiful, when Dria's your daughter? It's no wonder she's turned London on its ear! I can't thank you enough for Dria. When I think that she might never have come to England and I might never have met her, it makes my blood turn to solid ice! I really should write to Dria's Aunt Prudence, and thank her for having Estelle Richards for a friend, so that Dria came over with her and made me the luckiest man in the world."

After they'd gone to bed, Andrea turned to Reggie and hissed, "Weren't you laying it on a little thick? Sometimes you let that charm of yours run away with itself!"

Reggie was hurt. "Every word I said was true, so I

221

wasn't laying it on, as you so crudely put it, at all."

"Never mind that. Reggie, how could you have bought that new car? You know perfectly well that we can't afford it! It'll be repossessed, and you'll be lucky if you aren't arrested for nonpayment."

"But that's no problem at all! You're worrying about nothing, Dria. My new baby is already paid for. Your father was so impressed with it that he made up the difference!"

"Reggie, you didn't!" Andrea's shame nearly choked her. She wanted to hit him, and she might have if her parents hadn't been in the other bedroom with only one wall between them, certain to hear the resultant quarrel. The intensity of her feeling dismayed her. She'd been angry with Reggie plenty of times during their three years of marriage, but this was the first time she'd ever actually wanted to strike him.

"I don't see why you're so upset!" Reggie, too, kept his voice low. Quarreling where other people could hear you simply wasn't done. "He'll never miss it, and after all, a third of everything he has will eventually come to you. There's no reason you shouldn't have a smidgeon of it in advance."

Andrea turned her back on him, lying as far on her own side of the bed as she could. Reggie was asleep within two minutes—he never had a problem big enough to keep him awake—but she lay open-eyed for hours, trembling inside with the rage she felt against him. Why wouldn't he grow up and accept his responsibilities! Was she fated to spend all the rest of her life with a perpetually adolescent boy?

In spite of the disastrous first evening, the rest of Kate's and Adam's stay was pleasant. They went shopping and sightseeing, and Lady Madeline, on learning that the Wentworths were again in London, invited them all for a weekend. Andrea's spirits soared just from being on Caprice again. If her father hadn't been on Sir Robert's blue-ribbon hunter, she'd have beat him in the race they had.

Ned was there, and the way he looked at Andrea

222

wasn't lost on Kate. She married the wrong one, she thought sadly. If she was determined to marry an Englishman, she should have taken Edward Cavindish. A blind person could see that Ned loved her, even though he was meticulous about treating her as no more than a cousin-in-law. It was amazing that Andrea herself didn't realize how Ned felt about her, but Kate knew her daughter well enough to realize that Dria was completely oblivious to Ned's feelings toward her.

Neither Adam, nor Kate, had any idea that Andrea cried when she got home after seeing them off. Reggie, as might have been expected, hadn't been able to make it. She cried with humiliation, she cried from homesickness and loneliness, she cried because her life seemed to suddenly have become barren. She cried because the full realization of how much she wanted to see Hank again had broken through the wall of her defenses.

It was Ned who found her in tears, having come to ask if her parents had gotten away all right.

"Come back down to the country with me. Mother'll love to have you and you know that Father is always delighted to have you there to exercise and school Caprice. It'll take your mind off your parents having left."

"Thank you, Ned, but I can't do that. There's no way Reggie could get off from the bank, and my job is to stay with him and cook and clean and be the proper little housewife."

"Hang Reggie!" Ned said explosively. "Why don't you do what you want to, for a change?"

"Because one of us always doing what he wants is enough!" Andrea dredged up a laugh. "Two of us would be a disaster!"

She did let Ned take her out for lunch and a drink. She liked having someone concerned for her, other than her parents. She didn't get too much of that in her day-to-day life with Reggie. Still, it wasn't like her to feel so depressed. She didn't feel well, that was the trouble. She'd felt queasy for the last several days. She must be coming down with something, and when it developed and ran its course she'd be all right again.

15

Andrea's illness was diagnosed as one that would last several more months—eight, to be exact. The Harley Street specialist that Reggie insisted she consult as soon as she suspected the real cause of her queasiness and depression told her that she was already a month pregnant, and that she could expect her baby in May.

She was ecstatic. She wanted to dance in the streets, to shout out her news to all the passersby. The way she felt, you'd think that she was the first woman in the world ever to have a baby. She had to take it out in writing to Kate, and just realizing how happy the news would make her and her father made her cry so that her tears smeared the paper and she had to start all over again. She was going to present them with a grandchild; now she was as good as Wade; she was about to fulfill her duty as a Beddoes, as a Renault, as a Wentworth, and ensure the continuation of the clan.

Reggie took the news with his usual insouciance. He

was delighted that he was going to be a father. Every man wanted a son. His friends would envy him, his Aunt Madeline would be so delighted that she and Sir Robert would undoubtedly come through with a whacking check when the little nipper made his appearance, and certainly Adam Wentworth would send an even larger amount. The worries and responsibilities of parenthood never entered his mind. A child was someone to look up to you, something that made other people think of you as stable and settled; it was altogether an asset.

Andrea fought down her annoyance at Reggie's attitude. It was unfair of her to be annoyed because she was the one who had to suffer the morning sickness and later the growing discomfort of her expanding stomach and the awkwardness of her everyday movements. It never entered Reggie's mind that climbing two flights of stairs every time she left or entered their flat was taxing, as her girth continued to expand. Actually, she knew that the exercise was good for her. She was young and in excellent health, her body had been hardened by ranch life, she could have climbed six flights of stairs and laughed it off the way she laughed at herself now for getting just the least bit out of breath when she went up too fast.

She didn't laugh when she learned that Reggie had run up more debt, getting the Mercedes worked on. How could automobile parts be so expensive? Anyone would think they were made of solid gold!

She'd already cut their daily living expenses to the bone. Caroline had been a wonderful help there; she knew from years of experience how to live on next to nothing. She could make a soupbone last for three meals, serving the soup with French bread the first night, as stew the second night and on the third turning the rest into a casserole, thickened and with a biscuit crust on top. Andrea hadn't bought herself any new clothing since she'd learned of her pregnancy, except for a couple of those shapeless wrappers that were supposed to be maternity dresses and hide your condition from the world. Using the originals as patterns, she and Caroline made two more from material bought on sale. Reggie never noticed.

By dint of such penny-pinching economies, she'd managed to save enough to ensure that the specialist would be paid and that her baby would find an ample layette waiting when it was born. She relied heavily on baby-shower gifts there; Kate would be sure to send her heaps of things. Now she was determined to save enough more so that they could move into a larger, sunnier flat. A first-floor flat with a bit of a garden, she dreamed, so that their baby would have plenty of fresh air and a place to play on fine days. She was already looking for one, with Reggie's approval. He himself never got around to helping her look.

And she'd better look harder, Andrea thought, as she waited for the agent to show her more places on that morning in early March. Time was running away from her. So far everything she'd been shown had been either too expensive, or not suitable.

She was in luck today. The third place the agent took her to see was very nearly perfect. First floor, the bit of garden, a sunny bedroom that would be ideal for the nursery. It needed work; the paint was dingy and the living room would have to be repapered, but Caroline and Mort would help her with that. The flat would be cheaper if they did the work themselves. The thought of Mort wielding a large brush, painting interior walls instead of pictures, was amusing, but he'd do it. And Caroline would revel in climbing on a stepladder and hanging wallpaper. Caroline had sold one slender book of verses, but her success hadn't gone to her head, and Mort had done even better. He'd actually sold a painting to a collector who specialized in discovering new talent, and on the strength of that a gallery was going to set up a show for him in the fall.

"We'll take it," she told the agent, who looked relieved. She had been a nuisance to him, but it was so important to find exactly the right place!

"Your husband will have to sign the lease," the agent reminded her. Bother! "But I'll hold it for you until tomorrow. If he could be in my office at, say, ten tomorrow morning, we can take care of the whole thing."

Tomorrow was Saturday; that was a bit of luck. The bank was getting thoroughly out of patience with Reggie's legitimate and illegitimate absences, always chasing off after car parts or for conferences with other automobile enthusiasts. Ned had spoken to him about it, sharply, on several occasions. Even Sir Robert's influence wouldn't keep him working there much longer, if he didn't pay more attention to business.

Andrea was so excited at the prospect of getting the new flat redecorated and moving in well before the baby was born that she prepared an especially good dinner. She felt like splurging. This was a celebration. If there'd been time, she'd have invited Caroline and Mortimer. But they'd have a real celebration when they moved in, just the four of them. Thinking back, Andrea couldn't understand why she hadn't realized, during the first months of her marriage, that out of all the others only Caroline and Mort were friends worth having. She must have been bereft of her senses, until their financial situation had forced them to call a halt to their extravagant ways. The others, except for Owen, had all disappeared as soon as she and Reggie were on their uppers; only Caroline and Mort had been faithful.

She prepared a roast duck, Reggie's favorite, and bought a bottle of really good white wine to go with it. The day had turned out cold and dreary, and snow was falling heavily by the time she lighted the candles on the table in front of the cheerfully glowing coal fire in the grate. Snow, in March! But it had been that kind of winter; there were still patches of snow and ice on the streets. This, at least, would cover up the soot that had spoiled its whiteness, and maybe soon all of it would melt and spring would actually come.

"The flat is perfect, Reggie, it really is!" she said. "I'm going to do the nursery in yellow, to bring the sunshine in. And the garden is really quite large, all it needs is a bit of tending."

"It sounds good. We'll be at that bloke's office and sign for it, darling, if it's what you want." Reggie swallowed the mouthful of duck he'd just taken and smiled with appreciation. "Dria, you're getting better at duck. We should have it more often."

"Not at the price I have to pay!"

As always, Reggie chose to ignore any implication that they couldn't afford the best. "Romantic, isn't it?" he asked. "The candlelight was an inspiration. We'd better make the most of it while we can, before we have a squalling brat to interrupt us every time we get cozy!"

"Our child might cry, but he will not squall! I made a trifle, so don't stuff yourself, leave room for it."

"A trifle? Dria, you're surpassing yourself!"

Andrea preened. She felt like purring. Everything was going marvelously well. Reggie might tease her about squalling brats, but he was as pleased about the child as she was. And the flat really was a find!

"By the way, honey, can you let me have ten guineas? I had to have some repairs made on the car."

"Ten guineas! Reggie, are you mad? You didn't tell me there was anything wrong with the car; it seemed to run perfectly all right the last time I was in it."

"But it needed work, darling. Be a good girl and write me out a check."

Ten guineas! Maybe by some people's standards, it wasn't a great deal, but in their financial position it would make an uncomfortable dent in their budget. Reggie's extravagance was a constant source of worry to her. He didn't have the faintest conception of how to handle money, of how much just so much would buy. Some prankish fate had fashioned him to be a wealthy man, while at the same time it had endowed him with neither a fortune nor the aptitude for earning one.

"Don't pull such a long face! I know you have plenty stashed away in the bank!" Reggie's good humor had vanished; when he was crossed, he had a habit of turning into a sulky boy who'd been denied a treat.

Andrea's mouth compressed. "That money is to pay the specialist and to move us into the new flat. There's barely enough as it is."

"You can always touch your father for some more." Reggie's mouth, too, had gone flat, his eyes dark with anger. "He can afford it. If you don't want to ask him now, the doctor can wait for his fee; he knows our credit is good. Your father will send a whopping check when the baby comes, so why all the indignation over a paltry ten guineas?"

"I'll write the check." Andrea gave in. If Reggie owed it, then it had to be paid, but she wasn't going to ask her father for extra money to indulge her husband's hobby. Seething inside, she gave up the idea of an expensive pram, of repapering the new living room for several months.

"That's my girl!" Reggie was beaming again, now that he'd had his way. "It's well worth it, you'll see when I give you a spin! She runs like a dream now. We can't go around in a rattletrap, now can we?"

"Actually, we could do without a car at all! Other men take the trams to get to work!" Andrea pushed her plate aside. Her lovely celebration was ruined, her appetite gone.

Reggie looked at her with genuine shock. "Do without a car! You don't mean that, you're just out of sorts. Wait till you see how she runs now; you'll be ashamed of the childish way you're acting!"

As always, Reggie laid the blame for the unpleasantness on her. She was the one who was unreasonable, she was the one who insisted on their living like paupers when they could have lived the way they were entitled to live. Wentworth was several times a millionaire. No merchant in London would refuse them all the credit they wanted, and if they had the termerity to dun them, then Adam Wentworth would pay up if only Andrea would shake off that stiff-necked pride of hers. He supposed it was because she was an American; Englishmen knew how to live, they weren't forever toting up ha'pennies in their minds when they'd be rolling in money one of these days.

When he failed to cajole Andrea out of her sulks, he turned to the decanter for comfort. Andrea cleared away the dishes and washed them up herself. One of her economies had been to cut down their charwoman's visits to once a week. By the time she'd tidied the kitchen, Reggie had decided to seek more pleasant company. Andrea wasn't surprised. It was what he usually did if she didn't agree with anything he wanted. The living room was empty when she returned to it; he hadn't thought to tell her that he was going out. That, too, was only usual.

Andrea decided to go to bed. Her back ached, and she was tired. She didn't worry about Reggie. She was used to his lack of consideration by now, and she was asleep before he came home.

In the morning he acted as if nothing had happened. "Hadn't you better get ready, love? We want to sign that lease. Personally, I think the neighborhood is shoddy, not a decent address at all, but as long as you have your heart set on it, I suppose it'll do for a while." His tone implied that he was humoring her because he liked her to have her own way.

"It'll only take me a moment." It was a nasty day. A wet sleet had begun to fall. Andrea bundled herself up in her sable coat, the same one she'd had when she'd made her fateful trip to England, wrapped a warm woolen scarf over her hat, and struggled to put on her fur-lined boots. She didn't dare risk taking cold, it would be bad for the baby.

Wryly, amusement glinting in her eyes, she wondered what the agent would think when he saw her in the sable coat, when they were renting a flat in what was admittedly a rather shoddy neighborhood. She wouldn't explain it to him; let him draw his own conclusions.

The moment they stepped outside, the wind slashed sleet against her face and she felt her body shriveling inside the coat. Reggie had brought the car around from the mews, but her feet slipped on the icy walk as she crossed to get in.

"Careful, love! Can't have you falling," Reggie said cheerfully. Andrea didn't answer him. She had no intention of doing anything as foolish as falling at this stage of the game. She was only glad that they didn't have far to go. Driving in weather like this was dangerous; all of the vehicles on the streets were proceeding at a snail's pace. The draymen and hackmen huddled in greatcoats, their collars pulled up around their faces, and they kept firm hands on the reins as they attempted to keep their teams from slipping and going down.

"Reggie, you should have turned there!"

"There's loads of time. I just want to show you how this baby runs, so you'll know your ten guineas went for a good purpose."

"I don't want to see how it runs! I want to get to the agent's office and then back home!"

"But it'll only take a few minutes, Dria!" Reggie's face was wreathed with smiles as he turned onto a more sparsely traveled street. "Listen to that engine, don't you hear it purring? And just watch this, see how she picks up now!"

"Damn it, Reggie, stop acting like a little boy with a new bicycle! It's no day for such tricks! I'll take your word for it, you don't have to prove anything to me!"

Reggie paid no attention to her protests. Grinning, he bore down on the accelerator, and the Mercedes leaped ahead. Andrea pulled the scarf closer around her neck, shivering. Right at the moment, she'd have liked to see the first man to evolve the idea of motor-driven vehicles strung up by his thumbs. But then, it hadn't been his fault, whoever he'd been, that men like Reggie looked on automobiles as toys, possessions to be shown off and tinkered with to get more speed, more smoothness of performance.

He was driving too fast. The street was coated with ice that formed as the wet, rain-laced sleet struck the ground. Andrea opened her mouth to give vent to a sharp order that he slow down and turn around and get them to their destination, and then her eyes widened with shock and her mouth remained in an open, frozen O as a dray turned the corner right into their path.

Cursing, Reggie braked. The tires, failing to find any traction on the icy surface, sent the Mercedes into a skid. For a few incredible seconds Andrea thought that Reggie was going to bring it under control again, but then they slid sideways and crashed into the dray. Andrea thought that she screamed, but the sound didn't seem to come from her own throat. She felt herself being propelled through the air, felt a sickening jolt as her body landed on the iron-hard cobbles, and then a jagged, incredibly agonizing pain laced through her midsection to turn it to fire.

She lay there stunned, not believing that it had happened, refusing to believe it. Reggie's face was bent over hers; he was asking her something, but she couldn't understand the words. The drayman was cursing, the wheels of the overturned Mercedes were still spinning, and the drayhorse was down, floundering and screaming as it struggled in its tangled traces.

"Damned fool autocarist!" the drayman shouted. "Look what you've done! No sense, no brains, the lot of you ought to be banned from the road! Jet's leg is broken, that's what it is! Gawd, is yer missus hurt?" Another face, the drayman's face, hovered close above hers, red with cold, the expression filled with horror. "She's hurt, you bloody idiot! Gor, why doesn't somebody come?"

Yes, yes, somebody come! Andrea thought. The pain tore at her; she couldn't bear it. She was burning, she was freezing, the sleet froze and then melted as it struck her face. Oh, God, somebody come! Where was her mother, where was her father, she wanted them, she needed them, they wouldn't have let this happen to her.

In and out of consciousness, she never knew how long it was before a horse-drawn ambulance finally came, before she was lifted with excruciating pain and placed on a stretcher and covered with a rough, scratchy blanket. Then there was jolting, merciless jolting as the horses were set in motion. The downed drayhorse was still screaming. Why didn't somebody shoot it and put it out of its misery? The poor creature would have to suffer a great deal longer; this was London and nobody carried guns, even the bobbies didn't carry guns, only their whistles and their nightsticks. The baby was coming and it was too soon, it was only six months along. Mamma, Daddy, make it stop! Henry, can't you shoot that horse? Give me your gun, I'll do it . . .

"Pneumonia," Doctor Hertley told Kate. "Your daughter contracted pneumonia after she lost the infant, and of course her debilitated condition and her severe mental depression complicated matters. I must tell you that we despaired of saving her, but she has a fighting spirit that refused to let go. But I'm still not satisfied with her condition, not satisfied at all. She needs a long rest in a warm, dry climate. Spain, or Italy."

"Or Texas?" Kate asked. She'd come as soon as Edward Cavindish had cabled, before she'd known about the pneumonia. She and Adam had been stricken to learn about the loss of the baby, but they'd never thought of further complications. Andrea was so young, so vital, that she should have had a rapid recovery. Kate had been convinced that by the time she arrived Andrea would be on her feet again, and that her natural resilience would have mitigated the worst of her heartbreak. These things happened; if you were a Wentworth, you picked up from there and went on.

"Texas?" Doctor Hertley showed his astonishment. "But that's across the Atlantic, Mrs. Wentworth, practically at the other side of the world!"

"A sea voyage, under excellent care, should be beneficial. I'll engage a trained nurse if you think it's necessary, and we'll have a private railway car from New York to Texas," Kate told him. "And I assure you that the climate there will be warm and dry. Is she fit to travel?"

"Under the circumstances you describe, I believe that you are right. Much depends on whether or not she wishes to go, of course." Doctor Hertley was cautious. "You may see her now, if you wish. You understand that I thought it best to warn you that you'll find her changed, Mrs. Wentworth."

The nurse, or sister as they were called here in England, led Kate to a small private room in the nursing home. The nursing home was pleasantly furnished and well run, but nothing could mitigate the gloomy effect of the steady drizzle against the rain-spattered windows. No wonder the doctor thought that Dria needed a change of climate, if this was what a London spring was like!

Despite the warning, Kate was shocked at her first sight of Andrea. She was sitting up in bed, propped up against her pillows, but her only immediately recognizable feature was her long dark hair, plaited into pigtails and tied with ribbons. Her face was thin to the point of gauntness, her cheekbones stood out, her eyes were sunken and filled with apathy in a face so pale that for a moment Kate thought that the sister had made a mistake and brought her to the wrong room.

Then Andrea sat up straight and held out her hands, hands so thin and clawlike that Kate had to hide a wince as she took them in her own.

"Mama! I thought you'd never get here! Oh, Mama, I've wanted you so much!" It was such a cry of misery that Kate winced again as she folded her daughter gently in her arms.

"I'm here now, and everything's going to be all right. I'm sorry about your baby, Dria. Your father and I both are, but you'll be able to have more. I've talked with Doctor Hertley and he says that no internal damage was done. Next time, it'll be a different story. Do you want to talk about it, tell me how it happened?"

Two spots of red appeared in Andrea's cheeks, the red of a flaming anger. "It was Reggie's fault! He was showing off, driving too fast, we were on our way to sign the lease on our new flat but instead of taking me directly to the agent, he insisted on showing me how well that damned car ran after he'd spent ten guineas getting it worked on! I told him I didn't want to see how it ran, but he wouldn't pay any attention to me—he never does— and now my baby's dead!"

The bitterness and recrimination in her voice stunned Kate. She'd never heard Andrea talk like this. Granted that it was Reggie's fault, and knowing Reggie she thought that it probably was, still Dria had never shown such active hatred for another human being.

"Mother, I just can't bear it!" Andrea cried. "I've tried and tried, you can't imagine how hard I've tried to make my marriage work out! I've scrimped and I've saved, I've done nearly all of my own housework, I've gone dizzy

234

trying to balance our budget, but Reggie just won't grow up! I have to give in to him time and again when I know I'm right and he's wrong, in order to keep any kind of peace between us. He sulks like a little child when he doesn't have his own way; he thinks that he's entitled to have everything he wants just because he wants it. Lady Madeline spoiled him rotten because she felt sorry for him, and I'm stuck with the result."

Andrea's hands clutched at the sheet, twisting it. Her eyes were pools of tragedy.

"Mother, I wanted my baby, I wanted it so much! My little boy, it was a boy, did they tell you? My own little baby, I planned for him, I loved him! I was going to name him Adam, after Dad. Adam Jonathan. And now he's already buried, and I didn't even see him, he doesn't even have a marker yet. . . ."

Kate moved to put her arms around her and hold her close. "Oh, my dear!" she said, stricken. "Dria, don't! Don't grieve so, it's bad for you, I'm sure that Reggie loves you. . . ."

"That's just it. He does love me! But he killed my baby anyway, just because he wanted to show off. I'll never forgive him, don't ask me to forgive him, because I can't! Everything's spoiled, life is rotten, it's nothing but a dirty trick!"

"Hush, hush." Kate held Andrea's head against her breast and rocked her. "Darling, I know you don't believe me now, but I promise you that time will dull this first unbearable grief."

She struggled to find words that would bring her daughter some modicum of comfort. Her heart ached for her; she'd have given years of her own life to spare Dria this. She'd arrange for a marker, a beautiful one, perhaps an angel, suitable for a tiny child. Maybe that would help, a little.

"Doctor Hertley thinks you need a change of climate," she said carefully. "What would you say to the idea of coming back home with me for a while? We need to get some color in your face again, and there's nothing like a little Texas sun to do that!"

"Mama, if only I could!" The cry was torn from the depth of Andrea's heart. To see Texas again, to breathe the clean air, to feel the hot sun on her face and the wind in her hair as she galloped across country on Runner! She wanted to see the mountains, to breathe in the heady scent of piñon and ponderosa pine, she wanted to see the golden eagles soaring against a sky so blue that it hurt her eyes. She wanted to taste chili, tacos, tamales, she wanted to talk to the house servants and vaqueros in Spanish so rapid that you had to be born to it. She wanted to go home!

"Of course you can! I'll arrange it all with Reggie, and we'll leave just as soon as Doctor Hertley will release you from this nursing home! Your father will be beside himself to see you, Dria. So will Wade and Mike. You'll stay for at least the entire summer." She hesitated, not sure of how to feel her way. "Do you suppose that Reggie will want to come, too?"

"No! I don't want him!" Andrea snatched her hands from Kate's. "Maybe it's wicked of me, but right now I can't even bear to look at him!"

"That's understandable." This was no time to point out that a wife's first duty was to her husband, that the marriage ceremony stressed for better or for worse. "You've had a severe shock, and you're still far from well. I simply won't invite him, how will that be?" It was probably just as well if Reggie didn't go, the way Adam felt about him right now. She'd seen the desire to commit murder in his face when he'd received the cable. An accident, Edward had said, and he'd known immediately that it had been Reggie's fault, that that automobile had been the cause of it.

There was a soft rat-a-tat on the door, and then a head popped around the jamb, followed by the rest of Ned Cavindish's lanky body.

"Mrs. Wentworth! I knew you were coming, of course, but it's still a pleasant surprise to find you already here! You're just what Andrea needs to brighten up such a dismal day. I'm afraid that London isn't putting itself out to make visitors welcome, the way it keeps raining. Our

236

springs aren't always like this; we just happen to have an unusually bad one this year."

His handclasp was warm and firm as he took Kate's hand, and she felt a resurgence of her original liking for this cousin of Reggie's. Once again she thought what a shame it was that Dria hadn't fallen in love with Ned instead of with Reggie.

Now Ned crossed to Andrea's bed and leaned over to kiss her cheek. "How are you today, Dria? You're looking much better. I'm sorry I'm late." So he came every day! Kate wasn't surprised. He was still in love with Dria; it was evident in the way he looked at her with his worry over her carefully concealed behind a smile.

"I'll forgive you this time, as long as it was unavoidable. And you needn't send me any more flowers. Ned, I'm going home! Mother's going to spirit me off with her for a long visit! Isn't that wonderful?"

"It's wonderful indeed. And a jolly good idea, as well. You can use the rest. Just don't like it so much back there that you forget to come back! We'd all miss you." The understatement of the year, Kate thought. It was astounding that Andrea could be so blind where Ned was concerned. "Does Reggie know yet? How is he taking it?"

No matter how he took it, Kate thought, it would make no difference. Andrea was going home with her, and that was that.

Once Kate had made up her mind to something, it didn't take her long to set things in motion. In a matter of days, she'd arranged passage back to the States, she'd bought Andrea a new traveling wardrobe, she'd paid Doctor Hertley's fee in full and settled with the nursing home. She did not offer to pay for having the Mercedes repaired, or ask Reggie if he needed any extra cash.

Andrea's goodbyes to her husband were restrained. She turned her cheek to his kiss, and her face was impassive as he held her close. Reggie registered sadness and bewilderment and gnawing regret that he'd been the cause of Dria's illness, but it made no impression on Kate. She'd seen enough of him to know that Andrea's evaluation of him had been correct.

"Get well as fast as you can, darling!" Reggie begged. "I won't know what to do without you. I'd give anything to be going with you, but you know how it is. Bankers are heartless, always have been."

He stood on the pier and waved when the ship got underway, but after lifting her hand once, Andrea turned away from the rail. For the first time since Kate had arrived, there was animation in her face.

"I'm going home!" she said. "Pinch me, Mother, I'm still not sure that I'm not just dreaming it!"

TRAIL'S END

16

Andrea's body stiffened, and she drew a deep breath to steady herself. This was the moment she'd been dreading, but she knew that it had to be faced.

She sat down at her dressing table and examined herself in the mirror carefully. Her hair was hanging loose over her shoulders, caught back from her forehead with a wide pink ribbon. Her light summer dimity had been taken in, or else it would still have hung on her too-thin body like a grain sack. Her face was still too pale, in spite of the ocean voyage and the Texas sun. She reached for the rouge pot that Kate had supplied her with before they'd boarded the train in New York, telling her laughingly that she didn't want Adam to think he was looking at a ghost when he met them with the buckboard.

She let her hand drop before it touched the rouge pot. Her chin went up. She'd never used paint to prepare herself for Henry's scrutiny in all the years she'd known him, and she wasn't going to start now. He'd ridden in fifteen minutes ago. Kate herself had come to her room to tell her that Henry was asking for her. There was no point in delaying any longer.

If only her heart wouldn't pound so! It was ridiculous; it was only Henry she'd known for most of her life. They were old friends, nothing more. If Henry had had some notion that he was in love with her, that had been years ago when he'd been scarcely more than a boy. He certainly wouldn't feel the same way now, so there was no need to be making such a big thing of this.

She stood up and held her shoulders straight, and her step was firm as she entered the living room where her father and Henry were talking.

"Hello, Henry."

But this couldn't be Henry, it must be his older brother, except that that was silly—Henry didn't have an older brother, he had a younger brother and two sisters. Had he always been this tall, or had she just forgotten? His face, too, had changed; it was older, completely mature, the planes more sharply defined and harder. His eyes met hers and held them, with a force that made her breath catch in her throat.

"Hello, Dria. It's been a long time."

"Too long." Adam said. "Henry, this calls for a drink. Whiskey? Not for you, Dria. You'll settle for a small sherry."

"And so will I. It's much too early in the day for anything more potent." Kate rose to pour the drinks, her hands graceful as she handled bottles and glasses. Andrea was suddenly thankful that she wasn't doing the honors; she was sure that her hands would have trembled so hard that she would have spilled the drinks.

"You're looking good, after being so sick," Henry said. His voice was deep, more richly timbered than it had been before Andrea had gone away. She felt a momentary pang, as from an irreparable loss, and then she reminded herself that Henry was as much older now as she was, that they'd both changed, they were scarcely the same people they had been all that long time ago. "From what I've

242

been hearing, I was afraid they'd wheel you in here in one of those invalid chairs."

"Not Andrea," Adam said firmly. "She has too much gumption to let herself be an invalid. She's doing fine, Henry. You should have seen her when she first got here. Nothing but skin and bones. But Manuella's feeding her up, and we'll have our old Dria back before you know it."

"Speaking of feeding, you'll stay for lunch, of course? You'll have to, in any case, so that your horse can rest before the ride back."

"And speaking of horses, Dria, why doesn't Henry show you his new one? If I didn't already own Beau, I'd come near to being jealous. What tickles me is he bought him right out from under Wayne Bradshaw's nose. Wayne had his eye on him, but before he could talk Clay into paying the price Nat Engles wanted, Henry latched onto him. Wayne's fit to be tied."

Andrea gave her father an angry look. He was all but pushing her and Henry out of the house so they'd be alone. Why couldn't he realize that it was far too late to go on clinging to his old hopes?

But Henry's eyes were on her, questioning, and she could think of no excuse to refuse without making too much of it. They walked to the corral together, where young Pablo was still rubbing the animal down.

"He's a beauty, señor. I am glad that you're the one who got him, and not Señor Bradshaw."

"So am I." Henry tossed a coin to Pablo, who caught it in midair, his smile dazzling in his brown face. Henry took the cloth the boy had been using and continued the rubbing down. "I'll finish up. Skedaddle. He's sixteen and a half hands, Dria, and he's tough and fast. Not as good as Beau, of course, but if you were in any condition for a race I'd be willing to lay a bet that he could beat Runner even with my extra weight on him."

Andrea stroked the horse's nose, admiring him in spite of the turmoil inside her. He had four black stockings, and he did look fast. She'd love to try him herself, if only she were stronger. "I'm glad that Wayne didn't get him, too," she said.

"A man has to have some luck at getting what he wants." Henry's voice was rough and his eyes bored into hers. "It doesn't stand to reason that he should lose everything he has his heart set on."

Andrea's hand began to tremble and she dropped it back to her side. "Don't, Henry! I'm sorry I hurt you. I never meant to. I've been hurt, too, if that's any comfort to you."

"It isn't. If there's anything in the world I never wanted, it was for you to be hurt. What I can't get through my head is why the devil you had to go chasing off after rainbows!"

"I was young. Hank, I was so young! I just didn't know any better. I wanted so much out of life!"

"And all I ever wanted was right here. You, and a good ranch, and to raise our kids here in Texas."

Andrea turned away from him so that he couldn't see the tears that blinded her. She was still so weak! If she wasn't still so weak, she'd have been able to control these sudden tears. She blinked, her hands clenching, and then found the control she was fighting for.

"At least you don't hate me for it. I'm glad of that. You don't, do you?"

"It wasn't from lack of trying." Henry draped the cloth over the corral fence and gave his horse a slap on its rump to send it trotting away to the other end of the corral. He put his hands on Andrea's shoulders and turned her to face him. His face was grim, and the pain in his eyes cut right through to her heart. For a moment she thought he was going to take her in his arms and kiss her, and she didn't think she could bear it.

Instead, his fingers tightened so that she winced with pain, although she refused to cry out in protest. No matter how much he hurt her, she deserved it.

"Dria, why? Why in God's name did you go running off like that, all the way to England, and then marry a man you hardly knew? I can understand Georgia, you always wanted to go there and meet your relatives, but England! And the man's no good, Mike's let me know that. You threw your life away, and mine with it, and nothing can ever change it. . . ."

He broke off, and his hands dropped from her shoulders. "We'd better go back in. You look shaky."

She felt shaky. If only things could be the way they used to be, if only some miracle could turn time back, if only she'd never left Trail's End to go chasing after those rainbows!

But there weren't any miracles. She'd followed her own headstrong inclinations, and now it was too late.

"Yes, we'd better," she said. She felt a little as though she were dying, but by the time they reached the house she was able to act as if nothing was the matter, that Henry's being here meant nothing more than a visit from an old friend. That was all it could mean, after all.

She didn't see Henry alone again before he left, after an hour or two of small talk about local affairs, and then a late lunch. When he did leave, all he said was, "I'm glad you're back, Dria. I hope you'll feel better soon."

That was all there was. He'd come, and he was gone again before she'd gotten used to his presence. Andrea excused herself and went to her room because she was afraid that her control would snap.

"There's still something between them," Adam said to Kate. "The air was thick with it."

"Adam, she's married, no matter how much we wish it wasn't so. We can't do anything about it."

"Married, and to what!" Adam's voice was a deep growl. "Married to that young English puppy who isn't worth the air Henry breathes! When I think that Dria and Henry might already have been married, might have had one or two children by now, I could hang myself for ever letting her leave Trail's End!"

"Adam, even you can't run the whole world the way you want it. Andrea wasn't ready to get married, she knew Henry too well, so well from everyday contact that she couldn't see any romance in it. Leave it alone."

"There's such a thing as divorce. If Andrea finds out that she loves Henry, if she's had enough of Reggie Mansfield and England, she could get her freedom."

Divorce. The word hung between them, stark and ugly. Neither of them knew anyone who had been divorced. In nineteen nine, divorce was still a word that was spoken of in whispers, a scandal that shamed the family of anyone involved. At least it was in Texas, and that was the way Kate thought it should be. But still . . .

"Isn't that for Dria and Henry to decide?" she asked. "And Reggie, of course. As little as we like the idea, he still is involved. It isn't any of our business, Adam. Andrea will have to make her own decision, and we have no right to try to influence her one way or the other."

"You're right, as always." Adam reached out to gather her in his arms. "But damn it, Kate, I wish that just this once, you weren't!"

Back in her room, Andrea sank into her soft padded armchair and leaned her head against its back. She was still trembling, and she railed at herself for her weakness. The impact of seeing Henry again had been so much greater than she'd anticipated that she was still shaken, her hands still trembling and her heart beating too fast.

He'd changed so much! She'd left a boy, good-looking, fun to be with, someone she'd been more than fond of, but still a boy, hardly in his manhood. Now he was a man, completely a man, and a man that anyone would have to respect. She could still feel the compelling look in his eyes, still feel the heat that had spread through her body when she'd walked into the room and seen him standing there.

A stranger, someone she didn't know any more, but still familiar, oh, still so familiar! If she hadn't gone to Georgia, if her mother and father hadn't decided that they had to ship her out in order to keep peace in the Chinatis, what might have happened, how different her life might have turned out!

She stood up and took up her hairbrush and began to brush her hair furiously—anything to work off her sudden, frightening feelings. She had left the Chinatis, she had gone to Georgia and then to England, she had let herself be swept into marriage to Reggie, and there was no use in wondering about what might have happened if she hadn't.

Reggie was her husband, and although she'd become disenchanted with him, he was still her husband. She hadn't been able to forgive him for the accident that had cost her her baby, but that didn't mean that she could walk out on him, leave him permanently.

Reggie needed her. He had to have someone to try to keep him on an even keel, someone who'd curb his impulses and try to make him grow up. His charm was still there, that same boyish charm that had swept her off her feet when she'd first met him. He wasn't evil, or even bad; he was merely selfish and thoughtless. And selfishness and thoughtlessness wasn't enough reason to break up a marriage.

She stared at her reflection in the mirror, pressing her lips together in an effort to control their trembling. She knew that when she had to go back to Reggie, she'd go reluctantly. It might be her duty, but she was no longer at all sure that there was anything in their marriage that was worth salvaging. Reggie might still be able to stir her, to satisfy her bodily needs, but there should be more to marriage than that. And there should be more to marriage than being more a big sister, or a mother, than wife, because she was married to a perpetual adolescent.

She wished that Henry hadn't come today, but that in itself was childish. She couldn't stay in the Chinatis without seeing him. It was up to her to control herself, to remember that however much she wished otherwise, she wasn't free.

She dropped the brush and refused to put her face in her hands and give way to the tears that she felt rising in her throat. How long would it be before she could face the fact that her baby was dead, that it had never had a chance to live? It had been a boy; thinking of it was an agony to her, worse than the pain she'd endured when the child had wrenched itself from her body three months too soon, stillborn.

She was still trembling, her knees felt weak, and she had to sit down. She wasn't as strong as she'd thought she was. The pneumonia that had so nearly taken her life had left her so debilitated that it would be a long time before she was back to normal.

Resolutely, refusing to give in to her weakness, she got up and went to her writing desk by the window. She had to write to Reggie; she'd been putting it off ever since she'd arrived at Trail's End. And she wanted to write to Caroline, and to Ned. Three letters! She looked at her hand and wondered if it had the strength to write three letters.

All right. She'd start with one, and that one had to be to Reggie. What could she say to him, how should she begin? Dear Reggie, I'm having a wonderful time and I wish you were here? Her laugh was mirthless as she drew a sheet of creamy, embossed stationary toward her, her initials heavily engraved at the top. A. M. W. It was like an omen, those maiden initials of hers.

Just as resolutely, she covered the initials that stood for Andrea Marie Wentworth with her left hand, and began to write. "Dear Reggie: We had a pleasant voyage, and now that I'm back at Trail's End my strength is returning rapidly. How is the weather in London? It's sunny here, and beautifully warm. I'd almost forgotten how warm it is in Texas in the spring."

A page full of words, all of them trivial, but it was the best she could do. She folded the sheet of paper and inserted it in its matching envelope and addressed it, and then, not able to face writing another letter, she walked down to the corral to visit Roadrunner.

Runner hadn't forgotten her while she'd been away. The day she'd arrived back at Trail's End and insisted on walking down to see him he'd thrust his head over the bars of the corral and nuzzled her, whinnying with pleasure at seeing her again. His compact body was in splendid condition. True to his breed, he could still work all day without tiring, filled with spirit and stamina and just plain guts.

Runner's nose was velvety against her hand as he took the lump of sugar that she offered him, so delicately that she scarcely knew that it was gone. Tomorrow, she determined, her jaw set with all her old arrogant decisiveness, she was going to ride, even if she could only stay in the saddle for a couple of miles. She'd never get her strength back by lying around the house or sitting on the patio being coddled, and until her strength returned, she'd be subject to these fits of depression that were so hard to cope with. She hadn't returned to Trail's End to have everyone wait on her hand and foot, to have them tiptoe around her afraid of disturbing her.

"And you'd better behave yourself, Runner!" she told the Appy. "If you dump me off because I'm too shaky to hold you, I'll never forgive you!"

She looked at the sleek Appaloosa doubtfully. He'd been exercised regularly, of course, but he was still a lot of horse. The sugar gone, he tossed his head and pranced away from her, kicking up his heels, bringing his front feet down joltingly, a trick he had that she remembered all too well and one that had nearly shaken her teeth loose even when she'd been in the best of physical condition. On second thought, maybe she'd better take one of the other horses, something that wouldn't be as hard to handle.

Her chin went up, and her old stubborn look came into her face. No, by gosh! Runner was her horse, and he was the one she was going to ride! She was tired of being an invalid; she had to begin living again or she'd go mad. Stay in the saddle or get thrown, it was all the same. She'd be doing something, making an effort, and that was what counted!

She started as a shadow fell over her as she leaned her forearms on the top rail of the corral fence. "Dad! Why haven't you ever learned to clump around like other men, so that people could hear you coming?"

Adam really was amazing, she thought, as she studied him appreciatively. Looking at him, a stranger would never know that he was in his middle age. He still moved as silently and as lithely as a panther, and his face had none of the tell-tale sagging that so many men developed as they grow older. His eyes were as keen as they'd been in his youth, and there wasn't an ounce of excess weight on his strongly muscled body. No wonder Kate had fallen so desperately in love with him when he'd rescued her from that despicable saloon keeper who had kept her under bondage in payment of a debt that her father had owed, all those years ago, and that she was still as much in love with him today as she had been then.

But the smile that usually lighted up Adam's eyes whenever he looked at her was missing now, and his face was deadly serious.

"You and Hank didn't have much to say to each other," he told her.

Andrea stiffened. "What was there for us to say? I've been away for a long time, and I'm a married woman now, not the girl he used to know."

"You're the same girl. As for being married, something could be done about that if you decide that you don't want to go back to England." In spite of Kate's warning, Adam couldn't hold it back. "Good God, Andrea, it's your life that's on the line! You're still a young woman, hardly more than a girl. You can't go throwing away your whole future on a man you don't love any more, a man who isn't worth your love, just because of convention! Damn convention! Are a few wagging tongues any reason to spend all the rest of your life in misery?"

Andrea was very still. She felt as if her blood had stopped running through her veins. "Do you mean divorce?" she asked him at last.

"It isn't unheard of. You ought to know us well enough to know that if you decide to salvage your life, your mother and I and your brothers will back you to the limit. We never did give a damn what other people thought of us as long as we knew we were doing the right thing, and I pray to God that we never will. Life is for living, Dria, not for burying yourself under a heap of conventions that don't mean a thing except other people haven't the courage we have! Just get it in your mind that you don't have to go back unless you want to! I'm not going to try to influence you, no matter how much I'd like to, but I want you to know that whatever you decide will be all right with us."

Andrea felt the tears that she'd refused to shed back

in her room prickle behind her eyelids. But now, as she had before, she refused to give in to such weakness. Her eyes met Adam's steadily. "Thank you, Dad. That's good to know. And I promise you that I'll think about it."

Think about it! The very thought made her blood start to run through her body like wildfire. To be free, never to have to go back! Was it possible?

Looking at her father, she knew that it was. In her place, he'd have the courage to do whatever was necessary in order to find happiness. His courage, Kate's courage, the courage of all her ancestors permeated every drop of blood in her body. Yes, she would think about it, she would think about it very hard. Knowing that she had a choice and that her family would stand behind her made her feel as if a great weight had been dropped from her shoulders.

The talk at dinner that night was of affairs across the border, where the peons were stirring restlessly under the yoke of centuries of servitude.

There was a hot light of battle in Mike's eyes as he raised his voice to shout down his older brother.

"Certainly they're going to revolt! It's about time, isn't it? All they need is leadership, and the powder keg's going to blow up right in the dons' faces! I'm sorry, Constanza. I'm not trying to upset you, but it's true all the same. Maybe your father isn't as heavy-handed with his workers as most of the others, but there's going to be a revolution, and nothing can stop it."

"And knowing you, you'll be right in the thick of it!" Wade said, his eyes, so like Adam's, dark with foreboding. "It isn't our affair, Mike. I wish to God you'd stay out of it."

"What if George Washington had felt like that, or Thomas Jefferson, or Patrick Henry?" Mike retorted, his face unaccustomedly grim. "They were aristocrats, they were wealthy and privileged land owners, but they didn't skulk on their estates and say that our fight for independence from England was none of their affair! Right's right, and when it comes, you can just bet I'm going to do everything I can to help the cause along!

How many people like our own mine workers are still in Mexico, groaning under the dons' silver spurs? How many of them are just waiting for a leader to dredge up the guts to make a bid for freedom?"

"Freedom?" Adam's brows rose. "For all the freedom they've found on our side of the border, Mike, we'd do better to try to clean up our own mess!"

"Well, you've certainly done all you could, and had half the Big Bend on your neck for the stand you've taken against exploiting these people! And you're still trying, doing all you can. But we're talking about a few hundred or a few thousand, over here, where there are hundreds of thousands in Mexico who'll never have a chance unless they rise up against their masters. Our country abolished slavery a long time ago, and our own Martha Curtis Beddoes was right in the thick of it! What do you think she'd think of us if we turned our backs on other people who need our help?"

"Not much," Adam said briefly. "Nevertheless, Mexico is a different country, Mike, and our government won't look kindly on any Americans who take up arms against the established government there. You'll have to find some other way to help besides carrying a gun and shooting down every don you can draw a bead on."

Andrea shivered. Across the table, she saw that Constanza's face was very pale. Her father, Don Felipe, was one of those dons whom Mike was ranting against, one of the ones who would stand to lose everything they owned, including their lives, if the peons actually revolted.

"I'm sure that all of us, Constanza included, would like to see the peons' condition improved," Kate said firmly. "But this is hardly a pleasant subject for the dinner table, and I'd prefer it if you men would discuss it some other time."

Adam threw back his head and laughed. "You, Kate, to say that we men can discuss it! You'll be right in there, telling us what to think and how to act, if and when it comes."

Kate's laughter echoed his own. "I expect I will. I

never could be content to do my needlework and let men rule the world, could I?"

"What's the point of sweeping the subject under the rug?" Mike demanded hotly. "It's right on our doorstep, and we'd better be ready to face it! As for me——"

"Mike, knock it off!" Wade's voice was sharp. "You heard Mother, and with Andrea only just home and hardly well yet, you might make a little more effort to keep things pleasant around here!"

"Don't mind me." Andrea spoke with false demureness that made all of them, even Mike, laugh again. "I'm just a visitor to your country. The British aren't involved."

"Wash your mouth out with soap!" Mike hooted at her. "You, British! You're pure Texas, sister of mine! But all right, let's talk about something else. You aren't actually going to go back to that whippersnapper you married over there, are you?"

"Mike!" This time Kate's voice held more than a warning; it was a direct command. Mike subsided, and the rest of the meal passed in relative peace.

Andrea went with Constanza to the nursery after they'd finished their coffee and dessert, to look at little Philip as he lay sleeping in his cradle. Looking at the baby, holding him and cuddling him, still brought pangs of grief to her as her arms ached for the child she had never held, but this, too, was something that had to be faced and battled down. She couldn't spend the rest of her life avoiding children just because she had lost her own.

"He's so beautiful!" she told her sister-in-law. "And Wade and Dad are so proud of him! He does look like Dad, don't you think?"

"Sí. I think that he does, very much. But of course my father thinks that he looks exactly like him!"

"I'm glad that you named him for your father, anyway. If Don Felipe had any lingering doubts about your marrying Wade, seeing his grandson must have laid them to rest."

"It wasn't easy for him, Andrea. No Alvarez in history had ever married outside their pure Spanish bloodlines before. I'm so lucky that he loves me enough to have realized that I'd have died if he hadn't given his consent. Only it seems as if there's always controversy. Now Wade and Mike are at each other's throats over the problems in Mexico. If a revolution does come, think how much worse it will be! Wade will feel that it's his duty to help my father, and Michael will fight on the side of the peons, brother against brother."

Andrea put her arm around her. "Let's not borrow trouble! It might never happen at all. And if it does, it won't be the first time that brothers have been on different sides. It happened during our own Revolution, during the War Between the States; it's happened all down through history. But somehow people survived it, and families have gotten back together again. Just go on loving Wade and your baby, and we'll both pray that everything will turn out all right."

For all of us, she added silently. Not only for Wade and Michael and Constanza, but for herself as well. She'd been thinking about what her father had told her, about the possibility of a divorce. It was still too soon to make up her mind. She could only hope, and pray, for the courage and the wisdom to make the right choice when the time came.

17

Henry rode over again two days later. Andrea was on the patio alone when he came riding in. Constanza was in the nursery supervising Philip's mid-morning feeding and Kate was holdng a class at the workers' cottages, where she was teaching the younger children the rudiments of the alphabet, as determined as ever that no child was going to grow up at Trail's End without being able to read English so that they'd be better able to cope with their adult lives on the American side of the border. Adam and Wade were out on the range somewhere and nobody ever knew where Michael was. Up at the mining settlement again, just as likely, or out riding across country to visit friends whom he hoped to stir up about the plight of the Mexican peons.

There was a book lying open on Andrea's lap, but she wasn't reading. Her attention had wandered from the novel that Constanza had loaned her, and she gazed unseeingly out over the sun-drenched vista in front of her as she tried to resolve her own personal problems.

Her hand froze on the book as Henry came loping up the long drive to the house, and she rose to her feet, panicked at this unexpected visit. She didn't want to see him alone—she wasn't ready for it. What could they possibly find to say to each other? Two nights ago, when Henry had stopped by, they'd scarcely said hello and then goodbye before Henry had stalked out as if she were no more than the most casual acquaintance.

But there was no way to escape. She was still standing there, her fingers clutching the book so hard that her knuckles showed white, when Henry swung off his horse and handed the reins to young Carlos, who'd come running so fast that his bare feet stirred the dust, his teeth startlingly white against his brown face as he grinned a delighted welcome. *"Buenos días, Señor Stockton!"*

"Buenos días, Carlos." Henry flipped a quarter into the air and Carlos caught it, his smile widening and his eyes filled with worship. All of the Mexican workers liked Henry, just as they disliked Wayne Bradshaw, whose attitude toward them tried to deny his own heritage of half Spanish blood from his mother. He should have been proud of that heritage, the blood that had endowed him with his extraordinary handsomeness. Goodness knew that his father, Clay, wasn't anything to look at, in spite of his stocky strength and hawklike features. Wayne's dark, curling hair, his lithe build and gracefulness of movement, his inborn aristocratic manner had all come from Pilar Lopez.

"Good morning, Henry." With a great effort, Andrea managed to keep her voice from betraying her agitation. "I'm afraid that your ride has been for nothing. Dad and Wade are down on the south range, and Mike isn't anywhere around. Even Mother isn't here right now."

"I came to see you." Henry's voice was blunt as he stepped onto the patio and stood facing her, his eyes probing into hers so directly that she had to fight down her panic all over again. "Are you going to go back to that husband of yours in England, or are you going to use the sense God gave you and stay home?"

256

"I don't know. I haven't decided. How did you know that I was even thinking about staying?" Andrea was so surprised at the question that her reply was made in a voice as blunt as his.

"Mike rode over yesterday and talked to me. Now just simmer down, Dria. He wasn't talking because he likes to carry tales, he's almighty fond of you and he wants you to be happy, so he clued me in on a lot of things I'd only suspected. He figured I had a right to know."

"Divorce is a serious step, Hank. It's not only an admission of failure, but people aren't very modern around here when it comes to breaking up a marriage."

"Since when would that hold you back if you wanted to be free? If it would, you've sure changed a lot from the girl I used to know! Nobody around here would say a word. They wouldn't want to in the first place, and if they did they wouldn't dare. They'd have your father and your brothers, and me, to reckon with, and they'd know it."

Andrea's breath caught. "If you're telling me that you still love me, that you'd marry me if I got a divorce, have you thought of what it would mean to your parents, to your sisters? You can talk all you want, and I know that my real friends would be loyal to me, but there'd still be a stigma attached." Now that they'd brought everything out into the open, there was no use in holding anything back. "What about our children? A divorced mother!"

"They'd have the guts they were born with, that's what about our children! They'd be proud of you, proud that you had the courage to let go of a bad thing and find something better, the way anybody who isn't a coward would do! You haven't answered my question. Are you going back to England, or are you going to stay here so we can pick up the pieces before it's too late?"

"I don't know! Don't push me, Hank. So much has happened, I'm not capable of making a decision like that yet! I don't want to go back, I'd almost rather die than go back, but how can I be sure that it isn't still just depression because of the way I lost my baby? It was a boy, Hank, and I wanted him! I loved him and I wanted him and he died because Reggie was selfish and thoughtless, and I haven't had time to be sure that a divorce wouldn't be just a childish way of striking back at Reggie in anger, as irresponsible as he is!"

Henry winced at the reminder of why Andrea had come home, but then his expression became gentle. "I'm sorry, Dria. I have no right to push you, except that I love you so much that the thought of losing you all over again drives me *loco*. I only want you to promise me one thing. Don't go back to England because you think you have to because of a lot of ridiculous customs! Your life means more than that, your life as much as mine."

"That's what Dad told me, right after you left the other night. You weren't eavesdropping, by any chance?" Andrea's smile was forced at first, but then her old humor came into it and Henry's answering grin made her heart lighten. "Give me time," she added softly. "I can't be crowded or pushed, you ought to know that by now."

"You'll be here for the rest of the summer. If you can't make up your mind by then, don't bother on my account," Henry told her. "I had this crazy notion that you might still love me, that you realized what a mistake you made when you went traipsing off, but if the whole summer isn't time enough for you to decide, then I'm damned if I'd want you!"

He wasn't going to beg, or tell her that he couldn't live without her, or any such foolish thing as that. He was a man talking to a woman, demanding truth between them, a man any woman would be crazy not to grab if she had the chance or else spend the rest of her life regretting it. Andrea's stomach knotted.

"I'll make up my mind before that, Hank. A long time before that, and that's a promise."

"Good enough. I'll be around, Dria. How about we ride out together as soon as you feel up to it? Have you been on Runner yet, since you came home?"

"Yesterday." Darn it, she was going to have to tell the truth; at least he probably wouldn't go rolling on the ground laughing the way he would have three years ago. "I got too smart for my britches, and he threw me. My . . . never mind . . . still smarts. Let's put it this way. I didn't

258

land on my shoulder, rolling, the way Dad and Wade taught me. I'm just thankful that Runner decided to toss me where I didn't land in a patch of cacti!"

"Catch him all right, so you didn't have to walk home?"

"Yes, thank heavens. Dad would have had a fit if he knew I was thrown. I sneaked off; nobody knew I went out alone. Runner's a safe horse, you know that. He might throw you, but he never runs off and leaves you afoot afterwards. I think he was as surprised as I was when I went sailing out of the saddle. He was only cutting up a little for the fun of it; he didn't know that I'm not as strong as I always used to be so I could stick to him and make him behave."

"Well, you'll just have to learn again. Only don't try to take it too fast. You always did go rushing into things before you were ready."

He was standing very close to her and for an instant she thought he was going to reach out and touch her, perhaps even take her in his arms and kiss her. But he only pulled his hat down over his forehead again and turned to give a shrill, piercing whistle to let Carlos know that he was ready to leave.

"I'll come over in a couple of days and take you out. And don't go challenging me to a race because I won't take you up on it! You've got to get your strength back before it'd be any kind of a contest. But don't go getting the idea that I'll be a gentleman and let you win, once you're up to giving me a real race!"

She stood at the edge of the patio, the honeysuckle vine that shaded the south side of it permeating the air with its sweet, cloying fragrance, and watched him ride out. Her eyes were very bright, only partly from the tears that prickled just behind them.

Easy, she cautioned herself. Take it easy. Like Hank just said, I always did go rushing into things before I was capable of handling them. But not this time. This was important, far too important to go rushing in. She'd met disaster head-on by rushing into things before. She had all the rest of the summer to make sure.

The trouble was, watching Hank ride away, she didn't think that she needed the rest of the summer. If he hadn't left when he had, she might have gone rushing in again. And this time she had to be sure, absolutely and irrevocably sure, because she mustn't hurt Hank again. If she did, then she wasn't worth him and she never would be.

"Wasn't that Henry I just saw riding out?" Kate had returned to the house and entered through the kitchen so that Andrea wasn't aware of her presence until she spoke.

"Yes, it was. He's coming over again soon to take me riding."

"That will be nice. At least, with Henry with you, Runner won't throw you again." Kate's face was perfectly straight and Andrea smothered an exclamation of surprise. How had she known?

"You were trying so hard not to limp, Dria. And there was dirt on your riding skirt, in the back, that you missed when you brushed yourself off."

"That's a relief." Andrea burst into laughter. "For a minute there I felt as if I were eight years old again, and you not only had eyes in the back of your head but a special little bird that was a despicable tattletale!"

Their arms linked, they went into the coolness of the house. Kate refrained from making any other comment about her daughter's prospective ride with Henry. Andrea was a grown woman, not a little girl to be directed or ordered. Kate could only hope that whatever came of this prolonged visit home, Andrea would end up with all the happiness she deserved.

The party was Mike's idea. "Everybody in the Chinatis wants to see Dria, and we haven't had a real shindig for a long time. Why don't we have a barn dance?" Mike's eyes were shining with the enthusiasm he put into everything he did.

"Mike, Dria's being at home isn't a social visit," Kate reminded this youngest child of hers. "She's here to recuperate from a serious illness, not to entertain the entire region!"

But Adam backed Mike's suggestion. "Mike's right, Kate. A party would do Dria a world of good. We'll send out word." Looking at him, Kate knew that he had an ulterior motive, beyond just wanting to entertain his friends and show Andrea a good time. He wanted to remind Dria of the closeness of their community. He wanted, Kate thought wryly, to show Andrea where her roots were, to prove to her that this was where she belonged, rather than in England where such spontaneous gatherings were virtually unheard of.

However doubtful Kate was of Adam's motives, she didn't have the heart to demur when Andrea's face lighted up at the suggestion.

"Oh, let's!" Andrea exclaimed. "A real, old-fashioned country hoe-down! I want to see just everybody!"

And so it was settled, and two weeks from the evening of Mike's suggestion, people began arriving as early as mid-afternoon. In this region of widely scattered population, word was spread from mouth to mouth, one ranch sending it on to their next nearest neighbor until it had spread throughout the Chinati region. That everybody was invited was taken for granted. Large rancher or small landholder, rich man or whoever of their hired workers could be spared from their duties, everyone was welcome.

Andrea felt almost as though she were eighteen again as she caught her hair back at the nape of her neck and secured it with a blue ribbon tied in a bow. Her dress, a matching summer blue, was made of dotted swiss, with ruffles at the neckline and sleeves and hemline, a dress she'd worn when she'd actually been eighteen. Although its style was a little juvenile for a married woman, it was more suitable for this strictly informal affair than anything she had brought with her from London.

And who cared if it was too girlish for her? She felt young; she wanted to step back into the past and forget everything that had happened during the last three years. She'd dance with everyone who asked her, she'd dance with Hank, she'd feel as young as she looked, and if anyone thought that she wasn't behaving as decorously as a young matron should, that would be their problem, not hers!

Hank had ridden over nearly every day, and the hours they'd spent together had told her, over and over, that this was where she belonged, that she'd been a fool ever to leave. Tonight she wasn't going to think about Reggie or the problems that she'd have to face if she returned to London. Tonight she wasn't going to think about anything except having the best time it was possible to have.

The smell of the young steer that had been barbecuing in a deep pit ever since daybreak wafted in through her opened windows, along with the soft, melodious voices of the workers talking to each other in Spanish. The ground floor of the hay barn had been swept, and paper streamers had been hung between the rafters and entwined around every supporting post. Japanese lanterns were strung on the patio and hung on lines between the giant cottonwoods that provided shade for the house. In the kitchen, Manuella had had half a dozen girls busy for two days as they'd baked cakes and pies and dozens of loaves of bread, as she'd planned salads and basted two whole hams and overseen the plucking of dozens of chickens. The honor of Trail's End's hospitality was at stake, and if Manuella had anything to do with it, this affair would be talked about for a year.

There was a tremendous thump on Andrea's bedroom door, and Mike's voice, filled with laughter, rose in a demanding shout. "Are you decent? I've brought someone to meet you."

One last look at her reflection in the mirror assured Andrea that she was ready for inspection. She'd had to take in the waistline of the dress a little, but her illness-related thinness only accented her youthful appearance. "Come in!"

The door was flung back so hard that it banged against the wall, and Mike came in holding a girl by the hand. Andrea didn't need his introduction to know that she was meeting Lupe Mendoza at last.

"Come on, Lupe, she's only my sister, she isn't going to bite you! Here she is, Dria. I had to hogtie her to get her here. She tried to give me an argument, can you imagine that?"

Lupe's face was suffused with an embarrassed blush as Mike literally dragged her into the room. Andrea took one look at her and capitulated. No wonder Mike was so wrapped up in her! She was beautiful. Her skin was tanned by sixteen summers of Mexican and Texan sun, but Andrea could tell that without the tan she'd be almost as fair skinned as she and Kate. Her hair hung loose over her shoulders, a cloud of the darkest brown, and her eyes were limpid pools fringed by lashes that were incredible.

"Buenas noches," Lupe whispered. "We do not intrude?" Her face was so anxious when she looked at Andrea's dress that Andrea's heart melted. Lupe herself was dressed in her best, a full, tiered cotton skirt that came not quite to her ankles, a white cotton Mexican peasant blouse that tied at the neckline with a drawstring and exposed her shoulders and had short puffed sleeves that enhanced the childish roundness of her arms. Her shoes were woven Mexican huaraches, and in them her feet were bare. She didn't own a pair of stockings; she never had. She was frightened half to death to be in such exalted company, and yet she had the inborn graciousness and dignity of her heritage.

"Of course you aren't intruding! Come over here, I have a ribbon that just matches your skirt. Now let me see; shall we draw your hair back like mine or just put it around your forehead and behind your ears, like this? Mike, get out of here, we girls have to finish getting ready. Here, Lupe, use my brush. Our hair always gets tangled from riding, but Mike wouldn't think of anything like that; men are so dense it's a wonder we put up with them at all!"

Mike's grin widened. Dria liked Lupe, or else she wouldn't be dabbing her own perfume behind Lupe's ears, a scent that made Lupe's eyes widen with delight. He didn't have anything else to worry about, as long as Dria liked her. Kate and Adam had already expressed their approval of her, as well as Wade and Constanza, even if Lupe was an illiterate peon girl fresh over the border, whose English was still faltering. Lack of schooling meant nothing as long as intelligence was there, and all the other ingredients that would go to make up another Wentworth woman to be proud of.

"Your hair is beautiful. No, don't pull it back like mine, it's prettier the other way. There, you're perfect, let's go and join the party."

Lupe's hand was warm and trusting in hers as she took it. Now that she'd seen them together, Andrea knew that Mike's love for this girl was no passing crush; it was the real thing, something that would last a lifetime. It wouldn't be long before Adam had all the grandchildren he wanted, even if she didn't decide to stay here and marry Henry and . . . but she wasn't going to think about that now. Tonight she was a young girl again, eager for a party.

The patio was well filled with older people who were glad to sit in the wooden or high-backed wicker chairs and sip cooling drinks after their long rides. They'd come on horseback, in buckboards or buggies or wagons, many of them for long distances. In front of the barn near the barbecue pit, boards had been laid across sawhorses to make long tables, covered with sheets and decorated with bowls of fruit and flowers from Kate's gardens. That was where the younger people had congregated, their voices rising in the clear, purple evening as they laughed and exclaimed and the young men slapped each others' backs and showed off in front of the girls while they waited for the dancing and eating to begin.

Andrea paused to introduce Lupe to several of the older people, and then she fairly whooped with delight as she turned and ran full tilt into a man so tall and broad that she'd have known him in the dark.

"Uncle Jacob! Do you know Lupe Mendoza? Lupe, this mountain is my uncle, Jacob Renault. That means that Aunt Barbara and my cousins are somewhere around. How's Natalie, Uncle Jacob, as ornery as ever?"

"Twice as ornery." Jacob grinned. "I swear I don't know where we got her. You're looking a heap better than when you first got home, Dria. It's a good thing you're a married woman now, else there'd be sure to be another fight before this shindig's over. Lupe, it's good to see you again. Mike's over yonder somewhere, you want I should bellow for him?"

So Mike had taken Lupe to meet Uncle Jacob; just as she'd thought, he was serious about her.

"No thank you, *por favor*," Lupe murmured shyly.

Andrea squeezed her hand. "There's Natalie now. I can't get over how she's shot up."

"All arms and legs and big horse teeth." Jacob nodded. "Likely she'll grow into them, given time. And look at her dress! Barbara will have a fit."

She would indeed, Andrea had to admit, seeing the stains on Nattie's ruffled pink dress and a three-cornered tear in the skirt. Natalie's pointed face gave evidence of the beauty she'd develop into when she outgrew her colt-ishness, but right now she was still pure imp, and she drove Barbara to distraction. She and Jacob had twice as much trouble with Nattie as they did with both their boys put together. In Andrea's case, it was she and Mike who'd given their parents trouble; Wade had always been serious-minded and too busy going about a man's work even when he'd been twelve and thirteen to pull the tricks she and Mike had thought up.

She paused again as she saw Paula Ingram, or rather, Paula Bradshaw now, sitting in the corner of the patio talking with Mrs. Perkins, a woman more then twice her age. If Paula was here, then Wayne was here, too, and even though everyone knew that the party was open to everyone, she'd just as soon that he hadn't come.

That was silly, of course. Wayne was married now, just as she was, and there wouldn't be a fight between him and Hank tonight to spoil the party as her eighteenth birthday party had been spoiled. Drawing Lupe with her, she made her way to Paula, genuinely glad to see her.

As she came nearer she saw that there were shadows under Paula's eyes and that her face had a pinched look.

It didn't come from not feeling well, either, Andrea thought. Paula wasn't happy; no doubt Wayne didn't treat her the way he should. The circumstance of their marriage was known to Andrea by now; Mike lacked his mother's reservations when it came to people he liked and he'd always liked Paula, as a friend. The contempt and disgust in his voice, all aimed at Wayne, had left no doubt as to where he laid the blame.

Andrea only wondered why Wayne had married Paula even though she was pregnant. Knowing Wayne, it was a wonder that he hadn't simply left her to face the consequence alone. He'd even had the gall to try to deny responsibility, when everyone knew that Paula had never looked at any other boy ever since she'd been in short skirts.

But Wayne had come up against an insurmountable obstacle in his attempted denial. Clay Bradshaw had demanded that his son marry Paula. Having an illegitimate grandchild hadn't set well with him, especially if it should turn out to be a boy. Paula came from good stock, and Clay had no intention of relinquishing a flesh and blood grandson he could be proud of.

"Paula, I'm so glad you came! I've been hoping you'd ride over to see me. If it took a party to get you here, I'm twice as glad that we decided to have it!"

"Hello, Dria. I'm awfully glad to see you, too. You look just wonderful. Nobody would ever know you've been sick." There was wistfulness in Paula's voice, and Andrea mentally cursed Wayne.

"Lupe and I are on our way down to the barn. Come along with us."

Paula's face became more pinched than ever. "Not right now, Dria. I'm talking to Mrs. Perkins. I'll be down later."

Mrs. Perkins, her eyes avid in her pudding-like face, looked eager to draw Andrea into their conversation, and Andrea made her excuses quickly and escaped, taking Lupe with her. There were only a few people whom Andrea didn't care for, but the heavy, stupid woman was one of them because of her proclivity for malicious gossip. Come to think of it, she didn't care much for Mrs. Perkins's daughter, either; at eighteen, Belinda still possessed a vapid kind of prettiness, but her mind was as shallow as her mother's, and she was going to become just as fat and malicious as she grew older.

The sound of the fiddles tuning up in the barn drew her like a magnet. As she walked, still holding Lupe's hand, her eyes searched for Hank. She knew he was here, but where?

There he was, talking to Wade and Mike. She changed the direction of their steps to head for them, but before they'd covered half the distance another figure loomed in front of them and she felt Lupe's hand jerk in hers, a tremor running all the way from her hand up her arm and into her body.

Wayne! As big as life and just as handsome and arrogant as he'd ever been! Besides her, Lupe whispered something and withdrew her hand and ran toward Mike. Damn! Had Wayne's roving eyes discovered Lupe, had he been bothering her? She would swear that Lupe was terrified of him, and she knew that Clay Bradshaw had an interest in the mine and that Wayne was sent up to the encampment occasionally to check into how things were going. Any girl as pretty as Lupe would be sure to arouse Wayne's interest. If it were true, she hoped that Mike didn't get wind of it; there'd be trouble, bad trouble, if he ever found out that Wayne was bothering Lupe.

"Dria! If you aren't a picture for sore eyes! Married life must agree with you, you're even prettier than you were before you went running off and got yourself married!" Wayne grabbed both of her hands, holding them too tightly, making red flags of annoyance spring into her cheeks. "We're going to have to make up for lost time. How about starting with the first dance?"

"I'm sorry, Wayne. My first dance is already promised." She kept her voice even and disinterested. "Why don't you ask Paula? After all, she's your wife, even if you seem to have forgotten that she's here."

"Ouch! Your tongue is as sharp as it ever was, isn't it? The second dance, then. Paula doesn't like to dance, she'd rather sit with the older women and talk about how to keep milk from turning." The contempt in his voice when he mentioned Paula made Andrea writhe with anger.

"Not the second dance, either. And you can give me back my hands now, I might have use for them."

Still he didn't release her, and now her temper flared. "I said let go of me!" She tried to jerk her hands free, but he was too strong for her. If he didn't watch it, as soon as she had the use of them back she'd use one to smack that self-satisfied smile off his face!

It wasn't necessary to use such attention-calling tactics. Henry was already besides them, with Mike and Wade directly behind them, all three faces set in grim, watchful lines. Before their united front, even Wayne backed off. "I'll see you later, then, Dria," he said, as casually as if he hadn't just made her furious. "We'll have that dance together."

"Has he been bothering you, Dria?" Henry demanded.

"Nothing worth having a fuss about. He was just being his usual obnoxious self. Listen, Harvey Fletcher's calling for couples! Let's get in the first set!" Without waiting for him to reply she pulled him toward the barn, her eyes sparkling with excitement as the fiddles set her blood to racing.

A few feet away, Jacob's daughter Natalie scowled with disappointment. Darn, for a minute there she'd thought there was going to be some fun! Dria's other party had been a lot better, when Hank and Wayne had got in that fight that had turned into a free-for-all.

Still scowling, her gaze happened to fall on Gig Walstrom. Gig was a year or two older than she was, and goodness knew there wasn't anything good-looking about him. He was gangly and freckle-faced and his straw-colored hair always stood up in a cowlick in back. Even worse, he persisted in ignoring her. A look of determination came into Nattie's eyes and she moved toward him, lurching against him just as she came up to him.

"Clumsy! Whyn't you watch where you're going?" Nattie demanded.

268

"Hey, are you crazy or something? You bumped into me!" Gig protested, completely bewildered.

For an answer, Natalie doubled her fist and popped him in the eye.

"Ow! What in tunket did you do that for?" Gig howled.

Natalie's mocking laughter trailed after her. She darted into the barn, wove her way through the half-dozen sets on the floor and scrambled up the ladder that led to the hayloft.

Gig was right behind her, as she'd known he would be, his freckled face furious. Who'd she think she was, popping him one when he hadn't done anything? It was time she learned a lesson! He didn't even hear the laughing "Hey, boy, watch where you're going!" as he nearly tripped a swinging couple. Another few seconds and he, too, gained the ladder and swarmed up it into the loft.

Where was she? He strained his eyes, searching for her, but Natalie was nowhere in sight. He bent over, intent on ferreting her out where she was hiding under the hay and repaying her blow in kind.

"Gotcha!"

It wasn't Gig who spoke, but Natalie as the hay exploded and she popped up to grasp him around his knees and bring him tumbling down with her sprawling on top of him. Her hair was filled with wisps of straw, it clung to her dress, and the dust made a sort of halo around her.

The dust made Gig sneeze.

"God bless you." Natalie said. And in the same breath, "Have you ever kissed a girl?"

"Achew! 'Course I ain't! Why'd I want to kiss a girl?"

"You might learn something, that's why. Come on, kiss me."

A shadow fell over them, and Gig froze as Jacob Renault's huge hand reached out and grasped Natalie by the back of her dress.

"All right, Gig, skedaddle. Next time remember not

to go chasing girls into haylofts, there might not be any-body around to rescue you!" Jacob said.

Gig gulped and his legs came to life, and he lost no time in skedaddling. In the loft, Jacob looked at this twelve-year-old daughter of his with a mixture of sorrow and awe. Damned if he knew what he was going to do with her. Wallop her now, or wait till later, or tell her ma on her? One thing was sure, she was going to be a man-eater when she got a few more years on her. He only hoped that she'd wait that long!

Nattie grinned at him, not in the least purturbed at having been caught trying to seduce a boy. "Heck, Dad, couldn't you have waited another couple of seconds?" she asked him.

"Get out of this hayloft, and don't let me catch you up here again!" Jacob bellowed at her.

Nattie's grin became more impish than ever. "You bet, Dad. I won't let you catch me!"

Then she was gone, and before Jacob could get him-self back down the ladder she'd disappeared. Jacob sighed. He'd done all he could for tonight. If Gig didn't have sense enough to keep out of her way, he'd have to take care of himself.

The fiddles had changed to a waltz, and Henry's face was transfigured as the strains of "The Blue Danube" gave him a chance to have his arm where he wanted it, around Andrea.

"Have you been doing any thinking?" he asked her.

"A lot of thinking."

"And?"

"Henry, this isn't the time or place for a discussion like this."

"It's always time and the place. It's the only thing in the world that matters. You aren't going back to England. Say it, Dria!"

"People are looking at us! Mother and Dad went to a lot of trouble giving this party, don't do anything to embarrass them!" Thank heaven, the music was ending and Henry had to take his arm from around her, he had

270

to stop looking down into her eyes like that. "Do you want to set the whole region to talking?"

"Let them talk! They can't say anything that they won't all know is true, pretty soon." If only he wouldn't look at her like that! Her heart was pounding, and she was breathing too fast. She looked around for someone to rescue her, Mike or Lupe, but they were standing by themselves over in the corner under the loft, completely oblivious to anyone else.

Her eyes moved from them and settled on another figure, a girl of seventeen, who was also by herself, her face a picture of desolation as she watched Mike laugh down into Lupe's face and then tuck her hand under his arm and draw her away. It was Lucy Ingram, Paula's younger sister. She'd only been fourteen when Andrea had left the Big Bend, but even then Andrea had noticed, and been amused by, her obvious crush on Mike.

Now Andrea's heart twisted, because she recognized the look of utter despair on Lucy's face. Lucy wasn't a child any more, and she was in love with Mike, and Andrea had a very good idea that Lucy was one of those people who would never love more than once. Like Paula, she wasn't outstandingly pretty; her face was plain, although she had a pretty mouth and a sweet smile. Why was it that so many people had to be hurt because they loved someone? And usually the nicest people, the ones who least deserved to be hurt.

She continued looking around. Paula hadn't come down to the barn. But Wayne was here, pulling Belinda Perkins to her feet, encircling her waist with his arm, whispering something that made her simper up at him.

Stupid girl! She was as silly as her mother. Didn't she realize that she was making a spectacle of herself, letting Wayne take such liberties with her right in front of everybody? Belinda was beaming now, her face flushed with triumphant pleasure at Wayne's attention. Wayne was going too far. She was going to find Paula and get her down here to the barn if she had to drag her!

"I'll be back in a minute," she told Henry. "No, don't come with me!" She made her way through the milling crowd. There was Uncle Jacob, looking as if he'd just bitten into a particularly sour persimmon; whatever could have happened to make him look like that? It had nothing to do with Barbara, because she was just over there, laughing and talking and obviously having a wonderful time.

"Paula? She went into the house," Mrs. Perkins told Andrea when Andrea didn't find her on the patio. "I don't believe she feels very well. I wonder if she's breeding again? I wouldn't put it past Wayne Bradshaw to get her that way again so soon, would you?"

Andrea didn't dignify the question with an answer. Paula wasn't in the living room or the dining room. On a hunch, Andrea went to her own room, and found her friend there, a huddled figure of misery in the middle of the bed, her face pressed into the pillows.

"Paula!" Andrea put her hand on Paula's shoulder. "You aren't sick, are you?"

Paula's face was filled with shame and streaked with tears as she raised it. Unfortunately, she wasn't one of those girls who still look pretty when they cry. Her eyes were swollen, and her face was puffed.

"Oh, Andrea, I'm sorry! Only I just feel so awful! Wayne hasn't come near me all evening! I did go out to the barn, but he walked right past me and asked some other girl to dance. Everybody noticed it, they're all laughing at me, I can't go back out there!"

"I don't believe anyone noticed it, they're all too busy having a good time. You know Wayne, he just wasn't thinking."

"You don't understand. You're so pretty, and all the men have always been crazy about you, and you married a rich, glamorous Englishman! But I never thought I'd get married at all, and I only did because Wayne had to marry me and he hates me for it, he never comes near me any more, he hasn't come near me since little Davie was born. And I love him, and that makes it worse. I just don't know what to do!"

"Well, you shouldn't hide away in here like a kicked kitten! Don't let him know he's hurting you, and

272

don't let anyone else know it, either. Now let's get your face washed and your hair combed, and then you're going back out there with me and you're going to dance with anyone who asks you, and have a wonderful time!"

Paula shook her head. "I can't. Nobody would ask me, even if I did go out. Dria, you don't know how lucky you are! You were born to be happy, and I'll never be happy. All I have is Davie, and Wayne and Clay will teach him to have contempt for me and ignore me, just the way Wayne ignores his mother. Sometimes I think I can't stand it."

"Then don't let him get away with it! If he's going to make you miserable all the rest of your life, leave him!" Andrea told her. The vehemence of her voice surprised her. "No man in the world has the right to make his wife unhappy, just because they happen to be married. If you can't be happy with him, walk out on him! You're young, you'd be crazy to throw away all the rest of your life on a man who dosen't love anybody but himself."

Who was she to be talking to another girl like this? The advice she was giving Paula was the advice she should be giving herself. Yes, and taking! Trying to comfort Paula, trying to instill some backbone into her, she knew that she would never, not ever, throw away what was left of her life just because she'd been foolish enough to marry a man who was fundamentally as selfish as Wayne Bradshaw.

If she had had any doubt in her mind before tonight, seeing both Paula and Lucy so unhappy had made her realize that she'd be the worst fool in the world not to stay right here and divorce Reggie and marry Hank. It wasn't Mike's fault that Lucy was unhappy; there wasn't a mean or selfish bone in Mike's body. He'd just never noticed Lucy except as Paula's little sister. But men like Wayne and Reggie had no right to wives to make into doormats. She had no intention of becoming like either Paula or Lucy. Her own happiness was waiting for her; all she had to do was reach out and take it. If she didn't have the courage to do that, then she had no more backbone than Paula.

She could hardly wait to get Paula calm enough so that she could leave her and get back to Henry. She was going to tell him now, tonight, that she wasn't going back to England, that she was going to ask her father to help her set divorce proceedings in motion. She'd wasted enough of her life, thrown enough of it away just because she'd been too young and too foolish to know any better. Now she was going to begin to really live, to live with a vengeance, and she was going to wrest every last ounce of happiness there was to be had from life!

Henry was waiting for her just beyond the patio, and even in the dim light from the Japanese lanterns he saw her transformed face and knew what it meant. His arms went out to draw her into them in spite of all interested eyes watching them from the chairs where the older women were still gossiping.

"Not here, Hank," Andrea whispered. "Later when we can be alone."

Her blood raced through her body as she took his hand and drew him back toward the barn, where Harvey Fletcher was singsonging, "Swing on the corner like swingin' on a gate, now back to your partner and don't be late. . . ."

Back to your partner! That was exactly what she was doing, going back to her partner. She was three years late in getting back to him, but this time, it was going to be for good!

18

Andrea was seated at her writing desk by the window in her room when Constanza brought her two letters from England that Mr. Perkins had dropped off on his way to his own ranch from town. It wasn't unusual for neighbors to pick up other ranchers' mail and bring it along to them if it was on their way; often weeks passed between trips to town and the postmaster expedited delivery by asking if whoever stopped in would take along mail that otherwise wouldn't be picked up for several more days.

Andrea had a sinking feeling as she turned the letters over in her hand, even though neither of them was from Reggie.

The letter she was writing to Reggie, asking him to cooperate in the matter of the divorce, was only half completed. She'd found it more difficult to write than she'd thought it would be. It lay there on the desk, her neat, legible handwriting making the words on the paper seem stark and unfeeling. She wasn't that; she had no desire to hurt Reggie. He was what he was, and he probably couldn't help it any more than she could help being what she was. Should she start it over, reword it, to try to mitigate Reggie's shock when he received it?

She looked at the unopened letters. She recognized the heavy, cream-colored stationery that Lady Madeline used even before she noticed the crest on the envelope. The other was from Caroline, the envelope an inexpensive one that she'd picked up from some stationery counter in an ordinary shop.

Which should she read first? Eenie, meenie, miney, mo, her mind said, the childish rhyme dancing through her mind unbidden. She shook her head at herself and picked up the cream-colored one after first laying it aside in favor of Caroline's. As Lady Madeline was older, she must come first.

The words that leaped out at her from the paper shocked her and shook her to the core. Reggie wasn't well. Lady Madeline was worried about him. He'd lost a great deal of weight, his color was bad, he had no appetite and no interest in anything. He missed Andrea, he was grieving over her absence, but he felt that he had no right to beg her to come home before she wanted to, after what he had done. He blamed himself severely for what had happened. He didn't know that Lady Madeline was writing to her; in fact, he'd expressly forbidden her to write, but she felt that Andrea should know.

"If you are feeling quite well again, perhaps you might decide to return a little before you had planned," Lady Madeline had written. "Of course you must consider your own health, but I assure you that Reggie needs you as soon as you can see your way clear to return to him. I am quite at my wits' end to know how to help him. Even Robert is concerned for him; he remarked that Reggie looked ghastly the last time we prevailed on him to spend a weekend with us in the country."

It isn't true, Andrea thought. Reggie always could get around Lady Madeline. Her mind balked at accepting what she had read. It was just another of Reggie's tricks, to get her to come back. But Lady Madeline wouldn't lie, and if Sir Robert was worried about him, there must be something in it.

276

Still shaken, her sense of foreboding deepening, Andrea laid Lady Madeline's letter aside and opened the one from Caroline. It was almost as if she knew, before she started to read it, what Caroline would say.

Reggie was ill. There was no doubt of it, he was actually ill. He needed her. He was eating his heart out because he was afraid she would never come back to him. He looked awful—Andrea could have no idea of how bad he looked, nothing but skin and bones. He was drinking too much, he didn't eat, and he didn't sleep.

"Look, Dria, I know what a stinker he was when he got in that accident that cost you your baby. But the point is, he knows it, too, and it's driving him around the bend. He loves you, Dria. I never thought he could love anyone as much as he loves you. If you don't come back, I don't know what's going to happen to him. From the way it looks now, he'll either drink or starve himself to death; it's a tossup which will get him first. Mort's worried about him, really worried, and so am I. I think you'd better get yourself on home, honey. . . . "

Andrea read the letter a second time, wincing as the import of the words sank in. She laid it aside and reread Lady Madeline's. There was no doubt about it. Reggie was sick, and he was sick because of her. He might be able to pull the wool over Lady Madeline's eyes, but Sir Robert was no such doting uncle as she was an aunt, and Caroline knew him inside out and so did Mort. They wouldn't lie to her for his sake.

She sat there for nearly half an hour, her mind in turmoil. Oh, God! Why had it happened, why did he have to care so much, when she'd been convinced that he'd never care for anybody but himself? Why couldn't he have just gone on being his old, selfish, insouciant self?

She couldn't sit still any longer. Learning that Reggie was ill, that her absence was the cause of his illness, sent her hurrying from the house to the corral. She had to get outside, to ride, she had to let the wind blow her mixed-up emotions out of her head so that plain common sense could tell her what to do.

Kate was on the patio, working on a nightgown for

277

little Philip. Her fingers paused in their task of setting the tiny stitches. "Where are you off to, Dria?"

"I thought I'd ride up to the mining settlement and visit Lupe." It was the first thing that came into Andrea's head. She couldn't talk to anyone now, not even to Kate. She had to be alone, to think things out for herself.

Runner seemed to sense her mood as she turned him onto the narrow road, scarcely more than a track, that led to the settlement. Fortunately, he decided to attend to business rather than try cutting up just for the fun ot it, and he forged ahead with no further direction from his rider, sure of his destination and with no need for a guiding hand on his reins. As she'd told Kate that she was going to visit Lupe, she'd have to do it, but she wouldn't stay long; no one would think anything of it if she came back late, so she'd have time to come to a decision. She lifted her face into the wind, her heartbreak at the idea of leaving Trail's End, of leaving Hank for what would have to be forever, almost more than she could bear.

The people at the settlement were friendly. Except for a few who'd come since she'd left Texas three years ago, they all knew her, and she knew nearly all of them by name. The excitement of her arrival compelled her to take her mind off the two letters for this little time. There was a new bride to be congratulated, there were several new babies to be admired, there were injuries or illnesses to be sympathized with, before Lupe, who like the others had come out of her house to see who had arrived, led her into the hovel that she and her grandfather and her younger brother called home.

It was a hovel—there could be no other name for it, although it was no worse than any of the others scattered around it. These habitations weren't anywhere near as good as the jacals that most Mexicans lived in, and they were so far worse than the neat cottages at Trail's End that there was no comparison. The shacks at the settlement were hardly fit for human occupancy. Thrown up out of any material that came to hand, they were for the most part no more than rude shelters with roofs contrived from thatch made from brush. Some of the workers,

278

the less ingenious or the less capable, actually lived in caves in the sides of the mountain, grateful for even that much shelter from wind and weather.

The settlement itself had no saving graces. The only public building was the company store, at which all were compelled to do all their trading. Anyone caught bringing in any kind of goods from another source would have been discharged immediately, but there was little chance of that. The workers labored six days a week, a nine or sometimes a ten-hour day, for a dollar and a half a day, and it hadn't been many years since the directors had resisted all petitions to allow the workers even Sundays off.

And no wonder it was so bad here, Andrea thought grimly, when Clay Bradshaw held an interest in this particular mine. Adam and Kate had done all they could in trying to stir up public anger against the conditions the workers had to live in, but because of Clay's long-standing enmity toward Adam, he just dug his heels in all the more firmly and refused to mitigate the hardships. Adam himself had once held an interest, but he had decided years ago that he didn't have enough time to devote to it and sold out. He'd tried to buy in again when he'd seen how it was run after he no longer had a voice in the management, but Clay and the other stockholders steadfastly refused to let him come by as much as one share because they knew that his ideas of how it should be run would cut down on their profits.

The Mendoza shack consisted of one room in which both the cooking and the living were done, except for a tiny lean-to that they'd built and curtained off for Lupe's cot. As it was only a little after noon, neither Manuel, Lupe's grandfather, or young Jesus was there. Andrea would have liked to meet them, but there was no way she could stay until the day's shift was over.

Lupe gave her coffee served in a cracked pottery mug, the only piece of china in the place, while she herself drank from a battered tin cup. In spite of the troubles that weighed so heavily on her mind, Andrea was struck anew with the inborn Spanish hospitality with which these people welcomed guests. No matter how little they had, they offered the best the house could provide. If there was wine, it was served with graciousness as if it had been the best imported vintage, no matter how thin and sour it might be. If there was coffee, that was what was forthcoming. If there was only water, a glass or a cup was tendered with the same simple dignity.

In spite of her own warm liking for Lupe, it was obvious that the girl was embarrassed by this visit. Andrea did her best to draw her out, telling her about Georgia and Massachusetts and England. "But Texas is the best place of all. I wouldn't trade Texas for all the rest of the world put together! You and Mike are lucky, you'll never have to leave here, you'll probably always live in the Big Bend. I wish I'd never left. If I had it to do over, nobody would ever be able to persuade me to leave!"

Lupe's face flushed and she lowered her eyes. There was no way that Andrea could persuade her to admit that she and Mike were in love, although it was written all over the lovely girl's face that she literally worshipped Mike. If only there were some way she could get through to her, make her realize that as long as she and Mike loved each other, nothing else mattered. The fiasco she'd made of her own life brought it home to her all the more strongly.

She rose to leave after half an hour. "I've still some children to get acquainted with and gossip to catch up on." She smiled. "Be happy, Lupe. Nothing in the world is more important than being happy." The irony of her advice struck her. How she wished that it applied in her own case! But she'd already made her mistakes, while Lupe hadn't, and now she must face the consequences no matter how much she wished she didn't have to. Lupe never had to make the mistakes she had made, especially the mistake of thinking that because her family wasn't wealthy she wasn't good enough to marry Mike.

Sandwiched between admiring a curly-headed toddler who was proud of a deep scar on his knee and exclaiming over a small flock of hens, her fluency in Spanish and her ingeniously put questions gave her the answer to something that had been bothering her ever since the night of the barn dance. Yes, she was told, Wayne Bradshaw came to the settlement often, a great deal more often than the people liked. The mothers were concerned for their daughters. Two or three young girls, rebellious at the poverty in which they were forced to exist, had accepted trinkets from him in return for who knew what favors. Rosa's father had beaten her, but it did no good. And yes, Wayne looked at Lupe, although Lupe always managed to put herself in the center of a group of older women whenever he rode in and stay there until he had left.

They liked Mike, they looked on him as almost one of their own in spite of the fact that he was a Wentworth of Trail's End. They were too discreet to hint at it, but Andrea could see that they hoped that Mike and Lupe would marry.

It proved one thing to Andrea's satisfaction. Lupe wasn't to be seduced that easily. And with any luck maybe Mike would be able to persuade her to overcome her diffidence at the thought of marrying into such a distinguished family before trouble erupted between him and Wayne. For all his almost unreal handsomeness, Wayne was not a man to be dismissed as a fop or a weakling. He was lithe and strong and far from a coward, mean in a fight, and always ready to accept a challenge. If it came to a confrontation between them, Andrea wasn't sure that Mike, who was younger and several pounds lighter and who had never been too interested in learning how to be a dead shot as Wayne was, would come out on top.

The thought made her throat tighten. If anything happened to Mike, how would she be able to bear it? All of their lives Mike had been like the second half of her, they'd done everything together, they'd been like each other's shadows. If you looked for one of them, you'd find both, if you could find them at all, usually in some kind of a scrape with Henry getting them out of it with whole skins. A stab of pain shot through her as she remembered that Henry had used to call them "the terrible twins."

Henry and Mike! Her world, her life, was all wrapped up with both of them. Oh, God, if only she could stay here, if only she never had to leave them behind her! Her life was here, her heart was here, but because she'd been young and foolish she'd thrown it all away. She supposed she'd been so saturated with the stories of Martha Curtis Beddoes and of Prue and of the slave Rebecca who'd escaped her destiny and ended up a countess that she'd been convinced that if she, too, didn't have wonderful, romantic adventures, she would be wasting the only life she had. Now, too late, she realized that it had been her very longing for such storybook romance that had proved her undoing.

And now there was nothing she could do about it. And like herself, Mike would have to solve his own problems. She swung upon Runner and turned his head not toward home but deeper up into the mountains. She needed more time to think, to come to terms with herself and the thing that she already knew she had to do even if it tore the heart out of her body.

She stopped two hours later in a little glade where second-growth scrub trees were beginning to spring up again after the area had been denuded to feed the needs of the mine. She dropped Runner's reins over his head and threw herself face down on the ground, her head buried in her arms, and gave vent to the emotions that were tearing her apart. She cried for a long time, until she was almost too exhausted to lift her head to see if Runner was still nearby.

Her crying was over with now. It had served its purpose, let her release some of the tension that had made her feel as if she were going to burst. Now there was no more room for tears in her life. She'd face what had to be faced with her head held high and no trace of her inner feelings betrayed by word or expression. She was still her parents' daughter, and she would not betray the heritage of strength that had come down to her through the Beddoeses and the Renaults.

She'd ridden farther than she'd intended, and she'd have to push Runner fast to get back to the ranch before dark. Oh, God, how I'm going to miss all this, she cried out silently as she drew in a deep lungful of the clear, tangy mountain air. Her thought was so agonized that for a moment she thought she'd said it aloud.

Runner came at her whistle, just as she'd trained him

years ago. She remounted, swallowing down the lump in her throat at the knowledge that she'd have to leave him behind, as well as everything else that made life worth living. The Appaloosa needed no direction from her to turn his head toward home. Andrea paid little heed to the path he chose, her thoughts filled with the necessity of telling Henry and her parents that she was going to go back to England.

She was so deep in her thoughts that she almost missed seeing the doe pronghorn, its grayish-brown fawn close by her side. She knew from her childhood that these pronghorns used to run in herds of two or three hundred before the country had become so settled, but it had been years since she had seen one. The beautiful little antelopes were tan on their backs and sides with white patches on either side of their faces and at the base of their ears. They had black muzzles, and the bucks had a black spot on each jaw just under the ears. The bucks ran around three feet tall at their shoulders and were anywhere from four to five feet long. The does, of course, were smaller. This doe was grazing close enough to Andrea so that she could see its markings plainly. How lovely it was, how proud and free! A wave of envy of the beautiful creature swept over her. If she could live out her life in these mountains, as the doe and its fawn would, she'd ask nothing more of life.

She and Runner were so still that the doe moved closer to them. Once she lifted her head, but Andrea didn't move a muscle and she held Runner motionless. Sensing that it had nothing to fear from either horse or rider, the doe looked straight at her and then resumed its grazing. Like Runner, it had some sixth sense that told her that it was in no danger from this particular human.

A shadow passed across Andrea's face so swiftly that she scarcely had time to realize that it had been there, and she looked up, her breath expelling with sudden force. Automatically, her hand reached for the rifle that should have been in its saddle scabbard, but it wasn't there. She'd ridden out in such a rush that she hadn't thought to bring it; it hadn't occurred to her that she might need a firearm.

The doe, too, realized the danger. Her head came up

and she galvanized into motion as she raced back toward where she had left her fawn several yards away. The long white hair on her rump, that usually lay flat, now stood erect like a huge white pompom as she rushed to protect her fawn from the golden eagle that was already swooping down on it, its talons extended.

Andrea's heels dug into Runner's sides and she shouted as she sent him catapulting toward the scene of the danger. "Get away, damn you!" she shouted. She took off her broad-brimmed hat and waved it at the eagle, determined to drive it off before the doe had to defend its offspring. She knew that the doe would drive the eagle off, but there was the very real danger that she or the fawn would be severely lacerated by those wicked talons before she could put it to rout.

Damn those golden eagles! How could any creature so beautiful be such a menace, be so greedy that it would attempt to carry off a weight that it couldn't possibly handle! The eagles could carry only eight pounds for any distance, but that didn't stop them from mutilating calves and young sheep and goats, and they were the pronghorns' greatest natural enemy.

Runner reared, pawing at the air with his front hoofs as Andrea reached the fawn. The doe was already there, and as the eagle, deflected from its purpose, soared upwards again, she and the fawn were off like a flash, faster than a horse could run. Andrea's breath rasped in her throat. The eagle would return, make another swoop at the fawn, hopeful of catching it in its talons before the doe could drive it away. She set Runner into as fast a pace as he could go on this uneven footing, but she had little hope that she'd get there in time to help drive it off again.

The crack of a rifle made her spine stiffen, and she reined Runner around. Above her, the eagle plummeted toward the earth as Henry replaced his rifle in its scabbard and trotted toward her.

"That was close. Dria, what the hell are you doing way up here, and all alone? Your mother told me you'd gone up to the settlement, but they told me you'd left, heading this way, and I had one heck of a time tracking you!"

"I'm all right, Hank. I just lost track of time."

"I'll say you did! Look at you, there isn't a drop of color in your face! You're not as well as you think you are; you ought to have sense enough to be more careful! If anything happened to you . . ."

This was it. Andrea drew a deep breath to steady herself. She had to tell him, and there could be no better place than here high in the mountains with no other soul for miles around.

"Henry, I had letters from England this morning, one from Lady Madeline and one from Caroline Byron. Reggie's sick. Really sick, and it's because of me. I have to go back."

Henry's face registered utter incomprehension. "Go back? Dria you're out of your mind! He has family back there, friends, he'll be cared for. Of course you aren't going back, what kind of a crazy thing is that to say?"

"It's no good, Hank. They said—Lady Madeline and Caroline—that Reggie needs me, that I'm the only one who can make him pull out of it. They're afraid that he'll die if I don't go back. Don't make it any harder for me than it already is! Don't you see that it's tearing me apart, that I can hardly bear it? But he's my husband, I married him, and I made promises when I married him. For better or for worse, in sickness and in health!"

Her voice was agonized, her face so white that Henry was afraid that she, too, was ill, that she might collapse and fall off Runner right in front of his eyes. Still he couldn't hold back his bitter, demanding protests.

"It's our lives you're throwing away, don't you realize that? You don't love him! And from all you've told me, from all I've been able to find out, he isn't worth loving! You can't do it, I won't let you, just get the notion right out of your head! If he were any kind of a man, if he even began to deserve having you, it would be different, but he isn't; he'll never make you anything but miserable, and you know it. Your father's already consulting his lawyers about your divorce; you can't throw everything away for a man who isn't worth it!"

"I have no grounds for divorce." Andrea fought back her despair. "Not real grounds, Hank. There was only my own desire to be free. Granted that Reggie's selfish and thoughtless, he never meant to hurt me. And I had no idea that he loved me so much. How could we ever be happy, if I deserted him when he needs me so desperately? What if he actually died? It would always be between us! What kind of a wife could I be to you, a woman who lacks common loyalty to her husband!"

"So you're ready to throw our lives away just because you made a mistake when you were eighteen and married a man who'll never be worth the ground you walk on! That isn't just jealousy, Dria. Adam's told me what he thinks of Reggie, and I've never known Adam to make a mistake in a man's character. I can't accept it, and I won't. You belong to me, and all the wedding rings and marriage certificates in the world can never make you belong to anyone else. You told me you loved me, you told me you were never going back. You can't do it, I won't have it!"

"You aren't even trying to understand! I didn't know then that Reggie was sick! I had no idea that this would happen! I have to do what's right, no matter what it does to us, can't you understand that?"

She swayed in her saddle, and Henry was off his horse instantly to lift her down from Runner's back. In spite of her determination not to give in to weakness, Andrea found herself leaning against him for support, her legs too weak to hold her up.

Henry held her with one arm and took her hat off with his free hand. He dropped the hat to the ground and his hand brushed her dark hair back from her forehead. His voice was filled with agony that matched her own.

"Remember when you used to wear your hair in two pigtails when you rode? Once I told you you looked like an Indian squaw, and you told me that you were proud of it, that you were part Indian and that if I didn't stop teasing you, you'd tomahawk me. We couldn't have been more than eleven and fourteen. Your eyes were so filled with fire that I thought you meant it, and I was darned near scared."

Andrea remembered, blind with pain. "And you pulled one of my pigtails and took out your knife and said you were going to cut it off to teach me not to make

286

threats I couldn't carry out." Their lives were all wrapped up in each other's; they were interwoven, they'd been destined for each other, and she'd been too young, too stupid, to realize it! "Henry, don't! It doesn't change anything. I still have to go back."

"No!" Suddenly, without thinking, without being able to stop himself, he was shaking her until her head bobbed back and forth on her neck, until her hair flew wildly. And as suddenly as he'd started to shake her, he stopped and his arms drew her into an embrace so fierce that she felt the ground tilt under her feet, she felt as though she were sinking into an abyss with nothing but darkness at the bottom. His mouth on hers was ruthless, possessive, commanding, it was as fierce as the arms that held her. His hands were frantic as they tore at the buttons of her shirt, as they opened it, sought her breasts, cupped them. His mouth left her lips and seared her throat, her bare shoulders. His weight bore her to the ground, holding her down, powerless against him until one more searing kiss made her body go limp, to lie underneath his, trembling helplessly.

It was going to happen now, he was going to take her and every drop of blood in her body cried out that she wanted him to, that she'd die if he didn't. He was her man, she loved him, she'd never had him and if she never had him then she'd die without knowing the full meaning of love, her entire life would be pointless, sterile, she might as well never have lived at all.

She was jolted back to reality as Henry's open hand struck her across her face, so hard that her head rang and tears flooded her eyes. Stunned, disbelieving, she stared at him through a pain-filled blur.

"Damn you, Andrea Wentworth! Damn you to hell! You'd give yourself to me, you'd let me have one taste of everything we could have had, and then you'd leave me and go back to Reggie! All right, go back to him, but if you go, don't come back! You betrayed me once before when you went running off to Georgia and then to England, and I thought I was going to die of it, but I know now that I won't die. It's the end of it, Dria. Go if you have to, go if you want to, but don't ever come back!"

"Henry—"

"I don't want to hear it! Not unless you're going to say that you aren't going, that you're going to stay here and get your divorce and marry me. Well, Dria?"

Her words caught in her throat, strangled against the pain that consumed her, a pain a hundred times worse than the pain of her face where he had struck her. "Henry, I can't. God knows I want to, but I can't."

His eyes bored into hers for one more moment, and then he flung her away from him so hard that she rolled over and her face and hands dug into the ground and were scratched. He was on his feet, jamming his hat back on his head, and for a few rendingly piercing seconds she felt as if she had lived all this before.

"That's that, then." Without helping her up, without making any move at all toward her, he caught up his horse and swung into the saddle. Andrea still lay there on the ground, her breath rasping in her throat, her throat burning, her eyes, her face burning, and watched him ride away from her without looking back.

She lay there for a long time, so filled with despair that she wished that she could die before she had to get up and straighten her clothes and get on Runner and ride back down to Trail's End. He was gone, and she knew as surely as she knew the sun would set that she'd never see him again.

Runner came and nuzzled her, wondering why she didn't mount him and start for home. Slowly, Andrea sat up, and her numbed fingers struggled with the buttons that Henry had undone. She got to her feet and started to put her foot into the stirrup, but then she wrapped her arms around Runner's neck and wept with her face pressed against his silky hide. An hour ago, no more, she had thought she was done with crying. She had been mistaken.

The sun was already going down behind the horizon when she rode out of the mountains, leaving the world as dark as her heart. But she straightened her shoulders before she rode into the stableyard, and her face was outwardly calm as she went into the house to tell her family that she was going back to England.

ENGLAND

19

If Andrea hadn't felt such a sense of panic at meeting Reggie again she'd have had to laugh at the spectacle he presented with his arms so laden with flowers that he wasn't even able to take her in his arms and kiss her when he met her at the boat. Like an adolescent on his first date, he seemed filled with confusion, desperately anxious to make a good impression but having no idea what to do with his hands. He tried to put his arms around her, he looked bewildered when the flowers got in the way, and then he thrust the whole mass at a porter to get rid of them and enveloped her in an embrace that nearly crushed her.

For another panic-stricken moment she thought he was going to cry right there in the midst of a milling mob of total strangers, a thing unthinkable in any man and especially in an Englishman. But the moment passed. Reggie settled for kissing her with an ardor that brought disapproving stares from a brace of dowagers, and then he retrieved the flowers from the astonished porter and thrust them into her arms.

"Welcome home, darling. I've been waiting at this dock for hours! I thought the ship would never get across the Atlantic. I've been beside myself ever since you let me know that you were actually coming home."

He put his hand under her elbow and forced a way through the crowds, the porter following with her luggage. "Ned, lent me his car, but I had to park quite a distance away," Reggie told her, his voice anxious. "Are you sure you're up to the walk, or would you rather wait here till I fetch it around?"

"I'm perfectly well, Reggie." Andrea spoke through the roses that all but obscured her face. "Ned's car? Was . . . our car beyond repair, then?" Her hesitation was barely discernible, and she fought down the stab of pain that the mention of the car that had cost her baby his life sent cutting through her.

"Yes, it was badly damaged, rather. It wasn't worth repairing, even if I could have afforded it. I sold it for what it would bring, just as it was. Darling, I'd begun to wonder if you were an invalid after all, in spite of Hertley assuring me, over and over, that there was nothing to keep you from having a complete recovery."

Andrea's face felt stiff as she struggled to keep her smile in place. She didn't want to talk about her illness or Doctor Hertley or even skirt around the cause of her illness. That was behind them; they had to go on from here.

The flat smelled stale, unlived in. It was reasonably clean. The char had been there the day before and given it a dusting up, but there is an undefinable but very clear aura about any place that has gone unused, or nearly unused, for a long time. The first thing Andrea did was to put the roses in the tarnished silver-plated pitcher that Caroline had given them as a wedding present, and then she opened all of the windows. The air that came in smelled of dust and smoke, but she'd have to get used to that again. It was better than suffocating, even if not much better.

"You must have been out of your mind to buy so

many roses! The florist must have thought you were drunk." Suddenly embarrassed to be alone with him, she fussed with the bouquet, trying to make it look as if it wasn't too large for its container. The roses looked uncomfortable crowded so closely together, and she felt uncomfortable in this tiny flat, in too close proximity with a man she no longer loved but with whom she was going to have to live all the rest of her life. "He ought to be ashamed of taking advantage of you."

"I told him they were for the most beautiful woman in the world." Reggie's arms were around her, he strained her to him, his mouth found her forehead, her cheeks, her throat, and then at last her lips. "Oh, Lord, Dria, you're really home! I can't believe it, I have to go on holding you because I'm afraid you'll disappear."

He picked her up and carried her into the bedroom. His hands trembled with eagerness as he worked at buttons, at snaps. Andrea closed her eyes and willed herself not to think of that last time she'd been with Henry, when he'd been just as clumsy and eager before he'd struck her and told her that he never wanted to see her again. Tears stung and burned behind her eyelids as Reggie took her, clumsily and roughly in his eagerness until he caught the rhythm, his passion spending itself too quickly so that she felt she was being used.

But she had no right to protest. She was his wife; he had the right to make love to her whenever he wanted her, even like this in broad daylight. If her first unthinking passion for him was dead, she was still fond of him. Her bitterness at the accident had had time to fade. He hadn't done it on purpose, he'd wanted the baby, too. And he'd loved her and married her when she'd been at her lowest ebb, caring nothing for her background, for the heritage that Gregory Randolph had found so shameful that he had wanted to marry her secretly and hide away until Crissy should die so that she couldn't spread her malicious tales that would have disgraced him and his proud Southern family. She would always be grateful to him for that. If he was immature, irresponsible, then that was a part of him and something that she must learn to accept.

Whether their life together from now on would be reasonably smooth or miserable with dissension depended almost entirely on her.

Reggie's face was actually wet with tears as they fell apart. "Dria, you do love me! You do, I can tell. Oh, God, you'll never know how frightened I've been! I thought I'd lost you, I was afraid you'd never come back, I didn't know how I was going to get on without you!"

She gathered his head to her breast and smoothed his tumbled hair back from his forehead. "It's all right, darling, I'm here."

Reggie's smile was radiant, boyish, filled with happiness. "What we need right now is a good, stiff drink, to celebrate your return home! Or even two. Then we'll get dressed and go out to dinner, someplace posh. After all, this is your first day home and we have to do something special to mark the occasion."

He was so eager that she didn't have the heart to say no, even though she wondered whether he could afford a posh place for dinner. Knowing Reggie, it would be very posh indeed. She accepted the drink he brought her, drank it gratefully, and was glad to accept a second one before they were ready to leave the flat. It helped to dull the ache in her heart and to put thoughts of financial or any other troubles away in the back of her mind until some later time when she'd feel more able to cope with them.

Poor Reggie! He really did look bad. Caroline and Lady Madeline hadn't exaggerated when they'd written to her. He was thin, and he looked haggard under his gaiety. Pity for him made her kiss him as he locked the door behind them, and his joy in her spontaneous gesture made it well worth it.

She drank too much that night, letting Reggie urge drink after drink on her as he celebrated her return home to the hilt. They dined sumptuously on pheasant; Reggie ordered the finest wines, and they danced to soft music while he held her close, his cheek pressed against hers as though they were on their honeymoon instead of being an old married couple. If she'd been completely sober, the tab at the end of the evening would have horrified her.

But then they were in Ned's car again, and she was more concerned that Reggie should get it back to the flat without having an accident, after all he'd had to drink, than she was about the tab. And after that, there was a nightcap, and they made love again and had another nightcap. She'd survived her first day at home, and that was all that mattered.

It mattered the next day, after Reggie had gone to work and she had to cope both with her hangover and getting the flat livable again. Reggie came home that evening to find her pale and shaky, tired out from giving the kitchen the scrubbing that Mrs. Baker, the char, had neglected, from unpacking and rearranging drawers and closets, from shopping and getting some kind of a meal together.

"Darling, you overdid! Here, sit down, I'll bring you a drink."

Andrea shuddered. "I don't really think so. . . ."

Reggie laughed at her. "Trust me, Dria. I know what a hangover needs. Another drink, and you'll be surprised at how much better you'll feel! I don't mean that we should overdo it again, two nights in a row, but one or two more is exactly what's called for."

Surprisingly, he was right. After the first surge of nausea that the first swallow brought on, she did feel better. Reggie even managed to make her laugh, insisting on serving her at dinner with a napkin over his arm like a proper waiter. By the time they'd washed up the dishes together, and Reggie suggested, hopefully, that they make an early night of it, she was able to give herself to him with no outward hint that she didn't love and want him as much as he loved and wanted her.

She got through the next day, and the next. Every evening, when Reggie suggested a nightcap, she took it, grateful for the slight dulling of her senses, for the blessing of being able to go on pretending. If she pretended long enough and hard enough, maybe it would come true and she'd become reasonably happy. At least it helped her to put Henry from her thoughts, and Mike, and Trail's End.

When she was completely sober, the thought of them hurt so much it was unbearable.

She'd been back for three weeks, and was still wondering if she'd ever get used to it no matter how hard she tried, when Reggie came home one evening with a look on his face that made her heart sink. He'd been up to something; the signs were unmistakable. She'd seen that look on his face too many times in the past not to recognize it.

"Darling, I have a surprise for you. But you have to come outside to see it." His voice was boyish with enthusiasm, and Andrea had a sense that she'd lived through this scene before. Of course she had! It was when her mother and father had been visiting them, and Reggie had come home with this same look on his face.

The surprise was long and gleaming silver, its sheer magnificence relegating all the lesser vehicles parked at the curb to total insignificance.

"Reggie, you couldn't have!"

"But Dria, it was a steal! It was an absolute steal! And we can't do without a car forever. Now that you're back, we need it, for shopping, and getting around town, and going down to the country to visit Aunt Madeline and Uncle Robert. I can't go on imposing on Ned every time I have to have a car, now can I?"

"But a car like this! What is it, anyway?"

"Isn't that just like a woman! It's a Rolls, of course, can't you tell? It's a Rolls-Royce Silver Ghost! And it's ours, every glorious centimeter of it! Don't look so stricken, it isn't new, it's one of the first ones ever made, that's why I got such a fantastic buy on it. But it's in top condition, it's every bit as good as the later models, and there's nothing like a Rolls-Royce, they're the best, nothing else can touch them."

"I don't believe it! Even second-hand, what did you use for money?" Her voice was too sharp, almost shrill, and she took a deep breath to control it.

"I touched Owen for a bit of it," Reggie confessed. Then his face brightened. "But your mother took care of

Hertley's fee, and the nursing home, and we have no use for a larger flat now, so it wasn't actually more than we can afford."

Completely oblivious to her shock, he urged her into the car, climbed in himself, and started the engine.

"Listen to that! That's power, Andrea, that's six cylinders of power, a seven-litre engine of power! There'll never be another automobile like it. It's unbelievable that Henry Royce built his first machine right in his own shop back in '04, that he'd never had anything to do with building autocars before. He bought one, you see, and he decided that he could make a better one himself, and so he did. But he didn't come up with anything like this until Charles Rolls looked him out and went into partnership with him. The Honorable Charles Rolls had money, pots of it. They aren't making anything but Silver Ghosts now; that proves how good they are."

As far as Andrea was concerned, that didn't prove anything at all. The idea of Reggie buying such an expensive car was so shocking that she wouldn't have cared if there were dozens of more magnificent makes.

But she bit back the scathing remarks that rose in her throat. She mustn't start a quarrel. She and Reggie were married, they had to live together, it would be unbearable if they started right out quarreling, no matter how foolish he'd been. They'd manage somehow. She only wished that she didn't feel like shaking him and sending him to bed without his supper, as if he were the small boy he so resembled at times like this.

She let him take her for a spin, fighting against the nervousness that made her want to scream at him to stop the car so she could get out. Reggie didn't fail to notice her paleness.

"There, darling, that's one reason I bought the car. You have to get over being afraid. It's like falling off a horse, you have to get right back on before you lose your nerve and never ride again. I promise I'll be careful, not as much as a scraped fender. You'll soon see how right I was to buy the Ghost."

She'd never see how right it was, but she compressed

her lips and refrained from answering him. Reggie's insistence on owning a car was another thing she'd have to accept, if their marriage was to have any chance at all. All the same, resentment stirred inside her. Why was it always the woman who had to compromise, the woman who had to accept whatever her husband wanted?

The state of their finances, as she delved more deeply into it, appalled her. In spite of Reggie's off-hand assurances that the Ghost had cost practically nothing, she learned that he still owed nearly two hundred pounds on it. Compared to that, the charwoman's statement that he owed her several weeks back wages from right after she'd left for America dwindled into nothing.

"I kept on doing for him because I was sorry for him, like, you being sick and losing the baby and then going away and all," Mrs. Baker said. "But when 'e didn't give me over my wages I had to quit 'im. I 'ave my own family to think of, and where's the shillings to put in the gas meter to come from if I don't get my wages? I only came back to dust up the flat this last time because 'e knocked me up to tell me you were coming 'ome. I didn't like to think of you facing a filthy flat, but I 'ave to be paid, Mrs. Mansfield, you understand that."

Andrea paid her, her mouth set in a grim line. Still determined not to instigate a quarrel, she didn't mention it to Reggie when he came home that evening. Owing the charwoman, and then going out and buying all those outrageously expensive roses that had wilted so quickly in the early autumn heat! There was no way to keep the flat cool; situated as it was, between two taller buildings, it got hardly any breeze. The flat they'd been going to take had been so much airier.

She mustn't let herself think about that. The other flat would also have echoed with a baby's cooing and crying, smelled of drying napkins and baby talcum. They'd make do with this flat through the winter. Next spring, before the heat of the summer set in, she'd hunt for something else. It would be a sensible move, because getting away from the scene of so much unpleasantness would be a boost for their marriage. She was pleased with the idea, it gave her something to look forward to, but that was before she found out about the Ghost.

"You're cross with me," Reggie said, his eyes wary.

"Darling, I'm not cross, but I have to know where we stand. How much more do you owe, and on what?" She struggled to keep her patience. She'd known that Reggie was irresponsible, so she had no right to fly into a rage; all she could do was try to make sure that he didn't run up any more debts in the future.

"Nothing to speak of, I swear. And we'll be able to pay off the Ghost in no time at all, now that you're back and we'll have your allowance."

"There isn't any allowance! Whatever gave you that idea?"

Reggie looked astonished. "But Dria, after the way your mother saw how we were strapped, when she came to take you home, naturally I assumed she'd see that you wouldn't have to live so close to the bone when you came back! If she didn't have your father set up an allowance for you, then certainly they sent you back with a pocket-ful of cash!"

"They did not," Andrea told him. "They tried to give me a few thousand dollars, but they've already done far too much for us, paying for Mother's trip over and both our trips back, and as you pointed out, paying the doctor and the nursing home. I only accepted pocket money to see me through until I arrived."

Reggie looked at her as if she'd turned into some kind of a monster in front of his eyes. "I don't understand your reasoning. What's money for, if not to be spent and enjoyed? You're an heiress. . . ."

"I'm not an heiress while either my father or my mother are alive. We'll just have to make up a strict budget and stick to it." Andrea already had paper and pencil in front of her, and now she picked up the pencil. "Your other debts, Reggie?"

Sulkily, he tried to remember. There was a pair of shoes from a Piccadilly shop. "I was walking on the pavement, my others had holes clear through the soles," he defended himself. Andrea didn't say anything. She wrote down the sum, fifteen pounds. Seventy-five dollars for a pair of shoes? But they were the best, of course. She looked at him. She even tried to smile, because she suspected that her face looked grim.

He might owe a bit at the spirit shop. No, he didn't know how much, he didn't go around with a column of figures in his head like some bloody clerk. It was bad enough being one, trapped in that dreary bank all day, without thinking and acting like one. It wasn't much.

Not, Andrea thought the next day when she stopped around to ask for the bill, if thirty pounds wasn't much. The proprietor was unctuous. It was good of her to settle up, he'd had no intention of dunning them for such a paltry amount, the Mansfields' credit was good.

Further investigation showed just how good it was. There was an unpaid statement for three shirts, also of the finest quality, for two ties from a haberdasher whose prices were notorious for their absurdity, and for a suit that Andrea hadn't even seen yet because it hadn't been delivered, the alterations were only just now completed. Would Mrs. Mansfield care to take it with her, or should they send it around?

Andrea stared at the amount, her heart sinking even as her anger rose. It was only too apparent that certain shopkeepers still remembered who she was, the American heiress who had cut such a swath through quasi-smart London society three years ago before she had come to her senses and browbeaten Reggie into helping them tighten their belts.

She took the suit with her. The shop would have to wait for its money and be content with a little on account every month. No roast tonight, or any night until these bills were settled.

Reggie was contrite. "You know I have no head for figures. I can add them, but their meaning seems to escape me. Now you can understand why you'll have to ask your father for an allowance, can't you? Actually, we can't live on my salary, it simply can't be done."

"Yes, we can. We simply haven't tried. It's going to be pretty rough until we get caught up, but at least you have your new car and your new clothes, so we won't be running up any more on the red side of the ledger. And now that I'm back, you won't have any excuse to drink so much and we'll save on the liquor bills. I never realized it cost so much to be a souse!"

Reggie turned sullen. His attitude was that he'd be patient for a little while longer until she got over the notion of playing at being poor, but she'd better not take too long to admit that they had to have more money in order to live with any decency at all.

"I just can't seem to get through to him!" Andrea confessed to Ned over lunch. He'd called late in the morning to ask if she and Reggie could have dinner with him that evening, and finding her struggling with the budget, her forehead creased and shadows under her eyes that foretold an impending headache, he'd carried her off with him to a quiet restaurant that he particularly liked. "Didn't anyone ever teach him that two and two are four and that three pounds will not buy five pounds' worth of goods?"

She had Ned's complete sympathy. "Unfortunately, Reggie should have been born with a silver spoon in his mouth, but wasn't. Mother's family didn't have a bean, and while she did fairly well for herself when she let Father persuade her to marry him, her sister settled for a struggling barrister who had a predilection for taking cases for people who hadn't a bean, either. Her second marriage is a bit more solid, but her present husband can't see supporting a stepson who, as you so accurately put it, has never learned that two and two are four. And actually, his mother was fed up with him years ago, when she was continually harassed by tradespeople to pay accounts he'd run up when he was in public school. As a matter of fact, the school decided to forego the pleasure of his continued presence there, causing her extra embarrassment. She didn't raise too much objection when Reggie and his new stepfather had a serious falling out a couple of years before you came on the scene, and his stepfather showed him the door."

"I can't understand how he managed to survive!" Andrea said. "Not on credit, surely, because he couldn't have had any!"

"I'm afraid that my mother coddled him a bit too much; the welcome mat was always out for her sister's unfortunate boy, and he did make a charming house guest for friends of our family. Hostesses are rather cramped at finding extra, unencumbered, presentable and amusing men to balance their dinner tables, you know."

"But he isn't a footloose, carefree bachelor now!" Andrea's exasperation showed in her voice. "He's a married man, with responsibilities. Ned, I'm thinking of looking for a position myself. What do you think the owners of some of the posh shops I used to trade at would think if I walked in and asked for a post as a salesperson?"

Ned's face registered horror. "Andrea, you can't! Mother would never get over it! Look here, I can let you have a few quid. . . ."

Andrea shook her head and dredged up a rueful laugh. "I didn't actually mean it, I'm afraid. It's just that I get so tired of forever walking a tightrope, trying to balance creditor A against creditor B and still have enough over to pay the rent! But I'm doing it, even if I am a bit worse for the wear."

Going back to the cramped little flat after her lunch with Ned struck her, suddenly, like going back into a prison cell after having been given a weekend pass. She settled herself at the accounts again, trying to see where she could trim a pound off expenses here, a few shillings there. Her head was aching again. Now that autumn was well advanced, the coal smoke that hung low over the city suffocated her. The figures blurred in front of her eyes, and she threw down her pencil in exasperation when she realized that there was just no way she could cut down any more.

Reggie was particularly demanding that night. Long after he had at last given over fondling her and weighing her down with his arm after he'd finished a prolonged session of lovemaking, she lay staring into the darkness, her eyes burning with tears that she wouldn't shed. Reggie had been drinking, he must have had two or three before he'd come home from the bank, and he'd had two or three more during the evening, that was why he'd taken so long to come to completion that she'd had to fight against screaming and trying to throw him off.

Henry! The thought of him was an agony tearing at her body and soul. In all the years she'd known him, she'd never seen Henry drunk, never seen him take even a little too much. He was considerate, responsible, everything that Reggie was not. Her impression of being imprisoned built up in her until she felt that if she couldn't break out she'd disintegrate into a million pieces.

She had to get some sleep. Her head was throbbing, her nerves were screaming. Quietly, moving with actual stealth so that she wouldn't waken Reggie, she got out of bed and went into the living room and poured herself a stiff Scotch. She drank it neat, and it burned her throat all the way down. She poured another and sat curled up in a chair for another half-hour, sipping it. Then she went back to bed, her body just numbed enough so that she could doze off.

She'd seen Caroline two or three times since she'd come back, but she hadn't seen her for a few days. Caroline and Mort were more affluent now than they had been when she'd first known them, and she was embarrassed not to be able to pay her share when Caroline wanted to lunch at an expensive restaurant. But she took a bus the next afternoon and dropped in on her friend, unable to stand the flat another moment.

"You look rocky, love," Caroline told her. "Headache? Here, have some sherry, it's something Mort picked up and quite good. How's Reggie behaving himself?"

The sherry was too sweet for Andrea's taste, but after the first glass she felt better. "Tolerably. We haven't murdered each other yet, if that's what you're wondering."

"Reggie's all right, if only he'd grow up," Caroline said sympathetically. "I'd hoped that your being away so long would have given him a jolt so that he'd realize he had to straighten up if he didn't want to lose you. He did miss you dreadfully, he had me really worried. He loves

303

you, Dria." She refilled Andrea's glass. "Have another, it can't hurt. Did I tell you that Mort has a new client? He's contracted for three pictures; I feel positively wealthy! I'm glad you came over, you can help me celebrate. Finish your drink and we'll go out to lunch, my treat."

There was a cocktail before lunch, wine with the filet of sole, and another drink afterwards. Andrea enjoyed herself and she still felt mellow when she got back to the flat, but before Reggie got home, it had worn off. When Reggie made a grimace at the chopped meat patties she served for their supper, she went into the kitchen and fixed herself another drink.

Reggie had followed her, a habit he'd developed that drove her crazy. He was always on her heels, as if he was afraid to let her out of his sight.

"That's a good idea! Fix one for me, darling. Maybe it'll take the curse off that abomination I had to swallow. I'm sorry I was ugly about it, but a drink will fix you up and put you in the mood I want you in!"

He leered like a villain in a nickelodeon movie, and Andrea's nerves tightened. She had two more drinks before she went to bed, hoping that she'd be able to pretend that she was as eager for lovemaking as he was. But even the drinks didn't help much. It was Henry she wanted, Henry whom her heart and body and mind screamed out for while she endured Reggie's caresses and made a pretense of returning them. The walls of the trap she was in moved closer to her, threatening to crush her. And there was no way out. Even if she could find some way to leave Reggie without his destroying himself without her, Henry's last words to her echoed in her mind. Never come back!

The flat, the bills, Reggie. She began drinking every day, just enough to keep herself going without cracking up. If she kept her mind just a little blurred, it wasn't so hard to get through the days. The evenings, the nights, with Reggie, required a little more.

"You look like the devil," Caroline told her frankly when she stopped by shortly before Christmas. "What's that you're drinking? Scotch, in the middle of the afternoon? Don't tell me you're turning into a closet alcoholic!"

"Don't be ridiculous!" Andrea said shortly. "I have a headache, that's all."

"All the same, you'd better take it easy. We don't want you getting where Reggie was before you came back. Are you sure there isn't something wrong?"

"Nothing's wrong!" Andrea finished her Scotch and fought down the demanding desire to pour another. She wanted to scream that everything was wrong, that nothing would ever be right again, that she was no more alive and happy than a zombie going through the motions of living when she was really dead and only waiting for someone to bury her. She was so short with Caroline that Caroline left a few minutes later, and then she sat down and cried. Caroline was her only friend; what had possessed her to all but drive her away? She'd have to apologize. She'd do it tomorrow, she'd go over to Caroline's especially to make it up with her. Another drink calmed her, made the near quarrel seem not quite as bad, nothing that a few tactful words wouldn't heal.

Lady Madeline invited them down to the country for Christmas. They couldn't actually afford to go. They'd have to take gifts for Lady Madeline and Sir Robert, and Reggie would be outraged if she didn't manage something really nice, as well as something expensive and luxurious for himself.

Day after day, she combed the shops. She finally bought Reggie an angora sweater and charged it, but she'd almost given up in despair about Lady Madeline and settled for a bottle of scent when she passed a little shop on a side street. Its window was filled with a collection of china and little boxes and bits of statuary so jumbled together in total disorder that she almost passed it by. It was a china teapot that caught her eye. It was dusty. Everything in the window was dusty, and the window itself was so dirty that she had to squint to get a better look at what she was sure was a genuine Meissen teapot, its pattern exquisitely delicate.

Because of the junkshop atmosphere of the place, she still hesitated, until she told herself that the only way to be sure was to go in.

A bell jangled above the door when she entered, and the door itself squeaked on its hinges. The interior of the shop proved even more of a jumble than the window. Objects were pushed together helter-skelter on tables and shelves that hadn't seen a dustcloth for weeks, a layer of London grime overlaid most of the articles on display, and her footsteps left gritty prints on the dusty, uncarpeted floor.

The proprietor was a long time in appearing from behind a curtained-off doorway at the back. He was somewhere in his late middle years, taller than he seemed because of his stoop, his face red from either ill health or tippling. Watery blue eyes looked at her from behind steel-rimmed spectacles, and he was still chewing something so that he had to swallow before he could speak.

"You wanted to see something?"

"That teapot in the window, please."

He was so clumsy in extracting it from the rest of the jumble that she held her breath, certain that something would be broken before he finally turned back to her with it cradled in his hands, cradled so lovingly that her opinion of him changed for the better.

"Yes indeed, yes indeed. It's a beautiful piece. Meissen, very rare."

She took his word for it. There was no hint of cupidity in his watery gaze. "How much?"

He named a figure that was ridiculously low. For a moment her suspicions were aroused, but a closer examination of the teapot convinced her. Still, she was curious.

"It's very reasonable, for what it is. Why are you selling it at such a price?"

His shrug was eloquent. "I have to move some of the goods. Trade is slow, madam, and the rent has to be paid. After this month, you won't be able to buy anything in here at all. I am, unfortunately, going to have to close my doors. So if there's anything else you might like, this is the time to buy it, while I'm still here."

There wasn't anything else. She couldn't have afforded anything else even if she'd seen something she really wanted. She didn't look too closely, because there were pieces that were so lovely and rare that she had to hang onto her will power. It was a shame that Mr. Elias Smith, the name in chipped and scratched gold leaf on the window, was such a poor businessman that his shop had failed.

Mr. Smith packed the teapot lovingly, and Andrea's elation at discovering it was dampened by the thought of all those other exquisite pieces jumbled together with what was no more than trash. Under decent managership, Mr. Smith could have made a good thing of his establishment.

The teapot proved a tremendous success. Lady Madeline's delight was unfeigned. Sir Robert fondled the meerschaum pipe she had bought for him, and Reggie beamed over his sweater. Ned was there, aromatic wood fires leaped on the hearths, the odor of evergreens permeated the house. This was the way people were meant to live, the way her family lived, although in a different setting and culture. But it was all spoiled for Andrea because of Reggie's gift to her.

The gift was an evening wrap, blue velvet the exact color of her eyes. She didn't dare ask him how much it had cost; she knew from the label that the total of their indebtedness had taken an astronomical jump.

She drank too much on Christmas Day. Only Ned seemed to notice, and he looked concerned, although he was too well bred to comment on it. But he objected when, late in the afternoon, she proposed that they should go riding.

"Do you think you should, Andrea? You've celebrated a little too much, I'd suggest a nap before dinner instead."

"Don't be such a fuddy-duddy! It's a beautiful day, just crisp enough to make a good gallop enjoyable. Please, Ned! I want to go! It's been so long since I've ridden that I could scream!"

Ned gave in. With him on the rangy hunter that Reggie complained had too high a trot, and she on Caprice, they started out decorously enough. There was only a little snow on the ground, not enough to impede their progress, and the horses were eager for exercise.

The cold air after having been inside made Andrea's head feel light, and a wildness rose up in her. If only she could gallop forever, gallop to the ends of the earth, never have to go back to the flat and the bills and Reggie's maddening dependence on her!

"Race you!" she shouted.

"Andrea, don't! It's slippery up ahead, it isn't safe. . . ."

Andrea didn't even hear him. She lifted the reins and put Caprice to a gallop, faster and faster until the wind tore at her hair and seared her lungs, driving out the city smoke and making her giddier than ever. She rode with a reckless desperation, trying to blot out everything that she didn't want to think about. Caprice caught her mood and her hooves seemed to fly, scarcely touching the ground. She could almost imagine that she was on Runner, that she was racing with Henry, that the forfeit if she lost was to be a kiss, only she wasn't going to lose, she didn't like to lose, it was in her blood always to win.

"Faster!" she cried, her face flaming with excitement. Caprice responded. Andrea's laughter rang out, wild and mocking. And then Caprice's hooves struck a patch of half-melted ice, and she went down on her side, falling heavily. It happened so fast that only Andrea's instinctive horsemanship made her kick her feet out of the stirrups and throw herself sideways as Caprice fell, to land in a ball, rolling away from the mare's wildly threshing body as Caprice struggled to regain her feet.

"Andrea!" Ned pulled up beside her, and he was out of his saddle and trying to keep her from moving as she tried to sit up. "Be still, there may be broken bones!"

Still dazed, Andrea fought him off, striking and clawing at him. "Caprice!" she sobbed. "Oh, Caprice! Ned, let me up, damn it! She may have a broken leg!"

Ned was shaking, his face dead white. "You might have been killed! Are you sure you're all right?"

Andrea broke away from him and ran to where Caprice was now on her own feet, favoring her left front leg. Tears ran unchecked down her face as she knelt in the mud and ran her hands over the leg, probing for damage. "I don't think it's broken. Oh, God, Ned! She might have had to be shot! It was my fault, I made her fall, she might have had to be destroyed!"

"But it didn't happen." Ned had gained control of himself now. "You can see that it's only a bad sprain. Let me lift you up into my saddle, Dria, and we'll lead her home."

Lady Madeline's and Sir Robert's consternation when they returned with Andrea muddied and bruised, with Caprice still limping badly, made Andrea want to die of shame. She was shaking so hard from her fright about Caprice that Reggie immediately pressed a shot of brandy into her hand.

"Drink it, love," he urged. "There's a good girl, drink it all!"

Now that the first shock was wearing off, Andrea was beginning to ache. Her teeth clattered against the rim of the glass as she swallowed.

"A hot bath," Lady Madeline insisted. "She must have a good long soak and be tucked up in bed with a hot toddy."

When Andrea woke up the next morning, her mouth was so dry that she could hardly swallow, and she knew what some of the young men in Texas had meant when they'd claimed that a skunk had slept in their mouths. Her eyes were bloodshot, and her face looked puffy. Holding onto the edge of the dressing table for support, nausea churning in her stomach, she looked at herself with disgust. How long had it been since she'd gone through an entire day completely sober, since she hadn't reached for a drink every time she felt the weight of her problems grow a little heavier?

You're a lush! she told herself. You're destroying yourself, and you might have destroyed one of the most beautiful creatures that God ever put on earth. Caprice! If the animal had had to be shot, she would never have forgiven herself.

She wanted a drink. She needed a drink, she needed it so much that she began to tremble. It was late, nearly eleven; she'd overslept because she'd had too much to drink again after she'd fallen and Lady Madeline had insisted that she mustn't be disturbed. What was it Caroline had said to her a few weeks ago? A closet alcoholic!

The thought was frightening. She knew the story of her maternal grandfather, who had died in a fire caused because of his drunkenness. Had she inherited the taint in his blood?

Reggie came into their bedroom, a glass in his hand. He grinned that boyish grin of his at her and held it out to her. "I thought you might be able to use a hair of the dog that bit you."

Andrea looked at the glass, and she swallowed convulsively. She wanted to tell him to dump it down the bathroom sink, or drink it himself. She opened her mouth to say that she didn't want it. And then her trembling hands closed around the glass and she drank its contents without pausing for breath.

"That'll fix you up," Reggie said cheerfully. "How do you feel, now that you've had your eye-opener?"

She turned away from him, hating herself. "Awful."

"Think nothing of it. If you want breakfast, you'd better hurry, they'll be clearing away the sideboard any minute now. There's still some kidneys left."

Andrea's stomach knotted. Kidneys! Right at the moment she felt that she'd never want to eat again, but if she did want to eat, it would be a good Texas breakfast of steak and eggs. "I don't want anything, thanks."

"Another drink, then. You still look shaky. And no wonder, after a tumble like the one you took yesterday! Caprice is going to be fine, she's all bandaged and quite comfortable. Here, here, you aren't crying, are you? It was only an accident, it could have happened to anyone."

Especially if they were drunk, Andrea thought sickly. She had to get up and go into the bathroom to retch. When she came back, Reggie had another drink waiting for her.

"Here you go. This one will stay down," he promised her.

She drank it, shuddering, hating herself. She wished that it were poison. She was drinking too much, she'd been drinking too much ever since she'd come back from

Texas. It had become a way of life for her, and she knew it for what it was, a weakness. Kate and Adam would be appalled. She didn't like herself very much, either. But right now, this once more, she needed it, to help her over this rough spot of guilt that wouldn't stop gnawing at her. She'd nearly killed Caprice, and it was her fault because she'd been drunk.

The letter was from her mother and father, delayed en route so that it hadn't arrived until they had left for the country. It contained a check for a hundred pounds, not nearly as much as Adam would have liked to send but had refrained from sending because of Andrea's pride.

A hundred pounds! Nursing a dull hangover, Andrea turned the check over and over in her hands. Considering the present state of their bank account, it was a fortune. Which debt should she pay off first? Provided, of course, that Reggie wouldn't draw on it before she'd had a chance to pay off any of them!

She needed a drink, just a little one to help her think. The bottle of Scotch was nearly empty, but there was enough until she could get out to replace it. She'd buy another on her way back from depositing the check.

Her hand touched the bottle, and then withdrew. No! Damn it, no! She wasn't her grandfather, her mother's father who'd been a lush. What would Adam and Kate think of her if they could see her now? What would Grandfather Gaylord think, and Aunt Prudence and Naomi? More important, what did she think of herself?

Resolutely, she dressed and left the flat without touching the bottle. She'd get the check in the bank, and then she'd make up her mind what to do with the money, but not one cent of it was going to be spent on alcohol!

She never got to the bank. Halfway there, she got off the bus and took another one. Twenty minutes later she was in Mr. Smith's shop again.

"Mr. Smith, if you could come up with the money to pay next month's rent, and if you could find a partner who could get this place on its feet, what would you say?"

She was mad, but she wouldn't back off. She had a

very good idea that this was the lifeline that was going to save her from drowning, and she had to hang onto it with the last ounce of her strength.

The faded blue eyes looked at her through the steel-rimmed glasses that were nearly as smudged as his windowpanes. "Do you know someone who has that kind of money?"

"I have a little. And I can get more before we run out." Her father would advance all she needed. It would be a business loan, to be paid back at the prevailing rate of interest. "I'd have to be a full partner, of course."

"It would be a very bad investment. You would probably lose everything you put into it."

"Not if you'll give me my way in running it. Well, Mr. Smith?"

Mr. Smith took out his handkerchief, surprisingly immaculate, and dabbed at his eyes and nose. "God bless you," he said. "By this time next week, I would have been out of business, just another useless old man with nothing to do."

Andrea shuddered at the thought of what she would have been like in one more week, had she not determined to close the bottle and open her eyes to her own survival.

20

The explosion that evening when Andrea told Reggie what she'd done was even worse than she had expected.

"You've bought a half interest in a shop? What kind of a shop? How could you have been so crazy? What do you know about business? You've thrown our money away, that's what you've done! I bought those new tires today, on the strength of your father's check. Where's the money to come from now?"

"If you've already bought the tires, we'll have to pay for them. You'll just have to stop buying anything more for the Ghost, or for yourself, for that matter. Money is going to be much too tight for a while for either of us to spend on anything that isn't absolutely essential. But it will pay off, Reggie, I know it will! Mr. Smith is a genius at picking up genuine antiques."

"If your father will make you a loan, he'd have given you all you wanted outright and then there'd have been no danger of losing it. How did you dare do such a thing without consulting me? I'm your husband, I'm the one who should handle our affairs!"

It came out before she could stop herself. "And a sorry mess you've made of it! If I'm willing to work, to get us out of the hole your extravagance has got us into, you should be pleased instead of flying into a rage! If the venture succeeds, and I'm confident that it will, we'll be a good deal better off than we are now, we'll be able to afford some of those luxuries you think you can't live without!"

"How soon?" Reggie's voice held a tinge, just a tinge, of hopefulness.

"Not soon. A year, maybe, or two years, or even more. You don't build up a profitable business overnight, and there'll be the loan to repay."

"There's no need to repay it! Your father wouldn't dream of asking you to repay it!"

"And I wouldn't dream of accepting it unless I meant to repay it, every cent of it, with interest!"

"A shopkeeper, a common tradesman!" Reggie said. "I can't think what possessed you! Aunt Madeline will be horrified, and rightly so. I only hope that no word of it reaches the bank; I'd be humiliated. My wife in trade!"

"Reggie, this isn't the seventeenth or the eighteenth century, there's no disgrace in being in trade, as you put it. But there can be a profit, a very nice profit if it's gone about right."

"In a year, or two years!"

He turned his back on her in bed that night, after having had several drinks that did nothing to mitigate his displeasure. Andrea had to control her urge to give vent to an audible sigh of relief that she was to be spared his lovemaking. If only she didn't love Henry to the exclusion of all other men, she might have at least found relief from her tensions, and some degree of pleasure, in their marital relations, because Reggie was still attractive and when he set himself to it he could be charming. But there was Henry, and now that she was thoroughly disenchanted with Reggie, the thought of letting him or any other man touch her was repugnant to her. Not that she'd deny him, any time he wanted her. Wasn't there some old saying about having made your bed, now you must lie in it?

He didn't speak to her before he dragged himself off to work in the morning, nor did he eat the porridge and eggs she put on the table. Let him sulk, she thought. She didn't have time to coddle him any more. She ate her own breakfast, every mouthful, struggling to keep her mind off the bottle that Reggie had left on the counter. Then she bathed and dressed and for the first time in her life, she left to go to work.

The first thing she did on reaching the shop was to put a hand-lettered sign in the window. "Closed for alterations. Open soon under new management."

She worked harder in the following days than she'd ever worked in her life. With all the delicate things in the shop, she dared not hire a charwoman to help her with even the heaviest cleaning and scrubbing, and Mr. Smith had to be banished to his own living quarters over the premises because he himself was more like a bull in a china shop than a dealer in objets d'art. The floors were scrubbed until they were immaculate; every small pane in the old-world window gleamed. Every object that could be washed was washed, and her hands turned red and sore from the ammonia she used in the hottest water she could bear to give the glassware and crystal the shine that nothing else could achieve.

She was ruthless in her selection as to what should be saved for sale and what should go in the dustbin. "Mr. Smith, whatever made you stock this imitation cut glass? What possessed you to buy those silly carnival dolls?"

"I hoped to sell them. Expensive things, fine things, don't sell. At least, not here," Mr. Smith said, his face showing his frightened concern at the way she was throwing things away.

"They will now," Andrea promised him. And when she had finished, only about a third of the merchandise had been spared.

There was very little money left from the Christmas check but she plunged ahead and charged new display tables, new glass display shelves. She ordered an appallingly expensive rug for the floor, lengths and lengths of black velvet for the tables, which she draped in graceful folds. She returned to the flat every night exhausted, to face Reggie's sulking displeasure because she was making a charwoman of herself, because she wasn't providing him with decent meals, because she refused to part with an unnecessary penny for his whims.

"You don't have to drive the Ghost to work every day. Take the tram. Petrol is expensive. Everybody knows you own the Rolls. It isn't necessary to keep showing it off," she told him. "And you'd be better off without wine for lunch. You're drinking altogether too much as it is."

"I never knew you could be so hard! And speaking of drinking, you were doing plenty of it yourself just a short while ago, so you have no call to disapprove of mine. Every gentleman has a drink after dinner."

"Before, and during, and after," Andrea said tiredly. "Several after. It's your liver. I can't stop you from ruining it, but I'm darned if I'm going to pay for it when all that alcohol catches up with you!" Andrea's mouth was compressed. She hated herself when she was like this; she sounded like a shrew, but she was so tired she couldn't help it. There was only one good thing about those early days of preparation for reopening the shop. She was so tired that she went to bed as early as she could every night, and she slept, with no thought of having a drink, and she never woke up in the middle of the night to go and get one. A month ago, she'd have thought it was impossible; now she was simply too tired to care if she drank or not. It was rest and sleep she needed, not alcohol.

Adam's check, the exact amount she had asked for, arrived just when she didn't dare to charge another thing. The letter, signed by both Kate and Adam, expressed confidence in her and wished her all the luck in the world. And a few days later a letter from Naomi arrived, also expressing confidence in her and wishing her luck, and made her all the more determined to prove herself worthy of the blood that flowed in her veins.

Andrea and Naomi had corresponded sporadically ever since Andrea and Reggie had been married. Naomi was completely happy as the wife of the junior editor of a small-town newspaper. She and Kelvin had two children, a boy and a girl. Money, or its lack, seemed to have no place in Naomi's life. She was content with what she had, still so much in love with Kelvin that it glowed from the pages of her letters. If Andrea had been married to Henry rather than to Reggie, she could have lived in the meanest jacal and been as happy as her cousin. As it was, she had to have something else to fill her life; work, and enough money, she hoped, when the shop succeeded, to keep reasonable peace between her and Reggie.

She deposited the check, and as soon as it had had time to clear, she rousted Mr. Smith from his flat over the shop.

"Buy," she told him. "And remember, nothing but the best! Everything must be authentic, and unique of its kind."

Ned was nearly as doubtful of her enterprise as Reggie when he stopped in at the flat to see them a few days before Andrea was ready to open the shop for business. "A curio shop, Andrea? And one that was failing?"

"And antiques," Andrea corrected him. "Mr. Smith is a genius at ferreting out pieces that other dealers would never be able to find! He may not be much of a businessman, but he's a real genius in his field. Stop around at the shop next Friday and you'll see what I mean."

"Yes, stop around and see what's going to plunge us into bankruptcy!" Reggie's voice was sour. He'd already had more than he should have to drink, but he splashed another two fingers into his glass. It was going to be another of those nights, with Reggie at her because she was throwing away the money that Adam would have been glad to give her for their own personal use. Her knuckles whitened as she clenched her hands in her lap and fought down a sudden, overwhelming urge to have a few drinks herself. What if she failed, what if she was never able to pay Adam back, never able to get herself out of this bind?

Ned's concerned eyes on her face brought her back under control. "We're not going into bankruptcy," she said, her voice steady. "We may not become millionaires, but we're going to end up with a good, steady profit. Next Friday, Ned. You'll see our advertisement in the newspapers, if you use a magnifying glass."

He found it, not as small as Andrea had implied, but extremely conservative as befitted a fine shop. "Curios and antiques, only the finest and most rare. Smith and Wentworth, Hartwell Street, London." It was a good advertisement, he thought. Certainly it would attract only serious buyers.

At the moment that Ned was approving the advertisement, Andrea was surveying her business partner with dismay.

"No!" she said. "No, no, no! Take it off!"

Mr. Smith's face was a study in bewilderment. "But it's exactly right, it's exactly what I should wear now that we have such an elegant establishment!"

"It's wrong," Andrea said. Her heart ached for his disappointed bewilderment, but she had a sixth sense about these things. For Mr. Smith to appear in a morning coat and striped trousers wasn't at all the image of him that she wanted to project. He was the eccentric hunter, the genius sniffer-downer, a man so lost in his love for rare and costly objects that he cared nothing for his own appearance or what people might think of him. It was the role that suited him, and Andrea intended to play it up for all it was worth. The elegance, the graces, were her department. No prim black salesperson's dress for her, but the most chic of afternoon dresses that might have graced any drawing room in Mayfair. So exquisite, so chic, that they would shout of taste and money to indulge it through their sheer understatement. Like Kate, she would wear no jewels, both because she had no need of them and because they had no place in a business establishment unless they were in a display case. Like Kate, she would be the jewel, a jewel in a setting worthy of her.

She'd had to convince Mr. Smith that moving to a better location wasn't advisable. "Let them come to us!" she said. "And they will, Elias." She'd been calling him Eilas for weeks. She had become inordinately fond of him in the short time she'd known him. She had learned that the shop had been moderately successful while his wife had been alive, that she had taken care of display and sales. When she'd been carried off by pneumonia two years ago, Elias had been lost. He knew antiques and curios, but when it came to running the shop itself, he had been a total loss. Besides, without his beloved Helen, there had seemed little point in it. She had shared his love for the merchandise they had handled. With no wife to share it with, with no children, Elias's interest had waned to the dying point.

Andrea had changed all that. Her own love for the exquisite pieces, her boundless enthusiasm, had breathed new life into the bereft widower. His own enthusiasm had grown as he had watched, slightly befuddled but completely admiring, what Andrea was doing. Until now, on the morning they were to open, he had appeared in his newly purchased morning coat and striped trousers, beaming with pride and ready to give his all.

"Take it off," Andrea said again, a great deal more gently. "Just be yourself, Elias. That will impress our clients a whole lot more than imitating a Mayfair business tycoon."

"But my other suit isn't even pressed, I thought I'd be wearing this one!" Elias protested, blinking behind glasses that were incongruously smudged in contrast with all his elegance.

"All the better. You just putter around and look as if you were lost in some other world. Answer questions about origins and authenticity, but don't try to close a sale. You aren't interested in that. Do you see what I'm getting at?"

"I never was much interested in that," Elias said gloomily. "Why do you think I was ready to close my doors when you came into my life like a guardian angel?"

"Then let me go on being your guardian angel, and go and change into your nice rumpled suit," Andrea told him. "And don't you dare clean your glasses!"

A few minutes later, five minutes early for opening time, Ned stood in front of the shop window and wondered why he'd ever doubted that Andrea would make a whooping success of it.

There were only two items in the window, one of which was for sale, a slender bud vase, its lines so classically simple that just looking at it made Ned itch to buy it. It was placed slightly off center on a velvet-covered stand, and a gilt-framed mirror reflected its perfection and the perfection of the single red rose that it held. Ned's breath caught with awe.

He entered the shop, prepared now for what he would see, small groupings of objets d'art so beautifully arranged that anyone who observed them would picture them placed exactly like that in their own homes. There were no plate glass wall mirrors to distract potential purchasers by tempting them to study their own reflections. Everywhere he looked there was nothing but pure beauty, the most exquisite taste.

Andrea came toward him, both hands extended to take his, her face radiant with happiness at seeing him. "Ned! You did come! You're the first one to step over the threshold, and it's going to bring us luck, I know it is!"

"How much is that vase in the window?" Ned asked, his voice sounding just a shade strangled.

"You can't afford it. Send some of your wealthier friends!" Andrea laughed.

Ned blinked. Andrea's partner was puttering around a display at the back of the shop, his suit—a suit that could only be described as vintage—rumpled and not even as clean as it might have been. He was completely absorbed in his examination of a small figurine, so that he didn't even look up to acknowledge Ned's presence.

Andrea's voice was filled with mischief. "Ask him about the bud vase," she urged him.

Elias looked as if it took him a moment to come out of his absorption with the figurine. "The vase? Which vase? The one in the window? Yes, yes. Crystal. I unearthed it at the auction of the Dowager Countess of Argyle's personal belongings. It came from Italy over two hundred years ago. The price? Dear, dear, let me see. I'm afraid you'll have to ask my associate about that." He was immediately absorbed with the figurine again, an absorption that Ned perceived was entirely genuine. Dutifully, he returned to Andrea. He could not afford the vase. Perhaps if he dropped a hint in his father's ear, Lady Madeline might find it wrapped as her next birthday gift.

In spite of the uniqueness of Andrea's shop, progress was slow. Advertising was largely by word of mouth as one purchaser enthused to another about the most positively remarkable shop she'd yet discovered in London. The prices alone were steep enough to turn most prospective purchasers off. Andrea was not discouraged, she was only hard put to control her impatience to achieve the success she was sure would come.

The overhead was high. The landlord, seeing what the shop was now, raised the rent, and the pieces that Elias ferreted out to buy were dear. It wasn't in him to pretend that anything he was interested in was worth less than it should bring to the seller, and Andrea concurred in that. She herself wasn't interested in cheating people who for their own private reasons had to dispose of cherished family possessions. As she'd warned Reggie, it would take time.

It took her time, as well. There were not only the ordinary shop hours, but the hours she was obliged to spend after the doors were locked in cleaning and polishing and rearranging. Smith and Wentworth's proprietress could not be seen wielding a dustcloth during business hours; it would have destroyed the mystique.

Still, the profits were steady, if small, as word got around. But the profits also had to be equally divided between herself and Elias, and her half share didn't add up to much more than to help replace the stock and pay the rent. There was so little left over that Reggie's impatience, his disgust with her venture, steadily increased. He claimed—and Andrea admitted, ruefully, that he had a good deal of justice on his side—that she had no time left for him, that their social life had been nil ever since she had got the notion of being a shopkeeper in her head.

The fact that their debts were being paid off, that in another year they should be able to afford a larger flat, one in Mayfair again, meant nothing to Reggie. If he couldn't have it now, there was no point in it.

But Andrea loved the shop. She enjoyed every minute she spent in it, whether it was making a beautiful profit in selling a piece of rare china or an inlaid eighteenth-century snuffbox, or doing all the dusting and polishing that she couldn't trust to the char who came in to do the window and floors. Mr. Smith was an angel to work with. He left everything to her and he wasn't often in the shop at all, but out tracking down still more treasures. But the time always came when she had to lock the door behind her and go home, wondering what sort of mood Reggie would be in.

He'd been in a better mood for the last few weeks than he'd been in all winter. He hadn't even raised too much of a fuss when Andrea couldn't get away to spend weekends in the country, visiting Lady Madeline and Sir Robert. Once or twice he'd gone off without her, but then even that had stopped. If he was not at home some evenings when she got there after work, she didn't question him too closely when he did come in. He had to have some sort of a social life because he was that kind of a man, he'd always been gregarious, wanting other people around him. She supposed that he was seeing Owen Fitzgerald, going around to pubs with him where they could talk cars with other men who were automobile enthusiasts, from things he let drop across the breakfast table, and as long as she was too busy to have nights of her own out with him she certainly didn't begrudge him his pastime.

But there was the matter of the statement in the mail one evening when she came home to find that Reggie was out somewhere again. It pertained to repairs on the Ghost, and it came to forty-two pounds. Forty-two pounds! She had to ask him about that, ask him if it had been something absolutely vital.

He didn't get in until after midnight, and Andrea was too sleepy when she roused up just enough to glance at the bedside clock to see what time it was. She smelled liquor on his breath when he apologized for disturbing her. He and Owen must have made a night of it, it was after one in the morning.

She asked him in the morning, and she was struck speechless when he told her not to worry about it, that he'd take care of it himself. He even looked a little sheepish.

"I've been picking up a little extra work, doing accounts for private citizens," Reggie explained. "It's so bloody lonesome here with you working all hours, Dria. I thought I might as well put my extra time to use and pick up a bit in the process, so I wouldn't have to bother you for every little thing."

"But Reggie, that's wonderful!" she exclaimed.

Maybe he'd grown up a little at last. Reggie was pleased and he basked under her praise, wanting to make sure that she appreciated how good he was. "You're working so hard, I felt a bit guilty. I felt I wasn't doing my share, you know. So if I'm a bit late from now on you'll know what I'm about. Every little bit helps."

"It certainly does!" Andrea got up and walked around the table to kiss him. "I'm proud of you, Reggie."

It was nice to have something to be happy about. But the news from home, from Texas, wasn't good. Trouble was flaring up all over Mexico, just as her father and Wade had predicted before she'd come back to London. A man named Francisco Mandero had actually risen up to run against President Díaz, and the peons were solidly behind him. Their condition was so desperate that at last, after centuries of abuse, they were attempting to better their lot. In spite of the fact that at least eighty percent of them were illiterate, Mandero had rallied them to the cause.

But then, on June the tenth, Mandero had been arrested for sedition. He'd managed to escape and had taken refuge in Texas. Adam had seen him, listened to him speak, and Michael was enthusiastic about his cause and the political and agrarian reforms that he proposed. There had already been fighting in Mexico, and a man named Arango, the leader of a ring of cattle rustlers, was rallying more and more peons.

323

"Arango has a price on his head, so of course he has come out strongly for Mandero," Kate wrote. "He's changed his name and now calls himself Francisco Villa, after a former bandit who gained a good deal of notoriety. Many of the peons call him Pancho, and they're flocking to his call to fight for their rights. Michael is so stirred up that your father is having a hard time keeping him at home. Even so, he's disappeared several times, for days at a time, and he makes no secret of the fact that he's helping to run cattle from Mexican haciendas that have been raided, to the Texas border where they're sold to buy arms and ammunition. While Wade is sympathetic to the peons' cause, he disapproves of this outright stealing and he and Mike are at loggerheads.

"Outside of the dissension among your brothers, everything goes along here just as usual. Constanza and little Philip are well, and your father and I are never sick. How is your shop progressing? We will be glad to hear from you, although your father says that knowing you, you're probably already making great profits."

And her months of work were paying off, at last. Business at the shop had picked up so much that she'd begun to study the Flats to Let advertisements. Ned was good about driving her around. He had what he called "digs" in London, as he'd taken over nearly all of Sir Robert's business interests in town, a modest flat with a man to keep it in order and prepare such meals as he ate at home. Ned was the soul of patience, and she was glad of his help during her search because he knew more about good locations and what the price should be than she did.

She was thinking about these things as she relaxed with a cup of coffee in the little sitting room she'd contrived behind the shop, the alcove that Elias had spent so much time in before they'd gone into partnership. She had two comfortable upholstered chairs in there, and a gate-legged table and a bright rug on the floor and curtains at the one window. A gas plate accommodated the coffee pot, and when the shop was empty of customers, it was a delight to be able to rest and savor a cup of real American coffee.

The bell over the door jingled, a soft, melodious sound far removed from the nerve-grating bell that Elias had had there before she had taken over. She set down her cup and went out into the shop, and her face lighted up when she saw that it wasn't a customer, but Caroline.

"Caroline! How nice to see you! What are you doing in this neighborhood? Whatever it is, I'm glad you stopped by. Come on back and have some coffee, you look tired."

Caroline accepted her invitation gratefully even though she'd never acquired a taste for Andrea's version of coffee. "I am, rather. I've been shopping for Mort. His regular supplier was out of the canvas he needs and I had to search all over and I ended up just three blocks from here so I thought I'd pop in. Since you've become a business woman, I hardly ever see you any more."

"We'll make up for lost time as soon as Reggie and I find our new flat. I won't be working nights much after that; I'll soon be able to afford an assistant, so we'll be able to get together more often."

"You're doing well, then." Andrea could tell that Caroline was genuinely happy for her. There wasn't an envious bone in her friend's body. She was satisfied with her eccentric Mort, who was doing well enough himself to content her. "I don't know anyone who deserves it more, Dria. You've worked so hard!"

"And now I'm on the verge of cashing in on the fruits of my labor," Andrea said, her own contentment enveloping her. This wasn't the life she would have chosen for herself, running an exclusive antique shop in London, being tied to Reggie for all the rest of her life, but as long as she couldn't have Henry and Texas, then it was strictly up to her to make the best of what she could have.

She handed Caroline her coffee, and picked up her own. "To make it even better, Reggie's come around. He doesn't fight the idea of my being a shopkeeper any more, he's even taking on a little extra work himself, evenings, can you imagine? Doing private accounts. He doesn't earn much at it, I'm afraid, but it shows that he does have some ambition, after all. He's gone two or three nights a week when I get home, so his work must give satisfaction."

Caroline's face had stilled, taken on a tense, startled expression. Andrea stared at her, puzzled.

"Caroline, what is it? What did I say? Something's bothering you, so you might just as well tell me now because I'll dig it out of you."

"It's nothing, Dria." Caroline busied herself stirring her coffee, which didn't need stirring, and she didn't meet Andrea's eyes.

"Whatever it is, you can tell me! Is it Mort? You two aren't having trouble, are you? I always thought you were the happiest couple in London!"

"It isn't Mort, it's Reggie!" Caroline burst out. She looked as if she were about to cry. "Andrea, I've wanted to tell you, I just couldn't work up the courage, and I hate carrying tales. Besides, after you came back from Texas, I thought he'd broken off with her, that it was going to be all right. Only he isn't working those evenings he isn't home, Dria. He's seeing a woman."

Andrea's hand froze on the handle of her cup, and for a moment she didn't realize that she was about to snap it. She replaced the cup on its saucer very carefully, and it took an effort to make her fingers unclamp from the handle.

"Who is it?" Her voice was carefully controlled.

"Bea," Caroline whispered. "She was after him as soon as your ship sailed. She always wanted him, you know. She never forgave you for taking him away from her. They were together constantly all the time you were in America. I didn't even know it, until Mort happened to meet Owen one night a few weeks ago and let it drop. He had me fooled completely with that act of his, letting on that he was going to die of a broken heart if you didn't come back to him. And he did look dreadful. It was all his drinking, I suppose. And worrying that he'd lose out on all that money, if you didn't come back."

"But he must be working nights! He's bringing home extra money, he's paying for all those things he had done to the Rolls out of his own pocket!" Andrea's throat was tight. She found herself flexing the muscles in her fingers, still tense from clasping the handle of the coffee cup.

"She's quite well off, Dria. She's making pots, with her sculpture. Her studio is fabulous. She can afford to, well . . ."

"She's giving him money." Andrea's voice was flat. "That's what you can't bring yourself to say, isn't it? She's giving him money, and he's accepting it!"

Caroline didn't have to answer, the answer was there in her face.

"I hate being a tale-bearer!" she burst out again. "But you're my friend, you have the right to know. He's making a fool of you, Dria. And Bea's eating it up. I think I'd better go now, Mort's waiting for his canvas."

She rushed out of the shop and the bell over the door tinkled behind her. Andrea sat on where she was, staring at the wall in front of her chair, staring at nothing.

21

Reggie faced Andrea, and unlike his usual behavior when he'd been caught out, he didn't look in the least contrite or sheepish.

"What did you expect me to do while you lolled in the lap of luxury over there in Texas while I plodded away here in London without one extra shilling to rub against another? All right, I admit it. Bea came after me, and I didn't put up much resistance. I was sick of fish sandwiches and tea in our empty flat, sick of being alone. I enjoyed staying at Bea's studio flat. She's good company, she's lavish about her table, it was wonderful to go to the best restaurants again. You weren't exactly languishing away on your father's ranch, you know."

"And you not only warmed her bed, you let her pick up the tab for all this entertainment that kept you from being too lonesome without me."

"She can afford it, and she isn't parsimonious. She never gave it a second thought."

"And she's still picking up the tab, and slipping you a few extra quid on top of it." Andrea's voice was dangerously quiet. "All the time I've been working, struggling, driving myself into exhaustion to make things better for us, you've been providing Bea with male companionship and letting her pay you for the privilege! There's a word for men like you, Reggie. You're a gigolo. Or should I be a little less elegant in my language and call it by its right name? A male whore!"

Reggie's face flamed, but it was with anger, not with shame. "And why shouldn't I take what's offered? She's glad to pay me, if that's what you so crudely insist on calling it! She's a hell of a lot more fun to be with than you've been, ever since you decided that we had to live within our income! She has time for me, for one thing, and she respects me, for another. She respects me as a person, not as a money-grubbing little clerk in a bank! I don't see why you're raising such a fuss. I haven't asked you for a divorce, have I? Or even told you that I'm in love with Bea. I'm not, you know. I enjoy her company, she isn't all wrapped up in shillings and pence the way you are, she still enjoys the better things of life. And if she wants to share some of those things with me, you should be glad. After all, it takes some of the burden off your shoulders."

Andrea couldn't believe that he was saying these things. Her ears heard the words, but her mind refused to credit them.

She told him so, her face white with the fury that was consuming her.

"What kind of a marriage can we have, with you feeling perfectly free to indulge in extramarital affairs without the least shred of guilt? It isn't my idea of marriage, Reggie, and it never will be."

"You're letting your plebeian background show," Reggie told her contemptuously. "It's only what's done every day in the year. After all, I'm not demanding fidelity from you! If you want to find amusement with some other man, it's quite all right with me, as long as you keep it reasonably discreet and don't come up with a little bastard

329

to claim my name. There's no reason we shouldn't be civilized."

"There isn't any other man, and you know it! I've always been faithful to you." In the heat of her anger, Andrea discounted the fact that she'd been ready to ask for a divorce so that she could marry Henry, before she'd been tricked into believing that Reggie was mourning for her to the point of dying. She hadn't gone to bed with Henry, or with any other man. What Reggie had done was something entirely different. The fact that he hadn't done it for love, which would have been forgivable, made it all the worse.

Reggie laughed. "No? If you haven't, you're giving a reasonable facsimile of it, and with my own cousin Ned! You're seen everywhere with him, he hangs around your shop as if it were his second home, you buzz all around London with him in his car! You'd have a hard time convincing anybody that there isn't something in it, much less me! Of course, he's the one who'll inherit the title, as well as Sir Robert's estates, so I can hardly blame you for having second thoughts about settling for me!"

She couldn't stay here, continuing this shameful quarrel. There was no way to get past Reggie's defenses, his outrageous attacks. The walls of the flat were closing in on her; she couldn't breathe.

Reggie made no move to stop her when she left. He was already at the decanter, pouring himself a stiff drink. Wildly, she wondered whether he'd go to Bea after he'd had his drink, whether they'd laugh together over her naiveté. She had a very good idea that Bea had wanted her to learn about their affair, that Bea would relish Reggie's description of her reaction to it.

She didn't know how long she walked, only that it was for blocks. The pedestrians she passed on the streets looked at her strangely, and once a hack driver shouted at her to watch where she was going when she crossed directly in front of him without even realizing that she was doing it.

The near-accident brought her out of her daze. She didn't know where she was, she'd lost all sense of direction. She'd rushed out without her purse, without a hat or a wrap, and a fog was settling in. No wonder people were looking at her so strangely; she must look demented to them. She stopped, trying to locate herself, but the swirling mist made it seem as if she'd suddenly been dropped into the middle of a strange city on an alien planet.

There was another hack. Almost without thinking, she hailed it. The driver looked at her doubtfully, not sure that he wanted to pick her up. She didn't give him a chance to refuse, she simply scrambled inside and again without thinking gave him Ned's address. She didn't want to go back to her own flat; what if Reggie were still there? She couldn't bear to look at him, much less hear him go on defending himself and throwing completely unfounded accusations at her.

It took the driver some time to find the building. Andrea sat very still with her hands folded in her lap, trying to compose herself so that Ned wouldn't think that she'd gone suddenly mad when she appeared on his doorstep.

"Wait here," she told the hackman. She had no money, she'd have to ask Ned to pay him. The doorman looked at her warily before he recognized her. She'd been to Ned's flat two or three times, once to advise him on the color scheme for a redecorating project, once when he'd forgotten a list of flats that he was going to show her. The Honorable Edward Cavindish was not in. The doorman was certain of that.

"Then inform his man that I'm here." Andrea's voice was firm.

With an effort, she behaved as if it were the most natural thing in the world to ask Peters to pay off the cabbie and tell him that she would wait for his master to return.

As unusual as it was, especially since Edward Cavindish was such a conservative man, Peters admitted her and offered her a drink. She accepted it, not really wanting it but then drinking it off to quiet the chill that was making her tremble. It had turned cold along with the fog. Peters stirred up the coal fire in the grate. He was sorry, but he had no idea when his master would return;

he might be quite late, Peters had an idea that he'd gone to his club. Was Mrs. Mansfield quite sure that she didn't want him to summon a cab to take her home?

"I'll wait, thank you," Andrea said again.

Peters replenished her drink, respectful disapproval in every movement. Was there anything else he could bring her to make her comfortable? Would she like some biscuits to go with her brandy? Still disapproving, although the lady was the wife of Edward Cavindish's cousin, he left her and returned to his own domain off the kitchen.

Andrea sat with her head resting against the back of the wing chair in front of the fireplace. The brandy was warming her, she'd needed it. The shock of the scene she'd left behind her had chilled her as much as the wet, clinging fog. The new coal on the fire had warmed through and she rose to take the poker and strike it sharply so that it fell into smaller pieces. Blue flames crackled up between the coals, and she sat down again, her legs curled under her in the chair.

The effect of the warmth and the brandy, after she'd been so chilled, was soporific. Her battle with Reggie had exhausted her. Her eyes kept closing, and after the third or fourth time that they flew open to look at the clock, they closed again and stayed closed.

That was how Ned found her when he returned a little after ten. The doorman had told him that he had a visitor, but he was astonished to see that it was Andrea, so astonished that he spoke her name sharply. His voice woke her, and she looked at him half dazed, not remembering for a moment where she was or why she was here.

Then it all came flooding back and she was on her feet, her hands held out toward him in a childlike, pleading gesture that seemed to be begging him for help.

"I've had a row with Reggie. A bad row, Ned. Did you know that he's been having an affair with Beatrice Langton, that it's still going on?"

She was trembling again, her face too pale, her eyes too dark with the turmoil inside her. Ned stiffened,

332

and then took up the decanter of brandy and poured her another generous tot.

"Here, drink this. You look as if you need it."

The glass clattered against her teeth as she drank. She struggled for control. "Did you know?" she insisted.

"I've heard rumors," Ned said cautiously. "Naturally I didn't check them out."

"It's true. It's been going on for a long time, ever since my mother took me back to Texas to recuperate. She's keeping him, Ned! Oh, he still lives at home, he's been playing the part of the perfect, loving husband, I actually believed him, I thought that things were working out for us, and now this!"

She broke so suddenly that Ned was appalled. Her shoulders shook, and she was weeping wildly, stormily, all her pent-up frustration and disappointment bursting out at once.

He settled her in the wing chair again and urged her to finish her brandy. Then he went to the kitchen and told Peters that he wouldn't need him any more that evening, that he could take the rest of the night off and needn't return until morning. There was no telling how long it would take Andrea to regain control of herself, and it wouldn't do to have the family linen washed where even as discreet and loyal a servant as Peters might hear her voice raised in hysteria.

"I don't understand him, Ned. I just simply don't understand him!" Andrea cried when he returned to her. He pulled another chair up to the fire, so close that he could hold her hand. "He seems to think that it's perfectly all right! But it isn't all right, it can never be all right. Even if he broke with her now, even if he never resumed the affair, I could never feel the same about him. Not just because he's slept with another woman. I could forgive that. But the fact that he sees nothing wrong with it, that he has absolutely no shame at taking money from her, letting her subsidize all his foolish extravagances! There's something basically wrong with a man like that, and I can't cope with it. Do you understand what I'm talking about?"

"Of course I do." A muscle jerked in Ned's cheek. "He isn't the man for you, Dria. He never was. You deserve more than he could ever give you. Not money, but the fidelity, the love and cherishing that you're entitled to."

"I can't believe that I was so blind! I just can't believe it. If I hadn't been so wrapped up in making a sucess of the shop, I'd have suspected long ago and it wouldn't have been so much of a shock. I'm all in pieces. I'm sorry, but I am."

She began to cry again. Ned gave her more brandy. It was all he could think of to do.

"He said terrible things. He said that he wouldn't object if I had an affair. He said that everyone believes that I'm having an affair with you!"

"Stop it, Dria. He was just talking, you know how he is."

The anguish in Ned's voice made her stare at him. The brandy had taken effect, a great deal more effect than either she or Ned realized. She hadn't had anything to eat since the cup of coffee that she hadn't finished in the middle of the afternoon, when Caroline had told her about Reggie and Bea. Her eyes blurred so that Ned looked slightly out of focus.

"I shouldn't be here," she said. Was that her voice, so slurred? She knew that she shouldn't drink, she knew how close she had come to flushing her life down the drain after she'd returned to Reggie. "I had no right to barge in on you like this. If you'll call a cab, I'll go go home where I belong so you can get to bed."

But she didn't want to go home to the flat she shared with Reggie; it would never be home to her again. The measure of control she'd gained from the brandy crumbled and she turned an anguished face to Ned. "Ned, could you lend me some money so I can stay at a hotel tonight?"

"Nonsense. You can't go to a hotel in this state. You're still well known in London. The scandal would rock the whole city! Mother would be humiliated. I've a perfectly comfortable bed, the divan will do for me."

"I shouldn't. I don't know what I want to do! I can't seem to think. I'm sorry to be such a nuisance to you."

It was more than he could bear. He gathered her in his arms and let her cry; he brushed her tangled hair from her forehead; he kissed her temples. "You could never be a nuisance to me! You're my own darling Andrea, and who else should you come to when you're having trouble?"

Overcome by kindness, his genuine concern for her, Andrea's arms crept around his neck. His face was very close to hers, and she let her mouth touch the corner of his. She felt boneless, almost bloodless, except for her head. That was hurting. She didn't want to think any more, or feel any more.

"Take me to bed, Ned," she begged. "I want to go to bed."

He lifted her in his arms and she was limp in them. He carried her into his bedroom and deposited her in a chair while he turned down the spread and the sheets.

"There you are."

She tried to get to her feet, but she fell back into the chair again. Once again Ned picked her up, this time to lay her on the bed.

"My dress. I can't get my dress off and I'll have to wear it to get home tomorrow and it'll be all rumpled. Help me, Ned."

He helped her. His fingers trembled. He eased the dress off over her head. She managed her own shoes, but she got dizzy when she tried to remove her stockings and he had to do it for her. Dressed only in her petticoat and camisole, her arms went around his neck again.

"You're sweet, Ned. You're so sweet! Did I ever tell you how much I love you? I love you to pieces."

Ned's entire body was rigid with his overwhelming need for her. She was here, in his flat, in his bed, as he'd dreamed of her so many times, hating himself for dreaming it but helpless to stop himself. Looking down at her as she lay vulnerable, he fought the most difficult battle of his life. He could take her now. She'd been hurt, she was crying out for comfort, the comfort of the love he could give her. All he had to do was reach out and everything he wanted in life would be his. She wouldn't blame him tomorrow, when she had possession of her mind again. She wasn't that kind of a girl; she'd know that he'd taken her because he loved her; she'd understand. She might even turn to him again, cling to him now that her marriage to Reggie was on the rocks. Ned had seen it happen more than once; a void cried out to be filled, and proximity often turned into love.

There was only one hitch, and it was insurmountable. She'd feel dirty in the morning, dirty and cheap because that was the kind of girl she was. She wouldn't blame him, she'd blame herself. She might even think that she owed it to him to keep up the relationship for having let him think that she'd welcomed it! And he didn't want her that way. He wanted all of her, whole and untarnished and proud, given freely because she loved him.

"Go to sleep, Dria," he said. He drew the soft woolen blanket up around her shoulders and touched her cheek with his fingers. She was asleep before he went through to the living room and sat down in the chair she'd just vacated. He reached for the decanter of brandy, and then his hand fell away from it. Drinking wasn't going to do any good. One of them had to know what they were doing. He sat there staring into the dying fire, his face set, willing himself not to go back into the bedroom where Andrea lay sleeping, soft and warm and wanting comfort.

Andrea's first impression when she woke up in the morning was that her head was twice its normal size and that someone was pounding on it with a hammer to make it shrink back the way it belonged. She was nauseated and she had an uneasy feeling that it was a great deal later than she thought; she'd be late in opening the shop, she had to get up and get moving. She groped for the clock that she kept on the nightstand beside her bed, but her fingers couldn't find it. Her eyes were so blurred when she opened them to look for it that it took them a moment to focus and for her to realize that she wasn't in her own bed.

It came back to her then, in a rush that made her drop back onto the pillows and moan. Reggie, and Bea. She'd gone running to Ned. This was Ned's bed she was in, she'd stayed here all night. What would he think of her, imposing on him like this?

Ned heard her stirring, heard her agonizing little moan, and his head popped around the bedroom door. "The kettle's on the boil, I'll have tea for you in no time," he told her cheerfully. "And toast. Yes, definitely toast, dry toast. You don't look as if you could manage anything else."

"Ned, how can I apologize?" Andrea sat up again, realized that she was wearing nothing but her petticoat and camisole, and clutched at the sheet to cover herself. "I'll leave as soon as I get dressed. Oh!"

Her hand flew to her mouth as she struggled against retching. That would be the culmination of her humiliation at the way she'd behaved, to throw up all over Ned's bed after everything else she'd done!

Ned was beside her in an instant. "Here. Can you manage walking, or shall I carry you?"

She sagged against him, but she managed to keep on her feet while he supported her to the bathroom. The sounds of her retching humiliated her even further, but there was nothing she could do about it. The fumes of the brandy she'd consumed further sickened her. Unfortunately, she had nothing in her stomach to bring up after the brandy had been ejected. For a few minutes, she thought she was going to die. Only the thought of all the trouble it would cause Ned if she were to die here on his bathroom floor, only half dressed, enabled her to conquer her sickness.

White and shaking, she left the bathroom. Ned was waiting for her just outside, holding one of his robes. He held it while she thrust her arms through the sleeves, and he had to tie the belt because her still shaking fingers couldn't manage it.

"You'll feel better after you've had a cup of good,

hot tea," he assured her. "If you were anyone else I'd suggest another drink to settle your stomach, but I expect you might turn me down."

"Don't even mention it! I'll try the tea." Andrea's voice was as shaky as her hands, but she tried to laugh. "Oh, Ned, what a disaster I am! First I cry all over you, and now I'm sick! Whatever are you going to do with me?"

"Try to treat your hangover," Ned told her cheerfully. "What else should I do? Isn't that what friends are for?"

She thought she was going to bring up the first swallow of tea, but she managed to hold it down and then it was easier. She even nibbled at the slightly burned toast.

"Charcoal's good for what ails you," Ned assured her. "Settles your stomach. Feeling better now?"

She started, almost spilled the tea over Ned's robe when Peters appeared in the doorway. His face was correctly expressionless. "Would Mrs. Mansfield like more toast?"

"No, thank you, Peters. What we have will do admirably," Ned told him. Peters disappeared again as Andrea turned a stricken face to him.

"Ned, what will he think? What must he think?" she strangled.

"Peters isn't paid to think, he's paid to do for me." Ned's cheerfulness irritated her. "Don't worry, Dria. He'll never breathe a word of this."

Andrea was already on her feet. "I'll dress now. Will you call a cab for me?"

"Of course not. We can't have a cabbie pick you up at my apartment at eight-thirty in the morning. I'll drive you home."

It was a beautiful day, one of those days that poets eulogize. The sky was a soft, dulcet blue, with a few small puffs of white cloud, and even the air was crystal clear, most remarkable for London. The pedestrians making their way to their places of employment looked cheerful, their steps brisk. Andrea leaned back in Ned's little Austin and closed her eyes against all that beauty and cheerfulness.

"Ned, what shall I say to him?"

"That depends on you, doesn't it? On what you want. You either forgive him and accept him as he is, or you ask for your freedom." Ned fought to control his voice, but his knuckles were white on the steering wheel.

"Then I ask him for my freedom." She had, Andrea realized with surprise, already decided that before she'd asked Ned. Reggie would never change, and she would never be able to settle for what he had to offer, half a life, half a husband, and no self-respect.

"Do you want me to come up with you, for moral support if nothing else?"

"No, Ned. This is something I have to do myself. I'll thank you some other time for all you've already done for me."

The flat was empty, but there was ample evidence that Reggie had spent at least an hour or two there last night after she'd left. An empty, stained glass lay overturned beside the sofa, and the ashtray was overflowing. The room smelled stale; it looked as dismal as she felt, as if it somehow knew that things were never going to be the same again, that her marriage was at an end.

She opened the windows to air it out, and then bathed and changed. There was still the shop to see to; Elias would be worried.

Somehow she got through the day. She locked up promptly at closing time, denying herself the wishful wanting to stay on as she so often did just in order to delay the confrontation that lay ahead of her.

Reggie was at home and perfectly cheerful when she let herself into the flat. He'd even emptied the ashtray and carried his dirty glass to the kitchen. "You're early. No work tonight, for a change? Maybe we could have dinner out."

She stared at him as if she'd never seen him before. He bore no trace of the scene they'd had last night; he was choosing to act as if it had never happened. His face was boyish, open, filled with all the charm that had captivated her and swept her into her hasty marriage. Her throat felt tight.

"Reggie, stop it! I've come to a decision. I want a divorce."

His face changed so suddenly that he might not have been the same man. In all the years she'd known him, she'd never seen his expression so ugly.

"No. I won't hear of it."

"If you won't agree to an amicable settlement, then I'll have to fight for it."

"On what grounds? Infidelity? Don't be ludicrous. In the first place, you have no proof, and in the second place, you won't be able to get any! Word of mouth isn't evidence in a law court, Dria. And if you still want to try, it works both ways. If you charge me with having an affair with Bea, then I'll bring a counter-charge, accusing you of your affair with Ned."

"You're mad! You're stark, raving out of your mind! My affair with Ned! You know it isn't true. Ned would never dream of having an affair with me, his cousin's wife! Besides, he's all but engaged to Penelope Carruthers, you know that as well as I do!"

"But he isn't engaged to her, at least not formally, and even if he were, it would make no difference. Do you think that being engaged to someone suitable would stop any man from having an affair with the woman he can't have but whom he loves?"

For a moment Andrea was struck speechless. There was an acrid taste in her mouth.

"You're hallucinating! Ned and I are nothing more than friends; we never have been and we never will be."

Reggie's laughter turned her blood cold. "My cousin, my wonderful, perfect cousin! He wouldn't have any more compunction about betraying me than he would about stepping on an ant! My admirable, my sacrosanct cousin Edward Cavindish, the Honorable Edward Cavindish, heir to a baronetcy, rolling in luxury and money! He's always had everything, he's always had it all, so

340

why should he draw the line at having my wife as well?"

He hated Ned! It was all there, in his face, in his voice, in the vitriolic words that were pouring out of him. He was so jealous of Ned that it was a sickness in him, poisoning him! And she'd never known, she'd never even guessed!

"Andrea, don't be like this! I don't actually mind your having a little fling with Ned, as long as it amuses you. We must live and let live, mustn't we? And I really can't see why you're making such a fuss about Bea. You can't be so naive that you don't know that these things go on among all our friends. We aren't living in the dark ages. It isn't cause for divorce. After all, if Bea wishes to take a little of the financial pressure off us, she can well afford it. I needed the money, darling, but that doesn't mean that I don't still love you. I'd never divorce you for Bea, she's just an old friend, someone who keeps me amused when you're too busy for me, and you must admit that that's most of the time, lately. If you loved me, you'd want me to have some fun, you'd want me to have the things I want, as long as it doesn't take anything away from you!"

Andrea sat down because her knees had started to shake. She felt sick, much sicker than she'd felt this morning, only this was a worse kind of sickness, a sickness of the soul. Reggie actually didn't realize that he'd done anything wrong! Her weak, selfish, charming husband actually thought that she should accept the situation as it is, without protest!

"Come on, darling. Let's kiss and make up. I expect it isn't your fault that you were raised as a straight-laced American. You only need to grow up a little and see things in a more practical manner. Be a good girl and mix us some drinks, and we'll forget all about it."

Andrea got up from the sofa. Moving like a robot, she poured him a drink from the decanter, a good three fingers. She crossed the room to carry it to him. And then, very deliberately, she threw it in his face.

She left him gasping and spluttering with shock, and

as she had done the night before, she left the flat. Only this time, she remembered to take her hat and coat and purse.

Half an hour later she was in Ned's flat again, calm, composed, only the whiteness of her face testifying to the shock she'd undergone.

"He hates you, Ned. He hates you viciously. I felt I had to warn you. If I try to divorce him, he's going to strike at you. He had the audacity to say that you love me, that we're having an affair!"

Ned, too, was calm, but she could see a pulse throbbing in his temple.

"He's right, you know. Not about the affair, but in saying that I love you. I have ever since the first time I saw you, but it was already too late for me then, he already had you all wrapped up for himself. And I've loved you more every day I've lived since then. Divorce him! Let him do his worst. If he wants to make a fight of it, we can take whatever he throws at us. He can't hurt us, as long as we have each other."

Once again Andrea's legs threatened to go out from under her. She couldn't assimilate so much, so fast. "Ned, you don't know what you're saying! Think of what it would do to your mother, to your father, to say nothing of your own reputation. You'd be ruined! And there's Penelope."

"I love you," Ned said. "I love you and I want you and I don't give a damn about anything except getting you free from Reggie so that I can go on loving you and taking care of you all the rest of our lives."

She felt as if she wanted to cry, just to break down and cry for a very long time until she'd cried out all the bitterness, all the frustration that had been building up in her for months. Ned, dear dear Ned! How could she have been so blind, why hadn't she realized what she'd been doing to him all this time? She'd been completely selfish, so wrapped up in her own problems that she'd never given Ned a thought except to be grateful to him for his friendship, for all the help he'd always been ready to give her.

"I can't think now. Ned. Besides, I have things to do. I have to move out of the flat. I'll stay at the shop; the room behind it can be fixed up with a daybed perfectly well. There wouldn't be a bit of use in asking Reggie to move out, so it'll have to be me. After that, we'll see."

"I'll drive you. I'll go up with you while you pack your things, in case Reggie's there and wants to turn nasty."

"No. If he's there, he'd only pitch into you, and I don't want another scene tonight. I don't think I could take it. I'll stay at the shop tonight and collect what I need tomorrow after he's left for the bank."

"Let me take you to dinner, then," Ned urged. "You look rocky, Dria."

She shook her head. "Not tonight. I have tea and biscuits at the shop, and I'll stop somewhere and get a decent meal before I go there."

"You can stay here. Or at a hotel. I can't stand to think of you not being comfortable."

"Ned, if you'd ever spent nights rolled up in a blanket on the ground, where it gets so cold at night that your teeth chatter, you'd know that a night spent sleeping in a comfortable chair in my own shop poses no hardship! I've lived on dried jerky and coffee on hunting trips; I've gone without water when our canteens ran dry. I'm a Texan, one of those wild, uncivilized Texans, and you needn't worry about me at all."

"Tomorrow, then. I'll take you to dinner. We have to contact a good man to handle your divorce, and I think I know who to put in charge of it. I'll call him the first thing in the morning so we'll know something definitely by dinner time."

She let it go at that. Right now, she had to get out of here. Things were happening too fast; she couldn't take it in, she had to be alone so that she could think.

She let Ned kiss her. It was the first time he'd ever kissed her except for cousinly pecks on the cheek. His kiss was so sweet, so infinitely tender and yet so filled with fierce longing that she felt her heart would break.

343

Why did she always end up hurting the men who loved her, why wasn't she able to manage her life so that no one would be hurt, even herself?

She pulled away from his embrace as gently as she could. "Tomorrow, then," she agreed, because she knew that he wouldn't let her go until he was sure. "I'll be all right, Ned. Don't worry about me."

She had no idea of the lengths Reggie was prepared to go until a week later after she'd filed for the divorce and he'd been served with the papers. He came to the shop after Ned had brought her back from dinner and a play. Ned was determined to keep her cheerful, not to give her time to brood. His thoughtfulness, his tenderness, touched her deeply. If Reggie had inherited even a tenth of Ned's natural considerateness, they could have made a success of their marriage.

It was late when Reggie pounded on the shop door, nearly midnight. She was already in her nightgown and wrapper, ready to go to bed on the comfortable daybed she'd had delivered the day after she'd left him. Her hair was plaited for the night, hanging down over her shoulders and giving her the appearance of a girl still in her teens rather than a disillusioned married woman on the verge of divorce.

"Reggie, whatever is it, can't it wait until morning?" she asked when she unlocked the outer door.

Reggie's answer was to shoulder his way inside. He'd been drinking, but he wasn't drunk, the liquor had only put him in a belligerent mood.

"So you're going ahead with it!" he said, his voice so nasty that Andrea had a feeling of despair. He wasn't going to be reasonable. "I just came to advise you that it will accomplish nothing but to drag your name through the mud. Yes, and Ned's name, as well! You're not the only one who can hire a lawyer, you know. Bea's giving me enough to pay for the best, and there's enough evidence against you to make any judge throw your case out of court."

"What evidence? There is no evidence, because I've

344

had no affairs! I've been a faithful wife to you, and you know it!"

"Do you think anyone will believe that after my lawyer gets through with you? You've been seen with Ned, not just since you left me, but ever since you bought this damned shop!" Reggie swept his hand out in a furious gesture and a crystal bowl shattered against the wall from the force behind it. "You've been seen driving with him, looking for flats with him, you've spent the night with him at his digs!"

Andrea's face paled.

"That surprises you, doesn't it? Do you think I've been standing still while you prepared to scuttle me? Our investigator didn't have any trouble at all discovering that you spent the night with Ned! The doorman remembers you very well; he'll testify that you entered the building and didn't come out again! And Ned's man Peters will be called, and he'll be under oath. Oh, there's evidence enough, Andrea, evidence and to spare! Now are you going to come home where you belong and start behaving yourself?"

"Reggie, can't you realize that it's all over between us? There's no point in being vindictive."

"No point! I love you, you're trying to divorce me, and you say there's no point! What am I supposed to do, just sit back and let my cousin take you away from me without making any protest? Maybe you expect me to congratulate him! He's always had it all, and now he's taking you, as well!"

"That isn't true. We haven't had an affair, and I'm not planning to marry him. Go home, Reggie. I'm not even going to try to talk to you when you've been drinking."

Reggie's answer was to pick up an expensive porcelain figurine and hurl it against the wall, shattering it into a dozen pieces. "No divorce!" he shouted at her, his face red. He looked about twelve years old. The door slammed behind him, and Andrea leaned against it weakly after she'd relocked it. This man, this weak, selfish man, was her husband. She pitied him for what he was, for not being the man he could have been, but she couldn't go on being married to him. If she did, it would be the same as committing suicide, because she'd have no self-respect left.

TEXAS

22

Wade had arrived at Lajitas last night, just as the sun was going down. Now he squatted on his bootheels on the sand-duned island in the middle of the Rio Grande. He'd left the vaqueros he'd brought with him on the Texas side of the river. Cold-eyed and alert, they held their rifles in steady hands, trained on the islands, as they waited for their employer's son to transact his business.

Opposite Wade, the mustached revolutionist, the leader of the band that was equally alert and watchful on the Mexican side of the river, also squatted on his heels, his cruelly roweled Spanish spurs all but tearing a hole in his pantaloons. He'd stolen the boots and spurs, Wade surmised. The rest of his costume was typical of the Mexican peon, the loose, dirty white blouse, the drooping straw sombrero, the shapeless pantaloons.

A red bandana was laid out on the sand between them, weighted at the corners with stones. There was already a stack of gold coins in the center of the bandana, but the *bandido* was still not satisfied. Wade placed more coins on the stack and waited.

The *bandido* smiled, his white teeth startling against his darkly stubbled chin. *"Sí,"* he said. *"Gracias."*

"Por nada." Wade's voice was laden with ill-concealed sarcasm. He hadn't thought he'd have to pay so much for the steers that the bandit leader's men were holding on the other side of the river. Five hundred head, Don Felipe's own steers, a mere drop in the bucket to the three hundred and fifty thousand that had roamed and grazed on his huge holdings. Only five hundred head and all of them old, scrawny, well past their prime.

The bandit satisfied at last with the deal, stood up and gave a signal to his men. They started the small herd moving and pushed them into the river to swim and scramble across to the island. From the Texas side, Wade's men started across, to take over in getting the cattle the rest of the way. They weren't allowed to step on Mexican soil, and the bandits weren't allowed to cross over to Texas. This was the way it had to be done if it were to be done legally, under the watchful eyes of the rangers who were detailed to see that the letter of the law was kept. This island was neutral territory; beyond that, neither side could go.

How many such transactions took place even Wade couldn't be sure. Many of the dons had taken refuge in Texas, where their American friends were trying to salvage what they could of the huge herds they'd left behind them. But the pitifully few steers they managed to buy were as nothing compared to the prime cattle that were being driven across the river at other points, to be sold by the revolutionists in order to purchase guns and ammunition for their cause. Mike had been gone for three days now, and Wade knew that he'd gone down into Mexico to help in one of the raids that were stripping the great Mexican ranchers bare, cattle that would bring a high price when bought by Americans who had no compunctions about breaking the law as long as they could add to their herds below the market price. No amount of patrolling and policing was able to stop this illegal traffic in cattle; the border was long, and there simply weren't enough men to keep the situation under control.

Damn Mike, anyway! It was bad enough that he was breaking the law and stood a chance of being caught. What if he got himself killed in one of those raids? What would it do to Kate, to Adam? But there was no holding Mike back. His heart was with the revolutionists; he was determined to spend every ounce of his strength in aiding their cause. Adam couldn't have stopped him even if he'd tried. But being Adam, himself sympathetic to the desperate conditions that the peons were struggling against, he didn't forbid his younger son to do what he felt he must do.

Wade took off his Stetson and wiped the sweat from his forehead before he swung into his saddle. He'd done the best he could, but he was still seething because of the price he'd had to pay. He wondered what was left of Don Felipe's hacienda, if every piece of furniture in it had been carted off or wantonly destroyed, if it had been burned, hacked at, if it was occupied by hordes of men like these he had dealt with today; mutilated, rendered filthy, every mutilation and every act of destruction calculated as the peons struck back at their hated overlords in the only way they knew.

It was a long way home, and they had better get started. Constanza would be worried; she always worried, even though she knew that there was virtually no risk in these legitimate deals. Thank God that their children, little Philip and Consuela, their infant daughter, the image of Constanza, would never be caught in a revolution, that they were American citizens, born in Texas, that their heritage would be right here. Consuela was only two months old, but the thought of her being thirteen, fourteen, fifteen, the thought of her being the wife or daughter of one of the fabulously wealthy dons and falling into the revolutionists' hands turned his blood cold. At the very least they would be stripped of their heritage and fortunes, at the worst . . .

"Let's keep them moving," he told Pedro, the senior

vaquero. "It's going to be hot, we'll have to keep a slow pace."

"Sí, Señor Wade." Pedro touched the brim of his sombrero. There was no servility either in his gesture or in his voice. Pedro was his own man. If he hadn't come to Texas years ago, if he hadn't worked his way up to a position of importance and authority at Trail's End, he'd be one of those men back there who were already cantering away with their pockets jingling with the gold coins that Wade had left behind him.

Sighing, Wade settled himself for the long, gruelling drive back to the ranch, trying to project himself into the future when he'd arrive to find Constanza's welcome more than reward enough for this thankless task.

They swooped down on the hacienda, whooping and firing their rifles. There were nineteen of them—twenty, counting Lupe. Mike looked over his shoulder to make sure that Lupe was keeping well to the back, as he'd ordered her.

He didn't like it, that she'd insisted on coming along on this raid. He'd done his best to argue her out of it. He'd even ordered her to stay behind, and he'd thought she'd listened to him, that she'd realized how impossible it was for a girl to take part in such dangerous business. But there she'd come, popping up when they'd almost reached the border. The little devil must have more Indian than Spanish in her, he thought, to have tracked him so successfully without once letting him catch a glimpse of her.

At first he'd thought that she was a boy. She'd borrowed some of her brother's clothes that he'd left behind when he'd gone to fight for Mexico's freedom. Jesus was younger than she was, but because she was a girl she wasn't any bigger than he was, so the fit was reasonably good, if Mexican peon clothes could ever be thought of as fitting in any reasonable sense of the word. Her hair was braided and pinned up under her sombrero, and her feet were in a huaraches that were worn by both men and women. Even the lushness of her breasts, those breasts that drove him almost out of his mind trying to keep his thoughts and his hands off them, were hidden by the shapeless overblouse.

She refused to go back. Jesus was with the revolutionists. He was only fifteen, but he'd crept away from the settlement in the night two months ago, to go and fight for his suffering people. Her grandfather's heart was broken. If Jesus died for a lost cause, if the peons didn't win this revolution against their masters, it would kill Manuel. He was too old, already too broken by his own years of serfdom and by seeing his son and his daughter-in-law die, to survive more tragedy. If Jesus could help the cause, if Mike could fight for it, then so could she.

Mike had no time to think about Lupe any more; they were already bearing down on the *casa*. Lupe was hanging back, just as he'd ordered her, one of his own two Colt forty-fives in her hand. She wasn't to participate in any actual fighting unless it became certain that the fight was going against them.

Only sporadic gunfire was returned from the deeply embrasured windows of the adobe *casa*. Most of the workers would have run away long since to join the cause; only the family, if they hadn't already taken refuge in Mexico City or Texas, and a few exceptionally faithful retainers would still be here. And they wouldn't put up any more than a token resistance; a man would have to be a fool to get himself killed for an overlord who'd scurried for safety.

Just as he'd thought, a white rag on a stick was thrust out through one of the windows. Mike held up his hand. "Let them come out," he ordered. It didn't occur to him to wonder at the way these men accepted his leadership without question. El Gringo was smart, he could read and write, he could plan raids and attacks better than they could, and as long as he was fighting on their side, then it wasn't in their province to question El Dios who had sent him to lead them. They'd even accepted Lupe's presence, and no man had made a move toward her even after they'd all seen that she was young

353

and beautiful, a luscious armful. She was El Gringo's woman, she was sacrosanct just as long as El Gringo lived and led them.

They came out, their hands held high. There were only four of them, and one of them was a fat woman approaching middle years. The cook, without a doubt, because she wasn't well dressed enough to have been a ladies' maid or even a housemaid. This had been the easiest raid yet. The last time, there'd been a battle. They'd had to lay siege to the house for twenty-four hours before the defenders had decided to give up, and that not before one of his men had been killed and two wounded and two of the defenders had lost their lives.

One of his *bandidos* whistled through his teeth, a wide grin stretching from ear to ear. "The woman's mine, I saw her first!" he said. "She's old, but not too old!"

"That can wait," Mike said curtly. "I want them questioned, we have to find out if there are any cattle left, if there are any more armed men around. Even then, if the lady objects, leave her alone. She's a peon like you; we aren't warring against our own kind."

His men liked that kind of talk, it showed that El Gringo was a leader, that his heart was with their cause. Besides, maybe the fat *vieja* wouldn't object. Weren't they handsome and lusty, wouldn't any such old fat one be happy to oblige them? It was her patriotic duty, and besides they'd show her a better time than she'd had in many years.

They knew their jobs, and they went about them efficiently. The questioning went well. Vaqueros? Two or three, no more; maybe they'd already run away, or joined the revolutionists. There were steers, *sí*. Many steers. This *rancho* hadn't been raided before, it was not one of the *ranchos grandes* that other patriots were raiding. There was food, *sí*. Not much but some; the heroes were welcome to it.

The bandits swarmed into the barns and sheds. The machinery and farm tools were dragged out to sit in the weather, to rust, whatever was left of them after

354

rough dismantling and sabotage. The poultry in the kitchen yard was chased down amid racuous squawking and flying feathers, their necks wrung, their bodies flying off while brown hands still held onto their heads. The *casa* was searched, and clothing was dragged from chests and closets, blankets from beds. Mattresses were slashed, mirrors were smashed, any object of value that had been left behind when the don and his *señora* had fled was confiscated if it was small enough to carry, ruined or destroyed if it was not.

The *vieja* made no objections to helping them to prepare the slaughtered hens and roosters. Wine was brought out, much wine that the don hadn't had the time or the inclination to carry with him. It was good wine, and after all, wine doesn't travel well—jolting in a cart or wagon ruins it so that it has to be transported most carefully.

The whole project took a remarkably short time. Their bellies full, their spirits high because of the wine they had drunk, the larger body of the bandits rode off to round up all the cattle they could find, leaving only two behind to fire the *casa* and catch up with them later. Lupe's cheeks were flushed with excitement, her eyes shining, even though the destruction of so many beautiful things filled her with sadness. But one thing of beauty even now nestled in the hollow between her breasts, a locket that had been overlooked when the *casa*'s owners had left. It was gold, with seed pearls in the shape of a cross on the front and space for a picture inside. The picture was of a baby, its round eyes trusting as it looked back at Mike and Lupe when she opened the clasp.

"I'll take it out for you," Mike told her.

"No, leave it there. A baby is not our enemy, I like it," Lupe protested. "Michael, is it always this easy?"

Mike loved the way she said his name. She made the common, ordinary syllables into something beautiful, something special that was for him alone. He couldn't stand loving her the way he did without being married to her much longer. As soon as they got back from this raid, he was going to break down this stubbornness of hers and make her say yes. Her argument that she couldn't leave her grandfather didn't hold water. Manuel was too old to be working for the mining company, anyway. Adam would find a place for him at the ranch if he was too proud simply to live with Mike and Lupe. Or Kate would put him to tending her gardens; he could putter at his own pace and still earn his wages and keep.

"Keep it, then. But some day soon it will have to be replaced with a picture of our own baby."

Lupe tucked the locket back between her breasts, her eyes downcast, her face flushing even more warmly. If they hadn't had all these men around them, Mike would have taken her in his arms right then and driven away the last of her reluctance. He had to have her; he'd never have a moment's peace until she belonged to him.

Three days later he was slumped in his saddle, relaxed, as they drove the herd of steers, no more than four hundred, toward the border. They'd cross the river at a different point than they had after the last raid; they always chose a different point, miles away from any they had used before. Mike knew the lay of the land as well as he knew the palm of his hand. He had to outguess the patrols, and he had perfect confidence in his ability to do it.

He looked up and smiled as Lupe began to hum. They were riding side by side, so close that their stirrups often touched. These days and nights had been torment. Sleeping in the open, there was no chance to try to make love to Lupe, to try to break down her resistance. They could have put their blankets at some distance from the others but Lupe was no *vieja,* like the cook from the *rancho* they had raided. The woman was traveling with them, bestowing her favors first on one and then on another of the raiders. She had no place to go, and the opportunity to be taken across the river where she could search for work seemed a godsend to her so that the price she had to pay was inconsequential. That was what confession was for; the *padre* would understand, he'd give her absolution and she'd pay the penances with a glad heart just as long as she was in Texas and never had to place herself in servitude to another don again.

The first shot caught them by surprise. They'd become careless; the scouts that Mike always sent branching out ahead of them had been too busy counting their profits to keep a careful watch.

In an instant, everything was confusion. The cattle bawled and broke into ungainly galloping, tossing their horns and kicking up clouds of dust as they panicked, their eyes rolling. Men were shouting and cursing, firing back at the patrol that had discovered them.

"Spread out, there's only a handful of them!" Mike shouted as he brought his plunging horse under control. "We can fight them off, don't run, damn it!"

Two or three of his men wheeled their horses and took off, intent only on saving their own skins. After all, they had not always been bandits, they were peasants; fighting against soldiers was new to them and far different from raiding a poorly defended hacienda. But the rest rallied to Mike's cry. The battle was short but vicious. Three of Díaz's soldiers were down, and one of Mike's men was killed and two others wounded, but only superficially. The soldiers were the ones to retreat in the face of the bandits' determined defense. After all, many of them were peons, too, conscripted against their will and with no heart for fighting their own people.

"Round up those steers, all you can find in a hurry!" Mike ordered. His left forearm had begun to smart and throb. He hadn't felt the bullet when it had creased him, he'd been too caught up in the excitement of the battle. Now he saw that blood was welling up from the crease, but it was nothing to worry about; within a week it would have healed and in the meantime Lupe would wrap a rag around it and it wouldn't hamper him.

"Lupe!" He looked around, trying to locate her. She'd had her orders; in case of trouble she was to stay back, just as he'd instructed her before their onslaught at the *rancho*. "Lupe, come here, it's safe now, they've gone."

357

The dust that had been roiled up made it difficult to see. He squinted through it and called again.

"Michael?" The voice was faint, off to the left. He wheeled his horse, and as the dust began to settle he found her.

She was lying on the ground, her head raised, her eyes filled with bewildered shock. Her shoulder was bleeding, her shapeless shirt soaked with blood. Mike's cry of horror strangled in his throat as he knelt beside her, his hands frantic as he tore the bottom half from her shirt and tried to stanch the flow.

"I'm all right, Michael. It doesn't hurt," Lupe whispered. He winced. The wound was a bad one. The bullet had gone straight through but the bleeding filled him with panic. He wadded the rag and applied pressure, knowing that he was hurting her in spite of her reassurances.

"I'm sorry. I did fall back, but . . ." She closed her eyes, her small white teeth biting into her lower lip.

The *vieja* was there, tearing ruthlessly at her voluminous skirt to supplement the bandages. Her fat face streamed with tears as she crooned to the beautiful *muchacha,* the Gringo Roja's sweetheart. *"Pobre* little one!" she crooned.

Lupe's eyes were open again and she even managed to smile when they managed to control the flow of blood, but her face was so white that it frightened Mike. He'd seen wounds like this before. With care and expert nursing there was a good chance, but out here in the middle of nowhere, with no doctor, no medical supplies, there was nothing they could do except to try to keep the wound from bleeding again.

"She can't go on, she must rest, the little one," the *vieja* told him. "Let the others go on with the cattle, I'll stay with you and care for her."

"No," Lupe said. Her voice was weak but filled with determination. "I can go on." Her fear was for Mike, fear that the patrol would come back, that they'd get reinforcements and return to hunt down the bandits, and Mike would certainly be killed if he was alone with only her and the old woman.

Mike was torn with indecision. Moving her would be dangerous, but she had to have care. If he could get her to Kate, she'd be all right. A town, a doctor, would be better, but from where they were Trail's End was closer.

They let her rest for an hour. They didn't dare delay any longer. And then Mike sent the *vieja* on with the others in spite of her voluble protests against leaving Lupe, and lifted Lupe into his own saddle so that he could cradle her against his chest and support her, and he struck out alone. Even carrying Lupe, his horse would make the border in less than half the time than it would take the slow moving herd, even allowing for rest periods. Jacko, short for Jumping Jack, was a strong animal. Mike had trained him himself and named him because of his prowess at bucking before he'd finally tamed him. He'd never been more grateful for the quality of horseflesh on his father's ranch than he was now.

"Tell me if you get too tired, or if you're in pain," he told her, his voice harsh with his suffering for her.

"I'm all right," Lupe insisted again. They had to get moving, it wasn't safe here, nothing must happen to Michael because of her.

Michael stopped three times before sundown, so that she could rest. The others had filled both his canteen and Lupe's from their own, but he drank none of the water. It was for Lupe; he could manage without it in spite of the dryness of the desert air that dehydrated men even in cool weather. Twice, he gave Jacko a mouthful from his hat. The river wasn't far ahead, and then the horse could drink his fill.

It was easier after dark. His sense of direction was infallible; it had always been, even when he'd been a boy. More than once, when they'd been youngsters and gone off by themselves, he'd had to lead other boys home.

"Are you all right? Do you need to rest?" Mike checked the padded, clumsy bandage again. The wound hadn't reopened, but Lupe's face felt clammy against his fingers and his heart constricted.

He wrapped the serape that one of his men had given him for Lupe more closely around her, but she still shivered, although she insisted that she wasn't cold. They could stop and he could build a fire to warm her, but that would be dangerous—the fire might be seen. In his arms in the saddle, Lupe willed herself not so shiver. Her shoulder throbbed, and the pain was so intense that she bit her lips raw to keep from moaning.

It was an hour or two before sunrise when Lupe woke from a half-conscious state and realized that her wound had reopened. She could feel the blood running down inside her blouse. It was bleeding too fast; she should tell Mike to stop so that he could tend it, let her rest lying down until the bleeding stopped. But now that they were close to the border the danger was intensified. There might be patrols, both Díaz's soldiers and his bands of *rurales,* that had been the terror of the peons for years with their cruelty, were keeping a close watch to prevent Mexican cattle from being driven illegally across the river. If they were caught, she had no doubt that Mike would be shot out of hand. And if they were seen, they would certainly be caught; there was no way that even Jacko could outrun them, as tired as he was and carrying double.

She sank her teeth into her lower lip and kept silent, letting Mike think that she was still asleep. Nothing must happen to Mike, she mustn't be the cause of his death. They must go on.

Unaware of what was happening to Lupe, Mike had much the same thoughts in his mind. He should stop and let her rest, but as long as she was sleeping it was probaby better to press on. The sooner he could get her across the border and find help for her, the better her chances would be. The first streaks of dawn were lightening the eastern horizon; with daylight their danger would increase. His face grim, every sense alert, he kept Jacko at a steady pace, praying that Lupe wouldn't wake up and be in pain.

It was when every object looked gray in the first half light that he felt dampness seep through his sleeve on the arm that supported his burden. Fear congealed his own blood, turning it to ice. He reined Jacko to a stop and dismounted, lifting Lupe to the ground and laying her flat. He stripped off his leather gloves and his hands felt numb with his fear as he lifted Lupe's blouse and saw that she was bleeding hard.

She opened her eyes as he ripped a strip from his own shirt to wad and press against the wound. Intent on what he was doing, he didn't realize that she was conscious until she whispered his name.

"Michael?"

"Yes, darling? Lie still. I'll have the bleeding stopped soon." His voice was rough with his fear. In the increasing light he saw that her face was colorless, even her lips were white.

"I love you."

His heart twisted. "I love you, too. Hang on, darling. Am I hurting you?"

"No. It doesn't hurt. Only hurry."

"You have to rest. It's all right, it isn't much farther now. There's no one around, we're safe."

She closed her eyes again. Under his hands, the bleeding was lessening; he thought that he had it stopped. "Rest, Lupe." He kissed her forehead, her closed eyes. She seemed to be sleeping again, her breath shallow. He squatted on his heels, his eyes searching in every direction, alert for the least movement, the tiniest puff of dust that would herald the approach of other riders. Sleep was good for sick or wounded people, Kate always said that. It was going to be all right. He'd let her rest for an hour, two hours, and then they'd go on. It wasn't much farther now to the border.

It was an hour later that he realized that Lupe wasn't sleeping any longer, that she was dead.

Mike started when Manuel's shadow fell over him and the old man spoke. They'd buried Lupe ten days ago and he still couldn't bear to be near anyone, he couldn't bear any human companionship. His face was gaunt, his eyes were sunken and dull, he felt as dead as Lupe was. She was dead, and he'd killed her because he'd let her go on the raid. He should have turned back and taken her back to her grandfather when he'd discovered that she was following him. Or better, taken her to Kate, told Kate to keep her at the ranch, not to let her out of her sight. But he'd wanted her with him, he'd known the danger and he'd discounted it because he'd wanted her with him, because he'd loved her so much that the idea of having her with him twenty-four hours a day had over-ridden his common sense.

She was dead, and he'd killed her, and he was dying of his grief and his guilt. Kate couldn't reach him, or Adam. He kept to himself, untouchable, wanting no one, wanting only solitude to flay himself, to either learn to bear his grief or to die of it.

"Señor Michael."

Mike looked up. He'd ridden out alone, as he did every day in order to insulate himself from the grating presence of other people. Now his horse was standing patiently, its reins dropped over its head as it foraged for the sparse mountain growth, as Mike sat leaning against a rock in the secret, memory-laden place where he had so often brought Lupe when they'd ridden out together from the settlement. He felt closest to her here, almost as though she were with him; he could almost imagine that if he remounted Jacko and rode to the settlement she would be there, waiting for him to bring her back here for an hour, for two hours, until his importunings became too dangerous for her and she would insist on returning home.

"Yes, Manuel?" Adam had brought Lupe's grandfather to Trail's End the same day that Michael had ridden in, his face a death mask, with Lupe's body in his arms. Manuel was to make his home there; he'd been given a small adobe cottage for his own, and when his grief had dulled, he would work in the gardens. He would always have a home, he would be welcome and know that he was earning his own way. When Jesus came back

362

. . . Adam would not hint at the possibility that Manuel's grandson might never come back . . . he, too, would live at Trail's End, be one of Adam's vaqueros.

"You grieve, Señor Michael."

Michael didn't answer him. He wished that Manuel would go away. How had the old man found him, managed to trail him here?

"I, too, grieve. Grief is no stranger to me." There was infinite sadness, infinite resignation, in the old man's voice. "But you blame yourself, and this is wrong. It was not your fault that Lupe was killed. She was afraid, Señor Michael. She was afraid to stay alone at the settlement with only the women to protect her. They watched, but they could not be with her always. And he was clever, and patient, and he would have found a way to get to her. For months, he had been closing in on her, ever closer. And so she feared, and that is why she followed you."

For a moment the words didn't penetrate Mike's consciousness. He heard them but they didn't register in his mind. When he spoke, his voice was sharp, filled with disbelief.

"What are you talking about? Who could Lupe have been afraid of? Everyone loved her, no one would hurt her!"

"She was afraid, Señor Michael. Because of the other time, when he found her alone away from the settlement, when he forced her. Always after that, he came and watched, and waited, and tried to find her alone again where no one could protect her. She was fifteen, Señor, when it happened. A child. She nearly died of the shame. Only I knew—she wouldn't let me tell anyone. If there had been a priest, he might have helped her, but there s no priest at the camp, so she bore her shame and her ear alone, and kept her secret."

Mike was on his feet now, his hands on the old nan's shoulders. He shook him, until he realized what e was doing and stopped, his hands dropping to his sides nd clenching. *"Who?"* he demanded, and his hazel eyes ad turned black. *"Who hurt her, Manuel?"*

"It was Señor Wayne Bradshaw, Señor Michael.

Much time ago, when we had first come to the settlement. This is why she would not agree to marry you; she was ashamed, she could not tell you of it for her shame. And this is why she followed you on this last raid, because Señor Bradshaw had come to the settlement again, he had watched her, and she was afraid to stay. So it isn't your fault that she is dead, Señor Michael. You flay yourself for no reason. I promised her, she made me swear by the Holy Virgin, that I would never speak of this to anyone, but now I have had to tell you because she would want you to know that it wasn't your fault that she died."

The old man squatted on his heels beside Mike, still holding the hackamore of the donkey he had borrowed from one of the ranch children to ride and find the young man who was being eaten up by his grief. It was not his place to take one of the horses without asking permission, and he had not wanted to explain where he was going, but a donkey was all right to take, they were only the pets of the niños.

"She cried in the night, Señor Michael. She cried softly, but I heard her. Her shame would not let her give herself to you, although she loved you. Give herself to you tainted, as the peon girls are given to other men to marry after the don or his overseers have done with her. She was not like those other girls, she had pride, she loved the Holy Mother. And always she was afraid."

He was no longer talking to Michael, because Michael was already on his horse, spurring it to a blind gallop. The wild, reckless Michael, who had still always been so gentle that he would never touch a spur to a horse! Manuel looked after him sadly, shaking his head, his shoulders bent from his years of labor, his gnarled hands hanging limp at his sides. Perhaps he should not have told the young señor, but he was suffering and Lupe would not have wanted him to suffer.

Mike wasn't thinking as much as he was feeling, a blind, white rage that told him that he must find Wayne, that he must beat him senseless, hurt him more than he'd hurt Lupe, exact payment for what he had done until Wayne was a senseless, battered and whimpering hulk

364

Any horseman not as skilled and experienced at riding the treacherous mountain trails would have met with disaster from the speed he exacted from Jacko. He paid no heed to the trail, his reflexes worked with no conscious direction from his mind.

Wayne Bradshaw! That handsome, arrogant bastard who'd chased every skirt in the Chinatis, who'd caught more than his share and fed his ego on his mastery of them! He'd caught Lupe, forced her, raped her when she'd been no more than a child! Because of him, because of her fear of him, Lupe was dead.

His rage drove him on, blind, unthinking. When he saw the other horseman approaching, going up to the settlement, his mind was so blanked out with his hate that he nearly let Wayne pass by without recognizing him.

Wayne was in a good humor. He whistled as he rode, his broad-brimmed hat pushed back on his head to reveal his curly black hair, his dark eyes gleaming with anticipation. It was too bad that Lupe had got herself killed, chasing off after Mike Wentworth on one of those raids into Mexico. Crazy young bastard! How could a Wentworth, a member of the ruling class, be crazy enough to align himself with those revolting peons? It was a lost cause, anyway; Díaz's forces would crush the rebellion, crush the rebellion so thoroughly that they'd never dare to revolt again. That was the only way to handle them; crush them, force them back into the submission they owed their betters. Wade Wentworth, at least, knew which side of the fence he belonged on. He'd married one of them, but she was an aristocrat, and he was doing everything he could to salvage some of Don Felipe's assets. It was too bad that Michael didn't have as much sense.

His mood lightened again as he thought of Ruby, the peon girl who had finally, after weeks of coaxing, accepted the bauble he'd carried with him on every trip he made to the settlement, a cheap, gaudy bracelet with bangles on it, bits of colored glass that gleamed like jewels. She'd accepted it, delighted with it, and he knew that today she'd be looking for another bauble, and she'd be willing to pay for it in the coin that he wanted. She was only afraid that her father or her brothers would catch her. Not that they could do anything about it if they did; when a girl was ripe, it was time for the picking and he was Wayne Bradshaw, they wouldn't dare make a fuss, and even if they did who in authority would listen to them? A peon girl counted for nothing; it was only to be expected that the Bradshaws of the world would take what they wanted from them.

He'd made a mistake with Lupe. He shouldn't have forced her, she'd been too young, but she'd been so beautiful when he'd come on her as she'd been inspecting the snare she'd set for rabbits that he'd lost his head. He'd promised her anything she wanted, a red dress, a lace shawl, money.

But Lupe had only run away afterward, crying, her face filled with terror and revulsion, and he'd never been able to get close to her since. If he'd handled it right, if he'd had a little more patience, he'd have had her for as long as he wanted her, and it would have been well worth the patience because she'd grown even lovelier so that his loins ached every time he'd got a glimpse of her. What a waste it was that she was dead!

But still, Mike Wentworth had all but wrapped her up, and as long as Mike had his eye on her, it would have been more risky than it was worth to go on persuing her, anyway. And now there was Ruby, not as pretty but pretty enough, and even more lush of body.

He nodded to Mike as he clattered past him, wondering only vaguely why he was in such a tearing hurry. He was so wrapped up in his thoughts of the delight he'd take in Ruby's capitulation that he was startled when Mike reined his horse around and came pounding back up the track toward him.

"Wayne! Get off that horse!" Mike shouted, his voice strangled.

"What the hell! Mike, have you gone *loco*?"

It was all he had time to say. Mike left his own saddle and catapulted through the air and landed on him, his arms around him, to send both of them falling to the ground. Mike was beating him, smashing his face to pulp; he was blinded by the blood that ran into his eyes, and he knew that this was a fight for his life.

He fought back, blind instinct making him defend himself as Mike's fury exploded over him. But for all that he wouldn't have dreamed it possible, Mike was beating him, his fury giving him a raging strength that Wayne knew he couldn't overcome even though he was taller and heavier than his attacker.

With an almost superhuman effort, he threw Mike off and scrambled to his knees. Through his blood-blurred eyes he saw Mike tense to launch himself at him again, and again it was instinct that made his hand dart toward his holster.

His own fury-clouded vision cleared just enough for Mike to see what Wayne was doing. His reflex was so instantaneous that the sound of his own shot as he drew and fired surprised him. There were two reports in the still mountain air, but only one man fell; the other shot went wild, ricocheting off a rock.

Manuel, guiding his donkey in a plodding, careful descent, heard the gunshots and tried to kick the donkey into a faster pace, his heart beating painfully against his chest.

He came on the man sprawled face down in the trail, in another few moments. Manuel's breath came out in a deep, grateful sigh of relief. He couldn't see the man's face yet, but the horse that was standing nearby, having run only a short distance after the shots, wasn't Jacko.

Manuel dismounted, his movements slow because of the arthritis that racked his body. He turned Wayne Bradshaw over, put his gnarled hand over his heart, and laid his ear to his chest. There was blood, a great deal of blood, from a shoulder wound, but Señor Wayne was still breathing and there was still a faint heartbeat.

It took Manuel a long time to lift Wayne's inert body to his horse and arrange it face down over the saddle and secure it with Wayne's riata so that it wouldn't shift or slide off during the long trip down. Then, riding the donkey and leading the burdened horse, he turned their faces toward Trail's End. He should take Señor Wayne to his own ranch, but Trail's End was closer, and he didn't think that he had too long to get there before it would be too late. If it hadn't been for his memory of Lupe, he would have left her betrayer there to die, but Lupe wouldn't want Michael to be a murderer, not even in revenge for her.

ENGLAND

23

Andrea's heart was heavy as she left her lawyer's office. Her conference with him had brought out one thing clearly; if Reggie refused to consent to a divorce and Andrea persisted in filing, she didn't have a case.

"Mrs. Mansfield, all your husband has to do is tell the judge that he's willing to let bygones be bygones, that he's forgiven you for your own infidelities and wants you to come back to him. The testimony of the doorman at Mr. Cavindish's block of flats will be ruinous, to say nothing of the forced testimony of his man Peters. Peters will have to testify that he left you alone in the flat with Mr. Cavindish, and that you were still there, in his employer's bed, when he returned the next morning. You've been flat-hunting with Mr. Cavindish; how can we prove that the flat he's been helping you search for wasn't intended as a love nest? Your husband knew nothing of your search, and that alone will weigh heavily against you. My advice is not to bring suit, because you haven't a prayer of winning."

She knew that the lawyer was right. As long as Reggie acted the contrite and forgiving husband a divorce would not be granted. Nevertheless, she had no intention of returning to Reggie. She could not and would not go on living with him. With her lips compressed but her chin set firmly, she took a cab to the flat and instructed the driver to wait. She had to pick up the rest of her clothes. Outside of that, Reggie was welcome to everything the flat held; she wanted no reminders of her life with him, even if there had been space for anything more in the room she was now living in at the shop.

The condition of the flat was appalling. Reggie had always been meticulous about his own personal appearance and apparel, but outside of that, it never occurred to him to pick up a towel he'd dropped on the bathroom floor or to gather up the newspapers he scattered around or to do anything else that could even faintly be thought of as servants' work. There were dirty dishes on the kitchen table, crusted over with food, half a dozen dirty glasses were on various pieces of furniture in the living room, the bed was unmade, the drawers of the chest left pulled out. Every surface she touched was thick with London's grimy dust.

Andrea's mouth curled. It would seem that Bea's generosity didn't extend to paying Reggie's charwoman and that he had no intention of paying her out of his own pocket.

It took her only a few moments to pack. The flat depressed her; she felt that if she didn't get out of it and into the fresh air she'd suffocate.

The cab driver helped her carry her bags down. "Bit of a mess, isn't it?" he asked cheerfully.

"You could say that," Andrea agreed. She didn't offer any explanations. Let the man draw his own conclusions; there was no point in adding details to the story he'd probably tell his wife when he went home for his tea.

Elias was minding the shop when she arrived. He clucked when he saw her baggage. "You've definitely moved out, then," he said. She'd had to tell him that she was leaving Reggie, even though she hadn't filled him in on any of the details. "What did the lawyer have to say, Andrea?"

"No divorce. He says I couldn't win."

"But you're leaving him anyway."

"Yes, I am." Amazingly, a dimple appeared at the corner of her mouth and her eyes sparked with humor. "How do you feel about having a notorious woman as your partner, Elias? Do you want to bring our association to a close?"

Elias regarded her gravely. He saw no humor in the situation, but his own eyes were filled with sympathy. "I'm sorry you're having so much trouble. Of course I don't want to dissolve the partnership. It means everything to me, not only that we're making a profit but the knowledge that I'm no longer a failure that I don't have to join all the other old men on the scrap heap. I don't fancy myself sitting in the park on fine days, playing checkers with another has-been."

Andrea's smile disappeared. On impulse, she threw her arms around him and hugged him. "Elias, you're a jewel! I don't know what I'd do without you, either. It is a bit of luck that we have the shop, isn't it? Else I'd feel like I was on the scrap heap, too." She broke off, her eyes widening. "What have you done to that display!"

"I thought the ormulu clock would look nice with the shepherdess and the cloisonné box," Elias said meekly.

"No! You're a wonderful partner, Elias, as long as you stick to unearthing things for us to sell, but please don't go moving things around." The offending clock, a beautiful piece in itself, was removed to one of the display cases, and Andrea's simple arrangement of shepherdess, cloisonné box, and one Queen Anne candlestick was restored, one of Andrea's arrangements that sold so much of their goods when prospective buyers wanted to move them intact to their own homes. "What have you done with that small Oriental rug you brought in yesterday?"

"It's in the back. I put it on the floor beside your daybed," Elias confessed sheepishly.

Andrea started to protest and then held it back. The

dear man had never noticed that the rug was filthy, so filthy that it was a miracle that he'd detected its worth. It would have to be sent to be cleaned, and then she'd meant to hang it on the wall behind another display where it would set off the lacquered Chinese chest with one jeweled Buddha on it. Now she'd have to forego the fabulous price she could have got for it. Elias wanted her to have it; he'd been concerned because she had no rug on the floor of her living quarters. She couldn't hurt his feelings by pointing out the dollars and cents value of it.

Ned picked her up that evening after she'd locked up the shop. "How did your conference with the lawyer turn out?" he asked her immediately, his plain, kind face filled with concern.

"Not well," Andrea told him. "I have no case, I haven't a prayer of getting my freedom as long as Reggie doesn't want the divorce. I guess that's that, Ned. So I've simply moved out."

"But you can't live here at the shop while Reggie makes up his mind that you aren't going back to him! We'll find you a decent place, Dria. I don't want you here in any case, where Reggie can come bothering you after hours when no one's here."

Andrea considered what he'd said. She supposed that he was right. She wanted no repetition of the scene Reggie had made at the shop only three nights ago. She could refuse to unlock the door, but he could and probably would cause a disturbance by pounding on it and demanding entrance, and if there was anything she wanted to avoid, it was more notoriety. The newspapers, the ones that she thought of as scandal sheets, would make a field day of it. Mrs. Reggie Mansfield, the former Miss Andrea Wentworth of Texas, U.S.A. . . It hadn't been so long since she'd been the madcap heiress that the public would have forgotten. The thought sickened her.

They had dinner at a Chinese restaurant that featured Cantonese cuisine. Andrea's dimples came into play when Reggie told her where they were going.

"We'll have to make sure to read our fortune

cookies!" she told him. "Maybe they'll give us a hint of what's in our futures."

Ned's answer was to take her in his arms and kiss her. "I know what's in our futures, darling. We're going to be married and live happily ever after. It just might take a while longer than I'd hoped, until Reggie's convinced that holding out will gain him nothing."

Andrea felt guilty as she returned his kiss with a great deal more fondness than love. Because of her fondness for him, she gave him no inkling that she was almost glad of the delay. She needed a great deal more time to think. It would be only too easy to let herself marry Ned just because they got on together so well and enjoyed so many of the same things. She had never been meant to live alone. She needed a man, and a man she could look up to and respect, as well as one to share her bed.

There was no use in thinking about Henry; even if she could be free tomorrow, and go home to Texas, that part of her life was over. If she were to have any kind of a life at all, she would have to remarry, but the thought of marrying Ned when she knew that she didn't love him as he deserved to be loved seemed cheap and shoddy to her, because she'd be cheating him even if he never realized that he was being cheated.

On the other hand, she didn't want to hurt him by refusing him. It would be better to let things drift for a while, to have time to make him realize that she wasn't the girl he wanted unless all of her love came with her. There was no point in trying to send him away now. She knew he wouldn't go, at least as long as he thought that she needed him. But eventually Ned, like Reggie, would have to give up, unless time proved to her that she could make him happy as well as bring herself as much contentment as it would ever be possible for her to have.

Business at the shop fell off so gradually that at first she didn't realize that there was anything unusual about the slump. All businesses went through periods when sales weren't good. But a month after her conference with the lawyer, as she went over the shop figures, she realized that their profits for the last thirty days were infinitesimal.

She frowned as she rechecked the figures. At this rate it wouldn't be long until they were forced out of business. Competition in the antique field was fierce; their shop was small and not in a fashionable section of town; their drawing card was its very unorthodox setting and her own flare for arranging the pieces that Elias uncovered. If the novelty had worn off, if people were beginning to shop at the larger, more fashionable shops, it was the beginning of the end.

It was Caroline who told her, over another cup of Andrea's American coffee in the back room, the real cause for the slump in their business.

"You don't read the tabloids, Dria, and neither does Mr. Cavindish, so he wouldn't know about it, either. I doubt that any of his associates would mention the things to him that those rotten little sheets are printing."

"What are they printing?" Somehow Andrea managed to keep her hand from shaking as she handed Caroline her cup.

"Things about your alleged affair with Edward Cavindish," Caroline told her grimly. "And Reggie's behind it, Dria. He told Mort so right out when Mort ran into him a couple of days ago. He's giving them those pieces to print, he's playing every inch the wronged husband in hopes that you'll be forced to go back to him. Maybe it's the twentieth century, but this is still England, and flagrant extramarital affairs are still beyond the pale among the kind of people who buy from you. It might be all right for a man, if he kept it discreet, but not for a woman, and especially not for an American woman who already has a reputation for wildness, every bit of which is being dredged up and reprinted from your old madcap-heiress days."

The corners of Andrea's mouth tightened. "Thank you for telling me, Caroline. I wondered what was causing business to fall off."

"Of course I had to tell you! You're my friend, and Reggie's being an absolute rotter. Mort told him so to his face, but he only laughed. He wanted me to run straight to you and tell you, that's why he told Mort what he's doing. He wants you to know that you can't win."

"We'll see about that!" Andrea said. Now that her first shock at Reggie's latest perfidy was wearing off, her fighting blood was up. "Even the yellow press is bound to consider Reggie's tidbits as stale, after a while, and I can hang on until that happens."

After Caroline had left, she went over the figures again. She could hang on, for quite a while, until either Reggie or the tabloids got tired of their game. It would mean staying on here at the shop—a flat was out of the question until business picked up again, but that was no hardship. She only hoped that Elias wouldn't notice the decline in their sales, but there was little risk of that; Elias never looked at the books. If things got really bad, she could always defer the payments on the loan her father had given her. Reggie was dealing with the Wentworths, not with some spineless and helpless little woman who would crumple at the first sign of trouble.

She didn't tell Ned about Caroline's visit or the news she'd brought when she had dinner with him that night. There was no use in burdening him with more of her troubles; he was already involved in a great deal more than she wished he was.

They dined at a new place, an Italian restaurant that was gaining in popularity. It was exactly the sort of place that Andrea would have been enthusiastic about when she and Reggie had first been married. The lighting was dim, candles stuck in the necks of well-dribbled wine bottles provided the illumination for the checkered-clothed tables, garish paper flowers festooned the walls, and the food was excellent. She knew that Ned had chosen it because he wanted to divert her mind from her troubles, and she did her best to eat enough of the too-heavy pasta so that he wouldn't realize that she had no appetite.

"I have another flat for you to look at," Ned told her as they waited for their dessert, a kind of ice cream called spumone. "It's a trifle large for your needs right now, but you'll be needing a large place eventually, if you decide you like it enough to want to keep it. I can take you around to see it tomorrow morning, if you can persuade Elias to look after the shop for a couple of hours."

"I don't think so, Ned." How was she going to put him off without his guessing that something was wrong? "There isn't that much hurry, and I'm awfully busy right now."

"But I hate to think of you living in that one small room! It makes me feel selfish, sleeping in my own comfortable digs."

Andrea forced a laugh. "That's foolish of you. I'm perfectly comfortable, and think how convenient it is not to have to get to work in the morning because I'm already there!"

Her last word broke off, almost choking her, when she saw Reggie enter the restaurant with Beatrice Langdon on his arm. Ned's back was toward the door, so he didn't realize that some quirk of fate had made Reggie choose this same restaurant tonight. She hoped that the candlelight was dim enough so that Reggie, who could have no idea that they were here, wouldn't notice them. As soon as he and Bea were shown to a table, she'd make some excuse to leave.

Her hope was short-lived. Reggie, with his singleness of purpose, was looking only for an empty table but like nearly every woman who has ever entered a public place, Bea's eyes were darting around the room to see if anyone she knew was there, to notice what the other women were wearing and whether or not their escorts looked interesting. Bea herself was dressed in turquoise, a sheath-like dress that was Grecian in style and that set off her enticingly proportioned body to perfection. Andrea, well aware of the worth of clothing, knew that the dress had cost a small fortune and knew by the same token that Beatrice's fortunes, unlike her own, were going very well.

She winced, realizing that it was too late to retreat, as Bea touched Reggie's arm and said something to him with a laugh that set Andrea's teeth on edge even though they were too far away for her to hear what the other girl said.

"Ned, Reggie and Beatrice Langdon just came in. They're coming over to our table." Andrea just had time to warn him before Reggie loomed over them with Bea, her hand still possessively on Reggie's arm, evaluating her just as accurately as she had evaluated the sculptress seconds ago.

Andrea's heart sank even farther when she saw that in spite of the earliness of the hour Reggie was the worse for drink. Not that it would have been apparent to the casual observer; Reggie had always held his liquor well, but she knew him well enough to recognize the signs, the slightly reddened eyes, the belligerent set to his chin.

"Mrs. Reginald Mansfield, I presume!" Reggie said, bowing in a sardonic manner, his words laced with sarcasm. "And in the company of my esteemed cousin, Edward Cavindish, the wife-stealer! I can't say that I care for your choice of company, my dear. Nor for Ned's, either. But then, birds of a feather. . ."

"Reggie, you're drunk. Why don't you go to your table and have something to eat?" Andrea kept her voice even. She even forced a semblance of a smile. If there was anything she didn't want, it was a public scene in a crowded restaurant.

"Sorry. I just lost my appetite, seeing you two flaunting your affair in the face of decent society!" The fact that he was here with his mistress apparently had no meaning to him. In Reggie's case, what was sauce for the goose was definitely not sauce for the gander, or the other way around, as it were.

Ned had risen to his feet. "We were just leaving," he told Reggie. "Good evening, Miss Langdon. Might I suggest that you try to persuade Reggie to make an early night of it?"

Reggie's face changed, became vicious, a viciousness that was reflected in his voice. "You aren't going anywhere with my wife! Andrea, I've had enough of this, you're coming home with me where you damned well belong!"

"You're making a spectacle of yourself!" Ned told him, his face white with anger. "Please step out of our way."

The next instant, Reggie struck him full force in the face with his doubled fist. And then his own rage exploded, and in another instant the two men were battling with no holds barred. Women screamed as tables were overturned, men rose to their feet expressing shock and outrage. Waiters came rushing to break up the melee, but not before Reggie's mouth was dripping blood and one of his eyes was blackened. Given equal odds, Reggie would have been able to give a better account of himself, but the amount he'd had to drink before coming to the restaurant had slowed his reflexes, put him at just enough of a disadvantage so that Ned could have beaten him into the ground if the waiters hadn't intervened, two of them holding each man's arms behind his back as they were propelled forcibly toward the door.

"You haven't heard the last of this! I'll bring suit against you for assault!" Reggie shouted, struggling against his captors like a madman. "Wife-stealer, cad!"

Incredulously, Andrea saw that Beatrice Langdon was enjoying the disgraceful episode, that her eyes gleamed with malice as she looked at her before she turned to hurry after her escort.

The head waiter spoke authoritatively to Bea. "Madam, I suggest that you take your escort away from the premises. And you, sir," he looked at Ned, "will please to remain inside the door until your adversary has gone. If there is any further disturbance we will be forced to call in the police, and neither of us wants that."

One of the waiters who had helped eject Reggie came back, nursing his shin where Reggie had kicked him. Ned was still white with fury, but he stood where he was, now that he had been released from restraint, his mouth a thin, hard line. "Andrea, I'm sorry that a thing like this had to happen. A public brawl!" His distaste for the situation was written all over him. "They'll be well away by now, and I think we had better leave. But one thing is certain, there's no way you can go back to your shop tonight. With Reggie in this mood, he's as likely to go there searching for you as not. I'll take you to a hotel."

"No, not a hotel." She'd have to give her name at a hotel, explain her lack of luggage. "I'll spend the night with Caroline and Mort." She was filled with despair as Ned paid the check and added a generous gratuity to atone for the disturbance. She might have been eighteen again, watching Henry Stockton and Wayne Bradshaw battle over her until they were both bloody and staggering on their feet, watching other fights break out between boys she was only casually interested in. Except for one thing . . . when she'd been eighteen, some perverse little demon inside her had enjoyed seeing boys fight over her, had reveled in the fact that she had such power over the opposite sex. Now she was sickened and filled with shame and self-hate.

"Don't feel so badly about it, Dria. Reggie was drunk, that's all. As soon as he's sobered up, he'll realize what a fool he made of himself. Maybe it will even serve to make him realize that it's all over between you."

Ned's voice was filled with a forced heartiness that Andrea knew he didn't feel. It wasn't all over, it never would be, because Reggie was Reggie and he wouldn't give up. He'd either force her to come back to him or make her life so miserable that it wouldn't be worth living. And not only her life, but Ned's as well.

Caroline was almost as upset as she was when Ned dropped her off at the Byrons'. "I feel partly responsible," she said, her voice filled with contrition. "I should have warned you what Reggie was like before you married him, Mort and I should both have warned you. Only we liked him, he was a lot of fun, you know how charming he could be. None of us, of that crowd, were angels in those days, and we hoped that marrying you would settle him down and everything would be all right."

"There's no use in exhuming the past love," Mort told her. "I feel as rotten about it as you do, but this affair tonight will blow over. Andrea, you need a drink, Caroline needs a drink, I need a drink. And then you'd better get off to bed, you look done in."

Mort was mistaken about its blowing over. In the morning the tabloids made a big thing of it. Screaming black headlines proclaimed to all of London that there had been a brawl in a restaurant, that Andrea Wentworth Mansfield's estranged husband and his cousin had attempted to kill each other over the beautiful American heiress.

Andrea had spent a sleepless night deciding that this couldn't go on, that for Ned's sake, if not her own, she had to put an end to it. Ned's career was being jeopardized, his chances for standing for parliament ruined, as well as any chance he might have of marrying Penelope Carruthers and enjoying a contented life once Andrea had left the scene.

The headlines only served to cement her resolution. If she stayed on in London and went on seeing Ned, his reputation would be in shreds, and not only he but Lady Madeline and Sir Robert would be hurt, as well as Penelope. As much as it galled her to admit defeat and run, she knew that this chapter of her life had come to a close, that it was time to cut her losses and go home. She couldn't stake other peoples' future happiness in a game where all the cards were stacked against her. There was no way she could justify staying on in London just because she needed Ned's strong arm to support her, taking from him and giving nothing in return.

Henry Stockton's face superimposed itself over Ned's in her mind, and she winced. Going home would mean seeing him again, and she didn't know whether she could bear it.

But that was in the future, and she'd find the strength to bear it when it came. Right now, she had to leave England as soon as possible, before she had entirely ruined several people's lives.

ROSELAWNS

24

Once Andrea had made up her mind to act, she moved fast. She brought her personal effects from the shop and moved in with Caroline and Mort. While Mort arranged passage for her, she advertised for a new partner for Elias. With the shop well known now, she had several applicants, and she chose a young middle-aged woman who had all of the qualities she was looking for: taste, a quiet elegance, and a sense of design. She had to come down in the price she asked for her half of the business, but it was worth it to get the right person, one who would be able to keep Elias's shop afloat.

Ned's vehement protests were the hardest to bear. Telling him as kindly as possible but so firmly that he had to understand that she would never marry him taxed her inner resources to the limit. His pain hurt her to the quick.

The passage across the Atlantic dragged. Because of her circumscribed financial condition, she didn't travel first class but in the tourist section. Most of her fellow passengers were middle-aged couples who regarded the exotically beautiful young woman who was traveling alone with reserve and made few overtures toward friendliness. That suited her mood, which was bleak. No matter how unsatisfactory or even heartbreaking a marriage has been, ending it is a wrench. She kept to herself, using the solitary time by trying to make plans for the future, but she could think of nothing to plan for, to look forward to.

She broke her journey at Boston, to go on to Martin's Corners to visit Naomi. It wasn't just a delay tactic because she dreaded getting home to Texas and the problems that awaited her there. Naomi was like a sister to her, and it might be a long time before she had the opportunity to see her again.

"Andrea!" Naomi cried, when Andrea stepped down out of the public coach that was still the only link to Martin's Corners. Her face was alight as she threw her arms around her cousin and hugged her, laughing and crying at the same time. "Oh, Andrea, I thought you'd never get here! I've counted the days ever since you wrote me that you were coming! Do you know, I've met this stage every day for the last week, just in case you might be on it? I'm a silly goose, Kelvin said so, but what if you'd come earlier than we'd thought you would and there'd been no one to meet you?"

"I'd have found my way to your house. I couldn't have forgotten." Andrea extricated herself from Naomi's embrace, straightened her smart traveling hat, which had been knocked askew, and feasted her eyes on this girl she had longed to see so many times during the last few years.

Kelvin was there, already picking up Andrea's lighter cases, and leaving the rest for Mr. Blaisdel's son to bring along in a cart. Kelvin looked well, as serious and lean as ever but with an unmistakable air of contentment about him that only a happy marriage could bring about.

And there, peeking around her mother's skirts, was little Martha, Naomi's daughter, regarding her with grave, serious eyes from a face that was a replica of Naomi's own. And Jonathan, a year older, who looked so much like Uncle Rory that Andrea's heart caught, valiantly trying to pick up one of her larger cases to carry it home.

"No, darling, it's too heavy even for Daddy," Naomi told him. "Leave it, and say hello to your cousin Andrea."

"Hello, Dria. I'm glad you've come," Jonathan said gallantly, and his use of her nickname brought tears to her eyes. Naomi must have told the children about her, talked of her often, for him to say Dria.

Everything about the little town was familiar, bringing back memories of a happier time. They passed the *Clarion,* and Blaisdel's Feed and Seed Store and Hamilton's General Store, they paused to speak to one of the Tate girls, and then they were there, with Jonathan running ahead to throw open the door and Martha walking sedately beside her mother, only smiling shyly at Andrea every once in a while.

The saltbox house was just as she'd remembered it, and Andrea had an eerie feeling, as she stepped inside, that Aunt Emily knew that she was there. Give me some of your strength, she prayed, although the smile was still on her face. Lend me some of your courage that you passed on so generously to the first Martha, and Prudence, and Naomi!

The eerie feeling persisted as she felt the aura of the house. It was a happy house, filled with love and strength and serenity. She felt its healing properties, and she was glad that she had come.

How beatiful Naomi was, even lovelier now than she had been at Roselawns. Maturity became her. Her complexion had the clearness and glow of health, and her hazel eyes were serene. Andrea was glad for her, without a trace of envy, even though their marriages had turned out so differently.

Andrea was absorbed into the life of the family effortlessly. She helped Naomi dust and sweep; she made beds and took her turn at cooking and washing dishes. She worked beside Jonathan, keeping the yard clean, while little Martha trotted around gathering fallen twigs in her apron, determined to do her share.

There was no party for Andrea. Andrea didn't want one and Naomi had been intuitive enough not to arrange for one. What Andrea needed was to talk, to have someone to confide in, and Naomi was exactly the person to pour her doubts and fears out to.

"Of course you had to leave Reggie!" Naomi told her. "There was nothing else you could do. Things will work out for you, Dria. Someday you're going to be as happy as I am, I can feel it in my bones. You're still in love with Henry, aren't you? And he's never married."

"But I'm still married. Reggie won't allow a divorce."

"He can't hold out forever. Just hang on, Dria. And whatever you do, don't let him talk you into going back to him! You've made your quota of mistakes for one lifetime, you haven't any more coming."

Just talking to her made Andrea feel better, and she was enthralled to learn that Naomi, like the first Martha, was now writing for the *Clarion*.

"Nothing as wonderful and significant as my grandmother's abolitionist pieces, of course, but I am trying to promote better schools, and an education for everyone. Kelvin says my work is good. I'll never be famous, as Martha was, but I feel I'm doing something, no matter how little."

"I wish I had something significant to do. I'll feel like a parasite, back at Trail's End. What could be more useless than a married woman who isn't married, who has no children?"

"Andrea Wentworth, you stop that! You'll find something to do, something every bit as significant as my little pieces in the *Clarion*. Give yourself time, don't be so hard on yourself. Everybody in the world makes mistakes. Look at the one I almost made! If it hadn't been for you, I'd have married Gregory Randolph and been miserable all my life, and just look at me now. I have to thank you for that, so you see you've already done one significant thing!"

They both dissolved into laughter. It was wonderful to laugh again, to have a confidante, to feel a part of a closely knit family. It gave Andrea strength, lent her the courage and determination that she so sorely needed.

She only stayed for a week. The house was small, and her place wasn't here, no matter how welcome she was. But that seven days gave her renewed confidence, a sense of generations of strong and undefeatable people behind her.

Her next stop was in Georgia. She felt the need to return there, to face down those ghosts and put them to rest, even if it meant the chance that she might come face to face with Gregory again. Prudence, unlike Naomi, was aware of her imminent arrival, as Andrea had written to her the day she'd arrived in Boston. Once again her welcome was heartwarming, the assurances that she'd done the right thing in leaving Reggie an added source of strength.

"We all make mistakes, Andrea. The mistakes I made were so much worse than yours that it's a miracle I survived them. But I did, and so will you. It might take a little time, but it's worth waiting for."

"How is my grandfather? I want to see him before I go on to Texas."

"He isn't as well as you remembered him. After all, he's getting on, just as I am. He's retired now, still living in the same house in town."

"And Aunt Christine?"

Prudence's eyes were shadowed. "She doesn't change. Gay's situation is difficult. He had to send her to an institution for a few months after you left Georgia. He wasn't able to handle her; she'd have drunk herself to death if he hadn't, but she's never forgiven him. He'll be glad to see you, Andrea, but I think I'd better send him word that you're here, rather than have you visit him at his house. There's no telling what Chrissy's reaction might be if you showed up there."

"How can she be so bitter, so unforgiving, after all these years?" Andrea exclaimed.

"Crissy makes a career of it," Cleo, who had just brought in a plate of her famous gingerbread and a silver pot of coffee, said dryly. "You stay away from her,

Andrea. I knew from the day she was born that she'd be nothing but trouble, and I was right. How she could be Prudence's sister is more than I can fathom."

"She's had a hard life, Cleo." There was no reproach in Prue's voice, but only a reminder.

"So have a lot of people, but that doesn't turn them into demons!" Cleo's voice was flat. "She won't let anybody help her, she's as prickly as one of those cactus plants you have out in Texas. I never did hold with Gaylord Renault, with the things he did when he was young, but he managed to straighten himself out. Crissy didn't, and she never will. Prudence, drink your coffee. There's no use fretting about Crissy, it's out of your hands and there's nothing you or anybody else can do for her. Leave her to the Lord." Cleo helped herself to a piece of the gingerbread and marched back to the kitchen to supervise supper.

Andrea laughed. "Cleo never changes, does she?"

"No, and I thank God for it. She's still my strong right arm. I hope she lives to be a hundred, because I swear I don't know how I'll get along without her when she goes." Prudence picked up her coffee cup and forced a light, tinkling laugh. "There, there's no use in borrowing trouble from the future. One day at a time is all the good Lord ever expected us to handle."

One day at a time, Andrea thought, and once again she felt a resurging of her own inner strength. That's what she'd do, she'd live one day at a time and do the best she could, and maybe she'd end up being just a little bit worthy of this family of hers after all.

Crissy lay perfectly still in her bed, feigning sleep. In the rocking chair on the other side of the room, Beulah Jones nodded. Twice now the black woman's head had jerked up, cutting off a soft snore as she prodded herself awake to make sure that her charge was still quiet and not about to cause any trouble.

Not that Beulah expected any trouble. The Lord Himself knew where Christine Renault had got that bottle this afternoon. Beulah, as well as Mr. Renault, had searched every inch of the house and grounds after Mrs. Renault had come home from that institution where Mr. Renault had had to send her after all that scandal about Mr. Renault's niece that Crissy had brought down around their heads. Not just then, either, but they both made the search periodically to make sure that Crissy hadn't managed to come by another bottle and stash it somewhere. Mostly they were successful in their efforts to enforce Crissy's sobriety, but every once in a while she managed to outwit them and then there'd be the devil to pay, with Crissy drunk out of her mind and screaming filth at Mr. Renault and throwing things and sometimes even trying to attack him physically. More than once Beulah had seen scratches on his face that hadn't come from any razor blade.

Whenever Gaylord had to be away from the house, he had arranged for Beulah to come and sit with his wife because Crissy couldn't be trusted. The doctors at the institution had been able to dry her out, but they hadn't been able to drive out the demon that made her go on craving alcohol. She'd go for weeks at a time, sometimes even months, giving no trouble at all, and you'd think she was cured at last, and then something would set her off and she'd get herself a bottle somewhere and it would start all over again.

Beulah disliked her job of watching Mrs. Renault. She didn't like the woman, she never had. Crissy Renault still lived in the past; she had an inborn conviction that if your skin was black, she had the right to order you around as if you were dirt, as if black people were still slaves. If she hadn't been sorry for Gaylord Renault, Beulah would have refused to keep on coming in to do the laundry and the heavy cleaning and to sit with Crissy when Gay had to be away. It didn't matter if he paid her more than the going rate; no amount of money would have made it worth it.

But she was the only one who would come; the other women who did housework wouldn't come near the place. And she was sorry for Gaylord Renault. She'd heard tell that he'd been a hellion in his younger days, that he'd been as bad as the worst of the masters who'd thought they were kings of the earth just because they'd happened to be born white and rich and just own plantations and slaves. That was a long time ago, before Beulah's time, and Mr. Renault was a fine man now, and a man with a burden that touched Beulah's heart, so she went on helping him when he asked.

In a way, Beulah thought, it was a mercy that Crissy had picked today to pull another of her tricks and end up drunk. She'd gone to bed early in the afternoon, claiming that she had another of her headaches, and every time Gay had looked in she'd pretended that she was asleep, and all the time she'd had a bottle under her pillow. Gaylord hadn't discovered her ruse until she'd been so drunk that she'd forgotten to stop it up and hide it under her pillow again after her last pull at it, right from the bottle.

Beulah sniffed. If it was up to her, she'd let Mrs. Renault drink herself to death and have done with it. It wasn't as if the woman was happy; she wasn't, she was miserable and she made everybody close to her miserable, too. All the same, if she'd been going to do it, today had been as good a time as ever. Mrs. Amhurst had sent a message around to Beulah to let Mr. Renault know that his niece Andrea was at her place and that he should come to supper. She'd had to do it that way so that her sister Crissy wouldn't find out and raise the devil. Having Crissy drunk, sleeping it off, had made it that much easier for Gaylord to leave her this evening without her raising a fuss wanting to know where he was going.

She got up and crossed over to the bed and looked down at the sleeping woman. A little snort of exasperated satisfaction escaped her lips as she went back to the rocking chair. She folded her hands in her lap and rested her head against the padded headrest. From the looks of it, she wouldn't have any trouble out of Crissy tonight, she'd sleep right through until morning. For Mr. Renault's sake, she hoped so. She set the rocker into motion, back and forth, back and forth, until it gradually slowed as she, too, fell asleep. She'd had a hard day; she'd done Mrs. Jenning's washing and Mrs. Mason's ironing and washed the windows in Mrs. George's house. With Crissy sleeping away like that, it wouldn't hurt to catch a few minutes' catnap herself.

In the bed, Crissy still lay motionless, but her ears were strained for the slightest noise from the rocking chair. Five minutes, ten, fifteen, the minutes ticked away on the clock on the bureau with mind-screaming slowness.

Now! The black bitch was securely asleep. All she had to do was be quiet enough—the woman had ears like a cat. With agonizing caution she sat up and slipped her feet over the edge of the bed. Another second and she had her shoes in her hand and had reached the door. She inched it open, holding her breath, but the woman in the chair didn't stir.

Now she was out of the room and down the stairs, careful to avoid the one that creaked. The front door, and freedom, lay directly in front of her.

What a fool Gaylord was! It had never entered his mind that she knew that Andrea Wentworth was at Prue's, that she had overheard, from her open bedroom window, that Andrea had arrived yesterday. There was nothing the matter with her ears, and Beulah had a voice that carried even when she spoke in a low tone. Gay had been in the front yard spading around the flower-beds when Beulah had arrived to give him Prue's message, otherwise she'd have gone to the back door and Crissy wouldn't have been aware of Andrea's arrival.

That was what had set her off. She'd been glad, as the rage had enveloped her, that she still had that bottle in the attic, concealed above a rafter that she had to stand on a trunk to reach. She'd had the bottle for weeks, but she hadn't touched it, she'd been saving it against a time when she might need it, a time when she could elude her jailers and drink it without being discovered and having it taken away from her.

Andrea Wentworth, that beautiful, that fabulously

wealthy bitch, the daughter of Gaylord's bastard son! That nigger bitch, who had everything that Crissy should have had, everything that was her right by birth and that had been taken from her. And Prue was giving her house room, Prue had welcomed her! You'd think the chit would have had the sense to stay away after what had happened the last time she'd come to Georgia. Didn't she realize that niggers passing as whites weren't welcome here, didn't she know that her very presence was an insult to all the decent members of the family?

Even if she didn't, Prue knew, but Prue had never cared about things like that. Prue, who'd actually so defected from her social order as to pass Adam Wentworth off as her husband's son, pass him as white! Prue, who'd had all the best of everything while she, Crissy, had had nothing!

Crissy was still drunk so that she staggered a little as she walked down the street keeping to the deep shadows of the overhanging trees, but her mind had a frightening clarity. The bail of the can of kerosene she'd taken from the shed in the back cut into the palm of her hand, but she paid no attention to the pain. Old Jake Jefferson, who eked out a living with a brokendown cart and a horse that was even more decrepit by hauling junk away and collecting rags, lived in a shack at the edge of the black section of town, right on the outskirts. It was a long walk for a woman of Crissy's age and in her condition, but the alcohol that was still in her bloodstream kept her going, her determination to have revenge on everyone who had harmed her keeping her feet moving.

Old Jake was asleep, but the door of his shack wasn't locked. He was Beulah's great-uncle, and it gave Crissy a great deal of satisfaction that he was the one who supplied her with the bottles of cheap wine that fed her craving, right under the nose of the woman who was supposed to guard her. Nobody would ever find out that it was Jake who supplied her, that she had a secret place behind the fence post of the back yard, by the hollyhocks, where she left money and he left the bottles for her to pick up when no one was watching her. She'd dug out a hole in the ground and covered it with a rock, and because it was behind the fence post Gaylord never came across it while he was puttering around the yard.

Her nose wrinkled at the disorder of the place, but the accumulation of odds and ends that cluttered the shack only skirted the edge of her mind, an annoyance because she had to grope her way around them in the dark. Jake's cot was against the far wall, and from the smell around it he, too, had enjoyed a bottle of wine before he'd gone to sleep. Everyone liked Jake, who was invariably cheerful, but everyone also knew that the way he drank was a caution. But he never caused any trouble, and he was honest in his dealings, so he was left alone to do as he liked.

She shook his shoulder. "Jake, get up and harness your horse to the cart. Did you hear me, you lazy nigger? Get on your feet, or it'll be the worse for you!"

It took a moment for Jake's bemused mind to realize that it was Mrs. Renault who was shaking him. "Now, ma'am, I can't do that! This here's nighttime, and besides, you can't go no place in that old cart, it wouldn't be fittin'."

"Do as I tell you! There's fifty cents in it for you if you hurry."

Jake scratched his thick crop of white hair, mulling it over. Fifty cents! That was a heap of money, just to drive a crazy old woman someplace even if it was way after dark when a man and his horse deserved their rest. It would be clear profit and that was something to think about.

"Where we goin', Mrs. Renault?"

"You aren't going anywhere! The fifty cents is to rent the horse and cart. Hurry along, do you think I can stand here all night?"

"I can't go letting you take my horse and cart, ma'am!"

Crissy took the fifty-cent piece from her pocket and waved it tantalizingly in front of his face. "I won't be long. I'll have your horse and cart back here inside of two hours. I'll give you another fifty cents, I'll put it in the hole tomorrow. A dollar, Jake! Now get moving before I become angry!"

Jake got moving. He spend a good share of his life, when he'd been young, obeying white people, and even when he'd become older he'd gone on obeying them until he'd decided that he'd rather live from day to day being his own man than draw a weekly wage working for someone else. And Mrs. Renault was a Renault, and a Beddoes, so she was quality even if she was kind of crazy, and it wasn't his place to argue with her. A dollar would buy enough wine to keep him in a state of euphoria for days to come, but it wasn't only that that made him obey. That look in Mrs. Renault's eyes, gleaming like they were in the dark, she might hit him if he didn't do as she said, and then what would he do? He couldn't go hitting a white lady back, or push her out of his house.

"You take care, now! Ben's old, don't you go pushing him too hard!" Jake warned as Crissy climbed into the cart and flicked the lines.

The cool night air did nothing to cool the rage that was still flaming inside Crissy as she urged the horse along the deserted country road. It was time that Prue was taught a lesson, that she got her comeuppance for having got everything that Crissy had been denied. Look at the way Prue lived now, lived at Roselawns, which by rights belonged to Crissy as much as it belonged to her sister! Lived high on the hog because Burke was doing well as a doctor, even if he was in his seventies, and Rory managed to run the plantation at a profit.

The profits should be a third hers, no, half hers, because what right did Prue have to live there at all, after she'd married a Northerner, married an enemy, and a fortune into the bargain! It didn't matter that the fortune belonged to Adam; Adam had made it possible for Prue and Burke and Rory to move back to Roselawns, to resume their places as the leaders of Georgian society.

She knew her way, she could have traveled from

town to Roselawns with her eyes closed, she could have done it sleepwalking. Roselawns was her home, only they'd taken it away from her, just as Swanmere had been taken away. Everything had been taken away from her, while everything had been given to Prue, who deserved nothing, who deserved to be punished as she was going to be punished now.

Her mind only made more cunning by drink, Crissy tied the horse to a tree a good way from Roselawns and walked the rest of the way. Prue was in that house, and Rory and Burke and Gaylord and Andrea Wentworth. They were laughing and talking and having a wonderful time; they were probably laughing at her. Drinking expensive wine, not the sour or too-sweet, cloying stuff that Jake supplied her with because it was all she could afford to scrape out of the pittance Gaylord gave her for pocket money. There'd be candlelight, and Prue would be wearing Mother's pearls.

At the thought of the pearls Crissy began to shake, but she controlled herself and went on. She was as silent as a specter as she rounded the house to the back, feeling in her pocket for the matches that she'd picked up before she'd left her own house.

In the living room, Cleo put down the fresh pot of coffee that she had just brought from the kitchen house and checked to see that these people whom she loved had everything they needed. There was still plenty of brandy in the decanter, the silver dish of pralines that she'd supervised making that afternoon, was still nearly half full, there were matches in a cut glass container for the man's cigars.

Cleo took a praline from the silver dish. She'd never lost her sweet tooth, even though half of her own teeth were missing by now. "I'll just check the kitchen again to make sure that worthless girl banked the fire properly, and then I'll go on to bed, Prue. Good night, Andrea. Good night, Gaylord. Good night, Burke and Rory."

It was good to see them all together like this. Everything was as it should be. Why, then, did she have this uneasy feeling that something was wrong? Like a goose was walking over her grave, she thought as she returned through the dining room, her practiced eyes making sure that no crumb was left on the table and that every article on the sideboard was in its exact proper place.

Grudgingly, she conceded that Bella had done a good job in the dining room. Now if the kitchen was in as good order, she could get some rest.

She walked along the covered passageway between the house and the kitchen, savoring the coolness of the night air. She'd need a blanket before morning, her bones weren't as young as they'd used to be and they felt the cold and the damp.

For a moment, just as a cloud drifted across the face of the half moon and cut off what light there was, she thought that she saw something move over there by the oleander bushes. She stopped and squinted her eyes in that direction, but she saw no movement now. It had only been a shadow cast by the cloud, she told herself. She was getting as jumpy as a cat with fleas. Shaking her head at her case of the jitters, she resumed walking.

The kitchen was in order. Certainly it was, it had better be or those girls would feel the brunt of her anger come morning! It hadn't been easy, but she'd finally trained them to do things right, and that was a mercy because she was, she confessed to herself now that she was alone where no one could read her mind, getting too old to do it all by herself. It was a good feeling, knowing that you were leaving things in order when your time was coming to go to the Lord, knowing that because of your efforts things would still run smoothly for the ones you loved.

She'd been thinking a lot about Miss Martha and Miss Emily lately, even more than she usually thought about them. Her time was coming, that's why she thought about them so much. They were there waiting for her, and she'd be glad to go to them because she was getting just a mite tired. And she'd be able to tell them that she'd done her duty, that she'd done right by Prue and

Rory. If she felt just a little proud, then she guessed she had the right.

She retraced her steps to the main house where Prue had fixed up a room for her as a member of the family, with her own things around her. Cleo was fully aware that Prue wanted her within earshot in case she became ill in the night, that all of them watched her and made sure that she didn't overtax her strength. She didn't mind their solicitude toward her as long as it didn't get in the way of her doing her work and seeing that everything ran smoothly. She took a soft, fluffy blanket from the cedar chest at the foot of her bed and folded it at the bottom of the bed so that she could reach it if she became chilly during the night. The cedar smelled nice; she'd always liked that smell.

In her nightgown, her hair plaited in two tight braids, snow white now and thin, she got into bed and blew out the lamp on her bedside table. Yes, it was nice to know that they were all here, down in the living room, enjoying each other's company. Martha and Miss Emily would have liked Andrea, and they'd be glad that Adam had made his peace with Gaylord and that Andrea was so fond of her grandfather.

She closed her eyes, but the feeling of uneasiness that had plagued her for the past half-hour wouldn't let her relax and go to sleep. Something was wrong, she felt it in her bones.

She gave up. There was no use trying to sleep till she checked everything again. Pulling a flannel wrapper around her thin shoulders, she left her room and padded down the stairs again. She was being an old fool and she knew it, but she couldn't rest until she made sure.

She checked the dining room first, and then went noiselessly in her old felt slippers to glance into the living room where Gaylord was laughing at something Andrea had just said. Lord, Lord, the girl was a beauty, but even so she didn't have a patch on Prudence. Prue might be seventy-two, but she was still beautiful to look at. She held herself as erect as she had when she'd been a girl in her twenties, there was hardly a sag in her face, and her white hair gleamed like silver in the lamplight.

The feeling of uneasiness, of something wrong, still persisted in spite of the fact that she knew that the kitchen fire had been properly banked. Yet she could swear that she smelled smoke, and there shouldn't have been any smoke, the evening was so mild that no one touched a match to the wood laid in the fireplace.

No one in the room had noticed her standing there, for their attention was on each other. Andrea looked a great deal better than she had when she'd arrived. A day of rest, of having Prue tell her that she'd done right, had brought her old radiant glow back to her face and eyes. Cleo shook her head at herself, once again calling herself an old fool imagining things that weren't there.

Still, just as she started to climb the stairs to her room again something compelled her to turn around and step outdoors instead.

She knew, now, that her imagination hadn't played her false. The smell of smoke was stronger out here, and there was another smell mixed with it, one that couldn't be mistaken.

Kerosene! Moving faster than she had for at least five years, she ran around the corner of the house and then stopped for one blood-freezing moment while the shock of seeing flames lick up the side of the house held her in her tracks. The dining room wing was on fire, and someone had set it. There was no doubt of that in her mind even as she turned to run back into the house to give the alarm.

They came piling out, stunned, their faces registering their disbelief, but that only lasted for seconds. They all worked, every one of them, Andrea as hard as the others, never giving a thought to her own safety as she darted dangerously close to the flames that were licking up the sides of the house to throw bucket after bucket of water on it as fast as Burke could draw it from the well. And it was Andrea who was the first to see that the curtains at the open window had caught, and who rushed back inside to yank them from their rods and throw them

400

out of the window. Her face black with smoke, her hands and eyebrows singed, she ran out again to take her place in the bucket brigade.

"Get back, Grandfather, Uncle Rory!" Andrea commanded. "We're getting it under control, don't overexert yourselves!"

Cleo, too, got back, making sure that Gaylord and Rory fell back with her, her tongue lashing out at them to obey Andrea. "It ain't going to spread, I found it soon enough. Don't go keeling over, the girls and Andrea can do it now."

"Cleo, how did you happen to discover it? I thought you were in bed and asleep."

"I smelled it in my mind," Cleo told her. "There! It's out, Prudence. You all go back inside and have yourselves a drink. You girls, stay out here and watch that it doesn't start up again! It won't hurt to throw a few more bucketfuls of water on it, while you're out here. Andrea, you're pretty well singed, you get on inside, too, and let Burke have a look at you. Adam wouldn't like it if we sent you back to him with your pretty skin scarred."

Now that the excitement was all but over, Andrea realized that her hands were smarting. As soon as they were back in the light of the living room, Prudence exclaimed with dismay.

"Oh, my goodness! Andrea, you're lopsided! One of your eyebrows is half singed off! Burke, do something!"

"I intend to, as soon as we get her face and hands clean enough so I can get an estimate of the damage." Nearly as vigorous as he'd been forty years ago, Burke sent one of the housegirls scurrying for soap and water and clean towels. His hands, gnarled now with age, were surprisingly steady as he set about swabbing off Andrea's face and hands.

"Superficial," he pronounced. "But I'll bet it stings like fury for all that."

"It does, a little," Andrea admitted. Her relief at learning that she wasn't going to be scarred astonished her. Was she really that vain? At least, she consoled herself, she hadn't stopped to think twice before she'd dashed inside to snatch down the burning curtains. At the time her only thought had been to save this house that meant so much to the family. Roselawns! If it had been reduced to ashes she thought that she would have grieved almost as much as Prudence herself.

"However did it start?" she asked as Burke set about smoothing ointment on her hands and forehead.

Cleo came into the room. She looked, if it were possible, years older than she had earlier that evening. She was carrying something in her hand, an empty kerosene can.

"This," Cleo said. "One of the boys found it thrown into the bushes. Somebody set that fire."

They looked at each other, their stunned bewilderment reflected on all of their faces. Arson! But who could have done it, and why? As far as Prue and Burke and Rory knew, they had no enemies, there was no one in all of Georgia who would wish them ill.

It was Gaylord who broke the silence. "Crissy!" he said. "But how? She was sound asleep when I left her, she was drunk, and Beulah was there to guard her. All the same, I'd swear that that's my kerosene can. There's a dent in it, there toward the bottom. I checked it just last week to make sure that it wasn't leaking."

Rory had been slumped in his chair, but now he got to his feet. "I think maybe we'd better take a look, Gay. I'll have your horse hitched up."

Crissy was more than halfway back to town, urging Ben to the fastest pace she could get out of him. She was exultant because she had carried out her mission successfully. She'd fired the house, she'd fired Roselawns! She hoped that it burned to the ground, that nothing would remain of it but ashes. If she couldn't live there, then Prue couldn't, either! Let Prue see what it meant to be homeless, to lose everything as Crissy had done! She was only sorry that she hadn't dared wait until everyone in the house was asleep so that they'd all perish in the flames. But she hadn't dared wait, Gay would have come home and then she wouldn't have had a chance to get out of the house. This would have to do. With all of them in the living room it was certain to get a good enough start so that there would be no saving it.

She slapped the reins smartly on Ben's back. She had to get home and be in bed and presumably asleep before that black bitch set to guard her woke up. Her first elation was subsiding, and now fear possessed her, driving at her back like a demon. If Gay were to find out that she was the one who set the fire, he'd have her committed again, and she couldn't stand it. She'd never gotten over the last time, the way the doctors, the nurses, had treated her like dirt, had treated her as if they didn't know that she was a Beddoes, a Renault, that she was Quality. The humiliation of it, the degradation, being lumped in with insane and disgusting dregs of humanity, combined with her crawling, screaming need for alcohol, had nearly killed her. She couldn't go back there, she'd rather die.

"Get up! Get along there, stop that lagging!" Crissy screamed at the horse. When he didn't respond, her rage exploded. There was no whip in the whip socket, so she stood up and began flapping the reins as hard as she could, bringing them down sharply on the horse's back with all the strength she had.

Old Ben panicked. In all the years that Jake had owned him, he'd never felt a whip, he'd never been shouted at, he'd never known anything but kindness as both of them had ambled along at their slow, steady pace, never in a hurry. This screaming, rein-slapping woman who was belaboring him was entirely outside of his experience.

Old Ben laid his ears back and plunged, and then started to gallop as fast as his spavined legs could move, headed for home and Jake. The springless cart bounced in the ruts of the road, threatening to break apart.

"Whoa, whoa!" Crissy screamed. "Whoa up, damn you! What are you trying to do, kill me? I'll fix you. . . ."

They were at the sharp bend in the road where it turned toward town, and Ben took it too fast. Its wheel caught in a rut, the cart tilted, and Crissy went flying out of it. Ben went on running until he realized that the screaming woman was no longer in the cart that was clattering and bouncing behind him. Then he slowed to a slow but determined trot, and kept on going.

For a blinding second before blackness enclosed her, Crissy was a little girl again. She was standing up in the carriage, and Rory, a young and handsome Rory, had his arm around her to steady her. Roselawns lay directly in front of her, with its house people and field people lined up to welcome her.

"Oh, it's beautiful! It's a mansion. I didn't know we were so rich!" Crissy cried. "I love it! Are all those slaves ours? Papa, will I have one of my very own, a lady's maid? Will we have parties, and great balls? Oh, it's such fun to be rich!"

25

The whole county turned out for Crissy's funeral. It didn't matter that she had been a virtual recluse for years, that most of the younger people didn't even remember her. She had been a Beddoes, a Renault.

Out of respect for Crissy's hatred of her, Andrea didn't sit with the family during the services at the church, but in the last pew, anonymous among the other crowded mourners. The rumor that it was Crissy who had set fire to Roselawns had already spread throughout the county, and she shrank from adding fuel to the gossip by appearing with the family.

The service was a long one, but the minister, a Reverend Morton, dwelled almost entirely on Crissy's earlier life, on the Beddoes' and the Renaults' place in county society, on the hardships she had undergone during and immediately after the war. He mentioned that she had been in ill health for years but gave no hint as to the nature of her malady. It didn't matter, everyone knew anyway.

Prue's face was pale under her black mourning veil, but her back was erect and her expression only that of normal grief for the death of a sister. Rory looked as though he were carved from stone, and Burke was grave and calm. But Gaylord looked shriveled, years older than his seventy-five years and Andrea's heart ached for him.

Beside her, Cleo reached out to take her hand. The erect, incredibly wrinkled black woman had entered the church at the last moment, having spent the earlier part of the morning at Gaylord's house preparing for the crowds of sympathizers who would come in after the burial.

After the service was at an end and the long lines of mourners had filed past the casket to look at her, almost unbelievably young-looking and beautiful again in death, Andrea found herself standing directly behind Gregory Randolph and a pretty young woman who looked anxious, as though she weren't quite sure that she should be by his side. Andrea's breath caught, and then she forced herself to breathe naturally. It had been inevitable that she would see Gregory sooner or later, if she stayed at Roselawns for any length of time.

As though he felt her eyes on her, Gregory turned and looked directly at her. His face registered consternation, and something more, a tightening of his facial muscles that spoke of inner stress and pain.

"Good morning, Gregory." Andrea would be damned if she'd call him Mr. Randolph even if half the people who were still standing around were looking at them.

"Good morning, Andrea. Lillian, this is Mrs. Reginald Mansfield, from England." Andrea noticed with ironic amusement that he didn't designate her as a member of the Beddoes family.

The look that his wife gave her was stricken, filled with near panic, and Andrea's anger at Gregory mounted. Lillian wasn't sure that Gregory loved her, it was as plain as if it had been spelled out to her letter by letter.

406

Maybe she had jumped out of the frying pan into the fire when she'd run off to England and married Reggie, but from where she stood right now she'd a lot rather be in her own shoes than Lillian's.

"I'm very happy to meet you, Lillian," she said. "If you ever find yourself with some free time, you come on out to Texas, you'll find that you have friends at Trail's End."

She clasped Lillian's hand warmly before she turned back to Cleo. The two of them were not going on to the cemetery for the conclusion of the funeral, but directly to Gaylord's house, where they'd wait for the influx of mourners.

"Crissy hated me!" she burst out to Cleo as the two of them set coffee pots on the old coal-burning range. "She didn't even know me, and yet she hated me enough to try to burn down Roselawns just because I was in it!"

"She was sick, Andrea. The worst kind of sickness, the sickness of bitterness and jealousy. Nobody could have helped her. Prudence tried. I tried. Gaylord tried. Her sickness went too deep. We can only hope that the Lord has cured her now."

"Her life must have been miserable!" Andrea reached for the handerchief she had tucked into the bodice of the black dress that had been purchased so hastily for the funeral. "I'm sorry for her. I'm sorry it had to be like that for her."

"So am I. But I've been sorrier for Gay, all these years. I'm glad he has you, Andrea. Rosalind, too, of course, and Nelson and Jacob, but you're Adam's daughter and you have a special place in his heart. It's like you're the forgiveness for what he did all those years ago. It would be nice if you'd stay on for a few weeks, to help him over this last blow."

"Wouldn't that only add to the gossip?"

"Probably, but none of us care about that." Andrea noticed Cleo's use of the word "us" that very simply placed her as a member of the family, and in spite of her inner turbulance she felt comforted.

A smile sent Cleo's face into even more wrinkles and creases. "Miss Emily would have looked all those gossipers in the eye and made them shrivel down till they rattled in their skins. Martha, too. You stay, Andrea, at least for a little while. We're above gossip, what people think or say can't hurt us, and Gaylord needs you. And don't go blaming yourself for what Crissy did. She was bound to come to a bad end one way or another, I knew it from the time she could walk."

It was Cleo who gave Andrea courage to pass around trays of coffee and cake when the mourners began coming in. She had no reason to be ashamed, to hide herself away in the kitchen. If these people, the curiosity seekers rather than the genuine friends of the family, wanted to get a good look at her, Adam Wentworth's daughter and Gaylord's granddaughter, then let them. Watching from the kitchen doorway, Cleo was proud of her. Maybe she didn't look anything like Martha or Prudence, but she had their spirit, that unquenchable quality that no adversity could humble.

The last of the mourners finally left, and Andrea felt as though she'd been put through a wringer although she showed no indication of it. All of her concern was for her grandfather and Aunt Prue. As Cleo closed the door after the last straggler, Andrea went up to Gaylord and took his hand in both of hers.

"I'm going to stay on for another week or two, Grandfather. When I leave, why don't you come with me out to Texas? You could stay for a month or a year or forever. This house holds too many memories, so why not just close it up and come home with me?"

For the first time since he and Rory had found Crissy's body crumpled in the ditch beside the road, Gaylord smiled.

"Thank you, Andrea. In a way, I'd like to take you up on that, but I'm a little old to be uprooted."

"All the same, you could at least visit us for a while! The trip isn't hard any more. Grandfather Jonathan came out when he was old, back when it was a lot harder to get there."

"Jonathan was a better man than I am!" Gaylord said with a touch of ironic humor. "He always was. Don't worry about me, Andrea. I'm going to be all right."

He drew a deep breath, and his face lightened. "I'm not glad that Crissy's dead, much less that she died as she did, but for the first time in decades, I feel free. I have my lodge, I have friends here in town, and Prue and Burke and Rory at Roselawns, and Nelson and Rosalind visit me as often as they can, they don't always wait for a funeral." Both Nelson and his wife and three children and Rosalind and her husband and two children had already left for Roselawns, where Andrea and Gaylord would join them for supper tonight before Rosalind and her husband came back to spend the night with Gay in his house. "I love my garden and my flowers, and I have my books, my life will be full. Maybe in another year I'll pry myself away for that Texas visit, but right now I have a lot of catching up to do and I intend to do it. Am I shocking you?"

Andrea threw her arms around his neck and kissed him. "Shocking me? I'm proud of you! Gaylord Renault, you're worthy of being my grandfather, you're worthy of being Adam's father!"

"And it's about time, isn't it?" Gaylord's eyes twinkled with real humor. "It took me long enough, Dria, but I reckon I finally got to where you don't have to be ashamed of me any more."

Andrea stayed on at Roselawns for ten more days. Before she started out on the last leg of her journey home, the dining room wing had been repaired and repainted and no more curiosity seekers were driving out to crane their necks at the damage that Crissy had inflicted. Prudence was bearing up as wonderfully as Andrea had known she would, and when she visited Gaylord every day, helping Beulah Jones give his house a thorough cleaning and rearranging and disposing of Crissy's personal things. Andrea saw that her grandfather had shed he shriveled look he'd had at the funeral and seemed eager to start this final phase of his life.

"I'll never forgive myself for falling asleep that night and letting Mrs. Renault get away from me," Beulah told her. "And to think she got the cart and horse from my own great-uncle! He's all broken up about it, but he didn't know how to refuse her. She had a way of making people do what she wanted, and knowing Uncle Jake, he was probably half drunk."

"There's no use blaming yourself, Beulah. Nobody else does. Everybody knows how Christine was. And I know that my grandfather appreciates the way you helped look after her all those years. You aren't the only one Christine ever outsmarted. There was no way you could have known she wasn't asleep when she pretended she was."

"It's nice of you to say so, but I still feel bad about it. And so does Uncle Jake."

"What do you think about yellow curtains for the living room?" Andrea wanted to divert Beulah's mind from her feeling of guilt. "A nice bright yellow, to bring the sunshine in."

"This room's always been gloomy, with those heavy dark red drapes." Beulah brightened up. "Yellow curtains, yes, that would be nice. And Mr. Renault ought to have a bigger lamp for his reading chair—he isn't young any more, and that lamp doesn't give enough light for his eyes."

"And bigger vases for his flowers," Andrea said.

Gaylord entered the room at that moment. "Crissy didn't care for flowers in the house, she said they made a mess when they wilted and the petals dropped."

Andrea's voice was firm. "Well, now you can bring in the whole garden! I'm going to write to Elias to send you the biggest, most beautiful cut crystal vase he has. When I left, there was one that still might not be sold because it was so expensive. Now don't go making a fuss; Elias got a very good price on it and you have no idea of the markup on things like that! If it's still there, you're to have it, a present from me to you."

"I'll cherish it," Gay told her simply. "And I cherish you."

TEXAS

26

The train journey to Texas was like traveling back in time. As the lush, flat prairies gave way to rock and sand and cacti and cholla and all the other desert growth, Andrea felt as though she were traveling back to her girlhood. This country, this great American West, had its own special beauty even though it lacked the rolling greenness of other beautiful parts of the world. For at least the last five of her first eighteen years her only dream had been to leave it, to get out into what she'd thought of as the real world. Now, coming back, she wished with all her heart that she'd never left it!

Her father and Wade met her with the buckboard. She'd expected Kate, and she swallowed hard to cover her disappointment. Reading her face, Adam explained.

"Your mother has her hands full at the ranch, Dria, or she'd have been here come hell or high water. I guess you left England before you got her last letter. We've had a little trouble here. Wayne Bradshaw was shot, he nearly died, and Kate's still nursing him at Trail's End."

Andrea's shock jolted her. "Shot? I can understand someone shooting him, he probably had it coming, but why is Mother taking care of him?"

"Manuel brought him in. Lupe's grandfather. Trail's End was closer, and he was too near dead for Manuel to take him on home. Besides, he knew that Wayne's best chance was for Kate to tend him till we could get the doctor out there."

"I never knew that Manuel cared that much about Wayne." There was irony in Andrea's voice. All of the Mexicans disliked the Bradshaws, because of the airs Wayne put on, because of the way Clay treated his Mexican-born wife like someone beneath him.

"The circumstances were a little unusual," Wade told her, his voice so serious that she looked at him quickly before she looked back at her father. "It was Mike who shot him."

This time the shock went all through her. "Mike! But why?"

"Dria, Lupe's dead," Adam told her. His face was carefully expressionless, but she knew that what had happened had shaken him. "She went with Mike on a raid down into Mexico, to bring back cattle to sell for the revolutionist cause. They were surprised by some of Díaz's soldiers, and she was shot and she died before Mike could get her home."

Andrea's bewilderment drove all thoughts of her weariness after the long journey from her mind. "But what has that to do with Wayne?"

"Manuel told Mike, thinking to ease his guilt at having let Lupe go along on the raid, that she'd insisted on going because she was afraid of Wayne. It seems that Wayne caught her alone, soon after she and her grandfather and brother came to the settlement, and raped her." Adam had never found it necessary to mince words with any of his children, not even with Andrea. They'd been raised to face the world as it was, not to think of it in terms of fairy-tale perfection. "She always managed t

414

keep out of his reach after that, but lately, since she'd grown so much more desirable, he'd been after her again, doing his best to catch her alone.

"And so she went with Mike, to keep out of his reach while Mike would be away. And when Mike found out why she'd followed him, he shot Wayne. Apparently he thought that he'd killed him. He never came back to the ranch. We don't know where he is. And as I told you, Kate's been nursing Wayne. We thought for a few days that he was going to die, but she and Doc Mason managed to keep him breathing, and now it's better than an even chance that he's going to make it. So you can see why your mother couldn't take the chance of leaving him, even to meet you. She can't take any chance that he might die and make Mike a murderer."

Andrea's breath came out in a long sigh. "Then we'd better get moving," she said. "Mother will be tired by now, she'll need my help."

"Good girl," Adam said. He didn't elaborate. The reasons behind Andrea's unexpected telegram, received only four days ago, that she was on her way home, could wait. She'd tell them about it in her own good time. Adam was only glad that Reggie wasn't with her. He didn't like the man, and son-in-law or not, he didn't want him around. If Andrea had had more trouble with him and left him, then he'd back her to the limit no matter his distaste for divorce and how disgraceful it was still thought to be by a large portion of the civilized world.

Kate was thinner than Andrea had remembered her, fine-drawn from the constant strain of watching over Wayne day and night. She gathered Andrea in her arms and held her for long seconds before she spoke.

"I'm glad you're home, Andrea. We missed you."

"I've missed you, too. Mother, I hope Manuella has the biggest coffee pot we own on the stove! I could drink a gallon."

"Manuella's prepared for you, have no doubt." Kate smiled. Her silent glance at Adam told him that she'd had no word from Michael since he and Wade had gone to pick Andrea up. A muscle in Adam's jaw twitched, but he gave no further sign of his disappointment. Andrea's heart ached for both of them, on top of her own frantic worry about her brother. She loved Wade, and she'd always respected him even though she hadn't shown it when they were youngsters, but Mike! Her special brother whom she'd always been closer to than anyone! Their affinity toward each other was rare, and her heart caught as she realized how much he must be suffering.

Where was he? He thought he was a murderer. Knowing him as she did, Andrea was sure that he'd run not because he had been afraid of facing the consequence of his action, but to spare their mother and father the grief of seeing him tried and possibly hanged. The Wentworths were powerful, but the Bradshaws were also powerful, and Andrea had no doubt that if Wayne had died Clay would have thrown all his resources into trying to get Mike convicted.

There would be Mike's grief over Lupe, as well. Andrea's throat was so tight with unshed tears that she could hardly drink the coffee she'd asked for. Its heat, fresh from the stove, burned her throat less than the salt of the tears that seemed to be lodged there. Mike had loved Lupe as some men can love only one woman in their lifetime. He must be dying inside now that she was gone. Oh, God, if there were only some way she could help him!

But there was no way. No one knew where he was, and whatever he was suffering, he was suffering alone. Her job right now was to help her mother and father all she could, to ease the burden of Kate's nursing of Wayne, to give an outward appearance of faith that Mike would return to them. Her distaste for the actual care of Wayne Bradshaw would have to be pushed into the background. Right at the moment she felt like killing him with her own hands, finishing the job that Mike had started, than trying to make him well. Damn him! Oh, damn him, damn him!

She smiled at her mother over the rim of her cup and drained it and held it out to be refilled. "Where's Constanza? I haven't even seen her and the children yet."

"Philip has the measles. There's been an outbreak

among the workers' children. Constanza was up with him until nearly dawn. Before the epidemic, she helped me with Wayne, so she's fairly well worn out, too, between taking care of Philip and guarding to see that the baby doesn't contract it. We've both been helping the other children as much as we can, and no one but Carmelita is allowed near the baby, she hasn't left the house or come near any of the rest of us. Manuella takes her her meals on a tray. This has all been something like a siege. Another pair of hands will be welcome, and you'd better get a good night's sleep tonight, because I'll be putting you to work the first thing in the morning!"

For the next two weeks Kate's statement couldn't have been more true. Andrea was kept so busy that she scarcely had time to think, but she welcomed the constant work and the fatigue that followed. Both Adam and Kate were sorry that Gaylord hadn't elected to come home with her, but under the circumstances it was just as well that he hadn't, as everyone was too busy to have the time to devote to him that he deserved.

"Poor Crissy," Adam said, when Andrea told him how his younger half-aunt had died. "She was a tormented woman, Andrea. I'm glad that Prue's bearing up, and my father, too. Next summer I'll get back to Georgia to see them, it's been too long."

"Nothing would make him happier," Andrea told him. "He loves you, Dad. I think it's safe to say that he loves you more than his other children. Grandfather and I got along." There was a twinkle in her eyes in spite of the strain she'd been through as she added, "I might go so far as to say I'm the apple of his eye."

"And why wouldn't you be?" Kate demanded matter-of-factly. "You are of ours, too."

She could say that, after all the heartbreak Andrea had caused her, after she'd made such a mess of her life that she'd had to come home like a bad penny! Of the three Wentworth offspring, only Wade had seldom caused their parents trouble. But being a model child, Andrea realized with sudden insight, has nothing to do with how much your parents love you. It had started as far back as in Biblical days, with the story of the prodigal son. It gave her a sense of the continuity of families, of the deep ties that nothing could sever, and at the same time it made her feel that she could face anything that life threw at her.

Even Wayne Bradshaw, she told herself sourly, and his father. Wayne was showing steady improvement, but Clay still came to Trail's End every second day to check up on him and to use his suspicious eyes to detect any trace that Mike might have come back.

Now that Wayne could talk, he insisted that Mike's attack on him had been unprovoked, that he'd had no idea that Mike was going to draw on him. As long as there had been no witnesses, as long as the only evidence was Wayne's gun with only one bullet fired from it, as long as Michael wasn't there to defend himself, he was going to stick to that story and Clay was going to continue to brand Mike as a would-be murderer and never slacken in his efforts to find him and prosecute him to the limits of the law.

Neither Adam nor Kate, nor Andrea although the effort cost her more than she thought she could bear, allowed themselves to enter into argument with Clay or Wayne. Any such argument would be pointless and only add to Clay's old enmity toward them. Privately, they all wondered just how hard Clay was actually trying to find Mike. It might suit his purpose just as well if Mike never came back so that he could come up against no denial and could continue to spread his malicious invective to anyone who would listen.

It was hard to keep silent, when they knew the cause of the fight between Mike and Wayne and they knew that most of the Big Bend country would consider Mike justified in what he'd done. Lupe was dead, and they would not shame her memory by telling of Wayne's attack on her, not only because Mike would never forgive them, but because of Lupe herself, and her grandfather. And never having mentioned it, Wayne apparently believed that they knew nothing of it.

"Look, Dria, just because that hot-headed brother of yours picked a fight with me is no reason for you to treat me like a leper!" he burst out when it was Andrea's turn to sit with him. "You and I meant a lot to each other not too many years ago!"

"It was all in your own swelled head, Wayne," Andrea told him, not trying, this time, to keep her contempt out of her voice. "If I flirted with you it was because girls just naturally like to flirt, not because I liked you that much as a person, because I didn't. You were always a conceited, arrogant louse. It's too bad Mike didn't finish you off, except that your father would hound him to his death if he had!"

"You're mighty damned uppity!" Wayne snarled at her, his eyes filled with malice. "You Wentworths always did think you were a cut better than anybody else! What's so damned wonderful about you, anyway? Maybe I'm half Mex because of my mother, but you're part Indian, and that doesn't give you any reason to look down at me!"

Andrea regarded him thoughtfully. "I'm beginning to see," she said. "You're actually ashamed of being half Spanish, aren't you? And that makes you even more of a louse than I thought you were, because your mother's a lady and you ought to be proud of your Spanish blood! What made you think that anyone would look down on you because of your Mexican extraction? Wade married a Spanish girl; half the people in Big Bend have Spanish in them. You learned it from your father, of course. He's the only man I know who thinks that his wife isn't as good as he is just because she's Mexican!"

"Constanza's an aristocrat, another blasted aristocrat like your father!" Wayne burst out. His face was white, with red spots flaring over his cheekbones.

"Aristocrat! You make me sick, Wayne Bradshaw! There aren't any aristocrats in this country, unless it comes from the inside! Maybe you do have a reason to be jealous of us after all, because it's blamed sure that you don't have any of what it takes to be what you mistakenly think of as being an aristocrat, and you never will! I can't wait till you're strong enough to go home so I won't have to look at you any more! And when you do, tell Paula that she has all my sympathy!"

She couldn't bear to stay in the same room with him any more or she'd be sick. Damn him, he was here at Trail's End, safe, cared for, but where was Mike tonight? Not in a soft clean bed, being waited on hand and foot, of that she was certain. Wherever he was, he was broke, and hunted, and homesick, and completely alone. She left the room quickly before she could give in to the impulse to strike that supercilious look right off Wayne's face, and try to hit him hard enough when she did it so that his neck would be broken.

Instead of rejoining her mother and father in the living room, she went out onto the patio. There was a chill in the air at this time of night in spite of the warmth of the afternoon, but she needed the fresh air to wash the taste of Wayne Bradshaw out of her mouth. She stood looking at the stars that seemed to hang low enough to reach up and touch, and she wondered where it was all going to end. Mike missing, her own marriage at an end but no way to get a divorce. From where she stood right now the problems seemed insurmountable.

"Andrea? Shouldn't you have a wrap?" Kate had come out to the patio so quietly that Andrea hadn't heard her footsteps, and she started.

"I'm not cold, Mother. I won't stay out here very long, anyway. I just wanted some air. When do you think Wayne will be able to go home?"

"Very soon now. I confess it'll be a relief to be rid of him. The responsibility of keeping him alive wasn't something I relished."

"But he's going to be all right, because of you. And when Mike hears that he's still alive, he'll come home."

They had to believe that. It might take a long time, but word was bound to seep through to wherever Mike was, sooner or later, and then he'd know that he wasn't a murderer and that he could come back without causing trouble for his family. Pray God that by now, his reason would have taken over and he'd realize that he couldn't kill Wayne because Lupe was dead, that killing Wayne wouldn't bring her back and would only cause more trouble and heartbreak to everyone who loved him.

420

The things uppermost in both Andrea's and Kate's mind were left unspoken. There was always the possibility, the very distinct possibility, that Mike might be killed before he found out that he could come back. That was a war going on down in Mexico, a very real war. Díaz's soldiers and the revolutionists weren't using blank cartridges, and Mike was sure to be in the thick of it. It was where he would have gone, there was no other possibility. Freeing Lupe's people, taking revenge on the soldiers who had actually killed her, would be the only thing that he thought he had left to live for.

Kate touched Andrea's arm lightly before she returned indoors, a touch that brought tears to Andrea's eyes because of the love it managed to convey in such a simple gesture. She herself stayed outside for several more minutes, looking up into the sky. It was ironic that anyone could be as unhappy as she was on such a beautiful night. She'd been home for two weeks. She knew that Henry knew that she was back, but he hadn't come to the ranch, even though Kate had told her that he'd stopped in often before her return. There was only one reason why he didn't come any more, and that was because she was here.

Standing alone in the clear Texas night, Andrea relived those last moments she'd seen him, heard again the finality in his voice when he'd told her not to come back. The months that had passed since then had made no difference in the way he felt. He didn't want to see her, he never wanted to see her again. He was only a few miles way, by the Texas way of distance. He might be outside right now, looking up at the same stars she was looking at, but a thousand miles might as well separate them. He didn't want to see her, he wouldn't come here again as long as she was here, and that was a fact that she might as well face and get used to, because she'd have to live with it all the rest of her life.

And all for nothing, her heart wept! Reggie's illness had been feigned, a facet of his supreme selfishness and determination to get what he wanted. He'd deceived Lady Madeline and Caroline and Mort into thinking that he might die unless she came back to him, and all the time he'd been having an affair with Beatrice Langdon, an affair he kept right on having with her all the time Andrea had been working so hard to earn enough money to give him the kind of life he wanted!

He didn't love her. She doubted now that he'd ever loved her, not the way a woman wants to be loved, whole-heartedly, unselfishly, and for herself alone. They'd gotten along together, at first. Reggie had enjoyed her beauty, enjoyed showing her off, enjoyed her body, but it had always been the money that the Wentworth name stood for, the expectation that a third of Adam's fortune would come to her, that he had really wanted. Now that she'd left him, he was still determined to wait for it, because as her husband he would have a claim on it. In the meantime he'd go on sponging off Bea, or any other woman rich enough and beautiful enough to satisfy his needs and foolish enough to grant them.

She went inside a few minutes later, and to bed, but not to sleep. She was going to have to find something to do with her life. As much as she loved her family and this ranch, she didn't think that she could bear staying here, married and yet not married, with no real place of her own.

Perhaps she could get herself another shop in some large city. Her experience in London, with Elias, would stand her in good stead. It was something to think about, to discuss with Kate and Adam, as soon as Wayne was able to go home and she wasn't needed here any more.

Resolutely, she closed her eyes against the moon-light that flooded her room, and willed her mind to go blank. Tomorrow would be another full day, and she had to be in shape to do her full share to help Kate.

27

The two Bradshaw women, Paula and Pilar, Paula's mother-in-law, sat silently at the table at the Bradshaw ranch three weeks later. Wayne had been home for eighteen days, his recovery so rapid once he'd regained enough strength to get back on his feet that it was hard to believe that he had been near death a few weeks ago.

Clay was speaking, his face suffused with anger, his voice so loud that it made Paula wince.

"There she was, big as life and as arrogant as that father of hers, holding school on mine property! And not the Mex brats, which might have been expected, but she was talking to the men, teaching them their ABC's! Sneaked up there on a Sunday so's the men would be off work, determined to teach them to figure, and American history, so's they can get citizenship and vote!"

Paula's surprise was so great that she forgot her usual timorousness with her father-in-law, who held all women to be morons and expected them to be quiet while their menfolk were discussing matters of importance. "But I thought that Andrea was planning to leave the ranch, to start an antique shop somewhere! Belinda told me, when she rode over a couple of weeks ago."

Clay glared at her as though this latest dereliction were her fault. "Well, they've got another bee in their bonnet now! Citizenship for the Mexicans, hand them the right to vote just as if they were white! When I told her to pack up her slates and books and get the hell out of there, she looked at me as if I was dirt and refused to budge! She had the gall to tell me that they had the right to learn!" Clay almost choked on the piece of meat he'd just put into his mouth. "Damnation, Pilar, why can't you learn to cook meat so it's chewable? This steak is as tough as saddle leather!"

Pilar Bradshaw kept her eyes lowered as she murmured an apology. The steer that had been slaughtered for the table was old and tough. Outside of stewing it all day, there was no way to make it tender, and Clay refused boiled meat, or meat stewed up into any of the Spanish dishes that made it so palatable. Across from her, Paula also looked at her plate, but she felt her own anger rise at the way Clay spoke to his wife.

Wayne gulped down half a cupful of coffee to wash down his own meat and banged the cup back onto its saucer so hard that Paula winced again, expecting the china to break. "We aren't going to let them get away with it, are we? They have no right to go up there and teach those people!"

"Not only up there, but Kate's in the thick of it, going around to other ranches and giving lessons! The hell of it is, they have a lot of friends and they've talked them into allowing it! And Constanza's teaching the ones at Trail's End. Constanza! You'd think that she, at least, would know better, being an aristocrat who ought to know how to keep the peons in their place!"

"I didn't think that even the Wentworths would have the gall to try something like this!" Wayne speared another steak. It was hardly fit to eat, having lived at the Wentworths' spread for so long, getting used to really

424

good food, had brought home to him that the food at home was decidedly lacking in quality. He didn't follow that thought through to its logical conclusion, that the Wentworths were willing to pay for quality.

Paula's hand trembled as she placed her fork on her plate, her appetite ruined by all this shouting and show of bigotry. Had they forgotten that Wayne was half Mexican, that they were insulting Pilar by this kind of talk? But they never, either of them, paid any attention to Pilar. Clay had married her because she'd been the prettiest of the available Mexican girls and there hadn't been what he termed a "white" girl available when he'd decided that it was time he married and started raising a family so that his holdings would go down to people of his own name and blood. It made Paula tremble with rage, the way both Clay and Wayne treated Pilar as if she were no more than a piece of furniture, there for their convenience.

"I think they're doing the right thing!" Her voice spoke the words before she had time to think about the consequences, and now that they were out she was astonished at her own termerity. All the same, she wasn't going to apologize. The weeks without Wayne constantly putting her down and making her life miserable had strengthened her as she and Pilar had shared the house-work and the care of little Davie in perfect harmony, ignored by the autocratic head of the household.

"That's enough of that!" Clay roared at her. "I'll be damned if I'm going to be sassed at my own table! You keep your opinions to yourself, missy!"

"You're not my father, and you're not my keeper!" Paula's anger flared and she rose to her feet. "The fact that you're my father-in-law is my own foolish fault, but that doesn't necessarily make me half-witted! And the Wentworths are right, and I hope you won't be able to get any of the other owners to back you up in trying to stop them!"

"Get to your room and stay there!" Clay strangled. But Paula had already left the kitchen and was running to the room that she shared with Davie, the room that

Wayne had delegated her to three months before the baby had been born, as soon as she'd become too big with her pregnancy for him to exercise his marital rights. After Davie had been born, he hadn't asked her to return to his own bedroom, visiting her in hers only when his sexual needs demanded satisfying and something kept him from finding another, more attractive partner.

Her position in this house was becoming insupportable. When Wayne did come to her, he used her as casually as if she were a whore. If she protested, tried to refuse him in order to cling to some shred of dignity, he used force and it ended up in what amounted to rape, after which he left her without as much as a backward glance. She couldn't scream or fight him because it would frighten little Davie, and besides, what good would it do? Wayne was her husband, so he had a right to use her as he pleased.

She knew that things were never going to be any different between them, just as she knew that she wasn't going to be able to stand it much longer. Everybody, even the Paula Ingrams who threw their lives away on men who didn't deserve to be loved, had a breaking point, and hers was very near.

If only there were some way she could get away! She mulled it over, as she had a hundred times, as she lifted her son from his crib and rocked him, smoothing his dark hair and marveling that so far there wasn't a trace of her husband's evil disposition in him. He resembled her and her father more than he did Wayne, and that at least was a blessing.

Her arms tightened around Davie as her mind went over the same rutted route. She couldn't stay here, she had to get away and take Davie with her, but how? For a woman to leave her husband, in any decent circles, was virtually unheard of. Andrea Wentworth had done it, but the Wentworths had always been a law unto themselves.

David had fallen asleep again and she laid him back in his crib, brushing his hair back from his forehead, her fingers gentle. He was the only good thing that had come

426

out of her marriage. The trouble was, Clay Bradshaw thought so, too, and she knew that he would fight to keep his grandson. There was no telling the amount of trouble he could cause her and her parents if she simply left and took Davie with her.

She wished that she could talk to Andrea. Andrea was smart, she'd always been the smartest girl Paula knew. Adam Wentworth was even smarter, and Kate, and equally unafraid of people like the Bradshaws.

She made up her mind, her mouth compressed as her eyes stared into their own reflection in the mirror. With Clay and Wayne so up in arms about the Wentworths egging the Mexicans on to become naturalized citizens, they wouldn't pay any attention to her. She'd ride out to-morrow and go to Trail's End. She'd have to start very early, soon after sunrise, in order to make it there and back before dark. If Wayne or Clay found out where she'd been, it would go hard on her, but she clung to the conviction that after talking to Adam and Kate and Andrea she would be armed with the knowledge of how to fight them.

She was at the corral before it was full light. She wished that she dared to take some other horse, a faster mount than Daisy, the litle paint mare she'd brought with her when she'd married, but if one of the faster horses was missing, Wayne or Clay would be sure to demand why she'd taken it.

A shadow loomed across her as she reached out to open the corral gate, and she started. "Juan! I didn't hear you, you scared me out of a year's growth!"

Juan Bustamonte smiled, and her heart contracted. Ever since she'd married Wayne she'd been very much aware of the lithe, handsome vaquero, one of Clay's most trusted men. There was a quality about Juan that made him stand out from the other vaqueros, a dignity, a sure-ness of his own worth. But more than that, there was the way he had of looking at her, a look filled with respect and something more.

Juan liked her, both as a person and as a woman,

427

and Paula had had so little of that sort of admiration in her life that she couldn't fail to recognize it. At first it had embarrassed her. Admiration from the opposite sex was so strange to her that she didn't know how to handle it. But Juan never overstepped his place, never gave her any reason to think that he was forward; there was always the respect for her that made it impossible to fault him, and as the months went by she'd come to accept his unspoken friendship and to be grateful for it even though any real friendship between them was impossible. If either Clay or Wayne had ever guessed at his feelings toward her, he'd have been discharged on the spot.

Juan took the bridle she was carrying from her hand. "You're riding early today, Señora." He never called her by name. It was always Señora, always formally correct. "I'll saddle Daisy for you."

"Thank you, Juan." In spite of her hard-fought-for composure, Paula couldn't stop the flush that rose to her face. Lately, every time she saw Juan she felt that betraying flush, the sigh of emotions that up until today she had tried to deny even to herself.

The way he was looking at her now, his dark eyes warm, made her heart beat faster and her blood race warm in her veins. If Wayne had ever looked at her like that, even once, she would have been so deliriously happy that nothing else would have mattered.

But Wayne never looked at her like that, and he never had, and he never would, and she realized, with her heart turning cold in her breast, that her own love for Wayne had been killed, inch by inch, starting with the day he had married her and then left her alone in their hotel room in town on their wedding night while he'd gone out and got drunk and come back at three in the morning reeking of cheap perfume and the stale smell of sex with one of the saloon girls. He hadn't wanted to marry her, he'd been furious when his father had insisted on it, and that was the beginning of his petty revenge because she had trapped him.

"Are you going far? I can send one of the boys with you."

"No, thank you, Juan. It won't be necessary. Just saddle Daisy for me." She wanted to tell him to hurry but she didn't dare give any indication that this ride was more urgent than a simple desire for exercise and fresh air. If she told Juan where she was going he might try to talk her out of it because he'd know that it would cause trouble, and that would take even more time.

He helped her mount, although she needed no help. His hand lingered under her elbow just a fraction of a second longer than necessary, and the touch was like a caress. He checked the stirrups to make sure they were even, he checked the bridle to make sure that the bit wasn't too tight in Daisy's mouth. His eyes lingered on her face and Paula's breath caught in her throat. If only she'd known Juan before she'd fallen in love with the excitingly flamboyant Wayne, who had considered every girl in the Big Bend as fair game and no more than his just due!

She lifted the reins and turned Daisy. She was behaving like a schoolgirl with her first crush, and it wouldn't do. She was a married woman, and even if the Wentworths knew of some way she could fight the Bradshaws and get her freedom and keep Davie, anything between her and Juan was out of the question. Not because he was Mexican, but because he was a Catholic. He could never marry her, even if she were free a dozen times over. She swallowed past the hurt in her throat. She'd have to settle for freedom, even if it meant that she'd spend all the rest of her life regretting that she hadn't known Juan first.

Juan watched her ride away from him, and his face was also set and bleak. He should leave this place, ride away and never come back, but he knew that he'd never go as long as Paula was here. Even the pain of seeing her every day, of loving her so much that it was a constant torment to him, was better than never seeing her again.

His face still grim, he set about his day's work, calling young Pepe to help him hitch up a buckboard and load a roll of barbed wire to take to the north range to mend a section of fence that was broken. He could have sent someone else to do it, but today it suited him to be alone, with only the carefree and unobserving Pepe for company.

It was late in the afternoon when the work was near enough completed so that he could leave Pepe to finish up and begin to scour the brush for any strays that might have got through the break. Clay Bradshaw would be furious if every last head wasn't accounted for.

He topped a small rise and stood up in the stirrups, his eyes narrowed against the westering sun as he searched the terrain. The rough track that led toward Trail's End was directly below him, and he saw the billowing dust thrown up by a horse traveling fast before his eyes were caught by the movement of a slower rider a little distance ahead. He recognized the slower horse instantly. It was Paula's little paint, Daisy, and she was headed back home. Even as he held himself motionless, the faster horse cut down the distance between them, and he saw that it was Wayne on his powerful blaze-faced roan, and that Wayne was spurring the roan mercilessly with the cruel Spanish spurs he always used in order to overtake his wife.

Juan tensed. He didn't like the looks of things. Even from where he sat his own horse he could see that Wayne was in a fury, and it was certainly strange that Paula had been gone all day. She hadn't mentioned to him that morning, when he'd saddled her mare, that she was going anywhere but for a morning ride. If he'd known that she was going for any distance he'd have insisted on sending someone with her, even if it was only Pepe.

An exclamation burst from him as Wayne overtook his wife and reached out to grab Daisy's bit and haul her to a stop. In another second, he was off his own horse and dragging Paula from her saddle. Without thinking, Juan set spurs to his own horse and sent it galloping down the rise toward them.

Paula had been so deep in her thoughts that when Wayne had come thundering after her she'd felt nothing but complete shock when she'd realized that he was there.

431

Her heart pounded with panic as his hands dug into her shoulders so hard that it forced a cry of pain from her lips. His face lowering down into hers was black with fury.

"You've been to Trail's End, you've been visiting the Wentworths! Don't bother to lie about it, I saw your tracks when I passed by their turnoff. Just what the hell are you up to, you sneaking little bitch? You have no business going there, you have one hell of a nerve going to see those bastards!"

"Let go of me!" Her pain and shock drove her to a defiance that was ordinarily foreign to her. "Andrea's my friend, and I'll go to see her whenever I want to!"

"You ran to them to warn them that we're going to put a stop to this Mex citizenship business! You told us how you felt about it last night, but who'd have thought you'd actually dare go running to them with your warnings and your sympathy? You're my wife, damn it, you're a Bradshaw, and your loyalty belongs to us! You stay away from them, do you hear me? You damned well stay away from them! What did you tell them?"

"It's none of your business what I told them!" Paula's talk with Adam and Kate and Andrea had put backbone into her. She wasn't a slave, or a chattel, she was a woman with rights. If she'd made up her mind to leave Wayne, Adam would send a man to her father and tell him to go and get her. Adam himself, with enough men to back him up, would meet him there just in case Wayne or Clay got any idea that they could hold either her or her baby forcibly, and if they decided to make a court fight for Davie's custody, Adam would have the best lawyer that was at his disposal to represent her.

But she had no intention of telling Wayne that. She was alone with him out in the middle of nowhere, and in the mood he was in he could beat her severely. All the same, her own fury made her lash out at him.

"Your wife! That's funny, Wayne, that's the funniest thing I've heard in years! Those saloon girls in town are more your wives that I am. At least you go to bed with them. . . ."

Wayne's hand landed against her face with such

431

force that her head snapped back violently and her teeth bit into her tongue so that blood filled her mouth and nearly choked her. Her eyes blurred and her knees sagged so that if he hadn't been holding her up, she would have fallen. She screamed as he struck her again, and then again. The sides of her face were on fire, her head was exploding, and her screams strangled in her throat as the blows continued to rain on her face and head.

Wayne's fury at her defiance of him, at her taunts about his saloon whores, had sent him into such a blind rage that he hardly realized what he was doing. She was siding with the Wentworths against him, with that snobbish bitch who'd laughed in his face and told him what she thought of him. That aristocratic, stuck-up bitch who thought she was too good for him, who considered him the dirt under her feet! It had been rankling him ever since that scene he'd had with her, and this open defiance on Paula's part made a red haze appear in front of his eyes while the roaring sound of his own blood pounding in his ears kept him from hearing the horseman who bore down on him.

Juan catapulted from his horse and landed squarely on Wayne's back, bearing him to the ground with breath-shattering force. Paula fell to her knees, only half conscious, her mind only dimly aware of what was happening. As her eyes cleared a little, she saw two men, Wayne and another, fighting each other like two wild animals, each of their faces so contorted as to be scarcely recognizable.

"Juan!" The word tore itself from Paula's throat, already lacerated by her screams under Wayne's brutal assault. "Oh, my God, Juan!" She tried to struggle to her feet, but her legs wouldn't hold her up and she sank shuddering to the ground, her eyes riveted on the struggling figures in front of her.

Juan was lithe and quick—he had all the wiry strength that came from a lifetime spent in the saddle, handling cattle—but Wayne was taller, broader, and his strength had the bull-like proportions that were his heritage from his father. Both of them were blind with rage,

432

fighting to kill. Wayne's superior weight managed to throw Juan off just long enough for him to go for his gun. He drew and fired in one lightning-fast motion, and Paula's mouth opened in a soundless scream.

But as quick as Wayne was, Juan was quicker. He hurled himself forward from a crouching position, under the bullet that would have torn the life from his body, and closed with Wayne again. Once more they were down, straining, rolling over and over, while Juan strained to wrest the gun from Wayne's grip. Then there was one more shot, strangely muffled in the dust that had been stirred by their struggles, and Wayne's body fell sideways in what seemed to Paula to be slow motion before he collapsed.

On her hands and knees, she crawled toward him, still moving through a dust-obscured nightmare that wouldn't let up. Her hands reached out, touched the wound, came away covered with blood. She stared at them without comprehension until something snapped inside her head and she gathered up the folds of her riding skirt and began to press them against the wound to try to stanch the flow of blood.

"No, Señora, no!" Juan's voice came in gasps. He drew Paula's hands away and tore off his own shirt. "Let me. I didn't mean to, he was beating you. . . ."

His voice broke off and he pushed the hair that had fallen over his forehead back dazedly. Paula's breath rasped in her throat as she saw that Wayne's chest had stopped moving. Like someone in a dream, she laid her ear on his chest, but she could detect no heartbeat.

"It's no use, Paula." In the stress of the moment Juan called her by her given name for the first time. "He's dead."

They stared at each other, their faces white except for the still livid crimson smears on Paula's cheek when she'd listened for a heartbeat. Juan reached out and tried to wipe the blood away with his fingers, but it only smeared more.

A shudder passed through her, shaking her whole

body. "What are we going to do?" Her voice sounded like a stranger's, a croak in her aching, throbbing throat.

"Can you ride, if I lift you to your horse? Can you get back to the ranch? I have to get away; Señor Bradshaw will have me killed. You know that, Paula. I wouldn't have a chance, he'd never let me come to trial."

Bleakly, horribly, she knew that it was true. The way Clay felt . . . she corrected herself, shuddering . . . had felt about Wayne, he'd carry out his own execution against his son's killer without a second thought. The fact that Juan was a Mexican made it all the more certain. He'd feel no more compunction about stringing Juan up to the nearest tree than he would about stepping on a scorpion or tarantula.

"No! There's no way you can get away, Juan!" She fought to control her breathing, to get her thoughts in order. She had to think! "He'll track you down, he'll find you wherever you go, even if you go to the ends of Mexico! It was different when Mike Wentworth shot him, because he didn't die that time, he was content to have Mike remain a hunted exile. But you killed Wayne, you killed his son! He'll never give up until he finds you!"

Flies were already gathering on Wayne's chest, on his face and hands, and she turned away with nausea rising in her thoat. "We have to have help. We must go to Adam Wentworth; he'll help you, I know he will, he's a fair man and he'll believe me when I tell him how it happened. If you have a trial, a fair trial, I'll be able to testify for you. It's your only chance."

His face grim, his eyes bleak, but knowing that what Paula said was true, Juan caught up their horses. He lifted Paula into her saddle and steadied her until her trembling abated enough for her to take the reins that he pressed into her hand. Then he mounted his own. As they set their mounts into motion, turning them back toward Trail's End, buzzards were already circling in the rapidly darkening sky above them.

Without any word of explanation, he dismounted again and turned Wayne's body over on its face, took his slicker from his saddle roll and lashed it around his head

434

and shoulders, and then covered the whole body with a blanket. It was all he could do. He swung back into the saddle and caught up with Paula whose face was white and set as they headed for the only man in the Big Bend who was sure to help them.

28

Andrea was writing a letter to Caroline, a letter that was long overdue, when Carmelita came to her room to tell her that Manuel wanted to see her. She was finding the letter a hard one to write because it was difficult to get it all down without covering too many pages.

"After we got the whole story out of Paula and Juan Bustamonte, Dad decided to take Juan in to town, with an armed escort, that same night. If Clay Bradshaw had tracked him to Trail's End, there would have been a fight and just as likely someone else would have been killed. Paula was in a terrible state. She wanted to go with them, but we wouldn't allow that. She was already so shaken up that she might have said the wrong things and it could have been used against Juan later, at his trial. I think she's in love with Juan, and goodness knows, after being married to Wayne, I wouldn't blame her! Juan is a fine young man, and Dad is getting the best lawyer to be had to defend him.

"Of course Clay is wild. He came storming over here long before Dad got back, and he was frothing at the mouth. He wanted us to hand Paula over to him, and if Wade and Mother and I hadn't been armed, and if Dad hadn't expected it and posted armed vaqueros around the house, he'd have taken her by force. Clay was so wild that he swore he'd never let Paula on his ranch again and that he'd never let her have little Davie. Dad got a court order, and yesterday he and Mother and I rode over with a deputy to get the baby.

"Poor Pilar! I could have cried for her. She adores the baby, and no wonder. Both Clay and Wayne always treated her like dirt. Her face was as white as porcelain when we took Davie, and then just as we were leaving, she begged us to wait. She threw a few clothes into a bundle and came with us!

"Clay's sworn vengeance on us and the threats he made to Pilar don't bear repeating, but he can't touch her now. This morning Mother set out with her to take her to New Mexico to cousins she has there, to make her home with them. Mother will stay with her until she's well settled.

"The Ingrams came to take Paula home with them, they got here only about an hour after Clay had left, so Paula's all right, too. They stayed here until we'd retrieved the baby. Mr. Ingram will see that Clay can't get near either of them. Right now Paula is in town to testify at Juan's trial. Dad's there, too. He's kept half a dozen of our best men patrolling the jail to make sure that Clay wouldn't have a chance to take it by storm to get at Juan. That leaves Wade and me to hold down the ranch, along with Constanza and the children. It's going to be a long, hard-fought affair. Both Dad and Mr. Ingram have men guarding Paula at the hotel. The whole territory out here is taking sides, pro and con.

"Wade has his hands full keeping our armed patrols watching our buildings and fences and cattle. Last week they caught someone trying to poison one of the water tanks, and a section of fence was torn down, but we got

437

all the cattle back except for a few that were wantonly shot. Thus the patrols.

"Uncle Jacob is going to be furious that he's missing all the excitement. He's back in Georgia visiting his father, my Grandfather Gaylord whom I've written you about. We're trying to hold the lid down on a full-fledged range war, but it should settle down as soon as Juan is found innocent. I only hope that Paula hangs onto her courage and realizes that she'll be missing the best bet of her life if she doesn't marry him when all this is over. . . ."

"Yes, Carmelita?" Andrea bit the end of her pen, a habit she had when she was writing a letter and trying to think of what to say next.

"It's Manuel, Señora. He's on the patio, and he says he has to see you."

For Manuel to come to the house and ask to see her was so unusual that Andrea put the pen down on her unfinished letter and went out immediately.

Manuel stood with his shapeless old sombrero in his hands. He was covered with trail dust, another unusual circumstance, because ordinarily he wouldn't have dreamed of presenting himself to any member of the family without brushing his clothing off and washing his hands and face.

"Señora Andrea, there is a thing I must tell you. Today is Monday. . . ."

Of course it was Monday! Then Andrea understood. Every Monday morning, without fail, ever since he'd been brought to work and live here after Lupe had been killed, he rode up to the settlement to ask if any of the men who drove the wood-laden burro trains from Mexico back to the settlement had heard anything of his grandson Jesus. Manuel had never heard a word from the lad since he'd run away to join the revolutionists below the border, but he never gave up hope.

Andrea's face lighted up with a smile. "Manuel, is it Jesus, have you heard something about him?"

The old man shook his head. "Not Jesus, Señora. There is no word about Jesus. But there is word about Señor Michael. . . ."

The smile froze on Andrea's face and she felt as if

all the blood had been drained from it as well. She reached out to touch one of the pillars that held up the patio roof, for support.

"Tell me! What did you hear? Manuel, tell me!"

"It isn't a good thing that I have heard." Manuel looked down at his dusty huaraches, and Andrea's blood chilled so that she felt suddenly cold, as cold as if a winter wind were blowing on her. Her whole body had turned to ice. Mike was dead! That was what Manuel had heard, it must be that, and how was she going to bear it, how were her mother and her father and Wade going to bear it? Dead, hundreds of miles from home, they'd never even be able to recover his body. . . .

"Drunk." Manuel was saying. The word, out of context, penetrated the buzzing in her ears.

"What? I'm sorry, Manuel. What was that you just said?"

"Drunk," Manuel repeated patiently, his weathered face conveying his misery for the news he was forced to tell her. "Very drunk, Señora. This is what I was told, that Señor Michael is always drunk and that he is *loco* when he is drunk. Crazy. They call him, the rebels he rides with call him, El Rojo Loco."

Andrea drew a deep breath to steady herself. Mike was alive! Her relief was so great that it took several seconds for the rest of what Manuel had said to sink in.

Drunk? Always drunk? But that was insane. Mike didn't drink, he hardly drank at all. There'd always been plenty of liquor around the house. Scotch, bourbon, brandy, all the best labels, much of it imported from abroad. Although Adam, like Wade and Mike, drank very little, he insisted on the best. He enjoyed a drink before dinner after a long trail ride, a brandy after dinner, and Wade often joined him, but Mike had always left it strictly alone except for a token drink on some special occasion. Even at the parties and dances at neighboring ranches, when most of the other young men were inclined to overindulge, Mike had remained sober. He'd never needed alcohol to help him have a good time. His own love of life, his interest in other people, had made any additional stimulant unnecessary. Her heart sank, after its first soaring flight at what Manuel had told her. It was a mistake, it was someone else Manuel's friends had seen, someone they'd mistaken for Mike.

Even as she tried to convince herself, she knew that it wasn't true. Rojo meant red, and Mike's red hair would stand out anywhere. And everyone who had anything to do with the settlement knew Mike. He'd been hanging around there ever since he'd been old enough to straddle a horse and get himself up there, making himself one with the laborers, aligning himself with them. If the men who'd brought back the last train of wood said that it was Mike, then it was Mike.

"Where was he seen, Manuel?"

"A town." Manuel shook his head. "A little town, a few hovels. He was in the cantina, and he was drunk. But they told me, my friends told me, that he never stays in one place long. He comes, he goes. On raids, to fight, you understand? They told me, my friends told me, that every government soldier in Mexico wants to take him. He leads his men like a *loco,* like a madman, like he doesn't care if he gets killed or goes on living. And then, when the raid is over, he gets drunk again."

Manuel shook his head, the picture of dejection. "Señora, I didn't know whether to tell you or not. But Señor Wade is out on the range somewhere and Don Adam and Doña Catrina aren't at home, and I thought about it and I thought I had better tell you, to let you know that Señor Michael is still alive." He paused, shuffling his feet. "That he was alive a few days ago."

"Do you know where this town is, Manuel? Could you tell me how to get there?"

"Señora!" Astonishment made Manuel's head jerk up, and he looked at her with his eyes filled with consternation. "You cannot go there. There is a war, a revolution! The danger is great! It is a long way, and you are a woman."

"You know where it is! You must tell me, Manuel!"

"It is a long way, and he would not be there," the old man said stubbornly.

"But he might be there! Or someone may know where he went from there! How far is it?"

"Far." Manuel was clearly puzzling the matter of distance over in his head. Miles mean nothing to the Mexican peons; they measured distance according to how long it took to go to one place from another on a donkey. "Many days."

"Tell me the name of the town."

"Not a town, Señora. A few hovels. I have never been there. I have never heard of this place before, it was too far."

Andrea grasped his arm and pulled him inside the house. Ignoring his protests, his consternation at actually being inside the great *casa,* she literally hauled him into Adam's study, where she went directly to the bookcases and pulled an atlas from one of the shelves. She opened it on Adam's desk, flipping over the pages with hands that trembled with her haste.

Here! A map of Mexico. "Manuel, look. Where is the place? Can you show me on the map?"

"It would not be on the map, Señora. It is not large enough."

"But about where is it, the general location? Do you know, can you show me?"

Manuel studied the map, his face drawn up in intense concentration. He had never seen a map before. For all Andrea knew, this was the first time he had ever seen a book.

"Look." She pointed with her finger. "This is the Rio Grande. Here is Chihuahua, here is Coahuila. Do you understand?"

A light semed to dawn on Manuel's face. "Sí, Señora. El Rio Grande, Chihuahua, Coahuila."

"This is Monterrey." Andrea placed her right forefinger on the map. "You know Monterrey?"

Manuel's excitement was rising. *"Sí,* Señora. I have heard of Monterrey. I have never been there, but I have heard of it. I could find it, I think. But your brother is not there."

"Where, in relation to Monterrey, is he?"

"I do not know, Señora. They said, my friends said, that it was near Ciudad Viejo. Only not near."

"North or south of Ciudad Viejo?"

"South, I think." Manuel looked at her worriedly. "But you cannot go."

"I must go. I am going. Michael must be found and there is no one else. My father will be busy at Juan's trial for I don't know how long, and Wade is needed here. If Uncle Jacob were here, I'd ask him to go with me, but he's in Georgia, so I must go alone."

"Señora! Not alone! Think of the danger, think of the rebels, of the soldiers! How will you find your way?"

Andrea answered him by ripping the page with the map of Mexico out of the book. "I'll find it." Her chin was set, her hands and her eyes were steady. "And I'll find Mike, and I'll bring him home. Manuel, you must promise me that you won't tell anyone that I've gone, or where. You must swear it. Say that I've ridden to the Johnsons' place, when they wonder where I am and begin asking, but that won't be until tonight, when Wade comes in for supper and he and Constanza realize that I'm not at home. Say that I told you that I'm going to spend the night. I want a good head start, with a trail too cold to follow."

Manuel lifted his head and looked her directly in the eyes, and now his face had changed. It was set, resolute.

"I will tell them nothing, Señora, because I am going with you. You cannot go alone. You will search for Michael. I will search for him with you, and I will search for Jesus. *Por Dios,* pray that we will find them!"

Andrea looked at him for a full minute and then she nodded. "I'll be ready in half an hour."

"I am ready now, Señora. I have nothing to pack."

"Then saddle Runner, and a good strong horse for yourself." Andrea was through the door before she'd stopped speaking. Her mind was working like lightning. The kitchen first. Thank God for the custom of siesta, observed by all of the household help with Kate's permission. Manuella would be in her room, and by now Carmelita would also be resting. Constanza was with the children in the nursery, napping on a chaise longue while they took their afternoon naps, so that she would be near if one of them woke.

Bread and cheese, a bottle of wine. Cold chicken, left over from today's lunch. A bag of raisins, part of a side of bacon, not too much because Manuella mustn't realize that anything had been taken. Coffee, cornmeal. It would have to do. They'd have to depend on buying food along the way. A blanket for each of them, slickers, two tarps for ground covers if they had to sleep in the open and it chanced to rain.

The matter of arms was trickier. No one would think anything of it if her own rifle were gone, but how about Manuel? For good measure, she buckled on her holster.

After she was ready she snatched up her hat and her leather gloves and paused only long enough to scribble a note on a sheet of paper from her stationery box. Manuel had heard that one of the Johnson children was ill, and she had gone to see if she could help and taken Manuel with her.

She left the note on the dressing table where it would not be found until Carmelita was sent to ask why she hadn't come to supper. Then to the corral, where Manuel already had the horses saddled and waiting, canteens of water tied to the saddles. She carried an extra rifle for him. Trail's End boasted more rifles than hand guns so he had to do without. She transferred the heavy load of silver dollars she'd taken from the box of coins that Adam kept in his desk to the saddlebags. She could have taken gold coins as well, and paper money, but they would have been of little use to her where she was going.

They made up the saddle rolls rapidly, with the ease of long practice. A stab of conscience made her hesitate as she was about to swing into the saddle. Manuel was old, and the trip would be hard.

"Manuel, are you sure you want to come? I can manage alone."

"I am coming, Señora."

She didn't argue with him. He was determined, and he had a right to do as he wished. If she was frantic with

443

her need to find Michael, then he was just as frantic with his need to find his grandson. He would never have asked for a horse, or for permission to leave Trail's End, by himself, but now that Andrea was determined to ride into Mexico there was no way that she could forbid him to go with her. Of all his family, Jesus was the only one he had left. Pray God that he, like Michael, was still alive! She didn't mention, nor did Manuel, the almost impossibility of being able to find him. There had been word of Michael; at least with him they had some idea of where to start looking. With Jesus, they had none at all.

Silently, she finished mounting and just as silently, Manuel mounted Baldy. Compared to Runner, Baldy was nothing to look at. He was big-boned—his white face had given him his name—and he was almost as thickset as a plow horse, but he had stamina and, in case of need, speed that no one would have expected unless they'd had experience with him. He also had a vicious temper; that was why he was still in the corral. None of the vaqueros would ride him unless no other horse was available. Would Manuel be able to handle him?

Manuel's hand on the reins was firm. He spoke to the horse in Spanish, his voice soft but filled with authority. "Be good, *caballo*, or I will break your bones." Baldy laid his ears flat and stepped out, his eyes rolling, but he made no attempt to act up. Manuel could handle him. The Mexicans had a way with horses; they could control mounts that the American cowboys had to fight into submission. Perhaps it was because of the countless generations that they had lived so close to the land, almost as primitive as the beasts themselves, both of them having to submit to masters, so that they understood each other.

Andrea drew a deep breath as their slow, steady lope put distance between them and the ranch. With any luck no one at Trail's End would begin to worry about her until several days had passed. If a child were ill at the Johnsons', Constanza and Wade would expect her to stay as long as she could be of help. Wade was on the go from morning till night, covering every mile of

444

the ranch, watching for more sabotage because of the high feelings generated over Juan's trial. Kate wouldn't be back for days, and there was no telling when Adam would return. Constanza was wrapped up in the children, completely confident in Andrea's ability to take care of herself.

They gave all of the ranches and other habitations a wide berth. Andrea wanted no word to get back as to the direction they'd taken when she was finally missed. Here on her own home ground Manuel followed her lead without question. It would be different when they crossed the border into Mexico. Andrea knew a little of it from her trips with her family, but they would penetrate much deeper this time, and then the old man would be invaluable. No one would look at him twice; he looked no different from any old Mexican peon, a part of the landscape. He would be able to ask directions, to buy supplies, without exciting curiosity.

They slept out that first night, each rolled in a blanket against the chill of the desert after sundown, using their saddles as pillows. It was no hardship for Andrea; she'd slept out like this countless times when she'd traveled or gone on hunting trips with her father and brothers. Their hobbled horses moved about, making soft gentle noises as they foraged for whatever grass or brush they could find. Both animals were tough, bred to withstand scant food and water, part and parcel of the land they had been born to.

Manuel fell asleep as soon as he'd settled himself, his hip in the small depression he'd dug out to accommodate it. With the stoicism of his race, he knew that there was no use in lying awake worrying. Nothing could be done tonight; *mañana* was soon enough to look to what lay ahead of them. But Andrea's eyes remained open for a long time, looking up at the stars that were incredibly brilliant in the clear desert air.

Wherever Mike was, he could see these same stars. Unless, as Manuel had heard, he was too drunk to see them except for a blur that he had no interest in. Where was he? Would she find him in the hamlet somewhere near

445

Ciudad Viejo, or would he have disappeared again on one of his insanely reckless raids? For all she knew, she was already too late. He might be lying dead somewhere, his still open eyes staring sightlessly at these same stars.

She closed her eyes tightly. No! He wasn't dead. She'd know it if he were, she'd sense it. He was somewhere in Mexico, and she'd find him no matter how long it took, find him and bring him home. There was no reason now for him not to come home. Clay Bradshaw's enmity had turned from him and unleashed itself with full force against Juan.

Inevitably, her thought turned to Henry. Was he, too, out of doors tonight; did he, too, look up at the stars and wonder if she were looking at them?

Again, no! She wasn't going to think about that, either. Henry was lost to her. He'd made that clear the day she'd told him that she was going back to Reggie. Under the blanket, her hands clenched and she used the force of her will not to let tears come into her eyes or to bite down on her lower lip. What was done was done. If the door to a lifetime of happiness with Henry was closed to her, she was the one who had closed it when she'd left him for the second time, and it was up to her to find another door to open, another way to find fulfillment in her life.

Reggie! Her throat felt tight as she thought of him. The waste of what could have been a fine man hurt her. He was intelligent, handsome, fun to be with, he could have been anything, made anything he wanted of himself. Instead, he'd let his jealousy of his cousin warp him, ruin him. She'd loved him, perhaps not as much as she should have and still married him, but they could have made a good life together, they could have been happy if he hadn't had that idea that the world owed him whatever he wanted without any expenditure of effort on his part except exerting his charm.

It was daytime in England now. Was he at work at the bank, or had he thrown over the job he hated now that she'd left him and there was no reason for him to go on going through the motions of an industrious husband? Perhaps he'd given up their flat and moved in with Beatrice Langdon; perhaps he was letting her support him entirely while he played at being a wealthy young man around town. Could she have changed him if she'd tried harder? Should she have gone on trying, even in the face of his blatant infidelity?

Of course not! She couldn't throw away her own life on a man who was as seriously flawed as Reggie. Granted that she'd returned home to nothing. She must find a way to make something of that nothing. Helping the Mexican aliens become naturalized citizens was a good start. She'd never be a crusader like Martha, but when there was a job to be done, somebody had to do it, and doing something useful gave you a feeling that there was meaning to your life.

A gentle snore from the other blanket-wrapped figure told her that Manuel was right. This was the time for sleeping. Tomorrow was time enough to worry. She turned on her side so that the stars no longer could try to pry their way through her closed eyelids, and went to sleep.

They were on their way again as the first streaks of dawn appeared in the sky. They set a grueling pace, as fast as they dared to travel without exhausting their horses. Now Andrea's heritage came to her aid, enabling her to keep going hour after hour without undue fatigue or discomfort. And there was that other part of her heritage, the quality that wouldn't let her acknowledge the existence of the word quit. She didn't allow herself to worry about things back at home. She set her face forward toward her goal somewhere deep in the interior of Mexico. If it turned out to be a false goal, then she'd change direction and go on looking. If Mike was as well known as Manuel's friends said he was, someone would be able to give them a lead.

"Are you tired, Doña?"

Andrea noted Manuel's change of address toward her. At home he'd called her señora, merely a married woman. Now that they were away from the estate where Kate was doña, he had transferred that title to her. On this long trail where there were just the two of them, she was his patroness, she was Doña Andrea.

"No, Manuel. And you?"

"*Sí*. But we will go on. There will be rest in plenty once we have found Señor Michael and Jesus."

All the same, Andrea slowed their pace in spite of her own driving anxiety to hurry. She must remember that Manuel was old, that he was worn out from a lifetime of the most grueling labor and hardship.

By the time they crossed the border into Mexico miles from any habitation to make sure that their entrance would go unremarked she felt that she had spent her entire life in the saddle. She didn't know exactly where they were, but she knew that they were heading in the right direction.

It seemed that they traveled for eons without seeing a sign of human life. Then, when they did come upon a *rancho,* she almost wished that they'd passed it by far enough away so that she wouldn't have seen it.

The place, once a prosperous hacienda, was a scene of utter desolation. The hovels that had sheltered the peons who had labored for their master were deserted, half fallen down. Rusted-out pots and pans littered the pack earth dooryards, abandoned iron kettles, broken pottery bowls. The *casa* itself, when they approached it with caution, was weatherbeaten, its original whitewash streaked and dirty, its deeply embrasured windows broken, its heavy carved front door hanging by one hinge and gaping open. Furniture had been tumbled out to lie on the ground willy-nilly, broken, mutilated, vandalized beyond any human reason except the drive that the vandals had felt for revenge.

Machinery had been dragged from the outbuildings, dismantled, smashed, left in the open to rust so that it could never be used again. A lone, bedraggled chicken pecked in the dust, her feathers dirty and ragged, so scrawny that even a coyote might have passed it by in favor of finding a more palatable morsel.

They dismounted and tied their horses to a stunted

448

tree. "No one is there, I think," Manuel said. "Wait here, Doña, while I look inside the house."

But Andrea was right beside him, her gun in her hand, when he stepped over the threshold. Not a stick of furniture was left inside. The walls had been slashed with machetes, with knives, with anything that could be put to the purpose. Feathers wafted up and drifted in the air from the passage of their footsteps, from where mattresses and pillows had been slashed open. The floors, originally of patterned, colorful tile, were gouged and broken. It was vandalism, pure unadulterated vandalism. Every room was the same. There was nothing usable left. Like similar haciendas all over Mexico, this one had fallen victim to the revolution, and there was no hint as to whether the people who had lived here had escaped with their lives.

Andrea felt a shudder pass through her body, and an overwhelming need to be back in the fresh air. The walls of the house seemed to exude the hatred that had gone into its destruction. She'd heard about things like this, but this was the first time she'd seen it with her own eyes, and it brought home to her the weakness, the futility of words. Words might describe what she saw here but eyes, seeing it at first hand, made it real.

They circled the *casa,* moving warily to make sure that there was no one left living here in need of help. There was not, but they came across a new grave with rocks piled on it to keep marauding animals from digging it up and a rude cross made from two tree branches lashed together with rawhide implanted at its head. At least one human being had not escaped. Whether it was a man or a woman, a child, a peon or a member of the *patrón*'s family, they had no way of knowing. Manuel took off his sombrero and bowed his head, and his lips moved in a silent prayer that Andrea echoed. Then they went back to their horses and rode away from this scene of devastation.

It was mid-afternoon of the next day when they came upon a cluster of adobe buildings that passed for a town. The rutted road was the only street. Chickens and goats foraged in the barren dooryards of the adobe

449

jacals, getting what nourishment they could from the tufts of grass that sprouted haphazardly wherever a little moisture had gathered. There was one general store, hardly larger than the houses around it. The cantina was the most imposing building to be seen.

They watered their horses at the fountain that served both animals and humans and then tied them to the hitching post in front of the cantina. The inside of the place was murky and redolent with the smoke of thin brown cigarillos, with the smell of liquor and beer and of highly spiced, greasy chili. In spite of the fact that it was not yet sundown, half a dozen men were loafing at the scarred tables, bottles and glasses in front of them. They were rough and unshaven, four of them wearing the shapeless white pantaloons and loose overshirts of peons, but the other two wore bandoliers well filled with bullets and bristled with sidearms.

Bandits, Manuel's eyes warned Andrea without speaking. Many of the Mexican bandits, outlawed under Díaz's long regime, had flocked to the rebel cause, pitting their forces against Díaz and gathering more followers every week as other bandits and peons joined them. Probably they did some good; there was no doubt that Madero could use every man who would fight for him, but just as probably they still robbed anyone they saw fit, for their own enrichment. Brutal times spawn brutal men; it was the way of things and always had been since the beginning of time.

The proprietor was squat and swarthy, hardly more wholesome-looking than the two guerrillas. He brought them mescal and chili. If the chili couldn't compare with the delicious concoction that Manuella simmered all day in the huge cast-iron kettle in the kitchen at Trail's End, at least it was hot and filling, and Andrea ate it avidly, ignoring the grease that floated on the top of the bowl.

Ciudad Viejo? The proprietor and the peons shook their heads. They had never heard of it. Men like these, before the revolution, had seldom traveled more than twenty miles from the place of their birth. El Rojo Loco? They shook their heads again. But one of the bandits slouched over to their table, pushing his sombrero back on his head, chewing on his cigarillo as he regarded them, his eyes suspicious and probing.

He had heard of such a man. El Rojo Loco was somewhere to the south, he thought. While he talked, his eyes never left Andrea, noting the quality of her riding clothes, her obvious prosperity. Manuel's face was impassive, but Andrea knew that he was nervous about the bandit's inspection of her. That made two of them. They finished their meal quickly and stayed in the village only long enough to buy more supplies as well as a small bag of corn to supplement their horses' diet as they traveled.

They set Runner and Baldy to a fast pace once they had left the town behind them. "We had better hurry, Doña," Manuel said. "I did not like the way that bandit looked at you. He knew you are rich."

It was almost sunset when they topped a rise and saw the dust of two pursuing riders coming toward them. Grimly, Manuel unsheathed the rifle from his saddle scabbard, and Andrea did the same with hers.

"I am not a good shot," Manuel told her. "I will hold my fire unless it becomes necessary for me to shoot. Try not to kill them, Doña. Only wound them enough so that they will not go on following us, so that they will know that you aren't as easy to rob as they thought. If one or both were killed, maybe they have friends who would be angry and come hunting for us."

Andrea's mouth was dry as she watched the approaching riders cut down the distance between them. She knew that she could kill them. She was almost certain that she could only wound them, drive them off, as Manuel had suggested. Her aim was always true; her marksmanship was known throughout the whole of the Big Bend. But she had never shot at a human target in her life, never had to defend herself against molestation from marauding men who were as well armed as she was. What if she made a mistake, what if she actually killed a man? What if she panicked at the last second and her shots went wild?

"Now," Manuel urged her. The men were close enough so that they were sure they were the bandits from the cantina; both of them recognized their horses that had been tied outside. If further proof were needed, they had both drawn their own rifles and gave every appearance that they were confident that they would have no trouble in taking one old man and a woman.

Manuel squinted at them through the setting sun. *Gracias* to *Dios* that there were only two of them! His own rifle was at his shoulder, his finger on the trigger in readiness, but he waited for Andrea to fire because although he knew how to shoot a gun he had no real skill at firearms of any kind. Peons did not own guns, they were for the *patróns,* for the rich.

Andrea's mouth tasted metallic now. Her breath seemed to stop functioning, and she felt perspiration under her armpits and beading her forehead. *"Por Dios,* fire!" Manuel begged her.

At the last possible second, just as the oncoming riders came within rifle range, Andrea lifted her rifle to her shoulder and fired. Her aim was true. One of the bandits grasped his right arm where the bullet had plowed through it halfway to his shoulder.

Both men reined up, but after a short altercation the remaining bandit came on. He pulled up to fire a shot, but it went wild, careening harmlessly off a rock several feet from them. Once more Andrea's rifle cracked. This time the bullet took the oncoming rider's hat from his head, and he turned tail and galloped back to rejoin his comrade. For good measure, Andrea sent another bullet plowing into the ground directly under their horses' feet.

The deadly accuracy of her fire decided them. They reined their mounts around and headed back in the direction of the hamlet.

"We can only hope that they don't come back, bringing friends with them." Manuel's face was grim. "We had better go on, Doña. We must put more distance between ourselves and those robbers."

Although both Runner and Baldy were tired after their day's travel, they pushed on. They sought rocky ground, they veered their direction, they used every trick they knew to throw off would-be pursuers. The moon was already high in the sky when they decided that it was safe to make camp for the night. Even then, after a few mouthfuls of cold food because they didn't dare risk a fire, they took turns keeping watch until the rising sun streaked the sky.

They came to another settlement the next afternoon. This time, Andrea didn't ride in with Manuel. She concealed both herself and the horses in an arroyo, while Manuel, with a few of the silver dollars, walked in alone, only a peon who was too poor to own a horse or a burro. Even a horse like Baldy could cause trouble for them.

When Manuel returned hours later, he brought with him not only the information that men in the cantina knew of El Rojo Loco, but a complete change of clothing for Andrea, a peasant skirt, bright red and fully gathered, a white cotton peasant blouse, a pair of huaraches and a shawl.

He turned his back while she changed, using the time to dig out a hole large enough to bury her divided riding skirt, her leather vest and tailored shirt, her tooled boots and her leather gloves. Andrea felt only a momentary twinge of regret as she crushed her white hat so that it would fit in the hole on top of her other betraying clothing. Her father had brought her that hat from Dallas, when she was sixteen, along with a duplicate for Kate, and she treasured it.

When they set out again, Manuel drooping in his saddle but insisting that they must go on, they were no longer a wealthy young Americano lady and her servant, but a peon girl with her hair braided into one thick plait down her back and a shawl covering part of her face. From this time on until they had come to the end of their quest, they were a grandfather and his granddaughter, seeking relatives farther south after the hacienda where they had worked had been raided. The horses they rode had been stolen from the hacienda while the raid was still going on, to aid them in their flight to safety. Andrea's holster and sidearm were concealed under her full skirt, the rifles rolled up in the blankets in their bedrolls. If the worst happened and their horses were confiscated either by soldiers or *rurales* or bandits, they would still be armed and have enough money to buy burros and go on. No one would think to search for money under Andrea's skirt, tied to her waist in a sack gathered up from a rag torn from Manuel's shirt.

But Andrea had no intention of letting anyone get close enough to the horses to recognize their worth. The sight of Runner would be enough to make any soldier's or bandit's mouth water with greed to own him. Not only was he her horse, almost a part of her, but burros were too slow. Mike was somewhere to the south of them, and she had to find him as quickly as possible before he got himself killed. Resolutely, she turned her face toward the south, and went on.

29

Adam returned to Trail's End in an elated mood. Juan Bustamonte's trial was over, and the jury had found him innocent. It was a landmark decision; Clay Bradshaw had pulled out every stop in his effort to bring about a conviction. There was no doubt that without the lawyer Adam had procured for him, who had challenged and had dismissed every juror Clay had tried to plant on the jury and seen that only honest men, indicated by Adam himself, would render the verdict, that Juan would even now be listening to the sound of pounding as a gallows was built to hang him by the neck until he was dead.

There was also no least doubt that Clay's enmity toward Adam had doubled. The bitter man had left town before Adam and his small force of armed men, because Adam, Juan, Paula, and the Ingrams and the lawyer had stopped to celebrate with the best dinner the hotel could provide. Their celebration was extended by the men who came to congratulate them and insisted on buying drinks so they could toast their success in bringing real justice to the district.

Now Adam was eager to get home, his spirits high as he clattered into the stableyard and tossed his reins to Pepe before he strode to the house, as erect and vital as he had been twenty years ago.

If only Kate were here! But she hadn't returned from escorting Pilar to New Mexico, and so he'd have to do without her excited reaction, without the wild, yearned-for lovemaking that would have released the tensions that had built up during the bitterly fought trial.

But Andrea would be here, and Wade and Constanza. They'd have a celebration; Adam could already savor the rich, imported brandy with which they'd toast each other and their victory. The brandy made from his own peach orchard was of excellent quality, admired by all his friends, but tonight called for something special.

He turned as he reached the patio, looking for Juan, who he had supposed was right behind him. It had already been arranged between them; Juan was to work at Trail's End until the worst of the sensational, scandal-racked case had died down and he and Paula could be married. Adam wanted Juan where he could make sure that Clay Bradshaw couldn't get at him; for him to have set out seeking work, even in New Mexico or Colorado or Montana or any other place, would have been tantamount to suicide because Clay would have him tracked and shot down. Adam would explore possibilities and find a safe place for the young couple when the time came. In the meantime, Juan was to stay here.

"Come on, Juan. It's been a long ride, and I'm hungry and thirsty. Manuella will find something for us while we do some bragging to the others."

Juan's smile flashed. He'd only followed Adam to try to thank him here with no one else around for all he had done for him. It had never entered his mind that he was to come into the *casa* as a guest. "*Gracias,* Señor Wentworth."

It was well after dark. They'd pushed hard all day in order not to have to spend another night on the trail because of Adam's eagerness to get home. Adam steered Juan through the door. He entered the house quietly, as he always did, so that Wade and Constanza were taken by surprise when he appeared in the archway of the living room.

"Dad! You're back!" Wade rose from the deep leather chair and crossed the room to his father, his hand held out in welcome. Standing face to face, they were cut from the same piece of stone, with only Wade's younger face setting them apart. "I'm glad to see you! And Juan!" His face lighted up even more. "I don't have to ask how the trial went, if you're here. Not that I had any doubt as to the outcome. A not guilty verdict was the only possible one."

Constanza too had risen and come forward, her fair hair like a halo in the lamplight. "I'm proud of you, Father," she said. "And very happy."

"You ought to be proud of me!" Adam's grin erased any hint of conceit. "It was a real battle. I worked harder to have that verdict brought in than I ever worked on anything else in my life. And it was worth it, almost as much to me and the rest of this district as it is to Juan. Every right-thinking man in the Big Bend is proud of me tonight, proud of our court system, proud that we can force justice when it's necessary. This case will set a precedent. We ought to have set off firecrackers and skyrockets when it was over, just like the Fourth of July. Constanza, will you see if Manuella is still awake so that she can get us something to eat? Wade, Juan and I need a drink." He looked around, frowning for the first time since he'd come in. "Where's Andrea? She ought to have heard the ruckus by now and come in to congratulate us in the manner we deserve!"

"Andrea isn't here. She had word that there's sickness over at the Lazy J, and she took Manuel and rode over there three or four days ago to see if there was anything she could do. I expect she'll be coming back any time now, providing it isn't too serious. We've had our hands so full patrolling to make sure that none of Clay's men or his sympathizers did any more damage that I haven't spared a man to ride over and see how things are."

Now there was a faint trace of a frown between Constanza's eyebrows. "I think we should send someone the first thing in the morning. I'm a little worried, Wade. It isn't like Andrea not to have sent back word of how things are with the Johnsons, and when she'll be back. She left while I was in the nursery with the babies, and neither Manuella or Carmelita saw her leave. She only left a note in her room. It's strange that Manuel hasn't come back. The Johnsons would have sent a man with Andrea, when she wanted to leave."

"We'll do that, Constanza." Adam's smile at his daughter-in-law was fond. He'd always liked the girl, but since she'd married Wade, his liking had turned into love as real as that he had for his own children. She was a perfect wife for Wade, an exemplary mother to his grandchildren, and she had courage. "I'll send Sanchez as soon as it's daylight. But I doubt that there's anything to worry about. Andrea would have got word to you if there were. Wade, let me tell you how my man Collins made a monkey of the prosecuting attorney every time he tried to make a point. . . ."

In a few more minutes he was deep in a rehash of the trial, savoring the brandy and the cold meat and pie that Manuella brought in. Constanza let Wade pour her a small glass of sherry, and she leaned forward in her chair, as interested in Adam's account of the trial as her husband. Andrea was forgotten; it was foolish of her to be worried.

It wasn't until two mornings later, when Adam and Wade were both out on the range, that Constanza felt a sudden premonition of trouble when Carmelita told her that Sanchez was back and waiting on the patio to report to her.

The vaquero looked both disturbed and perplexed. He was still covered with trail dust and his shoulders sagged with weariness, pointing out the fact that he'd pushed his horse and himself to the limit on his return trip.

"Señora, she hasn't been there, she was never there

at all. There is no sickness at the Lazy J. They have heard nothing of her."

Constanza's hand went to her throat to still the pulse that was beating too hard there. "Sanchez, will you send one of the men, anyone you can find, to locate Señor Adam and Señor Wade? Have him tell them what you just told me. Then you must have something to eat, and rest."

"*Si*, Señora. I'll do it immediately. Señora, where do you think she can be?"

Constanza's face was as strained as her voice. "I don't know, Sanchez. But Señor Adam and Señor Wade will find her, wherever she is. Send the man now, please. And thank you for riding so fast."

Somehow, she had the feeling that it had been necessary for Sanchez to ride so fast. Wherever Andrea and Manuel were, she felt certain that they needed to be found as soon as possible.

Adam and Wade, astounded by the news, felt the same way. Riders were sent out, half a dozen of them, to contact every ranch, every house, where Andrea might possibly have gone. The mystery of her disappearance was impenetrable; there had been no message delivered to the ranch—they made sure of that before they did anything else. No one had brought mail, no rider had come in, and yet Andrea was gone, and Manuel with her.

The riders returned, trail-weary, one by one, with word that Andrea was not at any of the places they had gone to inquire about her. The mystery deepened. By now even Adam admitted that he was worried. His face was grim as he set about organizing an even more extensive search. God, but he wished that Kate were here! Only he didn't really wish that at all. For Kate to return to find Andrea still missing, with no clue as to where she might have gone, would only add to the problem.

Blast the girl! She'd aways been self-willed and wild, hell-bent on doing exactly as she pleased whenever she pleased, but she'd never pulled a trick like this before. When he got her back, Adam was going to have a few words to say to her, adult or not. She had to be somewhere, but rack his brain as he might, he couldn't come up with a single idea of where she might be.

Henry rode over on the third morning, looking as grim as Adam felt. He'd heard about Andrea's being missing and the search for her on the first day it had been instituted, but he'd waited, more tense than he was willing to admit, to hear that she'd either turned up of her own accord or been found. By now, even his iron will wasn't able to make him wait any longer.

"Where the hell could she be, Adam?" he demanded, his knuckles white as he grasped the cup of coffee that Manuella placed in front of him.

"If I knew that, I wouldn't be going crazy," Adam told him. "I'm going into town tomorrow, I'm going to send a wire to Santa Fe, just on the thousand-to-one chance that Andrea took it into her head either to go there or to get in touch with her mother. Only it doesn't seem likely. Kate would have let me know."

"I'll ride in with you." Henry's face was as expressionless as a stone statue's, but Adam detected the gnawing worry for Andrea in his eyes. That was another thing that kept him from feeling the peace with life that he should have felt, this rift between Andrea and Henry, both of them too proud to make the first move to heal it. Not that he blamed Henry. In the younger man's place he'd probably have been just as stiff-necked, at that age. And Andrea was still married to Reggie Mansfield, and Adam didn't doubt that she felt that she had no right to try to get Hank back again.

He was going to do something about that, as soon as he located Andrea. There had to be a way to get her her freedom, and he meant to leave no pebble unturned until he found it. If he had anything to say about it, and he knew that he was going to have a great deal to say about it, those two were going to end up married to each other the way they should have been in the first place, before Andrea had gone off on that tangent that had all but destroyed her life. It was bad enough that Mike was probably down in Mexico somewhere, and God knew where

460

he'd come back. He had no intention of losing Andrea, and losing Henry in the bargain.

The idea of getting in touch with Kate showed the measure of Adam's worry. For the last two days he'd been glad that she was away from home so that she wouldn't have to bear the burden of Andrea's disappearance. Now he wanted her at home, whether she knew anything about Andrea or not. Kate was smart, and her woman's brain might come up with something that he and Wade had missed. Constanza wasn't much help there, even if she was a woman; she'd been sheltered all her life, guarded, she could have no conception of any girl disappearing without a trace, much less of where she might have gone.

"Do you think she might have headed back to Georgia, or to England?" Henry asked.

"With only the clothes on her back? And what would she have wanted with Manuel?"

"That's the poser, isn't it?" Henry put down his cup. The coffee tasted bitter to him and the ham and eggs stuck in his throat, even though he was ravenous after his long ride, started in the middle of the night to make sure that he got to Trail's End before Adam had left the house. "Wherever she was heading, why would she take Manuel with her?"

He shoved his plate aside, his breakfast only half finished, his forehead creased with a frown. There had to be some connection, and it came to him so suddenly that he wondered why Adam or Wade hadn't thought of it.

"Doesn't Manuel ride up to the settlement every week, looking for news about Jesus?"

Adam almost choked on his own second cup of coffee. Damn him for an idiot! It was his turn to push the remainder of his breakfast aside. "Let's get going," he said. "It's the only lead I haven't chased down."

They rode in silence, pushing their horses, Henry on a fresh mount from Adam's corral. Adam cursed himself every step of the way. All this time wasted just because he hadn't had sense to make the connection that Henry had seen immediately!

Henry's eyes narrowed as they rode into the settlement. The company office was situated some distance from the hovels that the workers lived in, well away from the litter and the undesired proximity of the people that the managers considered so far beneath them, but he recognized the oversized roan that was tied outside. "Looks like Clay's here," he said. "And the mood he'll be in, after Juan was acquitted, I feel sorry for anyone he decides to take his temper out on. No wonder it's so quiet. There isn't a youngster in sight, or a woman."

He was right. Whenever Clay came to the settlement, they disappeared into their hovels or into the brush as soon as they saw him. All of these people were wary of the huge, evil-tempered man who looked on them as no better than animals.

Adam's smile was without humor. "We'll give him a wide berth. Let's try Señora Escalante, Hank. She'll know what we want to know, if anyone does."

Rosa Escalante was the oldest woman in the settlement, a withered grandmother with bright, curious eyes in a face that had been molded into lines of compassion for all humanity from her own years of hardship and the hardships of those around her. Everyone at the settlement came to her with their troubles, even if all she could offer was sympathy. She was in her tiny shack, sewing a patch on a pair of pantaloons while the small lad who owned them squatted on the floor beside her, his indecency covered by a piece of sacking that ordinarily served as a towel while he waited for Rosa to fix his pantaloons so that a sizable section of his buttocks wouldn't disgrace him by showing through the three-cornered tear.

"Señor Wentworth, Señor Stockton!" Rosa rose immediately, her face weathered in a smile that deepened her wrinkles. "I am happy to see you. We have already heard that you won Juan's case. It is a wonderful thing." Her Spanish was so rapid that only someone as familiar with the language as he was with his own could have followed what she was saying. "Let me bring you coffee, and I have tortillas."

"Thank you, Señora Escalante. Coffee will be welcome." To refuse her hospitality would be an insult.

The coffee was thick and bitter, served without sugar or cream, commodities that none of the settlement people could afford, but no worse than many such mugs that both Adam and Henry had drunk on the trail.

"Señor Bradshaw is here. He kicked at Ramon," Rosa warned them. "His face is as black as a thundercloud. Be careful of that man, Señor Wentworth. He has no love for you."

Still squatting on the floor, the boy Ramon uncovered his left leg, where a bruise was rapidly turning purple because he hadn't been quick enough to get out of Clay's way. Ramon looked proud; a bruise inflicted by Clay Bradshaw would be something to talk about for days, gaining him prestige and a great deal of sympathy.

Adam ruffled the boy's hair and slipped a silver dollar into his hand. "You can treat your friends while you tell them about it."

Ramon was on his feet instantly, his face looking like a sunrise on a clear summer day. "I'll watch your horses, Señor Wentworth. I'll take good care of them, nothing will happen to them!" The towel slipped to the floor, but his shapeless shirt preserved his dignity, just barely. "You can count on me."

Even as worried as he was, Adam couldn't suppress a smile. Charity was not to be tolerated, but watching the horses was a gift of reciprocated friendship that made accepting the silver dollar, more money than Ramon had ever held in his hand before, all right.

"Señora Escalante, Manuel was here last Monday. Was there any news for him?"

Rosa's face was immediately serious, and she nodded vigorously. "Sí. There was news, much news. Not about Jesus." She crossed herself. "There has been no word about Jesus since he left. But news, Señor Wentworth, for you! You did not know, he has not told you? This is something I do not understand."

Adam felt his blood turn cold. "I didn't know. I was in town, attending the trial. And I have not seen Manuel since I returned."

"You do not know!" Rosa was consternated. "But

the news was of your son Michael, Señor! The men who bring the wood heard of him. They heard that he was somewhere near Ciudad Viejo, that he goes there sometimes, that he is still alive! Manuel left here immediately, without even waiting for food or coffee, to tell you."

Adam's heart lurched. Beside him, he felt rather than saw the tenseness of Henry's body. What Rosa had told them made everything clear. When Manuel had returned to the ranch, Wade had not been at the house and so the old man had told Andrea. There was no doubt about it. Andrea, being Andrea, had immediately taken it into her head to go and find Mike, and Manuel had gone with her. She hadn't told anyone, even Constanza, because she'd known that Wade would go after her and try to make her come back and wait until the men could go searching for Mike.

Ramon was filled with pride and self-importance as they emerged from Rosa's shack. "No one has touched your horses, Señor. I let no one come near them." The fact that none of the women or children had ventured from their hovels to come near the horses had nothing to do with it. "And Señor Bradshaw left—his horse was gone when I came out." It was an important thing to have news to give to such men as Señor Wentworth and Señor Stockton. Only he, Ramon, had dared to show himself while Señor Bradshaw was still in the settlement; the others had still not dared come out in case he changed his mind and came back in a few moments, as he often did, to tell the supervisors something he had forgotten.

They were nearly down the mountain track before Adam broke the silence as they pushed their horses even harder than they had on their way up.

"Are you coming with me?"

"Yes."

"Good. I can't spare Wade from the ranch, and I don't want to take anyone else. A bigger party would attract too much attention, and we'll make faster time alone. I'll send a man to tell your folks that you'll be with me for as long as it takes. We'll give the horses a couple

464

of hours' rest while we get our gear together and I have a conference with Wade, and then we'll be on our way."

The words had hardly left his mouth when a shot rang out and Adam clutched at his shoulder before he slumped over and all but fell from the saddle. Henry cursed as he spotted the sniper, already taking aim for a second shot. Clay Bradshaw! They should have had the sense to watch out for him instead of assuming that he'd kept right on going, not wanting to have to speak to the man who had foiled all his efforts to send Juan to the gallows. His mind must have come unhinged to ambush them and shoot Adam down without any warning!

Even as those thoughts raced through Henry's mind in less than a split second, his own gun was in his hand and he threw down on Clay and fired. Clay fell heavily, struggled to his knees, and tried to raise his own gun again. Henry's finger was already squeezing the trigger for his second shot when Adam, with an effort that drained every drop of blood from his face, reached over and knocked his arm up and ruined his aim.

"No, Hank! He must be out of his mind! We can't kill him in cold blood now that he's already down!"

The effort that deflecting Henry's aim had cost him now took its toll. Adam slumped in his saddle again, and Henry, cursing, managed to dismount just in time to keep him from falling to the ground. He let Adam lie where he eased him down and whirled to give all of his attention to the man who was lying in the track in front of them.

"Drop it, Clay! Drop it or you're a dead man!" Henry shouted.

There was no need for his command. Clay had already dropped his gun, and now he was clutching at his leg, his face contorted. Henry approached him cautiously, wary of a trick. It wouldn't be the first time a man had used a ruse to get in a final, killing shot.

But Clay wasn't feigning. "My leg! It's torn to pieces! The bullet's in the bone!"

Henry picked up Clay's gun and threw it as far as he could, too far for a man with a mangled leg to crawl after it and retrieve it. "I'll get back to you," he said curtly.

Working with maximum efficiency, he stripped away Adam's shirt and used his bandana to make a pad to stanch the flow of blood, anchoring it with his own bandana. Then, cursing the necessity of doing all he could for the would-be murderer, he returned to Clay.

The wound, halfway between knee and thigh, was an ugly one. The bullet had torn through flesh and muscle diagonally as it had entered, before it had lodged against the bone. Henry's exploring fingers told him that much. Like all ranch-bred men, he knew something of injuries. Doctors were a long way away, and everyone had to learn rough-and-ready first aid. Squatting on his heels, working as efficiently as he had on Adam, he removed Clay's vest so he could get at his shirt to get it off to make a pad and then bind it as well as he could with Clay's bandana.

There was no way he could move the huge man without agravating his condition. He'd have to be carried the rest of the way down on a litter, or rather, in this case where there was such a distance to go, dragged on a travois behind a horse, the way the Indians transported goods or injured persons.

Clay's skin felt cold to him when he touched his forehead. Shock. Shaking his head, Henry caught up his horse and removed the bedroll blanket and wrapped it around the man. Then he placed his own canteen as well as Clay's beside him. It was all he could do. Clay would either survive, or he wouldn't. Right now Henry had to get Adam home.

Beau Noir stood firm, only his ears twitching and his eyes rolling nervously as Henry boosted Adam up into the saddle. Adam was just conscious enough to stay there by supporting himself with the saddle horn. There was no need to lead Beau; the magnificent black stallion followed Henry's mount, placing his feet carefully as though he knew that Adam was hurt and must be carried gently.

"Good boy," Henry said. "You keep that up and we'll get him home." Wherever the track was wide enough to allow it, he rode beside Beau, close enough so that he could reach out and grab Adam if Adam slipped into unconsciousness and started to fall. It was slow going, and

Henry had to combat his urge for haste. Getting there without setting Adam to bleeding again was more important than getting there fast.

It took a long time, and Adam was barely clinging to consciousness when they reached Trail's End. Vaqueros and yard workers came running to help as soon as they were spotted, their exclamations of amazement and dismay falling on deaf ears as Henry let them lift Adam gently from Beau Noir while he burst into the house shouting for Constanza.

Two days later, Henry set about the business of packing his gear for a long journey. Miles Claybourne, the gruff, overworked doctor who served too large an area, had said that Adam was out of danger, although it would be a long time before he was up and about again. Clay had been brought down the trail just as Henry had directed, sending men from Trail's End to see to it. The man still clung to life, but Claybourne doubted that he'd ever regain the full use of his leg, even if he pulled through. There had been too much muscle damage, and the doctor couldn't work miracles. Once again, a Bradshaw was fighting for his life at Trail's End, this time the father rather than the son. His voice cold, Wade agreed with Hank that as soon as Clay could be moved he was to be taken to town in a wagon. They would do what they could to preserve his life, but they wouldn't shelter him under Adam's roof a moment longer than necessary.

"You'll charge him with attempted murder, of course." It wasn't a question.

"We'll charge him." Wade's voice was hard, his face even harder. "And this will be another trial that he won't win! Hank, thanks for going to look for Andrea. I'd give anything I own to be able to go with you, but there's no way I can leave the ranch now. Are you sure you don't want some men to ride with you?"

"I'm sure. There's just one thing, Wade. Tell Adam I took his horse."

He had only one purpose when he rode out on Beau Noir, to find Andrea if he had to track her to Mexico City and beyond. He knew where she'd been headed when she'd run off to find Mike. Ciudad Viejo. That was all he needed to know. A girl who looked like Andrea, riding a horse like Runner, would be noticed wherever she went. All he had to do was keep going, and he'd come up with her sooner or later.

He touched Beau with his heel and rode out without looking back. Damn her, he thought. She'd caused him nothing but trouble ever since he'd first met her when he'd been no more than a cowlicked adolescent. If it wasn't for his friendship with Adam and Wade, he wouldn't make the effort to find her. She'd never be anything but trouble for him, she'd proved that, over and over, starting from the days when she'd almost driven him out of his mind by flirting with Wayne Bradshaw up until the time she'd gone back to that husband of hers in England. Even for Adam and Wade, what was he doing setting off to Mexico to find her?

It didn't matter what he thought he was doing. He told himself that he was going more for Mike than for Dria, more to bring them both back so that Adam and Kate could breathe easy. His thoughts were as black as Beau Noir's hide as he set as fast a pace as he dared without wearing even that magnificent animal out. He'd find her, and he'd bring her back and push her though her own front door, and then it would be up to Adam and Kate to control her. His going after her didn't mean anything except that it was a job that had to be done.

His face hard, he turned Beau southward, intent on only the one thing, to get it over with and then get back to his own life and begin hunting for a girl worth marrying. It was time he settled down and started raising a family. He wasn't about to spend all the rest of his life alone just because one girl had turned him bitter. He'd get married, and that would put an end to it, once and for all.

MEXICO

30

If Andrea hadn't been too numb with weariness to think, she'd have thought that she'd never been as tired as this is her life! The miles she and Manuel had put behind them had been endless. Her red skirt was bedraggled, her blouse was gray with trail dust, her feet felt gritty in their woven huaraches. There was dust and sand between her toes, there was grit between her teeth, even her scalp felt gritty. She knew that her face was as dirty as her hands. She'd have given the next year of her life for a bath, a real bath in her own flower-painted bathtub at Trail's End, with the water so hot that she could hardly sit in it, with a whole fresh cake of her favorite rose-scented soap.

The bath bore thinking about; her own bed, wide and soft, with clean, scented sheets and her down-stuffed pillows, didn't. Riding beside her, his shoulders slumped and his head almost resting on his chest, she knew that Manuel was even more tired than she was.

Even their horses bore little resemblance to the clean-limbed, sleek mounts that they had set out on. Now Runner's coat was matted and dirty, and his mane was tangled and filled with burrs and bits of brush. Only his spirit remained the same. He was indefatigable, and that at least was a blessing. If their horses had given out the way most horses would have on this last, endless and exhausting portion of their odyssey, they would have been afoot, their mission aborted somewhere, Andrea was no longer sure where, deep in Mexico.

Michael had not been at Ciudad Viejo, or at any of the little hamlets that were anywhere near it. He had been there, off and on, but it had been a long time since he had been seen. The peons, the bandits, that they had questioned had had the impression that the last time he had left those parts he had not intended coming back. It was getting too dangerous. The *ruvales* had been there searching for him. His reputation had grown, and there was a price on his head. No one knew where he might be now.

What direction had he taken? East, but that meant nothing. There were four directions; he might have turned off in any of them once he had left the town behind, or countless variations of any direction. How many men had been with him? None. El Rojo Loco did not travel with a band. When he decided to raid, to punish the oppressors, he searched out a band and made himself its leader. It was safer that way; a band was easier for the soldiers to find. He struck, he routed the enemy, he wreaked havoc on enemy-held towns, and then he faded away again, always alone.

"Go southeast," a sloe-eyed woman, plump, still pretty in spite of the fact that her first youth was behind her, told them. "I do not know for certain, but things he said to me made me think that he might go southeast."

Her face was soft when she spoke of Michael. It was obvious to Andrea that she thought of Mike half as a boy, a son, and half as a man she loved.

"You are his sister? Find him, *Señorita*. Find him and take him home, or else he will not live to see many more days. He is *loco,* mad." She'd fingered the Mexican

472

silver cross around her neck, her lips whispering a prayer, her eyes filled with desolation.

"Doña, the town is near." Manuel's voice jolted Andrea from her fatigue-sodden reverie. She straightened her back and patted Runner's neck. Mike wouldn't be there, any more than he had been at any of the other desolate, war-ravaged settlements where they had searched for him, but at least the horses would have a chance to rest and eat something other than withered grass and brush. And she would have a chance to wash, all over, so that she could feel like a human being again.

She wished that she dared give a boy a few centavos to brush Runner and Baldy and pick the burrs out of their manes, but the worse the horses looked, the safer they were. There had been too many covetous looks at them since this journey had begun. When they'd approached settlements of any size, where there might be either soldiers or rebel bands, they hadn't ridden the horses in at all, but Manuel had made her camp in hidden arroyos well outside of the towns while he walked in to make his inquiries. It wasn't only the horses that such men looked at with avarice in their eyes. Tired, bedraggled, dirty, Andrea was still a beautiful woman, and a man who faces constant danger of death has more than the normal amount of lust in his blood. Beauty, as well as any appearance of having more than a few centavos, was a thing that had to be well concealed from lustful eyes.

This settlement was like all the others they had visited. They didn't look in larger towns; Mike wouldn't be foolish enough, no matter how drunk or how crazy he was, to show himself where there were sure to be soldiers who would recognize him. His red hair, his wiry build, his obviously being a gringo, made him easily recognizable, and who could distinguish, in times like these, between friend and enemy? Even a good man, if he were hungry enough or desperate enough over the hunger of his family, might be tempted by the size of the award for his capture, preferably dead rather than alive.

There were only two horses and three burros hitched outside the cantina, so even Manuel thought that it would be safe for Andrea to enter it with him, as long as she kept her shawl well over her head so that her beauty would not be noticed. If there had been either soldiers or bandits in the cantina there would have been more horses.

Andrea examined the horses with her heart sinking. Neither of them bore any resemblance to Jumping Jack. Mike had named him because it had been so hard to break him to the saddle; he'd been the worst bucker that he'd ever broken. But once he'd gentled him, he'd developed into one of Trail's End's best mounts, and Mike had shortened the name to Jacko.

No, neither of these horses was Jacko. This town, too, was a dead one. But they still must eat and rest; they still must ask their questions. Mike had to be somewhere, and one of these days they'd either find him or find someone who knew where he was.

Unless they were too late. The words sneaked through the barrier that Andrea had erected against them, her defenses against them weak because of her tiredness. Unless he was already dead.

Every eye in the place turned toward them as they entered the dim room. Coming from the brighter light of the fast-waning afternoon, it took Andrea's eyes a moment to adjust. No candles or kerosene lamps had yet been lighted, although it was nearly dark inside, with only one small window in the front to provide illumination. Such commodities were expensive, and could not be wasted. A man needs but little light to lift a glass to his mouth—he already knows where it is.

All of the men in the cantina wore the pantaloons and shapeless overshirts of the peons. All but one, whose head was in his arms as he slumped asleep at a table, stared at the newcomers with quick suspicion until they saw it was only an old peon, a man like themselves, and a young woman who was probably his granddaughter. Wanderers, as so many were these days when thousands upon thousands had been displaced from the haciendas where they had lived and labored all of their lives, homeless people searching for relatives, looking for work. Men who were young and strong enough joined the rebel forces

474

unless the soldiers caught them first and conscripted them forcibly into the army. Women became camp followers or went or were taken to the larger cities to become washer-women or prostitutes, or to starve. That was the way things were.

"Chili," Manuel said. He didn't make the mistake of helping Andrea with her chair at the battered table. He slumped down first, the picture of weariness, and Andrea followed suit, keeping her head bent to conceal her face. "And mescal."

He was too tired to ask his questions now; he'd wait until after he'd eaten. *Por Dios,* but he was tired! And in all these hundreds of miles that they had traveled, there had been no trace of either Señor Michael or Jesus. There had been word of Michael, many times there had been word of him because Michael was someone that many people knew of. Jesus . . . Manuel sighed. Jesus was just another boy, too young to fight but fighting anyway, in-distinguishable from hundreds of others just like him. How many Jesus Mendozas of his age were there in Mexico? So many that Manuel could not even begin to think of the number. He himself had known a dozen, in his own small territory, before he had taken Jesus and Lupe across the border.

"Tequila!" The voice came from the peon slumped over his table. It was thick with sleep, thick with drink. "Another bottle, *por favor.*"

Sitting with her head still bowed, Andrea's heart leaped and every nerve in her body began to quiver. Her head jerked up as she stared at the man who had spoken. His back was toward her, and he was wearing a huge Mexican sombrero, but she knew that it was Mike, she'd know his voice among a thousand others.

She was on her feet at once, crossing the room and circling the table.

Bleary eyes, bloodshot, half glazed, looked up as she stood directly in front of him.

"Mike. Oh, Mike! At last, I've found you at last!"

For a moment, the eyes were confused. To Mike, still only half awake, much more than half drunk, the girl in front of him looked like any other Mexican girl in her torn red skirt and peasant blouse and with a shawl over her hair.

"Andrea?" Then his chair scraped back as he came to his feet, staggering, losing his balance and having to sit down again before he fell. "Good God, Andrea! What the hell are you doing here, dressed for a masquerade?"

Andrea was laughing and crying at the same time, fighting hysteria. "Looking for you, you idiot! Oh, Mike, I thought I'd never find you! Manuel and I have been looking and looking. . . ."

"Go home," Mike said. He groped for his glass and cursed when he found it empty. The proprietor put another bottle on the table in front of him, but when he pulled out the cork with his teeth and made to pour it, Andrea's hand was over the top of his glass.

"Mike, you've had enough. Look at you, you're drunk!"

Mike grasped her hand and removed it, his laughter more like a bark. "Drunk. Always drunk, unless I'm raiding. Have to stay sober then, have to know what I'm doing. That's why I don't raid often enough. Too long between drinks, too long sober. You don't want any of this, Dria. It's raw, it'll burn your pretty throat out. Go home where you can have some nice, expensive sherry."

"Mike, stop it! I've come to take you home. It's all right. You didn't kill Wayne, he didn't die. He's dead now, but you didn't kill him, Juan Bustamonte did."

"Good for him. Who's Juan?"

"You know who he is! He worked for Clay Bradshaw. He fought with Wayne when Wayne was beating Paula, and he killed him. It was an accident, pure self-defense. Dad got a fancy lawyer for him to get him off; the trial was just about to start when Manuel and I came looking for you. Do you understand what I'm telling you, Mike? You can come home now, there aren't any charges waiting for you."

"You're a few months too late, Dria. I can't go home. I'm a drunk. A downright, hopeless drunk, and that's all I'll ever be. Besides, I have more soldiers to kill. They killed Lupe; I'll kill them. It's simple. Get drunk, raid, get drunk. That's what I am now, Dria, a raider and a drunk."

"And from all we've heard, and now that I've seen you I know it's true, you'll soon be a dead raider! Mike, can't you understand what you're doing to Mother and Dad? It's killing them, not having you home, not even knowing where you are or whether you're dead or alive!"

"You can tell them I'm alive. If they knew what I am now, they'd probably wish I was dead. If I get killed fighting for justice, at least it will be an honorable death, one they can be proud of. It'd be easier on them than having me die of drink, back home." His hand trembled as he lifted his glass and drained its contents, the tremor of the habitual drunkard. Andrea's heart felt as if a huge hand were squeezing it.

"You aren't a drunkard! All you need is to get home where you belong and you'll be the same Mike you always were."

"Look, Dria, who do you think you're kidding? A drunk's a drunk. Ask our mother. Her father, our grandfather, was one, and she says that I look just like him. Whatever he was, I inherited it, and there's no use fighting it. We just never knew it before because I never had any reason to drink before. Now I do. Lupe's dead, and there are a lot more raids for me to make."

"And one more raid might kill you!" Andrea exploded.

"What's the difference? One or the other's going to get me, a bullet or the bottle. Tell Juan thanks for finishing my job for me. All this time, I've wondered if Wayne was dead, I've wondered if I'd have gone back that day and finished him off if I'd known he was still alive."

He shook his head, pushing his sombrero back on his head. She could see his hair now, that flaming, carroty hair that had made the Mexicans call him El Rojo. She had an almost overwhelming need to stroke that hair of his back from his forehead with her fingers. Her little brother, her Mike!

She sat down, hardly noticing that Manuel had joined them. The old man said nothing. This part of their quest was ended, and it was not his place to speak in the presence of his betters. Doña Andrea must persuade Michael to go home with her; it was not his place to give orders or even to ask.

"Mike, how did it happen? Wayne swore that you shot him down without warning. I called him a liar right to his face. Not that he didn't deserve shooting, but it just wasn't like you."

"I saw him on the road. He was on his way up to the settlement. Manuel had just told me what he did to Lupe. When I saw him, I went for him. Not with my gun. I was an idiot, it never even occurred to me! I wanted to get my hands on him, I wanted to beat him, to batter the life out of him. He drew on me, and then he was dead. Only he wasn't dead; Juan Bustamonte had to finish the job for me."

"Manuel found him and took him to Trail's End. Mother fought like a tigress to save his life so you wouldn't be a murderer. You owe her something for that, Mike."

"Damned right," Mike said. "I owe her the respect of staying the hell out of her life so she can't see what her baby son's turned into! Leave me alone, Dria. Go home. Tell them anything you like, only get out of here and leave me alone."

His face went slack even as he was speaking, and his head went slowly down on the table again. Andrea put her hands on his shoulders and shook him. She lifted his head and slapped both sides of his face. It was no use. He was unconscious; he'd have to sleep it off.

"I want a room," she told the open-mouthed proprietor. "Do you have a room?"

"You know him, you know he is El Rojo Loco? You are his woman?"

"I am his sister. I want a room immediately, and I want him carried there and put to bed. Quickly, do you understand?"

All pretense of being a peon girl, of being Manuel's granddaughter, had dropped from her now that she had found Mike. She had to get him sobered up, to take care of him, to talk him into going back with her. These people would not betray him, their awe of El Rojo was apparent; Mike was a hero to the peons, to the revolutionists.

"It is a pity. He would have killed many more soldiers," the man said, shaking his head. "But it will be as you say, Señorita. It would be a pity, as well, if he died. I will take you to my sister's house. That is where El Rojo stays when he is too drunk to raid. He cannot stay here in the cantina, you understand, where *rurales* or soldiers might come, although they have not come for a long time. They have already done all the killing and pillaging there was to be done in this place."

His eyes were sad with the same patient, suffering sadness that Andrea had seen in the eyes of so many peons since she had been in Mexico. "My sister's only son, only fifteen, they killed because he tried to protect his sister from them. My sister was beaten when she tried to keep them from taking Delores. My sister's husband went to fight Díaz, before this happened, and there was no man to protect them. I was held here in my cantina, forced to serve the soldiers, and they did not pay. *Sí,* it is a pity that you are going to take El Rojo home, but he has already avenged us, and it would be a pity if he, too, should die."

Shaking with reaction, Andrea followed as two of the peons lifted Mike between them and carried him down the dusty street to an adobe house on the outskirts of the settlement. Another two led the horses, Runner and Baldy and Mike's, away to conceal them in some safe place, out of the sight of any *rurales* or soldiers who might happen to pass this way. Pray God that they wouldn't come this way again! These people had suffered enough, and she had to get Mike to safety.

Alva Gomez met them at her door, her eyes wide both with astonishment at seeing Andrea and Manuel, and that same heart-wrenching sadness that made a lump come into Andrea's throat. Considering her brother's story of what had happened to her family, it was little wonder. How they suffered, these poor Mexican people, and how they would go on suffering until this revolution was over,

479

and how much more they would suffer if Díaz's forces should win!

The tiny *casa* had only three rooms, two bedrooms and a larger room serving as kitchen and living quarters. Most of the furniture had been hand-crafted of wood; the cooking was done outside on a grate over an open fire. Water was carried every day from the fountain in the plaza. Señora Gomez had attempted to brighten her house with flowered curtains at the windows and colorful cushions on the chairs, now faded and worn. A religious print, its colors garish, hung on the wall, Christ showing his bleeding heart; it was the only picture in the house.

It had been a prosperous house for a town like this before Alva's husband had gone to fight with the revolutionists, before her son had been murdered and her daughter taken away, she had no idea where, only for what purpose. Now she was alone, depending on her garden, on her chickens and her goats and whatever help her brother could give her. She had no hope that either her husband or her daughter would ever come back.

Still she made them welcome, her eyes filled with concern for the American girl who had come so far in search of her brother. Her house was their house; whatever she had to offer was theirs. Mike was put to bed in one of the tiny bedrooms. Alva bustled around preparing food, the inevitable chili beans, tortillas, hot, thick coffee. Andrea saw, when Alva measured the coffee, that the canister was now empty.

"You have come so far! You must be exhausted. After you have eaten, you must rest. El Rojo will be asleep for a long time, probably until tomorrow. I have seen him like this before. When he wakes, he will weed my garden and carry water for me. He is a great man, Señora Mansfield." Alva's use of her legal name gave Andrea a start. Manuel must have mentioned it while introductions were being made; she couldn't remember. It wasn't important, anyway. The only important thing was to get Mike sobered up so that she could talk some sense into him and persuade him to come home.

The cornhusk mattress in the other bedroom was

lumpy and hard, and rustled whenever she moved. There was a ragged sheet to cover the mattress, and a rough blanket. The pillow was thin. Andrea had never been so grateful for a bed in her life. She fell asleep, completely exhausted, as soon as she lay down, and when she awoke in the morning the sun was streaming through the window and falling across her face.

Alva heard her stirring and came in at once, carrying a pitcher of hot water. There was a sliver of soap and a clean rough towel.

"I have washed your clothing. They are there, over the chair," Alva told her. Her kindness made Andrea feel like crying. How could these people be so kind, when their own troubles were so overwhelming, when giving of the little they had might leave them in actual want? It must be true, she thought, that the meek would inherit the earth. Certainly they deserved it, far more than the wealthy and arrogant!

The aroma of coffee drew her to the outer room as soon as she had washed and dressed. "You should have rested longer!" Alva scolded her. "I am making coffee for El Rojo, too. My brother brought it last night, after you slept. Carlos is a good man. He would be fighting, but he is old, and he can serve best here where he can tend the needs of the rebels when they pass through hungry and tired. If they are hungry but have no money, he feeds them. If they are wounded, he brings them to me so I can tend them."

She filled a pottery mug and handed it to Andrea and pushed a small bowl of sugar toward her. "Carlos brought the sugar as well. It is better to have sugar in the coffee, when a man is sick from drink. There is only goat's milk for cream; I can bring you some fresh, it will take only a little moment."

"This is perfect, *gracias*." Andrea savored the coffee, with a scant teaspoon of sugar. "Mike isn't awake yet?"

"No. It will be many hours still, if it is as usual. But when he wakes, there will be coffee. I will make you a tortilla. Manuel is at the cantina, with my brother. He

481

wanted to see to your horses. Carlos says they are the finest horses he has ever seen."

"It was kind of the men to take care of them for us."

"*Por nada.* You are the sister of El Rojo." Andrea noticed, with gratitude, that Señora Gomez never completed the name that her people had given Mike, she never said El Rojo Loco. "The horses must be kept safe so that you can go back to the *Estados Unidos* where El Rojo will be safe, where his family will care for him."

Andrea finished her breakfast and went in to look at Mike. Sleeping, even dirty and with several days' stubble of beard on his face, he looked as young as he was, even younger; he looked like a boy again, the younger brother who had always been so smiling and carefree. There was an innocence in his sleeping face that made her feel like crying again. How could Mike, her little brother Mike, be El Rojo Loco? She left him to sleep, knowing that to wake him before he had slept off the effects of the tequila would gain her nothing.

An old woman had entered the house while she was in the bedroom. She smiled shyly as Alva explained that she had brought some chicken tamales for El Rojo. Whenever Mike was here, the people brought a little food, the best they had. "They have much gratitude toward him, Señora Mansfield. They have the wish to share what they have with him because he fights for us, he avenges our wrongs."

"Bella Linda," the old woman said, smiling at Andrea.

"*Gracias,*" Andrea said. The familiar words cut through her like a knife. Bella Linda! Where was the little red car now, the one that had been instrumental in bringing her and Reggie together? She'd loved that car, just as she'd hated the Mercedes, hated the Silver Ghost. To hear the words spoken now, here so deep in Mexico, in this desolate crossroads that led nowhere, brought home to her the shambles that both she and Mike had made of their lives.

But Mike's life didn't have to be a shambles! All he needed was to get back home, to pick up the threads where he had broken them off. It wouldn't be easy for him. He wasn't the same Mike who had left, a fugitive, to keep Adam and Kate from having to bear the shame of having a murderer for a son. There was no way for her to know the grueling experiences he had lived through since then, experiences that had changed him so that he could never be completely the old Mike again.

But he was young, so very young, a year younger than she was, and to leave him here to pursue his mad rush toward suicide, either from the bottle or a bullet, was unthinkable. He had to get back to Adam, to Kate, to their good common sense and steadying influence, and she had to make him go. There could still be a good life for him back there. Before Lupe had come to the settlement and he'd fallen so madly in love with her, he'd partnered Paula's sister Lucy at many of the local affairs. Give him a year, two years, and his interest in her might reawaken. Lucy loved him, and they could have a contented marriage, children. All he needed was time, time that would not be granted him if he stayed here.

A sound at the bedroom doorway made her look from the old woman to see Mike standing there, unsteady on his feet, bracing himself with his hands against the doorjambs. His eyes were squinted against the sunlight; his face was pasty under its stubble. When he spoke, his voice was thick.

"I didn't dream it. You're really here," he said. "I thought I was still dreaming when I heard your voice."

The old woman rose to her feet, trembling because of her awesome nearness to El Rojo. *"Buenos días,"* she said, bobbing her head. And then, filled with confusion, she hurried out. Mike continued to stare at Andrea as if he still couldn't believe his eyes.

"Mike! How do you feel?"

He took one hand from the doorjamb and rubbed it across his face with a scrubbing motion. "Like I'd been run over by a stampede. Is there anything to drink in this house?"

"Señora Gomez has made coffee; it's still hot and it's delicious. There's sugar, too." Andrea was already at his

483

side urging him to the bare wooden table, reaching for the coffee pot that was still beside her mug.

Mike's face tightened. "No, thanks. I'll just mosey on down to the cantina."

Andrea's grip on his arm tightened. "You'll do no such thing! Are you out of your mind? What would Mother and Dad think if they knew you woke up with a hangover and reached for a bottle again? It's time to sober up, Mike, we have to talk."

"There's nothing to talk about. Go home. You shouldn't have come down here in the first place, you're the one who's out of her mind, coming to find me when I didn't want to be found! You've seen me, you know how it is with me, so you might as well go on home. Thanks for your concern, but there's no way you can get me to go back."

"Because you're a drunk? A pitiful, hopeless alcoholic?" Andrea's words were brutal, and Mike winced, but she didn't care. "Oh, no, Mike, that isn't good enough! Don't you think I know? But of course you don't, I never had a chance to tell you, I never told even Mother and Dad! But I've been where you are, Mike. Back in England. I've gotten up in the morning and reached for the bottle, just as you do now! The only difference is, I realized what I was doing to myself, and I quit."

"Good for you." Mike's voice was sour. "I'm happy for you. Only don't expect me to do the same thing, because I can't. Like grandfather, like grandson."

"That's a lot of hogwash! All right, so you inherited a tendency toward alcohol! So did I, so I have some idea of what you're going through. But that doesn't mean that you have to give in to it, any more than I did! It can be licked, if you have the guts."

"Andrea, I'm sick. And I just damned well don't care any more."

"So was I sick. Not as sick as you are, probably, but sick enough. I had the shakes, just the way you're shaking now. I couldn't get started in the morning without a drink, I couldn't keep going without another. And I damned well didn't care, either, as long as the liquor held out, until I got a good look at myself in the mirror one day and realized that I was killing myself, that I was flushing my life down the drain.

"You needn't think that it was easy for me to quit. It wasn't. I was sick, and it hurt. I felt like I was coming apart at the seams. But I found something I wanted to do, something that I could do if I worked hard enough, and so I worked. I worked so long and so hard that I didn't have time to drink. And then one morning I woke up and I didn't want a drink that badly any more. I wanted one, but I could face not having it."

Retelling it, the first time she'd ever told anyone except Caroline, brought it back so vividly that she could feel the sickness in her throat again, she could feel the black despair settle over her like a suffocating blanket. If it hadn't been for her work, she might not have made it. Reggie hadn't understood. He'd assumed that every civilized person drank, that it was the ordinary way of life. She'd had to do it on her own, with no help from anyone. But Mike would have her, someone who understood.

One thing had emerged from that dreadful time when she had felt that she was fighting for her life. She wasn't a true alcoholic. Once she had put meaning into her life, she'd been able to have a drink without any desire to go on drinking until she'd numbed her mind. Her faith in herself had overcome her dependence on alcohol.

She didn't know how much worse off Mike was. She had the idea, and she prayed that it wasn't just wishful thinking, that Mike's need for alcohol stemmed from that same lack of direction, that same doubt of his own worth. He'd let Lupe be killed, he'd let his raging temper drive him to attacking Wayne and leaving him for dead, he felt that he'd betrayed everyone he loved, Lupe, his family, he'd felt that the only reason he had to go on living was to fight against the Mexican peons' oppressors.

Mike winced. "Dria, I didn't know, I never dreamed," he said. His face looked pastier than ever, tinged with an underlayer of unhealthy yellow.

She pushed him down into the chair and poured him a mug of coffee while Alva made an excuse to go out

485

into the yard, murmuring something about the goats, embarrassed to be a witness to this intimate scene between brother and sister.

Mike's hands shook so that he had to use both of them to hold the mug. He drank half of the coffee and then bolted for the door, and Andrea heard him being sick. The racking sound of his retching tore at her, and her own hand shook as she poured herself another mug of coffee.

When Mike came back in, his color was a little better. He sat down again opposite her.

"Dria, it's been hell," he said. His eyes were haunted. "I want to kill every soldier in the Mexican army, and yet I know that half of them, maybe more than half of them, don't want to be soldiers, that they're only peons who were forced into service. I killed a boy, Dria. He was only a boy; he looked something like Jesus, and he wasn't any older. When I looked down on him I wished I'd been the one who'd been killed, instead. I didn't know he was just a kid till it was too late.

"I have nightmares about it. How many other boys have I killed? I try to be careful, but there isn't always time to sort out the men from the boys when bullets are flying. I can't live with myself any more. That's why I drink, to blot it out. That's why I can't stop drinking."

Andrea's voice was gentle as she rose to draw him to his feet. Her Mike, who'd never even wear spurs on his boots because he couldn't bear to hurt a horse, tormented with guilt at having killed a boy who was trying to kill him!

"Come back to bed, Mike. You need more sleep. I understand, I promise you I do. We'll talk about it some more after you feel better; we'll talk it all out; you don't have to keep it all bottled up inside you any more."

With Mike asleep again, his face gaunt and covered with clammy perspiration, there was nothing for Andrea to do. She walked the length of the town's street. Some women doing their washing at the town fountain smiled at her, friendly and shy. A little girl offered her a fistful of bedraggled flowering weeds, already wilted. She accepted them as if they were hothouse roses, her throat tight.

When she went back to Señora Gomez's *casa* two hours later, Mike was gone. Alva looked at her apologetically.

"He has gone to the cantina, Señora Mansfield. I could not stop him. He is a man; a woman cannot order a man to stay at home."

"It's all right. Of course you couldn't stop him. I should have known that he'd get up and go to the cantina; I shouldn't have gone out."

Mike was sitting at one of the tables, a bottle in front of him and a half-empty glass in his hand. Manuel sat opposite him, his face filled with sadness, watching him as he drank.

"Mike, damn it, stop it!" Andrea said. "Didn't you hear a word I said to you? I won't have it! I know it's rough, God knows I know that, but you have to stop sometime! I'm not going back home without you, and I'm not going to cart you over the back of your horse, dead drunk, either! And speaking of horses, what happened to Jacko?"

"Shot out from under me," Mike told her, squinting down into his glass, his face expressionless. He'd loved that horse.

She took the glass from his hand. He didn't resist. "It isn't any use, Dria. Yes, I heard what you said to me. And I'm glad that you licked your problem, you'll never know how glad I am. But you're you and I'm me. If I can't persuade you to go home without me, you're going to be in Mexico a damned long time. And how is that going to help Kate and Adam? They must be going crazy, worrying about you, have you thought of that?"

She'd thought of it, although she'd tried not to. She'd told herself, whenever her conscience had pricked her, that when she brought Mike home it would more than make up for any worry they'd had about her.

"Come back to the house," she urged. "Get some food in you. You have to eat. You can go without another drink for one more hour, can't you?"

"One hour. And then you'll ask for two, and then you'll make it half a day, and then a day. I know you too well, Dria. But this time you can't win."

"If you can sober up to go on those raids of yours, you can sober up now."

"I'm not ready. I've only been here three days."

She wanted to take his shoulders in her hands and shake him until she shook some sense into his head. But she knew that she couldn't do that. Mike had never been one who could be forced, any more than she was. The fear that she might be here in Mexico for a long time, as he'd just said, made her frantic.

"How long is long enough? How long do you usually stay drunk?"

"Four, five days. A week. I don't keep a schedule, Dria. I stay until I get the urge to leave, to find one of the bands that are fighting and join them."

And lead them, she thought. El Rojo Loco!

"Doña, I think you had better return to Señora Gomez's *casa*." Manuel spoke softly, a warning in his voice. "I think it is not good for you to be in this place. I will escort you. Señor Wentworth, you had better come, too."

She followed the direction of his eyes and for the first time she noticed that here were half a dozen men at one of the other tables. They were not peons, the ones who had been here last night. One of them, a man with a drooping mustache that gave his scarred face a sinister look in spite of the fact that he was quite handsome, was watching her with a great deal of interest.

Carlos came over and made a pretense of wiping their table with a stained cloth. *"Cuidado!"* he said. Be careful. "They are bandits, but they are not good men, I think. Manuel is right. You should leave, Señor, and take your sister with you, and it would not hurt to bar the door."

"Un momento, Señorita. Do not be in a hurry to leave. If this señor does not desire your company, then you will have a drink with me instead, *sí?"* The man had moved so swiftly that his hand was on Andrea's arm even

488

as she stood up and moved toward the door, hoping that Mike would follow her.

"*Gracias,* but no, thank you. It is too early, and I do not wish a drink. Take your hand from my arm, *por favor.*"

"A little drink will not hurt. This *hombre* here" . . . he indicated Mike . . ."does not know how to treat a beautiful woman. But I, Pedro Lopez, know how to make a lady happy. I have not seen you before, Señorita. If I had known that you were in this detestable town, I would have come much sooner."

At his table, his companions were watching, some of them grinning. Andrea's temper flared. This was impossible! In all her life she had never been accosted by a stranger, much less one who assumed that she was free for the asking. "Remove your hand," she said, her voice like ice.

In Texas, in Georgia or Massachusetts or England, her expression and her tone of voice would have been enough. But this was Mexico, and as Carlos had said, these were not good men. The bandit had no way of knowing that she was anything but what she appeared to be in her peasant clothing, an ordinary peon girl who was prettier than most and fair prey. Beside her, Manuel's face had gone still, and she could feel his fear for her. "You will please to remove your hand, Señor. I am leaving."

"You heard what the lady said. Remove your hand."

Mike was still slumped in his chair, and his voice was a lazy drawl, almost indifferent, but there was an underlying quality in it that made the bandit stiffen.

"The woman is yours, *hombre?*" he asked.

"The lady is my sister, and you will get your filthy hand off her arm instantly!"

"*Por Dios,* what a funny joke! You are an Americano, the señorita is one of us! What is a woman between friends? You do not want her, so you can lend her to me for a small while, *sí?* I promise I will return her."

Mike got to his feet. Deeper inside the room, Lopez's companions were also on their feet, their hands hovering near their holstered guns. Andrea's breath caught. Carlos, his face pale, hurried to pour oil on troubled water.

"You do not want to do that, Señor. The señor tells the truth. The lady is his sister, and he is El Rojo Loco. You do not want to insult the sister of El Rojo."

The bandit's hand dropped from Andrea's arm as he turned his full attention to Mike. "El Rojo Loco," he said, his voice soft, almost a whisper. *"Sí.* It is possible, I see now that your hair is red. And certainly you must be *loco,* to speak to me as if I were a peon, as if you were a don!"

The cantina was electric with tension.

"You can test it out and see," Michael said. His own hands toyed with his glass. The bandit's face twitched, and just for an instant he hesitated. But his followers were watching him; his reputation and his pride were at stake. If he backed down he would no longer command their respect, he might no longer be their leader.

He made his decision. The Americano was drunk, his eyes were blurred, he himself had seen how his hand trembled as he poured himself a drink. Pedro Lopez cared little that El Rojo Loco fought for the peons. He himself fought, did he not? Where it was profitable, he fought. And after all, El Rojo was only one man, and an Americano, and all Americanos were rich and that made him his enemy even if the was so *loco* that he fought for the peons when he was rich.

He had heard of El Rojo; who had not, in this part of Mexico? He had heard that he was very rich as well as very crazy. If he, Pedro Lopez, killed him, he could collect the reward that the Federales had put on his head and then he, too, would be rich. If he killed him and took the woman he would be even richer because her family would pay a large fortune to get her back. After he had finished with her, of course. It could be arranged safely by a man as smart as he was. Then he would have no need to be a bandit any more, he could go to Mexico City and live like a don, with all the wine and rich food and a fine house and servants and all the beautiful women he had ever dreamed of.

For Andrea, time seemed to stand still. Mike was in no condition to have a shoot-out with anyone, let alone a man as dangerous as this one. And Manuel wasn't armed, and her own gun was back at Alva Gomez's *casa;* she had not thought that she would have any need of it in this town where her brother was looked upon as a hero, where everyone was their friend. Her breath stilled in her throat as she waited for either Mike or the man he had challenged to make his move.

31

Saddle-weary and hungry some of the time and thirsty a good deal of the time, Henry pushed Beau Noir southward. The trail had been a long one and had had many dead ends. Although he knew where Andrea and Manuel were heading, he had given up hope of overtaking them in spite of having Beau Noir under him. Runner was a good horse, too, nearly as good as Beau, and Manuel was riding Baldy. Beau Noir would have to sprout wings, like Pegasus, to overtake them.

Still he faced southward, avoiding patrols, avoiding roving bands of bandits. It slowed him down, but it was necessary. A man could be killed for a horse much less valuable than Adam's. By the same token, he could only hope that Andrea and Manuel had also had the sense to avoid such bands, not only because their horses would most certainly be stolen or confiscated, but because of what would undoubtedly happen to Andrea if she fell into the hands of a certain type of soldier or bandit. It was something that he didn't care to think about.

He couldn't help thinking about it, no matter how grimly he tried to tell himself that Andrea was no fool and that she'd keep well clear of trouble. How could Manuel protect her, an old man, a man who had never learned to use firearms, who knew nothing of fighting? A girl like Andrea would stick out like a sore thumb. News of her, of her beauty and of the horses that she and Manuel were riding was sure to spread, and men would be on the lookout for them. Unless she was being very careful.

When he got his hands on Mike he was going to tell him exactly what he thought of him for being reckless enough to build up a reputation that had seeped back to Texas and brought Andrea on this insane search for him. Friend or no friend, and he liked Mike better than he'd ever liked any other man of comparable age to his own, he'd have things to say to him that would make his ears burn. As for Andrea. . .

Damn it, how far was he behind them? He'd have to travel faster, even if it meant giving up some of the caution that had kept him well out of the reach of anyone who might want to make trouble for him. If Andrea succeeded in finding Mike, he had to catch up with them before they started back for Texas, because there was no telling what route they would take, and with a price on Mike's head the danger to Andrea would be doubled.

So he had to be with them, to help get them back safely across the border. And he knew that if Mike was still alive Andrea would find him, provided she was careful not to come to grief before she did. Dria was the most stubborn girl he'd ever known; if she set her mind to a thing, she carried it through no matter how crazy it was or how difficult. She didn't know the meaning of the word quit. How could she, with Adam and Kate for her mother and father?

He found out, only a few days out, that Andrea *was* being careful. A young American woman, very beautiful, had been seen in hamlets, at crossroads where there were only half a dozen houses. But then there were no more reports of such a young American woman. For a while Henry had been close to despair. Had something happened to her, was she already in the hands of the soldiers or bandits?

But the horses that Andrea and Manuel were riding were also noticed. He'd been a fool not to describe the horses sooner, but only to ask about an American girl traveling with an old man. The horses had been seen, but they were ridden by a Mexican girl, a peasant girl, traveling with her grandfather.

The relief he felt made him feel actually sick. At least she'd had that much sense. With her fluent Spanish, dressed as she was now, she would be a darned sight safer than she'd been when she'd been rigged up in her tailormade divided riding skirt and her tooled boots and her white hat that shouted to everyone who saw her that she was not only young and beautiful but wealthy as well. In Mexico, these days, it was not safe to be wealthy and travel with only one old peasant for escort.

Inquiries about Mike's whereabouts proved as futile as those he made about Andrea and Manuel. The farther south he traveled, the more people knew of Mike, although Henry had to use the name of El Rojo Loco before they knew whom he was talking about. For all Henry knew, Andrea and Manuel might have found out where Mike was by now and be on their way directly there, and he might save time by finding Mike before he found them. It was worth thinking about. If he was able to learn Mike's whereabouts, Andrea would be able to, too. So he asked, over and over, but Mike remained as elusive as a phantom. He'd been here, he'd raided there, east, west, north, south. He was just never where Henry happened to be at the same time that Henry was there.

Then he had a bit of luck, the first he'd had so far. Andrea and Manuel, or more accurately, Runner and Baldy, had passed through a small settlement only the day before, going southeast. It was getting along in the afternoon when Henry came by that bit of information. He was tired and hungry, and both he and Beau Noir needed rest, but now that he was so close behind the two elusive people

ple he was tracking, he felt the urge to push on, right through the night, after only a short respite. Beau could stand it, and if he were to lose them now, after coming so close to them, the frustration would be unbearable.

With a bowl of hot chili beans in his stomach and Beau refreshed with a generous measure of corn, Henry was in the saddle again. Born and raised in the southwest, he could travel at night as easily as he did in the daytime. Sometimes it was easier, with the stars to keep him on the right course in unfamiliar territory.

It was cold, but he was used to that, and Beau's steady pace kept him from feeling it much. Even as he kept pushing forward, his grudging admiration for Andrea strengthened. She'd done darned well for a girl, she'd covered a lot of territory. But if she and Manuel were only that far ahead of him, and they stopped for the night, he was bound to come up with them.

And then what? Knowing Andrea and her determination, he knew the answer. All three of them would go on together until they found Mike. There was no way this side of hell that he could make Andrea turn back before she found her brother.

It was going on toward noon, and both he and Beau were beginning to feel the toll of this last hard push without rest, when the tiny settlement came into view. It didn't look like much, and he hadn't caught up with his quarry yet; the chances were that if they'd stayed here last night they'd set out again early this morning.

The thought was discouraging. He couldn't ask even Beau to keep going without rest indefinitely. His best chance, if he found out that they were only a few hours ahead of him, was to try to buy a fresh horse and leave Beau here to rest, but what kind of horseflesh would be available in a town of this size? The chances were that any horse worth riding had already been confiscated by either the army or the rebels. And how safe would Beau Noir be if he left him here? He'd pose a temptation, even to honest peons, that would be hard to resist.

There was no use worrying about that now. First he had to find out whether Andrea and Manuel had actually been here, and how many hours they were ahead of him. The logical place to ask, the same place he'd asked in all the other little towns he'd passed through, was the cantina.

He swung off, tied Beau to the hitching rail, and pushed through the door. For a second, while his eyes adjusted, he was aware only that something was wrong, that there was some kind of trouble here. And in that second, a shot rang out, sending its deafening echoes reverberating against the walls, and he saw a girl dressed in typical Mexican dress grab a gun from the holster of one of a group of men who were standing in the middle of the room, while another man, dressed like a peon, pointed his own still smoking gun at a man who stood near the door. A second shot, a third, rang out before Henry could draw a breath.

"Hold it!" he barked. "Just hold it!"

Without thinking about it he'd spoken in Spanish. His words had the desired effect. The man by the door was out of it, lying crumpled on the floor clutching at his shoulder. El Rojo hadn't been too drunk, or too shaky, to outdraw Pedro Lopez and hit him, and the beautiful young Americano lady's aim had been as accurate after her lightning grab for a gun, because one of the other bandits was grasping his wrist, staring with stunned disbelief at the long gouge plowed through it the instant the second shot, from the gun she'd grabbed, rang out.

Now, with another Americano standing in the doorway with his gun thrown down on them, the odds weren't to their liking. Their guns dropped to the floor, and their hands went up.

Carlos Perez still stood frozen with the dirty cloth in his hand, his face filled with anguished astonishment. Manuel breathed a long sigh of thanksgiving. Andrea was staring at Henry as if he were a ghost.

"Hank! I was never so glad to see anyone in my life. However did you get here?"

"On a horse," Henry said laconically. "You didn't think I walked, did you? Mike, is that you? You look like the devil. What have you been doing to yourself?"

"Acting like a damned fool," Mike answered just as

496

laconically. "Putting Dria in danger because I didn't have the sense God gave me." A grin spread across his stubbled face, boyish, ashamed, and then he staggered and started to fall, clutching at the back of a chair to try to keep upright.

"Mike!" Andrea screamed. She got to him before Henry did because she was closer to him, but she staggered under his weight as she tried to support him. Blood was oozing from a hole near his shoulder.

"Sorry." Mike tried to go on grinning. "I wasn't quite fast enough, Dria. You were right. All that drinking like to have got me killed." And then he pitched forward, his legs giving out under him, into Henry's arms.

The next few minutes would always remain confused in Andrea's mind. She was dimly aware that Manuel had gathered up all of the bandits' guns, that Carlos was telling Hank where to carry Mike, to his sister's house, that the four uninjured bandits had gathered up their fallen leader and carried him outside while the one who was still cursing as he held his wrist followed them. There was the sound of a rapid departure as they loaded Pedro López on his horse and spurred away from town and the deadly guns behind them.

Fifteen minutes later, after Henry had stripped Mike's shirt off him and laid bare his wound, he shook his head, his face more grim than Andrea had ever seen it, and that was saying a lot.

"The bullet's still in there. Is there a doctor in this town?" He knew it was a foolish question even before he asked it. The town was too small to have a doctor, and if there had been one, he would have been forced to go tend the wounds of the federal troops.

Alva shook her head, wringing her hands. "No Señor, no doctor. We have never had a doctor. *Por Dios,* is he going to die?"

"Mike? It would take more than a bullet in his shoulder to kill him!" Henry made his voice sound certain. "But he has to have that bullet out. How about it, Mike? How do you feel about an amateur doing a little probing? Perez, hike back to your place and fetch me a bottle of tequila. Andrea, take this and stick the blade in that fire outside—get it good and hot. Manuel, when Carlos comes back, you and he will hold Mike's shoulders and Señora Gomez and Andrea will put their weight on his legs. While we're waiting for the tequila, Señora Gomez can see if she has something she can tear up for bandages. Mike, I may not be gentle, but I'll try to be quick, all right?"

"Depends on how much of that tequila I can get down before you go butchering me out."

"Not much. The tequila's to pour in the hole after the bullet's out. We can't have you drunk, Mike, at least not any drunker than you already are. We're going to have to ride out of here as soon as you can sit a horse. Those men are likely to come back, with friends."

Mike's eyes clouded with more than the pain he was feeling. "Right. We'll have to make tracks. Not only for Dria's sake, but those so and so's just might take it into their heads to make reprisals against Alva and Carlos for helping me if we're still here. Don't worry. I'll ride out even if you have to tie me on my horse."

"It's going to be rough. I never trained to be a surgeon," Henry warned him. "I think you're tough enough to take it."

"I'm glad somebody thinks so. It doesn't sound so easy when you're on the receiving end of the knife."

Andrea's face was as white as her brother's as she helped Alva hold Mike's legs when Henry went in after the bullet. In spite of Manuel and Carlos holding his shoulders, his back arched just once as the sterilized knife probed in. Then he set his teeth in his lower lip and closed his eyes and was still. Sweat beaded his forehead, but no sound escaped from him.

Henry's hand was steady. When something had to be done, it had to be done. They had to get out of town as soon as possible, and they couldn't do it with the bullet still in Mike's shoulder. It had to come out, and then Mike had to rest for a hour, and Henry only hoped that Beau Noir would hold up long enough for them to find some place to hole up, out in the brush, where the bandits would have their work cut out for them tracking them and Mike could have a day or two to recuperate and Beau get the rest he needed.

He grunted his satisfaction as the tip of the knife scraped against the bullet. "Hang on, Mike. This is the rough part."

"I'm not going anywhere. Get it out, damn it!"

The bullet dropped to the rumpled bed, ugly and bloody, and now Andrea was the one to close her eyes. Manuel was praying silently, his face lighting up as his prayer turned to one of gratitude. "I'll go see to the horses, Señor. It will take a small while to bring them."

"You do that. Mike, here comes the tequila." Henry tilted the bottle over the open wound and the room echoed with Mike's sudden cursing.

"What a damned waste!" he finished, grinning weakly. "Too bad some of it couldn't have splashed into my mouth!"

Henry slapped the cork back into the neck of the bottle. "You'll live without it. You'll have to. See if you can go to sleep, Mike. You're going to need your strength." He was already bandaging the wound, his hands steady and sure. Mike called him a name that made Señora Gomez blanch, even though he spoke in English.

When the bandaging was finished Alva drew the blanket over Mike and left the room, gathering what supplies she had on hand to send with them when they left. Andrea, feeling disgracefully shaky, stepped through the door to draw a few deep breaths of air.

There was a small crowd of people gathered in the dooryard. Each of them carried something. They were waiting silently, with inborn patience. "Señora, take this little cornmeal." "Señora, I have some chicken." "A small piece of cheese, it is not much."

Andrea's eyes filled with tears. *"Gracias. Un mil gracias!"* she said, almost choking on the words. She accepted their offerings, her heart filled with gratitude that went far beyond the worth of the gifts. What they had given would mean going without just that much for their own sustenance. The gifts were a tribute to Mike, carrying their

499

prayers for his safety. Andrea knew that even if Mike hadn't become a sort of folk hero to them, the gifts would still have been forthcoming. Mike's needs were greater than theirs, and they must do all they could. She had seen this characteristic before, but now it was brought home to her in a way she knew she would never forget.

To offer payment would have been an insult, but she could leave money with Alva, to be given or spent as the need arose. Alva would distribute it wisely, and it would be accepted, when they had need, just as she accepted what they had brought today, as a token of friendship.

She carried her armful of donations into the house. Henry was watching Mike, who had actually fallen asleep.

"I haven't thanked you for coming to find us. I want you to know that I appreciate it, Hank. I don't know what would have happened if you hadn't shown up when you did."

"It seems that I'm fated to haul you and Mike out of trouble, no matter how much I'd like to forget that you exist! I could hardly have left Mike down here, hell-bent to get himself killed, after I found out where he was, even if you hadn't been insane enough to come dashing down here after him all by yourself. And we aren't home yet. Did it ever enter your stubborn head that Mike wouldn't have been shot if you hadn't been here? Aren't you ever going to get any sense?"

Andrea's temper flared. "Yes, it's entered my head! But how could I have known that it would happen? If it were your brother who was trying to get himself killed somewhere in Mexico, you needn't try to tell me that you wouldn't have come looking for him!"

"I'm not a girl! Damn it, Andrea, sometimes I think your mother should have smothered you in your crib—it would have saved a lot of people a whole lot of trouble!"

"You hate me that much!" Andrea's shock showed in her face, which had gone white. "I know I've hurt you, I know you've suffered, but I've been hurt, too. Even if it is no more than I deserved, it did hurt! And it still hurts! I'm sorry I've caused you even more trouble, but I had no idea that you'd come looking for us. That was your own idea, and you can't blame me for it."

"I'm not blaming you. I did it for Adam and Kate, and for Mike. But having you here complicates things. You're not only a girl, but I never know what you're going to do next—I only know, from experience, that it'll be something that will smash things up again. You have a talent for leaving broken lives behind you, Dria. Just because you hurt yourself in the process doesn't make it any easier on the ones you destroy."

Andrea felt as if he had struck her. What could she say, when every word he'd said was true? Why did it always have to be like this between them, why couldn't they as much as see each other without hurting each other?

"Mike's hurt pretty bad, and if those bandits don't come looking for us, I miss my guess," Henry went on, his voice hard. "They'll be pretty sure we have money as well as good horses, for one thing, entirely outside of the revenge they'll be frothing at the mouth to exact. It's too bad that Mike's shot didn't kill the leader. Even wounded, he looked like a dangerous man."

Andrea's face was set. We'll make it. We have to make it!"

"We will if I have anything to say about it. But get one thing clear, Andrea. From now on, I'm in charge. If I want your opinion on how to proceed I'll ask for it, but it doesn't seem likely."

The blood drained from Andrea's face, but she bit back the hot retort that rose to her lips. Let Henry insult her, let him let her know, with every word he spoke and every cold look he gave her, just what he thought of her; her only concern had to be to get Mike safely back to Trail's End. She couldn't blame Henry for feeling as he did. She'd caused him nothing but grief and heartache ever since they'd discovered that she was a girl and he was a boy. Once they got back, he could walk out of her life and she wouldn't raise a hand to stop him. But all the same, it hurt. It hurt like the very devil.

And that, too, she would have to hide. He mustn't know how much he was hurting her, not for the sake of her pride but because it would only make matters worse. The only thing she could do for Henry now was to let him go free, never have to think about her again. She'd made her mistakes, and no matter how much she regretted them, she couldn't change them.

It was a little more than an hour later when Manuel returned with the horses. Mike woke reluctantly when Henry demanded it. "All right, I'm ready. Just haul me up, Hank. I'll make it from there."

Alva's face was pale, her eyes pools of untold suffering as she watched Henry and Manuel boost Mike onto the horse he had acquired after Jacko had been shot from under him. It wasn't much of a horse, compared to Jacko, but at least it had had sufficient rest while Mike had been in town, and it wasn't too old.

Henry's face was expressionless as he reached out to prevent Andrea from mounting Runner. "You've always wanted to ride Beau. Now you're getting your chance. He's done in, and you're the lightest." He handed her Beau's reins and mounted Runner himself. "*Adios,* Señora Gomez. *Adios,* Carlos."

"*Adios. Vaya con Dios.*" Alva was fingering her rosary. "Take care of Michael, Señor. And of Andrea."

Impulsively, Andrea leaned from the saddle to kiss her. "I'll never forget you. I'll never forget any of you. After this is all over, I'll come to see you again. I promise."

They touched their heels to their horses. In spite of his grueling trip with only two hours of rest, Beau lifted his head and stepped out. Andrea's slight weight on his back was as nothing to him, after carrying Adam and Henry. When Andrea looked back, the little crowd of well-wishers were standing in the middle of the dusty street, watching after them. She prayed that they could lie well enough so that the bandits would not think that they had given them either comfort or aid.

When she looked back again, they were dispersing toward their homes, and she breathed a silent prayer for their safety.

Mike's jaw was rigid as he gritted his teeth against the pain of the jolting, and his face was so white that

502

Andrea ached for him. "Are you all right?" she asked him.

"I'll be all right if I don't have to waste my breath answering foolish questions. Just keep riding." A ghost of a grin took the sting from his words. Andrea kneed Beau as close beside him as she could and held her peace as they followed Henry's lead.

It was a miracle that Mike could stay in the saddle at all. She could only hope that it would take the bandits a good long time to organize a pursuit, or better still, that they wouldn't come after them at all. That last was a forlorn hope; a look at Henry's face, as he glanced back to see how Mike was holding out, showed that he held no such wistful hope. A man like Pedro Lopez would not let the insult to his pride go unavenged.

Adam was going to have a few words to say to both her and Mike when they got home. Adam! For the first time since Henry had come into the cantina and kept them all from getting killed, Andrea wondered why it was Henry who had come after them, alone, instead of Wade or her father. The question struggled to make itself audible, but a look at Henry's face made her bide her time. She'd ask him when they camped for the night, and she set her mind against a conviction that she might not want to hear the answer.

"Hang on, Mike," she said.

"What the heck do you think I'm doing?"

He was hanging on, his hands clutching the pommel, his face glistening with sweat, his mouth a straight line under the stubble on his face. Henry's face, as well, was covered with a growth of stubble. By the time they got to Texas, even Kate or Adam wouldn't recognize them, two gaunt, bearded men and a bedraggled girl in an even more bedraggled peasant dress.

Henry changed their direction, heading toward rougher country where there would be more cover. Mike was slumped over his horse's neck, still hanging on although Andrea could see that he was only half conscious, as they climbed and wound their way among rocks and hills and brush where there was no trace of a trail.

503

She and Alva had got one arm back into his shirt by ripping it a little down the back, and her breath caught as she saw a splotch of tell-tale red that didn't come from the reflection of the setting sun. His wound had reopened and was bleeding again; he couldn't go on much farther. She touched Beau Noir with her heel to bring him up to Henry to tell him, but Henry was already guiding Runner off to the left, where a small box canyon would provide shelter and be as defendable a position as they could find before full blackness set in.

In another moment he lifted Mike from his horse and eased him to the ground. "Spread out a couple of blankets," he ordered Manuel. "Andrea, help me get this shirt off him. Where are those bandages Señora Gomez gave us?"

Andrea located the bandages in her saddle bag. She knelt beside her brother, whose eyes were closed and whose cheeks were sunken in. "Has he lost much more blood?"

"Enough. Not too much, I hope."

"I want a drink," Mike muttered.

Andrea brought his canteen. Mike drank a few swallows and made a gagging noise. "Water!" he said.

"Drink it and shut up. It's good for you," Henry told him gruffly. "What did you think it would be, tequila or mescal?"

"It didn't hurt to hope."

"There'll be coffee in the morning. I don't want to risk a fire tonight. The smell of the smoke would travel far even if the light couldn't be seen outside this canyon. It'll have to be a cold camp till I can see if we're being followed."

They ate the cold chicken that one of the women had given them and washed it down with water. Mike could only manage a few mouthfuls.

"You must sleep, Doña. Señor Henry and I will watch," Manuel's soft voice spoke at her elbow.

"I'll take my turn. You can have the first watch, then wake me. Henry's more tired than either of us." Andrea accepted the blanket that Manuel proffered and rolled

504

herself up in it, close beside Mike so that her body would lend some warmth to his.

She was still awake, too keyed up to sleep, in spite of her aching tiredness, when Henry came back, moving as silently as a cat. "Everything seems to be all right." Henry's voice was low so as not to disturb Mike, who had already fallen into an exhausted sleep. "Get some sleep, Manuel."

"No, Señor. Doña Andrea said that the first watch is mine, the second hers."

"She did, did she? I thought I'd made myself clear. . . ."

Andrea propped herself up on her elbow. "Henry, why did you come after us alone? Was Dad still in town at Juan's trial?"

"The trial is over. Juan was acquitted. He's at Trail's End; your father gave him a job."

"But if Dad was back, why didn't he or Wade—"

"Adam couldn't come. Clay took a pot shot at him, and he's laid up."

Andrea's gasp cut through him in spite of the harshness of his words. "Dad! How bad is he hurt?"

"Pretty bad, but he's tough. He'll make it. Worrying about you isn't going to help him recover. Go to sleep, if you're bound to take the second watch."

"Did they catch Clay?"

"They didn't have to chase him." Henry's voice was sardonic. "He wasn't going anywhere. I was lucky when I shot back at him."

"But how did it happen? Where—"

"Go to sleep. It's all over with; it'll keep until morning. They're both going to live, that's all you have to know tonight."

With that, Henry rolled up in his own blanket on the other side of Mike, to give him the added warmth of being between them. Andrea lay down again, shivering. She knew it would be no use to ask him any more questions tonight and besides, he needed all the sleep he could get. But her own mind kept asking questions silently, frantic with worry, until she too fell asleep because her exhausted body took over and demanded it.

It seemed as though she had only slept for a few moments when Manuel's hand on her shoulder brought her to instant alertness. "It is time, Doña. All is quiet."

Andrea wrapped her blanket around her and walked back to the mouth of the canyon. A glance at the stars told her that it was nearly midnight. Manuel had let her sleep more than the allotted time. She'd let Henry have more than his share as well, then. Two more hours of sleep before they had to start out again would do her.

She settled herself to wait out her watch, her back against the canyon wall. Somewhere in the near distance a coyote lifted his plaintive voice in a series of sharp barks, and another answered him. There were soft rustlings in the brush. She made sure that her rifle was where she could reach it instantly, her ears attuned to the night just as her eyes adjusted to the darkness so that she could see almost as well as if it had been twilight or coming on to daybreak. The sound of the coyotes barking was the loneliest sound in the world, and she had never felt so far from home.

Henry cursed her when she woke him a scant two hours before dawn. "If you give out on us, you'll keep going even if I have to tie you to your saddle!"

"I won't give out." She touched Mike's forehead and smothered a gasp. "Henry! He's hot! He has a fever."

Henry knelt beside her. "You're right. Let's hope we threw off those bandits. It looks like we're going to be here for a while."

TEXAS

32

The sea voyage had been pleasurable. Reggie had the gift of making friends, and he had enjoyed every minute of it. Getting the money for this last determined effort to get Andrea back hadn't been too difficult. Sir Robert hadn't been exactly keen on subsidizing the trip, but he'd dipped down into his pocket when he'd realized that now that Reggie had lost his position at the bank, he'd be moving in on him unless the wherewithal to go and patch it up with Andrea was forthcoming.

Reggie had thought it all out after Bea had so unreasonably told him to get out of her life and stay out. That had been a shock to him; he'd thought that Bea loved him enough to go on supporting him until he could find another position—something suitable, of course. She'd always been crazy for him, she'd have crawled on her hands and knees over broken glass for him, not so long ago.

And then, right out of the blue, she'd presented him

with his packed bags one morning when he'd waked up with a king-sized hangover and told him that she'd already confiscated his key to her studio digs and not to slam the door on his way out.

Maybe it had been his fault, a little. But how could he have known that she'd take it wrongly, just because he'd flirted, perfectly discreetly, with Mrs. Deerfield? Agnes Deerfield had invited them to a party at her house in Kensington, in celebration of Bea's completing the bust of the late Mr. Deerfield. Bea hadn't been enthusiastic about accepting the commission, especially since Albert Deerfield had been pudgy and quite without character and she'd had to work from photographs, but the widow had offered such a huge commission that she hadn't been able to turn it down. After all, she was providing for two now.

The Kensington party had been for the purpose of unveiling the bust, and that part of it had gone all right. Reggie had thought it was a good idea to butter the old girl up, because she had friends who had money and it could have resulted in more lucrative commissions for Bea.

But Bea hadn't taken it that way. She'd taken exception to the way Agnes Deerfield had monopolized him, quite as if she'd bought him, too, along with that disgusting bust.

There wasn't any doubt that Agnes would be only too pleased to take over Bea's role in Reggie's life. She wasn't fabulously wealthy, as wealth went in the class of people Reggie liked to run with, but she had a comfortable income from her husband's estate, and she could afford Reggie as well as Bea could, if not a little better.

As a matter of fact, Reggie had toyed with the idea after Bea had booted him out. Agnes wasn't bad-looking. A bit long in the tooth, she must be approaching forty, but her figure was still good, if a bit plump, and she knew how to dress to minimize her defects. He wouldn't have to be ashamed to be seen with her, and she could make him very comfortable indeed.

The trouble was, she was looking for a husband, no a young lover. He might have talked her around. He' never had much trouble in talking women around. Bu he'd far rather be Andrea's husband than Agnes's. So in the end he'd decided to gamble everything on this last chance for a reconciliation. Andrea had had time to calm down by now, and if he showed her that he was going to behave himself, there was a good chance that she'd take him back.

To prove how much he meant to change, he was willing to make a major concession and live in this Texas of hers, if she had her heart set on it. After all, with the Wentworth money, living on a ranch wouldn't be so bad. They could always travel, even go back to London every year and visit Aunt Madeline and look up any of their old friends they'd like to see. During the rest of the year he'd make a real stab at making himself useful at whatever men did on a ranch.

The train trip across the United States had been tolerable enough, although even with his education he'd been astonished by how wide and seemingly endless the country was. But this last stage of the journey was appalling.

He'd ended up at a cluster of weatherbeaten buildings that had the temerity to call itself a town. It was situated in the middle of nowhere, the end of the world, and he'd been dismayed to find that he had to continue by either buckboard or horseback if he wanted to go on to Trail's End. The natives of the town had looked at him as if he were a visitor from another planet, their barely concealed amusement at his superbly tailored British clothing showing how far removed they were from any kind of civilized culture.

"Better hire a buckboard. You'd have a mite of trouble trying to tote all that luggage on a horse."

And now he was in a buckboard, a vehicle of such discomfort that he found it difficult to believe. His driver, who professed to know the way, was so laconic that Reggie had long since given up trying to find out whether they weren't actually lost. He was covered with dust, his throat was filled with it, his spine felt as if it had been jolted right up through his neck. The idea that Andrea had been born and lived nearly all of her life in this place was

511

beyond comprehension. It seemed impossible that even Indians could ever have survived here where the sun was so bright that it hurt your eyes to look at the sky and the air was so dry that his skin felt as though it were cracking underneath the layers of choking dust that had settled on it.

"Is all of the road this bad?"

"Yup."

"Can't you try to avoid some of the ruts?"

"Nope."

There was no way to avoid the ruts. Reggie was certain that every inch of his body was black and blue. Adam Wentworth had given his ranch the wrong name; it shouldn't have been Trail's End, it should have been World's End. The best valet in London would have been unable to salvage his suit.

"Is it much farther?"

"Nope."

Reggie felt a flicker of hope, but six hours later, when he asked the same question, he received the same answer. He had no conception of a country where a day's ride to visit a neighbor was spoken of as just down the road a piece.

He braced his back and his legs and endured. The journey had to be over with sometime, even though at the moment he would not have wagered a ha'penny on it.

When the driver, who had introduced himself only as Ernie, pulled off the road and stopped, Reggie stared at him with disbelief.

"What are you doing?"

"Campin'. Sun's most down."

"Camping! You must be mad!"

"Nope. Ain't nothin' happened to make me mad. Even your fool questions don't make me mad." The grin on the lean face was friendly, even if somewhat pitying. "Reckon you can't help bein' ignorant, bein' as you're foreigner." It was the longest string of words he'd uttered since they had started out.

"Why can't we go on? You said it wasn't much farther."

"Horses need rest. Pile out, friend. You can spread your blanket over there."

Reggie was dismayed. "I have no blanket! I was unaware, when I started out on this journey, that I would have any need to carry along my personal blankets."

Ernie shook his head, muttering with disapproval. "You're more of a greenhorn than I figured. Well, I'll lend you one of mine. We'll just have to keep our feet closer to the fire. You can gather up some wood whilst I unhitch."

Reggie bowed to the inevitable. He searched the immediate vicinity gingerly, wary of snakes, and gathered up a respectable armload of small branches from the brush that grew everywhere. Ernie grunted when he returned.

"It'll do for a start. Better fetch a few more loads while I get the fire goin' and put the coffee pot on, if you want to sleep warm. Even if you don't, a fire'll keep the varmints away."

"Varmints?" Reggie looked around uneasily.

Ernie grinned. "Wolves," he said. He doubted that a *lobo* was anywhere within fifty miles, but this dude from England probably wouldn't know a wolf from a coyote, anyway. At least it would make him hump his stumps to fetch more wood. "Maybe a painter."

"Painter?"

"Mountain cat. Puma. Panther. Anyway, a cat bigger'n you'd want to have rubbin' against your ankles." Ernie poured water from a canteen into a battered coffee pot and propped it up on a rock close to the flames he already had going. That really got the greenhorn to move. He shook his head with disgust. No blankets! He wouldn't have allowed that even a foreigner from England would be that ignorant.

The meal that Ernie handed Reggie on a tin plate half an hour later was, incredibly, even worse than the one he'd had at the hotel back at the last fringe of civilization. The coffee was strong enough to walk by itself, and there were grounds in it. The frying-pan biscuits were as hard as rocks, the bacon was burned, and

513

Reggie had always disliked beans. But as a true Britisher, who was obliged to make the best of any circumstances without complaint, he ate it without remark. He supposed that he'd have to learn about things like this, if Andrea insisted that they live in Texas. But he hoped there would be very few such journeys as this.

He woke the next morning so stiff from sleeping on the ground that he could scarcely move. Ernie was grinning down at him.

"Still here? I figured you were in such a almighty hurry you might have started out walkin'. The fire's out. You want breakfast, rustle up some more wood whilst I hitch up."

Reggie clamped his mouth shut against the question that rose to his lips. Was it much farther? He already knew the answer to that; he didn't need to hear Ernie say "Nope."

The few ranch workers who were in the immediate vicinity of the house hurried to stare with astonishment at the man who climbed stiffly down from the buckboard that clattered to a stop near the corral. They'd never seen even Adam dressed as this man was dressed. At Trail's End, Adam wore Western garb, even though it was tailored to his measurements and as different from an ordinary cowhand's clothing as a piece of glass is from fine crystal.

Now that he had arrived at last, the sight of the gracious *casa* reassured Reggie and made him sure that the discomforts of this last stage of his journey had been worth while. The house was very large, and it spoke of wealth and culture even though its architecture was strangely exotic to an Englishman's eyes. He left Ernie and the dark-complexioned workers to take his pigskin luggage from the buckboard and walked on back to the house.

The massive, hand-carved double doors opened as he stepped onto a vine-shaded patio. A young woman stood there, a pretty young woman, no more than nineteen or twenty. Reggie sensed that she was some kind of a housemaid, even though she was not wearing a uniform.

but a full gathered skirt and a deep-necked white blouse and some kind of woven slippers on her bare feet.

The girl smiled, a smile that was warm and friendly. "Señor? Please to enter. What name shall I tell to Doña Kate?"

"Mr. Mansfield," Reggie instructed her, thankful that she spoke English, even though her accent was strong enough so that he'd had a little trouble understanding her. He expected that he'd get used to that. It if came right down to it, he supposed that he could learn the language, he'd done well at French when he'd been at school and Spanish was also a Latin language. "You may announce me to Mrs. Wentworth and to my wife."

The smile that had been there an instant ago vanished, and the girl's face became expressionless, but Reggie felt a dislike that he was at a loss to account for. Women, even of the servant class, invariably liked him and went out of their way to make things comfortable for him.

"*Sí*, Señor. You may wait here." She indicated a carved straight-backed chair in the central hallway, one of a pair that flanked a low chest that held a pottery bowl of some unfamiliar dried flowers. Reggie was taken aback. So he was to cool his heels in the entrance hall, rather than being shown into the drawing room at once! But probably the girl wasn't properly trained. You couldn't expect the same measure of culture in America that was taken for granted in England.

He was shocked five minutes later when Kate came to him in the hallway. She looked pale and tired, with fine lines of some deep-seated worry showing around her eyes. As always, she was immaculately dressed and every strand of her dark hair was in place, the chignon at the nape of her neck smooth and shining. But her eyes lacked warmth as she greeted him, and Reggie had the distinct impression that he was the last person on earth she wanted to see.

"You didn't let us know that you were coming."

Reggie decided to be frank; it almost never failed, specially with women. He used his most charming and boyish smile, certain that she would understand and sympathize.

"I rather expected that if I did, Andrea would see fit to be somewhere else when I arrived. As she's the one I came to see, I thought it wiser to arrive without advance notice. Where is she? Has she been told that I'm here?"

A faint smile flickered at the corners of Kate's mouth. It wasn't echoed in her eyes. "Even arriving without advance notice, Andrea is somewhere else. She is, we have reason to believe, somewhere in Mexico, but we have no idea where or when she'll be back. I'm afraid that your journey has been for nothing, unless you're prepared to stay indefinitely."

This was something that Reggie hadn't counted on, and he was shaken, but his recovery was almost immediate.

"In that case, I'll talk to you and your husband first, Mother Wentworth." He used the title deliberately, certain that it would make her expression softer.

It didn't. Kate only waited, and he plunged on, with just a trace of his beginning desperation in his voice.

"Our separation was a dreadful mistake. Certainly you must realize that. Andrea is my wife, and I still love her even though she left me."

Candor, he thought. Be repentant. "Oh, I don't claim that I was entirely blameless! I confess that I had a lapse, but I was more than willing to break off with my . . . friend . . . when Andrea let me know how much she objected. Frankly, I was amazed that she made so much of it. But once I learned how strongly she did object, I certainly would never have allowed such a thing to happen again. It was largely a misunderstanding between two different cultures, Mother Wentworth. I hadn't given any thought to the fact that such matter-of-fact things aren't as common here in America as they are in England."

He smiled again, his most boyish, please-forgive-me smile. "I expect I shouldn't be talking like this to you, Mother Wentworth. You probably don't consider it a fi subject for a lady, even though you are Andrea's mothe

516

and concerned about it. If I could talk to Andrea's father—"

"Adam isn't well. But if you insist on seeing him, you may, when he wakes up. I'll only ask you to be brief and not to tire him."

"Ill? What a pity! What seems to be the trouble, Mother Wentworth?"

If he says Mother Wentworth one more time, Kate thought, I'm going to scream. "It seems that he got in the way of a bullet, Reggie. And gunshot wounds are quite likely to make one feel unwell."

"Gunshot wounds!" Reggie's mouth fell open. "Good Lord, do you mean he's been shot?"

"Ambushed," Kate told him curtly.

The hair on the back of his neck rose. Visions of red Indians rose in his mind. But no one here at the ranch seemed to be worried about an attack, and his first thought was immediately replaced by another. How badly was Adam wounded? He really needed to get Adam on his side, man to man, and if Adam were too badly hurt to hear him out, it would make it that much harder. What a rotten bit of luck, to have Andrea gone and Adam under the weather!

"I'm most dreadfully sorry to hear that he's been hurt, Mother Wentworth." Kate's mouth compressed, but he failed to notice it. "And certainly I'll wait. I didn't come all the way to America in hope of reconciling with Dria just to turn around and go back again without seeing her."

Kate inclined her head. She'd have liked to order Reggie out, but Western hospitality made that impossible. He had come a long way, and he was still Andrea's husband, no matter how much she wished that he was not.

Almost as if she had been standing in the wings at a stage play, the girl who had admitted him to the house reentered the hall. "Will Mr. Mansfield be staying, shall I see to a room for him, Doña?"

"Yes, Carmelita. Put him in the west wing and see that he had everything he needs."

Carmelita indicated that he should follow her. The room she led him to was spacious and comfortably furnished with Spanish-style furniture. The pieces were expertly crafted and spoke of Adam's affluence.

A middle-aged Mexican man brought in his luggage and stacked it at the foot of the bed, leaving without a word or a glance in his direction. Odd, that. Andrea had told him, over and over, how friendly the Mexicans were, how they went out of their way to show friendliness, even to strangers.

A few moments later Carmelita returned with an earthenware pitcher of hot water and some towels and a fresh cake of soap. She placed them on the washstand without asking him if there were anything else he needed. Her eyes, which should have been soft and smiling, held that same hostility that he had noticed earlier when he'd told her who he was.

Reggie decided to ignore it. After all, she was only a servant. At least the water was hot. He'd stayed in a good many country houses where the bathing facilities were no better than this, although he had expected something more lavish in the way of plumbing here in America, even in so remote a place. All the Americans he'd ever come in contact with seemed to have a fetish about bathrooms. But as long as he could rid himself of the dirt and dust he'd collected in the buckboard, he was satisfied. Cleanliness was the first rule of a gentleman; how it was achieved had little bearing on the matter.

Kate was nowhere to be seen when he left his room, once more clean and clad in fresh clothing from his bags. He found his way to the enormous living room by himself. Its size impressed him, as used as he was to English country houses. Once again the furniture was in the Spanish style. With all of Adam's money they could have furnished it more conventionally, with Hepplewhite, with Chippendale, with Queen Anne or Duncan Phyfe. But his eyes lighted up at the sight of a Corot on the wall, and what on closer inspection proved to be a Vermeer. He was examining a first edition of the *Pickwick Papers* when Kate came to find him, although his mind was more occupied with how long Andrea would remain away and with the state of Adam's health than on the rare book itself.

"Adam is awake now. You may see him for a few moments."

He followed her into a bedroom that faced on a garden on its outside wall and on a stone-paved courtyard off the opposite side. There were flowerbeds there, and potted plants and wicker and wrought-iron furniture with colorful cushions, and a fountain splashing in the center. All this, in the middle of the wilderness! The more Reggie saw of Trail's End, the more willing he was to live here.

The room itself was exceptionally large and furnished like the rest of the house, reflecting Adam's preference for exquisitely crafted Spanish pieces. But its elegance was lost on Reggie, who was astounded to see that Adam already had another visitor who had not only been allowed access to him before he himself had been summoned, but was actually the man Ernie who had driven him from town in that abominable buckboard!

Adam was propped up against his pillows, his bare torso wrapped around with bandages. He nodded at Reggie and waved a careless hand at him and turned his full attention back to the buckboard driver.

"In a moment, Reggie. Ernie, is that a fact! You sure you have your facts straight?"

"As sure as I'm sittin' here. Widder Armstrong told it herself, how she seen Clay cryin' like a baby because he's lost his grandson as well as his son. Said he didn't have anything left to live for and he wouldn't care if his place burned to the ground. He's goin' crazy tryin' to decide whether to cut little Davie out of his will to spite Paula and Juan, or to try to fix it so's they'll never be able to benefit, only the boy. He's a broken man; he knows he's never going to have the use of his leg again. Danged if I don't almost feel sorry for him."

"You know something, Ernie? Danged if I don't, too!" Adam's face lit up with a slow grin.

"It isn't anything to laugh about!" Kate's voice was sharp. "Granted that Clay had every bit of his misfortune coming to him, he's still a bitter, lonesome human being.

Pilar's waiting to hear from me about whether he's going to be able to take care of himself or if she should come back to care for him. I'll have to tell her that he needs her, but it's her own decision whether to come back or not. In her place, I'm not sure that I would."

Adam's face was suddenly grave as he gave Kate a look filled with love. "You would. And so will she. I didn't mean to laugh at him, Kate. I was just a little carried away, seeing how his sins came to roost on his shoulders after all those years of shoving everybody else around. It's all going to depend on Clay himself whether he has anything left to live for. Paula isn't a vindictive girl; she'll see that Davie visits his grandparents frequently, if he doesn't go cutting up so that it's impossible to allow it."

"Too bad Hank couldn't have aimed a little higher, but then, as long as Clay's goin' to have to pull in his horns, I reckon there shouldn't anybody go wishin' him dead," Ernie said laconically.

"I agree with you there. Are they treating you all right out in the bunkhouse? You're perfectly welcome in the house, you old coyote. I don't know why you insist on bunking out there with the vaqueros."

"I get uneasy with all this magnificence around me." Ernie grinned. "Not that I blame you for havin' it, it just ain't my style. Besides, when I get to jawin', I don't always watch my language, and Mrs. Wentworth's a lady. They're treatin' me like a king out there, don't you worry. I'll be pullin' out first thing in the mornin'."

He got to his feet, and now he turned his grin on Reggie. "Don't go wanderin' around without somebody ridin' herd on you, young feller. You might run into a *lobo* or a rattler, and I don't guess they'd know what to make of you, so you might get hurt."

"Well, Reggie?" Adam asked when Ernie had left. "What brings you to Trail's End?" His voice was cold; it held a quality that Reggie didn't like. There was no welcome in his eyes, either, which were as cold as his voice.

"I thought it was time that Andrea and I made up our differences and got back together. We can hardly go on the way we are, and as long as she refuses to return to England, it was up to me to come here and see if we can't work things out." Reggie's voice was confidential, man to man, implying that as long as women were unreasonable, it was always the man who had to take matters in hand.

"You've already been told that Andrea isn't here. You'll just have to wait for her to come back. Her mother and I have no intention of trying to influence her."

Kate choked back her strangled amusement. No intention of trying to influence her, indeed! No wonder Adam was such a good poker player!

"I can appreciate that. But we still need to talk, Mr. Wentworth." Reggie didn't quite have the courage to call Adam Father Wentworth, Kate noticed with still more amusement. "I'd like you to know my side of the story."

"I didn't realize that there were sides. I understand that you were having an affair with another woman. A blatant and shameless affair, even taking money from her." Adam's opinion of a man who would take money from his mistress was plain on his face.

"But as I've already explained to Mother Wentworth"—Kate held her handkerchief to her mouth, almost breaking up at Adam's expression when Reggie used that term—"I simply didn't realize that Dria would object so strenuously! It's just that things are different over there, Mr. Wentworth. Most wives wouldn't have given it a second thought as long as they realized that their husband still loved them, and had no intention of putting her aside for the other woman."

"Here in America we expect a man to be faithful to his wife, as any decent man would be." Adam's tone was not encouraging.

"Andrea wasn't completely without fault, you know. There was her"—he hesitated, not quite daring to say affair," and went on—"her friendship with my cousin Ted."

"And it was just that—friendship, nothing more. I know my daughter, Reggie. She could no more be unfaithful to her husband than she could sprout wings and fly, and God knows she's no angel. Dria has her faults, but sleeping around isn't one of them. Now, if you don't mind, I want my supper. You'll just have to wait until Andrea returns and hash all this out with her. Kate, tell Manuella that if she sends me any more of that pap, I'll burn up her fiesta dress as soon as I can get out of this bed. I want a steak, a thick one, with plenty of hot sauce on it. And a bowl of chili beans, and a brandy with my coffee."

Reggie's heart sank. There was no doubt that he'd get no help from Adam. And with Andrea in very real danger . . . what the devil was she doing in Mexico, anyway, hadn't he heard, all the way across the country, that there was a war going on down there . . . he was faced with the distinct possibility that he might come out of this venture with nothing at all. It would be bad enough losing Andrea. He really was fond of her. Outside of her rather stuffy American notions, he liked her, he actually loved her, more than he'd ever loved any other woman.

If Adam and Kate hadn't known him for what he was, a thoroughly weak man, they might have felt a little sorry for him when they saw the woebegone expression on his face. But weakness was something that neither of them could tolerate, especially in a man who might become the father of their grandchildren. Andrea deserved better than Reggie, and they had no intention of lifting a hand to try to persuade her to take him back.

His own dinner, taken with Kate in a dining room which could seat thirty people with no sense of crowding, had little appeal for Reggie, although the food was excellent and well served and Kate made polite conversation as was required of a hostess even when a guest is unwelcome. She inquired after Lady Madeline and Sir Robert, she asked Reggie if he knew the name of a particular beautiful apricot-colored rose that Lady Madeline had in her garden. She refused to speculate on Andrea's return or her reaction to his showing up at Trail's End.

Reggie drank a little too much with his dinner, and retired to his room, exhausted emotionally as well as physically, shortly afterward. It was obvious that Kate had no wish for his company but only wanted to return to Adam.

What would he do, if Dria refused to listen to reason? Or worse still, if she never came back at all, if she got herself killed down there in that backward country south of the Texas border?

She would come back; she had to. He needed her. He was willing to make every concession she might demand. It was impossible that his mission shouldn't succeed, when he wanted it to succeed so very much. He'd court her all over again, if he had to, but she was going to come back to him, and then everything in his world would be as it should be.

MEXICO

33

Andrea sat with her back propped against a rock, her arms wrapped around her knees. Overhead, the stars made the midnight air almost as bright as if it had been daylight.

Despite the blanket wrapped around her shoulders, she was cold. The quietness of the night, with only a faint rustling in the brush when the breeze riffled through it and the occasional yelp of a coyote, gave her the eerie feeling that she and Henry and Mike were the only human beings left on earth.

Manuel had taken Despacio, the horse that had replaced Jacko, at daybreak, to make his way back to Dos Hermanos to buy more supplies and to find out whether the bandits had returned and were still searching for them. They'd been holed up in this box canyon for three days while Mike had alternately tossed and raved in the delirium of his fever or fallen into a stupor-like sleep that frightened her even more. They were running out of food, and there was scarcely any water left. She was thirsty in spite of the coldness of the night. Her throat was dry and her lips were cracked, and she was tormented by visions of Manuella's coffee, of tall glasses of milk chilled in the spring house, of the pitchers of water, all the water she could drink, that stood on her bedside table every night at Trail's End. Being hungry didn't bother her much; it was the thirst that was hard to bear, but what little water there was remaining in the canteens had to be saved for Mike.

She pressed her lips together, ignoring the pain that the cracks in them caused her. No word of her discomfort had passed from them. Hank was thirsty, too, and probably hungrier than she was, but he hadn't mentioned it and neither would she. When Manuel came back, she would have both water and food, and until he came back she'd simply do her best to ignore their lack.

If the old man didn't run into trouble, he should be back sometime tomorrow. How early depended on Despacio. The nag fitted his name, which meant slow, a nondescript horse that wouldn't have been given corral room at Trail's End, but that was the reason Manuel had taken him. Both Beau Noir and Runner stood out like sore thumbs, and even Baldy was of such outstanding value that he'd be sure to be recognized but Despacio wouldn't draw a second glance. By the same token, it was Manuel who had gone back to Dos Hermanos. One lone Mexican looking like any other old Mexican peon on a seedy horse could pass unnoticed where it would have been the height of folly for Hank to show himself.

As silently as Hank moved, Andrea heard his approach and lifted her head as he squatted on his heels beside her. He made no comment about her alertness, but he felt a grudging approval. No matter what grief Andrea had been to him ever since he'd known her, she was a thoroughbred. She hadn't even voiced the fear for Mike that would have plunged most women into hysterical tears.

"How is he?" she asked, her voice scarcely more than a whisper.

"Sleeping. His fever's still high."

528

He saw her stiffen, and he reached out and put his hand on her shoulder. It was a gesture that he couldn't control.

"He's tough, Dria. He's as tough as an old longhorn. He'll make it. The water Manuel's bringing will help."

"Of course he'll make it!" Andrea's voice was fierce. "We're all going to make it!" There was no hint of the nagging fear inside of her; what if something happened to Manuel, what if he didn't make it back? But even in the starlight Hank saw the expression in her eyes, and it was too much for him. Without a word, he drew her into his arms, and his embrace tightened as he felt how she was trembling.

"Don't break now, Dria! We've made it this far. You're cold. Go and get some sleep; wrap up in my blanket as well as your own, close to Mike. I can stand watch the rest of the night."

"No. You'll need your blanket. The wind isn't exactly balmy here in the mouth of the canyon." Andrea drew herself away. "I'm all right."

She didn't want his concern for her, she didn't want to be treated with kindness that held any trace of pity. She already owed him far more than she could ever repay, just for coming to look for her and saving her and Mike and Manuel from being killed or captured back in Dos Hermanos. Her mind shied away from what probably would have happened if he hadn't caught up with them just when he had.

But he'd done it out of friendship for Adam and Kate and for Mike, not for her. Her back was straight as she walked away from him, and Hank felt frustration surge over him as he watched her go. She might be cold and tired and thirsty and hungry, she might be terrified that Mike would die, but nothing would ever break that pride of hers. Cursing, he settled down where she'd been sitting, pulled his blanket around his shoulders, and prepared to wait out the rest of the night. He had only his thoughts to keep him company, and they were cold comfort.

The sun had been up for several hours, taking most of the chill off the air, when Manuel arrived, coming from the wrong direction. Both Hank and Andrea knew, the moment they spotted him urging Despacio as fast as he would go, that something was wrong.

"Doña, Señor, the bandits have been back to Dos Hermanos, and they are searching for you. They will be coming this way *dentro de un momento,* in a short time. This is not a good hiding place; they will be sure to find you. Pedro Lopez was not hurt as badly as we thought, and he is leading them and he is a very bad man. It is not safe here."

Andrea stiffened, and Henry's mouth tightened. "How many men?"

"Many, Señor. Twelve, fifteen, it is a large band." Manuel was frightened, but he looked to Henry for orders and he would obey no matter what Henry decided to do.

"Mike can't be moved. It might kill him. I'll have to ride out and lead them away from here. Beau Noir will give them a run they won't forget in a hurry." Hank's voice was grim.

"*Sí* Señor. We will take good care of Señor Mike while you lead them away." Manuel looked doubtful. For only one man to attempt to foil the bandits was foolhardy, to say the least. "I have brought food and water; there will be everything he needs."

"Keep out of sight. And keep quiet. Make sure that the mouth of the canyon is covered again after I leave. If I don't come back, as soon as Mike is fit to stay on his horse, take him and Andrea home."

"*Sí* Señor. I will do that." Manuel's face was filled with sadness but with resignation, as well, and the inborn ability to survive against overwhelming odds.

They watched as Henry gave Beau Noir a little of the water that Manuel had brought, using his hat as a container. There was a sardonic amusement in Henry's eyes as he replaced the hat on his head. "At least it'll keep my brains from frying as long as it doesn't dry out." The joke wasn't very funny. Now, in the winter, it didn't get that hot, even in the middle of the afternoon.

530

Andrea and Manuel watched him ride out. When the figures of horse and man disappeared in the distance, Manuel began piling brush back across the mouth of the canyon.

"Not yet, Manuel," Andrea said. She was already giving Runner a few swallows of water just as Henry had Beau, taking only a mouthful or two herself. Then she slipped Runner's bridle on and threw his saddle over his back.

"Doña, you must not! It is too dangerous, and Señor Henry will be angry!"

"He's going to need me if he's to lead the bandits away. They might not follow just one man, but if there are two of us, they might think that Mike was hurt badly enough to die, and they probably didn't even know that you were with us. But they can't fail to recognize Beau, and they'll be after the two of us and you and Mike will be a lot safer."

She swung into the saddle and touched Runner with her heel. After his long rest, the great horse was willing to go even though he'd had so little water. Fixing her eyes on the point where Henry had disappeared from sight behind a jumbled mound of rocky hills, she set out after him, confident that she'd catch up with him because he wouldn't be traveling fast, he'd be keeping his eye out for the first sight of the vengeance-minded bandits.

She was right. Henry heard her coming, and she heard his cursing before she got near enough to understand the words.

"I told you to stay in the canyon with Mike and Manuel! Damn you, Dria, won't you ever learn to take orders?"

"Not when they're wrong. It's going to take both of us to draw the bandits away, and you know it. Let's not waste time arguing when we could be putting more distance between ourselves and the canyon."

Henry's answer was to pull his hat lower over his eyes and start out again without even looking back to see if she were following.

Two hours later they saw the dust of a large band of

horsemen from a rise. "Let them get a good look at us," Henry said grimly. "And then, as long as you were pig-headed enough to cut yourself in on this deal, let's see how good you are at outriding bullets! And remember that we have to let them keep us in sight if we're going to draw them far enough away from Mike and Manuel so they won't have a prayer of finding them."

Andrea nodded. Her throat was dry again in spite of the water she'd had. She could go for a long time without any more, but she was worried about Runner and Beau. No matter how tough and strong a horse is, it has to have water or it will collapse and die.

Henry's voice was gruff to hide his own worry. "I'll bet on Beau and Runner. All right. They've recognized us. If you know any prayers, you'd better say them. Let's go!"

They wheeled their mounts and set them to a gallop, holding them in just enough so that Lopez and his desperadoes could keep them in sight. There was a rifle shot, but only one. Lopez wasn't fool enough to let his men waste ammunition when they were out of range. Manuel was right, he was a dangerous man, and he was one who would go to any lengths to avenge the insult to his honor. Henry hoped that Andrea did know some prayers.

It was a game of follow the leader, of hide and seek. Henry used every ounce of his years of experience, now slowing down, now spurting ahead, now disappearing in the rough, mountainous desolation ahead only to show themselves again and keep their pursuers coming.

Andrea kept up with him, her lips compressed, the light of determination in her eyes. Everything depended on their succeeding, their lives and Mike's and Manuel's. They had to conserve their horses' strength as much as possible and at the same time keep a fast enough pace not to get within firing range. They had to make sure that they didn't get far enough ahead so that Lopez might decide that keeping up the chase wasn't worth it. He might just take it into his head to search for Mike, to make sure that Mike was dead.

To make sure of holding Lopez's interest, Henry commanded Andrea to take cover behind a hill while he circled back and around and then got off a couple of shots that sent spurts of dust up from the ground only a few yards from their pursuers, an act of bravado that was sure to strengthen Lopez's determination to run them down and kill them. Even as he wheeled Beau and hightailed it to a safer distance, another shot came from the right, striking even closer to the bandits. Damn that girl! He'd told her to stay put! But at the same time that he cursed her for not obeying him he appreciated her strategy. Her shot had slowed them down and given him more time to put distance between them.

"If we'd dared to get just a little closer, we could have put two of them out of action," Andrea said. "Maybe next time—"

"The next time you'll damned well do as I say!" Henry lashed at her. "Keep moving. That shot of yours made them mad."

They kept moving, but their horses were tiring. Henry was more worried than he liked to admit, and he knew that Andrea was as well aware of their danger as he was. Gritting his teeth, he kept his eyes open for some place where they could take cover and make a stand if Beau and Runner gave out. From the way they were laboring it looked as though it was going to come down to that. There was only one comfort in the thought. They both had rifles that were more accurate and had a longer range than those the bandits carried, and Andrea was as good a shot as he was. But it was still thirteen or fourteen against two, and a man as battle-wise as Lopez would send some of his men to circle around them and move in while the others kept them busy.

It was well along in the afternoon now, and still there was no promising place to make a stand. If Henry had had any moisture left in his body, his forehead would have been beaded with the sweat of growing desperation. What would Adam think if he got Andrea killed instead of bringing her home? His own father wouldn't be any too happy about it if he never came back, either. Beau and

Runner couldn't keep going at this pace much longer, and if they slowed down to save their strength, the fresher horses behind them would overtake them.

A low rumbling to the east intruded on the thoughts that had to fight their way through their own horses' hoofbeats. His head jerked up, and his eyes narrowed. He'd been so busy keeping one jump ahead of Lopez and his men that he hadn't even noticed that the sky had darkened there to the northeast. Here where they were, the sun was still shining in a sky that was relentlessly blue, and he was reasonably certain that no rain would fall except in the mountains where the thunder had come from.

His experienced eyes studied the terrain. If he could pick out just the right spot, there was a chance, provided it was raining hard enough up in those mountains. There! It was as likely a place as ever, a deep dry wash some distance ahead. A glance back over his shoulder told him that even if what he was praying for came to pass, it would be touch and go.

He signaled for Andrea to demand the last burst of strength from Runner even as his own spurs touched Beau's flanks. Now was the time, and they weren't going to get a second chance.

The horses sensed their urgency and with heart-breaking effort they flattened out in a dead gallop. If they didn't go head over heels and break a leg, they'd make it, and then it all depended on that rain that wasn't falling here but that was certainly falling up above them.

They reached the wash and clattered across it, and Andrea gasped as she saw the wall of water bearing down on them. Another few seconds and they'd have been caught, swept away. Even Beau's strength, or Runner's, could never have withstood the force of that current, one of the flash floods that are a phenomenom of desert country as walls of water race down dry washes sweeping away everything in its path.

Andrea was trembling as she looked behind her to where the troop of bandits had pulled to a stop, thwarted by nature. There was no way they could cross that wash they wouldn't be able to cross it until the rain in the mountains abated and the wash dried up. Henry's grin at her was shaky.

"Let's keep going. If we get ourselves good and lost up in those mountains, even Lopez will have to give up. At least we've got ourselves a breathing space, and we won't have to push the horses any more. Do you think you can keep going?"

"As long as we have to!" Andrea said. She suited her action to her words, although Runner was giving her a fight as he tried to get back to the water. She beat against his sides with her heels, cursing the fact that her feet, with only the huaraches on them, had little effect.

Beau as well was frantic, wanting to drink, but Henry brought him under control and reined close to Runner and brought his hat down between Runner's eyes. "Get up there! Move!" Henry shouted.

They put distance between them and the flooded wash barely in time. Lopez and his men, recovered from their initial shock at their escape, were already raising their rifles to their shoulders.

They kept on going until they were at a safe enough distance to let the horses drink. Then they went on, ever winding upwards, deeper into the foothills and then the mountains that had saved their lives. The sun sank in the west, and they went on in the darkness, their horses stumbling, faltering, but able to keep moving ahead now that they had had their fill of water. Henry seemed to have eyes like a cat, so that he could see in the dark. It was raining, not hard now, but still a miserable, uncomfortable drizzle that soaked them to the skin. Henry wouldn't take the time for them to get their slickers out of their saddle rolls. They were already wet, so there would have been no point to it.

Andrea swayed in the saddle, so tired that she was afraid to close her eyes for fear she'd fall asleep and fall off. It seemed as if she had been in these mountains forever, that the night had lasted forever, that dawn would never again break over the earth. But she could keep going, she *would* keep going. She was so numb with fatigue that it took her a moment to realize that Henry had spoken to her.

"I think it's safe to stop now. Here's a likely place."

Runner had stopped with his nose on Beau's rump, and Andrea jerked her head up.

"End of the line," Henry told her.

She slid off Runner's back and stood leaning against him, her legs without feeling.

"There's an overcrop of rock over there. It's shelter of a sort. Get out of those wet clothes and wrap up in your blanket. I'll give the horses some corn," Henry directed her. She hadn't even remembered that they still had some corn in their saddlebags.

She lost no time in stripping out of the sodden peasant blouse and skirt. She'd never realized how uncomfortable, what a drag they could be, when they were wet. Her undergarments followed. She was thankful that the blankets only felt damp. They'd been protected by the tarps, standard gear for pack trips. She wrapped herself in her blanket and then sat down at the back of the shelter that Henry had indicated, hugging herself, her teeth chattering. Desolation swept over her in such a sudden, shattering wave that she began to cry before she had time to control herself.

Her bone-aching fatigue, her worry about Mike, her gnawing hunger, and the cold that had penetrated to her very marrow all descended on her at once. She was still shaking, her teeth chattering, and with tears running down her face when Henry returned from taking care of Beau and Runner.

"What the devil!" Henry said. "It's over now, Dria. We've shaken them off and there's no chance in the world that they'll be able to pick up our trail, or find Mike and Manuel, either."

"I'm all right," Andrea said. Her voice trembled; she wasn't all right.

Henry squatted down in front of her. "Snap out of it!" he ordered her. "You've been wonderful up till now a man couldn't have done better. Don't go female on me now."

His words didn't bring the response he'd hoped for, instant anger. "I am a female!" Andrea said. "I'm not made of stone like you are! Leave me alone! I'll be all right, just leave me alone!"

Henry stood up and started to step outside of the shelter. Andrea's head snapped up.

"Come back here! Are you out of your mind? You have to get out of your own wet clothes and wrapped up in your blanket!"

"I thought you wanted me to leave you alone."

Andrea's answer was to begin to cry again, great, shuddering sobs that shook her body. Instantly Henry was beside her, his arms reaching out and gathering her to him. He couldn't have helped himself if his life had depended on it.

"Go ahead and cry. No one ever had a better right. You've been through enough these last days to make a man cry, even a man made of stone like I am."

"You're getting me wet. I don't want you to catch pneumonia. I almost got Mike killed, maybe I have got him killed, and if you catch pneumonia and die, then I'll have killed you, too."

"It wouldn't be the first time." Henry's voice was rough, filled with all the pent-up emotions he'd held in check ever since Dria had gone running off to Georgia and then to England and ended up married to that Englishman. "You came near to killing me when you decided to go back to your husband! Speaking of killing people, I wanted to kill you then!"

"And I almost wish you had!" The admission burst out of its own accord. "Oh, Hank, I wished so many times that you had! Or that you'd beaten me and refused to let me go! It was the worst mistake I ever made in my life! I felt that I had to give Reggie another chance, even though I already knew that he was selfish and weak and that he'd never change enough so that I could love him again. But he'll never change, and I'll never go back to him again, but I'm still tied to him—he refuses to let me have a divorce. I've ruined our lives, Hank. I wish you'd

537

found someone else before I came back home for good. It would be easier for me if you were married; I wouldn't begrudge you your happiness, I swear I wouldn't. I never meant to hurt you. I loved you even if I had to grow up before I realized that you were the only man in the world for me!"

She broke off, shuddering, and Henry's arms tightened around her, holding her closer against him. "When we get back home I'll go away," Andrea said, without giving him a chance to say anything. Now that she had started to talk it was as if she couldn't stop. "It's the least I can do for you, for both of us! I can make some kind of life for myself far enough away so that we won't ever have to see each other again. You'll forget me and find someone else. . . ."

"Like hell," Henry said. His voice was rough, filled with rage. The tension of the last few days, the danger that they'd been through, holding the distinct possibility that either or both of them might have been killed and all their chances of having each other gone forever, burst over him in a flood that he was helpless to control. He released her and began to strip off his sodden clothing, working fast, making every movement count. Before Andrea realized what he was doing he'd taken both her blanket and his own and and borne her to the ground and rolled them both up in them, his arms relentless a he held her captive and helpless.

And then he was kissing her, his hands and hi mouth hard and hurting and demanding in their urgenc and the fury inside of him, and she welcomed the pai she reveled in it as she strained against him, wanting hin needing him as nature needs rain in order not to withe up and die. This lovemaking was like the relentless rai that had just fallen, a storm that had battered growir things to the earth but that would nourish their roots that they would grow again, absorbing the life-givir force without which they would perish.

Wrapped in the damp blankets, the night dark ar frigid around them, they were oblivious to their su roundings. They'd become two primitive creatures

538

Henry sought for and gained entry to the body that yearned for his, as she opened to receive him with a blinding burst of joy that made her breath catch and threatened to suffocate her with pure, wildly rapturous happiness. He was her man, he'd always been her man, she belonged to him just as if they'd been the only two people left on earth, and if he hadn't taken her now, this moment, she thought that she would have died.

It had never been like this with Reggie, not even when she'd thought that she loved him enough to spend the rest of her life with him. This was wild, all-consuming, primeval; it was a force that shook her to the core of her being, that threatened to burn her to ashes and yet that brought with it a strength and a depth of feeling that she had never dreamed existed. For the first time in her life she felt complete, a whole woman, the way only a woman with her chosen mate can ever feel, knowing that if she'd never had the joy of possessing and being possessed by him, she might as well never have been born.

The flood burst over her, inundated her, spread through every inch of her body. It brought a wild, triumphant cry from her lips as she arched against him to savor the last throbbing, swelling, and then exquisitely ebbing flow of the force that bound them together for all eternity.

And then they lay limp and exhausted, still holding each other, warm, content, caught up in the wonder of their long delayed fulfillment.

"Dria?"

"Yes, Henry?"

"I love you. Damn you. I love you!"

"Go ahead and damn me. I love you, too. It's all right, Henry. I'm not sorry, I'll never be sorry, and I don't want you to be, either. I'm only sorry I made such a mess of our lives."

"You don't have to go on making a mess of them. You can get rid of Reggie some way. Those lawyers of Adam's will find a way to get you your freedom. Now that I've had you, you needn't think that I'm going to let you go, not if I have to go over to England myself and see to it that Reggie signs the papers."

"You don't know him, Hank. He's vindictive. He hates his cousin Ned, for one thing, and if I try to force a divorce, he's going to ruin Ned's life with a scandal that he'll never be able to live down. He'll swear that I'm an adulteress. It isn't true—"

She broke off and laughed, the utter merriment of the sound startling him and making him draw her closer.

"It wasn't true, is what I meant to say! Because I am now, aren't I? It's funny, but I don't feel like an adulteress. I feel as if you're my husband, the only husband I ever had."

Her mouth was as sweet as honey as he kissed her. She drew away to trace the outline of his face, of his lips, with her fingertips.

"Reggie has proof that will stand up in court that I spent the night with Ned. I did, but not that way! As a matter of fact, I was drunk out of my mind, almost crazy from finding out that Reggie had been having an affair with a girl he knew before we were married, that he'd been having the affair with her all the time I was back in Texas, and that he hadn't broken it off even after I went back to him. But Ned . . . Edward Cavindish . . . was a perfect English gentleman. He put me to bed in his bed to sleep it off and he took the couch in the living room. Only the doorman of his building saw me go in and he knows I didn't come out, and Ned's valet knows I was there all night because I was still there, wearing Ned's robe, when he came back in the morning, and they'll be called as witnesses and it would be very nasty. Ned wants to make a career in the government, and you can see what a scandal like that would do to his chances."

"This Ned sounds like an all-right man, but he ought to be able to take care of himself. I can't see myself letting any cousin wreck my career. I'd take him apart and throw enough of the pieces away so that he couldn't be put back together with enough left to make trouble for anyone!"

"How? Ned can hardly fight Reggie physically; that would only add to the scandal and really wreck things for him. We have to face it, Hank. Reggie has me over a barrel. Unless I'm willing to sacrifice the most decent man I've ever known, there can't be a divorce. And even if I were willing to throw Ned to the wolves, there's a good chance that I couldn't win a divorce, with all the false evidence Reggie has stacked up against me. I'd have ruined Ned's life without gaining a thing."

"So you're going to stay married to that no-good Englishman because you admire his cousin! Of all the insane, ridiculous reasons, that's the most ridiculous I've ever heard! Do you think that Ned Cavindish would want you to throw your life away because of him? He doesn't sound like that kind of a man to me."

"No, he wouldn't. And that's one reason why I couldn't live with myself if I ruined his. He not only loved me and asked me to marry him, but he was a good friend to me. Don't you see, I've already hurt him a very great deal. I can't hurt him any more than I already have."

"In other words, you love me but everyone else is more important to you than I am."

"That isn't true! I do love you, I'd give anything if only I were free to marry you! If I thought that Reggie could be paid off, that he'd let me go if we gave him money, I'd throw my pride to the winds and ask Dad to give him anything he asked for. I don't care about my pride any more, I only care about us. But you don't know Reggie, Hank. He's weak, but he's capable of being vindictive. He hates Ned for having everything he never had, and he doesn't want anyone else to have me. I keep hoping that he'll become tired of waiting, that his mistress will persuade him to let me go so that he can marry her. As far as I can see, it's my only chance to get my freedom without ruining Ned's life and causing a scandal that would hurt Mother and Dad."

"And if he doesn't get tired of waiting? Where does that leave me? Am I supposed to still be hanging around years from now, until it's too late for both of us? I'm sick of waiting, I'm sick to my guts with it. I must have been crazy to let myself believe that things could work out between us, but I'm damned if I'll go on being crazy, not

541

even for you. I'm going to get you and Mike home, and then I'm lighting out. Don't wait for me to come back."

"Henry, you can't mean that! How can you leave your family, your ranch, everything you've known and loved all your life?"

"How could you have left me, not once, but twice? Two can play the same game. I'll probably come back sometime. I can't see living all the rest of my life away from Texas. But I reckon it's time I saw some of that big wonderful world out there that you were always raving about, and get to meet some of the women in it. When I come back, I'll bring a wife, and maybe a youngster or two. And if you're still waiting around for Reggie to let you have freedom, it won't be on my account."

Andrea turned her face to the hard, cold ground after he left her, too numb with misery even to cry any more. She didn't blame him, but what could she do? Without her integrity, she'd be only half a person, unable to function, unable even to live with herself.

Henry didn't mean it. He was angry, and justly so. But in the morning, he'd admit that she was right, they'd try to work something out, something that they could both live with.

In the morning Henry turned a cold face to her as he handed her a cup of coffee. He'd built a small fire, so he must be certain that they were no longer being pursued. There was no hint that he had changed his mind, and her heart sank. She couldn't beg him to understand and forgive her, beg him to wait for what might turn out to be years. Twice he'd watched her walk out of his life. Now it was going to be her turn to be left behind.

They rode out in silence. Henry's face was grim and he set a fast pace, and he didn't look at her as he led the way. They saw no one on their return journey. The bandits had given up, persuaded that there was no use in continuing the chase.

Manuel had dragged more brush to conceal the entrance to the box canyon, and the camouflage was

542

perfect that they nearly rode past the place. Henry nodded with satisfaction. Manuel knew what he was doing; there wasn't a sign that he and Mike had been discovered.

He glanced at Andrea, almost wincing at the pallor of her face as she steeled herself to find out whether Mike was dead or still alive. She'd been through a lot. It would just about finish her if Mike wasn't all right. He wanted to say something, some word of encouragement that would take that look off her face, but there was no point to it. Whatever was in there had to be faced. Wordlessly, he removed enough of the brush so that they could ride through.

Manuel was sitting slightly inside the enclosure, Mike's gun strapped around his hips and his rifle in his hands. "You have returned. I recognized the sound of your horses. Only the great dark one and Runner have hoofbeats like that. All is well, or you would not have come back."

He rose to help Andrea dismount, but she was already on the ground, searching his face with eyes that were afraid of what they would find there.

"He still lives, Doña. I made a little shelter for him with brush and my tarpaulin. He has roused several times to drink a little water, but I have not been able to persuade him to take food. Come, I will show you."

Mike lay under the rough shelter, his face still flushed with fever and much too thin under his growth of beard. He stirred as Andrea and Henry approached him, and opened his eyes. A trace of a grin appeared through the stubble, and Andrea's heart leaped. He was conscious and in his right mind in spite of the fever, he knew them!

"Wouldn't you know I'd be laid up so you'd have all the fun!" he said. "How many of them did you get?"

"None, and you ought to be glad of it, or else the rest of them would never have given up. We were lucky, we lost them when we got across a dry wash just in front of a flash flood. How about a drink while you're awake?"

Mike's smile turned bitterly wry. "Water! That's all this old grandmother hen's given me since you left. How about a little tequila for a change?"

"No. You need water, plenty of it, to bring that fever down. Alcohol dries you out, as you should know by now with all the experience you claim to have had."

Mike ran his tongue over his dry lips. "Water, then." His voice was resigned. "And you're right. I never thought I'd see the day again when I'd settle for water if there was something better to be had, but right now anything will do as long as it's wet."

Andrea's eyes were damp with suppressed tears as she held a canteen to his mouth, supporting his head and shoulders so that he could drink. Swallowing was painful for him, and he gasped for breath when he turned his head away.

"Try to take a little more," she begged him. "You have to get well, so we can go home."

"You and Hank go. Manuel and I will do just fine."

"Shut up. Patients aren't allowed to argue with their doctors." His forehead was much too hot when she touched it with her fingers. She looked at Henry, who was already kneeling to loosen the rude bandages so that he could look at the wound. She stifled an exclamation of dismay when she saw how puffy and red the area around it was, and Henry's face looked as though it was carved out of stone.

"Manuel, boil some water in the coffee pot. This needs a little cleaning up."

Andrea held Mike's hand while Henry swabbed the area with hot water to wipe bloody pus away. Mike's teeth were set into his lower lip, but he made no sound until Henry poured a liberal amount of tequila from the bottle into the wound.

"I hope someday I'll get to return the compliment, Hank. I wouldn't want you to die without knowing how it feels," he gasped before his eyes closed and he sank into semi-consciousness.

"Hang on, old boy," Hank said under his breath. "You're going to make it yet."

He looked at Andrea then. "You and Manuel had better start back to Texas. It'll be easier on both of us under the circumstances. If you made it all the way down here, you can make it back, now that nobody's looking for you any more."

"No." Andrea's voice was final. "I'll keep out of your way if that's the way you want it, but I'm not leaving Mike."

"Have it your way. You might as well settle in, because we're going to be here for a while."

Andrea nodded. Once again she had come to a place in her life where all she could do was to grit her teeth and endure.

TRAIL'S END

34

Natalie was thoroughly miffed. Here she'd kept after her father until he'd agreed to ride over to Trail's End the very day after they'd returned from Georgia, and Dria wasn't even here, and to make matters worse, Aunt Kate and Uncle Adam weren't very interested in her rapturous accounts of the beauties of her ancestral home, Swanmere.

She'd nagged at Jacob, back there when they'd been at Roselawns, until he'd taken her to see the house where he'd been born. Aunt Prudence and Uncle Rory and Uncle Burke were real nice, and they'd made almost as big a fuss over her as her tremendous ego could have wished for, and Roselawns was beautiful, but it didn't hold a candle to Swanmere, especially after the Randolphs had fixed it all up.

Gregory Randolph certainly was handsome. It was a danged shame that he was married. Even if he had been chicken enough to back out of marrying Dria just because of that drop of black blood, and even if Natalie was young enough to be his daughter, she'd have managed to latch onto him one way or another and see to it that he waited for her. She was already twelve, almost thirteen, and there wasn't anything wrong with a girl getting married at fifteen. Well, maybe sixteen; her mother and father might pull a fit if she wanted to get married at fifteen, but she'd have had Greg, and Swanmere. After all, she had more right to it than the Randolphs! Papa was a Renault, and the plantation had belonged to the Renaults since way before the war.

But Kate had only smiled indulgently when Natalie had raved on and on about Swanmere and how she was going to find a way to get it back from the Randolphs, and Uncle Adam, on his feet for the first time since that horrid Clay Bradshaw had shot him, had almost ignored her and then, to cap the insult, Papa had told her to run outside so the grownups could talk without her bending their ears with her nonsense. Suffering jumping catfish, she was grown up! That was the trouble with parents and aunts and uncles, they looked at you but they didn't really see you, they thought you were still a baby just because you'd been a baby a hundred years ago.

There was nothing to do out here. With Dria down in Mexico some place she might as well have stayed at home. Natalie kicked at the dirt with the toe of her boot as she leaned on the corral fence, and then things brightened a little because there was Juan Bustamonte and he was smiling at her and holding out something that was brown and lumpy and horny. Glory, but Juan was handsome! No wonder Paula Ingram was in love with him. It was just Nattie's luck that all the handsomest men were already taken by girls who'd had the luck to be born a few years before she had. Only she wouldn't really want Juan anyway, except to flirt with, because he wasn't rich, he only worked for Uncle Adam, and if she was going to get Swanmere back then she had to marry a rich man, the richer the better.

"See what I have for you, Señorita." Juan smiled. "Do you want it? Isn't it nice?"

Natalie squealed with pleasure, her grownup attitude

gone by the boards as she took the horned toad from his hands. Oh, it was darling! It was the biggest one she'd ever seen, its snubbed face comical as it blinked at her, its ruff of pointed horns around its neck perfect, its stub of a serrated tail feeling rough and bumpy against the palm of her hand. Darling little brown, lumpy creature! She used to catch them and keep them for pets when she was a little girl, but she hadn't had one for a long time now. Burke would make her a cage to keep it in until it got used to being a house pet, and at least catching flies for it would be something to do.

"Thank you, Juan!" Her smile at the handsome vaquero was dazzling, giving promise of the startling beauty that she would become in another few years. Then a little frown appeared between her eyebrows and she looked at him anxiously. "Are you sure that Paula won't want it, or little Davie?"

"Quite sure Señorita. Paula doesn't care much for our little brown friends and Davie's too little. I'll find him another one when he's big enough."

Natalie could feel the horned toad's heart beating against her hand but it made no attempt to escape. She'd bet that some of those kids in Georgia would have a hemorrhage if anybody ever handed them one of these; they wouldn't have any idea what it was, and they'd be scared spitless. She wasn't scared of anything, her father bragged that she had more spunk than all those back-east kids put together, because she was a Texan.

Juan's head went up as he was the first to hear the hoofbeats that heralded a rider's approach. "Señor Mansfield," he said. His voice had a peculiar flat quality that signified his dislike of Andrea's husband.

That had been a real shocker to Natalie, finding Reggie Mansfield here at Trail's End, fixing to cause Dria even more trouble by wanting her to go back to him. Nattie didn't like him. He was good-looking and he'd gone to a lot of trouble trying to charm her into being on his side, but her clear eyes saw right through his skin to the weakness and selfishness inside. Dria must have been out of her head to marry him when she could have come home from Georgia that time and married Hank instead. Natalie was very sure that she'd never make such a damned fool mistake when she grew up! Her husband was going to be both rich and handsome and good-natured, too, so that he'd always do what she wanted, but above all he was going to be strong, someone she could respect.

Instinctively, she put both her hands behind her as Reggie drew the horse to a stop and dismounted, tossing the reins to Juan. She shook her head just a trifle, but Juan saw and understood, and she knew that he'd follow her lead.

"Hello, Reggie." Her greeting, her smile, were sweetness personified. "Did you have a nice ride?"

"It's a bit difficult getting used to a Western saddle, but I think I'm getting the hang of it. Your uncle keeps good horses, Nattie."

The way he turned his charm on her made her sick. She'd bet he was like that to everything in skirts, whether they were six or sixty. Poor Dria! Imagine being tied to someone like Reggie for all the rest of her life!

"Look out!" she screamed. "It's a Gila monster!" At the same instant, she threw the horned toad at Reggie so that it landed on his neck, its scratchy tail scraping along the exposed skin of his chin.

Reggie screamed, his hand going up to fling it off, then going to his chin where he was sure he'd been bitten. Stupid greenhorn dude! Anybody who knew anything at all knew that if a Gila monster bit you, it didn't let go, you had one heck of a time prying it loose, they held on worse than a snapping turtle or a bulldog. Reggie's face was stark white, his eyes rolling with terror.

"Oh, my gosh, it got him!" Natalie shrieked. "Juan, he's been bitten, he's going to die for sure!"

Reggie began to run, terror lending wings to his feet. He burst into the living room where Jacob was just replenishing his brandy snifter from the decanter.

"Send for a doctor!" Reggie strangled. "I've bee bitten by a Gila monster!"

Jacob came near to dropping the decanter. Kat

was on her feet, her face almost as pale as Reggie's. Only Adam remained calm, his eyes probing into Natalie's as she entered directly behind Reggie, her face filled with an innocence with which he was all too familiar. He had to use control to keep the corners of his mouth from twitching.

"Jacob, we'll have to cauterize it. We can't wait for Doctor Mason to get here, it might take him two or three days. You'd better give Reggie that brandy, he's going to need it."

Reggie's face turned even whiter and his knees threatened to buckle. He wasn't a coward, and he was able to stand as much pain as most men but the thought of a red-hot iron or knife mutilating his face made his senses reel. Jacob thrust the brandy at him, and his hands shook as he grasped the glass, so that the rim clattered against his teeth and he choked as he swallowed too fast.

"Natalie, run to the kitchen and see if Manuella has a good fire going." Adam's face was grave. "Jacob, we'd better get Reggie on his bed. Kate, this isn't going to be pleasant; I suggest that you take Nattie out onto the patio or, better still, down as far as the corral before we operate. You'd better have some more brandy, Reggie."

Natalie stood rooted to the spot waiting for Reggie to faint. He looked as if he were going to be sick on the rug.

"Nonsense. You'll need me." Kate's voice was brisk. "Natalie, do as your uncle told you. Tell Manuella we'll need her sharpest knife. And then run and tell Juan to ride to town for the doctor as fast as he can."

Natalie felt a moment's compunction. Knowing Uncle Adam as she did, she was sure that he knew she was behind this contretemps and that Reggie was in no danger, but Aunt Kate and her father might just possibly be a little put out with her when they found out the truth. Then she saw her father's face, struggling to keep down a broad grin, and the twinkle in Kate's eyes. She hadn't fooled them, after all, but that was all right, she'd only wanted to scare Reggie, and she'd certainly succeeded in that. If it wouldn't spoil everything, she'd bust right out laughing.

Then Juan had to go and spoil it all by coming into the room with his cat-like tread, holding the horned toad in his hand.

"I caught it," Juan said. "We were mistaken, Señorita. It isn't a Gila monster, after all, it's only a horned toad."

"Oh!" Natalie's hand went to her mouth, and her eyes were wide circles of innocence. "Well, I thought it was a Gila monster. If I'd got a better look at it I'd have known it wasn't, it's nowhere near big enough and it hasn't got the pretty colors. How did I ever make such a stupid mistake?"

Juan's eyes reflected his amusement. "I, too, was mistaken for a moment, Señorita. We didn't have a very good look at it before the señor threw it off."

"Natalie!" Jacob boomed. Natalie fled.

Adam's laughter filled the room. "Jacob, when are you going to teach that daughter of yours to behave? Made a mistake!"

"I guess I'm never," Jacob rumbled. "I suppose I ought to whale her, but darned if I'm going to! This is the first good laugh I've had since we got back and found you laid up and Andrea missing."

"A joke!" Reggie was livid. Furious, he poured himself another generous tot from the decanter and downed it. "I fail to appreciate you Americans' sense of humor!" He glared at all of them, and then he, too, left the room to seek his bed until the nausea in his stomach subsided. He took the decanter with him without a by-your-leave.

"At least he has an excuse to overindulge this time." Adam's voice was dry. "If he doesn't stop drinking so much, his liver is likely to save Andrea the trouble of trying to get her freedom from him. Unfortunately, even the way Reggie drinks, it might take too long."

Outside the house, Natalie decided that it might be politic to have Juan saddle up a fresh horse for her and go for a nice long ride, long enough to give her father and Adam and Kate time to cool down. Not that the seemed angry about her joke, but sometimes they got it into their heads that she needed to be restrained. She had her eye on the paint that was standing by itself in the corner of the corral. She'd had her eye on him even before they'd gone to Georgia, only Uncle Adam said that he was too much horse for her, that she'd have to wait at least another year before he'd let her try him.

"Juan, saddle Cactus for me. I'm going for a ride."

"Cactus, Señorita?" Juan looked at her searchingly. "Don't you think another horse would be better?"

"Pooh! I've ridden Cactus lots of times!" Natalie lied. "And Uncle Adam said it was all right. Golly, couldn't you have just died laughing when Reggie thought he'd been bitten by a Gila monster?" Changing the subject was always a good idea when you wanted to get away with something. If the grownups found out afterwards that she'd ridden Cactus, and she was punished, it would be worth it.

"You are a very naughty little girl," Juan told her. "I will saddle Ranger for you."

Drat! She'd thought she could get away with it this time, but Juan wasn't stupid, like Reggie. Oh, well, Ranger wasn't so bad and she was in a hurry to put distance between herself and her father, so she didn't have time to argue with Juan.

"And I will accompany you," Juan said firmly. "On Cactus, Señorita. Then you will be able to see his tricks without the danger of having your neck broken. And yes, it was very funny when the señor thought he'd been bitten by a Gila monster."

Juan didn't care for Reggie any more than Nattie did, or Carmelita, or any of the other help at Trail's End. Reggie was never openly insulting to them the way Clay Bradshaw was, but they sensed that he considered them second-class citizens. Adam Wentworth and the Doña were going to help Juan get his American citizenship, just as they were helping so many others. He knew that he was man enough to be Paula's husband, but for her sake and Davie's, others must know it as well. Here in the Big Bend, with Adam Wentworth's help, the old days when

555

being a Mexican meant that a man wasn't as good as other men would soon be over.

Within minutes he and Nattie rode out together. Nattie was sulking a little because she wasn't on Cactus, and Juan was smiling as he thought how Paula would laugh when he told her about Reggie and the horned toad.

Natalie didn't sulk for long, because it wasn't in her nature. The two rode in perfect companionship. "See, Señorita, how Cactus lays his left ear back? That means that he's going to try to shy at that bush ahead. You must be ready so that you will not go sailing."

Cactus started to shy just as Juan had said, and Juan's firm hand brought him back under control. Natalie was filled with admiration. She hoped that Juan and Paula wouldn't move away from the Chinatis when they were married. She liked Juan—he didn't treat her like a child—and Paula was nice, and visiting them would give her a respite from being ordered around until she could get back to Georgia and the serious business of getting Swanmere back in the family.

"Let me try him now, Juan!" she begged an hour after they had started. "You've shown me all his tricks. I can handle him, I know I can!"

Juan considered it. It was true that Natalie was an expert horsewoman for her age; how could she have helped but be, born and raised on a Texas ranch? And Cactus had settled down now after the miles they'd put behind them. If he rode close to her and kept careful watch, it would probably do no harm.

Stirrups were readjusted and Natalie scrambled up into Cactus's saddle without assistance except that Juan held his head to make sure that he didn't take off at a full gallop as soon as she had one foot in the stirrup, as he had been trained. Remembering Reggie's outraged expression when the first horse he'd ridden at Trail's End had done that made Juan chuckle. It had been doubly funny because Reggie had been mounting in the English style with his back to the front of the horse, sending the horse into near panic and making it take off even faster. H

556

had to grant that the man was a capable horseman, else he'd have been hurt.

Natalie's hands on the reins were confident. She'd paid close attention to Juan's explanations of Cactus's foibles, and though he tried once to shy and another time to buck, considering that it was a slip of a girl on his back instead of a man, she controlled him well.

There was an estatic smile on Natalie's face. "Juan, the next time Reggie wants to ride, why not let him take Cactus?"

"I think it would be a very good idea, Señorita. Perhaps a few words from you as to what a remarkable animal he is. . . ."

They were in accord. They didn't want anything drastic to happen to Reggie, but a little punishment was sweet to contemplate. Both Nattie and Juan were extremely fond of Dria, and Reggie was out to cause her trouble, so why not let him see that it could work both ways?

They were just considering turning back when they saw a rider coming so fast that they drew rein. Nobody rode like that unless there was either trouble or news of such import that a man would push his horse for all it was worth, in this country where concern for the welfare of horses was almost greater than concern for the welfare of men.

The rider saw them and his horse went down on his haunches as he too drew up. "You're Natalie Renault!" he exclaimed. "I've got news for Adam Wentworth, I'm the last to pass it along. Andrea and Hank Stockwell have found Mike, and they're bringing him home. They're still thirty or forty miles back because Mike's hurt, riding in a buckboard. If you'll take the news on to Trail's End I can spare my horse and take it slow, I've been pushing him pretty hard."

Natalie whooped, her face flaming with excitement. Without a word she slammed her heels into Cactus's sides, wheeling him and taking off hell-bent-for-leather. With an exclamation Juan was after her. But Cactus was he faster horse and with only Natalie's lighter weight on his back he was soon left behind. He should have known better than to let her ride Cactus! If anything happened to her, it would distract from the joy of Mike's homecoming! His face set, Juan concentrated on trying to keep her in sight.

Jacob was on the patio enjoying a cigar and wondering if Nattie would have sense enough to get back in time for supper when he saw his daughter coming. Not only coming, but coming like streaked lightning and riding Cactus! He threw the cigar into the yard with an oath and stepped off the patio in time to grasp Cactus's bit when Nattie sent him rearing as she pulled him to a stop.

"Nattie, this time I'm going to give you a whaling, and don't think you can talk me out of it!" His hand descended on her shoulder as she slid out of the saddle, holding her fast.

"Damn it, leave go of me! They're coming, I've got to tell Uncle Adam and Aunt Kate!"

"Who's coming?"

Natalie's answer was to sink her teeth into his arm. Jacob yelped, but Natalie was already off and running. She burst into the living room screaming at the top of her lungs.

"They're coming! Dria and Mike and Hank are coming! They're still about thirty miles away, and Mike's been hurt so he's in a buckboard, but they're on their way!"

Kate was on her feet, her hand at her throat. Adam, too, got to his feet, his face showing more emotion that it usually did. "Nattie, are you sure?"

"Of course I'm sure, dang it! A rider told us, he's on his way, and here's Juan, he'll tell you, too!"

"*Sí*, it is true. The messenger told us. I do not know his name, but he will be here soon, you can ask him then what more he knows."

Kate looked at Adam. "I'm going to ride out to meet them."

"And I'm going with you!" Jacob boomed. He was still nursing his bitten arm, but his face was split with huge grin.

558

"Me, too!"

The next instant she was grasped so firmly that she had no chance even to bite and propelled toward Adam. "Adam, latch onto her and don't let her go. If she doesn't behave herself, send half a dozen men with her to take her home and see that she gets there."

The threat of missing this fateful homecoming was enough to subdue even Natalie. "I don't care! I rode Cactus and you said I couldn't handle him, Uncle Adam! I rode him good, and I beat Juan here with the news!"

"I am sorry I let her get away from me. Cactus was calmed before I let her try him, and I had no idea we would meet the rider with the news. But she rode Cactus well, Señor Jacob. Señor Wentworth, am I permitted to ride to the Ingrams and give them the news? They will want to know."

"Yes, of course. Go right along, Juan." Adam reached for the new decanter that had replaced the one that Reggie had taken to his room after his fright about the horned toad. No doubt by this time he'd drunk himself into a stupor and Adam saw no reason to wake him and tell him that Andrea was on her way home. He poured himself a stiff drink, but he only drank half of it. Damn this shoulder of his! He'd have to stay here, like an invalid, and wait while Kate and Jacob rode to meet the homecomers. "This is good news, Jacob. Don't worry, I'll keep an eye on Nattie."

Now that she knew she was to stay, Nattie barged in again with all her usual officiousness. "I'll tell Carmelita to fix a room for Lucy, Uncle Adam. Dria's going to be tired, and if Mike is sick, then Aunt Kate will be able to use some extra help around here. Lucy can ride back with Juan when he comes back from the Ingrams'. She'll be busting to come anyway, and she might as well be invited. I'll see that Dria's room is ready, too, and Mike's, and I'll send a man to tell the Stocktons that they're on their way." As competent as she was precocious, she walked from the room to take the reins of the household into her own hands until Kate should return. Jacob shook his head.

"Adam, what the devil am I going to do with her? She's too big for her britches."

"Leave her alone, as much as possible," Adam advised. "No matter how much trouble she gets into, I have a feeling that she's always going to land on her feet."

35

Reggie struggled out of a deep sleep, wondering why so many footsteps and raised, excited voices echoed throughout the house. You'd think that these people would have a little consideration for him. After all, he was a guest, even if an unwelcome one. Not only a guest, but a member of the family.

There wasn't even a bell in his bedroom for him to ring to summon someone to tell him what was going on. These Americans were totally uncivilized. No one brought him tea in the morning along with his hot water for washing, and no one collected his shoes at night to polish them.

His head aching as though it were going to explode, he groped for his dressing gown and house slippers. The sun streaming in through his windows hurt his eyes. He'd have to go to the kitchen himself and ask why his hot water hadn't been brought to his room so that he could make himself presentable for the day. He hoped that that abominable child and her father, Jacob, had left. He

561

didn't feel capable of enduring any more practical jokes.

Manuella looked up from where she was preparing a tray for someone as he entered the kitchen. That was odd; Adam was on his feet now, and nobody in this house had breakfast in bed unless they were too ill to come to the table.

"Carmelita hasn't brought my hot water."

"Señor?"

"My hot water." Reggie struggled to maintain his patience. These servants of Adam's had an infuriating habit of pretending not to understand the King's English when it suited their moods.

"It is there," Manuella said. "You will have to carry it yourself, we are too busy." She turned back to what she was doing. Seething, Reggie lifted the large kettle and poured water into one of the pitchers that were lined up on a shelf. He'd like to know what was going on, but he had no intention of giving the Mexican cook the satisfaction of having to ask.

He performed his morning ritual more hastily than usual, his curiosity gnawing at him. Presentable at last—at least Kate saw to it that his clothes were properly sponged and pressed—he made his way to the living room, where several voices were all raised at once, only to stop short in the archway and stare with total amazement as he saw that not only Adam and Kate and Jacob and Natalie were there, but Andrea, as well, and another man he had never seen before.

Andrea looked fine-drawn and exhausted, and she was wearing an outlandish costume of some sort, rather like the clothing that the housemaid Carmelita wore, except that it was torn and bedraggled and dirty. Andrea herself was dirty, her face and hands and the torn clothing covered with dust.

They didn't realize that he was there until the exclamation emerged from his mouth. "Andrea! So you've come back at last!"

They all turned to look at him, and Reggie encountered a pair of eyes looking at him from a face that was covered with a shaggy growth of beard with mor hostility than he had ever encountered, even Adam's and Kate's. He was the first one to speak, and his voice was soft and flat.

"So this is Reggie. I've waited a long time to meet him. Isn't anybody going to introduce us before I ask him a few questions that I want answers to?"

"Hank—"

"Not now, Dria. Mansfield, I understand that you have some sort of objection to letting Andrea have a divorce."

Reggie called up all of his dignity. "I can't see what concern it is of yours, Mr . . . ?"

"Hank." It was Adam who spoke this time, as quietly as Henry had spoken, but Henry subsided at the authority in his voice. Andrea put down the coffee cup she was holding and turned again to face her husband.

"The answer is no," she said. "I won't live with you again, Reggie, not ever." Her face was hard, harder than he had ever seen it. Seeing Reggie here, the last place she had ever expected to see him, had made her come to a lightning-quick decision. She was going to gamble, all or nothing, and she wasn't Adam's daughter for nothing. A week ago, two weeks ago, she might not have risked it, but having been with Hank, having tasted the ecstasy that being with him forever would be, made her determined to give it her best try. She couldn't let both their lives be ruined because Reggie wanted to play dog in the manger.

"I'm going to divorce you, Reggie. Or at least I'm going to make a darned good try at it! If you won't agree to let me go without a fight, then the next move is yours."

"If you don't care if your name is blackened, and if your family thinks so little of you that they don't care, either, have you given any thought of what the scandal I'll loose on the press will do to Ned? He'll be up for M.P. soon, and it will blast his chances." Backed into a corner by this determined woman in front of him, Reggie, too, decided to gamble.

"What are you going to use for money to pay your lawyers? Or are you actually stupid enough to believe that Lady Madeline and Sir Robert will advance it to you so that you can ruin their son? Bea's sent you packing, hasn't she? You wouldn't be here otherwise, you wouldn't have made the effort as long as she was keeping you in comfort while you tried to wear me down."

It was a shot in the dark, but she saw that it had struck home. She knew Reggie so well, she was all too aware of his disinclination to remove himself from any situation where he was comfortable and cared for.

All Reggie could do was try to bluff it out. He could see that Andrea meant every word she said. She'd never come back to him, but he ought to come out of this with something. It wasn't fair, it wasn't right, that he should have nothing at all.

"There are other sources of revenue. Your name is well known; the newspapers, the magazines, will jump at the chance to pay me for the story I can give them."

The words were hardly out of his mouth before Henry was on him. "You stinking bastard! You've come to the wrong part of the world if you think we'll put up with anything like that!" Reggie's head reeled from the force of the blow that Henry dealt him, and then he staggered as another caught the other side of his head. He raised his hands instinctively to defend himself, but he knew, despairingly, that he had no chance against this panther-lean man who was as tough as whipcord.

"Henry, stop it!" Andrea demanded. But it was Jacob who broke it up, thrusting his huge body between them, one hand on each of their shoulders as he held them apart.

"That's enough!" Jacob roared. "Quit it before I lose my temper! If I have to knock your heads together hard enough to put you both out, we never will get anywhere."

He gave Reggie a shove that sent him halfway across the room. Henry he treated more gently, but not much "Keep quiet, Hank. If we can't get this sorted out, the you can have your say, and get in your licks, too, for al of me."

Adam had sat unmoved through the brief interruption. Now he reopened the discussion.

"First you would have to get the story to the pres

564

or the magazines, providing that any would publish such libelous material without proof. How do you suppose to go about doing that?"

Jacob was enjoying himself. If this British clothes horse knew anything about poker, he'd know that he was up against two of the most expert bluffers in the world and that he didn't have a chance. He looked at Reggie expectantly, waiting for the next turn of the card.

"It shouldn't be too difficult. Such publications are happy to publish charges that are to be brought against anyone of your daughter's prominence; it isn't up to them to prove them. If you aren't inclined to come to a reasonable settlement, I'll simply accent the highest bid. Of course, if you want to be reasonable in the matter of a settlement—"

"And how do you propose to get in contact with these publications, in order to further your attempt at blackmail?" Adam's voice was almost disinterested.

"I still have enough money left to get back to New York." So far, Jacob thought, it was almost a draw. He looked at Adam expectantly.

"I'm glad to hear it. Of course, the first step of the journey will be to get yourself to town from Trail's End, and it's a long walk."

"Walk!" For the first time, Reggie was nonplussed.

"You're free to leave any time you wish," Adam told him. "But I have no intention of lending you a horse so that you can set your money-making schemes in motion, and horse-stealing is still a serious offense in Texas. I can assure you that if you were to take a mount without my permission, you wouldn't get far. Of course, a part of your purpose would be accomplished. You'd end up in town, but in jail. Then there would be a considerable delay while you were tried and served your sentence, which wouldn't be a short one."

There was a white line around Reggie's mouth. "Am I to understand, then, that I'm a prisoner here at your ranch?"

"Certainly not. As I told you, you're free to leave at any time you wish. On foot."

Henry had come to the end of his enforced patience. "I've had about enough out of this man. We don't take kindly to men like you around here. You aren't dealing with a helpless woman now, Mansfield—"

He broke off momentarily as Jacob choked. Andrea, helpless? That 'ud be the day!

"You're dealing with men. You don't go armed, but I'm sure that either Adam or Jacob will be happy to lend you a gun so I can take you outside and settle all this right now. We wouldn't want to get Kate's rug dirty, so just beyond the patio will do."

Kate smiled at him. "Thank you, Henry."

None of them realized that Wade had entered the room until he spoke. "Mike's well settled, Mother. You can go in now and see if I got him clean enough to suit you. And Hank, I take exception to your challenge to Reggie. Andrea's my sister, so it's my place to defend her."

Wade was tight-lipped and as grim as Henry, and Reggie realized that for all that he'd been conventionally courteous to him since his arrival, he was fully as deadly as this savage who proposed to shoot him.

"You're mad, the lot of you!" He knew how to handle firearms; back in England he'd had a good deal of experience at country estates during grouse-shooting season, or at trapshooting. But a duel, with hand guns, was something that he knew nothing about. "It would be nothing less than murder!"

"I think there are enough witnesses here to testify that it was a fair fight," Jacob said mildly.

Reggie clung to whatever shreds of dignity he could. "It's obvious that Andrea must have her freedom if she ever hopes to marry again. And it's just as obvious that unless I consent to a divorce she'll have a difficult time in obtaining one. A man's indiscretions are looked on more leniently than a woman's, especially if he claims remorse and says he wants nothing more than to patch things up. How much will you settle for, if I agree to be reasonable in my demands?"

"Your passage back to England, and not a cent more," Adam said flatly. His words left no doubt that

Reggie would get nothing more from the Wentworths except the privilege of going on living.

"And not even that, until the divorce has gone through," Wade put in, motioning for Andrea, who had been about to say something, to keep silent. "You will be our guest until then." His words cut the last inch of ground out from under Reggie's feet.

"Now, Wade, I don't see why you folks should be inflicted with him for all that time. Best he comes to my place, it'll be less strain on all of you. Andrea isn't going to want to stumble over him every time she turns around. Nattie'll keep him amused. I'll make it her special duty."

Reggie managed not to flinch. "It seems I have no choice."

"You don't have a hell of a lot, at that," Jacob agreed amicably. "Adam, you get in touch with those high-falutin' lawyers of yours and have them draw up an agreement that Reggie here isn't going to try raising any stink after his visit with us comes to an end. You can have them put in that he isn't to raise any stink about that cousin of his over in England, either. I reckon he'll sign it. They'll know how to go about making it a binding contract."

"Mike!"

Kate was on her feet, hurrying to put her arm around her younger son, who was supposed to be in bed. "What on earth are you doing up?"

"Looking after Dria's interests," Mike said. He looked at Reggie, studying him with such cold intensity that Reggie felt as if death had brushed his face. "I just wanted to get a good look at this *hombre* so I'll know him again if I have to go over to England after this is all over, just in case he feels safe enough there to break his word."

He was shorter than either Adam or Wade, nowhere near as broad and powerful as either of them, to say nothing of Jacob Renault, but still Reggie felt a stab of icy fear. This wounded man, scarcely more than a boy, was El Rojo Loco, who had taken it on himself to help right the wrongs of a people who meant nothing to him, much less his sister. He'd killed men in Mexico. How much

567

faster would he kill the man to do his sister an injury?

"I am not in the habit of breaking my word," he managed to get out.

"I'm glad to hear it. I never did think I'd care much for England. Tea makes me sick to my stomach. Uncle Jacob, are you going to hog that whole decanter of brandy, or can you spare a little for a thirsty man?"

"Mike . . ." There was both question and warning in Andrea's voice. Mike grinned at her as he downed the fiery liquid.

"No problem, Dria. One's enough." He handed the empty snifter back to his sister. "All right, Mother. I'll go back to bed now."

With one more hard look at Reggie he turned and went back to his room, with Kate hurrying after him to make sure that he hadn't done himself any damage. Andrea drew a deep breath and her eyes filled with smarting tears. Mike was all right. He wasn't going to turn into a lush, like their grandfather. Those days in the desert, with no alcohol available, had boiled it all out of his blood. He knew his problem now, and he knew his limit, just as she did. The hate and the guilt that had made him drink had been washed clean. Maybe he realized there were reasons to go on living. She hoped so.

Jacob nodded at Adam. "If it's all settled, we'll pull out the first thing in the morning. It would be a shame if Reggie got out of line and Hank here had to shoot him after all. It's always more pleasant if a girl doesn't have to marry the man who killed her husband, makes it easier if she doesn't have to explain to her children how it came about."

All of the fight went out of Reggie. He was beaten, and he knew it. He didn't know how to deal with people like these; they were entirely out of his experience with their hard eyes and harder confidence.

So it was back to England, empty-handed. It was a bitter blow. Reggie felt thoroughly sorry for himself. He needed someone to sympathize with him, to tell him how shabbily he'd been treated, to help mend his broken heart. Bea wouldn't take him back, he was sure of that. Bu there was Agnes Deerfield. She'd understand, she'd be as indignant as he was.

He brightened a little. Maybe it wouldn't be so bad. Agnes was desperate for a husband. She knew she was older than he was, she'd know how lucky she was to get him, she'd treat him the way he should be treated. She'd never turn on him, as Andrea had. He could be very comfortable indeed in the Kensington house, helping Agnes spend her money. She wouldn't object, as Andrea had, if he slipped now and then. She was a cultured, civilized Englishwoman who realized that a man isn't perfect, who'd be willing to overlook an occasional slip as long as she could hold onto him. At least he thought she would.

Natalie had been as quiet as a mouse ever since she'd slipped into the room where she had no business being, determined not to miss all the fun. But shucks, it was all over, except that Dria and Hank weren't looking at each other, so it didn't matter now if the grownups noticed her.

"I'll go and tell them to have our horses ready." She darted out of the room, and for once even Jacob didn't suspect an ulterior motive as he savored the victory over this young weakling who'd nearly cost Andrea her life back there in England through his selfishness and inconsideration. If he only knew it, Reggie was getting off easy. Imagine his gall, to think that he could outbluff Texans!

"We'll be riding out the first thing in the morning. Mr. Mansfield is coming with us," Natalie told the first vaquero she saw. "He's to ride Cactus."

"*Sí*, Señorita. I'll see to it." The brown face was as bland and innocent as Natalie's own, but there was a deep amusement in the vaquero's eyes.

Natalie returned to the house, well satisfied. Reggie wouldn't be hurt, of course. He was a good rider, even if that was all he was good for. But when Cactus turned his head sideways and jerked it a little, signifying that he was going to go straight up in the air and come down at a dead gallop heading in the opposite direction, she wasn't going to say a word. She was just sorry that Juan wouldn't with them to see the fun, but of course he'd wanted to ride over to the Ingrams' with the news that Mike and Dria were back because it would give him a chance to see Paula.

She was smiling as she made her way back to the house, first to go to the kitchen to make sure that Manuella had lunch preparations well under way and then to sit by Mike's bed so that she could start planting the idea in his head that he'd be a blamed fool if he didn't grab Lucy Ingram.

It was a good thing that she was so capable. Somebody had to take care of things! Once she'd taken care of the matter of Mike and Lucy, and Andrea had her divorce, she'd turn all of her efforts to persuading her mother and father to send her to boarding school in Savannah next fall. She could spend all the holidays with Aunt Prue and Uncle Burke. If she was going to get Swanmere back, she had to start learning how to be a Southern lady as soon as possible.

In the living room, Henry finished off the drink Jacob had poured for him and shook his head at the offer of a refill. "It's too early for me. I was just washing the taste of Reggie Mansfield out of my mouth."

He looked around. "Dria? Where is Dria?"

"I expect she's gone to her room to clean up," Kate told him. "I won't say that she doesn't need a bath and change of clothing! You'll see her later, Hank. You'll stay the night, of course? It's a little late to ride all that way especially without any rest. Wade can supply you with everything you'll need, you're about of a size."

"No, I think I'll go on home. I've been away for long time. I just wanted to see Dria before I leave."

"I'll go and tell her, then."

But Andrea wasn't in her room when Kate went looking for her, and a subsequent search showed that she was nowhere in the house. Kate's brows knit with perplexity. She'd noticed—how could she have failed notice?—that Andrea and Henry had acted like two strange dogs bent on ignoring each other ever since she met them on the road. They'd hardly exchanged to words. But where on earth could she be, even if she was avoiding Henry?

"I might as well get going, then," Henry said, his mouth flat, when she returned to the living room with the news that Andrea wasn't to be found. "If she doesn't want to talk to me, that's that."

He was in a grim mood as he swung up on his own horse. It felt odd not to have Beau under him, but at least his chestnut was well rested and eager to go. The sooner he left Trail's End behind him, and put Andrea out of his mind, the better. She'd made herself clear enough down there in Mexico. She didn't love him enough to risk hurting anyone else in order to get her freedom. Ever since he'd known her, for too many years, she'd always put something or someone ahead of him. She was almighty fond of Edward Cavindish, that was certain. Maybe now she'd go back to England and marry him.

He was three miles down the road when he reined Jasper to the left and then cut diagonally back toward Trail's End. An idea of where Andrea might be had popped into his head, and he knew he wouldn't rest until he'd checked it out, even if it was only so he could tell her that she could go on back home now, Kate and Adam were worried about her and he wouldn't be there.

She was there. He saw her horse first, not Runner but a little piebald, bridled but without a saddle. She'd ground-ied him and he was cropping the browned grass under the peach trees. If she hadn't still been wearing that bright red skirt he'd have had more trouble locating her because she was deeper in the orchard, sitting on the ground with her cheek pressed against one of the trees.

She heard his footsteps as he came near her, and lifted her head. Her face was strained and pale.

"Your mother's looking for you. You'd better get back to the house. What the devil are you doing here, anyway?"

"I just wanted to be alone, to think." The look she gave him was stricken, and tears filled her eyes although she was making a gallant effort not to let them overflow.

"What are you crying about now?" Henry's voice was

rough. "Not Reggie. You're rid of him, and it won't be long before you can go back to Ned Cavindish."

"I'm not going back to Ned Cavindish! And yes, I am crying about Reggie! It's such a waste, Hank! He could have been a real man, the kind of man I thought I was marrying, instead of what he is now. I'm sorry for Lady Madeline and Sir Robert, and I'm sorry for the years I wasted on him, but I'm the sorriest of all for him, even if he doesn't deserve it. I guess I should hate him, but I don't. I just feel empty, now that I'm finally rid of him."

"From what you've told me, Ned Cavindish is everything that Reggie isn't. And also from what you've told me, he'd be damned glad to see you if you went back there."

"Hank Stockton, don't you dare be jealous, don't you dare! There's nothing to be jealous of, and you know it You've already made it plain that you don't want any part of me!"

"No, I don't want any part of you! I want all of you every last finger and toe and every last thought in you head! I'll always be jealous! It's your own fault, for bein you. If that makes me a damned fool, then I'm a damne fool, but that's the way it is. You go running off from m when I wanted to talk to you, and I find you here in th orchard, our special place, crying about another man, or you can't even live with!"

"You won't even try to understand!" Andrea was c her feet now, her face filled with rage. "Would you l happier if I told you I was crying over you?"

"Yes, I would!"

"All right, then, I'm crying over you! How wou you expect me to feel, when you've hardly looked at r or spoken to me ever since that night——"

She broke off, the agony and the glory of that nig after they'd shaken off the bandits washing over her. Sh been so happy, happier than she'd ever dreamed that a human being could be, and then Hank had turned on l because of her integrity, because she couldn't buy her o happiness at the expense of someone else!

"Dria, why do we have to go on cutting each othe

pieces? Why can't you accept me for what I am, a man who loves you so much that he's never going to be reasonable where you're concerned, a man who's going to be jealous of you till the day he dies!"

"Then why can't you accept me for what I am, a girl who makes mistakes but who doesn't want to hurt anyone deliberately? Oh, Hank, what's the use? Even if we made it up now, it doesn't look like a very promising future for us, does it?"

"Adam and Kate made out all right, and both of them are just as strong-minded as we are."

"But we aren't my mother and father. We're us."

"Then we can find our own way to make out. No, damn it! Don't you open that mouth of yours to argue with me!"

Andrea had no opportunity to open her mouth to argue with him, because he very effectively stopped her mouth with his own. She stiffened, and she struggled for a moment, but then she went limp in his arms. She never wanted to be anywhere else, as long as she lived.

She knew that their life together wasn't going to be serene. But she wouldn't die of boredom, either. There would be battles, but she'd give as good as she took. As long as the battles always ended like this, life would be very much worth living.

Dozing against the bunkhouse wall where the reflected sun warmed his old bones, Manuel saw Hank and Andrea ride back in together, and he nodded. This love between them was a good thing. He, too, knew that they would not always be as content with the world and each other as they were at this moment, but to have troubles together was better than to be alone.

Life was long and life was hard, but it was longer and harder, alone. He, Manuel, knew that from bitter and heartbreaking experience, and he was glad that these two would never have to experience it. Because of people like Adam and Kate and Andrea and Henry, life would be less bitter and heartbreaking for many of his people.

573

And so they deserved all the happiness they were able to find.

Andrea and Hank saw Manuel by the bunkhouse. They both raised their arms in salute.

"He survived the rigors of that trip incredibly well," Dria remarked.

"Better than we nearly did," Hank said and tightened his hold on Andrea's waist as he helped her down from her horse.

"Oh, Hank," Dria said, winding her arms around his neck and not caring who saw. "When I think of all the years and places I've been chasing after dreams that could never come true anywhere but right here in your arms . . ."

"And that's where I aim to keep you, Dria." His lips closed over hers, sealing the promise that would last their lifetime, fulfilling all of their desires and dreams of glory.

PULSE-RACING, PASSIONATE HISTORICAL FICTION

CARESS AND CONQUER by Donna Comeaux Zide (82-949, $2.25)
Was she a woman capable of deep love — or only high adventure? She was Cat Devlan, a violet-eyed, copper-haired beauty bent on vengeance, raging against the man who dared to take her body against her will — and then dared to demand her heart as well. By the author of the bestselling SAVAGE IN SILK.

PASSION AND PROUD HEARTS by Lydia Lancaster (82-548, $2.25)
The bestseller that brought Lydia Lancaster to national fame, this is the epic historical romance of the remarkable Beddoes family, joined by love and promise, divided by hate and pride, played out against and paralleling the historic sweep of the decades surrounding the Civil War.

DESIRE AND DREAMS OF GLORY by Lydia Lancaster (81-549, $2.50)
In this magnificent sequel to Lydia Lancaster's PASSION AND PROUD HEARTS, we follow a new generation of the Beddoes family as the headstrong Andrea comes of age in 1906 and finds herself caught between the old, fine ways of the genteel South and the exciting changes of a new era.

GARNET by Petra Leigh (82-788, $2.25)
For the love of a man, she sheared her long hair and bound her curving body into the uniform of a British ensign. No war would keep Garnet Mallory from the man she wanted. Disguised, she searched for him across Europe, only to discover that hers was not the only charade; that love itself often wears a mask.

LOVE SO BOLD by Annelise Kamada (81-638, $2.50)
Lillian was the wife of a brutal, sadistic noble — who was an intimate of the King. And James was bound by memories and guilt to another woman. In 14th Century England, such a love was doomed, but this was a love that would not surrender, a love so bold it obeyed no law but its own.

ADVENTURE...DANGER...
ROMANCE!

SWEET BRAVADO by *Alicia Meadowes* (89-936, $1.95)

It was not a marriage made in heaven! It was a union decreed in her will by Aunt Sophie. She planned to end the feud between two branches of her family by naming joint heirs. Valentin, Viscount of Ardsmore, and Nicole Harcourt, daughter of his disgraced uncle and a French ballet dancer, would inherit Aunt Sophie's fortune only if they married each other. And wed they did. But Aunt Sophie's plan for peace had stirred up a new battle between the fiery little French girl, who wanted love — and fidelity — from her new husband, and the virile viscount, who expected his wife to want only what he wanted to give. Fun and suspense abounds in this delightful Regency Romance featuring a warm and witty heroine and a story brimming with laughter, surprise, and True Love.